Collected
Stories

Also by Cynthia Ozick

The Bear Boy

Collected Stories

Cynthia Ozick

Weidenfeld & Nicolson
LONDON

First published in Great Britain in 2006
by Weidenfeld & Nicolson

10 9 8 7 6 5 4 3 2 1

The Pagan Rabbi, Envy; or, Yiddish in America, The Dock-Witch, The Doctor's Wife,
The Butterfly and the Traffic Light and Virility first appeared in *The Pagan Rabbi and
Other Stories* (Knopf, 1971). A Mercenary, Bloodshed, An Education and Usurpation
first appeared in *Bloodshed and Three Novellas* (Knopf, 1976). Levitation, Shots and
From a Refugee's Notebook first appeared in *Levitation: Five Fictions* (Knopf, 1976).
Helping T. S. Eliot Write Better first appeared in *Fame and Folly: Essays* (Knopf, 1996).
At Fumicaro first appeared in *New Yorker* (August 1984); Actors in *New Yorker*
(October, 1998) and What Happened to the Baby? in *Atlantic* (forthcoming).

A CIP catalogue record for this book
is available from the British Library.

Hardback ISBN-97 8 02978 5122 6
ISBN-0 297 851225 5

Typeset by Deltatype Ltd, Birkenhead, Merseyside

Printed in Great Britain by Clays Ltd, St Ives plc

Weidenfeld & Nicolson

The Orion Publishing Group Ltd
Orion House
5 Upper Saint Martin's Lane
London, WC2H 9EA

The Orion publishing group's policy is to use papers that are
natural, renewable and recyclable products and made
from wood grown in sustainable forests. The logging and
manufacturing processes are expected to conform to the
environmental regulations of the country of origin.

www.orionbooks.co.uk

To David Miller,
alchemist

Contents

The Pagan Rabbi

Rabbi Jacob said: 'He who is walking along
and studying, but then breaks off to remark,
"How lovely is that tree!" or "How beautiful is that
fallow field!" – Scripture regards such a one
as having hurt his own being.'

– from The Ethics of the Fathers

When I heard that Isaac Kornfeld, a man of piety and brains, had hanged himself in the public park, I put a token in the subway stile and journeyed out to see the tree.

We had been classmates in the rabbinical seminary. Our fathers were both rabbis. They were also friends, but only in a loose way of speaking: in actuality our fathers were enemies. They vied with one another in demonstrations of charitableness, in the captious glitter of their scholia, in the number of their adherents. Of the two, Isaac's father was the milder. I was afraid of my father; he had a certain disease of the larynx, and if he even uttered something so trivial as 'Bring the tea' to my mother, it came out splintered, clamorous, and vindictive.

Neither man was philosophical in the slightest. It was the one thing they agreed on. 'Philosophy is an abomination,' Isaac's father used to say. 'The Greeks were philosophers, but they remained children playing with their dolls. Even Socrates, a monotheist, nevertheless sent money down to the temple to pay for incense to their doll.'

'Idolatry is the abomination,' Isaac argued, 'not philosophy.'

'The latter is the corridor to the former,' his father said.

My own father claimed that if not for philosophy I would never have been brought to the atheism which finally led me to withdraw, in my second year, from the seminary. The trouble was not philosophy – I had none of Isaac's talent: his teachers later said of him that his imagination was so remarkable he could concoct holiness out of the fine line of a serif. On the day of his funeral the president of his college was criticized for having commented that, although a suicide could not be buried in consecrated earth, whatever earth enclosed Isaac Kornfeld was *ipso facto* consecrated. It should be noted that Isaac hanged himself several weeks short of his thirty-sixth birthday; he was then at the peak of his renown; and the president, of course, did not know the whole story. He judged by Isaac's reputation, which was at no time more impressive than just before his death.

I judged by the same, and marvelled that all that holy genius and intellectual surprise should in the end be raised no higher than the next-to-lowest limb of a delicate young oak, with burly roots like the toes of a gryphon exposed in the wet ground.

The tree was almost alone in a long rough meadow, which sloped down to a bay filled with sickly clams and a bad smell. The place was called Trilham's Inlet, and I knew what the smell meant: that cold brown water covered half the city's turds.

On the day I came to see the tree the air was bleary with fog. The weather was well into autumn and, though it was Sunday, the walks were empty. There was something historical about the park just then, with its rusting grasses and deserted monuments. In front of a soldiers' cenotaph a plastic wreath left behind months before by some civic parade stood propped against a stone frieze of identical marchers in the costume of an old war. A banner across the wreath's belly explained that the purpose of war is peace. At the margins of the park they were building a gigantic highway. I felt I was making my way across a battlefield silenced by the victory of the peace machines. The bulldozers had bitten far into the park, and the rolled carcasses of the sacrificed trees were already cut up into logs. There were dozens of felled maples, elms, and oaks. Their moist inner wheels breathed out a fragrance of barns, countryside, decay.

In the bottom-most meadow fringing the water I recognized the tree which had caused Isaac to sin against his own life. It looked curiously like a photograph – not only like that newspaper photograph I carried warmly in my pocket, which showed the field and its markers – the drinking-fountain a few yards off, the ruined brick wall of an old estate behind. The caption-writer had particularly remarked on the 'rope'. But the rope was no longer there; the widow had claimed it. It was his own prayer shawl that Isaac, a short man, had thrown over the comely neck of the next-to-lowest limb. A Jew is buried in his prayer shawl; the police had handed it over to Sheindel. I observed that the bark was rubbed at that spot. The tree lay back against the sky like a licked postage stamp. Rain began to beat it flatter yet. A stench of sewage came up like a veil in the nostril. It seemed to me I was a man in a photograph standing next to a grey blur of tree. I would stand through eternity beside Isaac's guilt if I did not run, so I ran that night to Sheindel herself.

I loved her at once. I am speaking now of the first time I saw her, though I don't exclude the last. The last – the last together with Isaac – was soon after my divorce; at one stroke I left my wife and my cousin's fur business to the small upstate city in which both had repined. Suddenly Isaac and Sheindel and two babies appeared in the lobby of my hotel – they were passing through: Isaac had a lecture engagement in Canada. We sat under scarlet neon and Isaac told how my father could now not speak at all.

'He keeps his vow,' I said.

'No, no, he's a sick man,' Isaac said. 'An obstruction in the throat.'

'I'm the obstruction. You know what he said when I left the seminary. He meant it, never mind how many years it is. He's never addressed a word to me since.'

'We were reading together. He blamed the reading, who can blame *him*? Fathers like ours don't know how to love. They live too much indoors.'

It was an odd remark, though I was too much preoccupied with my own resentments to notice. 'It wasn't what we read,' I objected. 'Torah tells that an illustrious man doesn't have an illustrious son. Otherwise he wouldn't be humble like other people. This much scholarly stuffing I retain. Well, so my father always believed he was more illustrious than anybody, especially more than your father. *Therefore,*' I delivered in Talmudic cadence, 'what chance did I have? A nincompoop and no *Sitzfleish*. Now you, you could answer questions that weren't even invented yet. Then you invented them.'

'Torah isn't a spade,' Isaac said. 'A man should have a livelihood. You had yours.'

'The pelt of a dead animal isn't a living either, it's an indecency.'

All the while Sheindel was sitting perfectly still; the babies, female infants in long stockings, were asleep in her arms. She wore a dark thick woollen hat – it was July – that covered every part of her hair. But I had once seen it in all its streaming black shine.

'And Jane?' Isaac asked finally.

'Speaking of dead animals. Tell my father – he won't answer a letter, he won't come to the telephone – that in the matter of the marriage he was right, but for the wrong reason. If you share a bed with a Puritan you'll come into it cold and you'll go out of it cold. Listen, Isaac, my father calls me an atheist, but between the conjugal sheets every Jew is a believer in miracles, even the lapsed.'

He said nothing then. He knew I envied him his Sheindel and his luck. Unlike our fathers, Isaac had never condemned me for my marriage, which his father regarded as his private triumph over my father, and which my father, in his public defeat, took as an occasion for declaring me as one dead. He rent his clothing and sat on a stool for eight days, while Isaac's father came to watch him mourn, secretly satisfied, though aloud he grieved for all apostates. Isaac did not like my wife. He called her a tall yellow straw. After we were married he never said a word against her, but he kept away.

I went with my wife to his wedding. We took the early train down especially, but when we arrived the feast was well under way, and the guests far into the dancing.

'Look, look, they don't dance together,' Jane said.

'Who?'

'The men and the women. The bride and the groom.'

'Count the babies,' I advised. 'The Jews are also Puritans, but only in public.'

The bride was enclosed all by herself on a straight chair in the centre of a spinning ring of young men. The floor heaved under their whirl. They stamped, the chandeliers shuddered, the guests cried out, the young men with linked arms spiralled and their skullcaps came flying off like centrifugal balloons. Isaac, a mist of black suit, a stamping foot, was lost in the planet's wake of black suits and emphatic feet. The dancing young men shouted bridal songs, the floor leaned like a plate, the whole room teetered.

Isaac had told me something of Sheindel. Before now I had never seen her. Her birth was in a concentration camp, and they were about to throw her against the electrified fence when an army mobbed the gate; the current vanished from the terrible wires, and she had nothing to show for it afterwards but a mark on her cheek like an asterisk, cut by a barb. The asterisk pointed to certain dry footnotes: she had no mother to show, she had no father to show, but she had, extraordinarily, God to show – she was known to be, for her age and sex, astonishingly learned. She was only seventeen.

'What pretty hair she has,' Jane said.

Now Sheindel was dancing with Isaac's mother. All the ladies made a fence, and the bride, twirling with her mother-in-law, lost a shoe and fell against the long laughing row. The ladies lifted their glistering breasts in their lacy dresses and laughed; the young men, stamping two by two, went on shouting their wedding songs. Sheindel danced without her shoe, and the black river of her hair followed her.

'After today she'll have to hide it all,' I explained.

Jane asked why.

'So as not to be a temptation to men,' I told her, and covertly looked for my father. There he was, in a shadow, apart. My eyes discovered his eyes. He turned his back and gripped his throat.

'It's a very anthropological experience,' Jane said.

'A wedding is a wedding,' I answered her, 'among us even more so.'

'Is that your father over there, that little scowly man?'

To Jane all Jews were little. 'My father the man of the cloth. Yes.'

'A wedding is not a wedding,' said Jane: we had had only a licence and a judge with bad breath.

'Everybody marries for the same reason.'

'No,' said my wife. 'Some for love and some for spite.'

'And everybody for bed.'

'Some for spite,' she insisted.

'I was never cut out for a man of the cloth,' I said. 'My poor father doesn't see that.'

'He doesn't speak to you.'

'A technicality. He's losing his voice.'

'Well, he's not like you. He doesn't do it for spite,' Jane said.

'You don't know him,' I said.

He lost it altogether the very week Isaac published his first remarkable collection of responsa. Isaac's father crowed like a passionate rooster, and packed his wife and himself off to the Holy Land to boast on the holy soil. Isaac was a little relieved; he had just been made Professor of Mishnaic History, and his father's whims and pretences and foolish rivalries were an embarrassment. It is easy to honour a father from afar, but bitter to honour one who is dead. A surgeon cut out my father's voice, and he died without a word.

Isaac and I no longer met. Our ways were too disparate. Isaac was famous, if not in the world, certainly in the kingdom of jurists and scholars. By this time I had acquired a partnership in a small book store in a basement. My partner sold me his share, and I put up a new sign: 'The Book Cellar'; for reasons more obscure than filial (all the same I wished my father could have seen it) I established a department devoted especially to not-quite-rare theological works, chiefly in Hebrew and Aramaic, though I carried some Latin and Greek. When Isaac's second volume reached my shelves (I had now expanded to street level), I wrote him to congratulate him, and after that we corresponded, not with any regularity. He took to ordering all his books from me, and we exchanged awkward little jokes. 'I'm still in the jacket business,' I told him, 'but now I feel I'm where I belong. Last time I went too fur.' 'Sheindel is well, and Naomi and Esther have a sister,' he wrote. And later: 'Naomi, Esther, and Miriam have a sister.' And still later: 'Naomi, Esther, Miriam, and Ophra have a sister.' It went on until there were seven girls. 'There's nothing in Torah that prevents an illustrious man from having illustrious daughters,' I wrote him when he said he had given up hope of another rabbi in the family. 'But where do you find seven illustrious husbands?' he asked. Every order brought another quip, and we bantered back and forth in this way for some years.

I noticed that he read everything. Long ago he had inflamed my taste, but I could never keep up. No sooner did I catch his joy in Saadia Gaon than he had already sprung ahead to Yehudah Halevi. One day he was weeping with Dostoevsky and the next leaping in the air over Thomas Mann. He introduced me to Hegel and Nietzsche while our fathers wailed. His mature reading was no more peaceable than those frenzies of his youth, when I would come upon him in an abandoned classroom at dusk, his stocking feet on the windowsill, the light already washed from the lowest city clouds, wearing the look of a man half-sotted with print.

But when the widow asked me – covering a certain excess of alertness or irritation – whether to my knowledge Isaac had lately been ordering any books on horticulture, I was astonished.

'He bought so much,' I demurred.

'Yes, yes, yes,' she said. 'How could you remember?'

She poured the tea and then, with a discreetness of gesture, lifted my dripping raincoat from the chair where I had thrown it and took it out of the room. It was a crowded apartment, not very neat, far from slovenly, cluttered with dolls and tiny dishes and an array of tricycles. The dining table was as large as a desert. An old-fashioned crocheted lace runner divided it into two nations, and on the end of this, in the neutral zone, so to speak, Sheindel had placed my cup. There was no physical relic of Isaac: not even a book.

She returned. 'My girls are all asleep, we can talk. What an ordeal for you, weather like this and going out so far to that place.'

It was impossible to tell whether she was angry or not. I had rushed in on her like the rainfall itself, scattering drops, my shoes stuck all over with leaves.

'I comprehend exactly why you went out there. The impulse of a detective,' she said. Her voice contained an irony that surprised me. It was brilliantly and unmistakably accented, and because of this jaggedly precise. It was as if every word emitted a quick white thread of great purity, like hard silk, which she was then obliged to bite cleanly off. 'You went to find something? An atmosphere? The sadness itself?'

'There was nothing to see,' I said, and thought I was lunatic to have put myself in her way.

'Did you dig in the ground? He might have buried a note for goodbye.'

'Was there a note?' I asked, startled.

'He left nothing behind for ordinary humanity like yourself.'

I saw she was playing with me. 'Rebbetzin Kornfeld,' I said, standing up, 'forgive me. My coat, please, and I'll go.'

'Sit,' she commanded. 'Isaac read less lately, did you notice that?'

I gave her a civil smile. 'All the same he was buying more and more.'

'Think,' she said. 'I depend on you. You're just the one who might know. I had forgotten this. God sent you perhaps.'

'Rebbetzin Kornfeld, I'm only a bookseller.'

'God in his judgment sent me a bookseller. For such a long time Isaac never read at home. Think! Agronomy?'

'I don't remember anything like that. What would a Professor of Mishnaic History want with agronomy?'

'If he had a new book under his arm he would take it straight to the seminary and hide it in his office.'

'I mailed to his office. If you like I can look up some of the titles—'

'You were in the park and you saw nothing?'

'Nothing.' Then I was ashamed. 'I saw the tree.'

'And what is that? A tree is nothing.'

'Rebbetzin Kornfeld,' I pleaded, 'it's a stupidity that I came here. I don't know myself why I came, I beg your pardon, I had no idea—'

'You came to learn why Isaac took his life. Botany? Or even, please listen, even mycology? He never asked you to send something on mushrooms? Or having to do with herbs? Manure? Flowers? A certain

kind of agricultural poetry? A book about gardening? Forestry? Vegetables? Cereal growing?'

'Nothing, nothing like that,' I said excitedly. 'Rebbetzin Kornfeld, your
husband was a rabbi!'

'I know what my husband was. Something to do with vines? Arbours?
Rice? Think, think, think! Anything to do with land – meadows – goats –
a farm, hay – anything at all, anything rustic or lunar—'

'Lunar! My God! Was he a teacher or a nurseryman? Goats! Was he a
furrier? Sheindel, are you crazy? *I* was the furrier! What do you want from
the dead?'

Without a word she replenished my cup, though it was more than half
full, and sat down opposite me, on the other side of the lace boundary
line. She leaned her face into her palms, but I saw her eyes. She kept
them wide.

'Rebbetzin Kornfeld,' I said, collecting myself, 'with a tragedy like
this—'

'You imagine I blame the books. I don't blame the books, whatever
they were. If he had been faithful to his books he would have lived.'

'He lived,' I cried, 'in books, what else?'

'No,' said the widow.

'A scholar. A rabbi. A remarkable Jew!'

At this she spilled a furious laugh. 'Tell me, I have always been very
interested and shy to inquire. Tell me about your wife.'

I intervened: 'I haven't had a wife in years.'

'What are they like, those people?'

'They're exactly like us, if you can think what we would be if we were
like them.'

'We are not like them. Their bodies are more to them than ours are to
us. Our books are holy, to them their bodies are holy.'

'Jane's was so holy she hardly ever let me get near it,' I muttered to
myself.

'Isaac used to run in the park, but he lost his breath too quickly.
Instead he read in a book about runners with hats made of leaves.'

'Sheindel, Sheindel, what did you expect of him? He was a student, he
sat and he thought, he was a Jew.'

She thrust her hands flat. 'He was not.'

I could not reply. I looked at her merely. She was thinner now than in
her early young-womanhood, and her face had an in-between cast,

poignant still at the mouth and jaw, beginning to grow coarse on either side of the nose.

'I think he was never a Jew,' she said.

I wondered whether Isaac's suicide had unbalanced her.

'I'll tell you a story,' she resumed. 'A story about stories. These were the bedtime stories Isaac told Naomi and Esther: about mice that danced and children who laughed: When Miriam came he invented a speaking cloud. With Ophra it was a turtle that married a blade of withered grass. By Leah's time the stones had tears for their leglessness. Rebecca cried because of a tree that turned into a girl and could never grow colours again in autumn. Shiphrah, the littlest, believes that a pig has a soul.'

'My own father used to drill me every night in sacred recitation. It was a terrible childhood.'

'He insisted on picnics. Each time we went farther and farther into the country. It was a madness. Isaac never troubled to learn to drive a car, and there was always a clumsiness of baskets to carry and a clutter of buses and trains and seven exhausted wild girls. And he would look for special places – we couldn't settle just here or there, there had to be a brook or such-and-such a slope or else a little grove. And then, though he said it was all for the children's pleasure, he would leave them and go off alone and never come back until sunset, when everything was spilled and the air freezing and the babies crying.'

'I was a grown man before I had the chance to go on a picnic,' I admitted.

'I'm speaking of the beginning,' said the widow. 'Like you, wasn't I fooled? I was fooled, I was charmed. Going home with our baskets of berries and flowers we were a romantic huddle. Isaac's stories on those nights were full of dark invention. May God preserve me, I even begged him to write them down. Then suddenly he joined a club, and Sunday mornings he was up and away before dawn.'

'A club? So early? What library opens at that hour?' I said, stunned that a man like Isaac should ally himself with anything so doubtful.

'Ah, you don't follow, you don't follow. It was a hiking club, they met under the moon. I thought it was a pity, the whole week Isaac was so inward, he needed air for the mind. He used to come home too fatigued to stand. He said he went for the landscape. I was like you, I took what I heard, I heard it all and never followed. He resigned from the hikers finally, and I believed all that strangeness was finished. He told me it was absurd to walk at such a pace, he was a teacher and not an athlete. Then he began to write.'

'But he always wrote,' I objected.

'Not this way. What he wrote was only fairy tales. He kept at it and for a while he neglected everything else. It was the strangeness in another form. The stories surprised me, they were so poor and dull. They were a little like the ideas he used to scare the girls with, but choked all over with notes, appendices, prefaces. It struck me then he didn't seem to understand he was only doing fairy tales. Yet they were really very ordinary – full of sprites, nymphs, gods, everything ordinary and old.'

'Will you let me see them?'

'Burned, all burned.'

'Isaac burned them?'

'You don't think I did! I see what you think.'

It was true that I was marvelling at her hatred. I supposed she was one of those born to dread imagination. I was overtaken by a coldness for her, though the sight of her small hands with their tremulous staves of fingers turning and turning in front of her face like a gate on a hinge reminded me of where she was born and who she was. She was an orphan and had been saved by magic and had a terror of it. The coldness fled. 'Why should you be bothered by little stories?' I inquired. 'It wasn't the stories that killed him.'

'No, no, not the stories,' she said. 'Stupid corrupt things. I was glad when he gave them up. He piled them in the bathtub and lit them with a match. Then he put a notebook in his coat pocket and said he would walk in the park. Week after week he tried all the parks in the city. I didn't dream what he could be after. One day he took the subway and rode to the end of the line, and this was the right park at last. He went every day after class. An hour going, an hour back. Two, three in the morning he came home. "Is it exercise?" I said. I thought he might be running again. He used to shiver with the chill of night and the dew. "No, I sit quite still," he said. "Is it more stories you do out there?" "No, I only jot down what I think." "A man should meditate in his own house, not by night near bad water," I said. Six, seven in the morning he came home. I asked him if he meant to find his grave in that place.'

She broke off with a cough, half artifice and half resignation, so loud that it made her crane towards the bedrooms to see if she had awakened a child. 'I don't sleep any more,' she told me. 'Look around you. Look, look everywhere, look on the windowsills. Do you see any plants, any common house plants? I went down one evening and gave them to the garbage collector. I couldn't sleep in the same space with plants. They are like little trees. Am I deranged? Take Isaac's notebook and bring it back when you can.'

I obeyed. In my own room, a sparse place, with no ornaments but a few pretty stalks in pots, I did not delay and seized the notebook. It was a tiny affair, three inches by five, with ruled pages that opened on a coiled wire. I read searchingly, hoping for something not easily evident. Sheindel by her melancholy innuendo had made me believe that in these few sheets Isaac had revealed the reason for his suicide. But it was all a disappointment. There was not a word of any importance. After a while I concluded that, whatever her motives, Sheindel was playing with me again. She meant to punish me for asking the unaskable. My inquisitiveness offended her; she had given me Isaac's notebook not to enlighten but to rebuke. The handwriting was recognizable yet oddly formed, shaky and even senile, like that of a man outdoors and deskless who scribbles in his palm or on his lifted knee or leaning on a bit of bark; and there was no doubt that the wrinkled leaves, with their ragged corners, had been in and out of someone's pocket. So I did not mistrust Sheindel's mad anecdote; this much was true: a park, Isaac, a notebook, all at once, but signifying no more than that a professor with a literary turn of mind had gone for a walk. There was even a green stain straight across one of the quotations, as if the pad had slipped grasswards and been trodden on.

I have forgotten to mention that the notebook, though scantily filled, was in three languages. The Greek I could not read at all, but it had the shape of verse. The Hebrew was simply a miscellany, drawn mostly from Leviticus and Deuteronomy. Among these I found the following extracts, transcribed not quite verbatim:

Ye shall utterly destroy all the places of the gods, upon the high mountains, and upon the hills, and under every green tree.

And the soul that turneth after familiar spirits to go a-whoring after them, I will cut him off from among his people.

These, of course, were ordinary unadorned notes, such as any classroom lecturer might commonly make to remind himself of the text, with a phrase cut out here and there for the sake of speeding his hand. Or I thought it possible that Isaac might at that time have been preparing a paper on the Talmudic commentaries for these passages. Whatever the case, the remaining quotations, chiefly from English poetry, interested me only slightly more. They were the elegiac favourites of a closeted Romantic. I was repelled by Isaac's Nature: it wore a capital letter, and smelled like my own Book Cellar. It was plain to me that he had lately grown painfully academic: he could not see a weed's tassel without finding a classical reference for it. He had put down a snatch of Byron, a smudge of Keats (like his Scriptural copyings, these too were quick and fragmented), a pair of truncated lines from Tennyson, and this unmarked and clumsy quatrain:

> And yet all is not taken. Still one Dryad
>   Flits through the wood, one Oread skims the hill;
> White in the whispering stream still gleams a Naiad;
>   The beauty of the earth is haunted still.

All of this was so cloying and mooning and ridiculous, and so pedantic besides, that I felt ashamed for him. And yet there was almost nothing else, nothing to redeem him and nothing personal, only a sentence or two in his rigid self-controlled scholar's style, not unlike the starched little jokes of our correspondence. 'I am writing at dusk sitting on a stone in Trilham's Inlet Park, within sight of Trilham's Inlet, a bay to the north of the city, and within two yards of a slender tree, *Quercus velutina*, the age of which, should one desire to measure it, can be ascertained by (God forbid) cutting the bole and counting the rings. The man writing is thirty-five years old and ageing too rapidly, which may be ascertained by counting the rings under his poor myopic eyes.' Below this, deliberate and readily more legible than the rest, appeared three curious words:

Great Pan lives.

That was all. In a day or so I returned the notebook to Sheindel. I told myself that she had seven orphans to worry over, and repressed my anger at having been cheated.

She was waiting for me. 'I am so sorry, there was a letter in the notebook, it had fallen out. I found it on the carpet after you left.'

'Thank you, no,' I said. 'I've read enough out of Isaac's pockets.'

'Then why did you come to see me to begin with?'

'I came,' I said, 'just to see you.'

'You came for Isaac.' But she was more mocking than distraught. 'I gave you everything you needed to see what happened and still you don't follow. Here.' She held out a large law-sized paper. 'Read the letter.'

'I've read his notebook. If everything I need to fathom Isaac is in the notebook I don't need the letter.'

'It's a letter he wrote to explain himself,' she persisted.

'You told me Isaac left you no notes.'

'It was not written to me.'

I sat down on one of the dining-room chairs and Sheindel put the page before me on the table. It lay face up on the lace divider. I did not look at it.

'It's a love letter,' Sheindel whispered. 'When they cut him down they found the notebook in one pocket and the letter in the other.'

I did not know what to say.

'The police gave me everything,' Sheindel said. 'Everything to keep.'

'A love letter?' I repeated.

'That is what such letters are commonly called.'

'And the police – they gave it to you, and that was the first you realized what' – I floundered after the inconceivable – 'what could be occupying him?'

'What could be occupying him,' she mimicked. 'Yes. Not until they took the letter and the notebook out of his pocket.'

'My God. His habit of life, his mind . . . I can't imagine it. You never guessed?'

'No.'

'These trips to the park—'

'He had become aberrant in many ways. I have described them to you.'

'But the park! Going off like that, alone – you didn't think he might be meeting a woman?'

'It was not a woman.'

Disgust like a powder clotted my nose. 'Sheindel, you're crazy.'

'I'm crazy, is that it? Read his confession! Read it! How long can I be the only one to know this thing? Do you want my brain to melt? Be my confidant,' she entreated so unexpectedly that I held my breath.

'You've said nothing to anyone?'

'Would they have recited such eulogies if I had? Read the letter!'

'I have no interest in the abnormal,' I said coldly.

She raised her eyes and watched me for the smallest space. Without any change in the posture of her suppliant head her laughter began; I have never since heard sounds like those – almost mouselike in density for fear of waking her sleeping daughters, but so rational in intent that it was like listening to astonished sanity rendered into a cackling fugue. She kept it up for a minute and then calmed herself. 'Please sit where you are. Please pay attention. I will read the letter to you myself.'

She plucked the page from the table with an orderly gesture. I saw that this letter had been scrupulously prepared; it was closely written. Her tone was cleansed by scorn.

'"My ancestors were led out of Egypt by the hand of God,"' she read.

'Is this how a love letter starts out?'

She moved on resolutely. '"We were guilty of so-called abominations well-described elsewhere. Other peoples have been nourished on their mythologies. For aeons we have been weaned from all traces of the same."'

I felt myself becoming impatient. The fact was I had returned with a single idea: I meant to marry Isaac's widow when enough time had passed to make it seemly. It was my intention to court her with great subtlety at first, so that I would not appear to be presuming on her sorrow. But she was possessed. 'Sheindel, why do you want to inflict this treatise on me? Give it to the seminary, contribute it to a symposium of professors.'

'I would sooner die.'

At this I began to attend in earnest.

'"I will leave aside the wholly plausible position of so-called animism within the concept of the One God. I will omit a historical illumination of its continuous but covert expression even within the Fence of the Law. Creature, I leave these aside—"'

'What?' I yelped.

'"Creature,"' she repeated, spreading her nostrils. '"What is human history? What is our philosophy? What is our religion? None of these teaches us poor human ones that we are alone in the universe, and even without them we would know that we are not. At a very young age I understood that a foolish man would not believe in a fish had he not had one enter his experience. Innumerable forms exist and have come to our eyes, and to the still deeper eye of the lens of our instruments; from this minute perception of what already is, it is easy to conclude that further forms are possible, that all forms are probable. God created the world not for Himself alone, or I would not now possess this consciousness with which I am enabled to address thee, Loveliness."'

'Thee,' I echoed, and swallowed a sad bewilderment.

'You must let me go on,' Sheindel said, and grimly went on. '"It is false history, false philosophy, and false religion which declare to us human ones that we live among Things. The arts of physics and chemistry begin to teach us differently, but their way of compassion is new, and finds few to carry fidelity to its logical and beautiful end. The molecules dance inside all forms, and within the molecules dance the atoms, and within the atoms dance still profounder sources of divine vitality. There is nothing that is Dead. There is no Non-life. Holy life subsists even in the stone, even in the bones of dead dogs and dead men. Hence in God's fecundating Creation there is no possibility of Idolatry, and therefore no possibility of committing this so-called abomination."'

'My God, my God,' I wailed. 'Enough, Sheindel, it's more than enough, no more—'

'There is more,' she said.

'I don't want to hear it.'

'He stains his character for you? A spot, do you think? You will hear.' She took up in a voice which all at once reminded me of my father's: it was unforgiving. '"Creature, I rehearse these matters though all our language is as breath to thee; as baubles for the juggler. Where we struggle to understand from day to day, and contemplate the grave for its riddle, the other breeds are born fulfilled in wisdom. Animal races conduct themselves without self-investigations; instinct is a higher and not a lower thing. Alas that we human ones – but for certain pitifully primitive approximations in those few reflexes and involuntary actions left to our bodies – are born bare of instinct! All that we unfortunates must resort to through science, art, philosophy, religion, all our imaginings and tormented strivings, all our meditations and vain questionings, all! – are expressed naturally and rightly in the beasts, the plants, the rivers, the stones. The reason is simple, it is our tragedy: our soul is included in us, it inhabits us, we contain it, when we seek our soul we must seek in ourselves. To *see* the soul, to confront it – that is divine wisdom. Yet how can we see into our dark selves? With the other races of being it is differently ordered. The soul of the plant does not reside in the chlorophyll, it may roam if it wishes, it may choose whatever form or shape it pleases. Hence the other breeds, being largely free of their soul and able to witness it, can live in peace. To see one's soul is to know all, to know all is to own the peace our philosophies futilely envisage. Earth displays two categories of soul: the free and the indwelling. We human ones are cursed with the indwelling—"'

'Stop!' I cried.

'I will not,' said the widow.

'Please, you told me he burned his fairy tales.'

'Did I lie to you? Will you say I lied?'

'Then for Isaac's sake why didn't you? If this isn't a fairy tale what do you want me to think it could be?'

'Think what you like.'

'Sheindel,' I said, 'I beg you, don't destroy a dead man's honour. Don't look at this thing again, tear it to pieces, don't continue with it.'

'I don't destroy his honour. He had none.'

'Please! Listen to yourself! My God, who was the man? Rabbi Isaac Kornfeld! Talk of honour! Wasn't he a teacher? Wasn't he a scholar?'

'He was a pagan.'

Her eyes returned without hesitation to their task. She commenced: '"All these truths I learned only gradually, against my will and desire. Our teacher Moses did not speak of them; much may be said under this head. It was not out of ignorance that Moses failed to teach about those souls that are free. If I have learned what Moses knew, is this not because we are both men? He was a man, but God addressed him; it was God's will that our ancestors should no longer be slaves. Yet our ancestors, being stiff-necked, would not have abandoned their slavery in Egypt had they been taught of the free souls. They would have said: 'Let us stay, our bodies will remain enslaved in Egypt, but our souls will wander at their pleasure in Zion. If the cactus-plant stays rooted while its soul roams, why not also a man?' And if Moses had replied that only the world of Nature has the gift of the free soul, while man is chained to his, and that a man, to free his soul, must also free the body that is its vessel, they would have scoffed. 'How is it that men, and men alone, are different from the world of Nature? If this is so, then the condition of men is evil and unjust, and if this condition of ours is evil and unjust in general, what does it matter whether we are slaves in Egypt or citizens in Zion?' And they would not have done God's will and abandoned their slavery. Therefore Moses never spoke to them of the free souls, lest the people not do God's will and go out from Egypt."'

In an instant a sensation broke in me – it was entirely obscure, there was nothing I could compare it with, and yet I was certain I recognized it.

And then I did. It hurtled me into childhood – it was the crisis of insight one experiences when one has just read out, for the first time, that conglomeration of figurines which makes a word. In that moment I penetrated beyond Isaac's alphabet into his language. I saw that he was on the side of possibility: he was both sane and inspired. His intention was not to accumulate mystery but to dispel it.

'All that part is brilliant,' I burst out.

Sheindel meanwhile had gone to the sideboard to take a sip of cold tea that was standing there. 'In a minute,' she said, and pursued her thirst. 'I have heard of drawings surpassing Rembrandt daubed by madmen who when released from the fit couldn't hold the chalk. What follows is beautiful, I warn you.'

'The man was a genius.'

'Yes.'

'Go on,' I urged.

She produced for me her clownish jeering smile. She read: '"Sometimes in the desert journey on the way they would come to a watering place, and some quick spry boy would happen to glimpse the soul of the spring (which the wild Greeks afterwards called naiad), but not knowing of the existence of the free souls he would suppose only that the moon had cast a momentary beam across the water. Loveliness, with the same innocence of accident I discovered thee. Loveliness, Loveliness."'

She stopped.

'Is that all?'

'There is more.'

'Read it.'

'The rest is the love letter.'

'Is it hard for you?' But I asked with more eagerness than pity.

'I was that man's wife, he scaled the Fence of the Law. For this God preserved me from the electric fence. Read it for yourself.'

Incontinently I snatched the crowded page.

'"Loveliness, in thee the joy, substantiation, and supernal succour of my theorem. How many hours through how many years I walked over the cilia-forests of our enormous aspiring vegetable-star, this light rootless seed that crawls in its single furrow, this shaggy mazy unimplanted cabbage-head of our earth! – never, all that time, all those days of unfulfilment, a white space like a desert thirst, never, never to grasp. I thought myself abandoned to the intrigue of my folly. At dawn, on a hillock, what seemed the very shape and seizing of the mound's nature –

what was it? Only the haze of the sun-ball growing great through hoarfrost. The oread slipped from me, leaving her illusion; or was never there at all; or was there but for an instant, and ran away. What sly ones the free souls are! They have a comedy we human ones cannot dream: the laughing drunkard feels in himself the shadow of the shadow of the shadow of their wit, and only because he has made himself a vessel, as the two banks and the bed of a rivulet are the naiad's vessel. A naiad I may indeed have viewed whole: all seven of my daughters were once wading in a stream in a compact but beautiful park, of which I had much hope. The youngest being not yet two, and fretful, the older ones were told to keep her always by the hand, but they did not obey. I, having passed some way into the woods behind, all at once heard a scream and noise of splashes, and caught sight of a tiny body flying down into the water. Running back through the trees I could see the others bunched together, afraid, as the baby dived helplessly, all these little girls frozen in a garland – when suddenly one of them (it was too quick a movement for me to recognize which) darted to the struggler, who was now underwater, and pulled her up, and put an arm around her to soothe her. The arm was blue – blue. As blue as a lake. And fiercely, from my spot on the bank, panting, I began to count the little girls. I counted eight, thought myself not mad but delivered, again counted, counted seven, knew I had counted well before, knew I counted well even now. A blue-armed girl had come to wade among them. Which is to say the shape of a girl. I questioned my daughters: each in her fright believed one of the others had gone to pluck up the tiresome baby. None wore a dress with blue sleeves."'

'Proofs,' said the widow. 'Isaac was meticulous, he used to account for all his proofs always.'

'How?' My hand in tremor rustled Isaac's letter; the paper bleated as though whipped.

'By eventually finding a principle to cover them,' she finished maliciously. 'Well, don't rest even for me, you don't oblige me. You have a long story to go, long enough to make a fever.'

'Tea,' I said hoarsely.

She brought me her own cup from the sideboard, and I believed as I drank that I swallowed some of her mockery and gall.

'Sheindel, for a woman so pious you're a great sceptic.' And now the tremor had command of my throat.

'An atheist's statement,' she rejoined. 'The more piety, the more scepticism. A religious man comprehends this. Superfluity, excess of custom, and superstition would climb like a choking vine on the Fence of the Law if scepticism did not continually hack them away to make freedom for purity.'

I then thought her fully worthy of Isaac. Whether I was worthy of her I evaded putting to myself; instead I gargled some tea and returned to the letter.

'"It pains me to confess,"' I read, '"how after that I moved from clarity to doubt and back again. I had no trust in my conclusions because all my experiences were evanescent. Everything certain I attributed to some other cause less certain. Every voice out of the moss I blamed on rabbits and squirrels. Every motion among leaves I called a bird, though there positively was no bird. My first sight of the Little People struck me as no more than a shudder of literary delusion, and I determined they could only be an instantaneous crop of mushrooms. But one night, a little after ten o'clock at the crux of summer – the sky still showed strings of light – I was wandering in this place, this place where they will find my corpse—"'

'Not for my sake,' said Sheindel when I hesitated.

'It's terrible,' I croaked, 'terrible.'

'Withered like a shell,' she said, as though speaking of the cosmos; and I understood from her manner that she had a fanatic's acquaintance with this letter, and knew it nearly by heart. She appeared to be thinking the words faster than I could bring them out, and for some reason I was constrained to hurry the pace of my reading.

'"—where they will find my corpse withered like the shell of an insect,"' I rushed on. '"The smell of putrefaction lifted clearly from the bay. I began to speculate about my own body after I was dead – whether the soul would be set free immediately after the departure of life; or whether only gradually, as decomposition proceeded and more and more of the indwelling soul was released to freedom. But when I considered how a man's body is no better than a clay pot, a fact which none of our sages has ever contradicted, it seemed to me then that an indwelling soul by its own nature would be obliged to cling to its bit of pottery until the last crumb and grain had vanished into earth. I walked through the ditches of that black meadow grieving and swollen with self-pity. It came to me that while my poor bones went on decaying at their ease, my soul would have to linger inside them, waiting, despairing, longing to join the free ones. I cursed it for its gravity-despoiled, slow, interminably languishing purse of flesh; better to be encased in vapour, in wind, in a hair of a coconut! Who knows how long it takes the body of a man to shrink into gravel, and the gravel into sand, and the sand into vitamin? A hundred years? Two hundred, three hundred? A thousand perhaps! Is it not true that bones nearly intact are constantly being dug up by the paleontologists two million years after burial?" Sheindel,' I interrupted, 'this is death, not love. Where's the love letter to be afraid of here? I don't find it.'

'Continue,' she ordered. And then: 'You see I'm not afraid.'

'Not of love?'

'No. But you recite much too slowly. Your mouth is shaking. Are you afraid of death?'

I did not reply.

'Continue,' she said again. 'Go rapidly. The next sentence begins with an extraordinary thought.'

'"An extraordinary thought emerged in me. It was luminous, profound, and practical. More than that, it had innumerable precedents; the mythologies had documented it a dozen dozen times over. I recalled all those mortals reputed to have coupled with gods (a collective word, showing much common sense, signifying what our philosophies more abstrusely call Shekhina), and all that poignant miscegenation represented by centaurs, satyrs, mermaids, fauns, and so forth, not to speak of that even more famous mingling in Genesis, whereby the sons of God took the daughters of men for brides, producing giants and possibly also those abortions, leviathan and behemoth, of which we read in Job, along with unicorns and other chimeras and monsters abundant in Scripture, hence far from fanciful. There existed also the example of the succubus Lilith, who was often known to couple in the mediaeval ghetto even with pre-pubescent boys. By all these evidences I was emboldened in my confidence that I was surely not the first man to conceive such a desire in the history of our earth. Creature, the thought that took hold of me was this: if only I could couple with one of the free souls, the strength of the connection would likely wrest my own soul from my body – seize it, as if by a tongs, draw it out, so to say, to its own freedom. The intensity and force of my desire to capture one of these beings now became prodigious. I avoided my wife—"'

Here the widow heard me falter.

'Please,' she commanded, and I saw creeping in her face the completed turn of a sneer.

'"—lest I be depleted of potency at that moment (which might occur in any interval, even, I assumed, in my own bedroom) when I should encounter one of the free souls. I was borne back again and again to the fetid viscosities of the Inlet, borne there as if on the rising stink of my own enduring and tedious putrefaction, the idea of which I could no longer shake off – I envisaged my soul as trapped in my last granule, and that last granule itself perhaps petrified, never to dissolve, and my soul condemned to minister to it throughout eternity! It seemed to me my soul must be released at once or be lost to sweet air forever. In a gleamless dark, struggling with this singular panic, I stumbled from ditch to ditch, strained like a blind dog for the support of solid verticality; and smacked my palm against bark. I looked up and in the black could not fathom the size of the tree – my head lolled forward, my brow met the trunk with all its gravings. I busied my fingers in the interstices of the bark's cuneiform. Then with forehead flat on the tree, I embraced it with both arms to measure it. My hands united on the other side. It was a young narrow weed, I did not know of what family. I reached to the lowest branch and plucked a leaf and made my tongue travel meditatively along its periphery to assess its shape: oak. The taste was sticky and exaltingly bitter. A jubilation lightly carpeted my groin. I then placed one hand (the other I kept around the tree's waist, as it were) in the bifurcation (disgustingly termed crotch) of that lowest limb and the elegant and devoutly firm torso, and caressed that miraculous juncture with a certain languor, which gradually changed to vigour. I was all at once savagely alert and deeply daring: I chose that single tree together with the ground near it for an enemy which in two senses would not yield: it would neither give nor give in. 'Come, come,' I called aloud to Nature. A wind blew out a braid of excremental malodour into the heated air. 'Come,' I called, 'couple with me, as thou didst with Cadmus, Rhoecus, Tithonus, Endymion, and that king Numa Pompilius to whom thou didst give secrets. As Lilith comes without a sign, so come thou. As the sons of God came to copulate with women, so now let a daughter of Shekhina the Emanation reveal herself to me. Nymph, come now, come now.'

"'Without warning I was flung to the ground. My face smashed into earth, and a flaky clump of dirt lodged in my open mouth. For the rest, I was on my knees, pressing down on my hands, with the fingernails clutching dirt. A superb ache lined my haunch. I began to weep because I was certain I had been ravished by some sinewy animal. I vomited the earth I had swallowed and believed I was defiled, as it is written: 'Neither

shalt thou lie with any beast.' I lay sunk in the grass, afraid to lift my head to see if the animal still lurked. Through some curious means I had been fully positioned and aroused and exquisitely sated, all in half a second, in a fashion impossible to explain, in which, though I performed as with my own wife, I felt as if a preternatural rapine had been committed upon me. I continued prone, listening for the animal's breathing. Meanwhile, though every tissue of my flesh was gratified in its inmost awareness, a marvellous voluptuousness did not leave my body; sensual exultations of a wholly supreme and paradisal order, unlike anything our poets have ever defined, both flared and were intensely satisfied in the same moment. This salubrious and delightful perceptiveness excited my being for some time: a conjoining not dissimilar (in metaphor only; in actuality it cannot be described) from the magical contradiction of the tree and its issuance-of-branch at the point of bifurcation. In me were linked, *in the same instant*, appetite and fulfilment, delicacy and power, mastery and submissiveness, and other paradoxes of entirely remarkable emotional import.

'"Then I heard what I took to be the animal treading through the grass quite near my head, all cunningly; it withheld its breathing, then snored it out in a cautious and wisp-like whirr that resembled a light wind through rushes. With a huge energy (my muscular force seemed to have increased) I leaped up in fear of my life; I had nothing to use for a weapon but – oh, laughable! – the pen I had been writing with in a little notebook I always carried about with me in those days (and still keep on my person as a self-shaming souvenir of my insipidness, my bookishness, my pitiable conjecture and wishfulness in a time when, not yet knowing thee, I knew nothing). What I saw was not an animal but a girl no older than my oldest daughter, who was then fourteen. Her skin was as perfect as an eggplant's and nearly of that colour. In height she was half as tall as I was. The second and third fingers of her hands – this I noticed at once – were peculiarly fused, one slotted into the other, like the ligula of a leaf. She was entirely bald and had no ears but rather a type of gill or envelope, one only, on the left side. Her toes displayed the same oddity I had observed in her fingers. She was neither naked nor clothed – that is to say, even though a part of her body, from hip to just below the breasts (each of which appeared to be a kind of velvety colourless pear, suspended from a very short, almost invisible stem), was luxuriantly covered with a flossy or spore-like material, this was a natural efflorescence in the manner of, with us, hair. All her sexual portion was

wholly visible, as in any field flower. Aside from these express deviations, she was commandingly human in aspect, if unmistakably flowerlike. She was, in fact, the reverse of our hackneyed euphuism, as when we say a young girl blooms like a flower – she, on the contrary, seemed a flower transfigured into the shape of the most stupendously lovely child I had ever seen. Under the smallest push of wind she bent at her superlative waist; this, I recognized, and not the exhalations of some lecherous beast, was the breathlike sound that had alarmed me at her approach: these motions of hers made the blades of grass collide. (She herself, having no lungs, did not 'breathe'.) She stood bobbing joyfully before me, with a face as tender as a morning-glory, strangely phosphorescent: she shed her own light, in effect, and I had no difficulty in confronting her beauty.

'"Moreover, by experiment I soon learned that she was not only capable of language, but that she delighted in playing with it. This she literally could do – if I had distinguished her hands before anything else, it was because she had held them out to catch my first cry of awe. She either caught my words like balls or let them roll, or caught them and then darted off to throw them into the Inlet. I discovered that whenever I spoke I more or less pelted her; but she liked this, and told me ordinary human speech only tickled and amused, whereas laughter, being highly plosive, was something of an assault. I then took care to pretend much solemnity, though I was lightheaded with rapture. Her own 'voice' I apprehended rather than heard – which she, unable to imagine how we human ones are prisoned in sensory perception, found hard to conceive. Her sentences came to me not as a series of differentiated frequencies but (impossible to develop this idea in language) as a diffused cloud of field fragrances; yet to say that I assimilated her thought through the olfactory nerve would be a pedestrian distortion. All the same it was clear that whatever she said reached me in a shimmer of pellucid perfumes, and I understood her meaning with an immediacy of glee and with none of the ambiguities and suspiciousness of motive that surround our human communication.

'"Through this medium she explained that she was a dryad and that her name was Iripomoňoéià (as nearly as I can render it in our narrowly limited orthography, and in this dunce's alphabet of ours which is notoriously impervious to odoriferous categories). She told me what I had already seized: that she had given me her love in response to my call.

'"'Wilt thou come to any man who calls?' I asked.

'"'All men call, whether realizing it or not. I and my sisters sometimes come to those who do not realize. Almost never, unless for sport, do we come to that man who calls knowingly – he wishes only to inhabit us out of perversity or boastfulness or to indulge a dreamed-of disgust.'

""Scripture does not forbid sodomy with the plants,' I exclaimed, but she did not comprehend any of this and lowered her hands so that my words would fly past her uncaught. 'I too called thee knowingly, not for perversity but for love of Nature.'

""I have caught men's words before as they talked of Nature, you are not the first. It is not Nature they love so much as Death they fear. So Coryĺyĺyb my cousin received it in a season not long ago coupling in a harbour with one of your kind, one called Spinoza, one that had catarrh of the lung. I am of Nature and immortal and so I cannot pity your deaths. But return tomorrow and say Iripomoňoéià.' Then she chased my last word to where she had kicked it, behind the tree. She did not come back. I ran to the tree and circled it diligently but she was lost for that night.

"'Loveliness, all the foregoing, telling of my life and meditations until now, I have never before recounted to thee or any other. The rest is beyond mean telling: those rejoicings from midnight to dawn, when the greater phosphorescence of the whole shouting sky frightened thee home! How in a trance of happiness we coupled in the ditches, in the long grasses, behind a fountain, under a broken wall, once recklessly on the very pavement, with a bench for roof and trellis! How I was taught by natural arts to influence certain chemistries engendering explicit marvels, blisses, and transports no man has slaked himself with since Father Adam pressed out the forbidden chlorophyll of Eden! Loveliness, Loveliness, none like thee. No brow so sleek, no elbow-crook so fine, no eye so green, no waist so pliant, no limbs so pleasant and acute. None like immortal Iripomoňoéià.

"'Creature, the moon filled and starved twice, and there was still no end to the glorious archaic newness of Iripomoňoéià.

"'Then last night. Last night! I will record all with simplicity.

"'We entered a shallow ditch. In a sweet-smelling voice of extraordinary redolence – so intense in its sweetness that even the barbaric stinks and wind-lifted farts of the Inlet were overpowered by it – Iripomoňoéià inquired of me how I felt without my soul. I replied that I did not know this was my condition. 'Oh yes, your body is now an empty packet, that is why it is so light. Spring.' I sprang in air and rose effortlessly. 'You have spoiled yourself, spoiled yourself with confusions,' she complained, 'now by morning your body will be crumpled and withered and ugly, like a leaf in its sere hour, and never again after tonight will this place see you.' 'Nymph!' I roared, amazed by levitation. 'Oh, oh, that damaged,' she cried, 'you hit my eye with that noise,' and she wafted a deeper aroma, a leek-like mist, one that stung the mucous membranes. A white bruise disfigured her petally lid. I was repentant and sighed terribly for her injury. 'Beauty marred is for our kind what physical hurt is for yours,' she reproved me. 'Where you have pain, we have ugliness. Where you profane yourselves by immorality, we are profaned by ugliness. Your soul has taken leave of you and spoils our pretty game.' 'Nymph!' I whispered, 'heart, treasure, if my soul is separated how is it I am unaware?'

"'Poor man,' she answered, 'you have only to look and you will see the thing.' Her speech had now turned as acrid as an herb, and all that place reeked bitterly. 'You know I am a spirit. You know I must flash and dart. All my sisters flash and dart. Of all races we are the quickest. Our very religion is all-of-a-sudden. No one can hinder us, no one may delay us. But yesterday you undertook to detain me in your embrace, you stretched your kisses into years, you called me your treasure and your heart endlessly, your soul in its slow greed kept me close and captive, all the while knowing well how a spirit cannot stay and will not be fixed. I made to leap from you, but your obstinate soul held on until it was snatched straight from your frame and escaped with me. I saw it hurled out onto the pavement, the blue beginning of day was already seeping down, so I ran away and could say nothing until this moment.'

"'My soul is free? Free entirely? And can be seen?'

"'Free. If I could pity any living thing under the sky I would pity you for the sight of your soul. I do not like it, it conjures against me.'

"'My soul loves thee,' I urged in all my triumph, 'it is freed from the thousand-year grave!' I jumped out of the ditch like a frog, my legs had no weight; but the dryad sulked in the ground, stroking her ugly violated eye. 'Iripomoňoéià, my soul will follow thee with thankfulness into eternity.'

"'I would sooner be followed by the dirty fog. I do not like that soul of yours. It conjures against me. It denies me, it denies every spirit and all my sisters and every nereid of the harbour, it denies all our multiplicity, and all gods diversiform, it spites even Lord Pan, it is an enemy, and you, poor man, do not know your own soul. Go, look at it, there it is on the road.'

"'I scudded back and forth under the moon.

"'Nothing, only a dusty old man trudging up there.'

""'A quite ugly old man?'

""'Yes, that is all. My soul is not there.'

""'With a matted beard and great fierce eyebrows?'

""'Yes, yes, one like that is walking on the road. He is half bent over under the burden of a dusty old bag. The bag is stuffed with books – I can see their ravelled bindings sticking out.'

""'And he reads as he goes?'

""'Yes, he reads as he goes.'

""'What is it he reads?'

""'Some huge and terrifying volume, heavy as a stone.' I peered forward in the moonlight. 'A Tractate. A Tractate of the Mishnah. Its leaves are so worn they break as he turns them, but he does not turn them often because there is much matter on a single page. He is so sad! Such antique weariness broods in his face! His throat is striped from the whip. His cheeks are folded like ancient flags, he reads the Law and breathes the dust.'

""'And are there flowers on either side of the road?'

""'Incredible flowers! Of every colour! And noble shrubs like mounds of green moss! And the cricket crackling in the field. He passes indifferent through the beauty of the field. His nostrils sniff his book as if flowers lay on the clotted page, but the flowers lick his feet. His feet are bandaged, his notched toenails gore the path. His prayer shawl droops on his studious back. He reads the Law and breathes the dust and doesn't see the flowers and won't heed the cricket spitting in the field.'

""'That,' said the dryad, 'is your soul.' And was gone with all her odours.

"'My body sailed up to the road in a single hop. I alighted near the shape of the old man and demanded whether he were indeed the soul of Rabbi Isaac Kornfeld. He trembled but confessed. I asked if he intended to go with his books through the whole future without change, always with his Tractate in his hand, and he answered that he could do nothing else.

""'Nothing else! You, who I thought yearned for the earth! You, an immortal, free, and caring only to be bound to the Law!'

"'He held a dry arm fearfully before his face, and with the other arm hitched up his merciless bag on his shoulder. 'Sir,' he said, still quavering, 'didn't you wish to see me with your own eyes?'

""'I know your figure!' I shrieked. 'Haven't I seen that figure a hundred times before? On a hundred roads? It is not mine! I will not have it be mine!'

'"If you had not contrived to be rid of me, I would have stayed with you till the end. The dryad, who does not exist, lies. It was not I who clung to her but you, my body. Sir, all that has no real existence lies. In your grave beside you I would have sung you David's songs, I would have moaned Solomon's voice to your last grain of bone. But you expelled me, your ribs exile me from their fate, and I will walk here alone always, in my garden' – he scratched on his page – 'with my precious birds' – he scratched at the letters – 'and my darling trees' – he scratched at the tall side-column of commentary.

'"He was so impudent in his bravery – for I was all fleshliness and he all floppy wraith – that I seized him by the collar and shook him up and down, while the books on his back made a vast rubbing one on the other, and bits of shredding leather flew out like a rain.

'"The sound of the Law,' he said, 'is more beautiful than the crickets. The smell of the Law is more radiant than the moss. The taste of the Law exceeds clear water.'

'"At this nervy provocation – he more than any other knew my despair – I grabbed his prayer shawl by its tassels and whirled around him once or twice until I had unwrapped it from him altogether, and wound it on my own neck and in one bound came to the tree.

'"'Nymph!' I called to it. 'Spirit and saint! Iripomoňoéià, come! None like thee, no brow so sleek, no elbow-crook so fine, no eye so green, no waist so pliant, no limbs so pleasant and acute. For pity of me, come, come.'

'"'But she does not come.

'"'Loveliness, come.'

'"She does not come.

'"'Creature, see how I am coiled in the snail of this shawl as if in a leaf. I crouch to write my words. Let soul call thee lie, but body . . .

'". . . body . . .

'". . . fingers twist, knuckles dark as wood, tongue dries like grass, deeper now into silk . . .

'". . . silk of pod of shawl, knees wilt, knuckles wither, neck . . ."'

Here the letter suddenly ended.

'You see? A pagan!' said Sheindel, and kept her spiteful smile. It was thick with audacity.

'You don't pity him,' I said, watching the contempt that glittered in her teeth.

'Even now you don't see? You can't follow?'

'Pity him,' I said.

'He who takes his own life does an abomination.'

For a long moment I considered her. 'You don't pity him? You don't pity him at all?'

'Let the world pity me.'

'Goodbye,' I said to the widow.

'You won't come back?'

I gave what amounted to a little bow of regret.

'I told you you came just for Isaac! But Isaac' – I was in terror of her cough, which was unmistakably laughter – 'Isaac disappoints. "A scholar. A rabbi. A remarkable Jew!" Ha! He disappoints you?'

'He was always an astonishing man.'

'But not what you thought,' she insisted. 'An illusion.'

'Only the pitiless are illusory. Go back to that park, Rebbetzin,' I advised her.

'And what would you like me to do there? Dance around a tree and call Greek names to the weeds?'

'Your husband's soul is in that park. Consult it.' But her low derisive cough accompanied me home: whereupon I remembered her earlier words and dropped three green house plants down the toilet; after a journey of some miles through conduits they straightway entered Trilham's Inlet, where they decayed amid the civic excrement.

Envy; or, Yiddish in America

Edelshtein, an American for forty years, was a ravenous reader of novels by writers 'of' – he said this with a snarl – 'Jewish extraction'. He found them puerile, vicious, pitiable, ignorant, contemptible, above all stupid. In judging them he dug for his deepest vituperation – they were, he said, 'Amerikaner-geboren.' Spawned in America, pogroms a rumour, *mama-loshen* a stranger, history a vacuum. Also many of them were still young, and had black eyes, black hair, and red beards. A few were blue-eyed, like the *cheder-yinglach* of his youth. Schoolboys. He was certain he did not envy them, but he read them like a sickness. They were reviewed and praised, and meanwhile they were considered Jews, and knew nothing. There was even a body of Gentile writers in reaction, beginning to show familiarly whetted teeth: the Jewish Intellectual Establishment was misrepresenting American letters, colouring it with an alien dye, taking it over, and so forth. Like Berlin and Vienna in the twenties. *Judenrein ist Kulturrein* was Edelshtein's opinion. Take away the Jews and where, O so-called Western Civilization, is your literary culture?

For Edelshtein Western Civilization was a sore point. He had never been to Berlin, Vienna, Paris, or even London. He had been to Kiev, though, but only once, as a young boy. His father, a *melamed*, had travelled there on a tutoring job and had taken him along. In Kiev they lived in the cellar of a big house owned by rich Jews, the Kirilovs. They had been born Katz, but bribed an official in order to Russify their name. Every morning he and his father would go up a green staircase to the kitchen for a breakfast of coffee and stale bread and then into the schoolroom to teach *chumash* to Alexei Kirilov, a red-cheeked little boy.

The younger Edelshtein would drill him while his father dozed. What had become of Alexei Kirilov? Edelshtein, a widower in New York, sixty-seven years old, a Yiddishist (so-called), a poet, could stare at anything at all – a subway car-card, a garbage can lid, a streetlight – and cause the return of Alexei Kirilov's face, his bright cheeks, his Ukraine-accented Yiddish, his shelves of mechanical toys from Germany – trucks, cranes, wheelbarrows, little coloured autos with awnings overhead. Only Edelshtein's father was expected to call him Alexei – everyone else, including the young Edelshtein, said Avremeleh. Avremeleh had a knack of getting things by heart. He had a golden head. Today he was a citizen of the Soviet Union. Or was he finished, dead, in the ravine at Babi Yar? Edelshtein remembered every coveted screw of the German toys. With his father he left Kiev in the spring and returned to Minsk. The mud, frozen into peaks, was melting. The train carriage reeked of urine and the dirt seeped through their shoelaces into their socks.

And the language was lost, murdered. The language – a museum. Of what other language can it be said that it died a sudden and definite death, in a given decade, on a given piece of soil? Where are the speakers of ancient Etruscan? Who was the last man to write a poem in Linear B? Attrition, assimilation. Death by mystery not gas. The last Etruscan walks around inside some Sicilian. Western Civilization, that pod of muck, lingers on and on. The Sick Man of Europe with his big globe-head, rotting, but at home in bed. Yiddish, a littleness, a tiny light – oh little holy light! – dead, vanished. Perished. Sent into darkness.

This was Edelshtein's subject. On this subject he lectured for a living. He swallowed scraps. Synagogues, community centres, labour unions underpaid him to suck on the bones of the dead. Smoke. He travelled from borough to borough, suburb to suburb, mourning in English the death of Yiddish. Sometimes he tried to read one or two of his poems. At the first Yiddish word the painted old ladies of the Reform Temples would begin to titter from shame, as at a stand-up television comedian. Orthodox and Conservative men fell instantly asleep. So he reconsidered, and told jokes:

Before the war there was held a great International Esperanto Convention. It met in Geneva. Esperanto scholars, doctors of letters, learned men, came from all over the world to deliver papers on the genesis, syntax, and functionalism of Esperanto. Some spoke of the social value of an international language, others of its beauty. Every nation on earth was represented among the lecturers. All the papers were given in Esperanto. Finally the meeting was concluded, and the tired great men wandered companionably along the corridors, where at last they began to converse casually among themselves in their international language: '*Nu, vos macht a yid?*'

After the war a funeral cortège was moving slowly down a narrow street on the Lower East Side. The cars had left the parking lot behind the chapel in the Bronx and were on their way to the cemetery in Staten Island. Their route took them past the newspaper offices of the last Yiddish daily left in the city. There were two editors, one to run the papers off the press and the other to look out the window. The one looking out the window saw the funeral procession passing by and called to his colleague: 'Hey Mottel, print one less!'

But both Edelshtein and his audiences found the jokes worthless. Old jokes. They were not the right kind. They wanted jokes about weddings – spiral staircases, doves flying out of cages, bashful medical students – and he gave them funerals. To speak of Yiddish was to preside over a funeral. He was a rabbi who had survived his whole congregation. Those for whom his tongue was no riddle were spectres.

The new Temples scared Edelshtein. He was afraid to use the word *shul* in these palaces – inside, vast mock-bronze Tablets, mobiles of outstretched hands rotating on a motor, gigantic dangling Tetragrammatons in transparent plastic like chandeliers, platforms, altars, daises, pulpits, aisles, pews, polished-oak bins for prayerbooks printed in English with made-up new prayers in them. Everything smelled of wet plaster. Everything was new. The refreshment tables were long and luminous – he saw glazed cakes, snowheaps of egg salad, herring, salmon, tuna, whitefish, gefilte fish, pools of sour cream, silver electric coffee urns, bowls of lemon-slices, pyramids of bread, waferlike teacups from the Black Forest, Indian-brass trays of hard cheeses, golden bottles set up in rows like ninepins, great sculptured butter-birds, Hansel-and-Gretel houses of cream cheese and fruitcake, bars, butlers, fat napery, carpeting deep as honey. He learned their term for their architecture: 'soaring'. In one place – a flat wall of beige brick in Westchester – he read Scripture riveted on in letters fashioned from 14-carat gold moulds: 'And thou shalt see My back; but My face shall not be seen.' Later that night he spoke in Mount Vernon, and in the marble lobby afterwards he heard an

adolescent girl mimic his inflections. It amazed him: often he forgot he
had an accent. In the train going back to Manhattan he slid into a
miniature jogging doze – it was a little nest of sweetness there inside the
flaps of his overcoat, and he dreamed he was in Kiev, with his father. He
looked through the open schoolroom door at the smoking cheeks of
Alexei Kirilov, eight years old. 'Avremeleh,' he called, 'Avremeleh, *kum
tsu mir, lebst ts' geshtorben?*' He heard himself yelling in English: Thou
shalt see my asshole! A belch woke him to hot fear. He was afraid he
might be, unknown to himself all his life long, a secret pederast.

He had no children and only a few remote relations (a druggist cousin
in White Plains, a cleaning store in-law hanging on somewhere among
the blacks in Brownsville), so he loitered often in Baumzweig's apartment
– dirty mirrors and rusting crystal, a hazard and invitation to cracks, an
abandoned exhausted corridor. Lives had passed through it and were
gone. Watching Baumzweig and his wife – grey-eyed, sluggish, with a
plump Polish nose – it came to him that at this age, his own and theirs, it
was the same having children or not having them. Baumzweig had two
sons, one married and a professor at San Diego, the other at Stanford, not
yet thirty, in love with his car. The San Diego son had a son. Sometimes
it seemed that it must be in deference to his childlessness that
Baumzweig and his wife pretended a detachment from their offspring.
The grandson's photo – a fat-lipped blond child of three or so – was
wedged between two wine glasses on top of the china closet. But then it
became plain that they could not imagine the lives of their children. Nor
could the children imagine their lives. The parents were too helpless to
explain, the sons were too impatient to explain. So they had given each
other up to a common muteness. In that apartment Josh and Mickey had
grown up answering in English the Yiddish of their parents. Mutes.
Mutations. What right had these boys to spit out the Yiddish that had
bred them, and only for the sake of Western Civilization? Edelshtein
knew the titles of their Ph.D. theses: literary boys, one was on Sir
Gawain and the Green Knight, the other was on the novels of Carson
McCullers.

Baumzweig's lethargic wife was intelligent. She told Edelshtein he too
had a child, also a son. 'Yourself, yourself,' she said. 'You remember
yourself when you were a little boy, and *that* little boy is the one you love,
him you trust, *him* you bless, *him* you bring up in hope to a good
manhood.' She spoke a rich Yiddish, but high-pitched.

Baumzweig had a good job, a sinecure, a pension in disguise, with an office, a part-time secretary, a typewriter with Hebrew characters, ten-to-three hours. In 1910 a laxative manufacturer – a philanthropist – had founded an organization called the Yiddish-American Alliance for Letters and Social Progress. The original illustrious members were all dead – even the famous poet Yehoash was said to have paid dues for a month or so – but there was a trust providing for the group's continuation, and enough money to pay for a biannual periodical in Yiddish. Baumzweig was the editor of this, but of the Alliance nothing was left, only some crumbling brown snapshots of Jews in derbies. His salary cheque came from the laxative manufacturer's grandson – a Republican politician, an Episcopalian. The name of the celebrated product was LUKEWARM: it was advertised as delightful to children when dissolved in lukewarm cocoa. The name of the obscure periodical was *Bitterer Yam*, Bitter Sea, but it had so few subscribers that Baumzweig's wife called it Invisible Ink. In it Baumzweig published much of his own poetry and a little of Edelshtein's. Baumzweig wrote mostly of Death, Edelshtein mostly of Love. They were both sentimentalists, but not about each other. They did not like each other, though they were close friends.

Sometimes they read aloud among the dust of empty bowls their newest poems, with an agreement beforehand not to criticize: Paula should be the critic. Carrying coffee back and forth in cloudy glasses, Baumzweig's wife said: 'Oh, very nice, very nice. But so sad. Gentlemen, life is not that sad.' After this she would always kiss Edelshtein on the forehead, a lazy kiss, often leaving stuck on his eyebrow a crumb of Danish: very slightly she was a slattern.

Edelshtein's friendship with Baumzweig had a ferocious secret: it was moored entirely to their agreed hatred for the man they called *der chazer*. He was named Pig because of his extraordinarily white skin, like a tissue of pale ham, and also because in the last decade he had become unbelievably famous. When they did not call him Pig they called him *shed* – Devil. They also called him Yankee Doodle. His name was Yankel Ostrover, and he was a writer of stories.

They hated him for the amazing thing that had happened to him – his fame – but this they never referred to. Instead they discussed his style: his Yiddish was impure, his sentences lacked grace and sweep, his paragraph transitions were amateur, vile. Or else they raged against his subject matter, which was insanely sexual, pornographic, paranoid, freakish – men who embraced men, women who caressed women, sodomists of every variety, boys copulating with hens, butchers who drank blood for strength behind the knife. All the stories were set in an imaginary Polish village, Zwrdl, and by now there was almost no American literary intellectual alive who had not learned to say Zwrdl when he meant lewd. Ostrover's wife was reputed to be a high-born Polish Gentile woman from the 'real' Zwrdl, the daughter in fact of a minor princeling, who did not know a word of Yiddish and read her husband's fiction falteringly, in English translation – but both Edelshtein and Baumzweig had encountered her often enough over the years, at this meeting and that, and regarded her as no more impressive than a pot of stale fish. Her Yiddish had an unpleasant gargling Galician accent, her vocabulary was a thin soup – they joked that it was correct to say she spoke no Yiddish – and she mewed it like a peasant, comparing prices. She was a short square woman, a cube with low-slung udders and a flat backside. It was partly Ostrover's mockery, partly his self-advertising, that had converted her into a little princess. He would make her go into their bedroom to get a whip he claimed she had used on her bay, Romeo, trotting over her father's lands in her girlhood. Baumzweig often said this same whip was applied to the earlobes of Ostrover's translators, unhappy pairs of collaborators he changed from month to month, never satisfied.

Ostrover's glory was exactly in this: that he required translators. Though he wrote only in Yiddish, his fame was American, national, international. They considered him a 'modern'. Ostrover was free of the prison of Yiddish! Out, out – he had burst out, he was in the world of reality.

And how had he begun? The same as anybody, a columnist for one of the Yiddish dailies, a humorist, a cheap fast article-writer, a squeezer-out of real-life tales. Like anybody else, he saved up a few dollars, put a paper clip over his stories, and hired a Yiddish press to print up a hundred copies. A book. Twenty-five copies he gave to people he counted as relatives, another twenty-five he sent to enemies and rivals, the rest he kept under his bed in the original cartons. Like anybody else, his literary gods were Chekhov and Tolstoy, Peretz and Sholem Aleichem. From this, how did he come to *The New Yorker*, to *Playboy*, to big lecture fees, invitations to Yale and MIT and Vassar, to the Midwest, to Buenos Aires, to a literary agent, to a publisher on Madison Avenue?

'He sleeps with the right translators,' Paula said. Edelshtein gave out a whinny. He knew some of Ostrover's translators – a spinster hack in dresses below the knee, occasionally a certain half-mad and drunken lexicographer, college boys with a dictionary.

Thirty years ago, straight out of Poland via Tel Aviv, Ostrover crept into a toying affair with Mireleh, Edelshtein's wife. He had left Palestine during the 1939 Arab riots, not, he said, out of fear, out of integrity rather – it was a country which had turned its face against Yiddish. Yiddish was not honoured in Tel Aviv or Jerusalem. In the Negev it was worthless. In the God-given State of Israel they had no use for the language of the bad little interval between Canaan and now. Yiddish was inhabited by the past, the new Jews did not want it. Mireleh liked to hear these anecdotes of how rotten it was in Israel for Yiddish and Yiddishists. In Israel the case was even lamer than in New York, thank God! There was after all a reason to live the life they lived: it was worse somewhere else. Mireleh was a tragedian. She carried herself according to her impression of how a barren woman should sit, squat, stand, eat and sleep, talked constantly of her six miscarriages, and was vindictive about Edelshtein's sperm-count. Ostrover would arrive in the rain, crunch down on the sofa, complain about the transportation from the Bronx to the West Side, and begin to woo Mireleh. He took her out to supper, to his special café, to Second Avenue vaudeville, even home to his apartment near Crotona Park to meet his little princess Pesha. Edelshtein noticed with self-curiosity that he felt no jealousy whatever, but he thought himself obliged to throw a kitchen chair at Ostrover. Ostrover had very fine teeth, his own; the chair knocked off half a lateral incisor, and Edelshtein wept at the flaw. Immediately he led Ostrover to the dentist around the corner.

The two wives, Mireleh and Pesha, seemed to be falling in love: they had dates, they went to museums and movies together, they poked one another and laughed day and night, they shared little privacies, they carried pencil-box rulers in their purses and showed each other certain hilarious measurements, they even became pregnant in the same month. Pesha had her third daughter, Mireleh her seventh miscarriage. Edelshtein was griefstricken but elated. '*My* sperm-count?' he screamed. '*Your* belly! Go fix the machine before you blame the oil!' When the dentist's bill came for Ostrover's jacket crown, Edelshtein sent it to Ostrover. At this injustice Ostrover dismissed Mireleh and forbade Pesha to go anywhere with her ever again.

About Mireleh's affair with Ostrover Edelshtein wrote the following malediction:

> *You, why do you snuff out my sons, my daughters?*
> *Worse than Mother Eve, cursed to break waters*

for little ones to float out upon in their tiny barks of skin,
you, merciless one, cannot even bear the fruit of sin.

It was published to much gossip in *Bitterer Yam* in the spring of that year – one point at issue being whether 'snuff out' was the right term in such a watery context. (Baumzweig, a less oblique stylist, had suggested 'drown'.) The late Zimmerman, Edelshtein's cruellest rival, wrote in a letter to Baumzweig (which Baumzweig read on the telephone to Edelshtein):

> Who is the merciless one, after all, the barren woman who makes the house peaceful with no infantile caterwauling, or the excessively fertile poet who bears the fruit of his sin – namely his untalented verses? He bears it, but who can bear it? In one breath he runs from seas to trees. Like his ancestors the amphibians, puffed up with arrogance. Hersheleh Frog! Why did God give Hersheleh Edelshtein an unfaithful wife? To punish him for writing trash.

Around the same time Ostrover wrote a story: two women loved each other so much they mourned because they could not give birth to one another's children. Both had husbands, one virile and hearty, the other impotent, with a withered organ, a *shlimazal*. They seized the idea of making a tool out of one of the husbands: they agreed to transfer their love for each other into the man, and bear the child of their love through him. So both women turned to the virile husband, and both women conceived. But the woman who had the withered husband could not bear her child: it withered in her womb. 'As it is written,' Ostrover concluded, 'Paradise is only for those who have already been there.'

A stupid fable! Three decades later – Mireleh dead of a cancerous uterus, Pesha encrusted with royal lies in *Time* magazine (which photographed the whip) – this piece of insignificant mystification, this *pollution*, included also in Ostrover's *Complete Tales* (Kimmel & Segal, 1968), was the subject of graduate dissertations in comparative literature, as if Ostrover were Thomas Mann, or even Albert Camus. When all that happened was that Pesha and Mireleh had gone to the movies together now and then – and such a long time ago! All the same, Ostrover was released from the dungeon of the dailies, from *Bitterer Yam* and even seedier nullities, he was free, the outside world knew his name. And why Ostrover? Why not somebody else? Was Ostrover more gifted than

Komorsky? Did he think up better stories than Horowitz? Why does the world outside pick on an Ostrover instead of an Edelshtein or even a Baumzweig? What occult knack, what craft, what crooked convergence of planets drove translators to grovel before Ostrover's naked swollen sentences with their thin little threadbare pants always pulled down? Who had discovered that Ostrover was a 'modern'? His Yiddish, however fevered on itself, bloated, was still Yiddish, it was still *mamaloshen*, it still squeaked up to God with a littleness, a familiarity, an elbow-poke, it was still pieced together out of *shtetl* rags, out of a baby *aleph*, a toddler *beys* – so why Ostrover? Why only Ostrover? Ostrover should be the only one? Everyone else sentenced to darkness, Ostrover alone saved? Ostrover the survivor? As if hidden in the Dutch attic like that child. *His* diary, so to speak, the only documentation of what was. Like Ringelblum of Warsaw. Ostrover was to be the only evidence that there was once a Yiddish tongue, a Yiddish literature? And all the others lost? Lost! Drowned. Snuffed out. Under the earth. As if never.

Edelshtein composed a letter to Ostrover's publishers:

Kimmel & Segal
244 Madison Avenue, New York City

My dear Mr Kimmel, and very honoured Mr Segal:

I am writing to you in reference to one Y. Ostrover, whose works you are the company that places them before the public's eyes. Be kindly enough to forgive all flaws of English Expression. Undoubtedly, in the course of his business with you, you have received from Y. Ostrover, letters in English, even worse than this. (I HAVE NO TRANSLATOR!) We immigrants, no matter how long already Yankified, stay inside always green and never attain to actual native writing Smoothness. For one million green writers, one Nabokov, one Kosinski. I mention these to show my extreme familiarness with American Literature in all Contemporaneous avatars. In your language I read, let us say, wolfishly. I regard myself as a very Keen critic, esp. concerning so-called Amer.-Jewish writers. If you would give time I could willingly explain to you many clear opinions I have concerning these Jewish-Amer. boys and girls such as (not alphabetical) Roth Philip/ Rosen Norma/ Melammed Bernie/ Friedman B. J./ Paley Grace/ Bellow Saul/ Mailer Norman. Of the latter having just read several recent works including political I would like to remind him what F. Kafka, rest in peace, said to the German-speaking, already very comfortable, Jews of Prague, Czechoslovakia: 'Jews of Prague! You know more Yiddish than you think!'

Perhaps, since doubtless you do not read the Jewish Press, you are not informed. Only this month all were taken by surprise! In that filthy propaganda *Sovietish Heymland* which in Russia they run to show that their prisoners the Jews are not prisoners – a poem! By a 20-year-old young Russian Jewish girl! Yiddish will yet live through our young. Though I doubt it as do other pessimists. However, this is not the point! I ask you – what does the following personages mean to you, you who are Sensitive men, Intelligent, and with closely-warmed Feelings! Lyessin, Reisen, Yehoash! H. Leivik himself! Itzik Manger, Chaim Grade, Aaron Zeitlen, Jacob Glatshtein, Eliezer Greenberg! Molodow-sky and Korn, ladies, gifted! Dovid Ignatov, Morris Rosenfeld, Moishe Nadir, Moishe Leib Halpern, Reuven Eisland, Mani Leib, Zisha Landau! I ask you! Frug, Peretz, Vintchevski, Bovshover, Edelshtat! Velvl Zhbarzher, Avrom Goldfaden! A. Rosenblatt! Y. Y. Schwartz, Yoisef Rollnick! These are all our glorious Yiddish poets. And if I would add to them our beautiful recent Russian brother-poets that were killed by Stalin with his pockmarks, for instance Peretz Markish, would you know any name of theirs? No! THEY HAVE NO TRANSLATORS!

Esteemed Gentlemen, you publish only one Yiddish writer, not even a Poet, only a Story-writer. I humbly submit you give serious wrong Impressions. That we have produced nothing else. I again refer to your associate Y. Ostrover. I do not intend to take away from him any possible talent by this letter, but wish to WITH VIGOROUSNESS assure you that others also exist without notice being bothered over them! I myself am the author and also publisher of four tomes of poetry: *N'shomeh un Guf, Zingen un Freyen, A Velt ohn Vint, A Shtundeh mit Shney*. To wit, 'Soul and Body', 'Singing and Being Happy', 'A World with No Wind', 'An Hour of Snow', these are my Deep-Feeling titles.

Please inform me if you will be willing to provide me with a translator for these very worthwhile pieces of hidden writings, or, to use a Hebrew Expression, 'Buried Light'.

Yours very deeply respectful

He received an answer in the same week.

Dear Mr Edelstein:

Thank you for your interesting and informative letter. We regret that, unfortunately, we cannot furnish you with a translator. Though your poetry may well be of the quality you claim for it, practically speaking, reputation must precede translation.

Yours sincerely

A lie! Liars!

Dear Kimmel, dear Segal,

Did you, Jews without tongues, ever hear of Ostrover before you found him translated everywhere? In Yiddish he didn't exist for you! For you Yiddish has no existence! A darkness inside a cloud! Who can see it, who can hear it? The world has no ears for the prisoner! You sign yourself 'Yours'. You're not mine and I'm not Yours!

Sincerely

He then began to search in earnest for a translator. Expecting little, he wrote to the spinster hack.

Esteemed Edelshtein [she replied]:

To put it as plainly as I can – a plain woman should be as plain in her words – you do not know the world of practicality, of reality. Why should you? You're a poet, an idealist. When a big magazine pays Ostrover $500, how much do I get? Maybe $75. If he takes a rest for a month and doesn't write, what then? Since he's the only one they want to print he's the only one worth translating. Suppose I translated one of your nice little love songs? Would anyone buy it? Foolishness even to ask. And if they bought it, should I slave for the $5? You don't know what I go through with Ostrover anyhow. He sits me down in his dining room, his wife brings in a samovar of tea – did you ever hear anything as pretentious as this – and sits also, watching me. She has jealous eyes. She watches my ankles, which aren't bad. Then we begin. Ostrover reads aloud the first sentence the way he wrote it, in Yiddish. I write it down, in English. Right away it starts. Pesha reads what I put down and says, 'That's no good, you don't catch his idiom.' Idiom! She knows! Ostrover says, 'The last word sticks in my throat. Can't you do better than that? A little more robustness.' We look in the dictionary, the thesaurus, we scream out different words, trying, trying. Ostrover doesn't like any of them. Suppose the word is 'big'. We go through huge, vast, gigantic, enormous, gargantuan, monstrous, etc., etc., etc., and finally Ostrover says – by now it's five hours later, my tonsils hurt, I can hardly stand – 'all right, so let it be "big". Simplicity above all.' Day after day like this! And for $75 is it worth it? Then after this he fires me and gets himself a college boy! Or that imbecile who cracked up over the mathematics dictionary! Until he needs me. However I get a little glory out of it. Everyone says, 'There goes Ostrover's translator.' In actuality I'm his pig, his stool (I mean that in both senses, I assure you). You write that he has no talent. That's your opinion, maybe you're not wrong, but let me tell you he has a talent for pressure. The way among *them* they write careless novels, hoping they'll be transformed into beautiful movies and sometimes it happens – that's how it is with him. Never mind the quality of his Yiddish, what will it turn into when it becomes English? Transformation is all he cares for – and in English he's a cripple – like, please excuse me, yourself and everyone of your generation. But Ostrover has the sense to be a suitor. He keeps all his translators in a perpetual frenzy of envy for each other, but they're just rubble and offal to him, they aren't the object of his suit. What he woos is *them*. Them! You understand me, Edelshtein? He stands on the backs of hacks to reach. I know you call me hack, and it's all right, by myself I'm what you think me, no imagination, so-so ability (I too once wanted to be a poet, but that's another life) – with Ostrover on my back I'm something else: I'm 'Ostrover's translator'. You think that's nothing? It's an entrance into *them*. I'm invited everywhere, I go to the same parties Ostrover goes to. Everyone looks at me and thinks I'm a bit freakish, but they say: 'It's Ostrover's translator.' A marriage. Pesha, that junk-heap, is less married to Ostrover than I am. Like a wife, I have the supposedly passive role. Supposedly: who knows what goes on in the bedroom? An unmarried person like myself becomes good at guessing at these matters. The same with translation. Who makes the language Ostrover is famous for? You ask: what has persuaded *them* that he's a 'so-called modern'? – a sneer. Aha. *Who* has read James Joyce, Ostrover or I? I'm fifty-three years old. I wasn't born back of Hlusk for nothing, I didn't go to Vassar for nothing – do you understand me? I got caught in between, so I got squeezed. Between two organisms. A cultural hermaphrodite, neither one nor the other. I have a forked tongue. When I fight for five hours to make Ostrover say 'big' instead of 'gargantuan', when I take out all the nice homey commas he sprinkles like a fool, when I drink his wife's stupid tea and then go home with a watery belly – *then* he's being turned into a 'modern', you see? I'm the one! No one recognizes this, of course, they think it's something inside the stories themselves, when actually it's the way I dress them up and paint over them. It's all cosmetics, I'm a cosmetician, a painter, the one they pay to do the same job on the corpse in the mortuary, among *them* . . . don't, though, bore me with your criticisms. I tell you his Yiddish doesn't matter. Nobody's Yiddish matters. Whatever's in Yiddish doesn't matter.

The rest of the letter – all women are long-winded, strong-minded – he did not read. He had already seen what she was after: a little bit of money, a little bit of esteem. A miniature megalomaniac: she fancied herself the *real* Ostrover. She believed she had fashioned herself a genius out of a rag. A rag turned into a sack, was that genius? She lived out there in the light, with *them*: naturally she wouldn't waste her time on an Edelshtein. In the bleakness. Dark where he was. An idealist! How had this good word worked itself up in society to become an insult? A darling word nevertheless. Idealist. The difference between him and Ostrover was this: Ostrover wanted to save only himself, Edelshtein wanted to save Yiddish.

Immediately he felt he lied.

With Baumzweig and Paula he went to the 92nd Street Y to hear Ostrover read. 'Self-mortification,' Paula said of this excursion. It was a snowy night. They had to shove their teeth into the wind, tears of suffering iced down their cheeks, the streets from the subway were Siberia. 'Two Christian saints, self-flagellation,' she muttered, 'with chains of icicles they hit themselves.' They paid for the tickets with numb fingers and sat down towards the front. Edelshtein felt paralysed. His toes stung, prickled, then seemed diseased, grangrenous, furnace-like. The cocoon of his bed at home, the pen he kept on his night table, the first luminous line of his new poem lying there waiting to be born – *Oh that I might like a youth be struck with the blow of belief* – all at once he knew how to go on with it, what it was about and what he meant by it, the hall around him seemed preposterous, unnecessary, why was he here? Crowds, huddling, the whine of folding chairs lifted and dropped, the babble, Paula yawning next to him with squeezed and wrinkled eyelids, Baumzweig blowing his flat nose into a blue plaid handkerchief and exploding a great green flower of snot, why was he in such a place as this? What did such a place have in common with what he knew, what he felt?

Paula craned around her short neck inside a used-up skunk collar to read the frieze, mighty names, golden letters, Moses, Einstein, Maimonides, Heine. Heine. Maybe Heine knew what Edelshtein knew, a convert. But these, ushers in fine jackets, skinny boys carrying books (Ostrover's), wearing them nearly, costumed for blatant bookishness, blatant sexuality, in pants crotch-snug, pencilling buttocks on air, mustachioed, some hairy to the collarbone, shins and calves menacing as hammers, and girls, tunics, knees, pants, boots, little hidden sweet tongues, black-eyed. Woolly smell of piles and piles of coats. For Ostrover! The hall was full, the ushers with raised tweed wrists directed all the rest into an unseen gallery nearby: a television screen there, on which the little grey ghost of Ostrover, palpable and otherwise white as a washed pig, would soon flutter. The Y. Why? Edelshtein also lectured at Ys – Elmhurst, Eastchester, Rye, tiny platforms, lecterns too tall for him, catalogues of vexations, his sad recitations to old people. Ladies and Gentlemen, they have cut out my vocal cords, the only language I can freely and fluently address you in, my darling *mamaloshen*, surgery, dead, the operation was a success. Edelshtein's Ys were all old people's homes, convalescent factories, asylums. To himself he sang,

Why	Farvos di Vy?
the Y?	Ich reyd
Lectures	ohn freyd
to spectres,	un shey dim tantsen derbei,

aha! spectres, if my tongue has no riddle for you, Ladies and Gentlemen, you are spectre, wraith, phantom, I have invented you, you are my imagining, there is no one here at all, an empty chamber, a vacant valve, abandoned, desolate. Everyone gone. *Pust vi dem kalten shul mein harts* (another first line left without companion-lines, fellows, followers), the cold study-house, spooks dance there. Ladies and Gentlemen, if you find my tongue a riddle, here is another riddle: How is a Jew like a giraffe? A Jew too has no vocal cords. God blighted Jew and giraffe, one in full, one by half. And no salve. Baumzweig hawked up again. Mucus the sheen of the sea. In God's Creation no thing without beauty however perverse. *Khrakeh khrakeh.* Baumzweig's roar the only noise in the hall. 'Shah,' Paula said, '*ot kumt der shed.*'

Gleaming, gleaming, Ostrover stood – high, far, the stage broad, brilliant, the lectern punctilious with microphone and water pitcher. A rod of powerful light bored into his eye sockets. He had a moth-mouth as thin and dim as a chalk line, a fence of white hair erect over his ears, a cool voice.

'A new story,' he announced, and spittle flashed on his lip. 'It isn't obscene, so I consider it a failure.'

'Devil,' Paula whispered, 'washed white pig, Yankee Doodle.'

'Shah,' Baumzweig said, *'lomir heren.'*

Baumzweig wanted to hear the devil, the pig! Why should anyone want to hear him? Edelshtein, a little bit deaf, hung forward. Before him, his nose nearly in it, the hair of a young girl glistened – some of the stage light had become enmeshed in it. Young, young! Everyone young! Everyone for Ostrover young! A modern.

Cautiously, slyly, Edelshtein let out, as on a rope, little bony shiverings of attentiveness. Two rows in front of him he glimpsed the spinster hack, Chaim Vorovsky the drunken lexicographer whom too much mathematics had crazed, six unknown college boys.

Ostrover's story:

Satan appears to a bad poet. 'I desire fame,' says the poet, 'but I cannot attain it, because I come from Zwrdl, and the only language I can write is Zwrdlish. Unfortunately no one is left in the world who can read Zwrdlish. That is my burden. Give me fame, and I will trade you my soul for it.'

'Are you quite sure,' says Satan, 'that you have estimated the dimensions of your trouble entirely correctly?' 'What do you mean?' says the poet. 'Perhaps,' says Satan, 'the trouble lies in your talent. Zwrdl or no Zwrdl, it's very weak.' 'Not so!' says the poet, 'and I'll prove it to you. Teach me French, and in no time I'll be famous.' 'All right,' says Satan, 'as soon as I say Glup you'll know French perfectly, better than de Gaulle. But I'll be generous with you. French is such an easy language, I'll take only a quarter of your soul for it.'

And he said Glup. And in an instant there was the poet, scribbling away in fluent French. But still no publisher in France wanted him and he remained obscure. Back came Satan: 'So the French was no good, *mon vieux? Tant pis!*' 'Feh,' says the poet, 'what do you expect from a people that kept colonies, they should know what's good in the poetry line? Teach me Italian, after all even the Pope dreams in Italian.' 'Another quarter of your soul,' says Satan, ringing it up in his portable cash register. And Glup! There he was again, the poet, writing *terza rima* with such fluency and melancholy that the Pope would have been moved to holy tears of praise if only he had been able to see it in print – unfortunately every publisher in Italy sent the manuscript back with a plain rejection slip, no letter.

'What? Italian no good either?' exclaims Satan. '*Mamma mia*, why don't you believe me, little brother, it's not the language, it's you.' It was the same with Swahili and Armenian, Glup! – failure, Glup! – failure, and by now, having rung up a quarter of it at a time, Satan owned the poet's entire soul, and took him back with him to the Place of Fire. 'I suppose you'll burn me up,' says the poet bitterly. 'No, no,' says Satan, 'we don't go in for that sort of treatment for so silken a creature as a poet. Well? Did you bring everything? I told you to pack carefully! Not to leave behind a scrap!' 'I brought my whole file,' says the poet, and sure enough, there it was, strapped to his back, a big black metal cabinet. 'Now empty it into the Fire,' Satan orders. 'My poems! Not all my poems? My whole life's output?' cries the poet in anguish. 'That's right, do as I say,' and the poet obeys, because, after all, he's in hell and Satan owns him. 'Good,' says Satan, 'now come with me, I'll show you to your room.'

A perfect room, perfectly appointed, not too cold, not too hot, just the right distance from the great Fire to be comfortable. A jewel of a desk, with a red leather top, a lovely swivel chair cushioned in scarlet, a scarlet Persian rug on the floor, nearby a red refrigerator stocked with cheese and pudding and pickles, a glass of reddish tea already steaming on a little red table. One window without a curtain. 'That's your Inspiring View,' says Satan, 'look out and see.' Nothing outside but the Fire cavorting splendidly, flecked with unearthly colours, turning itself and rolling up into unimaginable new forms. 'It's beautiful,' marvels the poet. 'Exactly,' says Satan. 'It should inspire you to the composition of many new verses.' 'Yes, yes! May I begin, your Lordship?' 'That's why I brought you here,' says Satan. 'Now sit down and write, since you can't help it anyhow. There is only one stipulation.

The moment you finish a stanza you must throw it out of the window, like this.' And to illustrate, he tossed out a fresh page.

Instantly a flaming wind picked it up and set it afire, drawing it into the great central conflagration. 'Remember that you are in hell,' Satan says sternly, 'here you write only for oblivion.' The poet begins to weep. 'No difference, no difference! It was the same up there! O Zwrdl, I curse you that you nurtured me!' 'And still he doesn't see the point!' says Satan, exasperated. 'Glup glup glup glup glup glup glup! Now write.' The poor poet began to scribble, one poem after another, and lo! suddenly he forgot every word of Zwrdlish he ever knew, faster and faster he wrote, he held on to the pen as if it alone kept his legs from flying off on their own, he wrote in Dutch and in English, in German and in Turkish, in Santali and in Sassak, in Lapp and in Kurdish, in Welsh and in Rhaeto-Romanic, in Niasese and in Nicobarese, in Galcha and in Ibanag, in Ho and in Khmer, in Ro and in Volapük, in Jagatai and in Swedish, in Tulu and in Russian, in Irish and in Kalmuck! He wrote in every language but Zwrdlish, and every poem he wrote he had to throw out the window because it was trash anyhow, though he did not realize it. . . .

Edelshtein, spinning off into a furious and alien meditation, was not sure how the story ended. But it was brutal, and Satan was again in the ascendancy: he whipped down aspiration with one of Ostrover's sample aphorisms, dense and swollen as a phallus, but sterile all the same. The terrifying laughter, a sea-wave all around: it broke towards Edelshtein, meaning to lash him to bits. Laughter for Ostrover. Little jokes, little jokes, all they wanted was jokes! 'Baumzweig,' he said, pressing himself down across Paula's collar (under it her plump breasts), 'he does it for spite, you see that?'

But Baumzweig was caught in the laughter. The edges of his mouth were beaten by it. He whirled in it like a bug. 'Bastard!' he said.

'Bastard,' Edelshtein said reflectively.

'He means *you*,' Baumzweig said.

'Me?'

'An allegory. You see how everything fits. . . .'

'If you write letters, you shouldn't mail them,' Paula said reasonably. 'It got back to him you're looking for a translator.'

'He doesn't need a muse, he needs a butt. Naturally it got back to him,' Baumzweig said. 'That witch herself told him.'

'Why me?' Edelshtein said. 'It could be you.'

'I'm not a jealous type,' Baumzweig protested. 'What he has you want.' He waved over the audience: just then he looked as insignificant as a little bird.

Paula said, 'You both want it.'

What they both wanted now began. Homage.

Q. Mr Ostrover, what would you say is the symbolic weight of this story?

A. The symbolic weight is, what you need you deserve. If you don't need to be knocked on the head you'll never deserve it.

Q. Sir, I'm writing a paper on you for my English class. Can you tell me please if you believe in hell?

A. Not since I got rich.

Q. How about God? Do you believe in God?

A. Exactly the way I believe in pneumonia. If you have pneumonia, you have it. If you don't, you don't.

Q. Is it true your wife is a Countess? Some people say she's really only Jewish.

A. In religion she's a transvestite, and in actuality she's a Count.

Q. Is there really such a language as Zwrdlish?

A. You're speaking it right now, it's the language of fools.

Q. What would happen if you weren't translated into English?

A. The pygmies and the Eskimos would read me instead. Nowadays to be Ostrover is to be a worldwide industry.

Q. Then why don't you write about worldwide things like wars?

A. Because I'm afraid of loud noises.

Q. What do you think of the future of Yiddish?

A. What do you think of the future of the Dobermann pinscher?

Q. People say other Yiddishists envy you.

A. No, it's I who envy them. I like a quiet life.

Q. Do you keep the Sabbath?

A. Of course, didn't you notice it's gone? I keep it hidden.

Q. And the dietary laws? Do you observe them?

A. Because of the moral situation of the world I have to. I was heartbroken to learn that the minute an oyster enters my stomach, he becomes an anti-Semite. A bowl of shrimp once started a pogrom against my intestines.

Jokes, jokes! It looked to go on for another hour. The condition of fame, a Question Period: a man can stand up forever and dribble shallow quips and everyone admires him for it. Edelshtein threw up his seat with a squeal and sneaked up the aisle to the double doors and into the lobby. On a bench, half-asleep, he saw the lexicographer. Usually he avoided him – he was a man with a past, all pasts are boring – but when he saw Vorovsky raise his leathery eyelids he went towards him.

'What's new, Chaim?'

'Nothing. Liver pains. And you?'

'Life pains. I saw you inside.'

'I walked out, I hate the young.'

'You weren't young, no.'

'Not like these. I never laughed. Do you realize, at the age of twelve I had already mastered calculus? I practically reinvented it on my own. You haven't read Wittgenstein, Hersheleh, you haven't read Heisenberg, what do you know about the empire of the universe?'

Edelshtein thought to deflect him: 'Was it your translation he read in there?'

'Did it sound like mine?'

'I couldn't tell.'

'It was and it wasn't. Mine, improved. If you ask that ugly one, she'll say it's hers, improved. Who's really Ostrover's translator? Tell me, Hersheleh, maybe it's you. Nobody knows. It's as they say – by several hands, and all the hands are in Ostrover's pot, burning up. I would like to make a good strong b.m. on your friend Ostrover.'

'*My* friend? He's not my friend.'

'So why did you pay genuine money to see him? You can see him for free somewhere else, no?'

'The same applies to yourself.'

'Youth, I brought youth.'

A conversation with a madman: Vorovsky's *meshugas* was to cause other people to suspect him of normality. Edelshtein let himself slide to the bench – he felt his bones accordion downwards. He was in the grip of a mournful fatigue. Sitting eye to eye with Vorovsky he confronted the other's hat – a great Russian-style fur monster. A nimbus of droshky-bells surrounded it, shrouds of snow. Vorovsky had a big head, with big kneaded features, except for the nose, which looked like a doll's, pink and formlessly delicate. The only sign of drunkenness was at the bulbs of the nostrils, where the cartilage was swollen, and at the tip, also swollen.

Of actual madness there was, in ordinary discourse, no sign, except a tendency towards elusiveness. But it was known that Vorovsky, after compiling his dictionary, a job of seventeen years, one afternoon suddenly began to laugh, and continued laughing for six months, even in his sleep: in order to rest from laughing he had to be given sedatives, though even these could not entirely suppress his laughter. His wife died, and then his father, and he went on laughing. He lost control of his bladder, and then discovered the curative potency, for laughter, of drink. Drink cured him, but he still peed publicly, without realizing it; and even his cure was tentative and unreliable, because if he happened to hear a joke that he liked he might laugh at it for a minute or two, or, on occasion, three hours. Apparently none of Ostrover's jokes had struck home with him – he was sober and desolate-looking. Nevertheless Edelshtein noticed a large dark patch near his fly. He had wet himself, it was impossible to tell how long ago. There was no odour. Edelshtein moved his buttocks back an inch. 'Youth?' he inquired.

'My niece. Twenty-three years old, my sister Ida's girl. She reads Yiddish fluently,' he said proudly. 'She writes.'

'In Yiddish?'

'Yiddish,' he spat out. 'Don't be crazy, Hersheleh, who writes in Yiddish? Twenty-three years old, she should write in Yiddish? What is she, a refugee, an American girl like that? She's crazy for literature, that's all, she's like the rest in there, to her Ostrover's literature. I brought her, she wanted to be introduced.'

'Introduce me,' Edelshtein said craftily.

'She wants to be introduced to someone famous, where do you come in?'

'Translated I'd be famous. Listen, Chaim, a talented man like you, so many languages under your belt, why don't you give me a try? A try and a push.'

'I'm no good at poetry. You should write stories if you want fame.'

'I don't want fame.'

'Then what are you talking about?'

'I want—' Edelshtein stopped. What did he want? 'To reach,' he said.

Vorovsky did not laugh. 'I was educated at the University of Berlin. From Vilna to Berlin, that was 1924. Did I reach Berlin? I gave my whole life to collecting a history of the human mind, I mean expressed in mathematics. In mathematics the final and only poetry possible. Did I reach the empire of the universe? Hersheleh, if I could tell you about reaching, I would tell you this: reaching is impossible. Why? Because when you get where you wanted to reach to, that's when you realize that's not what you want to reach to. Do you know what a bilingual German-English mathematical dictionary is good for?'

Edelshtein covered his knees with his hands. His knuckles glimmered up at him. Row of white skulls.

'Toilet paper,' Vorovsky said. 'Do you know what poems are good for? The same. And don't call me cynic, what I say isn't cynicism.'

'Despair maybe,' Edelshtein offered.

'Despair up your ass. I'm a happy man. I know something about laughter.' He jumped up – next to the seated Edelshtein he was a giant. Fists grey, thumbnails like bone. The mob was pouring out of the doors of the auditorium. 'Something else I'll tell you. Translation is no equation. If you're looking for an equation, better die first. There are no equations, equations don't happen. It's an idea like a two-headed animal, you follow me? The last time I saw an equation it was in a snapshot of myself. I looked in my own eyes, and what did I see there? I saw God in the shape of a murderer. What you should do with your poems is swallow your tongue. There's my niece, behind Ostrover like a tail. Hey Yankel!' he boomed.

The great man did not hear. Hands, arms, heads enclosed him like a fisherman's net. Baumzweig and Paula paddled through eddies, the lobby swirled. Edelshtein saw two little people, elderly, overweight, heavily dressed. He hid himself, he wanted to be lost. Let them go, let them go—

But Paula spotted him. 'What happened? We thought you took sick.'

'It was too hot in there.'

'Come home with us, there's a bed. Instead of your own place alone.'

'Thank you no. He signs autographs, look at that.'

'Your jealousy will eat you up, Hersheleh.'

'I'm not jealous!' Edelshtein shrieked; people turned to see. 'Where's Baumzweig?'

'Shaking hands with the pig. An editor has to keep up contacts.'

'A poet has to keep down vomit.'

Paula considered him. Her chin dipped into her skunk ruff. 'How can you vomit, Hersheleh? Pure souls have no stomachs, only ectoplasm. Maybe Ostrover's right, you have too much ambition for your size. What if your dear friend Baumzweig didn't publish you? You wouldn't know your own name. My husband doesn't mention this to you, he's a kind man, but I'm not afraid of the truth. Without him you wouldn't exist.'

'With him I don't exist,' Edelshtein said. 'What is existence?'

'I'm not a Question Period,' Paula said.

'That's all right,' Edelshtein said, 'because I'm an Answer Period. The answer is period. Your husband is finished, period. Also I'm finished, period. We're already dead. Whoever uses Yiddish to keep himself alive is already dead. Either you realize this or you don't realize it. I'm one who realizes.'

'I tell him all the time he shouldn't bother with you. You come and you hang around.'

'Your house is a gallows, mine is a gas chamber, what's the difference?'

'Don't come any more, nobody needs you.'

'My philosophy exactly. We are superfluous on the face of the earth.'

'You're a scoundrel.'

'Your husband's a weasel, and you're the wife of a weasel.'

'Pig and devil yourself.'

'Mother of puppydogs.' (Paula, such a good woman, the end, he would never see her again!)

He blundered away licking his tears, hitting shoulders with his shoulder, blind with the accident of his grief. A yearning all at once shouted itself in his brain:

EDELSHTEIN: Chaim, teach me to be a drunk!

VOROVSKY: First you need to be crazy.

EDELSHTEIN: Teach me to go crazy!

VOROVSKY: First you need to fail.

EDELSHTEIN: I've failed, I'm schooled in failure, I'm a master of failure!

VOROVSKY: Go back and study some more.

One wall was a mirror. In it he saw an old man crying, dragging a striped scarf like a prayer shawl. He stood and looked at himself. He wished he had been born a Gentile. Pieces of old poems littered his nostrils, he smelled the hour of their creation, his wife in bed beside him, asleep after he had rubbed her to compensate her for bitterness. *The sky is cluttered with stars of David. . . . If everything is something else, then I am something else. . . . Am I a thing and not a bird? Does my way fork though I am one? Will God take back history? Who will let me begin again. . . .*

OSTROVER: Hersheleh, I admit I insulted you, but who will know? It's only a make-believe story, a game.

EDELSHTEIN: Literature isn't a game! Literature isn't little stories!

OSTROVER: So what is it, Torah? You scream out loud like a Jew, Edelshtein. Be quiet, they'll hear you.

EDELSHTEIN: And you, Mr Elegance, you aren't a Jew?

OSTROVER: Not at all, I'm one of *them*. You too are lured, aren't you, Hersheleh? Shakespeare is better than a shadow, Pushkin is better than a pipsqueak, hah?

EDELSHTEIN: If you become a Gentile you don't automatically become a Shakespeare.

OSTROVER: Oho! A lot you know. I'll let you in on the facts, Hersheleh, because I feel we're really brothers, I feel you straining towards the core of the world. Now listen – did you ever hear of Velvl Shikkerparev? Never. A Yiddish scribbler writing romances for the Yiddish stage in the East End, I'm speaking of London, England. He finds a translator and overnight he becomes Willie Shakespeare. . . .

EDELSHTEIN: Jokes aside, is this what you advise?

OSTROVER: I would advise my own father no less. Give it up, Hersheleh, stop believing in Yiddish.

EDELSHTEIN: But I don't believe in it!

OSTROVER: You do. I see you do. It's no use talking to you, you won't let go. Tell me, Edelshtein, what language does Moses speak in the world-to-come?

EDELSHTEIN: From babyhood I know this. Hebrew on the Sabbath, on weekdays Yiddish.

OSTROVER: Lost soul, don't make Yiddish into the Sabbath-tongue! If you believe in holiness, you're finished. Holiness is for make-believe.

EDELSHTEIN: I want to be a Gentile like you!

OSTROVER: I'm only a make-believe Gentile. This means that I play at being a Jew to satisfy them. In my village when I was a boy they used to bring in a dancing bear for the carnival, and everyone said, 'It's human!' – They said this because they knew it was a bear, though it stood on two legs and waltzed. But it was a bear.

Baumzweig came to him then. 'Paula and her temper. Never mind, Hersheleh, come and say hello to the big celebrity, what can you lose?' He went docilely, shook hands with Ostrover, even complimented him on his story. Ostrover was courtly, wiped his lip, let ooze a drop of ink from a slow pen, and continued autographing books. Vorovsky lingered humbly at the rim of Ostrover's circle: his head was fierce, his eyes timid;

he was steering a girl by the elbow, but the girl was mooning over an open flyleaf; where Ostrover had written his name. Edelshtein, catching a flash of letters, was startled: it was the Yiddish version she held.

'Excuse me,' he said.

'My niece,' Vorovsky said.

'I see you read Yiddish,' Edelshtein addressed her. 'In your generation a miracle.'

'Hannah, before you stands H. Edelshtein the poet.'

'Edelshtein?'

'Yes.'

She recited, *'Little fathers, little uncles, you with your beards and glasses and curly hair. . . .'*

Edelshtein shut his lids and again wept.

'If it's the same Edelshtein?'

'The same,' he croaked.

'My grandfather used to do that one all the time. It was in a book he had, *A Velt ohn Vint*. But it's not possible.'

'Not possible?'

'That you're still alive.'

'You're right, you're right,' Edelshtein said, struck. 'We're all ghosts here.'

'My grandfather's dead.'

'Forgive him.'

'He used to read you! And he was an old man, he died years ago, and you're still alive—'

'I'm sorry,' Edelshtein said. 'Maybe, I was young then, I began young.'

'Why do you say ghosts? Ostrover's no ghost.'

'No, no,' he agreed. He was afraid to offend. 'Listen, I'll say the rest for you. I'll take a minute only, I promise. Listen, see if you can remember from your grandfather—'

Around him, behind him, in front of him Ostrover, Vorovsky, Baumzweig, perfumed ladies, students, the young, the young, he clawed at his wet face and declaimed, he stood like a wanton stalk in the heart of an empty field:

> *How you spring out of the ground covered with poverty!*
> *In your long coats, fingers rolling wax, tallow eyes.*
> *How can I speak to you, little fathers?*
> *You who nestled me with lyu, lyu, lyu,*

lip-lullaby. Jabber of blue-eyed sailors,
how am I fallen into a stranger's womb?

Take me back with you, history has left me out.
You belong to the Angel of Death,
I to you.
Braided wraiths, smoke,
let me fall into your graves,
I have no business being your future.

He gargled, breathed, coughed, choked, tears invaded some false channel in his throat – meanwhile he swallowed up with the seizure of each bawled word this niece, this Hannah, like the rest, boots, rough full hair, a forehead made on a Jewish last, chink eyes—

At the edge of the village a little river.
Herons tip into it pecking at their images
when the waders pass whistling like Gentiles.
The herons hang, hammocks above the sweet summer-water.
Their skulls are full of secrets, their feathers scented.
The village is so little it fits into my nostril.
The roofs shimmer tar,
the sun licks thick as cow.
No one knows what will come.
How crowded with mushrooms the forest's dark floor.

Into his ear Paula said, 'Hersheleh, I apologize, come home with us, please, please, I apologize.' Edelshtein gave her a push, he intended to finish. '*Littleness*,' he screamed,

I speak to you.
We are such a little huddle.
Our little hovels, our grandfathers' hard hands, how little,
our little, little words,
this lullaby
sung at the lip of your grave,

he screamed.

Baumzweig said, 'That's one of your old good ones, the best.'

'The one on my table, in progress, is the best,' Edelshtein screamed, clamour still high over his head; but he felt soft, rested, calm; he knew how patient.

Ostrover said, 'That one you shouldn't throw out the window.'

Vorovsky began to laugh.

'This is the dead man's poem, now you know it,' Edelshtein said, looking all around, pulling at his shawl, pulling and pulling at it: this too made Vorovsky laugh.

'Hannah, better take home your uncle Chaim,' Ostrover said: handsome, all white, a public genius, a feather.

Edelshtein discovered he was cheated, he had not examined the girl sufficiently.

He slept in the sons' room – bunk beds piled on each other. The top one was crowded with Paula's storage boxes. He rolled back and forth on the bottom, dreaming, jerking awake, again dreaming. Now and then, with a vomitous taste, he belched up the hot cocoa Paula had given him for reconciliation. Between the Baumzweigs and himself a private violence: lacking him, whom would they patronize? They were moralists, they needed someone to feel guilty over. Another belch. He abandoned his fine but uninnocent dream – young, he was kissing Alexei's cheeks like ripe peaches, he drew away . . . it was not Alexei, it was a girl, Vorovsky's niece. After the kiss she slowly tore the pages of a book until it snowed paper, black bits of alphabet, white bits of empty margin. Paula's snore travelled down the hall to him. He writhed out of bed and groped for a lamp. With it he lit up a decrepit table covered with ancient fragile model aeroplanes. Some had rubber-band propellers, some were papered over a skeleton of balsa-wood ribs. A game of Monopoly lay under a samite tissue of dust. His hand fell on two old envelopes, one already browning, and without hesitation he pulled the letters out and read them:

Today was two special holidays in one, Camp Day and Sacco and Vanzetti Day. We had to put on white shirts and white shorts and go to the casino to hear Chaver Rosenbloom talk about Sacco and Vanzetti. They were a couple of Italians who were killed for loving the poor. Chaver Rosenbloom cried, and so did Mickey but I didn't. Mickey keeps forgetting to wipe himself in the toilet but I make him.

Paula and Ben: thanks so much for the little knitted suit and the clown rattle. The box was a bit smashed in but the rattle came safe anyhow.

Stevie will look adorable in his new blue suit when he gets big enough for it. He already seems to like the duck on the collar. It will keep him good and warm too. Josh has been working very hard these days preparing for a course in the American Novel and asks me to tell you he'll write as soon as he can. We all send love, and Stevie sends a kiss for Grandma and Pa. *P.S.* Mickey drove down in a pink Mercedes last week. We all had quite a chat and told him he should settle down!

Heroes, martyrdom, a baby. Hatred for these letters made his eyelids quiver. Ordinariness. Everything a routine. Whatever man touches becomes banal like man. Animals don't contaminate nature. Only man the corrupter, the anti-divinity. All other species live within the pulse of nature. He despised these ceremonies and rattles and turds and kisses. The pointlessness of their babies. Wipe one generation's ass for the sake of wiping another generation's ass: this was his whole definition of civilization. He pushed back the aeroplanes, cleared a front patch of table with his elbow, found his pen, wrote:

Dear Niece of Vorovsky:

It is very strange to me to feel I become a Smasher, I who was born to being humane and filled with love for our darling Human Race.

But nausea for his shadowy English, which he pursued in dread, passion, bewilderment, feebleness, overcame him. He started again in his own tongue—

Unknown Hannah:

I am a man writing you in a room of the house of another man. He and I are secret enemies, so under his roof it is difficult to write the truth. Yet I swear to you I will speak these words with my heart's whole honesty. I do not remember either your face or your body. Vaguely your angry voice. To me you are an abstraction. I ask whether the ancients had any physical representation of the Future, a goddess Futura, so to speak. Presumably she would have blank eyes, like Justice. It is an incarnation of the Future to whom this letter is addressed. Writing to the Future one does not expect an answer. The Future is an oracle for whose voice one cannot wait in inaction. One must do to be. Although a Nihilist, not by choice but by conviction, I discover in myself an unwillingness to despise survival. Often I have spat on myself for having survived the death-camps – survived them drinking tea in New York! – but today when I heard carried on your tongue some old syllables of mine I was again wheedled into tolerance of survival. The sound of a dead language on a live girl's tongue! That baby should follow baby is God's trick on us, but surely we too can have a trick on God? If we fabricate with our syllables an immortality passed from the spines of the old to the shoulders of the young, even God cannot spite it. If the prayer-load that spilled upwards from the mass graves should somehow survive! If not the thicket of lamentation itself, then the language on which it rode. Hannah, youth itself is nothing unless it keeps its promise to grow old. Grow old in Yiddish, Hannah, and carry fathers and uncles into the future with you. Do this. You, one in ten thousand maybe, who were born with the gift of Yiddish in your mouth, the alphabet of Yiddish in your palm, don't make ash of these! A little while ago there were twelve million people – not including babies – who lived inside this tongue, and now what is left? A language that never had a territory except Jewish mouths, and half the Jewish mouths on earth already stopped up with German worms. The rest jabber Russian, English, Spanish, God knows what. Fifty years ago my mother lived in Russia and spoke only broken Russian, but her Yiddish was like silk. In Israel they give the language of Solomon to machinists. Rejoice – in Solomon's time what else did the mechanics speak? Yet whoever forgets Yiddish courts amnesia of history. Mourn – the forgetting has already happened. A thousand years of our travail forgotten. Here and there a word left for vaudeville jokes. Yiddish, I call on you to choose! Yiddish! Choose death or death. Which is to say death through forgetting or death through translation. Who will redeem you? What act of salvation will restore you? All you can hope for, you tattered, you withered, is translation in America! Hannah, you have a strong mouth, made to carry the future—

But he knew he lied, lied, lied. A truthful intention is not enough. Oratory and declamation. A speech. A lecture. He felt himself an obscenity. What did the death of Jews have to do with his own troubles? His cry was ego and more ego. His own stew, foul. Whoever mourns the dead mourns himself. He wanted someone to read his poems, no one could read his poems. Filth and exploitation to throw in history. As if a dumb man should blame the ears that cannot hear him.

He turned the paper over and wrote in big letters:

EDELSHTEIN GONE,

and went down the corridor with it in pursuit of Paula's snore. Taken without ridicule a pleasant riverside noise. Bird. More cow to the sight: the connubial bed, under his gaze, gnarled and lumped – in it this old male and this old female. He was surprised on such a cold night they slept with only one blanket, gauzy cotton. They lay like a pair of kingdoms in summer. Long ago they had been at war, now they were exhausted into downy truce. Hair all over Baumzweig. Even his leg-hairs gone white. Nightstands, a pair of them, on either side of the bed, heaped with papers, books, magazines, lampshades sticking up out of all that like figurines on a prow – the bedroom was Baumzweig's second office. Towers of back issues on the floor. On the dresser a typewriter besieged by Paula's toilet water bottles and face powder. Fragrance mixed with urinous hints. Edelshtein went on looking at the sleepers. How reduced they seemed, each breath a little demand for more, more, more, a shudder of jowls; how they heaved a knee, a thumb; the tiny blue veins all over Paula's neck. Her nightgown was stretched away and he saw that her breasts had dropped sidewise and, though still very fat, hung in pitiful creased bags of mole-dappled skin. Baumzweig wore only his underwear: his thighs were full of picked sores.

He put EDELSHTEIN GONE between their heads. Then he took it away – on the other side was his real message: secret enemies. He folded the sheet inside his coat pocket and squeezed into his shoes. Cowardly. Pity for breathing carrion. All pity is self-pity. Goethe on his deathbed: more light!

In the street he felt liberated. A voyager. Snow was still falling, though more lightly than before, a night-coloured blue. A veil of snow revolved in front of him, turning him around. He stumbled into a drift, a magnificent bluish pile slanted upwards. Wetness pierced his feet like a surge of cold blood. Beneath the immaculate lifted slope he struck stone – the stair of a stoop. He remembered his old home, the hill of snow behind the study-house, the smoky fire, his father swaying nearly into the black fire and chanting, one big duck, the stupid one, sliding on the ice. His mother's neck too was finely veined and secretly, sweetly, luxuriantly odorous. Deeply and gravely he wished he had worn galoshes – no one reminds a widower. His shoes were infernos of cold, his toes dead blocks. Himself the only life in the street, not even a cat. The veil moved against him, turning, and beat on his pupils. Along the kerb cars squatted under humps of snow, blue-backed tortoises. Nothing moved in the road. His own house was far, Vorovsky's nearer, but he could not read the street sign. A building with a canopy. Vorovsky's hat. He made himself very small, small as a mouse, and curled himself up in the fur of it. To be very, very little and to live in a hat. A little wild creature in a burrow. Inside warm, a mound of seeds nearby, licking himself for cleanliness, all sorts of weather leaping down. His glasses fell from his face and with an odd tiny crack hit the lid of a garbage can. He took off one glove and felt for them in the snow. When he found them he marvelled at how the frames burned. Suppose a funeral on a night like this, how would they open the earth? His glasses were slippery as icicles when he put them on again. A crystal spectrum delighted him, but he could not see the passageway, or if there was a canopy. What he wanted from Vorovsky was Hannah.

There was no elevator. Vorovsky lived on the top floor, very high up. From his windows you could look out and see people so tiny they became patterns. It was a different building, not this one. He went down three fake-marble steps and saw a door. It was open: inside was a big black room knobby with baby carriages and tricycles. He smelled wet metal like a toothpain: life! Peretz tells how on a bitter night a Jew outside the window envied peasants swigging vodka in a hovel – friends in their prime and warm before the fire. Carriages and tricycles, instruments of Diaspora. Baumzweig with his picked sores was once also a baby. In the Diaspora the birth of a Jew increases nobody's population, the death of a Jew has no meaning. Anonymous. To have died among the martyrs – solidarity at least, a passage into history, one of the marked ones, *kiddush ha-shem*. A telephone on the wall. He pulled off his glasses, all clouded over, and took out a pad with numbers in it and dialled.

'Ostrover?'

'Who is this?'

'*Yankel* Ostrover, the writer, or Pisher Ostrover the plumber?'

'What do you want?'

'To leave evidence,' Edelshtein howled.

'Never mind! Make an end! Who's there?'

'The Messiah.'

'Who is this? Mendel, it's you?'

'Never.'

'Gorochov?'

'That toenail? Please. Trust me.'

'Fall into a hole!'

'This is how a man addresses his Redeemer?'

'It's five o'clock in the morning! What do you want? Bum! Lunatic! Cholera! Black year! Plague! Poisoner! Strangler!'

'You think you'll last longer than your shroud, Ostrover? Your sentences are an abomination, your style is like a pump, a pimp has a sweeter tongue—'

'Angel of Death!'

He dialled Vorovsky but there was no answer.

The snow had turned white as the white of an eye. He wandered toward Hannah's house, though he did not know where she lived, or what her name was, or whether he had ever seen her. On the way he rehearsed what he would say to her. But this was not satisfactory, he could lecture but not speak into a face. He bled to retrieve her face. He was in pursuit of her, she was his destination. Why? What does a man look for, what does he need? What can a man retrieve? Can the future retrieve the past? And if retrieve, how redeem? His shoes streamed. Each step was a pond. The herons in spring, red-legged. Secret eyes they have: the eyes of birds – frightening. Too open. The riddle of openness. His feet poured rivers. Cold, cold.

> Little old man in the cold,
> come hop up on the stove,
> your wife will give you a crust with jam.
> Thank you, muse, for this little psalm.

He belched. His stomach was unwell. Indigestion? A heart attack? He wiggled the fingers of his left hand: though frozen they tingled. Heart. Maybe only ulcer. Cancer, like Mireleh? In a narrow bed he missed his wife. How much longer could he expect to live? An unmarked grave. Who would know he had ever been alive? He had no descendants, his grandchildren were imaginary. *O my unborn grandson* . . . Hackneyed. *Ungrandfathered ghost* . . . Too baroque. Simplicity, purity, truthfulness.

He wrote:

Dear Hannah:

You made no impression on me. When I wrote you before at Baumzweig's I lied. I saw you for a second in a public place, so what? Holding a Yiddish book. A young face on top of a Yiddish book. Nothing else. For me this is worth no somersault. Ostrover's vomit! —

that popularizer, vulgarian, panderer to people who have lost the memory of peoplehood. A thousand times a pimp. Your uncle Chaim said about you: 'She writes.' A pity on his judgment. Writes! Writes! Potatoes in a sack! Another one! What do you write? When will you write? How will you write? Either you'll become an editor of *Good Housekeeping*, or, if serious, join the gang of so-called Jewish novelists. I've sniffed them all, I'm intimate with their smell. Satirists they call themselves. Picking at their crotches. What do they *know*, I mean of *knowledge*? To satirize you have to know something. In a so-called novel by a so-called Jewish novelist (*'activist-existential'* – listen, I understand, I read everything!) – Elkin, Stanley, to keep to only one example – the hero visits Williamsburg to contact a so-called 'miracle rabbi'. Even the word *rabbi*! No, listen – to me, a descendant of the Vilna Gaon myself, the *guter yid* is a charlatan and his *chasidim* are victims, never mind if willing or not. But that's not the point. You have to KNOW SOMETHING! At least the difference between a *rav* and a *rebbeh*! At least a *pinteleh* here and there! Otherwise where's the joke, where's the satire, where's the mockery? American-born! An ignoramus mocks only himself. *Jewish* novelists! Savages! The allrightnik's children, all they know is to curse the allrightnik! Their Yiddish! One word here, one word there. *Shikseh* on one page, *putz* on the other, and that's the whole vocabulary! And when they give a try at phonetic rendition! Darling God! If they had mothers and fathers, they crawled out of the swamps. Their grandparents were tree-squirrels if that's how they held their mouths. They know ten words for, excuse me, penis, and when it comes to a word for learning they're impotent!

Joy, joy! He felt himself on the right course at last. Daylight was coming, a yellow elephant rocked silently by in the road. A little light burned eternally on its tusk. He let it slide past, he stood up to the knees in the river at home, whirling with joy. He wrote:

TRUTH!

But this great thick word, Truth!, was too harsh, oaken; with his finger in the snow he crossed it out.

I was saying: indifference. I'm indifferent to you and your kind. Why should I think you're another species, something better? Because you knew a shred of a thread of a poem of mine? Ha! I was seduced by my own vanity. I have a foolish tendency to make symbols out of glimpses. My poor wife, peace on her, used to ridicule me for this. Riding in the subway once I saw a beautiful child, a boy about twelve. A Puerto Rican, dusky, yet he had cheeks like pomegranates. I once knew, in Kiev, a child who looked like that. I admit to it. A portrait under the skin of my eyes. The love of a man for a boy. Why not confess it? Is it against the nature of man to rejoice in beauty? 'This is to be expected with a childless man' — my wife's verdict. That what I wanted was a son. Take this as a complete explanation: if an ordinary person cannot

The end of the sentence flew like a leaf out of his mind . . . it was turning into a quarrel with Mireleh. Who quarrels with the dead? He wrote:

Esteemed Alexei Yosifovitch:
    You remain. You remain. An illumination. More than my own home, nearer than my mother's mouth. Nimbus. Your father slapped my father. You were never told. Because I kissed you on the green stairs. The shadow-place on the landing where I once saw the butler scratch his pants. They sent us away shamed. My father and I, into the mud.

Again a lie. Never near the child. Lying is like a vitamin, it has to fortify everything. Only through the doorway, looking, looking. The gleaming face: the face of flame. Or would test him on verb-forms: *kal, nifal, piel, pual, hifil, hofal, hispael*. On the afternoons the Latin tutor came, crouched outside the threshold, Edelshtein heard *ego, mei, mihi, me, me*. May may. Beautiful foreign nasal chant of riches. Latin! Dirty from the lips of idolators. An apostate family. Edelshtein and his father took their coffee and bread, but otherwise lived on boiled eggs: the elder Kirilov one day brought home with him the *mashgiach* from the Jewish poorhouse to testify to the purity of the servants' kitchen, but to Edelshtein's father the whole house was *treyf*, the *mashgiach* himself a hired impostor. Who would oversee the overseer? Among the Kirilovs with their lying name money was the best overseer. Money saw to everything. Though they had their particular talent. Mechanical. Alexei Y. Kirilov, engineer. Bridges, towers. Consultant to Cairo. Builder of the Aswan Dam, assistant to Pharaoh for the latest Pyramid. To set down such a fantasy about such an important Soviet brain . . . poor little Alexei, Avremeleh, I'll jeopardize your position in life, little corpse of Babi Yar.

Only focus. Hersh! Scion of the Vilna Gaon! Prince of rationality! Pay attention!

He wrote:

The gait – the prance, the hobble – of Yiddish is not the same as the gait of English. A big headache for a translator probably. In Yiddish you use more words than in English. Nobody believes it but it's true. Another big problem is form. The moderns take the old forms and fill them up with mockery, love, drama, satire, etc. Plenty of play. But STILL THE SAME OLD FORMS, conventions left over from the last century even. It doesn't matter who denies this, out of pride: it's true. Pour in symbolism, impressionism, be complex, be subtle, be daring, take risks, break your teeth – whatever you do, it still comes out Yiddish. *Mamaloshen* doesn't produce *Wastelands*. No alienation, no nihilism, no dadaism. With all the suffering no smashing! No INCOHERENCE! Keep the latter in mind, Hannah, if you expect to make progress. Also: please remember that when a goy from Columbus, Ohio, says 'Elijah the Prophet' he's not talking about *Eliohu hanovi*. Eliohu is·one of us, a *folksmensch*, running around in second-hand clothes. Theirs is God knows what. The same biblical figure, with exactly the same history, once he puts on a name from King James, COMES OUT A DIFFERENT PERSON. Life, history, hope, tragedy, they don't come out even. They talk Bible Lands, with us it's *eretz yisroel*. A misfortune.

Astonished, he struck up against a kiosk. A telephone! On a street corner! He had to drag the door open, pulling a load of snow. Then he squeezed inside. His fingers were sticks. Never mind the pad, he forgot even where the pocket was. In his coat? Jacket? Pants? With one stick he dialled Vorovsky's number: from memory.

'Hello, Chaim?'

'This is Ostrover.'

'Ostrover! Why Ostrover? What are you doing there? I want Vorovsky.'

'Who's this?'

'Edelshtein.'

'I thought so. A persecution, what is this? I could send you to jail for tricks like before—'

'Quick, give me Vorovsky.'

'I'll *give* you.'

'Vorovsky's not home?'

'How do I know if Vorovsky's home? It's dawn, go ask Vorovsky!'

Edelshtein grew weak: 'I called the wrong number.'

'Hersheleh, if you want some friendly advice you'll listen to me. I can get you jobs at fancy out-of-town country clubs, Miami Florida included, plenty of speeches your own style, only what they need is rational lecturers not lunatics. If you carry on like tonight you'll lose what you have.'

'I don't have anything.'

'Accept life, Edelshtein.'

'Dead man, I appreciate your guidance.'

'Yesterday I heard from Hollywood, they're making a movie from one of my stories. So now tell me again who's dead.'

'The puppet the ventriloquist holds in his lap. A piece of log. It's somebody else's language and the dead doll sits there.'

'Wit, you want them to make movies in Yiddish now?'

'In Talmud if you save a single life it's as if you saved the world. And if you save a language? Worlds maybe. Galaxies. The whole universe.'

'Hersheleh, the God of the Jews made a mistake when he didn't have a son, it would be a good occupation for you.'

'Instead I'll be an extra in your movie. If they shoot the *shtetl* on location in Kansas send me expense money. I'll come and be local colour for you. I'll put on my *shtreiml* and walk around, the people should see a real Jew. For ten dollars more I'll even speak *mamaloshen*.'

Ostrover said, 'It doesn't matter what you speak, envy sounds the same in all languages.'

Edelshtein said, 'Once there was a ghost who thought he was still alive. You know what happened to him? He got up one morning and began to shave and he cut himself. And there was no blood. No blood at all. And he still didn't believe it, so he looked in the mirror to see. And there was no reflection, no sign of himself. He wasn't there. But he still didn't believe it, so he began to scream, but there was no sound, no sound at all—'

There was no sound from the telephone. He let it dangle and rock.

He looked for the pad. Diligently he consulted himself: pants cuffs have a way of catching necessary objects. The number had fallen out of his body. Off his skin. He needed Vorovsky because he needed Hannah. Worthwhile maybe to telephone Baumzweig for Vorovsky's number,

Paula could look it up – Baumzweig's number he knew by heart, no mistake. He had singled out his need. Svengali, Pygmalion, Rasputin, Dr (jokes aside) Frankenstein. What does it require to make a translator? A secondary occupation. Parasitic. But your own creature. Take this girl Hannah and train her. His alone. American-born but she had the advantage over him, English being no worm on her palate; also she could read his words in the original. Niece of a vanquished mind – still, genes are in reality God, and if Vorovsky had a little talent for translation why not the niece? – Or the other. Russia. The one in the Soviet Union who wrote two stanzas in Yiddish. In Yiddish! And only twenty! Born 1948, same year they made up to be the Doctors' Plot, Stalin already very busy killing Jews, Markish, Kvitko, Kushnirov, Hofshtein, Mikhoels, Susskin, Bergelson, Feffer, Gradzenski with the wooden leg. All slaughtered. How did Yiddish survive in the mouth of that girl? Nurtured in secret. Taught by an obsessed grandfather, a crazy uncle: Marranos. The poem reprinted, as they say, in the West. (The West! If a Jew says 'the West', he sounds like an imbecile. In a puddle what's West, what's East?) Flowers, blue sky, she yearns for the end of winter: very nice. A zero, and received like a prodigy! An aberration! A miracle! Because composed in the lost tongue. As if some Neapolitan child suddenly begins to prattle in Latin. Not the same. Little verses merely. Death confers awe. Russian: its richness, directness. For 'iron' and 'weapon' the same word. A *thick* language, a world-language. He visualized himself translated into Russian, covertly, by the Marranos' daughter. To be circulated, in typescript, underground: to be read, read!

Understand me, Hannah – that our treasure-tongue is derived from strangers means nothing. 90 per cent German roots, 10 per cent Slavic: irrelevant. The Hebrew take for granted without percentages. We are a people who have known how to forge the language of need out of the language of necessity. Our reputation among ourselves as a nation of scholars is mostly empty. In actuality we are a mob of working people, labourers, hewers of wood, believe me. Leivik, our chief poet, was a house painter. Today all pharmacists, lawyers, accountants, haberdashers, but tickle the lawyer and you'll see his grandfather sawed wood for a living. That's how it is with us. Nowadays the Jew is forgetful, everybody with a profession, every Jewish boy a professor – justice seems less urgent. Most don't realize this quiet time is only another Interim. Always, like in a terrible

Wagnerian storm, we have our interludes of rest. So now. Once we were slaves, now we are free men, remember the bread of affliction. But listen. Whoever cries Justice! is a liberated slave. Whoever honours Work is a liberated slave. They accuse Yiddish literature of sentimentality in this connection. Very good, true. True, so be it! A dwarf at a sewing machine can afford a little loosening of the heart. I return to Leivik. He could hang wallpaper. I once lived in a room he papered – yellow vines. Rutgers Street that was. A good job, no bubbles, no peeling. This from a poet of very morbid tendencies. Mani Leib fixed shoes. Moishe Leib Halpern was a waiter, once in a while a handyman. I could tell you the names of twenty poets of very pure expression who were operators, pressers, cutters. In addition to fixing shoes Mani Leib was also a laundryman. I beg you not to think I'm preaching Socialism. To my mind politics is dung. What I mean is something else: Work is Work, and Thought is Thought. Politics tries to mix these up, Socialism especially. The language of a hard-pressed people works under the laws of purity, dividing the Commanded from the Profane. I remember one of my old teachers. He used to take attendance every day and he gave his occupation to the taxing council as 'attendance-taker' – so that he wouldn't be getting paid for teaching Torah. This with five pupils, all living in his house and fed by his wife! Call it splitting a hair if you want, but it's the hair of a head that distinguished between the necessary and the merely needed. People who believe that Yiddish is, as they like to say, 'richly intermixed', and that in Yiddishkeit the presence of the Covenant, of Godliness, inhabits humble things and humble words, are under a delusion or a deception. The slave knows exactly when he belongs to God and when to the oppressor. The liberated slave who is not forgetful and can remember when he himself was an artefact, knows exactly the difference between God and an artefact. A language also knows whom it is serving at each moment. I am feeling very cold right now. Of course you see that when I say liberated I mean self-liberated. Moses not Lincoln, not Franz Josef. Yiddish is the language of auto-emancipation. Theodor Herzl wrote in German but the message spread in *mamaloshen* – my God cold. Naturally the important thing is to stick to what you learned as a slave including language, and not to speak their language, otherwise you will become like them, acquiring their confusion between God and artefact and consequently their taste for making slaves, both of themselves and others.

Slave of rhetoric! This is the trouble when you use God for a Muse. Philosophers, thinkers – all cursed. Poets have it better: most are Greeks and pagans, unbelievers except in natural religion, stones, stars, body. This cube and cell. Ostrover had already sentenced him to jail, little booth in the vale of snow; black instrument beeped from a gallows. The white pad – something white – on the floor. Edelshtein bent for it and struck his jaw. Through the filth of the glass doors morning rose out of the dark. He saw what he held:

'ALL OF US ARE HUMANS TOGETHER
BUT SOME HUMANS SHOULD DROP DEAD.'

DO YOU FEEL THIS?

IF SO CALL TR 5–2530 IF YOU WANT TO
KNOW WHETHER YOU WILL SURVIVE IN
CHRIST'S FIVE-DAY INEXPENSIVE
ELECT-PLAN

*

'AUDITORY PHRENOLOGY'
PRACTISED FREE FREE

*

(PLEASE NO ATHEISTS OR CRANK CALLS
WE ARE SINCERE SCIENTIFIC SOUL-SOCIOLOGISTS)

*

ASK FOR ROSE OR LOU
WE LOVE YOU

He was touched and curious, but withdrawn. The cold lit him unfamiliarly: his body a brilliant hollowness, emptied of organs, cleansed of debris, the inner flanks of him perfect lit glass. A clear chalice. Of small change he had only a nickel and a dime. For the dime he could CALL TR 5–2530 and take advice appropriate to his immaculateness, his transparency. Rose or Lou. He had no satire for their love. How manifold and various the human imagination. The simplicity of an ascent lured him, he was alert to the probability of levitation but disregarded it. The disciples of Reb Moshe of Kobryn also disregarded feats in opposition to nature – they had no awe for their master when he hung in air, but when he slept – the miracle of his lung, his breath, his heartbeat! He lurched from the booth into rushing daylight. The depth of snow sucked off one of his shoes. The serpent too prospers without feet, so he cast off his and weaved on. His arms, particularly his hands, particularly those partners of mind his fingers, he was sorry to lose. He knew his eyes, his tongue, his stinging loins. He was again tempted to ascend. The hillock was profound. He outwitted it by creeping through it, he drilled patiently into the snow. He wanted to stand then, but without legs could not. Indolently he permitted himself to rise. He went only high enough to see the snowy sidewalks, the mounds in gutters and against stoops, the beginning of business time. Lifted light. A doorman fled out of a building wearing earmuffs, pulling a shovel behind him like a little tin cart. Edelshtein drifted no higher than the man's shoulders. He watched the shovel pierce the snow, tunnelling down, but there was no bottom, the earth was without foundation.

He came under a black wing. He thought it was the first blindness of Death but it was only a canopy.

The doorman went on digging under the canopy; under the canopy Edelshtein tasted wine and felt himself at a wedding, his own, the canopy covering his steamy gold eyeglasses made blind by Mireleh's veil. Four beings held up the poles; one his wife's cousin the postman, one his own cousin the druggist; two poets. The first poet was a beggar who lived on institutional charity – Baumzweig; the second, Silverman, sold ladies' elastic stockings, the kind for varicose veins. The postman and the druggist were still alive, only one of them retired. The poets were ghosts, Baumzweig picking at himself in bed also a ghost, Silverman long dead, more than twenty years – *lideleh-shreiber* they called him, he wrote for the popular theatre. 'Song to Steerage': *Steerage, steerage, I remember the crowds, the rags we took with us we treated like shrouds, we tossed them away when we spied out the shore, going reborn through the Golden Door. . . .* Even on Second Avenue 1905 was already stale, but it stopped the show, made fevers, encores, tears, yells. Golden sidewalks. America the bride, under her fancy gown nothing. Poor Silverman, in love with the Statue of Liberty's lifted arm, what did he do in his life besides raise up a post at an empty wedding, no progeny?

The doorman dug out a piece of statuary, an urn with a stone wreath.

Under the canopy Edelshtein recognized it. Sand, butts, a half-naked angel astride the wreath. Once Edelshtein saw a condom in it. Found!

Vorovsky's building. There is no God, yet who brought him here if not the King of the Universe? Not so bad off after all, even in a snowstorm he could find his way, an expert, he knew one block from another in this desolation of a world.

He carried his shoe into the elevator like a baby, an orphan, a redemption. He could kiss even a shoe.

In the corridor laughter, toilets flushing; coffee stabbed him.

He rang the bell.

From behind Vorovsky's door, laughter, laughter!

No one came.

He rang again. No one came. He banged. 'Chaim, crazy man, open up!' No one came. 'A dead man from the cold knocks, you don't come? Hurry up, open, I'm a stick of ice, you want a dead man at your door? Mercy! Pity! Open up!'

No one came.

He listened to the laughter. It had a form; a method, rather: some principle, closer to physics than music, of arching up and sinking back. Inside the shape barks, howls, dogs, wolves, wilderness. After each fright a crevice to fall into. He made an anvil of his shoe and took the doorknob for an iron hammer and thrust. He thrust, thrust. The force of an iceberg.

Close to the knob a panel bulged and cracked. Not his fault. On the other side someone was unused to the lock.

He heard Vorovsky but saw Hannah.

She said: 'What?'

'You don't remember me? I'm the one what recited to you tonight my work from several years past, I was passing by in your uncle's neighbourhood—'

'He's sick.'

'What, a fit?'

'All night. I've been here the whole night. The whole night—'

'Let me in.'

'Please go away. I just told you.'

'In. What's the matter with you? I'm sick myself, I'm dead from cold! Hey, Chaim! Lunatic, stop it!'

Vorovsky was on his belly on the floor, stifling his mouth with a pillow as if it were a stone, knocking his head down on it, but it was no use, the laughter shook the pillow and came yelping out, not muffled but increased, darkened. He laughed and said 'Hannah' and laughed.

Edelshtein took a chair and dragged it near Vorovsky and sat. The room stank, a subway latrine.

'Stop,' he said.

Vorovsky laughed.

'All right, merriment, very good, be happy. You're warm, I'm cold. Have mercy, little girl – tea. Hannah. Boil it up hot. Pieces of flesh drop from me.' He heard that he was speaking Yiddish, so he began again for her. 'I'm sorry. Forgive me. A terrible thing to do. I was lost outside, I was looking, so now I found you, I'm sorry.'

'It isn't a good time for a visit, that's all.'

'Bring some tea also for your uncle.'

'He can't.'

'He can maybe, let him try. Someone who laughs like this is ready for a feast – *flanken, tsimmis, rosselfleysh*—' In Yiddish he said, 'In the world-to-come people dance at parties like this, all laughter, joy. The day after the Messiah people laugh like this.'

Vorovsky laughed and said 'Messiah' and sucked the pillow, spitting. His face was a flood: tears ran upside down into his eyes, over his forehead, saliva sprang in puddles around his ears. He was spitting, crying, burbling, he gasped, wept, spat. His eyes were bloodshot, the whites showed like slashes, wounds; he still wore his hat. He laughed, he was still laughing. His pants were wet, the fly open, now and then seeping. He dropped the pillow for tea and ventured a sip, with his tongue, like an animal full of hope – vomit rolled up with the third swallow and he laughed between spasms, he was still laughing, stinking, a sewer.

Edelshtein took pleasure in the tea, it touched him to the root, more gripping on his bowel than the coffee that stung the hall. He praised himself with no meanness, no bitterness: prince of rationality! Thawing, he said, 'Give him *schnapps*, he can hold *schnapps*, no question.'

'He drank and he vomited.'

'Chaim, little soul,' Edelshtein said, 'what started you off? Myself. I was there. I said it, I said graves, I said smoke. I'm the responsible one. Death. Death, I'm the one who said it. Death you laugh at, you're no coward.'

'If you want to talk business with my uncle come another time.'

'Death is business?'

Now he examined her. Born 1945, in the hour of the death-camps. Not selected. Immune. The whole way she held herself looked immune

– by this he meant American. Still, an exhausted child, straggled head, remarkable child to stay through the night with the madman. 'Where's your mother?' he said. 'Why doesn't she come and watch her brother? Why does it fall on you? You should be free, you have your own life.'

'You don't know anything about families.'

She was acute: no mother, father, wife, child, what did he know about families? He was cut off, a survivor. 'I know your uncle,' he said, but without belief: in the first place Vorovsky had an education. 'In his right mind your uncle doesn't want you to suffer.'

Vorovsky, laughing, said 'Suffer'.

'He likes to suffer. He wants to suffer. He admires suffering. All you people want to suffer.'

Pins and needles: Edelshtein's fingertips were fevering. He stroked the heat of the cup. He could feel. He said, '"You people"?'

'You Jews.'

'Aha. Chaim, you hear? Your niece Hannah – on the other side already, never mind she's acquainted with *mamaloshen*. In one generation, "you Jews". You don't like suffering? Maybe you respect it?'

'It's unnecessary.'

'It comes from history, history is also unnecessary?'

'History's a waste.'

America the empty bride. Edelshtein said, 'You're right about business. I came on business. My whole business is waste.'

Vorovsky laughed and said, 'Hersheleh Frog Frog Frog.'

'I think you're making him worse,' Hannah said. 'Tell me what you want and I'll give him the message.'

'He's not deaf.'

'He doesn't remember afterwards—'

'I have no message.'

'Then what do you want from him?'

'Nothing. I want from you.'

'Frog Frog Frog Frog Frog.'

Edelshtein finished his tea and put the cup on the floor and for the first time absorbed Vorovsky's apartment: until now Vorovsky had kept him out. It was one room, sink and stove behind a plastic curtain, bookshelves leaning over not with books but journals piled flat, a sticky table, a sofa-bed, a desk, six kitchen chairs, and along the walls seventy-five cardboard boxes which Edelshtein knew harboured two thousand copies of Vorovsky's dictionary. A pity on Vorovsky, he had a dispute with the publisher, who turned back half the printing to him. Vorovsky had to pay for two thousand German-English mathematical dictionaries, and now he had to sell them himself, but he did not know what to do, how to go about it. It was his fate to swallow what he first excreted. Because of a mishap in business he owned his life, he possessed what he was, a slave, but invisible. A hungry snake has to eat its tail all the way down to the head until it disappears.

Hannah said: 'What could I do for you' – flat, not a question.

'Again "you". A distinction, a separation. What I'll ask is this: annihilate "you", annihilate "me". We'll come to an understanding, we'll get together.'

She bent for his cup and he saw her boot. He was afraid of a boot. He said mildly, nicely, 'Look, your uncle tells me you're one of us. By "us" he means writer, no?'

'By "us" you mean Jew.'

'And you're not a Jew, *meydeleh?*'

'Not your kind.'

'Nowadays there have to be kinds? Good, bad, old, new—'

'Old and new.'

'All right! So let it be old and new, fine, a reasonable beginning. Let old work with new. Listen, I need a collaborator. Not exactly a collaborator, it's not even complicated like that. What I need is a translator.'

'My uncle the translator is indisposed.'

At that moment Edelshtein discovered he hated irony. He yelled, 'Not your uncle. You! You!'

Howling, Vorovsky crawled to a tower of cartons and beat on them with his bare heels. There was an alteration in his laughter, something not theatrical but of the theatre – he was amused, entertained, clowns paraded between his legs.

'You'll save Yiddish,' Edelshtein said, 'you'll be like a Messiah to a whole generation, a whole literature, naturally you'll have to work at it, practise, it takes knowledge, it takes a gift, a genius, a born poet—'

Hannah walked in her boots with his dirty teacup. From behind the plastic he heard the faucet. She opened the curtain and came out and said: 'You old men.'

'Ostrover's pages you kiss!'

'You jealous old men from the ghetto,' she said.

'And Ostrover's young, a young prince? Listen! You don't see, you don't follow – translate me, lift me out of the ghetto, it's my life that's hanging on you!'

Her voice was a whip. 'Bloodsuckers,' she said. 'It isn't a translator you're after, it's someone's soul. Too much history's drained your blood, you want someone to take you over, a dybbuk—'

'Dybbuk! Ostrover's language. All right, I need a dybbuk, I'll become a golem, I don't care, it doesn't matter! Breathe in me! Animate me! Without you I'm a clay pot!' Bereaved, he yelled, 'Translate me!'

The clowns ran over Vorovsky's charmed belly.

Hannah said: 'You think I have to read Ostrover in translation? You think translation has anything to do with what Ostrover is?'

Edelshtein accused her, 'Who taught you to read Yiddish? – A girl like that, to know the letters worthy of life and to be ignorant! "You Jews", "you people", you you you!'

'I learned, my grandfather taught me, I'm not responsible for it, I didn't go looking for it, I was smart, a golden head, same as now. But I have my own life, you said it yourself, I don't have to throw it out. So pay attention, Mr Vampire: even in Yiddish Ostrover's not in the ghetto. Even in Yiddish he's not like you people.'

'He's not in the ghetto? Which ghetto, what ghetto? So where is he? In the sky? In the clouds? With the angels? Where?'

She meditated, she was all intelligence. 'In the world,' she answered him.

'In the marketplace. A fishwife, a *kochleffel*, everything's his business, you he'll autograph, me he'll get jobs, he listens to everybody.'

'Whereas you people listen only to yourselves.'

In the room something was absent.

Edelshtein, pushing into his snow-damp shoe, said into the absence, 'So? You're not interested?'

'Only in the mainstream. Not in your little puddles.'

'Again the ghetto. Your uncle stinks from the ghetto? Graduated, 1924, the University of Berlin, Vorovsky stinks from the ghetto? Myself, four God-given books not one living human being knows, I stink from the ghetto? God, four thousand years since Abraham hanging out with Jews, God also stinks from the ghetto?'

'Rhetoric,' Hannah said. 'Yiddish literary rhetoric. That's the style.'

'Only Ostrover doesn't stink from the ghetto.'

'A question of vision.'

'Better say visions. He doesn't know real things.'

'He knows a reality beyond realism.'

'American literary babies! And in your language you don't have a rhetoric?' Edelshtein burst out. 'Very good, he's achieved it, Ostrover's the world. A pantheist, a pagan, a goy.'

'That's it. You've nailed it. A Freudian, a Jungian, a sensibility. No little love stories. A contemporary. He speaks for everybody.'

'Aha. Sounds familiar already. For humanity he speaks? Humanity?'

'Humanity,' she said.

'And to speak for Jews isn't to speak for humanity? We're not human? We're not present on the face of the earth? We don't suffer? In Russia they let us live? In Egypt they don't want to murder us?'

'Suffer suffer,' she said. 'I like devils best. They don't think only about themselves and they don't suffer.'

Immediately, looking at Hannah – my God, an old man, he was looking at her little waist, underneath it where the little apple of her womb was hidden away – immediately, all at once, instantaneously, he fell into a chaos, a trance, of truth, of actuality: was it possible? He saw everything in miraculous reversal, blessed – everything plain, distinct, understandable, true. What he understood was this: that the ghetto was the real world, and the outside world only a ghetto. Because in actuality who was shut off? Who then was really buried, removed, inhabited by darkness? To whom, in what little space, did God offer Sinai? Who kept Terach and who followed Abraham? Talmud explains that when the Jews went into Exile, God went into Exile also. Babi Yar is maybe the real world, and Kiev with its German toys, New York with all its terrible intelligence, all fictions, fantasies. Unreality.

An infatuation! He was the same, all his life the same as this poisonous wild girl, he coveted mythologies, spectres, animals, voices. Western Civilization his secret guilt, he was ashamed of the small tremor of his self-love, degraded by being ingrown. Alexei with his skin a furnace of desire, his trucks and trains! He longed to be Alexei. Alexei with his German toys and his Latin! Alexei whose destiny was to grow up into the world-at-large, to slip from the ghetto, to break out into engineering for Western Civilization! Alexei, I abandon you! I'm at home only in a prison, history is my prison, the ravine my house, only listen – suppose it turns out that the destiny of the Jews is vast, open, eternal, and that Western Civilization is meant to dwindle, shrivel, shrink into the ghetto of the world – what of history then? Kings, Parliaments, like insects, Presidents like vermin, their religion a row of little dolls, their art a cave smudge, their poetry a lust – Avremeleh, when you fell from the ledge over the ravine into your grave, for the first time you fell into reality.

To Hannah he said: 'I didn't ask to be born into Yiddish. It came on me.'

He meant he was blessed.

'So keep it,' she said, 'and don't complain.'

With the whole ferocity of his delight in it he hit her mouth. The madman again struck up his laugh. Only now was it possible to notice that something had stopped it before. A missing harp. The absence filled with bloody laughter, bits of what looked like red pimento hung in the vomit on Vorovsky's chin, the clowns fled, Vorovsky's hat with its pinnacle of fur dangled on his chest – he was spent, he was beginning to fall into the quake of sleep, he slept, he dozed, roars burst from him, he hiccuped, woke, laughed, an enormous grief settled in him, he went on napping and laughing, grief had him in its teeth.

Edelshtein's hand, the cushiony underside of it, blazed from giving the blow. 'You,' he said, 'you have no ideas, what are you?' A shred of learning flaked from him, what the sages said of Job ripped from his tongue like a peeling of the tongue itself, *he never was, he never existed*. 'You were never born, you were never created!' he yelled. 'Let me tell you, a dead man tells you this, at least I had a life, at least I understood something!'

'Die,' she told him. 'Die now, all you old men, what are you waiting for? Hanging on my neck, him and now you, the whole bunch of you, parasites, hurry up and die.'

His palm burned, it was the first time he had ever slapped a child. He felt like a father. Her mouth lay back naked on her face. Out of spite, against instinct, she kept her hands from the bruise – he could see the shape of her teeth, turned a little one on the other, imperfect, again vulnerable. From fury her nose streamed. He had put a bulge in her lip.

'Forget Yiddish!' he screamed at her. 'Wipe it out of your brain! Extirpate it! Go get a memory operation! You have no right to it, you have no right to an uncle, a grandfather! No one ever came before you, you were never born! A vacuum!'

'You old atheists,' she called after him. 'You dead old Socialists. Boring! You bore me to death. You hate magic, you hate imagination, you talk God and you hate God, you despise, you bore, you envy, you eat people up with your disgusting old age – cannibals, all you care about is your own youth, you're finished, give somebody else a turn!'

This held him. He leaned on the door frame. 'A turn at what? I didn't offer you a turn? An opportunity of a lifetime? To be published now, in youth, in babyhood, early in life? Translated I'd be famous, this you don't understand. Hannah, listen,' he said, kindly, ingratiatingly, reasoning with her like a father, 'you don't have to like my poems, do I ask you to *like* them? I don't ask you to like them, I don't ask you to respect them, I don't ask you to love them. A man my age, do I want a lover or a translator? Am I asking a favour? No. Look,' he said, 'one thing I forgot to tell you. A business deal. That's all. Business, plain and simple. I'll pay you. You didn't think I wouldn't pay, God forbid?'

Now she covered her mouth. He wondered at his need to weep; he was ashamed.

'Hannah, please, how much? I'll pay, you'll see. Whatever you like. You'll buy anything you want. Dresses, shoes—' *Gottenyu*, what could such a wild beast want? 'You'll buy more boots, all kinds of boots, whatever you want, books, everything—' He said relentlessly, 'You'll have from me money.'

'No,' she said, 'no.'

'Please. What will happen to me? What's wrong? My ideas aren't good enough? Who asks you to believe in my beliefs? I'm an old man, used up, I have nothing to say any more, anything I ever said was all imitation. Walt Whitman I used to like. Also John Donne. Poets, masters. We, what have we got? A Yiddish Keats? Never—' He was ashamed, so he wiped his cheeks with both sleeves. 'Business. I'll pay you,' he said.

'No.'

'Because I laid a hand on you? Forgive me, I apologize. I'm crazier than he is, I should be locked up for it—'

'Not because of that.'

'Then why not? *Meydeleh*, why not? What harm would it do you? Help out an old man.'

She said desolately, 'You don't interest me. I would have to be interested.'

'I see. Naturally.' He looked at Vorovsky. 'Goodbye, Chaim, regards from Aristotle. What distinguishes men from the beasts is the power of ha-ha-ha. So good morning, ladies and gentlemen. Be well. Chaim, live until a hundred and twenty. The main thing is health.'

In the street it was full day, and he was warm from the tea. The road glistened, the sidewalks. Paths crisscrossed in unexpected places, sleds clanged, people ran. A drugstore was open and he went in to telephone Baumzweig: he dialled, but on the way he skipped a number, heard an iron noise like a weapon, and had to dial again. 'Paula,' he practised, 'I'll come back for a while, all right? For breakfast maybe,' but instead he changed his mind and decided to CALL TR 5–2530. At the other end of the wire it was either Rose or Lou. Edelshtein told the eunuch's voice, 'I believe with you about some should drop dead. Pharaoh, Queen Isabella, Haman, that pogromchik King Louis they call in history Saint, Hitler, Stalin, Nasser—' The voice said, 'You're a Jew?' It sounded Southern but somehow not Negro – maybe because schooled, polished: 'Accept Jesus as your Saviour and you shall have Jerusalem restored.' 'We already got it,' Edelshtein said. *Meshiachtseiten!* 'The terrestrial Jerusalem has no significance. Earth is dust. The Kingdom of God is within. Christ released man from Judaic exclusivism.' 'Who's excluding who?' Edelshtein said. 'Christianity is Judaism universalized. Jesus is Moses publicized for ready availability. Our God is the God of Love, your God is the God of Wrath. Look how He abandoned you in Auschwitz.' 'It wasn't only God who didn't notice.' 'You people are cowards, you never even tried to defend yourselves. You got a wide streak of yellow, you don't know how to hold a gun.' 'Tell it to the Egyptians,' Edelshtein said. 'Everyone you come into contact with turns into your enemy. When you were in Europe every nation despised you. When you moved to take over the Middle East the Arab Nation, spic faces like your own, your very own blood-kin, began to hate you. You are a bone in the throat of all mankind.' 'Who gnaws at bones? Dogs and rats only.' 'Even your food habits are abnormal, against the grain of quotidian delight. You refuse to seethe a lamb in the milk of its mother. You will not eat a fertilized egg because it has a spot of blood on it. When you wash your hands you chant. You pray in a debased jargon, not in the beautiful sacramental English of our Holy Bible.' Edelshtein said, 'That's right, Jesus spoke the King's English.' 'Even now, after the good Lord knows how many years in America, you talk with a kike accent. You kike, you Yid.'

Edelshtein shouted into the telephone, 'Amalekite! Titus! Nazi! The whole world is infected by you anti-Semites! On account of you children become corrupted! On account of you I lost everything, my whole life! On account of you I have no translator!'

The Dock-Witch

That spring it fell to me – as family pioneer, I suppose – to do a great deal of seeing-off. Which was a bit odd, considering how we are a clan of inlanders; for generations we have hugged those little southern Ohio hamlets that surprise the tourist who expects only another cornfield and is rewarded, appropriately, only by another cornfield – but this one marvellously shelters a fugitive post office and a perfectly recognizable dry goods store. We have long lived in these places contentedly enough, in summer calling across pleasantly through rusting screens from veranda to veranda, in winter warming our hands on hymnals in the overheated church. We have little dark lakes of our own, and we can travel, if we wish, to a green-sided river for a picnic, but otherwise water is not in our philosophies.

My own lodging is a seventeenth-floor apartment in a structure of thirty-one storeys. I am a little low-down in that building, as you will calculate – perhaps there is still some adducent Ohioan matter in me that continues to seek the earth. The earth, however, is covered over with a stony veneer and is paced by a doorman costumed like the captain of a ship. There is something nautical about my house – from my windows I can see the East River, and I know that if I follow it downtown far enough I will find the mouth of the wide sea itself.

I am the only one of my family to turn Easterner. At first it was shrugged off as rebellion, then concentrated on ferociously as betrayal, and finally they wrote me long letters about the good old dry heat of home, and how I would surely get rheumatism up so high at night in damp air, and about how this or that farm was being taken over for 'development'. There were progress and prosperity to be had at home, they wrote, and girls of my own kind, and, above all, the clear open purity of the land. I always answered by telling my salary. In those early days I had what the partners ritually called promise, and was paid in jagged leaps upwards, like a graph of our national affluence – I was only two or three years out of Yale Law, more dogged than precocious, a mad perfectionist who chewed footnotes like medicinal candy. The firm I worked for in turn worked for a group of immense, mystically integrated shipping companies. We younger men grinding away in the back offices were all from landlocked interior towns; the cluster of our lawyerly heads slogging over our crowded-together desks looked like a breezeless patch of dun wheat. In the lunch-jokes we traded (pressed hard, we mostly ate out of paper bags at our desks) we snubbed landlubbers and talked about the wondrous Queens, whose formidable documents passed through our days like tender speckled sails. We all said we felt the sea in those papers more intensely than any sailor below decks; we toiled for the sea through the conscientious tips of our ball-point pens. Of course we said much of this in self-mockery, and some wag always found the opportunity to hum 'polish up the handle on the big front door' from Pinafore, but there was a certain spirit in which we really believed it. Those fabled white-thighed ships in the harbour not many streets west of our offices meant commerce and passengers, and we were the controlling godlets of commerce and passengers. Our pens struck, and the ships would begin the subtle, gigantic tremor of their inmost sinews; our pens struck again, and the engines would die in the docks. Talk of being lord of the waves! Curiously, I never had any desire to journey anywhere at all in those days. On the one hand, I didn't dare; to take a vacation and go blithely off to look at the world would have been to lose my place in line, and if I knew anything at all, I knew I was headed for the captain's table, so to speak, of that firm. And on the other hand, it was enough to smell the salt scent rising out of the mass of sheets on my blotter, each crowned with a printed QUEEN MARY, QUEEN ELIZABETH, QUEEN WILHELMINA, QUEEN FREDERICA, QUEEN EKENEWASA – it was the salt of my own loyal sweat.

The ships themselves, of course, we never saw; they were brawny legends to us. Now and then, though, we would get to hear what we supposed was an actual captain. Whenever a captain showed up in our offices he was sure to be heard, and he was sure to be angry – usually at one of us. He would spend half an hour bawling at some tangled indiscretion of ours perpetrated in triplicate sheafs, and we could catch his vibrations through the partners' Olympian oak doors – shouts of wrath; but the shouts always disappointed. If you didn't understand to begin with that it was a captain in there, you might think it was the head of a button-manufacturers' union, or a furniture company, or a cotton farm. All that monsoon of rage was only about cargoes delayed on trains, or cargoes arrived three weeks too soon, or cargoes – mostly this – unpaid for. Or else it was a complaint about registry or tariffs, or a quarrel over tankers. It was no use visualizing commanders of triremes or galleons – almost all the captains we heard yelling through those oak doors were tanker-types, and when they came out, still vaguely snarling but mainly mollified (it was hardly coincidence that afterwards one of us would feel the threat of getting fired), they all turned out to be rather short, flabby men wearing business suits and not very shiny brown shoes. My doorman had more of the salt about him than any of them.

Ah, well, the secret of it all was this: they were captains in our fancy only. What they really were, those furious ordinary men, was executives of the shipping line come to unravel a mix-up in the charter contract. It was nothing but contracts, after all – landlubber stuff. The farmers down near Clarksburg used to growl just that way, no different, over market-prices, subsidies, transport. And the captains – this was the worst of it – the glorious captains, those princes and masters whom we never saw and whose ships we only imagined, were, like us, only employees. They had no sway over the schemes of the sea, which belonged to our calm partners behind their doors and to the plain farmer-tanker sorts who ran the lines with their brown-shod feet set squarely on a dry expensive rug.

But if you avoided the shipping executives and the freight forwarders and stuck to the names of the Queens and kept your pen charging through that stupendous geography of paperwork – Porto Amélia, Androko, Funchal, Yokohama, Messina, Kristiansand, Reykjavik, Tel Aviv, and whatnot – you could preserve your sea-sense and all its luminous briny tenets. There was a period one spring when, I remember, I used to read Conrad far into the night and every night, novel after novel, until I felt that, if I had not been a seaman in my last incarnation, I was sure to be one in my next. And when, in the morning, groping groggily at my desk, I confronted a fresh envelope full of contradictory demands and excruciatingly detailed sub-clauses, it seemed like a plunge into the wave of life itself: Aruba, Suez, Cristobal, and all the rest crept up my nostrils like some unbearable siren's perfume, all weedy, deep, and wild. Those days a hot liquid of imagination lived in the nerve of my joy.

Still, I never actually boarded a ship until my uncle Al, a feed-man in

Chillicothe, decided the time had come for Paris and Rome to experience him. He was a thrifty person, but not unprogressive; he had opted in favour of sea travel and against flying because aunt Essie had always thought the Wright brothers blasphemous. 'If God had wanted people to fly, you and I would be flapping this minute,' Al quoted her. She was dead three years, and my uncle's trip was a kind of memorial to Essie's famous wanderlust. She had once stayed overnight in Quebec, and it seemed to her it would be interesting to spend a week or so in a place where everyone acted insane; she meant the effect on her of a foreign language. Al said he himself wouldn't mind if he never set foot out of Chillicothe and environs, but it was for the sake of Essie he was going out to look at those places. 'She would have wanted me to,' he said, squinting through my windows at the river. There were no children to leave the money to; he was resolved to get rid of it himself. 'Is that the ocean out there?' he asked. 'It's the East River.' 'Phew, how can you live with the smell?' he wondered.

The next day – it was a Saturday – we took a taxi to the piers. Al let me pay the fare. There was a longshoremen's strike on, so we had to carry the bags aboard ourselves. The ship was Greek, compact and confined. The patchy white paint on the walls of the tubular corridors was sweating. 'Why, the downstairs powder room at home's bigger than this,' Al said, turning around in the box of his room. He was sharing it with another passenger, who had not yet arrived; all we knew of him was his name, Mr Lewis, and that he was from Chicago. 'Big city guy,' my uncle said in a worried voice. Mr Lewis came so late that the visitors' leaving-signal, something between a gong and a whistle, had already been blown twice: he had only one little canvas bag, with a sort of tapestry design involving roses and a calligraphic letter L on the sides – he swung it between a pair of birch crutches. He told my uncle he was a retired cabinetmaker and had arthritis. His true name was Laokonos, and he was going to Patrai to meet his brother's family. Mr Lewis had an objectionably strong accent, and I could see my uncle meant to patronize him all the way across. 'Goodbye, have a good trip,' I said. 'Fine,' my uncle said, 'will do. You bet. Thanks for putting me up and all. I'll remember you in my will,' he joked.

The signal hooted a third time and I went down the gangplank and onto the covered pier – it was really a concrete roof with a solid concrete floor and open sides. It felt like the inside of a queer sort of warehouse, not like a pier at all. You could not even see the water – the bulk of the ship, pressed close against the margins of the sidewalk, obscured it – but the wind was tangible and shot through with an ecstatic gritty taste. I thought I would wait to watch the ship move off into the water. It was a small, pinched, stingy, disappointing thing, apparently without a single sailor anywhere on board; then it occurred to me that the owners might have been too poor to afford proper sailors' dress, and passengers, visitors, and mariners were all indistinguishably civilian. Anyhow most were Greeks. On the pier all the people waiting for the ship to shudder into action and farewell were talking Greek. There we stood in a patient heaving jostling bunch, raggedly crushed up against the barricade at the end of the sidewalk under that warehouse canopy, staring at a long piece of peeling sunlit hull. The top part of the ship was hidden by the roof of the pier, the middle part was cut off by the sidewalk, and what we had framed for us was a quarter-mile of flank, without even the distinction of a porthole. The Greeks went on strangling themselves with their jabber, which seemed to knock them in the teeth as they spoke; meanwhile the ship did not stir. It was not what I had imagined a dock scene to be, and after half an hour of that mute vigil it struck me that the intelligent thing to do would be to vanish. My uncle was irretrievably encased somewhere in the marrow of this grimy immobile crab, and in any event there was not even a deck with a rail for him to lean over while we mutually waved and mouthed – nothing of the sort.

'You think something's wrong? The engine?' one of the visitor-Greeks beside me asked in perfectly acceptable New York English. 'My mother's on there, going to see relatives, you shoulda seen her cry when I brought in the fruit. Who you got on?' 'My uncle,' I said, reduced to a Greek with relatives. 'Ever been down here before?' the Greek asked – 'how come they take so long to get going?' 'Bet they sprung a leak,' someone volunteered. 'The cook's got indigestion, by mistake he ate what they serve the passengers.' 'There was a mutiny, they found out the captain ain't Greek.' 'A Turk, they threw him to the sharks.' 'Believe me, when you get back over there in a clean suit of clothes, they're worse than sharks, they think you're an American you're a millionaire.' A local segment of the crowd gave a cheerful howl at this: there was a camaraderie of seers-off I had not suspected. 'Excuse me,' I said, attempting a passage through. 'You leaving?' 'What you want to leave for?' 'She's gonna take off!' 'You'll miss when she starts!' they cried at me from all around. And then, dropped with a startling clarity among the duller voices, a voice unlike the others: 'Don't go. It's a mistake to go so soon.

There's always a delay, even with the Queens, and if you go you won't see the milky part.'

The cocky tone of this – and then the shimmering word 'Queens', which secreted all my private visions – held me. I looked and looked. 'Milk?' I called like a fool.

'The wake. It's like a rush of milk expressed from the pith of Mother Sea.'

She was two yards from where I stood clamped by the laughing mob, a woman of forty or so, small, puffed out by an overstarched dress. It was grey but a little childish for her age and face. Her slivery eyes were darkly ringed like a night-bird's. 'If you see someone off you should see it *through*,' she chirped back at me.

I said helplessly, 'I've waited—'

'So have we all. You're *supposed* to wait. It's part of the sacred rites of the pier. And when she heaves off you're supposed to give a great yell. I'll bet this is only your first time. I'll bet you're a dryfoot. Midwesterner?' she wondered from afar.

A growl was prepared under our feet. The concrete rumbled like a dentist's drill. 'She's starting!' 'She's going!' 'I can see her move. She's moving!' The mangy rectangle of ship-side glared back at us without a sign of motion; as if to set it an example, the mob began to mill. Then, with a kind of gentle hiccup, the hull commenced to tingle visibly, almost to twitch, like the rump of a horse. A jungle-roar came out of her and struck our faces. 'There!' 'Can you see anybody?' 'The deck's on the other side.' 'There ain't no deck.' 'Look for a porthole.' 'Porthole's too low down.' 'Oil, that's what it is. I told you oil.'

A metal smell, the fragrance of some heavy untrustworthy machine, assaulted the wind. The water was all at once revealed, a vomit of snow. It piled itself on itself, whorl on whorl, before it melted into a toiling black, like an ominous round well or dark-blooded eye. The creamy wake ran swiftly after the stern. Without warning she was off and out, and we saw the whole of her, stacks, strakes, and all, grumbling outwards. The farther she went the better she looked. She smoothed herself down into an unflecked unsoiled whiteness; she rode with her head up, like something royal, and the Greeks shrieked and waved. Then she made a wide turn, trailing out of the harbour into the shining platter of openness, and we could spy, on her other haunch, a tiny deck filled with tiny figures. My uncle and Mr Lewis must have been among those wee dolls.

But I had had enough, and walked the long dim concrete route out to Canal Street for a taxi, peculiarly saddened.

It was only a week after this that my young cousin's senior class came through, thirty fastidious crew-hatted girls from Consolidated High, headed for a tour of 'Scotland, the Hebrides, England, and Wales': thus spake the tour pamphlet. 'Not Ireland?' I said. 'George, *nobody's* interested in *Ireland*,' my cousin said (she was really my first cousin once removed); 'we're going to see an actual *stool* that Robert Burns sat on. It's in a museum in Edinburgh. Did you know there's a big castle, like an old king's castle, right in the middle of Edinburgh? It's in the catalogue, want to see its picture? I don't know how you can stand New York. Mama thinks you're crazy to live in such a place, full of killers with daggers.' She made a pirate's face and handed me a goblet of champagne. They were giving themselves a party. All over the ship – it was a students' ship, and German – there were parties. A gang of boys had hauled the canvas off a lifeboat and were drinking from green bottles, their knees flattened under the seats. The ship smelled of some queer unfamiliar disinfectant, as though it were being scoured desperately into a state of sanitation. The students did not seem to mind the smell. Their bunks were piled with suitcases and stuffed knapsacks. 'We're landing at Hamburg first, and then we have to go *back*wards to Southampton,' my cousin explained. 'It's cheaper to do it backwards. The champagne's all gone, you want some beer?' She went to get me some, but forgot to come back. The senior class of Consolidated High began to scream out a song. They screamed and screamed, and though I had promised my cousin's mother I would take care of Suzy as long as she was in New York, I felt suddenly superfluous and wandered off on my own. The disinfectant followed like a bad cloud. In a corner of a cabin two levels down, jammed into the angle of a bunk, I saw the starched woman. She was eating a piece of orange layer cake, and there were four shouting students squatting beside her. 'Who're you seeing off now?' she addressed me out of the din. 'Your sister?'

'Don't have a sister.'

'Brother? Don't have a brother. Have some cake instead?'

I squeezed into the cabin and accepted a bit of icing on a paper plate. 'Who're *you* seeing off?' I asked her.

'The sailors. What do you do?'

'Fine,' I said.

'I didn't say how, I said what. I can see you're fine – you have very fine skin, you're not a sailor anyhow. My God, it's noisy on this one. I'm about ready for the dock. Will you wait till the end today?'

'The end of what?' I said; I thought her too friendly and too obscure.

'Of the dock part. You've got to see her go.'

'I saw her go last time.'

'You don't talk of time when you talk of Greek sailors. Greek sailors are tineless. Greek sailors are immortal, I bet you work in an office. Something dry, no leaks.'

'A law office,' I admitted.

'Makes sense, but I don't like lawyers. Wouldn't be one for anything. I'd be a sailor if I were a man. I suppose you're thinking I'm an old maid – well, I'm not. I've got a couple of married daughters, would you believe that?'

I politely muttered that the fact was hardly credible.

'I know,' she agreed. 'I've kept my youth.' We struggled through the ship together, and finally out of it and down the gangplank, while I observed for myself that this last remark of hers was almost justified. 'If you see someone off you should see it *through*,' she said emphatically, in the same confident voice as last time. She had a long but all the same jolly face: long earlobes stuck through with long wooden earrings, a long square nose, a long hard chin. She wore her hair too long. The first quick look you gave her took off fifteen years, and turned her into a girl, not pretty, but rather of the 'interesting' category, which I had always found boring; the second look, not so quick, put the years right back on, but assured you of something wise and pleasant. We waited for the ship's wake to form, and then waited for her to find a dairy metaphor that did for it. 'Butter-churn,' she said at last – 'the ocean's butter-and-eggs route. I *don't* like adolescents. They can't concentrate. Sailors can concentrate – well, maybe it's because they *have* to,' she conceded. 'Do you have to go back now?'

'I'm past my lunch hour.'

'Poor you. A little drudge. Do you see that drugstore down there – no, the one across, over there.' She pointed along Canal Street. 'That's my husband's. He's been a pharmacist around here for just about forever. A drudge worse than you, and been one longer. I doubt whether he's ever walked two blocks to the piers for the thrill of the thing. *I* do it practically every day. You like the water, don't you?'

This startled me. 'Yes,' I said.

'Well, law leaves *me* all at sea too,' she cracked, and fell into a tumble of laughter. She darted into the dark little store when we came to it. 'In the afternoons I help out sometimes,' she piped from the doorway.

After that it was a neighbour from home I put up, and then two members of the Clarksburg Post Office; and the Mayor actually. It seemed to me the whole timid town was emptying itself out, via my apartment and the docks, to throw itself on the breast of Europe. I could scarcely account for the miracle of all that fit of travelling that had fallen on the state of Ohio. As for the traffic that passed through my hands in particular (and my towels and my sheets), I soon began to understand how word had gotten back that I was, though crazy to live in such a place, cheaper than any hotel in the same place, and that I could 'afford' it. This was the price I paid for having boasted so frequently of my grand salary, which now – after a weekend of restaurant dinners and taxi fares for a pair of honeymooners, children of the brother-in-law of a treasured friend of my great-aunt-by-marriage – hardly seemed so grand. The price my visitors paid was something else, and perhaps worse – word got back to *me*, ever so mildly, that in Ohio I was considered a dull unlively half-dead sort, a snob, preoccupied with my own vanity, a New York careerist. They wrote me off as a lifelong bachelor-to-be, without a heart.

On my side I thought them all wretchedly ungrateful, and if I kept my threshold open for them it was to study their ingratitude. They streamed in, earmarked by every cliché of inland dress, the men's trouser-legs ludicrously billowing, the women very large in their backward-brimmed hats and tunicked flowered rayon suits and chalky white shoes, all of them gloved and looking out cautiously from narrow-nosed, sun-fearful, flaky faces. I despised their slow voices and I was certain they privately jeered at mine, with its acquired pace hard-won at Yale. We made briskly poisonous parties of it; I had the satisfaction of noting plainly how the headwaiters shared my contempt for them. The truth was, I suppose, that I courted and fed on my contempt, glad to see what I was well out of. The women asked pityingly whether I had never been abroad, and when I admitted I hadn't, the men laughed through cigar mist and said, 'Now then, y'see, I've always maintained there's no one more provincial than a New Yorker. Never seen the Eiffel Tower? Never seen Rome? Well I tell you, George, go ahead and have a look at Rome. One thing about Rome, it's worth a whole roll of film.'

That spring I saw the inside of all sizes and varieties of ships and ship-cabins, the greasy and the glittering, wherein I nuzzled elbow-to-elbow with my recent guests, all of us gripping our modest drinks in an unconfident little group and sick to death of one another's shafts. By then they had stopped asking when I was going to get some sense into my head and come back home to live in the real America; but by then the relief that always followed the self-indulgence of my scorn for them had begun to take hold. Standing, secretly frightened, in their narrow travelling-closets, they stood for everything I had escaped. They went on their foolish ritual tours and thought themselves worldly, and by Christmas would have forgotten it all if it had not been for the ritual colour slides they showed as ritual proofs of the journey. And I, meanwhile, took *them* as ritual proofs of my own journey – of how perilously near I had been to becoming a boarder of ships, instead of a seer-off. The passenger inexorably returns to his town in the stupid marrow of the land; the man on the dock quivers always at the edge of possibility. What I had attained, in my short stride from midland to brink, was width, endlessness. Waving vainly on the pier, I waved goodbye to all my dead ends. When at last the ship ground vibrating out through its scribble of spume, headed not really for its destination but more essentially for the way back, something like prayerfulness ascended in me, I thought at first it was only pleasure, that the burdensome visitors were gone; but then I knew it was the peace of clinging to the rim of infinity, without the obligation of resuming the limits of my old land-sewn self.

Through it all I never missed glimpsing the starched woman, with her long head and her deceptive long-haired girlishness; it was like being startled by a constantly yielding keyhole; sometimes I caught a curious view of her in someone's cabin, noiselessly clinking her earrings in an abyss of noise, and now and then I saw her leaning, always in a festive mob, holding on to a cookie, over a deck-rail, or threading in rope sandals through a slender corridor with a slender searching eye. Then the leaving-gong would clamour, and often enough I would find her beside me in the dock crowd, thirsting downwards into the white whirl excreted by the outgoing ship. She was always dressed with a noticeable cleanness and stiffness – her sleeves and skirts were as rigid as a dark linen sail. 'Whipped cream,' she said of the wake, and then as usual we walked out with self-gratified wise sadness into the noon glister of Canal Street, until the black doorway of the drugstore sucked her suddenly in.

Or she would not be there. And then – the day after I had seen someone off and she was not there – I would leave my office at lunchtime and take my sandwich in my paper bag with me and walk west to the docks, along Canal Street, past the hardware marts spread outwards on all the sidewalks, and choose a pier alongside which lay a white liner, and look for her. And there she would be, laughing seriously among strangers, eating cake, stamping her feet with their visible clean toes on the concrete, all for farewell to the departing voyagers. Or else would not.

She would not be there more often than she would be there, and on those days I was always disappointed. I circled the cement dock-floor awhile, chewing my sandwich at the side of an idle Cunarder, and tramped back, inflamed by regret and belching mustard, to my desk and its spotted documents. The Queens did not satisfy me then; I had the itch of curiosity. She was never there to see anyone in particular off, I had learned; no one she knew ever went abroad; she was there for the sake of the thing itself – but I never could fathom what that thing was: was it the ships? the sailors? the polyglot foreignness? Was it only an afternoon walk she took to the nearest bustling place? Was she a madwoman? I began to hope, for the colourfulness of it, that she might really be cracked; but whenever we conversed, she was always decently and cheerfully sound – though, it must be said, not like others. She was a little odd.

She asked me one day whether I was good at cross-examination.

'We don't do much of that in our office. Mostly it's desk work. We don't go to court hardly at all – the idea is we try to keep the clients *out* of court,' I explained.

'Haven't you ever been to a trial?'

'Oh, I've *been* to 'em.'

'But never broke a witness down?'

I smiled at this brutality of hers. 'No. Really, I'm not a trial lawyer. I just sit at a desk.'

'You're a passive intellectual.'

'No, I'm not. Not really.'

'Well, I'm glad you're not the sort who tries to get things out of people – admissions.'

'You don't have to admit anything to me,' I promised.

'I wouldn't anyhow,' she said. 'I'm the sort who doesn't tell things. If you tell things you don't get to keep them.'

'*I* don't like to keep things,' I said.

'Do you like to keep people?'

'I guess not. If I did I wouldn't always be sending them off.'

'You're not sending anyone off today,' she observed. 'And you were here day before yesterday, and you didn't send anyone off then either.'

'True,' I said.

'Are you keeping someone back?'

I had to laugh, though not pleasantly. 'I guarantee you my apartment's empty right now.'

'I want to see it. Your apartment. You said you can see the water from it?'

'Not this water – just the river.'

'All water is one,' she announced. 'I want to see. No one's there at all?'

'I don't keep anyone. Really. Not even a mistress.'

She looked offended at this. 'I have married daughters. I told you. And a husband. They're my wake. You understand? When you live you leave a wake behind you, and it always follows you, whatever you do. What you've been and where you've been are like a milk that streams out past you all the time, you can't get free of them. Mortality issues its spoor.'

I was suddenly angry; she was lecturing me with platitudes, as though I were a boy. 'Well, don't worry,' I said. 'I haven't invited you to be kept!'

'You haven't,' she agreed. 'But you will. Oh, you will, you will.'

I said, exasperated, 'Are you a clairvoyant?'

'Don't sneer. Everyone is who goes along with Nature. You're not made of wood.'

I touched the side of her dress, which extended as crisply as the hide of a tree. 'No,' I said, 'but *you* are. Why do you dress like this? Why don't you ever wear anything soft?'

'To armour myself. If I were soft you'd want to keep me.'

'Oh, go to the devil.'

'And the deep blue sea,' she said, turning her hard back on me.

I stayed away, after that, for almost a whole week. I did not even know her name (though she knew mine), and still I disliked her. She was a triviality, a druggist's wife, a crank who hung around the docks, and I thought myself absurd for having given so many lunch hours to her queer company. I kept my sandwich on my desk and rattled papers while I ate it; my colleagues did the same; I had already, as a consequence of having sacrificed all those bright noons to the docks, fallen a little behind them. We were in an unacknowledged race. The more documents one digested, the more one was digested by the firm: I had to remind myself that my whole ambition was assimilation into that mystical body. But I felt vaguely enervated. The race seemed not quite to the purpose; yet I hardly

knew what was more to the purpose. My colleagues struck me as silly
now when they whistled *Pinafore* or snickered out their little jokes about
tanker-types. I withdrew from them – I don't think they noticed at first –
and immersed my unexpectedly bored brain in the Queens' sheets. But
now they seemed not so much like sails as – well, sheets. They fluttered
under my hands with the limpness of unruly bedclothes. Their salt
emanation I knew to be no more and no less than human sweat. I gave up
reading at night; I gave up sticking at home nights. I put on my oldest
pair of shoes and scuffed along the riverside – to reach it I had to dare
the Drive that swarmed on its ledge. The car lights smacked my eyes and
I ran for my life across that wild road with its wild shining herds. Up from
the stinking water came the noises of melted garbage sloshing against the
artificial bank. Rarely I saw a barge creep by. The river was not enough.

On Friday night – the end of that same week of abstinence – I walked
crosstown and took a bus that sliced inexorably towards the lowest part of
the city, where the harbour lay pining. A pungent mist crowded the air. It
was dark down there, a dark patrolled by the scowls of guards. They
would not let me out onto the piers, so I prowled the cobbled sidewalks,
looking down alleys; once I saw a pair of rats the size of crouched
penguins, one hurrying after the other in a swift but self-aware
procession, like a couple of priests late for divine service. The docks were
curiously uninhabited, except by a row of the smaller sort of ship, bleak
cut-outs with irregular edges as if chewed out by bad teeth – the
mammoth prideful ones were all out at sea, or else dispersed among the
world's more fortunate ports. I longed sorely for one of these: one of the
radiant Queens – it was for these I had made this night-time pilgrimage,
hoping for the smell and signal of deep deep ocean. The loneliness of
that place was excruciating; now and then a derelict lurched by, or a
hushed criminal sliding forth on an errand of rape. For the first time I
had an unmistakable desire to go on a voyage – I was aware of it as surely
as of a taste: I had to have the marrow of a fleck of salt. I had to search
into the inmost corridor of my urgency. I scurried eastwards, then south
(imitating the pace and gait of those sacerdotal rats), to the death-lit
Battery. The terminal was as brilliantly electric as some hell. A ferry
stood panting in its slip, and I boarded it on the run, just as the gate
began to close. The dock and the stern split apart and the tame water
dandled and puddled between them, nearly under my feet. A froth spit
up all the way, stronger and stronger. The wind on the deck was harshly
warm. I sank my gaze into that harbour-pool, and pulled a rope of sea-

smell into a gluttonous lung; it was not enough. It was not the Thule of depths, it was not ocean enough, it was not savage enough. It was not salt enough.

Returning from Staten Island I slept on one of the side-deck benches; a drunk and I tenderly shared shoulders. The ferry was as bright as a wedding-palace or carousel. It was full of music borne by lovers embracing transistor radios. Once when the drunk's head fell from my shoulder, I awoke and saw in the blackness beyond the ferry's aureole a fantastic parade, majestically decorous – I thought it was a galaxy of rats riding the top of the water; I glimpsed pointed alert ears. But it was sails. I saw the sails of galleons, schooners, Viking vessels, floating full and black; dark kites.

On Saturday morning I kept away; it seemed to me I had a fever, though my thermometer registered normal. All the same I wallowed and rooted in my hot bed all day, rising out of it only to drink ice water. I drew the blinds so as to shut out the river; I was frighteningly parched. In the evening I poured whisky into the cold water, and then a little water into much whisky. On Sunday, though feeling no better, in an atavistic fit I went to church. The text was Jonah: 'For thou hadst cast me into the deep, in the midst of the seas; and the floods compassed me about: all thy billows and thy waves passed over me.' Afterwards I vomited in the vestry.

The next day, at noon (but I had brought no lunch), I was too impatient to walk, so I hailed a taxi for the piers, but leaped out of it in the middle of Canal Street, within a block's sighting of the wharf buildings. We had been halted by thickening traffic; I could not endure it. The rest of the way I ran, I ran up the stairs and into the long concrete hall. Everything was as usual – the mob, the noise, the familiar screeches of goodbye. Dimly from the bowels of a dim-grey ship I heard the leaving-gong. It was a Jewish ship heading for the Holy Land – it had an unhealed gash in its prow and along part of its visible side. All around were Orthodox sectarians wearing black hats and long black coats and antic beards, some of them clownishly red. They were weeping as though the broken wall of the ship were some ancient holy ravaged mortar. I flagged my arms like a fleeing ostrich through their cries and forced myself into the stream descending the gangway. A huge-breasted woman in a robust white uniform, robustly striped at the wrists, called to me to desist, but I pushed harder against the breasts pressing downwards against my climb. Still struggling I was freed into the ship, heard a wired voice command departure, and began to comb the passageways for my stiff prey. Almost instantly I found her; she was leaning against the door of a public lavatory, gleaming with splendid tears; her long face looked varnished. The gong struck again, the voice in the loudspeakers hoarsened and coarsened. 'Why are you crying, for God's sake?' I said. 'Everyone else is,' she said, 'everyone all over the place.' 'Quick, let's hop off or we'll end up in Jerusalem.' I pulled her by the sleeve – the starch of it scratched my palm – and we flew downwards. In a moment the hastening ship began to moan itself loose from the dock. The onlookers sent out a tremor of ecstasy. They joined themselves neck to neck and kicked out, kicked in, spun: they were dancing the ship towards the sacred soil. 'Let's dance, too,' I said: I was overjoyed at the miracle of having seized her in the pinch of my will. 'No, no,' she said, 'I don't dance, dancing makes me simply creak, I'm an antique for goodness' sake, I'm not young.' I lifted her in the air – but she was as heavy as a beam – and flung her down again, out of breath. 'See?' she said. 'I told you.' 'What's your name?' I demanded; 'all weekend I remembered that I don't know your name.' 'Undine.' 'Undine?' 'Call me Undine,' she insisted. 'I will if you want me to. What does the druggist call you?' 'Sylvia,' she replied, 'a name for a stick. A stick-in-the-mud name.' 'Undine,' I said.

That afternoon we became lovers. She peered down from the windows of my apartment. 'I like it up so high,' she squealed – 'you said you could see the river, though.'

'There it is.'

'That little dirty string?'

'All water is one,' I said, mimicking her.

She looked at me meditatively. '*I* taught you that.' And then, rattling the sash: 'Oh, I like it up so high! I miss being up high. Where I live now it's low.'

'That window's not made to open,' I explained, 'we're air-conditioned, can't you tell?'

'Sure I can tell. Air out of a machine. That's abnormal. It isn't natural, I'm against it.'

'Come back to the bed,' I begged, 'it's all right here.'

'They'll miss you at your office.'

'They're all drudges at my office.'

'I taught you that.'

'Teach me, teach me,' I said.

'I'll teach you fashion first. You don't like my clothes.'

'I'm against clothes, they're not natural. You're not fashionable anyhow – your clothes are like bark. I peel bark, that's what I do.'

'I know you do. I knew you would.'

'You're a clairvoyant.'

She laughed with an eerie autumnal clarity, like a flutter of leaves. 'No I'm not. I just go along with the tide. If I see a tidal wave I just mount it, that's all.'

'I'm the tide,' I said.

'I'm a wave.'

'I'm the crest of the wave.'

'I'm the trough.'

'We coruscate.'

'Like a fish's back.'

'We rock, we tumble, we turn.'

'I can see all the world's water from here, it's so high.'

'You stay down,' I ordered her.

She stayed all that night, and all the next day and all the next night. Early on the third day I put on a business suit – how strange it felt on my liberated, my sharpened, skin! – and came into my office as in a trance. My colleagues looked oddly nonhuman, like some unfamiliar species of sea-animal; the papers languishing on my desk seemed to have rotted. 'You didn't answer the telephone,' they accused, 'were you away? An emergency?'

'I think I was sick,' I said, and at once believed it.

'You look thin,' they said, 'how thin you've gotten.'

In the mirror in the washroom I examined my thinness. It was true, I had grown very thin.

'Are you staying in for lunch?' they asked me. 'Or are you going out like week before last?'

'Sure,' I said, unsure of either.

'We had a man over from one of the Queens the other day. You missed some real roars, boy. A tycoon.'

'A typhoon?' I said.

'Are you sick? You look sick,' they said, giggling.

'I'd better go home again,' I agreed, and went. The apartment smelled of decay. She was gone; she had turned off the air-conditioner and the refrigerator. My pillow smelled of rot. The milk had soured; so had the wine and the cream; two or three peaches were black. A bowl of blueberries had been transformed into an incredibly beautiful flower, all gilded over with mould.

I lay in my bed, exhausted by desire for desire; spiralled in reverie, I dreamed our three-days' lovemaking. I thought how she had slid from her parchment sheath and how all my pulse had mingled with hers. 'Undine,' I pronounced to myself, depleted. The belt of her dress was coiled, on a chair; I reached out a languid hand and unfurled it. It was stiff, like frozen linen, like the side of a fossil-tree. But her waist had been flesh, and as pliant as a tongue. I hid the belt under my pillow; she had returned to her husband – this made me spring up. In half an hour I was beating Canal Street with truculent shoe-soles. I stamped and scudded, afraid to go over to the other side. Across the street, between two hardware vendors, the drugstore squatted like a dark fly. No one went in and no one came out. I wondered what sort of a living they could make in a place like that. A truck blinded the road and I ran in front of it; horns sang at me, for no reason I was still alive; I bought the first object my hand seized – a washboard. Clutching it like a lyre, I entered the drugstore. Behind a fly-flecked cardboard-crowded counter she stood holding (I thought) a real lyre, laughing her confident laugh. 'We're working on a lipstick display. Isn't it nice? Look—' Her instrument turned into a thin tray fluted with golden tubes, each bloody at the tip. I read the names of all the lipsticks: Purple Fire, Crimson Ice, Silver Gash, Heart's Wound. 'The pharmacist is out,' she said; 'I mean he's in the cellar. He's bringing up cartons. Cosmetics. Woman's weakness since Cleopatra. Nothing touches *my* face, let me tell you – only water. If you wait you can meet him.'

'Please,' I said, 'come back to the apartment.'

'Suppose your cousins are there? Or your brother? Or your uncle?'

'You know I don't have a brother. No one's there,' I swore. 'No one. No one's expected. The place is empty.'

'I shut off all the fake cold, did you notice?'

'Come back with me, Undine.'

'Sylvia. *He* calls me Sylvia. He used to be all right but now he's all dried up, he's practically not there. I don't love him. I don't know why I stay here. Where else would I stay? It isn't as though we had any children.'

'Your daughters? Your married daugh—'

Out of a hole in the flooring in the back part of the store a big tan box floated upwards; behind it (seeming to paddle up, as out of a whirlpool)

Undine's husband emerged. 'My husband's name is George too, did I tell you that?'

He was clearly disappointed that I was not a bona fide customer, we shook hands, and then he lifted the very hand he had given me and parted the fingers to make horns behind his head. 'She met you down there?' he asked. 'At the docks? She always hangs around there. Eventually I get to see 'em all. Don't think I mind, it's all the same to me, buddy.' He glared at my washboard. 'Did you pay for that thing?'

'It's his, honey, he bought it next door. We don't sell that item,' Undine said.

'Well, then put it on the order book, I don't mind the competition. One hundred thousand items in stock. Hairpins to Sal Hepatica. Paregoric to pair-of-garters. We don't do much prescription business, though. They all go uptown to those cut-rate places. Robbers, they cheat on the Fair Trade Law, cut off their nose to spite their face.'

'I hate my nose,' Undine said. 'It's too long. I look like Pinocchio with it, don't I?'

'Quit fooling around,' George said. 'You want to go out with him, go out with him. I got plenty to do here, I don't need help either.'

'Let's see if there's a ship going off,' she assented, 'one with real sails,' and I followed her out of the store.

'Why do you treat him like that?' I asked.

'Oh, I don't know. Because I want to. Because he looks just like the Devil. Doesn't he look just *exactly* like the Devil, I mean really and truly?'

I considered it; she was perfectly correct. He was all points, like the ears of a rat – he was the driest, thinnest man I had ever seen. For some reason I felt cooled towards her. Her toes in her rope sandals looked too straight, too rigid. The tops of her sleeves jutted straight up from her shoulders. Her hem was like a rod.

'All the sails have come in by now. Did you read about it in the papers? From all over the world. They train sailors on those old sailing ships. Replicas. That's how they teach them about ropes and things. There's a Viking one from a movie they made. Did you see about it in the papers? Every single country's sent a sailing ship into New York harbour. It's a show, didn't you read about it?'

I said hoarsely, 'I haven't seen a newspaper in three days.'

'Well, they came before that. They started to come in last week. It's thrilling, don't you think it's thrilling?'

'I don't want to go to the docks. I want you to come home with me,' I said, but I hardly knew now whether I meant it. Guilt over her husband ground in my throat. 'Why did you say you had daughters?'

She stopped. 'Oh, you're a liar.'

'*I* haven't told any lies.'

'You said you never cross-examine. You said you never pry. You said you don't try to *get* things out of people.'

'What's that got to do with daughters or no daughters?'

'Of *course* I've got daughters,' she said sullenly. 'I have a husband, don't I? – They're married, I told you, and gone away.'

'All right,' I said. 'I misunderstood.'

'I don't want you any more.'

'I don't want you either.'

'You're a drudge. You look exactly like the Devil yourself.'

'I've lost weight,' I said, defending my body.

'You might have a cancer. Cancers always begin that way. – Look at the sails!'

We had come to the end of an alley opening on the water: a thousand dazzlements cluttered the sky. Sails, sails – it was as if some suddenly domesticated goddess had reached down to hang an aeon's worth of laundry. Or it was as if a flight of enormous gulls had paused in silence to expose their perfect bellies to the equal perfection of the daylight's brilliance. The harbour seemed very still. 'If it's a show,' I said, 'where's everybody? If it's a flotation museum, where are the visitors?' 'Shush,' said Undine, 'it's just maritime business, who said the public was invited?' 'Where are the sailors?' '*I* don't know. Ashore maybe. Asleep. Don't ask me, maybe we're having a hallucination. Look at this one!' Almost from the utmost stretch of our fingertips a great enamelled bow rose, as curved and naked as a scimitar, shining wetly in the sun-gaze, like a nude breast: above the bare cutwater stood thirty-seven white-clad sentries, stiff at attention in the clear air – it was a full-rigged ship under plain sail. 'Look at the masts!' Undine cried – 'they're like a forest. Big heavy trunks, then branches and twigs.' 'I don't like the hull,' I said, 'it looks too fragile. Potential sawdust. Give me steel every time.' 'Oh, that's wicked!' she said – 'steel comes out of a furnace, and then out of a machine, it isn't natural—' 'Sawdust,' I insisted, squinting upwards at the empty prow. It seemed to me there should have been a figurehead there.

She stomped after me reluctantly, scowling, kicking heavily, banging at things with my washboard. All the way uptown she would not speak to me; she spat at the doorman when he turned his glorious captain's coattails; she scratched her nails savagely on the elevator's grey metal walls. She would not come into the bed. 'I'm hungry,' she said. 'You switched off everything and spoiled all the food,' I complained. She sidled out of the kitchen frowning with contempt, grasping a tiny silver coffee spoon – then she went to the bedroom window and stabbed the handle through the glass. It did not shatter; it only gulped out a little hole, like a mouth, with creases and cracks and wrinkles radiating outwards. 'Air,' she said in triumph, and at last, at last, we made love.

But she was as weighty as a log. The mattress descended under her, groaning. She raised her legs and thrust them on my shoulders, and it was as though I had dived undersea, with all the ocean pressing on my arched and agonized spine. I felt like a man with a yoke, carrying on its ends a pair of buckets under a spell – the left one held the Atlantic, the right one the Pacific. When I slid my hand under her nape to lift her mouth to my gasping mouth, it seemed to me her very neck was a cord of wood. Her hair oppressed the pillow, each strand a freight, a weight, a planet's burden of gravity. How heavy she had become! Her tongue lying on my tongue exhausted me. I toiled over her unrefreshed, unspeakably wearied, condemned to a slavery of sledging logs.

'What's the matter?' she whispered. 'Don't you love me? Are you tired?'

With convulsed breath I told her I loved her.

'You satisfy me,' she said.

She stayed the night. We ate nothing, drank nothing; we never left the bed. In the morning I said I would go out. 'No, no,' she commanded. She snatched her belt from under the pillow, where she had discovered it, and buckled her wrist to the bedpost. 'I'm attached,' she said. 'I can't leave, and neither can you. I've got to stay forever, and so do you.'

'My job,' I said.

'No.'

'Your husband,' I appealed.

'I don't have a husband.'

'Undine, Undine—'

'Come on me again,' she said. 'Come aboard, I want you.'

'We'll starve. We'll perish. They'll find our bodies—'

'I don't have a body. Don't you want me?'

'I want you,' I wept, and heaved myself into the obscuring billows of my bed. She made me sweat, she made me a galley slave, my oar was a log flung into the sea of her.

'No more!' I howled; it was already dawn.

'But you satisfy me,' she said reasonably. 'Don't I satisfy you?'

I kissed her palms, her mouth, her ears, her neck, for gratitude, for torment, for terror. 'Let's go for a walk,' I begged.

'Where? I'm welded here, I told you.'

'Anywhere. I'll take you home. We'll walk all the way.'

'It's miles and miles. Will you carry me?'

'I've carried you miles and miles already.'

'I don't want to go home.'

'Then wherever you want.'

'I have no home. I'm homeless. I'm adrift.'

'Wherever you want, Undine! Only to leave here awhile. Air.'

'But I broke the window for you, didn't I?' she said innocently.

'We'll go look at the sailing ships,' I proposed.

She had hold of my hair. She licked my eyelids. 'No. No, no, no.'

'Never mind,' I said, practical and purposeful. 'Put on your clothes.'

'I have no clothes.'

'Where did you drop them?' I looked all around the room; they were not there, except for her starched belt, which still waggled stiffly from the bedpost. But on the chair I saw the washboard – she had brought it all the way from Canal Street.

'Here,' she said, grabbing it. 'I'll play you a tune. Can you sing?'

'No.' For the moment I forgot that I had been in the Clarksburg church choir.

She drubbed her nails back and forth across the washboard.

'That sounds terrible. Stop it. Put on your clothes.'

'I have no husband, I have no daughters, I have no house, I have no body, I have no clothes,' she sang. 'Your love is all I have.'

I said in a fury, 'Then I'll go out alone.'

'All right,' she said mildly. 'Where?'

'To work. You know what I want?' I said. 'I want to go to my office and put in a good day's work, that's what.'

It was true; all at once I had a rapturous craving for work. In the street I passed a crew of diggers, sunk to their waists in a ditch, wearing yellow helmets. I envied them violently. Their backs were glazed, their vertebrae protruded like buried nuggets, under the lips of their helmets they lifted sweated wine-dyed lips. They grunted, quarrelled, cursed, barked (a few yards away it all turned into a liturgy), and all the while their spines dipped downwards, straining for the bottom of the ditch. They had nothing to do but devote themselves to the ditch. They were like a band of monks, ascetic, dedicated, their shining torsos self-flagellated.

The sight of them deflected my feet. I hated my office. I hated its swarming susurrant documents – they were all abstract, they were no more than buying and selling, they were only cadaverous contracts. The rest was myth and fantasy – the captains, the salt spray, the Queens. All mist, all nothingness. What I wanted then was work – shovels, pitchforks. I thought then of those inland towns and farms I had left behind where the work was real and not a figment, where the work could be felt in the spine; work was earth and earth was work. I thought, for want of earth, I would go down to the docks and hire myself out for a longshoreman or, better yet, a sailor. I felt I had given myself out too long to fancies, and, just as I was meditating on this very notion – how passion is no more palpable than the spume's lace and lasts no longer – I came to the drugstore, and went in, and had the horrified sense of looking into a mirror.

'We got 'em now,' said my double, 'a whole new shipment. Arrived today.'

'Shipment of what?' But I was shrill as a parrot.

'Them.' The druggist pointed to a pile of cheap washboards. 'I maintain if they got something next door, we got to take it in too, otherwise the competition smothers you.'

'But you look like me,' I said.

He was indifferent to this.

'Like *me*,' I insisted, stretching my eyelids, exposing my face. I could scarcely believe I had grown so spare, for he was as dry as a length of hay, and his skin was blotched and fulvous, and his jaw was sharp as a pin. His eyes were at the same time shrewd and hopeless, like those of a man resigned to his evil, though he might covertly despise himself for it.

'Look at me!' I said.

'Don't shout,' he warned in a voice of dignity. 'This is a professional pharmacy, ethical. Where's she at now?'

'In my bed.'

'Don't be too sure of that, buddy.'

'It's where I left her.'

'You left her there don't mean she's still there.'

'I don't like your looks,' I said.

'Then how come you zoomed all the way downtown to check on 'em? Listen,' he offered, 'I got a glass in the back, Sylvia uses it sometimes.' He led me past the prescription counter – it was scabbed with dust and antique droplets – and then down two steps to a small rear cubicle. A long piece of stained mirror clung to the wall. We stood side by side in front of it. 'See?' he sneered. 'Peas in a pod.'

I was staring at two straw-like creatures with pointed chins and ears and flickering eyes. 'A pair of Satans,' I cried.

'Well, we got different occupations,' he said soothingly. 'What kind of work you do?'

'A sailor,' I said. 'I'm going to ship out as soon as I get my papers.' But at the word 'papers' I suffered a chill.

'I used to be a sailor. Pharmacist's mate, SS *Wilkinson*. I been everywhere.'

'I haven't been anywhere.'

'With me it came out the opposite. She made me stick in one place. She got me rooted to this hole and I can't get out. I never get out. See that?' He waved a dry arm at a bundle in a corner. It was a narrow campbed tangled up in dirty blankets. 'I even sleep here. It's like the hold of a ship back here.'

'Where does your wife sleep?'

He gave a scornful smirk. 'You can answer that one better than me, buddy.'

'Look here,' I said, all business. 'I want to get rid of her. Get her out of my hair, will you?'

'Had enough? Too bad. That means she's only just getting started on you.'

'Quit grinning,' I yelled.

'I got to grin, why not? She runs her course.'

'How long?'

'How should I know? Depends how long she gets something out of it. With me it was only a year or so—'

'A year? One year? But you've got children, daughters, grown children—'

'*She's* the one with the daughters, not me. *She's* got daughters all over.'

'She said two. A couple, she said.'

'A couple of thousand, for all I know about it.'

'She said married!'

'Listen, she'll call anything a marriage. A blink, and it's a wedding.'

'Isn't she your wife?'

'Why not?'

I fled.

It was late when I arrived, even though I had not stopped for breakfast. My colleagues were already immersed at their desks; their papers shimmered and shuddered. From the partners' office came whip-sounds of bleating winds: a quarrel. 'It's over you,' they told me. 'They want to fire you. Old Hallet's holding out for you, though. Says your stuff's been very good up till now. Advocates mercy.'

'The reason I'm here,' I said bravely, 'is to resign.'

They tittered. 'Now you won't have to.'

'I have my pride,' I said.

'You leaving? Where've you been? You look like the devil, my God, you look like hell,' they said.

'If a woman comes here, don't let on you've seen me,' I pleaded.

'Little odd stout woman?' one of them said. 'Youngish and oldish both? Nice firm breasts? Nice hard belly? Nipples like carvings? She's already been.'

Terrified, I crept back from the door. '*Been* here?'

'Turned up an hour ago asking for you. Dishabille, so to speak.'

'Please!' I said out of a burning lung.

'Naked. Nude. In her birthday suit, George. Fine figure, straight as a pole.'

'Asking for me?'

'Asking for George.'

'Where is she?' I whispered.

'Lord knows. We sent for an ambulance, y'know. Had to. Not that a law firm's no place for loons, mind you—'

The shouts from the partners' office swelled; I heard my name.

'She was carrying a lyre. She was covering her modesty with it.'

'A washboard you mean,' I said.

'*There's* a loon for you. Poor poor George – it's *pos*sible to tell the difference, y'know.'

'It was only a washboard,' I persisted.

'A lyre,' they said. 'It looked like the real thing, that's the nuttiest part of the whole show. Made out of a turtle-shell, green all over. Phosphorescent sort of. Could've been dragged up out of the bottom of the sea, from its looks. Think she swiped it from a museum? If they don't get her on disorderly conduct they'll get her for that. Poor George. A friend of yours?'

I ran from them, choking.

She was waiting for me in my apartment: I was scarcely surprised. 'That was mean,' she said; in a shower of her long hair she squatted on my bed. 'They took me into a sort of truck. You let them do that! I had an awful time running away from them. They would've thrown me into prison!'

'You're out of your mind,' I said, 'going up there like that. You've lost me my job.'

'What do you care? You didn't want it anyhow.'

This was incontrovertible, though I wondered how she had guessed. 'Come here,' she commanded.

'You can't just go up into offices stark naked.'

'Who said I did? Oh, for goodness' sake, don't lecture, I only went up there to look for you. It's your fault, you shouldn't have gone away.'

'You can't *do* a thing like that in a civilized country. You'll probably get us into the papers. For all I know the police'll be up here in a minute.'

'I wasn't stark naked.'

'They said you were.'

'You believe everyone but me! I bet you'd even believe George, and George is about as steady as a leaf on a stem.'

'They said you didn't have anything *on*,' I said.

'I was in a hurry. Didn't I *tell* you I wanted you? You had no business running off. I couldn't find my clothes, that's all.'

'A stupid stunt.'

'Now you're in a rage again. Always in a rage.'

'I'm not—'

'Besides, I was covered up anyhow.'

'With what?'

'You're cross-examining again,' she accused. 'It's none of your affair. I covered up what's supposed to be covered up in a civilized country, that's all.'

'Where's that lyre thing?'

'Don't be stupid. How should I know? Come here, I want you.'

She tossed up a smooth leg. Against my will I went to her. 'They said you stole it.'

'Where on earth would I get a lyre? A funny thing like that? You're insulting.' She reached under my pillow, laughing crossly. There it was: the ancient little hand-harp. 'On my way up to your office I passed a pawnshop and saw it in the window and bought it.'

'Went into the pawnshop without any clothes on?'

'Oh, don't *dig* like that. Mind your own business. Look, I'll sing some more, all right? Do you know Greek? I'll sing you a Greek song.'

'*You* don't know Greek,' I said.

'Oh, don't I? I know all the languages. I know Greek, I know Walloon, I know Orangutan—'

But when she began to sing it was in German:

> *Meine Töchter sollen dich warten schön;*
> *meine Töchter führen den nächtlichen Reihn*
> *und wiegen und tanzen und singen dich ein.*

Her voice was coarse; it recalled a plank of fresh-cut wood thumped against the grain, and it was somehow blurred, like a horn heard from afar, or as if her lung had been afflicted by a fog. 'You don't sound like yourself,' I complained.

'A cold,' she assented. 'Don't interrupt.'

'Stop,' I said, 'I don't like it.'

'Are you one of those people who think every unfamiliar language makes a bad noise? You ought to have more sense than that,' she said, 'a man like you.'

This shamed me, so I listened mutely. But now she was continuing in new syllables I could not recognize, very short and rough. 'What language is that?'

'Phoenician,' she answered.

'Oh come on, is it Arabic?'

'I just told you, it's Phoenician. It's about the sea when the waves are especially high and the rowers can't see over their tops.'

I was annoyed. The dark queer burr in her throat had begun to arouse me, and I could not bear to be teased just then. I wanted to get rid of her. 'All right,' I said, 'you found an old song-sheet wrapped in an old scroll in an old jar in an old cave, is that it? Fine. Now go home, will you?'

'It wasn't like that at all. I just happened to pick up the words one time.'

'On the docks, I know. From the current crop of Phoenician sailors. Go home, Undine.'

'I have no home.'

'Then just go away.'

'You'll be sorry if I do.'

'Damn it, I want to get some sleep.'

'I won't bother you. Come into the bed.'

'No.'

'Come here,' she insisted.

'Go away. It's *my* apartment. I didn't invite you here.'

'Yes you did.'

'Ages ago. It doesn't count.'

'Last week.'

'It feels like an aeon.'

'Come here,' she said again. She dipped two fingers into the strings of the lyre and provoked a vicious ripple. 'Because if you don't, do you know what I'm liable to do? I'm just liable to throw this thing right through that window.'

'I want to be let alone,' I said.

She threw the lyre through the window. It penetrated sideways, and cleanly, like the cut of a knife, with a soft clear click of struck sound – a thin pale note came out as it hit, and the pane and the lyre went gyrating downwards to the street together; I was in time to glimpse the two objects still gleaming and braiding in air. They fell not far apart, between two cars in the road.

'You could've killed someone down there!'

'I warned you, didn't I?'

I went to her docilely enough then; it was as though she had broken something in me – some inner crystal, through which up to the moment of its shattering I had been able to see rationality, responsibility; light. I saw nothing now; her mouth became a wide-open window, and I hurled myself through it, whirling my tongue like a lyre, I stretched the strings of her hair and webbed them and plucked at them; they seemed in my teeth as tough as rope. I was blind and faint, but her body took me ravenous for it; no sooner did I slip into consolation than a gong of lust pealed me alert. All the same the dreaded faintness returned, it kept returning, I awoke to her and it returned, I could not endure it, I was drained, behind my heated eyeballs it grew ladder-like and dark.

It was night.

'I want to sleep,' I moaned.

'Tired already? Ah, little man-darling.' And would not release me; and I had to tense again for the plunge. All that night it was a dream of plunging and diving; the undersea of her was never satiated, the dive was bottomless, plummeting, vast and vast. 'Soon, soon,' she promised me, 'soon you'll sleep, you'll see, trust me, always rely on me, I keep faith with everyone, don't I?' She crooned; and the warp of her voice lifted me alive like a tree. 'Aren't you happy now? Aren't you glad I stayed?' she asked me. 'Yes, yes,' I always replied, swimming in the wake of gratefulness.

At three o'clock – a blessed little nap had momentarily reposed her, and she lay in my arms while my open scared eyelids flickered like flies – the telephone rang. 'It's nobody,' she reprimanded with a yawn, but she passed the receiver to me, wreathing my member with the cord to hold it captive.

'That you, George?'

It was my uncle Al.

'Listen, George,' he said, 'I made it back sooner'n I thought I was ever going to – didn't like it over there. Neither did Nick. You wouldn't remember him, little gimpy foreign guy, this Greek I went over with, same cabin and all? This fella Lewis? Fact is he's with me now. I don't like to call you in the middle of the night, George boy, that's the truth—'

'Where are you, Al?'

'Down at the docks. My God, George, you ought to see what they got going down here – spooky enough to give you the creeps, about a hundred of them old wooden tubs all over the place, out of a goddam story-book, sheets out like a pack of Hallowe'eners. Back home we got bathtubs better-looking than some of that. Say listen, George, the truth is I'd like to know if you could put up the two of us for the night? Me and this Greek fella, he's not a bad little guy—'

'You mean you want to come up here right *now*?' I said.

'Well, yeah. Just stepped off the boat. Managed to get a spot back on this little Eye-tie job, accommodation's a little on the spaghetti side, but you don't waste a cent—'

'Look, Al,' I said, 'maybe you could get yourself a hotel room around about there, it's pretty late—'

'That's the *point*, kid, Nick here with his arthritis and all, it's kind of late to go looking around, couple of strangers in town—'

'I don't know, Al,' I said, 'this place is sort of a wreck at the moment. I mean it's sort of a wreck.'

Undine pulled on the telephone wire. 'Don't talk any more. I want you. Come back,' she called.

'Oh, come on, it's all in the family. We don't mind a little mess. Unless you got a lady-friend up there?' he hooted.

'No, look, all right,' I said. 'That's fine. Sure, Al, you come on over,' I said.

Her nostrils had turned rigid. Her neck twisted up like a root. 'What did you do that for? *We* don't want anybody.'

'I owe it to my uncle. He's bringing along that Greek too. You'll have to leave now,' I told her.

'But you said I made you happy!' she wailed.

'I *tried* to put him off, didn't I? You heard me.'

'All I heard was you said the place was a wreck. It's not, it's perfectly nice. I like it.'

'It was a way of telling him not to come, that's all. *You* heard. I couldn't help it, he insisted.'

She leaned her breasts against the bedpost, meditating; but her arms strove backwards. 'You don't want me really?'

'Enough is enough,' I said.

'Enough,' she said – and with an easy slap broke off the knob of the bedpost – 'is enough' – and with a stray sliver of window-glass shredded the bedclothes. Bits of rubber foam twinkled upwards.

'Undine—'

'A wreck, you're right, a wreck,' she cried – she was solemn and slow. She cradled the shade of a lamp, tender as a nursemaid, then crushed it under her naked toes, and used the brass lamp-pole to smash the frame of the bed. Her blows were cautious, regular, and accurate. She hewed the arm off a chair and the arm demolished the bureau. Drawer-knobs in flight mobbed the air. In all the rooms the floorboards sprang up groaning. Vases went rolling, limbs of little tables disported. Piece by piece the air-conditioner released its diverse organs; in the kitchen the ice-trays poured and clattered, the stove-grates ground the refrigerator door to a yellowish porcelain dust, the ceiling was pocked with faucet-handles embedded like silvery pustules. She slashed the sofa pillows, and crowing and gurgling with fury and bliss felled the toilet-tank. Mound by mound she heaped it all behind her – barrows rose suddenly up at her heels like the rapid wake of disappearing civilizations. A cemetery grew at her thrust. She destroyed with a marvellous promiscuity – nothing mattered to her, nothing was too obvious to miss or too minuscule to ignore. She was thorough, she was strong. I waited for the end, and there was no end. What had been left large she reduced; what had been left small she pulverized. The telephone (I thought of calling the police, but reserved this for the neighbours) was a ragged hillock of black confetti.

Finally she went away.

I lay down in the wreckage and slept moderately until my uncle and the Greek arrived. There was no door for them to come through: they simply came in, trampling sawdust.

'Good Lord,' Al said. 'Sweet Jesus. Was it burglars?'

'A bitch,' I said.

'A witch?' said the Greek, hobbling from waste to waste on polished crutches.

'We always say back home that this here's one dangerous city to live in,' Al said. 'If you had half a brain, George boy, you'd come on home. Practically all of Europe's just the same. No good. I saw that Mediterranean, and I didn't like the smell. You got to go deep inside a country, away from the shore line, if you want decency.'

'There is no witches,' Mr Lewis said boldly.

'The boy knows that,' my uncle said. 'Here come the police.'

The neighbours came too; there was a confusion, in which the Greek forgot his English, all but the odd word 'witch'; they took him off to the station house, and my uncle loyally followed to post bail. 'Superstitious little runt,' he explained, enjoying the crowd.

Morning was not yet; I ran through crepuscular streets, liberated. Now and again I stopped before a display window to pose and observe my reflection; it seemed to me I had none. How thin I must have become! I ran and ran, into the seeping dye of dawn. I felt an insupportable vigour. My feet scooped up miles – the miles themselves appeared to have been exorcised by my vigour and my glee, and grew improbably briefer. In an instant I was on Canal Street, half an instant afterwards I was scudding past the drugstore – it looked intact, and fleeing it I wondered whether the druggist's mirror might deliver up my lost reflection. But I could no longer halt, I ran on, I ran to the grey piers, I ran to the morning-tipped sails wind-full in the harbour. All the way I jogged her name in my teeth.

I knew where to look for her.

'Undine!' I shrieked into that deserted alley I remembered.

'Sylvia!' howled the druggist. His bits of hair stood aloft in peaked tufts, his jagged ears bristled, his triangular chin poked the bone of his chest. He was so wafer-like that I feared for him to show me his profile; I was certain he would vanish into a line. 'You too?' he said when he recognized me.

'She's left me,' I croaked.

'And me,' he informed me.

We hugged one another; we danced on the edge of the pier; we babbled at our luck.

'Will she come back?' I asked him.

'Who knows? But I bet not. Not after this time, I bet. She's all worn out, it looked like.'

'Did she tell you where she's going?'

'To visit her daughters, she said.'

'Where are they?'

'India, she said. Also Africa.'

Triumphantly I took this in. 'Did you ever see her off before?'

'One time I did. But after that she came back. She went on a Queen, that was the trouble – they caught her, scraped her right off. And anyhow she said she hated the thing, all cold metal, like riding a spoon, she said. Don't shoot me so many questions, buddy. I ain't your teacher.'

'I only want to know if you can see her.'

He squinted into the yolk-coloured sky. 'Not yet. Look for yourself.'

'But there are so many ships, I can't tell—'

'She might not be aboard yet.'

We skimmed up and down the alley, sniffing at the water. It brightened under the dawn; it spun out slavering columns of red.

'See that two-master? She ain't on that one.'

'I can't – no, that's right, not on that one.'

Down to the horizon, into the very bottom of the sun, the flotilla stood, bark after bark after bark, the galleys and galleons, the schooners and sloops, the single high Norsemen's vessel, the junks and the dhows and the xebecs and the feluccas, with their painted whimsical hulls and their multitudinous sails in rows and banks and phantasmal tiers, paper-white geometries clambering like petals out of the masts, and the water galloping and spitting beneath their tall arched bows.

The druggist's glance hopped from ship to ship.

Then I – too shy of what I sought to look so far – spied her: she hung nearly over our heads, she was an eave shadowing our heads, her hair streamed backwards over her loins, her left hand clasped a lyre, her right hand made as if to pluck it but did not, her spine was clamped high upon the nearest prow. Although her eyes were wide, they were woodenly in trance: I had never known her in so pure a sleep.

'Undine!'

'Sylvia!' mocked the druggist.

'She doesn't answer.'

'She won't,' he responded with satisfaction. 'You can go on home now, buddy.'

'She won't answer?'

'Use your eyes, buddy. Does she look like she will?'

I saw the long and delicate grain in her thighs, the nodules in her straight wrists, the knots that circled and circled about her erect and exact nipples, the splintered panel that cleft her flank. (I recalled a mole in that place.) 'Look at that,' said the druggist, pointing to the notch, 'she's getting old. More'n a century, I'd say. Want to bet she doesn't make it back? Falls right plump into the Atlantic? Her rigging's weak, she looks glued on, water'll wash her right off.'

I pleaded with him: 'She won't answer?'

'Try her.'

I flung back my neck and shouted up: 'Undine—'

A figurehead does not breathe.

'Go on back, boy,' said the druggist.

'And you?' I asked him; but did not leave off gaping into the flock of sails that seemed to spring from her immutable shoulders like a huge headdress of starched fans. They gasped and vaguely hissed, and she beneath them strained her back to meet the prow's grand arch, and threw into their lucidities her stiff gaze.

'I got my business to take care of,' he told me. 'Build it up a bit now maybe. Hire somebody with better customer-visibility. *She* never let me hire anybody.'

'She wrecked my apartment,' I confided. 'She lost me my job.'

'That's the least of it. Believe me, buddy, the least. That's the stuff you can fix up.'

'I guess I can fix up my apartment,' I said dejectedly.

'You going for a sailor, like you said?'

'No.' And spotted panic in me.

'Going back to wherever you come from?'

I considered this; I thought of the fields of home. 'No,' I said after a moment.

'Well, so long, buddy, I wish you luck with things when you find out.'

I said in the voice of a victim, 'Find out what?'

But he had turned his side to me, and, though I stared with all my strength, I could no longer see him.

The Suitcase

Mr Hencke, the father of the artist, was a German, an architect, and a traveller – not particularly in that order of importance. He had flown a Fokker for the Kaiser, but there was little of the pilot left in him: he had a rather commonplace military-like snap to his shoulders, especially when he was about to meet someone new. This was not because he had been in the fierce and rigid Air Force, but because he was clandestinely shy. His long grim face, with the mouth running across its lower hem like a slipped thread in a linen sack, was as pitted as a battlefield. Under a magnifying glass his skin would have shown moon-craters. As a boy he had had the smallpox. He lived in a big yellow-brick house in Virginia, and no longer thought of himself as a German. He did not have German thoughts, except in a certain recurring dream, in which he always rode naked on a saddleless horse, holding on to its black moist mane and crying '*Schneller, schneller*'. With the slowness of anguish they glided over a meadow he remembered from childhood, past the millhouse, into a green endlessness hazy with buttercups. Sometimes the horse, which he knew was a stallion, nevertheless seemed to be his wife, who was dead. He was sorry he had named his son after himself – what a name for a boy to have come through Yale with! If he had it to do over again he would have called him John.

'Where am I to put my bag?' he asked Gottfried, who was paying the truckmen and did not hear. His father saw a grey-green flash of money. The truckmen began setting up rows of folding chairs, and he guessed that Gottfried had tipped them to do it. Gottfried had organized everything himself – hired the loft, turned it into a gallery, and invited the famous critic to come and speak at the opening. There was even a sign swinging from the loft-window over West Fifty-Third Street: Nobody's

Gallery, it said – a metaphysical joke. Gottfried was not Nobody – the proof was he had married Somebody. Somebody had an unearned income of fifty thousand a year: she was a Chicago blueblood, a beautiful girl, long-necked, black-haired, sweetly and irreproachably mannered, with a voice like a bird. Mr Hencke had spent two whole dinners in her company before he understood that she had no vocabulary, comprehended nothing, exclaimed at nothing, was bored by nothing. She was totally stupid. Since she had nothing to do – there was a cook, a maid, and a governess – she could scarcely improve, and exhausted her summers in looking diaphanous. Mr Hencke was retired, but his son could never retire because he had never worked. Catherine liked him to stay at home, jiggle the baby now and then, play records, dance, and occasionally fire the governess, whom she habitually suspected of bad morals. All the same he went uptown to Lexington Avenue every day, where he rented an apartment next door to a Mrs Siebzehnhauer, called it his studio, and painted timidly. Through the wall he could catch the bleatings of Mrs Siebzehnhauer's Black Forest cuckoo clock. Sometimes he felt tired, so he put in a bed. In this bed he received his Jewish mistress.

The famous critic had already arrived, and was examining Gottfried's paintings. He poked his wheezing scrutiny so close to each canvas that the fashionable point of his beard dusted the bottom of the frame. Gottfried's paintings tramped solidly around the walls, and the famous critic followed them. He was not an art critic; he was a literary critic, a 'cultural' critic – he was going to say something about the Meaning of the Work in Terms of the *Zeitgeist*. His lecture-fee was extremely high; Mr Hencke hoped his opinion would be half so high. He himself did not know what to think of Gottfried's labours. His canvases were full of hidden optical tricks and were so bewildering to one's routine retinal expectations that, once the eye had turned away, a whirring occurred in the pupil's depth, and the paintings began to speak through their after-image. Everything was disconcerting, everything seemed pasted down flat – strips, corners, angles, slivers. Mr Hencke had a perilous sense that Gottfried had simply cut up the plans for an old office building with extraordinarily tiny scissors. All the paintings were in black and white, but there were drawings in brown pencil. The drawings were mostly teasing dots, like notes on a score. They hurtled up and down. The famous critic studied them with heated seriousness, making notes on a paper napkin he had taken from the refreshment table.

'Where am I to put my bag?' Mr Hencke asked Catherine, who was just then passing by with her arm slung through the arm of Gottfried's mistress.

'Oh, put it anywhere,' said Genevieve at once.

'Papa, stay with us this time. You can have the big room upstairs,' Catherine said, mustering all her confident politeness.

'I have a reservation at such a very nice hotel,' said Mr Hencke.

'Nothing could be nicer than the big room upstairs. I've just had the curtains changed. Papa, they're all yellow now,' Catherine said with her yielding inescapable smile, and through her father-in-law's conventionally gossamer soul, in which he believed as thoroughly as any peasant, there slipped the spider-thread flick of one hair of the horse's mane, as if drawn across his burlap cheek: not for nothing was he the father of an artist, he was susceptible to yellow, he still remembered the yellow buttercups on the slope below the millhouse.

'Kitty, you're hopeless,' said Genevieve. 'How can you think of shutting up a genuine bachelor at the top of your stuffy old house?'

'Not bachelor, widower,' said Mr Hencke. 'Not exactly the same thing.'

'The same in the end,' said Genevieve. 'You can't let them stuff you up, you have to be free to come and go and have people in and out if you want to.'

'It's a nice house. It's not stuffy, it's very airy. You can even smell the river. It's an elegant house on an elegant street,' Catherine protested.

'A very fine house,' Mr Hencke agreed, though he secretly despised New York brownstone. 'Only I feel Gottfried is not comfortable when I am in it. So for family peace I prefer the hotel.'

'Papa, Gottfried promised not to have a fight this time.'

'What in the world do they find to fight about?' Genevieve asked.

'Papa thinks Gottfried should have a job. It isn't *necessary*,' Catherine said.

'It isn't necessary for Rockefeller either,' Mr Hencke said. 'You don't see any of the Rockefellers idle. Every Rockefeller has a job.'

'Oh, you Lutherans,' Genevieve said. 'You awful Lutherans and your awful Protestant Work Ethic.'

'Papa, Gottfried's *never* idle. You don't know. You just don't know. He goes to his studio every day.'

'And sleeps on the bed.'

'My goodness, papa, you don't think Gottfried would be having this whole huge show if he never did any *work*, do you? He's a real worker, papa, he's an artist, so *what* if he has a bed up there.'

'Now, now,' Genevieve said, 'that isn't fair, all the Rockefellers have beds too, Kitty's right.'

'I wish you would tell me where to put my bag,' Mr Hencke said.

'Put it over there,' Genevieve suggested. 'With my things. See that chair behind the bar – where the barman's standing – no, there, that man putting on a white jacket – I left my pocketbook on it, under my coat. See it, it's the coat with all that black-and-white geometry all over it? Someone's liable to think it's one of Gottfried's things and buy it for nine hundred dollars,' Genevieve said, and Catherine laughed like a sparrow. 'You can lay your suitcase right on top of my nine-hundred-dollar coat, it won't be in the way. God, what a mob already.'

'We sent programmes to *every*body,' Catherine said.

'Don't think they're coming completely for Gottfried,' Mr Hencke said.

'Papa, what do you mean?'

'He means they're coming to hear Creighton MacDougal. Look, there's that whole bunch – not that way, over there, near the stairs – from *Partisan Review*. I can always tell *Partisan Review* people, they have faces like a mackerel after it's been caught, with the hook still in its mouth.'

'They might be dealers,' Catherine said hopefully. 'Or museum people.'

'They're MacDougal people. Him and his notes, get a load of that. I can hardly wait to hear him explain how Gottfried represents the existential revolt against Freud.'

'Gottfried put in something about Freud in the programme. Did you see the programme yet, papa? He did a sort of preface for it. It's not really *writing*, it's just quotations. One of them's Freud, I think.'

'Not Freud, dear, Jung,' Genevieve said.

'Well, I knew it was some famous Jewish psychiatrist anyway,' Catherine said. 'Come on, Gen, let's go get papa a programme.'

'I'll get one, don't trouble yourself,' Mr Hencke said. 'First I'll put away my bag.'

'Jung isn't a Jew,' Genevieve said.

'Isn't? Don't you mean wasn't? Isn't he dead?'

'He isn't a Jew,' Genevieve said. 'That's why he went on staying alive.'

'I thought he was dead.'

'Everybody dies,' Mr Hencke said, looking into the crowd. It resembled a zoo crowd: it had taken the form of a thick ragged rope and was wandering slowly past the long even array of Gottfried's paintings, peering into each one as though it were a cage containing some unlikely beast.

'Like a concentration camp,' Genevieve said. 'Everybody staring through the barbed wire hoping for rescue and knowing it's no use. That's what they look like.'

Catherine said, 'I certainly hope some of them are dealers.'

'You don't want me to put my bag *on* your overcoat, Genevieve,' Mr Hencke said. 'I must not crush your things. I'll put the bag just there behind the chair, that will be best.'

'You know what Gottfried's stuff reminds me of?' Genevieve said.

Mr Hencke perceived that she was provoking him. Her earlier reference to why he chose a hotel over his son's house – what she had said about his having people in and out – clearly meant prostitutes. He was stupendously offended. He never frequented prostitutes, though he knew Gottfried sometimes did. But Gottfried was still a young man – in America, curiously, to be past thirty-seven, and even a little bald in the back, like Gottfried, hardly interfered with the intention to go on being young. Gottfried, then, was not only a very young man, but gave every sign of continuing that way for years and years, while poor Catherine, though socially and financially Somebody, was surely – at sex – a Nobody. Her little waist was undoubtedly charming, her stretched-forward neck (perhaps she was near-sighted and didn't realize it?) was fragrant with hygiene. Her whole body was exceptionally mannerly, even the puppet-motion of her immaculate thighs under her white dress: so Gottfried sometimes went to prostitutes and sometimes – on grand occasions, like the opening of Nobody's Gallery – Genevieve came from whatever city it was in the Midwest – Cincinnati, or Boise, or Columbus: maybe Detroit.

'Shredded swastikas, that's what,' Genevieve announced. 'Every single damn thing he does. All that terrible precision. Every last one a pot of shredded swastikas, you see that?'

He knew what she meant him to see: she scorned Germans, she thought him a Nazi sympathizer even now, an anti-Semite, an Eichmann. She was the sort who, twenty years after Hitler's war, would not buy a Volkswagen. She was full of detestable moral gestures, and against what? Who could be blamed for History? It did not take a philosopher (though he himself inclined towards Schopenhauer) to see that History was a Force-in-Itself, like Evolution. There he was, comfortable in America, only a little sugar rationed, and buying War Bonds like every other citizen, while his sister, an innocent woman, an intellectual, a loyal lover of Heine who could recite by heart *Der Apollogott* and *Zwei Ritter* and *König David* and ten or twelve others, lost her home and a daughter of eleven in an RAF raid on Köln. Margaretchen had moved from Frankfurt to Köln after her marriage to a well-educated shampoo manufacturer. A horrible tragedy. Even the great Cathedral had not been spared.

'I was *sure* it was Freud Gottfried used for the quotation thing,' Catherine demurred.

'Gottfried would never quote Freud, Kitty, it would only embarrass him. You know what Freud said? "An abstinent artist is scarcely conceivable" – he meant sex, dear, not drink.'

'Gottfried practically never drinks.'

'That's because he's a mystic and a romantic, isn't he stupid? Kitty, you really ought to do something to de-sober Gottfried, it would do his work so much good. A little less Apollo, a little more Dionysus.'

Catherine tittered exactly as if she had seen the point of some invisible joke: but then she noticed that the truckmen had forgotten to set up the speaker's table, so she excused herself very politely, gaping out at her father-in-law her diligently attentive smile with such earnestness and breeding that his intestines publicly croaked. The father of the artist hated his daughter-in-law, and could not bear to share a roof with her even for a single night; her conversation depressed him and gave him evil sweated dreams: sometimes he dreamt he was in his sister's city, and the bomb exploded out of his own belly, and there rolled past him, as on a turntable in the brutalized nave, his little niece laid out dead, covered only by her yellow hair. Across the room Catherine was supervising the placing of the lectern: he heard it scrape through the increasing voices.

Meanwhile Genevieve still pursued. 'Mr Hencke, you know perfectly well that Jung played footsie with the Nazis. It's public knowledge. He let all the Jewish doctors get thrown out of the psychological society after the Nazis took it over, and he stayed president all that while, and he never said a word against any of it. Then they were all murdered.'

'*Gnädige Frau,*' he said – and dropped his suitcase to the floor in a kind of fright. Since his wife died he had not once spoken a syllable of German, and now to have such a strangeness, such a familiarity, pimple out on his tongue with a design of its own – and with what terrifying uselessness, a phrase out of something sublimely old-fashioned, a stiff staid long-ago play, *Minna von Barnhelm* perhaps, a phrase he had never said in his whole life – 'What do you want from me?' he appealed. 'I'm a man of sixty-eight. In sixty-eight years what have I done? I have harmed no one. I have built towers. Towers! No more. I have never destroyed.'

He raised his suitcase – it was as heavy as some icon – and walked through the chatter to the refreshment table and set it down behind the chair thickened and duplicated by the pattern of Genevieve's coat. The barman handed him a glass. He received it and avoided the walls, no space of which was unmarked by his son's Aztec emissions. He took a seat in a middle row and waited for the speaker to come to the lectern. At his feet lay a discarded leaflet. It was the programme. He saw that the topic of the lecture would be 'In His Eye's Mind: Hencke and the New Cubism'. Then he skipped a page backwards and under the title 'Culled by Hencke' he read a trio of excerpts:

'Schuppanzigh, do you think I write my quartets for you and your puling fiddle?' – *Beethoven, to the violinist who wailed that the A-minor quartet was unplayable.*

'It is better to ruin a work and make it useless for the world than not to go the limit at every point.' – *Thos. Mann.*

'For the people gay pictures, for the cognoscenti, the mystery behind.' – *Goethe.*

All three items had the touch of Genevieve. He looked for the quotation from Jung and found there was none. To Catherine, Beethoven and Freud were just the same, burdens indistinguishable and unextinguishable both. Undoubtedly Genevieve had told her that Schuppanzigh was another Jewish psychiatrist persecuted by the Nazis and that Goethe was a notorious Gauleiter. As for that idiot Gottfried, he read the gallery notes in the *Times*, nothing more, and had a subscription to *Art News* – he was two parts Catherine's money to one part Genevieve's brain, and too cowardly altogether to stir the mixture. Catherine, like all foolish heroines, believed that Genevieve (Smith '48, *summa cum laude*, Phi Beta Kappa) was devoted to her (Miss Jewett's Classes '59, graduated 32 in a class of 36) out of sentiment and enthusiasm. 'Genevieve loves New York, she can't keep away from it' was one of Catherine's sayings: alas, she uttered it like an epigram. They had met at Myra Jacobson's. Myra Jacobson (also Smith '48) was a dealer, one of the very best – she *made* reputations, it was said; last year (for instance) she made Julius Feldstein the actionist – and Catherine offered her a certain sum to take on

Gottfried, but she refused. 'You must wait till he's *ripe*,' she told Catherine, who cried and cried until Genevieve appeared like Polonius from behind a Jackson Pollock and gave her an orange handkerchief to blow with. 'Now, now,' Genevieve said, 'don't bawl about it, let me go look at him, you can't tell if he's ripe unless you squeeze.' Genevieve was escorted to Gottfried's studio next door to Mrs Siebzehnhauer, beheld the bed, beheld Gottfried, and squeezed. She pressed hard. He was not ripe. He was still a Nobody.

Hence Nobody's Gallery: Genevieve's invention. It was, of course, to mock Gottfried, who knew he was being mocked, and for spite agreed. Gottfried, like most cowards, had a dim cunning. But Catherine was infinitely grateful: a show was a show. Creighton MacDougal came terribly dear, but you would expect that of a man with a beard – he looked, Catherine said in another epigram, like God.

Applause.

God stood at the lectern, drew a glass of water from an aluminium spigot, sucked up the superfluous drops through the top part of his beard (the part that without the beard would have been a moustache), crackled an oesophagus lined with phlegm, and began to talk about Melville's White Whale. For ten minutes Mr Hencke was piously certain that the great critic was giving last week's lecture. Then he heard his son's name. 'The art of Fulfilment,' said the critic. 'Here, at last, is no Yearning. No alabaster tail-fin wiggles beckoningly on the horizon. There is no horizon. Perspective is annihilated. The completion-complex of the schoolroom and/or the madhouse is master at last. Imagine a teacher with his back to the class, erasing the blackboard. He erases and erases. Finally all is clear black once again – except for a scrap of the foot of a single letter, the letter "J" – "J", ladies and gentlemen, standing for Justice, or for Jesus – one scrap of the foot, then, of this half-remaining letter "J", which the sweep of the eraser has passed by and left unobliterated. At this point it is the art of Gottfried Hencke I am illustrating precisely. The art of Gottfried Hencke rises from its seat, approaches the blackboard, and with a singular motion, a swift, small, and excruciatingly exact motion, wets its pinkie and smears away the foot of the "J" forever. That, ladies and gentlemen, is the meaning of the art of Gottfried Hencke. It is an art not of hunger, not of frustration, but of satiation. An art, so to speak, for fat men.'

Further applause: this time tentative, as by vulgarians who mistake the close of the first movement for the end of the symphony.

The aluminium spigot squeals. God thirsts. The audience observes the capillary action of facial hair.

'Ladies and gentlemen,' continued the critic, 'I too am a fat man. I cleverly mask not less than two chins, not more than three. Yet I was not always thus. Imagine me at seventeen, lean, bold, arrogant, aristocratic. Imagine snow. I run through the snow. Whiteness. The whiteness, ladies and gentlemen, of Melville's very Whale, with which I began my brief causerie. All men begin at the crest of purity and hope. Now consider me at twenty-four. I have just flunked out of medical school. Ladies and gentlemen, it was my wish to heal. To heal, my beauties. Consider my tears. I weep in my humiliation before the dean. I beg for another chance. "No, my son," says the dean – how kind he is! how good! and his wife is a cripple in a wheelchair – "you will have a long hard row to hoe. Give it up." Now for thirty years I have tried to heal myself. Allegories, ladies, beauties; allegories, you darling gentlemen: trust me to serve you fables, parables, the best of their kind in season. The art of Gottfried Hencke is an intact art. Was there ever a wound in it? It is healed. It has healed itself, we all heal ourselves, thank you, thank you.'

God waved fervently through the exalted shimmer of the final applause.

With inscrutable correctness, as though mediating a bargain in a bazaar, Catherine introduced her father-in-law to Creighton MacDougal. Mr Hencke was moved. He felt stirred to hope for his son, and for his son's son, who had so far struck him as practically an imbecile. He undertook to explain to the critic about the old planes. 'No, no,' he said, leaning into a pair of jelly-red eyes, 'the Fokker was the fighter as everyone knows, but the Hansa-und-Brandenburger did everything – strafed, bombed, a little aerial fighting, now and then a little reconnaissance over the water to look for your ships. Everything. Very versatile, very reliable. At the end we used a lot of them. In the beginning we didn't even have the Fokker. All we had was the Rumpler-Taube, very beautiful. She was called that because she resembled a lovely great dove. Maybe you know her from the old movies. My daughter-in-law claims she saw one once in a movie at the Museum of Modern Art. I have a little fear of my daughter-in-law – spoils the stock, bad mental genes – a grandson two years old, very pretty boy, nothing mental. You won't mention this, yes? I say it in private. I have a liking for your face. You show a little of my father – the old school, as you say, very strict. Boys nowadays don't stand for that. We had also very strict teachers with the planes. All professors. They knew everything about an engine. The best teachers they gave us. I suppose in an emergency I could still fly something like a Piper Cub. We had the double wing in those days. The biplane, no closed cockpits. We had leather helmets. When it rained it was like needles on the eyeballs. We could go only a thousand feet – the height of the Empire State Building, yes? In the core of a cloud you are quite unaware it's a cloud, to you it's simply fog. Those helmets! In the rain they smelled like a slaughterhouse.'

An intense young lady who had just written a book review took the critic away from him: he wiped his mouth. A long thread of detached mucous membrane lifted from its right corner. He snuffed up the odour of his own breath. It confessed that his stomach was not well. On the refreshment table there was a bowl of apples. He thought how one of these would clean the stink from his teeth. The bowl stood next to a platter of cheese sandwiches at the end of the table, near the chair with Genevieve's coat on it. But the coat was not on the chair. It was on Genevieve. She was whispering to Gottfried over the apples. He saw that she intended to leave before Gottfried, to fool Catherine. It was an assignation.

'Gottfried!' he called.

His son came.

'You're not going home?'

'Not for hours, papa. There's a little band coming in. Catherine thought we ought to have some dancing.'

'I mean afterwards. Afterwards where are you going?'

'Home. Home, papa, where else at that hour? Catherine says you won't come with us. She says you're insisting on a hotel again.'

'You're not going to the studio first?'

'Tonight, you mean?'

'After the band. After the band you're going to the studio with the bed in it?'

'I can't possibly do any work tonight, papa. Not after all this. Listen, what did you think of MacDougal?'

'The man misunderstands you entirely,' Mr Hencke said. 'I talked to him privately, you observed that?'

'No,' Gottfried said.

'I want you to take me to your studio,' Mr Hencke said.

'That's a change,' Gottfried said. 'You never want to see my things.'

'You have something worth showing?'

'Oh, for God's sake,' Gottfried said. 'All ye who seek my monument, look around you. Don't you like a single thing on the wall?'

'I want to see what you keep in your studio.'

'Well, I've got a new thing going over there,' Gottfried said. 'If you're interested.'

'A new thing?'

'It's only one-quarter finished. The whole right bottom corner. Seems I've finally worked up the courage to try something in colour. Cerulean blue compressed into a series of interlocked ovals and rectangles. Like sky enclosed in the nucleus of the atom. Actually I'm pretty hopeful about it.'

'Tell me, Gottfried, who said that?' his father asked.

'Who said what?'

'The sky in the atom. Genevieve? Genevieve's words, hah? A brilliant lady. Very metaphorical. I want to see this sky. Explain to Genevieve that I am always glad to look at any evidence of my son's courage.'

'All right, papa, don't get rough. I'll call for you in the morning if you want. It's so damn perverse of you not to come to the house.'

'No, no, I have no interest in your house. I abominate high stoops – a barbarism. Tonight I want to see your studio.'

'Tonight?'

'After the band.'

'That's absurd, papa. We'll all be dead tired later on.'

'Good, then we will take advantage of the convenience of the bed.'

'Papa, don't get rough. I mean that. Don't get rough with me *now*, you hear?'

'When I myself was a very young man of thirty-seven I addressed my father with respect.'

'God damn you, you want to break it up. You really want to break it up. Finally you want to. Why? You kept out of it long enough, a whole year, now all of a sudden it bothers you.'

'A year and a half,' his father said. 'And still you like to call it a new thing. A new thing you call it.'

'Do you *need* to break it up? You have to? What's it to you?'

'Poor, poor Catherine,' his father murmured.

'Poor, poor Catherine,' Genevieve said, coming up behind Gottfried. She was devouring a cheese sandwich, and bits of bread mottled her mouth and sprinkled down on the breast of her coat. Mr Hencke confronted its design: a series of interlocked ovals and rectangles, dark and light. Looked at one way, they presented a deep tubular corridor, infinitely empty, like two mirrors facing one another. A shift of the mind swelled them into a solid, endlessly bulging, endlessly self-creating squarish sausage.

'He's trying to break it up,' Gottfried told her.

'Foolish, foolish boy,' said Genevieve, sticking out a cheesy tongue at the father of the artist.

'Are you listening?' said Gottfried.

'Yes, dear. I didn't know the dear knew anything.'

'You liar. Big innocent wide-eyes. I told you I told him. I had to tell him because he guessed.'

'I am Gottfried's confidant,' Mr Hencke said.

'Mine too,' said Genevieve, and embraced the father of the artist. The very slight fragrance of the pumpernickel crumbs on the underpart of her chin – a chin just, just beginning to slacken: a frail lip-like turn of skin pouting beneath it – made a flowery gash in his vision. Some inward gate opened. He remembered still another field, this one furry with kümmel, a hairy yellow shoulder of a field shrugging at the wind. A smear of joy worsened his stomach: at home one used to take caraway for a carminative. 'Childe Roland to the Dark Tower came,' Genevieve recited, 'and broke it up. Gottfried, I vouch for your father. He has never destroyed.'

My Hencke marvelled.

'I am a deceiver,' Genevieve cried, 'I too need a confidant, I need one more than Gottfried. Gottfried's papa, let me tell you about my extraordinary life in Indianapolis, Indiana. My husband is an intelligent and prospering Certified Public Accountant. His name will not surprise: Lewin. A memorable name. Kagan would also be a memorable name, so too Rabinowitz or Robbins, but *his* name is Lewin. A model to youth. Contributor to many charities. Vice-president of the temple. Now let me tell you about our four daughters, all under twelve years. One is too young for school. One is only in kindergarten. But the two older ones! Nora. Bonnie. At the top of their grades and already reading *Tom Sawyer*, *Little Women*, and the *Encyclopaedia Britannica*. Every month they produce a family newspaper of one page on an old Smith-Corona in the basement of our Dutch Colonial house in Indianapolis, Indiana. They call it *The Mezuzzah Bulletin* – the idea being that they tack it up on the doorpost. They all four have the Jewish brain.'

'Everyone's *looking* at you,' Gottfried said angrily.

'That's because I'm wrapped in one of your satiated paintings. Mr Hencke, did you know that some of the most avant-garde expressionism comes from the Seventh Avenue silkscreen people? But I want to confide some more. Gottfried's papa, some more confidences. First let me describe myself. Tall. Never wear low heels. Plump-armed. Soft-thighed. Perfectly splendid young woman. Nose thin and delicate, like a Communion wafer. Impression of being both sleek and amiable. Large, healthy, indestructible teeth. Half a dozen gold inlays, paid for by Lewin, the Certified Public Accountant. Excellent husband. Now your turn, Mr Hencke. I've undressed myself for you. It's your turn, that's only fair. Your brother-in-law the shampoo manufacturer that Kitty once mentioned – the one who lives in Cologne, whose house was bombed out?'

Mr Hencke begged, 'What do you want from me? Why do you talk about yourself that way?'

'Tell about him. Confide in me the nature of the shampoo. What did he make it out of? Not now. I mean during the war. Not the war you flew in, the war after that. He was making shampoo in Cologne all the while you were an American patriot architect, raising towers, never destroying. Please discuss your brother-in-law's shampoo. What were its secret ingredients? Whose human fat? What Jewish lard?'

'Genevieve, shut up. Shut up, will you please? Leave my father alone.'

'Poor, poor Catherine,' Genevieve said. 'I just fixed everything up with her. I told her I was going to make the midnight plane home and you had this inspiration and had to stay up all night with it at the studio.'

'Just shut up, all right?'

'All right, dear. I'll see you when Mrs Siebzehnhauer's cuckoo caws two.'

'Skip it. Not tonight.'

'Who says not? Gottfried's papa?'

'I have nothing against you, believe me,' Mr Hencke said. 'I admire you very much, Genevieve. I have absolutely no animus.'

'What a pity,' said Genevieve, 'every man should have a nice little animus.'

'My God, Genevieve, leave him alone.'

'Goodbye. I'm going back to Nora Lewin, Bonnie Lewin, Andrea Lewin, Celeste Lewin and Edward K. Lewin, all of Indianapolis, Indiana. First I have to say goodbye to poor, poor Catherine. Goodbye, Mr Hencke. Don't worry about yourself. As for me, I am sleek and amiable. My gold inlays click like castanets manufactured in Franco Spain. My breasts are like twin pomegranates. Like twin white doves coming down from Mount Gilead, OK?' She kissed the father of the artist. The hairy kümmel valley was photographed by flash bulb on the flank of his pancreas. 'Your cheek is like barbed wire. Your cheek has the ruts left by General Rommel's tanks.'

The artist and his father watched her go from them, picking at crumbs.

'A superior woman,' Mr Hencke said. He felt a remarkable control. He felt as though he had received a command and disobeyed it. 'A superior race, I've always thought that. Imaginative. They say Corbusier is a secret Jew, descended from Marranos. A beautiful complexion, beautiful eyelashes. These women have compulsions. When they turn up a blonde type you can almost take them for our own.'

His son said nothing.

'Do you enjoy her, Gottfried?'

His son said nothing.

'I would guess you enjoy her, yes? Imaginative. I would guess enjoyment. Superconsciousness.'

Still his son held on. Mr Hencke passionately awaited the confessional tears. He conjured them. They did not descend.

He said finally, 'Does she boss you much?'

'Never,' Gottfried said. 'Never, never. I think you broke it up, papa. God damn you to hell, papa.'

His arms clutched across his back, the father of the artist observed the diminishing spoor of visitors. In her bride's dress Catherine glimmered at the top of the stairwell, speaking elegant goodbyes learned at Miss Jewett's. Creighton MacDougal winked and saluted and snapped his heels like a Junker officer. A wonderful mimicry spiralled out of his head: the buzz of a biplane. Simultaneously a saxophone opened fire.

'Dance with me, papa!' said Catherine. 'Oh, no, you're just so out-of-date. Nowadays you're not supposed to even *touch*.' She taught him how; he had never seen her so clever. 'Mr MacDougal had to leave, but you know what he said? He said you were a fine person. He said' – her laugh broke like a dish – 'you were a natural hermit, and if you ever decided to put up a pillar to sit on top of, it would last a thousand years.'

Mr Hencke copied her but did not touch. 'Have there been sales?'

'Not yet, but after all it's only the *opening*. And even if there aren't any that's not the point. It's just so Gottfried can feel encouraged. You have to be noticed in this world, you know that, papa? Otherwise you don't feel you really exist. You just don't understand about Gottfried. No, papa, nobody *ever* dips at the end any more. It's so out-of-date to do that. I mean Gottfried works every minute he can. You make him feel awful when you talk the way you did before about Rockefeller. My goodness, papa, he's even going to work when we get through here, he's going over to the studio right afterwards.'

'I think not. I think he will be far too tired,' said the father of the artist.

'But he *told* me he wanted to work tonight. He really meant it, papa. It's not as if I'm the only one he said it to, he's been saying it to everyone—' A scream leaped out of the bowl of apples. 'Oh, look, what's the matter with Genevieve?' Catherine, inquisitive as a child, ran.

He delayed and envisioned wounds. In his heart she bled, she bled. He stepped away. He kept back. He listened to her voice – such a coarse voice. The voice or the bass fiddle? A biblical yell, as by the waters of Babylon. Always horrible tragedy for the innocent. She was not innocent. He suspected what wounds. The saxophone machine-gunned him in the small intestine.

Catherine twitched back. 'Someone's stolen Genevieve's pocketbook! She had it lying just like that on a chair, only it was all covered up with her coat, and there was this hundred dollars in it, and her driver's licence, and the plane ticket, and a million other things like that. With all these *people*, you wouldn't think there'd be a thief—'

He was bewildered. 'Hurt? She's hurt?'

'Well no, she didn't even *leave* yet, she was just starting to go. It's not as if somebody mugged her in the street or held her up or anything. I mean they just *took* it. It was just lying there, so they took it. Can you imagine anybody acting like that?' A vividness disrupted but lit her; his daughter-in-law exulted. She assumed the sheen her wealth deserved: he descried in her at the moment of adventure those canny cattle-buccaneers who had sired her temperament. Booty-getting cannot be bred out: she was just then a true heiress, and the father of the artist was for the first time nearly proud his son had chosen her. What Gottfried had seen, he now saw. Crime rejoiced her, crime loosened the puppet-strings of her terrifying civility. Crime made her intelligent. He himself knew what it was to be one whom crisis exalts. He had once landed with half a wing shot off: his hero's wound afterwards seemed sweeter to him than any crisis of lovemaking he was ever to endure.

'Gottfried thinks it must have been one of the truckmen,' Catherine said. Ah, she hugged herself.

'Absolutely it was the truckmen,' Mr Hencke assented. 'There was no one else here like that.'

'The barman?'

'The barman perhaps,' Mr Hencke once again agreed.

'But it couldn't be the barman, the barman's still *here*. If it was the barman we could catch him red-handed. A thief always disappears as fast as he can.'

'Then the truckmen,' Mr Hencke said. 'The truckmen without question.'

'All right, but you know what *I* think, papa?'

'No.'

Catherine sucked her lip until it gleamed. 'Well, the way that weird man *argued* about his fee when we hired him – I guess you don't say hired for a critic, but I don't know what else we did if we *didn't* hire him – anyhow he didn't think he was getting enough, especially since that little FM station W-K-Something-Something sent over a couple of men to pick up his speech on a tape-recorder, and he said he doesn't even get royalties from it, so what *I* think' – her beautiful shivery laugh broke and broke, if no longer like a plate then like surf – 'is Mr MacDougal decided to raise his own fee, hook or crook!'

'It was the truckmen,' Mr Hencke said with the delicacy of finality.

'I'm just *fooling*. You always agree with Gottfried, papa. I mean on fundamentals. I don't know why you argue about everything else.'

'Genevieve must be given some money to go home with.'

'She's terrifically upset, did you see her? You wouldn't think she could get so upset. She says her husband always tells her not to be highstrung and to carry cheques—'

'Tell Gottfried to give her some money,' Mr Hencke said.

'Oh, papa, *you* tell him. If it's something important he never pays attention to any of my ideas.'

He looked for Gottfried: there he was, quarrelling with the barman, who said he had seen no one and knew nothing.

Genevieve stood chewing on a glove.

'Don't fight with him, Gottfried, it's perfectly irretrievable. It's so silly, and really it's my own stupid fault. Ed'll kill me, not for the money but like they say for the principle. *You* know. He thinks I'm a terrible slob that way, he's a great one for believing in foreseeable actions. I lost the Buick last year, and the year before I lost the baby in the parking lot.

God, how I hate people of principle. All the persecutors of the world have been people of principle.'

'Genevieve invokes History always,' Mr Hencke said.

She unexpectedly ignored this; at once he regretted it. She said hoarsely, 'I'm simply resigned. I'll never get it back. OK, OK, so it's irretrievable.'

'That is true of so much in life,' Mr Hencke said.

Gottfried darkly turned. 'Papa, what do you want?'

The barman escaped.

'I want you to give Genevieve money.'

'Money?'

'Under the circumstances.' The father of the artist tenderly uncovered his teeth.

Gottfried repeated: 'Money?'

'For Genevieve. It's the least you can do, Gottfried.'

'I don't give Genevieve money, papa.'

He saw the damp creases under his son's nose. Even in America youth is not eternal.

'Ah, but you ought to, Gottfried. Nothing comes free in this life.' He felt obscurely delighted by Gottfried's pale charged mouth. His son resembled a pretty little spotted horse spitting disappointing hay. 'Aeroplane rides to Indianapolis, Indiana don't come free in this life,' he finished in a brief mist of his own laughter.

'Well, look at that,' Genevieve said. 'Gottfried's papa wants to get rid of me. You were perfectly right about that, Gottfried, he wants to get rid of me.'

'No, no,' Mr Hencke protested. 'Only of the band. What ugly music. Saxophones frighten. Such a loud lonely forest sound. Why don't you dismiss them, Gottfried? There are no guests left, I think.'

'Democracy,' Genevieve divulged: Catherine was dancing violently with the barman.

'I see how it is done,' Mr Hencke said. 'They move but don't touch. Touching is no longer the fashion. Catherine thinks she is dancing with the thief, yes? Gottfried, give Genevieve some money.'

'Catherine can do it,' Gottfried muttered; he swam towards his wife as through some thick preventing element.

'He is nearly inaudible when he feels he has been insulted,' his father noted. 'Did he say he would?'

'It was going to be over pretty soon anyway. How I hate a brouhaha,' Genevieve said, staring after Gottfried.

'What an amusing word. After so many years I don't know all the words. Ah, a brilliant lady like yourself, you're bored with my plain-hearted son.'

'I'm bored with Kitty. I'm bored with New York.'

'And with art. With art too?' He paused desperately. 'My son would not say whether it has been a success. He would not say whether there has been enjoyment.'

'I wish,' Genevieve said, 'I just hadn't lost that damn pocketbook. The Certified Public Accountant gave me his last warning. It's the guillotine next.'

'Please, please,' Mr Hencke said, 'thieves and pickpockets occur everywhere.'

'I don't *care* about the money,' Genevieve said sourly.

'Dear lady, you care about dignity.'

'Yes,' Genevieve said, 'that's it.'

'Sit down,' Mr Hencke said, and scratched towards her the guilty chair. On this chair the stolen pocketbook had lain, and over it Genevieve's patterned coat. The chair was empty. Listlessly Genevieve gathered up the hem of her coat and sat down.

'My bag,' Mr Hencke said, picking it up and putting it at her feet.

'Well, I guess you're lucky they didn't take that too.'

'Dignity,' Mr Hencke said. 'Dignity before everything. I subscribe to that. Persons tend to assume things about other persons. For example, my son believes I came to New York entirely for this occasion – you understand – to see the gallery, to see the work. For the cognoscenti the mystery behind, yes? In reality tomorrow morning I will be early on a ship. I'm going for a beautiful trip, you know.'

'To Germany?' But she seemed detached. She watched the stairwell swallow the musicians. Catherine was using Gottfried's back for a desk, writing something. Her pen wobbled like a plunged and nervous dagger.

'Not Germany. Sweden. I admire Scandinavia. Exquisite fogs. The green of the farmland there. Now only Scandinavia is the way I remember Germany from boyhood. Germany isn't the same. All factories, chimneys.'

'Don't speak to me about German chimneys,' Genevieve said. 'I know what kind of smoke came out of those damn German chimneys.'

His eyes wept, his throat wept, she was not detached, she was merciless. 'I didn't have the heart to tell Gottfried I'm travelling again. Don't tell him, hah? Let him think I came especially. You understand, hah, Genevieve? To see his things, let him think that, not just passing on the way to travel somewhere else. I have the one bag only to mislead. I confess it, purposely to mislead. In my hotel room already there are four other bags.'

'I bet you say Sweden to mislead. I bet you're going to Germany, why shouldn't you? I don't say there's anything wrong with it, why shouldn't you go to Germany?'

'Not Germany, Sweden. The Swedes were innocent in the war, they saved so many Jews. I swear it, not Germany. It was the truckmen, I swear it.'

'I suppose it *was* one of the truckmen,' Genevieve said languidly.

'The most logical ones were the truckmen. I swear it. Look, look, Genevieve, I'll show you,' he said, 'just look—' He turned the little key and threw open his suitcase with so much wild vigour that it quivered on its hinges. 'Now just look, look through everything, nothing here but my own, here are my shirts, not all, I have so many more in my other bags in the hotel, here I have mostly, forgive me, my new underwear. Only socks, see? Socks, socks, shorts, shorts, shorts, all new, I like to travel with everything new and clean, undershirt, undershirt, shaving cream, razor, deodorant, more underwear, toothpaste, you see this, Genevieve? I swear it must have been one of the truckmen, that's only logical. Please, I swear it. Genevieve,' Mr Hencke said, forcing his fingers rigidly through the depth of his new undershorts, 'see for yourself—'

Catherine in her white dress (the wife of the artist was seen in a white dress) jerked into view: she hung like a marionette in the margins of his eye's theatre. 'Really, Genevieve, Gottfried's so funny sometimes, he has plenty of money in his wallet, but he made me write you this cheque, he absolutely insisted. Good grief, he's got cheques of his own. Can you still make the twelve o'clock plane, Gen? – because look, if you can't, you can easily stay overnight with us, why don't you, that nice room's all ready and papa isn't staying—'

'Oh, no,' Genevieve said, jumping up, 'I'll never stay overnight!'

She seized the cheque and ran down the long stairs. The interlocked series of ovals and rectangles scorched into grey. In his tenuously barbule soul, for which he had ancestral certitude, the father of the artist burned in the foam of so much kümmel, so many buttercups, so much lustrous yellow, and the horse's mane so confusing in his eyes like a grid, and why does the horse not go faster, faster?

'My goodness,' Catherine said, 'why've you got your suitcase open and everything rumpled up like that? Papa, did they steal from you too?' she gave out in her politest, most cultivated, most ventriloquist tone. 'Tonight what criminals we've harboured unawares!' – it sounded exactly like a phrase of Genevieve's.

The Doctor's Wife

The Doctor's three sisters had gathered to make salads in the house of the sister who had the biggest kitchen. They were preparing for the doctor's fiftieth birthday. Quite logically, the sister who had the biggest kitchen also had the biggest house; but she was not the richest sister. Alas, none of them was rich, not a single one, though Sophie – the sister who had the biggest house – perhaps should have been. Her husband was a puffy-necked, mostly bald dentist with intact teeth of his own, which he was always lifting up to the light in perpetual melancholy glinting laughter. He had the sort of fat-lidded marble eyes that make anyone look prosperous, but he liked to gamble at the harness races, and, worse yet, he liked to dance. In the winter he shut up his practice for half a month at a time to take part in dance contests, dance marathons, dance exhibitions. In the summer he went alone to resort hotels with celebrated orchestras. He was short, still blond at the back of the head, and he had a lewd tongue, but was as scholarly as any adolescent about the newest step. Except for the doctor, the dentist was the poorest of them all – two of his boys were in expensive colleges, and sometimes he had to ask his assistant to wait a week or two until he could find the money to catch up with the salary he owed her.

The other brothers-in-law were a teacher and a photographer. The teacher, a bleak stern man who hated his job, was married to Frieda. They lived with five bickering children in a cramped apartment at the bottom of a two-family house. Olga was the youngest of the sisters and had only one little girl, who was either sickly or dull, and was never seen to blink at her father's flashbulbs. The photographer, a big, hairy, muscular fellow, actually had the temperament of a child, but his noisy football-coach mannerisms belied this. He was constantly daydreaming.

His business was mostly baby portraits, yet he hoped for fame and harangued the doctor with his theories of photographic satire.

The doctor was really very poor, but he was the sisters' saint.

Frieda loved her husband. Sophie and Olga did not love theirs.

Sophie and Olga were extraordinarily alike. Everyone swore that Sophie, with her mirror-like grey eyes, was the family beauty, whereas Olga's hair would not curl and her bosom was monstrous. But otherwise they were very nearly psychological twins. Both were bored by babies, both were artistic, both were discontented, both loathed housekeeping. They had both decided long ago that they were superior to Frieda, who was humdrum and without talent. Before her marriage Frieda had been a nurse, and even now her face was always steamy, as though she had just emerged from sterilizing bedpans. Frieda's tedious motto was to make the best of things, and this to Sophie and Olga smacked of slavishness. Sophie and Olga considered themselves rebels, but while Sophie escaped to her piano and her watercolour box, Olga read religious philosophy. She was attracted to all manner of arcane cults, and, though Sophie laughed at her, she was almost as tolerant as Frieda: Olga was their baby.

The doctor was the oldest. He was unmarried, and did not differentiate among the sisters or their husbands. He accepted it that the dentist was a rough sort who gambled and danced and was unfaithful to Sophie every summer, that the photographer fell into terrifying fits of vanity and humiliation and raged over Olga's superstitiousness, and that the teacher was so stingy that Frieda was made to buy the cheapest cuts of meat and walked right through the soles of her shoes. Sometimes he confused the husbands, called them by the wrong names, and mixed up their occupations and their vices.

The doctor, it seemed, was not very attentive to his sisters. This was because they were women, and women have no categories. He did not notice his sisters as individuals, but he noticed what they were. They were free. They were free because they were unfree; they were exempt from choices. They did not have to *be* anything; it was enough that they were women. Their bodies were their life's blueprints: they married, became pregnant, nursed their infants, fussed over the children's homework. The doctor marvelled that the three little persons in this one room had borne, all together, nine new souls. One day they would attend the children's weddings and then they would have nothing to do but grow comfortably old. What lives! He sat in the chair that caught the best light from the fluorescent rod over the sink and watched Frieda chop celery in a wooden bowl that had belonged to their grandmother half a century ago. Everything they did struck him as play. Here was Sophie licking mayonnaise from a big stirring-spoon, and there was Olga peeping over her chest and counting dishes.

'Tuna, tuna, salmon, tuna, salmon. It's monotonous. It's fishy,' Olga said.

'Egg salad next,' Frieda promised, chopping so hard that the loose fat on her arms quivered. She had a roly-poly but spry and tidy little figure, and the ends of her blouse were always tucked in exactly. Her complexion was open-pored and very red. 'What's wrong with fishy? Caviar is fishy. King and queens and movie people eat caviar, don't they? Fish is brain food anyhow.'

'Then Pug doesn't need any. Pug's the Smartest Man in the World,' Sophie said.

The doctor folded up his newspaper and looked at the clock.

'Pug, aren't you the Smartest Man in the World?'

'No, he's not,' Olga said. 'He's the Third Smartest.'

'So who's the First and Second Smartest?' Sophie demanded.

'A man named Sidney Morgenbesser is Second and a man named Shemayim is First.'

'Good God, Sidney *who?*'

'They're philosophers,' Olga said. 'One's at Cambridge, Massachusetts and one's at Columbia University in New York. I read about them. They're antispiritual.'

'Is she right, Pug?' Sophie asked.

The doctor smiled. He had a very little air of self-regard, but he kept it hidden, even from himself. He had never heard of Sidney Morgenbesser or Shemayim. 'Well, in that case maybe it's only Fourth for me,' he said. 'Olga's ahead of me. Olga knows all the philosophers.'

'Not personally,' Olga said.

'Carnally,' Sophie explained. 'Pug, where are you *going?*'

'I have house calls tonight.'

'On Thursday? I thought you did house calls on Wednesday,' Olga said.

'This is a different house call, puss, ask him what *kind* of house. Probably the kind all you bachelors go to now and then, right, Pug?'

'Leave the boy be,' Frieda said. 'Where's that mayonnaise spoon, I just *had* it—'

'Don't you dare have house calls tomorrow night,' Sophie warned. 'Miss your birthday and we'll see you never have another.'

'Soph, you've *licked* it, wash it off first.'

'I don't believe in germs,' Sophie said. 'I believe in what I can see.'

'Do you believe in radio waves?' Olga said. 'You can't see them and they're there.'

'Now don't start with your spooks. Thank God it's broken anyhow – the radio. I've had two whole nights without WPAP and Art Kane's Swinging Doodlers Direct from Miami Beach. Speaking of radios.'

'Stop that, Soph, you like to dance yourself,' Frieda said, sponging the spoon with detergent.

Olga suddenly giggled. 'Where's Saint Vitus gone tonight?'

'To the movies.'

'Because *I'm* here,' Olga said. 'He's afraid to meet Dan in case Dan comes to call for me. Which he will.'

'You should put a mask on Dan,' Sophie suggested, 'and introduce him as somebody else. Then they might start speaking again.'

'It wouldn't work,' Olga said. 'If they haven't spoken for two years – *is* it two years? – they'll never speak. Anyhow Dan won't.'

'With a mask,' Sophie said, 'you could introduce Dan as Sidney Morgenfresser.'

'Besser.'

'Besser late than never,' the doctor said, and put on his jacket. 'I've got to be off. What time do you want me tomorrow night?'

'Oh, wait, don't you want to see the cake?' Olga cried.

'I'll see it tomorrow, won't I?'

'Oh, but *look*. Look what it says. Frieda did it with a tube thing that you squeeze. It's going to have five candles—'

'One for each decade,' Sophie intervened.

'Pug can do arithmetic, stupid. Look what it says!'

He read, among pink sugar-roses, LOVE TO OUR DEAR DOCTOR PUG FOR PUGNACITY.

'Isn't it smart! Sophie thought of it but Frieda didn't like it.'

Frieda said, 'If there's one word that *doesn't* describe—'

'My God, Frieda, that's the point, it's teasing, it's a joke. Good God, the way you fight jokes, *you're* the pugnacious one.'

'Wonderful,' the doctor said, but he was embarrassed by the 'Doctor'. After so many years they never let him rest with it. They savoured his degree, they munched on his title. If someone asked after him, they never said simply 'my brother' – it was always Doctor Pug. His name was Pincus but they were ashamed of it. His father said Doctor Pug too; he howled at his son but boasted to the laundryman. They esteemed him the way peasants esteem the only lettered person in a village. The ignorance, the pitiful ignorance!

He went back to his office and found the waiting room full, though he had made no appointments. He was still belching from the fat-soaked dinner Sophie had given him. It was forced on him because the sisters thought it would be a treat to have him there the one night they were all working together. At Frieda's house, despite the inconvenience and squeezing-in at table, he ate well. But Sophie's dishes were only yearnings: she tried to imitate those coloured family scenes of splendid dining in the life-insurance advertisements, and approximated only the order of the forks. It was like chewing paint. She had fed him beef tonight that was all muscle. He had lied about the house calls, otherwise they would have kept him longer – house calls started early.

As usual, his patients had divided the room between them. The Negroes all sat on one side, near the door, and the Italians angrily on the other, monopolizing the magazine bench. The magazines were tattered, which was odd, since he never noticed that anyone read them. His practice embraced only the poorest. The neighbourhood had been decaying since Adam left Eden. For a long while it had been inhabited mainly by old immigrants, but now it was sulkily mixed; the crouching Italians peered over their tomato plants in the lots on the corners and saw the moving vans bringing the Negroes' sticks and shreds. Some of the Italians told him they would not come back if he took the Negroes for patients. But most stayed, because if they said they had no money to pay he charged them only fifty cents for the visit and promised he would collect it next time. But next time he always forgot.

Among these people there were surprisingly few physical diseases. An old Sicilian had a cataract. An adolescent girl with skin luminous as dyed silk who came in clinging to her aunt had a tiny cyst at the margins of the breast tissue. But the most ordinary complaints were headache, backache, sleeplessness, fatigue, obscure travelling pains. It was the old recurrent groan of life. It was the sound of nature turning on its hinge. Everyone had a story to tell him. What resentments, what hatreds, what bitterness, how little good will! Wives and husbands despised one another, grandchildren were spiteful, the money went on liquor, the children were marrying haughty strangers, the daughter-in-law was a cold-hearted wretch, the fathers left home in the middle of the night. Bedlam, waste, misery – it was humanity seething in its old pot.

The doctor was writing a prescription for phenobarbital for a woman who believed she had a hole in her lung (but the truth was her son had been married for twelve years and still had no bambini) when there was a knock on the window. He thought it was a branch of the elm and told the woman to take the medicine three times a day and the feeling of the hole would go away. 'Maybe they should stitch it up, the hole?' she asked. Her face was like a hound's: the ears were pulled down into abnormal lengths by pendent glass cylinders. 'Your lungs are perfectly sound, Mrs Filletti,' he said, and heard the window crack.

The dentist was weeping under the elm, holding a fistful of stones.

'Irwin!' the doctor called down.

'Pug, I'm lonely. Pug, I'm terribly lonely.'

'Irwin, I can't hear you. Come up, will you?'

'You've got people?'

'A few left.'

'I can't come up, I might be recognized. I'm a professional in this town same as you,' the dentist sobbed.

'Do you want money?' he said through the window.

'Please, don't shame me. Listen, what's money to me? I want happiness, happiness.'

'All right, go over to the house and I'll see you in a little while.'

'Don't try to send me where Dan is, Pug. That's all over. A finished relationship. You can't reconcile oil and water, Pug.'

'I mean my house, not yours.'

'Your old man puts his nose in everything.'

'Irwin, I have patients.'

'So do I, so do I! They act as if you're the only professional in the family. Look, hurry up, I've got the car, we'll ride around.'

The doctor took his time, bandaged a boy who had been beaten in a lot fight, listened to half a dozen more tragedies, inscribed *t.i.d.* on his pad with such pressure that his forefinger began to ache, shut off the lights, locked up and went down to the dentist's enormous globular car, which he had bought twenty per cent down and could not afford.

They rode through streets smelling of lilac. It was a May night. The car was crackly with candy wrappers and somehow this, and the lilacs which every spring struck him as some new marvel of the senses he had never before passed through, reassured and caressed the doctor; for a moment he thought that perhaps everything was really temporary, his life now was only a temporary accommodation, he was young, he was preparing for the future, he would beget progeny, he would discover a useful medical instrument, he would succour the oppressed, he would follow a Gandhi-like figure in a snow-white loincloth, he would be saved; the childlike fragrance radiated a conviction that his most intense capacities, his deepest consummations, lay ahead. His brother-in-law, wiping dirty moist furrows across his scorched and unshaven chin, turned off into a neighbourhood once rich and glorious, with huge houses set on huge hilly lawns, and trees thick as a forest. The houses were now all converted to apartments and bleated television noise. The lawns were striped and spotted with wagons and trucks, and children's wagons and trucks filled the spaces between them. Voices of night-time quarrellers sprang from house to house like terrible peregrinating angels. 'Life is transient,' the doctor said. 'Everything changes, what difference does it make to you?'

'But they did it out of malice,' his brother-in-law said. 'They did it out of spite. When I came in the house there he was. They know he's my enemy, and there he was.'

'Irwin, you have no enemies. You're your own enemy, like everybody else.'

'Am I? I'm my own enemy? *I* didn't ask him to come to my house. *They* did. *I* went to a movie.'

The doctor said with a smile, 'You should have gone to a double feature. You went to a single feature and it wasn't long enough, you see? Otherwise he would have been gone by the time you got back. He only came to call for Olga.'

'Olga's a fool. She's a vicious fool too. Don't get the wool pulled over you by that damn malicious laugh she puts on, it's poison. And Sophie's worse. Sophie actually let him into the house. I can't stand the sight of him, I do everything I can to avoid him, isn't it enough I have to look at him tomorrow night? I'm a man of peace. Peace, peace, peace—'

'So is Dan,' the doctor said. He concentrated; he meditated; he speculated; he could no longer remember the cause of the estrangement. Was it money? Jealousy? Surrender? Failure? A promise subverted?

'What *he* is, he's a hunter, a primitive hunter. He still stalks the jungles. Me, I'm sick and tired of being his prey. Listen, Pug, all I want is one very simple thing, all I want is to be happy, is that too much for a human being to ask?'

'You've got the boys, you've got Sophie.'

'The boys think they're smarter than me. Even the little fellows. All right, I admit it, they're smarter, it's true, I don't deny it. When the other two were home Christmas I said something and they laughed in my face and started talking biochemistry like I didn't exist. And Sophie, Sophie used to be a gorgeous woman, before we were married we used to go on in a certain way for hours. Right after your grandmother's funeral we did it, even then. It was a fantastic attraction, I'm telling you. Between me and Sophie it was something special, fantastic. Not that she ever let me go the limit, as they say, but she let me feel under her bra and sometimes down under, you know. Then, afterwards, we got married, nothing. I says let's go to Pug and get his advice, she says no, it's my brother, I'd die. Last summer in the mountains, place called Shady Green, very bad toilets, up there they throw down anything and everything, they don't care, even Kotex, they wouldn't hesitate to throw down a dead body if you ask me, anyhow there was this girl, not old, not young, maybe thirty-two-three, with her it was like it was with Sophie at the beginning. Same physical type, short waist, big hips, a lot of silly talk, you know what I mean—'

He stopped the car in a cave of blossoming trees. The din from the houses and the lawns crowded with vehicles prodded them like a horn. Under the leaves sound and shape seemed in heat; then demonically mated.

'I'm telling you the truth, Pug, sometimes I don't think I can live with it any more. I want something, I have this hollow feeling in me all the time, no, I mean it's more like a full feeling, there's something I want to get rid of inside me and I don't know what. Like if I could suddenly vomit it up I'd feel better, you know?'

The doctor said, 'You should pay more attention to your practice, Irwin. Not because you owe a lot, that's not the issue. Work helps a person, Irwin.'

'For a distraction it helps. That's my trouble, I'm not like you, I don't *want* distraction. I want to pull the rotten core out of me and look at it. I want to be happy, that's all. How do you get to be happy?'

'I don't know,' the doctor said.

'Listen, you know why I go to the track, say? I don't go for distraction, whatever you want to call it. Just the opposite, I go because it scares me there. I'm scared stiff of losing, I get these dunning letters from the kids' bursars. I get so damn scared. But when I'm scared it's like I *feel* myself, you know what I mean? I start believing in my own existence, you know what I mean? It's like dancing. God, I'm forty-six, I start doing some of those bits I'm so out of breath I think I'm getting a heart attack. But I start feeling my heart *beat*, I know it's there, and I figure well, if I have a heart I have a body, if I have a body I'm alive. I figure if I'm alive there's something to be alive for.'

'There *is* something to be alive for,' the doctor said.

'Well, what? Go ahead, what? You tell me.'

'I don't know,' the doctor said.

'And to Sophie, I mean this as true as I'm sitting here, to Sophie you're God! Go on, if you're God tell me what I'm alive for.'

'Nobody can answer that question.'

'You mean nobody can *ask* it. Who asks such a thing? Go on, tell me, you know somebody else who asks a question like that, what he's alive for? There's this power in me, Pug, it's eating me up. I think it's sex. Maybe I need more sex, or maybe different sex. You think I need more sex, Pug? Look, I'm not asking anything personal, but what happens when a nice guy like you wants a woman? Except for the toilets you ought to try Shady Green, Pug, honest to God.'

The doctor's father was awake and waiting for him. He was a stringy tottering old man, in an incessant fury, run down, paralysed in random places – a patch on the throat, a piece of the lip, his left shin, two fingers of his left hand, a single toe on the right foot. His fury rose with him in the morning and went to bed with him at night; fury was his wife. 'Where you've been? Where you've been?' he yelled at his son, and his gums – he had already put his teeth in a glass of water mixed with a powder – looked clean, ruddy, healthy and shining.

'I took a ride with Irwin.'

'Took a ride, took a ride! His father can rot in the house. You know what I ran out of today? You didn't bring? You never bring! Citrus! I got no grapefruits, I got no lemons, I got no Sunkist. Go, go, take a ride!'

'I'll buy some oranges tomorrow,' the doctor said.

'Tomorrow isn't today, tomorrow I could be dead. Go take a ride with a professional bum! You know you missed somebody, you weren't here? Three somebodies you missed. Olga, Dan, and the little stupid. What a stupid! God forbid, four years old, eyes like a sheep. You think it's right Dan should take the child out this time of night? He went to drive Olga, why? She couldn't come later on with Frieda? Frieda's got no looks, I'll admit it, but a *mensch*, she drives a car. He went to drive Olga, he took the child. I tell you that's why she's got no brain – abuse! Day and night they abuse her. Olga feeds her something? Nose in the book, that's all she knows. Religion religion. She thinks if she'll read a book she'll find out why God puts wax in the ears. A pox on religion and a pox on God! What good did God ever do me? How many strokes I got with or without God?'

'What did they want?'

'Who?'

'Olga and Dan.'

'You they want. You should be a middleman, a magician, the foot on the button so the button shouldn't break off. You'll call them up.'

'Not tonight.'

'So they'll call you. Goodnight, goodnight, my angel, my darling! A doctor and he leaves me to die without Vitamin C.'

'I'll get oranges, don't worry. Go to bed, pop, don't worry.'

'First look in my eye.'

The doctor looked.

'Idiot, stupid, the other eye, darling. You see bloodshot? You see swollen?'

'Nothing wrong with it.'

'I took a bath, I got soap in it! And he says nothing wrong. An angel! A darling! A doctor!'

The doctor went into his room and, still wearing his jacket, lay down on the bed. Then he realized the window was shut, so he got up with a whistle of disgust, opened it, and fitted an old screen into the sash. The air had altered. It felt clotted, sluggish, hot, partisan and impassioned, like the breathing of a vindictive judge. He hung his jacket on the doorknob and returned to the bed and blew into the pillow. Then, turning on his back to face the ceiling with its crafty stains, he began, quite consciously, to grieve: he thought how imperceptibly, how inexorably, temporary accommodation becomes permanence, and one by one he counted his omissions, his cowardices, each of which had fixed him like an invisible cement, or like a nail. What he had not done accumulated in his mouth from moment to moment – the pity of so many absences worked in him the way a gland works, emitting, filling, discharging, and his mouth overflowed with saliva, it ran down his chin and along his neck, the quilt under his neck became wet. At twenty he had endured the stunned emotion of one who senses that he has been singled out for aspiration, for beauty, for awe, for some particularity not yet disclosed. At thirty he believed all that had been a contrivance of his boy's imagination (exasperation over growing old is at no time more acute or melancholy than at thirty), but he was still delighted by his energies, he knew he had a vulgar talent for compassion just as, say, Sophie had a talent, equally vulgar, for copying landscapes; he saw himself, in fact, as an open plaza, already well-trodden, waiting to be overcome by a conquest, by an invasion of particularities, by those purposeful scrapings that would mark the tiles as a place where plainly something has happened. At forty he was still without a history – his sisters were having their last babies, his father his first strokes – and he became guilty and cynical about his own nature, and began to despise himself because he had put his faith in the possibility of significant, of miraculous, event. Too late he made up his mind to marry, but fell in love, as men of that age will, with a picture. He recognized the person in a biography of Chekhov (aha, who was also a doctor, a bachelor up to the last minute): a photograph, captioned Family and Friends, date 1890, location Sadovaya Kudrinskaya Street, under a grape-trellis – the young Chekhov, his sister, his sister's friend, his three brothers, his white-bearded father, his mother in a ribboned cap but with her ears showing, a schoolboy called Seryozha in a uniform with an over-sized hat, holding a looped twig – and there, there, second row, far left, with smooth hair, spacious forehead, a perfect pointed chin, smiling merely with half her mouth, thereby causing a vale, a dimple (oh, remarkable!), in her left cheek – his beloved. Her name in the caption was Unknown Friend. Today, if alive (since in the photograph she looked no more than nineteen or twenty), she was ninety-three or -four; but then, when the doctor was forty, and she, in her tormenting anonymity, sitting nameless, Unknown, next to Lika Mizinova (Chekhov's sister's friend), drew the side of her lip in at him and took his soul, *then* she was – if alive – only eighty-three or -four. With this Unknown Friend, this eternally dimpling girl (a withered old woman, a great-grandmother by now, somewhere in the Soviet Union; an embittered spinster émigré living in a basement apartment in Queens, New York; or, more likely, dead; dead!), the doctor was in love. He sought, he said (but only to himself – this was his wretched secret), the style of that face, sharp chin, narrow Slavic eyes vaporously Tatar yet clamouring impudence, and that neck slightly straining, anticipatory, the shoulders under their white scarf nervously hunched. If she spoke he would not understand. There was no other like her. The original was a crone or buried, and at fifty, sweating on his back in his own stark bed, the doctor resolved to throw away the biography with its deeply perilous photograph. (Actually he could not throw it away because he did not own it to begin with – it was a library book, he had kept it overdue, he paid his fine, now and then he passed it on the T-shelf – perversely catalogued under 'Tchekhov' – and visited surreptitiously with Unknown Friend's sly shy eyes.) What he meant by this was that he must throw illusion away. All the photographs of hope and self-deception – out! Everything imprinted, laminated, sealed, without fruit, without progress or process – out! Immobility, error, regret, grief – out!

For the second time that night he heard a bang on the window. To himself, released, joyful, he confessed all that was necessary: that his life was a bone, that he had nobody and nobody had him, that he was unmarried because he had neglected to look for a wife, that the human race – husbands, wives, children – was a sink, a drainpipe, a sewer, that reconciliation was impossible, that his waiting room would remain divided, that his brothers-in-law would remain divided, that his sisters were no more than ovum-bearing animals born to enact the cosmic will, that he himself was sterile by default, and would remain sterile; and that all the same it was possible to be happy. At which, another whack on the pane – whack, clump; the dentist summoning him once more for philosophy, for solace, for justice. Jumping up from his bed, he wondered how he would explain his stupendous discovery – that the worthlessness of everything was just what gave everything its worth. Divine overwhelming exquisite beautiful irrationality! Nonsense holy and pellucid! – for an instant he wrested a comely logic from the character of this nonsense, then it eluded him, then (meanwhile his brain roared like a sunflower) he seized it again, for one noble static sliver of a second he grasped all things – why we are here, the meaning of the alimentary canal, who Zeus was – then wisdom shook itself like a drop off a dog and he lost it.

A bag of knuckles hit the window. Lightning without thunder, bewildered blinks of a golden eyelid, and great lucent dice hammering.

In the course of this marvel the telephone rang.

'We've got another sign, Pug. *Another* sign.'

'Dan? I heard you stopped by,' the doctor said.

'Yeah, yeah, you remember the time with the radio waves?'

'That's all over, Dan, take it easy,' the doctor said.

'I'm crippled, I'm wounded, I'm bled, I'm dead. *Who's* it over for? For me? She read somewhere they interfere with the radioactive emanations of the human spirit? Hey Pug, I wake you, you sleeping yet?'

'It's finished, no harm done, why bring it up all over again?' the doctor said.

'Yeah, ask me why. Six months with the shades pulled down and crawling under the windows so's not to get hit by the radio waves coming in? You think I forgot? Sneaking under the windows? I'm dead, she's killed me, she's my murderer. – Hey, tell the truth, you weren't asleep, Pug?'

'No. No, I'm still up.'

'I mean I wouldn't like to wake you, but it's not *one* sign tonight, Pug, it's two. First when Filth-Face Irwin showed before he was supposed to. Ancient gypsy evil omen; the Unexpected Guest. Then she brings up for Sign Number Two the Egyptian plagues. Murrain I don't see, I says, frogs and locusts I don't see. Hail! she says. It's hailing, I swear to God it's hailing, Pug. Ack-ack. In May.'

'Yes. This part of town too. I hear it.'

'It takes two omens to start the action off. An old Chaldean saying, pal. Listen, old socko, so you know what now?'

'All right, Dan. Don't blow up. She needs consolation. You see yourself she needs consolation. Whatever it is, she'll get over it same as always.'

'Sure she will, same as always, then starts the next thing. Come on, boy, *count* – Rosicrucian, Galilee Scientist, Old Believer, Theosophical Analyst, Chapel Roller, Judas Praiser, Speaker in Tongues, and on top of it keeps strict kosher – you name it, she's been there. You people don't realize what I have to put up with, that featherbrain Sophie, what's *she* see? And Frieda tells me to my face I make it all up. You people try to sweep it under the Bible, the old man worst of all. Tells me I damaged the kid tonight, because I wanted to get Olga in early! Goddam fool, your old man, what does he know about it? She says she has to be in by ten o'clock to sing her goddam night office, and I go along with her on it, what'm I supposed to do? I'm the one that's stuck with her – if not for the kid I'd make tracks, I swear. All I need's the contacts, I could sell my photosatire idea to *Life*, I know that, believe me. Believe me I know how good I am. What kind of contacts d'you get with a nut wife? Astral bodies? You people don't realize, if I wasn't ten years dead I'd make Stieglitz look like Johnny One-Note.'

'What do you mean, "night office"?'

'It's a correspondence course on how to be a nun right in your own home, guaranteed no convent necessary. Goddam her to hell, she takes four-hundred-and-fifty out of the joint account to pay these fakers and doesn't say a word. All night I'm trying to tell her the Unexpected Guest doesn't count, Ice-Eyes Irwin's the host in that house allegedly. Some host – he threw me out, Pug, he threw me out. God, I'd like to crack up that blue-jaw mug of his. Then it starts to hail, and that's the camel's back, Pug. Omen Number Two, she's starting her vows as of immediately. She was undecided, now she's positively decided, the heavens have spoken. As of immediately she's a nun, only bite your tongue, I'm not supposed to let on to anybody except Pug. Doctor Pug does not revile. So from now on she's a celibate and I'm supposed to be a celibate too. Like whaddayacallem, Abelard and Heloise, who if I took their picture I'd show 'em hanging on to Krafft-Ebing by the goddam fly-leaves—'

'Let me speak to Olga,' the doctor begged. 'Calm down, Dan, what's the good of shouting at her? Let me speak to – oh. Olga? Hi, puss, pop mentioned you were here—'

'Frieda said to stop about the fruit, he was complaining he's out of fruit,' Olga said, patient, reasonable. 'Frieda's going to bring him oranges I think, she told me to tell him not to worry about the fruit, but you know Dan, the way Dan was carrying on after Irwin showed up, it was upsetting and I forgot.'

Olga gave her frail mocking giggle.

The doctor did not wait to hear it out. 'What's this about being a nun?'

'Oh, that's Dan's talk,' she said with scorn. 'He's against the Constitution, he doesn't believe in freedom of religion. He's too literal-minded for mysticism, he takes every metaphor seriously. My goodness, Pug, I was *born* somebody's sister. You can *call* me Sister if you want to, I don't mind.'

'It's not true, Olga?' he said.

'Did you ever read *The Kreutzer Sonata*, it's by Tolstoy? I just want to be chaste, Pug, that's all.'

'Olga, a married woman *is* chaste.'

'I mean *really* chaste. I just want one thing, purity, is that a sin? Dan acts like it's a terrible sin. He never reads *anything*, he can't understand. "Purity of heart is to will one thing," that's Kierkegaard who said it, but all Dan can do is scream at me all day. You *know* what I mean, don't you, Pug? I mean chaste like you're chaste. It isn't true what Sophie says, is it? About you? I *know* it isn't true.'

'What?'

'About going to houses—'

There was a scramble. The doctor's mouth gorged saliva. 'Olga? Olga? Dan, why did you – Dan?'

'You see? You see? Am I lying, am I making it up? You people don't realize, this is what's dragging me down in the world, it's sucking my blood, I'm the dregs, I'm a failure, ten years I'm stone dead—'

They kept it up for an hour, and he stood victimized, his ear clammy, inwardly spinning, rattling like a gong, burning against the instrument, his throat a cornucopia of garbage, his chest a vessel under sail beaten and beaten, taking it in and taking it in. What they spewed he chewed. His brother-in-law shot grievances like beads across an abacus and went on adding them up in a pitch of torment which tomorrow would deliver him to the doctor whimpering for an electrocardiogram, his hand over his broad left nipple. And Olga, a mouse of persistence, a beam of inflexibility, tapping her small, laughing, modest voice, through it all tittered Universal Love. Egotism, egotism! She was a secretive girl who aspired beyond her probabilities. She was unintelligent, hiddenly arrogant yet ordinary, plain, fat-legged, sycophantic, but her eyes were round and brown; she had the power of permanent spite. The world supposed her to be only another one of these domestic bundles rolling between stove and mattress – never mind: her vision declared her Joan the Maid. Hence the smile, the laugh, the slow fawning of her patience: if only they knew!

The hail left off, the clouds wheezed on, a bold tongue of a moon licked the top of the sky.

At noon the next day the doctor remembered his father's oranges.

He admired the carts, how one fitted into another, and how the plastic handles were blue, green, and red, each from a different supermarket, but long since strayed from home, so that he saw 'Finast' and 'A & P' and 'Bohack' nested together like ingenious silver cages, peaceful, twinkling. He pulled one out of its system of stubborn interlockings and tested it, drawing it this way and that, trying little turns: it rolled without resistance on its fat rubber wheels, and he was pleased that the handle was blue, and that it had a special compartment formed by a grid that could fold away flat. He took his cart and trundled it into an indoor garden. Everything delighted and awed him: cucumbers banked two feet high, their waxy skins glinting droplets, a blazing pyramid of apples, the lettuces like garlands of faint green roses, the sober maroon shining eggplants, the celery with their flowery heads, the mushrooms heaped in oval crates of the thinnest and most pungent wood, the attendant in his carrot-stained apron with its string tied in front and his crayon over his ear, the bits of onion-peel skittering on the linoleum floor, the three sizes of tan paper bags each in its proper bin, the women wandering, plucking, weighing, pinching, filling their carts. It seemed to the doctor he had come upon a diligent and orderly little farm, where everyone reaped serenely, and ladies wearing trousers had faces full of thanksgiving for such plenitude, for such roundness, for such births of colour and depths of brightness. The oranges in their slatted pine buckets were redolent of some spectacular sultanate. How thick, ardent, and multitudinous they were! And what a wonder their mysterious navels, through which protruded sometimes the little plump shoulders of the sections inside, pouting with juice!

'Pug,' said Frieda, 'you skeleton, not even a sandwich today? Look at you. What are you doing here? I caught you just in time, you would've bought everything I bought!'

The doctor hated to be scolded for not eating lunch.

In Frieda's cart there were six splendid oranges.

'Didn't Olga tell you I was coming down to do the shopping today? Suppose I didn't bump into you, pop would be drowning in double of everything.'

'Frieda, you don't buy him enough and he runs out of things.'

'You, you never notice prices,' she said indulgently. 'The radishes are orchids and as far as their oranges go it's Tiffany's here today. They think their potatoes are diamond chips! Honeydew seventy-nine cents each! Cantaloupe forty-nine! Oh, oh, look at *this* beautiful one—'

Maternally she picked up a grizzled melon, squeezed the stem-depression, sniffed it, shut her eyes at the hummingbird sweetness, and restored it to the rack like a baby prince.

'Too much, too much. Marvin wouldn't like it. Marvin says he wishes we all took after you and never ate anything, we could save a lot that way. Why're you skipping lunch again? Why?' she demanded.

'I'm not hungry. I didn't sleep much,' he admitted.

'The hail,' Frieda said. 'Wasn't that something? It woke us too. All the kids yowled, wasn't it something? Come home with me, I'll feed you right now, Marvin's at a meeting.'

'I have to get back to the office,' he said.

'At least take a nap!'

'I'll be all right.'

'It'll be like last year, I know it, we all know it. You'll fall asleep at your own party and we'll have our hands full with Sophie crying again.'

'No, no, I'll be all right,' he said.

'At least come on time—'

'I'll try. It depends.' He counted out half a dozen more oranges and five grapefruits brilliant as planets. 'I'll do my best,' he said.

'You let them eat you alive, those people. Low-class people, deadbeats. Prescribe soap. (They're eleven cents each, that fruit, too early in the season.) Listen, you're a GP in the sticks, not a Madison Avenue psychoanalyst. You want to act like their analyst, charge 'em, charge 'em through the nose. (Get the cherry tomatoes, they're down to thirty-nine cents a box.) You let them *eat* you enough, don't you?'

'Don't worry, Frieda, I'll be there by eight. By nine at the latest.'

'We'll be lucky if you'll come ten. We'll congratulate ourselves. Only one thing, Pug, don't get mad—'

'Looks like we're in the way here,' the doctor said. Carts butted and crashed. They retired under the eave of a shelf of soda bottles. The ladies in trousers glowered.

'—but stop off home first and change your tie, all right? Put on a nice dark one, maybe a grey, you know the one, the grey with the thin stripe?'

He protested, 'If you want me *early*—'

'There's this girl,' Frieda said vaguely. 'Now don't get mad, she was transferred to Marvin's school only last month, she's not just a teacher, she's the guidance counsellor for the whole school. Pug, just once don't say no. She's only thirty-three or so, Marvin says she's very sweet-looking.'

'Frieda, Frieda,' the doctor said, 'what do I want with a girl? I thought it was just the family tonight.'

'Marvin asked her, she accepted, she's coming. It's done. Nobody says you have to *marry* her,' Frieda retorted, and he saw in the snap of her rough nostril-caps the superior conjectures of a matchmaker.

But he said dimly again, 'What do I want with a girl?' The executioners' eyes of the ladies in trousers startled him. The garden grew corrupt and vicious: he was surrounded by organic matter destined to rot, and just then, seizing his cart to join the queue in the cashier's aisle, he discovered a cyst of fresh peanut butter on the underpart of its fair blue handle. He cleaned his fingers with the edge of a paper bag, then with the hide of an eleven-cent peach, and knew that his birthday was pretext, that deceit ruled him, pretence sapped him, egotism devoured him, hope and dignity were fugitive. They meant, even now, to marry him off.

All the rest of that day an imagined chin inhabited the private side of his eyelids: the daring chin of Unknown Friend, which he dutifully glued to the unimaginable face of the guidance counsellor.

In his office he attempted unions. He made everyone stand up, said it was an urgency of ventilation, dragged the magazine bench into the centre of the room, redistributed the chairs, shuffled the lamps, announced that it was imperative for them all to sit as near the open window as possible, and waited for the mingling to begin. Piously they obeyed him, but the Italians chose the far side of the window and the blacks the opposite. He had shifted the dividing-line from diagonal to vertical: he felt like a trickster, a fascist. A wind flapped over the magazines and plucked up the pages leaf after leaf, an unseen reader, uncovering four-colour refrigerators, washing machines, television sets, toasters. The Italians, some of them negroid, looked at their shoes; the Negroes, some of them olive, looked at their fingernails. There was a flurry, not yet an epidemic, of rubella, and the doctor rejoiced at the simplicity of a rash. A rash is a friend, a brother, it erupts, mildly pruritic, in the epidermises of all nations and races, it declares human-ness. He wrote the same prescription for everyone – a lotion, a unifying lotion, sending diverse men to diverse drugstores with a single purpose, alleviation, reconciliation, unexceptionable evidence for the equality of skins.

Mr Gino Angeloro told him confidentially that the niggers with their dirty habits were spreading the disease from yard to yard.

Mrs Nascentia Carpenter told him confidentially that the wops with their wormy tomato plants were spreading the disease from block to block.

He went home and changed his tie.

His father was already gone from the house – they had arranged it that Frieda and Marvin would drive him to Sophie's, a chancy trip in Marvin's second-hand little English car: the five children and Marvin's guitar vying in the back seat, his father thin and barking, lunging against the strings.

In the empty corridor outside his bedroom the doctor knotted his tie, from a distance, in his dresser mirror, surveying himself: his already distinct hunch, his hair beginning to cloud over everywhere (as though his scalp were sweating a creeping white mist), the flat bony beak of his angled forehead: this glimpse of what he had become – while he was not even noticing; behind his own back – filled his mouth again, and as he was going out he stopped at the kitchen sink and abundantly spat into it.

When he arrived they called (Sophie's joke) 'No surprise!' and 'Happy birthday!' and he saw all of yesterday's salads, undermined, burrowed into, in a row on a fresh tablecloth, and DOCTOR PUG gleaming greasily on the cake. He was late, they had all eaten, paper plates tumbled with pumpernickel crusts littered the coffee table; but they applauded him, the children shrieked, the guitar slammed a chord, a turmoil of laughter, kisses, cries of 'Speech!' churned and crimped the air. The doctor, unmoved, hiding his coldness, thanked them: 'I've come this far and I'm still an honest man, at least I've got an honest body, it always tells the truth – after half a century my hair is greyer than pop's, I've got a fine hump coming up like a tree between my shoulders, I guess I'm too tough to please any cannibal,' and the children shouted at the comedy of it. The photographer posed him, aimed elaborately, displayed finesse, temperament, commanded him immobile under lights that bloodied his eyes without mercy, then he was presented with the cake to blow at, cut up, give out – he held the knife like a dagger in the act of murder, icing tinged his cuffs and smeared his eyebrows, he felt at last a little dirty, whitened and wizened, a tired waiter gone to seed. The dentist and the photographer passed within inches (elbows lifted so as not to touch), ostentatious in a common silence, each invisible to the other; meanwhile Olga fed a slice of cake – the top said TORPUGF – into the automatic jaws of her little girl: the dullness of the child's eyes deepened and deepened, like a voluptuous ember. Finally the dentist took him aside and showed him a new letter, received that morning, from his oldest boy – 'See, what'd I tell you, Pug? Smart! Look at those grades! I tell him follow in your uncle's footsteps, make Phi Beta Kappa, get the key! You want to get into med school like Pug? Get your key! I tell them both that, not just Richy, I tell Petey the same thing.' Frieda brought him a plate of herring salad. Against the farthest wall, under a watercolour of Sophie's called Moonlight and Pines, serious, mild, his glasses blinking, Marvin was talking to a strange young woman, but the big guitar obscured her. His father was asleep in a pocket of the sofa, his head stiff and to the side, like the bust of a minor Roman official, his mouth a stone yawn, his gums glabrous, glistening, vibrant – his teeth were in his hand. The photographer began to try out his latest ideas for political satire – catch, with camera on the *qui vive*, the Russian ambassador in the urinal, the President smacking the First Lady, the Defence Secretary working out in boxing gloves. He was bullied, cornered, inextricable; then Sophie flew up – 'Pug! I nearly forgot to introduce you, come on!' – she wore cheap Chinese slippers strewing flakes of cardboard gold, and her heated smile was chipped, hazy.

But Marvin was already playing in earnest. He played like a warlock, his guitar was his life, he had the knack of a demon piper. The children went mad, the dentist went mad, even Olga's flawed little girl was snatched by spasms of bliss – she circled and circled, raised her dress, stared at her knees shuddering, screeched like a night-time cat. The teacher threw his white pick on the floor and dipped his naked fingers into the strings, as into a harp, or a pool crisscrossed by contending wakes, or a barred cell; and jounced, bounced, trounced his classes, the living he had to ply from πr^2, the head of the department, the principal, the wild boys who smoked at the back of the room: jounced them, bounced them, trounced them, until he was worn with the flogging, until he was cleansed for the sake of this shiver, this shimmer – then, in a splatter, like the steely water that shoots from a diver penetrating, the true and absolute music stuttered: a stick on spokes. The teacher tweezed it, struck it, beat it out, and the children rolled in panting heaps on the carpet, spent, belly-hurting with glee. Sophie shut her piano. Envy made her shut it with the plain grace of someone just back from a failed foreign tour – if not for the sting of this guitar (it nosed out into the room, a rapid loud gigantic subtle insect, billion-legged, nylon-winged, no-waisted, with quick insinuating antennae), she would even now be flourishing the long, Continental gigolo-thrills of Massenet's Elegy: it was her best piece.

So Frieda took him instead. 'Pug? Come and meet Gerda.'

He followed her. The seat of his pants was cruelly plucked; his buttock was pinched hard. 'My angel, this time don't be so foolish, darling. A nice female, I seen her myself, I keep my eyes open, bloodshot don't prevent!' said the doctor's father, wide awake. With the gesture of a gloved cavalier he opened his fist and thrust his teeth back into his face; all alone they smirked. 'You'll like her you'll marry her, if not not, only why not like? To like is easy. Someone the same as your sisters, only nice, educated – good girls, good enough! If she'll read too much you'll tell her to cut it out. Enough is enough, fifty years old is enough, get married! Tomorrow we'll make a wedding, sonny, darling, doctor, fool, idiot, maniac—'

Frieda persuaded him into the kitchen for orange juice.

Then 'Pug,' said Frieda, 'this is Miss Steinweh. Gerda, please meet my brother, Doctor Pincus Silver.'

'Steinway?' the doctor inquired.

'A very distant relative of the instrument people, collateral branch entirely, but about me I'm afraid there's nothing piano, not even my legs,' said the guidance counsellor: a humorist.

They sat together on the sofa, watching the Virginia reel.

'You have a big practice?'

'Fairly large,' the doctor said, concealing poverty.

'My cousin Morris is a pharmacist. He says all doctors could use handwriting analysis.'

'Do you find,' the doctor asked desperately, 'that more students are college-motivated nowadays?'

'Come see come saw. Who's that?' – Miss Steinweh pointed. 'The bald one doh-see-dohing with the kids? The clown. I know him.'

'My brother-in-law. Irwin Sherman.'

'A professional also?'

'A dentist—'

'I thought so. Talk about small worlds. He's the one that gave my girlfriend the runaround last year in the mountains. Said he wasn't married, then she looks in his pocket where he keeps his keys and finds a wedding ring. He's married to *that* one?' – Miss Steinweh pointed.

'No, that's my sister Olga. Sophie is Irwin's wife.'

'She's very attractive. Believe it or not, I never knew Marv was musical. In school he's a hundred per cent geometry, very quiet. Did his wife know?'

The doctor was confused.

'About the mountains? His *wife*. That he was going around saying he wasn't?'

'Wasn't—'

'Married. Look at him. A clown, thinks he's still a kid.' Miss Steinweh pointed. 'Which reminds me, many happy returns of the day.'

'Thank you,' said the doctor, feeling choked.

'I hear you're still a bachelor. At your age. Well, look, never mind, I have the same attitude. Either it's Mister Right or it's nobody.'

The doctor exerted himself. He ignored the nervous cramp in his calf. He did what his sisters expected: his voice turned effortful, high. Life! he cried. Life, life, where are you, where did you go, why didn't you wait for me? Let me live! he cried. 'Oh you,' he said in a voice that was new, light, aggressive yet dim, hopeful, 'you're scarcely in *my* boat, Miss Steinweh—'

'Gerda. You don't think thirty-six is old? Believe me it's not young. Everyone says my trouble is I have an MA, it's in clinical psychology. I tell them it was a slip I made. Believe me I treat it like a slip, I don't let it show.' Miss Steinweh laughed and pointed at her thighs, over which lay, presumably, her underwear. 'Actually, I'm reconciled, I really am. Are you?'

'Reconciled?' he said. He was aware of a collapse. His voice was heavy, heavy.

'To being a bachelor.'

'Oh, but I'm not,' the doctor said.

'You aren't?'

'No, no, I'm not.'

'I figure by age fifty a person would be reconciled.'

'No,' the doctor said urgently, 'I don't mean that. I mean I'm not what you think. I'm not—' how heavy, heavy his voice was, his breath! – 'I'm not a bachelor.'

'You're not? But Frieda—' Miss Steinweh pointed at Frieda. Far off, in the kitchen, she was washing the cake knife. 'Frieda *told* me you were.'

'Frieda doesn't know. Neither does Marvin. Nobody does.'

'I don't get it,' said Miss Steinweh, and for the first time the doctor took her in. Already the misery of having yielded whipped her mouth. She was like his sisters, lost: his father with the acumen of chronic insult had already recognized the daughter of his spirit, the failed daughter of the failed pedlar; his father with his tradesman's cleverness had already descried the yielding and the loss. Miss Steinweh was dark like dark Olga, but her eyes were grey like Sophie's, and under them the doctor observed a certain ruffling, a certain gathering-up, a suggestion of the drawstring; under her chin the same, a weariness of the mould, a pucker, a yielding, a loss of earliness. And in spite of this she had long girlish hair, and girlish glasses, and an abrupt girlish nod, and a girlish forefinger pointing: she was a sunset, it was the last hour before her night, the warmth of her last youth was ebbing, she was at the excruciating fulcrum of transition. The doctor pitied her. What had happened to him would happen to her. He saw her fifty and alone, less than his sisters, sculptured in cosmetics, her birth canal desolate, her red tides shrinking, vanishing; her powerful cheeks malevolent. 'Is it a joke?' she said. 'I can take a practical joke, believe me.'

'I have a wife,' the doctor said.

'You're married?'

'Yes,' he said.

'And they don't know about it? Your sisters? Your father? I don't get it.' She flung him a crafty look. 'Then why tell *me*?'

But he was craftier still. 'The compulsion of contrast. You don't remind me of my wife. My wife is different from you. She's different from Sophie, she's different from Olga. God knows she's not like Frieda.'

'A secret marriage?' said Miss Steinweh, leaning near. 'How long has it been?'

He picked (he put it to himself) a number. He was cunning enough, he was the scion of cunning, cunning was his sister, cunning was the primeval gene. 'A dozen years. It had to be, it has to be. Who could take my father? Every one of us is poorer than the next—'

'Poor?' she intervened, and pointed at his breast pocket. 'You said you have this big practice.'

'This big, big, poor, poor practice,' he said.

'You could have waited till it grew,' she said practically. 'Grew financially, I mean.'

'There are things in this world that don't grow. They're born a certain way and they stay the way they were when they came.' He stopped to notice Olga's little girl in her glowing dance, weaving through the weavers of the reel, solitary, on the trail of something private: a gem always just ahead of her, radiant, summoning. 'You can't have remorse over something that never was. You measure life by what's happened to you, not by what didn't happen. You think my sisters can grow? You think my father can grow? Can a stone grow? Who waits for a stone to grow?' He considered her. 'You don't believe me?'

'I don't get it. Just on account of your father it was? Couldn't he come to live with you?'

The doctor covered his face. A live violence entered his throat. 'I – cannot – live with my father,' he said.

This made her strange; she whispered. 'What you're telling me,' she said, 'is it – it's not just – *you* know, just an arrangement—'

'A marriage,' he said solemnly, and peered at her. 'We have a bona fide marriage certificate. We have children.'

'Children!' said Miss Steinweh, and did not point.

'Three,' he said. 'Eleven, nine, and four. Two girls and a boy.'

'And she *takes* it – she stands for it? Your wife? What kind of a marriage is that? What kind of a father are you?'

He said, 'Normal. Everything normal. No secret husband, no secret father. It's easy. One night a week I take the train to New York. Twenty-minute trip. My sisters think I do house calls. Every weekend I take the train. The families of travelling salesmen have it worse.'

'And they don't know? You've never told them? Your sisters, your father? Why don't you tell them?'

'It's too late,' he said. 'Too hazardous. My father's been having this

series of vascular constrictions, I'm not confident he could survive a bad
surprise – a shock.'

'You could tell your sisters,' Miss Steinweh persisted, 'and tell them
not to tell your father.'

'It would get to him. Things always get to him.'

'But why didn't you tell everybody to begin with!'

—By default, by default! he cried. He said humbly, 'I wanted a
different life.'

'It's different all right!' said Miss Steinweh, in the tone of one who
laughs: but did not laugh, did not nod; she looked at the doctor. 'What is
she like?'

'My wife?'

'Yes. A person like that.'

'Very young. Years younger than myself. Far younger than you.' It did
not pass him how this hurt her. 'An émigré. A fugitive. Suffered horrible
privations getting through. Very shy. Never learned English well. Speaks
Russian like a bird.'

'Russian?'

'The children are completely bilingual. Except for that, and whatever is
deposited in my wife's brain – she never mentions her memories, only
the snow and the Moscow skating – we have nothing Russian in the
apartment. Oh, a samovar, but we bought it in New York. We bought it
on Delancey Street,' the doctor said. 'She's older than she was when I
first saw her, but she's still a beautiful girl. A soul in her.' The teacher
loosed a sudden coruscation out of his guitar and the doctor trembled in
its resonance.

'*Now* I see,' said Miss Steinweh. 'She doesn't know what she's mixed
up with. She doesn't know the ways of the country. She's absolutely in
your hands, she's at your mercy.'

'She belongs to me,' the doctor admitted.

'It's not nice,' Miss Steinweh said. 'It's awful. You should bring her into
your own town. You should introduce her to your sisters.'

'Oh – my sisters!' the doctor said.

She stood up and went on greedily looking at him. 'Are you happy that
way?'

'We are both very happy.' Then a resplendent word discharged itself
like a ghost: beatific; but he did not use it. 'Both of us are happy. The
children are well.'

'As long as the children are well,' she said, 'that's the main thing, the children are well.' He was amazed. She was jeering at him. 'What pigs you all are – pigs, fakers, otherwise why would I be here, I don't have days to waste out of my life! Pigs! I don't have nights!'

When the dentist spotted her coming his way on her shaky high heels, immediately his neck puffed red and he importuned his brother-in-law to play a rhumba.

The doctor watched the dentist and the guidance counsellor dance. Miss Steinweh danced well – she was not so expert as the dentist, but she was not afraid of him. Her arms were thick but sinuous. Across the width of Sophie's living room, layered with Sophie's brutish copies of Van Gogh and Degas, she looked kind. She danced with the dentist and was kind to him.

Then the photographer captured the doctor again and began to outline another idea he had to make him famous.

Virility

You are too young to remember Edmund Gate, but I knew him when he was Elia Gatoff in knickers, just off the boat from Liverpool. Now to remember Edmund Gate at all, one must be a compatriot of mine, which is to say a centagenerian. A man of one hundred and six is always sequestered on a metaphysical Elba, but on an Elba without even the metaphor of a Napoleon – where, in fact, it has been so long forgotten that Napoleon ever lived that it is impossible to credit his influence, let alone his fame. It is harsh and lonely in this country of exile – the inhabitants (or, as we in our eleventh decade ought more accurately to be called, the survivors) are so sparse, and so maimed, and so unreliable as to recent chronology, and so at odds with your ideas of greatness, that we do indeed veer towards a separate mentality, and ought in logic to have a flag of our own. It is not that we seclude ourselves from you, but rather that you have seceded from us – you with your moon pilots, and mohole fishermen, and algae cookies, and anti-etymological reformed spelling – in the face of all of which I can scarcely expect you to believe in a time when a plain and rather ignorant man could attain the sort of celebrity you people accord only to vile geniuses who export baby-germs in plastic envelopes. That, I suppose, is the worst of it for me and my countrymen in the land of the very old – your isolation from our great. Our great and especially our merely famous have slipped from your encyclopaedias, and will vanish finally and absolutely when we are at length powdered into reconstituted genetic pore – mixed with fish flour, and to be taken as an antidote immediately after radiation-saturation: a detail and a tangent, but I am subject to these broodings at my heavy age, and occasionally catch myself in egotistical yearning for an ordinary headstone engraved with my name. As if, in a population of a billion and a quarter, there could be space for that entirely obsolete indulgence! – and yet, only last week, in the old Preserved Cemetery, I visited Edmund Gate's grave, and viewed his monument, and came away persuaded of the beauty of that ancient, though wasteful, decorum. We have no room for physical memorials nowadays; and nobody pays any attention to the pitiful poets.

Just *here* is my huge difficulty. How am I to convince you that, during an interval in my own vast lifetime, there was a moment when a poet – a plain, as I have said, and rather ignorant man – was noticed, and noticed abundantly, and noticed magnificently and even stupendously? You will of course not have heard of Byron, and no one is more eclipsed than dear Dylan; nor will I claim that Edmund Gate ever rose to *that* standard. But he was recited, admired, worshipped, translated, pursued, even paid; and the press would not let him go for an instant. I have spoken of influence and of fame; Edmund Gate, it is true, had little influence, even on his own generation – I mean by this that he was not much imitated – but as for fame! Fame was what we gave him plenty of. We could give him fame – in those days fame was ours to give. Whereas you measure meanly by the cosmos. The first man to the moon is now a shrivelling little statistician in a Bureau somewhere, superseded by the first to Venus, who, we are told, lies all day in a sour room drinking vodka and spitting envy on the first to try for Pluto. Now it is the stars which dictate fame, but with us it was *we* who made fame, and we who dictated our stars.

He died (like Keats, of whom you will also not have heard) at twenty-six. I have this note not from Microwafer Tabulation, but from the invincible headstone itself. I had forgotten it and was touched. I almost thought he lived to be middle-aged: I base this on my last sight of him, or perhaps my last memory, in which I observe him in his underwear, with a big hairy paunch, cracked and browning teeth, and a scabby scalp laid over with a bunch of thin light-coloured weeds. He looked something like a failed pugilist. I see him standing in the middle of a floor without a carpet, puzzled, drunk, a newspaper in one hand and the other tenderly reaching through the slot in his shorts to enclose his testicles. The last words he spoke to me were the words I chose (it fell to me) for his monument: 'I am a man.'

He was, however, a boy in corduroys when he first came to me. He smelled of salami and his knickers were ravelled at the pockets and gave off a saltiness. He explained that he had walked all the way from England, back and forth on the deck. I later gathered that he was a stowaway. He had been sent ahead to Liverpool on a forged passport (these were Czarist times), from a place full of wooden shacks and no sidewalks called Glusk, with instructions to search out an old aunt of his mother's on Mersey Street and stay with her until his parents and sisters could scrape up the papers for their own border-crossing. He miraculously found the Liverpudlian aunt, was received with joy, fed bread and butter, and shown a letter from Glusk in which his father stated that the precious sheets were finally all in order and properly stamped with seals almost identical to real government seals: they would all soon be reunited in the beckoning poverty of Golden Liverpool. He settled in with the aunt, who lived tidily in a grey slum and worked all day in the back of a millinery shop sewing on veils. She had all the habits of a cool and intellectual spinster. She had come to England six years before – she was herself an emigrant from Glusk, and had left it legally and respectably under a pile of straw in the last of three carts in a gypsy caravan headed westwards for Poland. Once inside Poland (humanely governed by Franz Josef), she took a train to Warsaw, and liked the book stores there so much she nearly stayed forever, but instead thoughtfully lifted her skirts onto another train – how she hated the soot! – to Hamburg, where she boarded a neat little boat pointed right at Liverpool. It never occurred to her to go a little further, to America: she had fixed on English as the best tongue for a foreigner to adopt, and she was suspicious of the kind of English Americans imagined they spoke. With superior diligence she began to teach her great-nephew the beautiful and clever new language; she even wanted him to go to school, but he was too much absorbed in the notion of waiting, and instead ran errands for the greengrocer at three shillings a week. He put pennies into a little tin box to buy a red scarf for his mother when she came. He waited and waited, and looked dull when his aunt talked to him in English at night, and waited immensely, with his whole body. But his mother and father and his sister Feige and his sister Gittel never arrived. On a rainy day in the very month he burst into manhood (in the course of which black rods of hairs appeared in the trench of his upper lip), his aunt told him, not in English, that it was no use waiting any longer; a pogrom had murdered them all. She put the letter, from a cousin in Glusk, on exhibit before him – his mother, raped and slaughtered; Feige, raped and slaughtered; Gittel, escaped but caught in the forest and raped twelve times before a passing friendly soldier saved her from the thirteenth by shooting her through the left eye; his father, tied to the tail of a Cossack horse and sent to have his head broken on cobblestones.

All this he gave me quickly, briefly, without excitement, and with a shocking economy. What he had come to America for, he said, was a job. I asked him what his experience was. He reiterated the fact of the greengrocer in Liverpool. He had the queerest accent; a regular salad of an accent.

'That's hardly the type of preparation we can use on a newspaper,' I said.

'Well, it's the only kind I've got.'

'What does your aunt think of your leaving her all alone like that?'

'She's an independent sort. She'll be all right. She says she'll send me money when she can.'

'Look here, don't you think the money ought to be going in the opposite direction?'

'Oh, I'll never have any money,' he said.

I was irritated by his pronunciation – 'mawney' – and I had theories about would-be Americans, none of them complimentary, one of which he was unwittingly confirming. 'There's ambition for you!'

But he startled me with a contradictory smile both iron and earnest. 'I'm very ambitious. You wait and see,' as though we were already colleagues, confidants, and deep comrades. 'Only what *I* want to be,' he said, 'they don't ever make much money.'

'What's that?'

'A poet, I've always wanted to be a poet.'

I could not help laughing at him. 'In English? You want to do English poetry?'

'English, righto. I don't *have* any other language. Not any more.'

'Are you positive you have English?' I asked him. 'You've only been taught by your aunt, and no one ever taught *her*.'

But he was listening to only half, and would not bother with any talk about his relative. 'That's why I want to work on a paper. For contact with written material.'

I said strictly, 'You could read books, you know.'

'I've read *some*.' He looked down in shame. 'I'm too lazy. My mind is lazy but my legs are good. If I could get to be a reporter or something like that I could use my legs a lot. I'm a good runner.'

'And when,' I put it to him in the voice of a sardonic archangel, 'will you compose your poems?'

'While I'm running,' he said.

I took him on as office boy and teased him considerably. Whenever I handed him a bir of copy to carry from one cubbyhole to another I reminded him that he was at last in contact with written material, and hoped he was finding it useful for his verse. He had no humour but his legs were as fleet as he had promised. He was always ready, always at attention, always on the alert to run. He was always *there*, waiting. He stood like a hare at rest watching the typewriters beat, his hands and his feet nervous for the snatch of the sheet from the platen, as impatient as though the production of a column of feature items were a wholly automatic act governed by the width of the paper and the speed of the machine. He would rip the page from the grasp of its author and streak for the copy desk, where he would lean belligerently over the poor editor in question to study the strokes of this cringing chap's blue pencil. 'Is that what cutting is?' he asked. 'Is that what you call proofreading? Doesn't "judgment" have an "e" in it? Why not? There's an "e" in "judge", isn't there? How come you don't take the "e" out of "knowledgeable" too? How do you count the type for a headline?' He was insufferably efficient and a killing nuisance. In less than a month he switched from those ribbed and reeky knickers to a pair of grimy trousers out of a pawnshop, and from the ample back pocket of these there protruded an equally ample dictionary with its boards missing, purchased from the identical source: but this was an affectation, since I never saw him consult it. All the same we promoted him to proofreader. This buried him. We set him down at a dark desk in a dungeon and entombed him under mile-long strips of galleys and left him there to dig himself out. The print-shop helped by providing innumerable shrdlus and inventing further typographical curiosities of such a nature that a psychologist would have been severely interested. The city editor was abetted by the whole reporting staff in the revelation of news stories rivalling the Bible in luridness, sexuality, and imaginative abomination. Meanwhile he never blinked, but went on devotedly taking the 'e' out of 'judgment' and putting it back for 'knowledgeable', and making little loops for 'omit' wherever someone's syntactical fancy had gone too rapturously far.

When I looked up and spotted him apparently about to mount my typewriter I was certain he had risen from his cellar to beg to be fired. Instead he offered me a double information: he was going to call himself Gate, and what did I think of that? – and in the second place he had just written his first poem.

'First?' I said. 'I thought you've been at it all the while.'

'Oh no,' he assured me. 'I wasn't ready. I didn't have a name.'

'Gatoff's a name, isn't it?'

He ignored my tone, almost like a gentleman. 'I mean a name suitable for the language. It has to match somehow, doesn't it? Or people would get the idea I'm an impostor.' I recognized this word from a recent fabrication he had encountered on a proof – my own, in fact: a two-paragraph item about a man who had successfully posed as a firewarden through pretending to have a sound acquaintance with the problems of water-pressure systems, but who let the firehouse burn down because he could not get the tap open. It was admittedly a very inferior story, but the best I could do; the other had soared beyond my meagre gleam, though I made up for my barrenness by a generosity of double negatives. Still, I marvelled at his quickness at self-enrichment – the aunt in Liverpool, I was certain, had never talked to him, in English, of impostors.

'Listen,' he said thickly, 'I really feel you're the one who started me off. I'm very grateful to you. You understood my weakness in the language and you allowed me every opportunity.'

'Then you like your job down there?'

'I just wish I could have a light on my desk. A small bulb maybe, that's all. Otherwise it's great down there, sure, it gives me a chance to think about poems.'

'Don't you pay any attention to what you're reading?' I asked admiringly.

'Sure I do. I always do. That's where I get my ideas. Poems deal with Truth, right? One thing I've learned lately from contact with written material is that Truth is Stranger than Fiction.' He uttered this as if fresh from the mouths of the gods. It gave him a particular advantage over the rest of us: admonish him that some phrase was as old as the hills, and he would pull up his head like a delighted turtle and exclaim, 'Now that's perfect. What a perfect way to express antiquity. That's true, the hills have been there since the earth was just new. Very good! I congratulate you' – showing extensive emotional reverberation, which I acknowledged after a time as his most serious literary symptom.

The terrible symptom was just now vividly tremulous. 'What I want to ask you,' he said, 'is what you would think of Edmund for a poet's name. In front of Gate, for instance.'

'*My* name is Edmund,' I said.

'I know, I know. Where would I get the idea if not from you? A marvellous name. Could I borrow it? Just for use on poems. Otherwise it's all right, don't be embarrassed, call me Elia like always.'

He reached for his behind, produced the dictionary, and cautiously shook it open to the Fs. Then he tore out a single page with meticulous orderliness and passed it to me. It covered Fenugreek to Fylfot, and the margins were foxed with an astonishing calligraphy, very tiny and very ornate, like miniature crystal cubes containing little bells.

'You want me to read this?' I said.

'Please,' he commanded.

'Why don't you use regular paper?'

'I like words,' he said. 'Fenugreek, an herb of the pea family. Felo-de-se, a suicide. I wouldn't get that just from a blank sheet. If I see a good word in the vicinity I put it right in.'

'You're a great borrower,' I observed.

'Be brutal,' he begged. 'Tell me if I have talent.'

It was a poem about dawn. It had four rhymed stanzas and coupled 'lingered' with 'rosy-fingered'. The word Fuzee was strangely prominent.

'In concept it's a little on the hackneyed side,' I told him.

'I'll work on it,' he said fervently. 'You think I have a chance? Be brutal.'

'I don't suppose you'll ever be an original, you know,' I said.

'You wait and see,' he threatened me. 'I can be brutal too.'

He headed back for his cellar and I happened to notice his walk. His thick round calves described forceful rings in his trousers, but he had a curiously modest gait, like a preoccupied steer. His dictionary jogged on his buttock, and his shoulders suggested the spectral flutes of a spectral cloak, with a spectral retinue following murmurously after.

'Elia,' I called to him.

He kept going.

I was willing to experiment. 'Edmund!' I yelled.

He turned, very elegantly.

'Edmund,' I said. 'Now listen. I mean this. Don't show me any more of your stuff. The whole thing is hopeless. Waste your own time but don't waste mine.'

He took this in with a pleasant lift of his large thumbs. 'I never waste anything. I'm very provident.'

'Provident, are you?' I made myself a fool for him: 'Aha, evidently you've been inditing something in and around the Ps—'

'Puce, red. Prothorax, the front part of an insect. Plectrum, an ivory pick.'

'You're an opportunist,' I said. 'A hoarder. A rag-dealer. Don't fancy yourself anything better than that. Keep out of my way, Edmund,' I told him.

After that I got rid of him. I exerted – if that is not too gross a word for the politic and the canny – a quiet urgency here and there, until finally we tendered him the title of reporter and sent him out to the police station to call in burglaries off the blotter. His hours were midnight to morning. In two weeks he turned up at my desk at ten o'clock, squinting through an early sunbeam.

'Don't you go home to sleep now?' I asked.

'Criticism before slumber, I've got more work to show you. Beautiful new work.'

I swallowed a groan. 'How do you like it down at headquarters?'

'It's fine. A lovely place. The cops are fine people. It's a wonderful atmosphere to think up poems in. I've been extremely fecund. I've been pullulating down there. This is the best of the lot.'

He ripped out Mimir to Minion. Along the white perimeter of the page his incredible handwriting peregrinated: it was a poem about a rose. The poet's beloved was compared to the flower. They blushed alike. The rose minced in the breeze; so did the lady.

'I've given up rhyme,' he announced, and hooked his eyes in mine. 'I've improved. You admit I've improved, don't you?'

'No,' I said. 'You've retrogressed. You're nothing but hash. You haven't advanced an inch. You'll never advance. You haven't got the equipment.'

'I have all these new words,' he protested. 'Menhir. Eximious. Suffruticose. Congee. Anastrophe. Dandiprat. Trichiasis. Nidificate.'

'Words aren't the only equipment. You're hopeless. You haven't got the brain for it.'

'All my lines scan perfectly.'

'You're not a poet.'

He refused to be disappointed; he could not be undermined. 'You don't see any difference?'

'Not in the least. – Hold on. A difference indeed. You've bought yourself a suit,' I said.

'Matching coat and pants. Thanks to you. You raised me up from an errand boy.'

'That's America for you,' I said. 'And what about Liverpool? I suppose you send your aunt something out of your salary?'

'Not particularly.'

'Poor old lady.'

'She's all right as she is.'

'Aren't you all she's got? Only joy, apple of the eye and so forth?'

'She gets along. She writes me now and then.'

'I suppose you don't answer much.'

'I've got my own life to live,' he objected, with all the ardour of a man in the press of inventing not just a maxim but a principle. 'I've got a career to make. Pretty soon I have to start getting my things into print. I bet you know some magazine editors who publish poems.'

It struck me that he had somehow discovered a means to check my acquaintance. 'That's just the point. They publish *poems*. You wouldn't do for them.'

'You could start me off in print if you wanted to.'

'I don't want to. You're no good.'

'I'll get better. I'm still on my way. Wait and see,' he said.

'All right,' I agreed, 'I'm willing to wait but I don't want to see. Don't show me any more. Keep your stuff to yourself. Please don't come back.'

'Sure,' he said: this was his chief American acquisition. 'You come to me instead.'

During the next month there was a run on robberies and other nonmatutinal felonies, and pleasurably and with relief I imagined him bunched up in a telephone booth in the basement of the station house, reciting clot after clot of criminal boredoms into the talking-piece. I hoped he would be hoarse enough and weary enough to seek his bed instead of his fortune, especially if he conceived of his fortune as conspicuously involving me. The mornings passed, and, after a time, so did my dread – he never appeared. I speculated that he had given me up. I even ventured a little remorse at the relentlessness of my dealings with him, and then a courier from the mail room loped in and left me an enormous envelope from an eminent literary journal. It was filled with dozens and dozens of fastidiously torn-out dictionary pages, accompanied by a letter to me from the editor-in-chief, whom – after a fashion – I knew (he had been a friend of my late and distinguished father): 'Dear Edmund, I put it to you that your tastes in gall are not mine. I will not say that you presumed on my indulgence when you sent this fellow up here with his sheaf of horrors, but I will ask you in the future to restrict your recommendations to *simple* fools – who, presumably, turn to ordinary foolscap in their hour of folly. PS In any case I never have, and never hope to, print anything containing the word "ogdoad".'

One of the sheets was headed Ogam to Oliphant.

It seemed too savage a hardship to rage all day without release: nevertheless I thought I would wait it out until midnight and pursue him where I could find him, at his duties with the underworld, and then, for direct gratification, knock him down. But it occurred to me that a police station is an inconvenient situation for an assault upon a citizen (though it did not escape me that he was still unnaturalized), so I looked up his address and went to his room.

He opened the door in his underwear. 'Edmund!' he cried. 'Excuse me, after all I'm a night worker – but it's all right, come in, come in! I don't need a lot of sleep anyhow. If I slept I'd never get any poems written, so don't feel bad.'

Conscientiously I elevated my fists and conscientiously I knocked him down.

'What's the idea?' he asked from the floor.

'What's the idea is right,' I said. 'Who told you you could go around visiting important people and saying I sicked you on them?'

He rubbed his sore chin in a rapture. 'You heard! I bet you heard straight from the editor-in-chief himself. You would. You've got the connections, I knew it. I told him to report right to you. I knew you'd be anxious.'

'I'm anxious and embarrassed and ashamed,' I said. 'You've made me look like an idiot. My father's oldest friend. He thinks I'm a sap.'

He got up, poking at himself for bruises. 'Don't feel bad for me. He didn't accept any at all? Is that a fact? Not a single one?' I threw the envelope at him and he caught it with a surprisingly expert arc of the wrist. Then he spilled out the contents and read the letter. 'Well, that's too bad,' he said. 'It's amazing how certain persons can be so unsympathetic. It's in their nature, they can't help it. But I don't mind. I mean it's all compensated for. Here *you* are. I thought it would be too nervy to invite you – it's a very cheap place I live in, you can see that – but I knew you'd come on your own. An aristocrat like yourself.'

'Elia,' I said, 'I came to knock you down. I *have* knocked you down.'

'Don't feel bad about it,' he repeated, consoling me. He reached for my ear and gave it a friendly pull. 'It's only natural. You had a shock. In your place I would have done exactly the same thing. I'm very strong. I'm probably much stronger than you are. You're pretty strong too, if you could knock me down. But to tell the truth, I sort of *let* you. I like to show manners when I'm a host.'

He scraped forward an old wooden chair, the only one in the room, for me to sit down on. I refused, so he sat down himself, with his thighs apart and his arms laced, ready for a civilized conversation. 'You've read my new work yourself, I presume.'

'No,' I said. 'When are you going to stop this? Why don't you concentrate on something sensible? You want to be a petty police reporter for the rest of your life?'

'I hope not,' he said, and rasped his voice to show his sincerity. 'I'd like to be able to leave this place. I'd like to have enough money to live in a nice American atmosphere. Like you, the way you live all alone in that whole big house.'

He almost made me think I had to apologize. 'My father left it to me. Anyway, didn't you tell me you never expected to get rich on poetry?'

'I've looked around since then, I've noticed things. Of America expect everything. America has room for anything, even poets. Edmund,' he said warmly, 'I know how you feel. RIP. I don't have a father either. You would have admired my father – a strapping man. It's amazing that they could kill him. Strong. Big. No offence, but he restrained himself, he never knocked anyone down. Here,' he pleaded, 'you just take my new things and look them over and see if that editor-in-chief was right. You tell me if in his shoes you wouldn't publish me, that's all I want.'

He handed me Gharri to Gila Monster: another vapid excrescence in the margins. Schuit to Scolecite: the same. But it was plain that he was appealing to me out of the pathos of his orphaned condition, and from pity and guilt (I had the sense that he would regard it as a pogrom if I did not comply) I examined the rest, and discovered, among his daisies and sunsets, a fresh theme. He had begun to write about girls: not the abstract Beloved, but real girls, with names like Shirley, Ethel, and Bella.

'Love poems,' he said conceitedly. 'I find them very moving.'

'About as moving as the lovelorn column,' I said, 'if less gripping. When do you get the time for girls?'

'Leonardo da Vinci also had only twenty-four hours in his day. Ditto Michelangelo. Besides, I don't go looking for them. I attract them.'

This drew my stare. 'You attract them?'

'Sure. I attract them right here. I hardly ever have to go out. Of course that sort of arrangement's not too good with some of the better types. They don't go for a poet's room.'

'There's not a book in the place,' I said in disgust.

'Books don't make a poet's room,' he contradicted. 'It depends on the poet – the build of man he is.' And, with the full power of his odious resiliency, he winked at me.

The effect on me of this conversation was unprecedented: I suddenly began to see him as he saw himself, through the lens of his own self-esteem. He almost looked handsome. He had changed; he seemed larger and bolder. The truth was merely that he was not yet twenty and that he had very recently grown physically. He remained unkempt, and his belly had a habit of swelling under his shirt; but there was something huge starting in him.

About that time I was asked to cover a minor war in the Caribbean – it was no more than a series of swamp skirmishes – and when I returned after eight weeks I found him living in my house. I had, as usual, left the key with my married sister (it had been one of my father's crotchets – he had several – to anticipate all possible contingencies, and I carried on the custom of the house), and he had magically wheedled it from her: it turned out he had somehow persuaded her that she would earn the gratitude of his posterity by allowing him to attain the kind of shelter commensurate with his qualities.

'Commensurate with your qualities,' I sing-songed at him. 'When I heard that, I knew she had it verbatim. All right, Elia, you've sucked the place dry. That's all. Out.' Every teacup was dirty and he had emptied the whisky. 'You've had parties,' I concluded.

'I couldn't help it, Edmund. I've developed so many friendships recently.'

'Get out.'

'Ah, don't be harsh. You know the little rooms upstairs? The ones that have the skylight? I bet those were maids' rooms once. You wouldn't know I was there, I promise you. Where can I go where there's so much good light? Over at the precinct house it's even worse than the cellar was, they use only forty-watt bulbs. The municipality is prodigiously parsimonious. What have I got if I haven't got my eyesight?

> *Take my pen and still*
> *I sing. But deny*
> *My eye*
> *And Will*
> *Departs the quill.'*

'My reply remains Nil,' I said. 'Just go.'

He obliged me with a patronizing laugh. 'That's very good. Deny, Reply. Quill, Nil.'

'No, I mean it. You can't stay. Besides,' I said sourly, 'I thought you gave up rhymes long ago.'

'You think I'm making it up about my eyes,' he said. 'Well, look.' He darted a thick fist into a pocket and whipped out a pair of glasses and put them on. 'While you were gone I had to get these. They're pretty strong for a person of my age. I'm not supposed to abuse my irises. These peepers cost me equal to nearly a month's rent at my old place.'

The gesture forced me to study him. He had spoken of his qualities, but they were all quantities: he had grown some more, not upwards exactly, and not particularly outwards, but in some textural way, as though his bigness required one to assure oneself of it by testing it with the nerve in the fingertip. He was walking around in his underwear. For the first time I took it in how extraordinarily hairy a man he was. His shoulders and his chest were a forest, and the muscles in his arms were globes darkened by brush. I observed that he was thoroughly aware of himself; he held his torso like a bit of classical rubble, but he captured the warrior lines of it with a certain prideful agility.

'Go ahead, put on your clothes,' I yelled at him.

'It's not cold in the house, Edmund.'

'It is in the street. Go on, get out. With or without your clothes. Go.'

He lowered his head, and I noted in surprise the gross stems of his ears. 'It would be mean.'

'I can take it. Stop worrying about my feelings.'

'I'm not referring just to you. I left Sylvia alone upstairs when you came in.'

'Are you telling me you've got a *girl* in this house right now?'

'Sure,' he said meekly. 'But you don't mind, Edmund. I know you don't. It's only what you do yourself, isn't it?'

I went to the foot of the staircase and shouted: 'That's enough! Come down! Get out!'

Nothing stirred.

'You've scared her,' he said.

'Get rid of her, Elia, or I'll call the police.'

'That would be nice,' he said wistfully. '*They* like my poems. I always read them aloud down at the station house. Look, if you really want me to go I'll go, and you can get rid of Sylvia yourself. You certainly have a beautiful spacious house here. Nice furniture. I certainly did enjoy it.

Your sister told me a few things about it – it was very interesting. Your sister's a rather religious person, isn't she? Moral, like your father. What a funny man your father was, to put a thing like that in his will. Fornication on premises.'

'What's this all about?' But I knew, and felt the heat of my wariness.

'What your sister mentioned. She just mentioned that your father left you this house only on condition you'd never do anything to defame or defile it, and if you did do anything like that the house would go straight to her. Not that she really needs it for herself, but it would be convenient, with all those children of hers – naturally I'm only quoting. I guess you wouldn't want me to let on to her about Regina last Easter, would you? – You see, Edmund, you're even sweating a little bit yourself, look at your collar, so why be unfair and ask me to put on my clothes?'

I said hoarsely, 'How do you know about Regina?'

'Well, I don't really, do I? It's just that I found this bunch of notes from somebody by that name – Regina – and in one or two of them she says how she stayed here with you over Easter and all about the two of you. Actually, your sister might be a little strait-laced, but she's pretty nice, I mean she wouldn't think the family mansion was being desecrated and so on if *I* stayed here, would she? So in view of all that don't you want to give your consent to my moving in for a little while, Edmund?'

Bitterly I gave it, though consent was academic: he had already installed all his belongings – his dictionary (what was left of it: a poor skeleton, gluey spine and a few of the more infrequent vocabularies, such as K, X, and Z), his suit, and a cigar box filled with thin letters from Liverpool, mostly unopened. I wormed from him a promise that he would keep to the upper part of the house; in return I let him take my typewriter up with him.

What amazed me was that he kept it tapping almost every evening. I had really believed him to be indolent; instead it emerged that he was glib. But I was astonished when I occasionally saw him turn away visitors – it was more usual for him to grab, squeeze, tease and kiss them. They came often, girls with hats brimmed and plumed, and fur muffs, and brave quick little boots; they followed him up the stairs with crowds of poems stuffed into their muffs – their own, or his, or both – throwing past me jagged hillocks and troughs of laughter, their chins hidden in stanzas. Then, though the space of a floor was between us, I heard him declaim: then received a zephyr of shrieks; then further laughter, ebbing; then a scuffle like a herd of zoo antelope, until, in the pure zeal of fury, I floundered into the drawing room and violently clapped the doors to. I sat with my book of maps in my father's heavy creaking chair near a stagnant grate and wondered how I could get him out. I thought of carrying the whole rude tale of his licentiousness to my sister – but anything I might say against a person who was plainly my own guest would undoubtedly tell doubly against myself (so wholesome was my father's whim, and so completely had he disliked me), and since all the money had gone to my sister, and only this gigantic curio of a house to me, I had the warmest desire to hold on to it. Room for room I hated the place; it smelled of the wizened scrupulousness of my burdensome childhood, and my dream was to put it on the market at precisely the right time and make off with a fortune. Luckily I had cosy advice from real-estate friends: the right hour was certainly not yet. But for this house and these hopes I owned nothing, not counting my salary, which was, as my sister liked to affirm, beggar's pay in the light of what she called our 'background'. Her appearances were now unhappily common. She arrived with five or six of her children, and always without her husband, so that she puffed out the effect of having plucked her offspring out of a cloud. She was a small, exact woman, with large, exact views, made in the exact image of a pious bird, with a cautious jewel of an eye, an excessively arched and fussy breast, and two very tiny and exact nostril-points. She admired Elia and used to ascend to his rooms, trailing progeny, at his bedtime, which is to say at nine o'clock in the morning, when I would be just departing the house for my office; whereas the poetesses, to their credit, did not become visible until romantic dusk. Sometimes she would telephone me and recommend that I move such-and-such a desk – or this ottoman or that highboy – into his attic to supply him with the comforts due his gifts.

'Margaret,' I answered her, 'have you seen his stuff? It's all pointless. It's all trash.'

'He's very young,' she declared – 'you wait and see,' which she reproduced in his idiom so mimetically that she nearly sounded like a Glusker herself. 'At your age he'll be a man of the world, not a house-hugging eunuch.'

I could not protest at this abusive epithet, vibrantly meant for me; to disclaim my celibacy would have been to disclaim my house. Elia, it appeared, was teaching her subtlety as well as ornamental scurrility – 'eunuch' had never before alighted on Margaret's austere tongue. But it was true that since I no longer dared to see poor Regina under our old terms – I was too perilously subject to my guest's surveillance – she had dropped me in pique, and though I was not yet in love, I had been fonder of Regina than of almost anyone. 'All right,' I cried, 'then let him be what he can.'

'Why that's *everything*,' said Margaret; 'you don't realize what a find you've got in that young man.'

'He's told you his designs on fame.'

'Dear, he doesn't have to tell me. I can *see* it. He's unbelievable. He's an artist.'

'A cheap little immigrant,' I said. 'Uncultivated. He never reads anything.'

'Well, that's perfectly true, he's *not* effete. And about being a foreigner, do you know that terrible story, what they did to his whole family over there? When you survive a thing like that it turns you into a man. A fighter. Heroic,' she ended. Then, with the solemnity of a codicil: 'Don't call him little. He's big. He's enormous. His blood hasn't been thinned.'

'He didn't *survive* it,' I said wearily. 'He wasn't even there when it happened. He was safe in England, he was in Liverpool, for God's sake, living with his aunt.'

'Dear, please don't exaggerate and *please* don't swear. I see in him what I'm afraid I'll never see in you: because it isn't there. Genuine manliness. You have no tenderness for the children, Edmund, you walk right by them. Your own nieces and nephews. Elia is remarkable with them. That's just a single example.'

I recited, 'Gentleness is the True Soul of Virility.'

'That's in very bad taste, Edmund, that's a very journalistic way to express it,' she said sadly, as though I had shamed her with an indelicacy: so I assumed Elia had not yet educated her to the enunciation of this potent word.

'You don't like it? Neither do I. It's just that it happens to be the title of the manly artist's latest ode,' which was a fact. He had imposed it on me only the night before, whereupon I ritually informed him that it was his worst banality yet.

But Margaret was unvanquishable; she had her own point to bring up. 'Look here, Edmund, can't you do something about getting him a better job? What he's doing now doesn't come near to being worthy of him. After all, a police station. And the hours!'

'I take it you don't think the police force an influence suitable to genuine manliness,' I said, and reflected that he had, after all, managed to prove his virility at the cost of my demonstrating mine. I had lost Regina; but he still had all his poetesses.

Yet he did, as I have already noted, now and then send them away, and these times, when he was alone in his rooms, I would listen most particularly for the unrelenting clack of the typewriter. He was keeping at it; he was engrossed; he was serious. It seemed to me the most paralysing sign of all that this hollow chattering of his machine was so consistent, so reliable, so intelligible, so without stutter or modest hesitation – it made me sigh. He was deeply deadly purposeful. The tapping went on and on, and since he never stopped, it was clear that he never thought. He never daydreamed, meandered, imagined, meditated, sucked, picked, smoked, scratched or loafed. He simply tapped, forefinger over forefinger, as though these sole active digits of his were the legs of a conscientious and dogged errand boy. His investment in self-belief was absolute in its ambition, and I nearly pitied him for it. What he struck off the page was spew and offal, and he called it his career. He mailed three dozen poems a week to this and that magazine, and when the known periodicals turned him down he dredged up the unknown ones, shadowy quarterlies and gazettes printed on hand-presses in dubious basements and devoted to matters anatomic, astronomic, gastronomic, political, or atheist. To the publication of the Vegetarian Party he offered a pastoral verse in earthy trochees, and he tried the organ of a ladies' tonic manufacturing firm with fragile dactyls on the subject of corsets. He submitted everywhere, and I suppose there was finally no editor alive who did not clutch his head at the sight of his name. He clattered out barrage after barrage; he was a scourge to every idealist who had ever hoped to promote the dim cause of numbers. And leaf by leaf, travel journals shoulder to shoulder with Marxist tracts, paramilitarists alongside Seventh-Day Adventists, suffragettes hand in hand with nudists – to a man and to a woman they turned him down, they denied him print, they begged him at last to cease and desist, they folded their pamphlets like Arab tents and fled when they saw him brandishing so much as an iamb.

Meanwhile the feet of his fingers ran; he never gave up. My fright for him began almost to match my contempt. I was pitying him now in earnest, though his confidence remained as unmoved and oafish as ever. 'Wait and see,' he said, sounding like a copy of my sister copying him. The two of them put their heads together over me, but I had done all I could for him. He had no prospects. It even horribly developed that I was looked upon by my colleagues as his special protector, because when I left for the trenches my absence was immediately seized on and he was fired. This, of course, did not reach me until I returned after a year, missing an earlobe and with a dark and ugly declivity slashed across the back of my neck. My house guest had been excused from the draft by virtue of his bad eyesight, or perhaps more accurately by virtue of the ponderous thickness of his lenses; eight or ten of his poetesses tendered him a party in celebration of both his exemption and his myopia, at which he unflinchingly threw a dart into the bull's-eye of a target-shaped cake. But I was myself no soldier, and went only as a correspondent to that ancient and so primitive war, naïvely pretending to encompass the world, but Neanderthal according to our later and more expansive appetites for annihilation. Someone had merely shot a prince (a nobody – I myself cannot recall his name), and then, in illogical consequence, various patches of territory had sprung up to occupy and individualize a former empire. In the same way, I discovered, had Elia sprung up – or, as I must now consistently call him (lest I seem to stand apart from the miraculous change in his history), Edmund Gate. What I mean by this is that he stepped out of his attic and with democratic hugeness took over the house. His great form had by now entirely flattened my father's august chair, and, like a vast male Goldilocks, he was sleeping in my mother's bed – that shrine which my father had long ago consecrated to disuse and awe: a piety my sister and I had soberly perpetuated. I came home and found him in the drawing room, barefoot and in his underwear, his dirty socks strewn over the floor, and my sister in attendance mending the holes he had worn through the heels, invigilated by a knot of her children. It presently emerged that she had all along been providing him with an allowance to suit his tastes, but in that first unwitting moment when he leaped up to embrace me, at the same time dragging on his shirt (because he knew how I disliked to see him undressed), I was stunned to catch the flash of his initials – 'E. G.' – embroidered in scarlet silk on a pair of magnificent cuffs.

'Edmund!' he howled. 'Not one, not two – two *dozen!* Two dozen in the past two months alone!'

'Two dozen what?' I said, blinking at what had become of him. He was now twenty-one, and taller, larger, and hairier than ever. He wore new glasses (far less formidable than the awful weights his little nose had carried to the draft board), and these, predictably, had matured his expression, especially in the area of the cheekbones: their elderly silver frames very cleverly contradicted that inevitable boyishness which a big face is wont to radiate when it is committed to surrounding the nose of a cherub. I saw plainly, and saw it for myself, without the mesmerizing influence of his preening (for he was standing before me very simply, diligently buttoning up his shirt), that he had been increased and transformed: his fantastic body had made a simile out of him. The element in him that partook of the heathen colossus had swelled to drive out everything callow – with his blunt and balding skull he looked (I am willing to dare the vulgar godliness inherent in the term) like a giant lingam: one of those curious phallic monuments one may suddenly encounter, wreathed with bright chains of leaves, on a dusty wayside in India. His broad hands wheeled, his shirttail flicked; it was clear that his scalp was not going to be friends for long with his follicles – stars of dandruff fluttered from him. He had apparently taken up smoking, because his teeth were already a brown ruin. And with all that, he was somehow a ceremonial and touching spectacle. He was massive and dramatic; he had turned majestic.

'Poems, man, poems!' he roared. 'Two dozen poems sold, and to all the best magazines!' He would have pulled my ear like a comrade had I had a lobe to pull by, but instead he struck me down into a chair (all the while my sister went on peacefully darning), and heaped into my arms a jumble of the most important periodicals of the hour.

'Ah, there's more to it than just that,' my sister said.

'How did you manage all this?' I said. 'My God, here's one in *The Centennial!* You mean Fielding accepted? Fielding actually?'

'The sheaf of horrors man, that's right. He's really a very nice old fellow, you know that, Edmund? I've lunched with him three times now. He can't stop apologizing for the way he embarrassed himself – remember, the time he wrote you that terrible letter about me? He's always saying how ashamed he is over it.'

'Fielding?' I said. 'I can't imagine Fielding—'

'Tell the rest,' Margaret said complacently.

'Well, tomorrow we're having lunch again – Fielding and Margaret and me, and he's going to introduce me to this book publisher who's very interested in my things and wants to put them between, how did he say it, Margaret? – between something.'

'Boards. A collection, all the poems of Edmund Gate. You see?' said Margaret.

'I *don't* see,' I burst out.

'You never did. You haven't the vigour. I doubt whether you've ever really *penetrated* Edmund.' This confused me, until I understood that she now habitually addressed him by the name he had pinched from me. 'Edmund,' she challenged – which of us was this? from her scowl I took it as a finger at myself – 'you don't realize his level. It's his *level* you don't realize.'

'I realize it,' I said darkly, and let go a landslide of magazines: but *The Centennial* I retained. 'I suppose poor Fielding's gone senile by now. Wasn't he at least ten years older than Father even? I suppose he's off his head and they just don't have the heart to ship him out.'

'That won't do,' Margaret said. 'This boy is getting his recognition at last, that's all there is to it.'

'I know what he means, though,' Edmund said. 'I tell them the same thing, I tell them exactly that – all those editors, I tell them they're crazy to carry on the way they do. You ought to hear—'

'Praise,' Margaret intervened with a snap: 'praise and more praise,' as if this would spite me.

'I never thought myself those poems were *that* good,' he said. 'It's funny, they were just an experiment at first, but then I got the hang of it.'

'An experiment?' I asked him. His diffidence was novel, it was even radical; he seemed almost abashed. I had to marvel: he was as bemused over his good luck as I was.

Not so Margaret, who let it appear that she had read the cosmic will. 'Edmund is working in a new vein,' she explained.

'Hasn't he always worked in vain?' I said, and dived into *The Centennial* to see.

Edmund slapped his shins at this, but 'He who laughs last,' said Margaret, and beat her thimble on the head of the nearest child: 'What a callous man your uncle is. Read!' she commanded me.

'He has a hole in the back of his neck and only a little piece of ear left,' said the child in a voice of astute assent.

'Ssh,' said Margaret. 'We don't speak of deformities.'

'Unless they turn up as poems,' I corrected; and read; and was startled by a dilation of the lungs, like a horse lashed out of the blue and made to race beyond its impulse. Was it his, this clean stupendous stuff? But there was his name, manifest in print: it was his, according to *The Centennial*, and Fielding had not gone senile.

'Well?'

'I don't know,' I said, feeling muddled.

'He doesn't know! Edmund' – this was to Edmund – 'he doesn't know!'

'I can't believe it.'

'He can't believe it, Edmund!'

'Well, neither could I at first,' he admitted.

But my sister jumped up and pointed her needle in my face. 'Say it's good.'

'Oh, it's good. I can see it's good,' I said. 'He's hit it for once.'

'They're *all* like that,' she expanded. 'Look for yourself.'

I looked, I looked insatiably, I looked fanatically, I looked frenetically, I looked incredulously – I went from magazine to magazine, riffling and rifling, looking and looting and shuffling, until I had plundered them all of his work. My booty dumbfounded me: there was nothing to discard. I was transfixed; I was exhausted; in the end it was an exorcism of my stupefaction. I was converted, I believed; he had hit it every time. And not with ease – I could trace the wonderful risks he took. It *was* a new vein; more, it was an artery, it had a pump and a kick; it was a robust ineluctable fountain. And when his book came out half a year later, my proselytization was sealed. Here were all the poems of the periodicals, already as familiar as solid old columns, uniquely graven; and layered over them like dazzling slabs of dappled marble, immovable because of the perfection of their weight and the inexorability of their balance, was the aftermath of that early work, those more recent productions to which I soon became a reverential witness. Or, if not witness, then auditor: for out of habit he still liked to compose in the attic, and I would hear him type a poem straight out, without so much as stopping to breathe. And right afterwards he came down and presented it to me. It seemed, then, that nothing had changed: only his gift and a single feature of his manner. Unerringly it was a work of – yet who or what was I to declare him genius? – accept instead the modest judgment of merit. It was a work of merit he gave me unerringly, but he gave it to me – this was strangest of all – with a quiescence, a passivity. All his old arrogance had vanished. So had his vanity. A kind of tranquillity kept him taut and still, like a man leashed; and he went up the stairs, on those days when he was seized by the need for a poem, with a languidness unlike anything I had ever noticed in him before; he typed, from start to finish, with no falterings or emendations; then he thumped on the stairs again, loomed like a thug, and handed the glorious sheet over to my exulting grasp. I supposed it was a sort of trance he had to endure – in those dim times we were only just beginning to know Freud, but even then it was clear that, with the bursting forth of the latent thing, he had fallen into a relief as deep and curative as the sleep of ether. If he lacked – or skipped – what enthusiastic people call the creative exaltation, it was because he had compressed it all, without the exhibitionism of prelude, into that singular moment of power – six minutes, or eight minutes, however long it took him, forefinger over forefinger, to turn vision into alphabet.

He had become, by the way, a notably fast typist.

I asked him once – this was after he had surrendered a new-hatched sheet not a quarter of an hour from the typewriter – how he could account for what had happened in him.

'You used to be awful,' I reminded him. 'You used to be unspeakable. My God, you were vile.'

'Oh, I don't know,' he said in that ennui, or blandness, that he always displayed after one of his remarkable trips to the attic, 'I don't know if I was *that* bad.'

'Well, even if you weren't,' I said – in view of what I had in my hand I could no longer rely on my idea of what he had been – 'this! This!' and fanned the wondrous page like a triumphant flag. 'How do you explain *this*, coming after what you were?'

He grinned a row of brown incisors at me and gave me a hearty smack on the ankle. 'Plagiarism.'

'No, tell me really.'

'The plangent plagiarism,' he said accommodatingly, 'of the plantigrade persona. – Admit it, Edmund, you don't like the Ps, you never did and you never will.'

'For instance,' I said, 'you don't do *that* any more.'

'Do what?' He rubbed the end of a cigarette across his teeth and yawned. 'I still do persiflage, don't I? I do it out of my pate, without periwig, pugree, or peril.'

'That. Cram grotesque words in every line.'

'No, I don't do that any more. A pity, my dictionary's practically all gone.'

'Why?' I persisted.

'I used it up, that's why. I *finished* it.'

'Be serious. What I'm getting at is why you're different. Your stuff *is* different. I've never seen such a difference.'

He sat up suddenly and with inspiration, and it came to me that I was observing the revival of passion. 'Margaret's given that a lot of thought, Edmund. *She* attributes it to maturity.'

'That's not very perspicacious,' I said – for the sake of the Ps, and to show him I no longer minded anything.

But he said shortly, 'She means virility.'

This made me scoff. 'She can't even get herself to say the word.'

'Well, maybe there's a difference in Margaret too,' he said.

'She's the same silly woman she ever was, and her husband's the same silly stockbroker, the two of them a pair of fertile prudes – she wouldn't recognize so-called virility if she tripped over it. She hates the whole concept—'

'She likes it,' he said.

'What she likes is euphemisms for it. She can't face it, so she covers it up. Tenderness! Manliness! Maturity! Heroics! She hasn't got a brain in her head,' I said, 'and she's never gotten anything done in the world but those silly babies, I've lost count of how many she's done of *those*—'

'The next one's mine,' he said.

'That's an imbecile joke.'

'Not a joke.'

'Look here, joke about plagiarism all you want but don't waste your breath on fairy tales.'

'Nursery tales,' he amended. 'I never waste anything, I told you. That's just it, I've gone and plagiarized Margaret. I've purloined her, if you want to stick to the Ps.' – Here he enumerated several other Ps impossible to print, which I am obliged to leave to my reader's experience, though not of the parlour. 'And you're plenty wrong about your sister's brains, Edmund. She's a very capable businesswoman – she's simply never had the opportunity. You know since my book's out I have to admit I'm a bit in demand, and what she's done is she's booked me solid for six months' worth of recitations. And the fees! She's getting me more than Edna St Vincent Millay, if you want the whole truth,' he said proudly. 'And why not? The only time that dame ever writes a good poem is when she signs her name.'

All at once, and against his laughter and its storm of smoke, I understood who was behind the title of his collected poems. I was confounded. It was Margaret. His book was called *Virility*.

A week after this conversation he left with my sister for Chicago, for the inauguration of his reading series.

I went up to his attic and searched it. I was in a boil of distrust; I was outraged. I had lost Regina to Margaret's principles, and now Margaret had lost her principles, and in both cases Edmund Gate had stood to profit. He gained from her morality and he gained from her immorality. I began to hate him again. It would have rejoiced me to believe his quip: nothing could have made me merrier than to think him a thief of words, if only for the revenge of catching him at it – but he could not even be relied on for something so plausible as plagiarism. The place revealed nothing. There was not so much as an anthology of poetry, say, which might account for his extraordinary burgeoning; there was not a single book of any kind – that sparse and pitiful wreck of his dictionary, thrown into a corner together with a cigar box, hardly signified. For the rest, there were only an old desk with his – no, my – typewriter on it, an ottoman, a chair or two, an empty chest, a hot bare floor (the heat pounded upwards), and his primordial suit slowly revolving in the sluggish airs on a hanger suspended from the skylight, moths nesting openly on the lapels. It brought to mind Mohammed and the Koran; Joseph Smith and the golden plates. Some mysterious dictation recurred in these rooms: his gift came to him out of the light and out of the dark. I sat myself down at his desk and piecemeal typed out an agonized letter to Regina. I offered to change the terms of our relationship. I said I hoped we could take up again, not as before (my house was in use). I said I would marry her.

She answered immediately, enclosing a wedding announcement six months old.

On that same day Margaret returned. 'I left him, of *course* I left him. I had to, not that he can take care of himself under the circumstances, but I sent him on to Detroit anyhow. If I'm going to be his manager, after all, I have to *manage* things. I can't do all that from the provinces, you know – I have to *be* here, I have to see people . . . ah, you can't imagine it, Edmund, they want him everywhere! I have to set up a regular office, just a *little* switchboard to start with—'

'It's going well?'

'Going well! What a way to put it! Edmund, he's a phenomenon. It's supernatural. He has *charisma*, in Chicago they had to arrest three girls, they made a human chain and lowered themselves from a chandelier right over the lectern, and the lowest-hanging one reached down for a hair of his head and nearly tore the poor boy's scalp off—'

'What a pity,' I said.

'What do you *mean* what a pity, you don't follow, Edmund, he's a celebrity!'

'But he has so few hairs and he thinks so much of them,' I said, and wondered bitterly whether Regina had married a bald man.

'You have no right to take that tone,' Margaret said. 'You have no idea how modest he is. I suppose that's part of his appeal – he simply has no ego at all. He takes it as innocently as a baby. In Chicago he practically looked over his shoulder to see if they really meant *him*. And they *do* mean him, you can't imagine the screaming, and the shoving for autographs, and people calling bravo and fainting if they happen to meet his eyes—'

'Fainting?' I said doubtfully.

'Fainting! My goodness, Edmund, don't you read the headlines in your own paper? His audiences are three times as big as Caruso's. Oh, you're hard, Edmund, you admit he's good but I say there's a terrible wall in you if you don't see the power in this boy—'

'I see it over you,' I said.

'Over me! Over the world, Edmund, it's the world he's got now – I've already booked him for London and Manchester, and here's this cable from Johannesburg pleading for him – oh, he's through with the backwoods, believe you me. And look here, I've just settled up this fine generous contract for his next book, with the reviews still piling in from the first one!' She crackled open her briefcase, and flung out a mass of files, lists, letterheads, schedules, torn envelopes with exotic stamps on them, fat legal-looking portfolios, documents in tiny type – she danced them all noisily upon her pouting lap.

'His second book?' I asked. 'Is it ready?'

'Of course it's ready. He's remarkably productive, you know. Fecund.'

'He pullulates,' I suggested.

'His own word exactly, how did you hit it? He can come up with a poem practically at will. Sometimes right after a reading, when he's exhausted – you know it's his shyness that exhausts him that way – anyhow, there he is all fussed and worried about whether the next performance will be as good, and he'll suddenly get this – well, *fit*, and hide out in the remotest part of the hotel and fumble in his wallet for bits of paper – he's always carrying bits of folded paper, with notes or ideas in them I suppose, and shoo everyone away, even me, and *type* (he's awfully fond of his new typewriter, by the way) – he just types the glory right out of his soul!' she crowed. 'It's the energy of genius. He's *authentic*, Edmund, a profoundly energetic man is profoundly energetic in all directions at once. I hope at least you've been following the reviews?'

It was an assault, and I shut myself against it. 'What will he call the new book?'

'Oh, he leaves little things like the titles to me, and I'm all for simplicity. – *Virility II*,' she announced in her shocking business-magnate voice. 'And the one after that will be *Virility III*. And the one after that—'

'Ah, fecund,' I said.

'Fecund,' she gleamed.

'A bottomless well?'

She marvelled at this. 'How is it you always hit on Edmund's words exactly?'

'I know how he talks,' I said.

'A bottomless well, he said it himself. Wait and see!' she warned me.

She was not mistaken. After *Virility* came *Virility II*, and after that *Virility III*, and after that an infant boy. Margaret named him Edmund – she said it was after me – and her husband the stockbroker, though somewhat puzzled at this human production in the midst of so much literary fertility, was all the same a little cheered. Of late it had seemed to him, now that Margaret's first simple switchboard had expanded to accommodate three secretaries, that he saw her less than ever, or at least that she was noticing him less than ever. This youngest Edmund struck him as proof (though it embarrassed him to think about it even for a minute) that perhaps she had noticed him more than he happened to remember. Margaret, meanwhile, was gay and busy – she slipped the new little Edmund ('Let's call *him* III,' she laughed) into her packed nursery and went on about her business, which had grown formidable. Besides the three secretaries, she had two assistants: poets, poetasters, tenors, altos, mystics, rationalists, rightists, leftists, memoirists, fortune-tellers, peddlers, everyone with an *idée fixe*, and therefore suitable to the lecture circuit clamoured to be bundled into her clientele. Edmund she ran ragged. She ran him to Paris, to Lisbon, to Stockholm, to Moscow; nobody understood him in any of these places, but the title of his books translated impressively into all languages. He developed a sort of growl – it was from always being hoarse; he smoked day and night – and she made him cultivate it. Together with his accent it caused an international shudder among the best of women. She got rid of his initialled cuffs and dressed him like a prizefighter, in high laced black brogans and tight shining T-shirts, out of which his hairiness coiled. A long bladder of smoke was always trailing out of his mouth. In Paris they pursued him into the Place de la Concorde yelling '*Virilité! Virilité!*' '*Die Manneskraft!*'

they howled in Munich. The reviews were an avalanche, a cataclysm. In the rotogravure sections his picture vied with the beribboned bosoms of duchesses. In New Delhi glossy versions of his torso were hawked like an avatar in the streets. He had long since been catapulted out of the hands of the serious literary critics – but it was the serious critics who had begun it. 'The Masculine Principle personified, verified, and illuminated.' 'The bite of Pope, the sensuality of Keats.' 'The quality, in little, of the very greatest novels. Tolstoyan.' 'Seminal and hard.' 'Robust, lusty, male.' 'Erotic.'

Margaret was ecstatic, and slipped a new infant into her bursting nursery. This time the stockbroker helped her choose its name: they decided on Gate, and hired another nanny to take care of the overflow.

After *Virility IV* came *Virility V*. The quality of his work had not diminished, yet it was extraordinary that he could continue to produce at all. Occasionally he came to see me between trips, and then he always went upstairs and took a turn around the sighing floors of his old rooms. He descended haggard and slouching; his pockets looked puffy, but it seemed to be only his huge fists he kept there. Somehow his fame had intensified that curious self-effacement. He had divined that I was privately soured by his success, and he tried bashfully to remind me of the days when he had written badly.

'That only makes it worse,' I told him. 'It shows what a poor prophet I was.'

'No,' he said, 'you weren't such a bad prophet, Edmund.'

'I said you'd never get anywhere with your stuff.'

'I haven't.'

I hated him for that – Margaret had not long before shown me his bank statement. He was one of the richest men in the country; my paper was always printing human-interest stories about him – 'Prosperous Poet Visits Fabulous Patagonia.' I said, 'What do you mean you haven't gotten anywhere? What more do you want from the world? What else do you think it can give you?'

'Oh, I don't know,' he said. He was gloomy and sullen. 'I just feel I'm running short on things.'

'On triumphs? They're all the time comparing you to Keats. Your pal Fielding wrote in *The Centennial* just the other day that you're practically as great as the Early Milton.'

'Fielding's senile. They should have put him away a long time ago.'

'And in sales you're next to the Bible.'

'I was brought up on the Bible,' he said suddenly.

'Aha. It's a fit of conscience? Then look, Elia, why don't you take Margaret and get her divorced and get those babies of yours legitimized, if that's what's worrying you.'

'They're legitimate enough. The old man's not a bad father. Besides, they're all mixed up in there, I can't tell one from the other.'

'Yours are the ones named after you. You were right about Margaret, she's an efficient woman.'

'I don't worry about that,' he insisted.

'*Something's* worrying you.' This satisfied me considerably.

'As a matter of fact—' He trundled himself down into my father's decaying chair. He had just returned from a tour of Italy; he had gone with a wardrobe of thirty-seven satin T-shirts and not one of them had survived intact. His torn-off sleeves sold for twenty lira each. They had stolen his glasses right off his celebrated nose. 'I like it here, Edmund,' he said. 'I like your house. I like the way you've never bothered about my old things up there. A man likes to hang on to his past.'

It always bewildered me that the style of his talk had not changed. He was still devoted to the insufferably hackneyed. He still came upon his clichés like Columbus. Yet his poems . . . but how odd, how remiss! I observe that I have not even attempted to describe them. That is because they ought certainly to be *presented* – read aloud, as Edmund was doing all over the world. Short of that, I might of course reproduce them here; but I must not let my narrative falter in order to make room for any of them, even though, it is true, they would not require a great deal of space. They were notably small and spare, in conventional stanza-form. They rhymed consistently and scanned regularly. They were, besides, amazingly simple. Unlike the productions of Edmund's early phase, their language was pristine. There were no unusual words. His poems had the ordinary vocabulary of ordinary men. At the same time they were immensely vigorous. It was astonishingly easy to memorize them – they literally could not be forgotten. Some told stories, like ballads, and they were exhilarating yet shocking stories. Others were strangely explicit love lyrics, of a kind that no Western poet had ever yet dared – but the effect was one of health and purity rather than scandal. It was remarked by everyone who read or heard Edmund Gate's work that only a person who had had great and large experience of the world could have written it. People speculated about his life. If the Borgias, privy to all forms of foulness, had been poets, someone said, they would have written poems like that. If Teddy Roosevelt's Rough Riders had been poets, they would have written poems like that. If Genghis Khan and Napoleon had been poets, they would have written poems like that. They were masculine poems. They were political and personal, public and private. They were full of both passion and ennui, they were youthful and elderly, they were green and wise. But they were not beautiful and they were not dull, the way a well-used, faintly gnarled, but superbly controlled muscle is neither beautiful nor dull.

They were, in fact, very much like Margaret's vision of Edmund Gate himself. The poet and the poems were indistinguishable.

She sent her vision to Yugoslavia, she sent it to Egypt, she sent it to Japan. In Warsaw girls ran after him in the street to pick his pockets for souvenirs – they came near to picking his teeth. In Copenhagen they formed an orgiastic club named 'The Forbidden Gate' and gathered around a gatepost to read him. In Hong Kong they tore off his underwear and stared giggling at his nakedness. He was now twenty-five; it began to wear him out.

When he returned from Brazil he came to see me. He seemed more morose than ever. He slammed up the stairs, kicked heavily over the floors, and slammed down again. He had brought down with him his old cigar box.

'My aunt's dead,' he said.

As usual he took my father's chair. His burly baby's-head lolled.

'The one in Liverpool?'

'Yeah.'

'I'm sorry to hear that. Though she must have gotten to be a pretty old lady by now.'

'She was seventy-four.'

He appeared to be taking it hard. An unmistakable misery creased his giant neck.

'Still,' I said, 'you must have been providing for her nicely these last few years. At least before she went she had her little comforts.'

'No. I never did a thing. I never sent her a penny.'

I looked at him. He seemed to be nearly sick. His lips were black. 'You always meant to, I suppose. You just never got around to it,' I ventured; I thought it was remorse that had darkened him.

'No,' he said. 'I couldn't. I didn't have it then. I couldn't afford to. Besides, she was always very self-reliant.'

He was a worse scoundrel than I had imagined. 'Damn you, Elia,' I said. 'She took you in, if not for her you'd be murdered with your whole family back there—'

'Well, I never had as much as you used to think. That police station job wasn't much.'

'Police station!' I yelled.

He gave me an eye full of hurt. 'You don't follow, Edmund. My aunt died before all this fuss. She died three years ago.'

'Three years ago?'

'Three and a half maybe.'

I tried to adjust. 'You just got the news, you mean? You just heard?'

'Oh, no. I found out about it right after it happened.'

Confusion roiled in me. 'You never mentioned it.'

'There wasn't any point. It's not as though you *knew* her. Nobody knew her. I hardly knew her myself. She wasn't anybody. She was just this old woman.'

'Ah,' I said meanly, 'so the grief is only just catching up with you, is that it? You've been too busy to find the time to mourn?'

'I never liked her,' he admitted. 'She was an old nuisance. She talked and talked at me. Then when I got away from her and came here she wrote me and wrote me. After a while I just stopped opening her letters. I figured she must have written me two hundred letters. I saved them. I save everything, even junk. When you start out poor, you always save everything. You never know when you might need it. I never waste anything.' He said portentously, 'Waste Not, Want Not.'

'If you never answered her how is it she kept on writing?'

'She didn't have anybody else to write to. I guess she had to write and she didn't have anybody. All I've got left are the ones in here. This is the last bunch of letters of hers I've got.' He showed me his big scratched cigar box.

'But you say you saved them—'

'Sure, but I used them up. Listen,' he said. 'I've got to go now, Edmund, I've got to meet Margaret. It's going to be one hell of a fight, I tell you.'

'What?' I said.

'I'm not going anywhere else, I don't care how much she squawks. I've had my last trip. I've got to stay home from now on and do poems. I'm going to get a room somewhere, maybe my old room across town, *you* remember – where you came to see me that time?'

'Where I knocked you down. You can stay here,' I said.

'Nah,' he said. 'Nowhere your sister can get at me. I've got to work.'

'But you've *been* working,' I said. 'You've been turning out new poems all along! That's been the amazing thing.'

He hefted all his flesh and stood up, clutching the cigar box to his dinosaurish ribs.

'I haven't,' he said.

'You've done those five collections—'

'All I've done are those two babies. Edmund and Gate. And they're not even my real names. That's all I've done. The reviews did the rest. Margaret did the rest.'

He was suddenly weeping.

'I can't tell it to Margaret—'

'Tell what?'

'There's only one bundle left. No more. After this no more. It's finished.'

'Elia, what in God's name *is* this?'

'I'm afraid to tell. I don't know what else to do. I've *tried* to write new stuff. I've tried. It's terrible. It's not the same. It's not the same, Edmund. I can't do it. I've told Margaret that. I've told her I can't write any more. She says it's a block, it happens to all writers. She says don't worry, it'll come back. It always comes back to genius.'

He was sobbing wildly; I could scarcely seize his words. He had thrown himself back into my father's chair, and the tears were making brooks of its old leather cracks.

'I'm afraid to tell,' he said.

'Elia, for God's sake. Straighten up like a man. Afraid of what?'

'Well, I told you once. I told you because I knew you wouldn't believe me, but I *did* tell you, you can't deny it. You could've stopped me. It's your fault too.' He kept his face hidden.

He had made me impatient. 'What's my fault?'

'I'm a plagiarist.'

'If you mean Margaret again—'

He answered with a whimper: 'No, no, don't be a fool, I'm through with Margaret.'

'Aren't those collections yours? They're not yours?'

'They're mine,' he said. 'They came in the mail, so if you mean are they mine *this* way—'

I caught his agitation. 'Elia, you're out of your mind—'

'She wrote every last one,' he said. 'In Liverpool. Every last line of every last one. Tante Rivka. There's only enough left for one more book. Margaret's going to call it *Virility VI*,' he bawled.

'Your aunt?' I said. 'She wrote them all?' He moaned.

'Even the one – not the one about the—'

'All,' he broke in; his voice was nearly gone.

He stayed with me for three weeks. To fend her off I telephoned Margaret and said that Edmund had come down with the mumps. 'But I've just had a cable from Southern Rhodesia!' she wailed. 'They need him like mad down there!'

'You'd better keep away, Margaret,' I warned. 'You don't want to carry the fever back to the nursery. All those babies in there—'

'Why should he get an infant's disease?' she wondered; I heard her fidget.

'It's just the sort of disease that corresponds to his mentality.'

'Now stop that. You know that's a terrible sickness for a grown man to get. You know what it does. It's awful.'

I had no idea what she could be thinking of; I had chosen this fabrication for its innocence. 'Why?' I said. 'Children recover beautifully—'

'Don't be an imbecile, Edmund,' she rebuked me in my father's familiar tone – my father had often called me a scientific idiot. 'He might come out of it as sterile as a stone. Stop it, Edmund, it's nothing to laugh at, you're a brute.'

'Then you'll have to call his next book *Sterility*,' I said.

He hid out with me, as I have already noted, for nearly a month, and much of the time he cried.

'It's all up with me.'

I said coldly, 'You knew it was coming.'

'I've dreaded it and dreaded it. After this last batch I'm finished. I don't know what to do. I don't know what's going to happen.'

'You ought to confess,' I advised finally.

'To Margaret?'

'To everyone. To the world.'

He gave me a teary smirk. 'Sure. The Collected Works of Edmund Gate, by Tante Rivka.'

'Vice versa's the case,' I said, struck again by a shadow of my first shock. 'And since it's true, you ought to make it up to her.'

'You can't make anything up to the dead.' He was wiping the river that fell from his nose. 'My reputation. My poor about-to-be-mutilated reputation. No, I'll just go ahead and get myself a little place to live in and produce new things. What comes now will be *really* mine. Integrity,' he whined. 'I'll save myself that way.'

'You'll ruin yourself. You'll be the man of the century who fizzled before he made it to thirty. There's nothing more foolish-looking than a poet who loses his gift. Pitiful. They'll laugh at you. Look how people laugh at the Later Wordsworth. The Later Gate will be a fiasco at twenty-six. You'd better confess, Elia.'

Moodily he considered it. 'What would it get me?'

'Wonder and awe. Admiration. You'll be a great sacrificial figure. You can say your aunt was reticent but a tyrant, she made you stand in her place. Gate the Lamb. You can say anything.'

This seemed to attract him. 'It *was* a sacrifice,' he said. 'Believe me it was hell going through all of that. I kept getting diarrhoea from the water in all those different places. I never could stand the screaming anywhere. Half the time my life was in danger. In Hong Kong when they stole my shorts I practically got pneumonia.' He popped his cigarette out of his mouth and began to cough. 'You really think I ought to do that, Edmund? Margaret wouldn't like it. She's always hated sterile men. It'll be an admission of my own poetic sterility, that's how she'll look at it.'

'I thought you're through with her anyhow.'

Courage suddenly puffed him out. 'You bet I am. I don't think much of people who exploit other people. She built that business up right out of my flesh and blood. Right out of my marrow.'

He sat at the typewriter in the attic, at which I had hammered out my futile proposal to Regina, and wrote a letter to his publisher. It was a complete confession. I went with him to the drugstore to get it notarized. I felt the ease of the perfect confidant, the perfect counsel, the perfect avenger. He had spilled me the cup of humiliation, he had lost me Regina; I would lose him the world.

Meanwhile I assured him he would regain it. 'You'll go down,' I said, 'as the impresario of the nearly-lost. You'll go down as the man who bestowed a hidden genius. You'll go down as the saviour who restored to perpetual light what might have wandered a mute inglorious ghost in the eternal dark.'

On my paper they had fired better men than I for that sort of prose.

'I'd rather have been the real thing myself,' he said. The remark seemed to leap from his heart; it almost touched me.

'Caesar is born, not made,' I said. 'But who notices Caesar's nephew? Unless he performs a vast deep act. To be Edmund Gate was nothing. But to shed the power of Edmund Gate before the whole watching world, to become little in oneself in order to give away one's potency to another – *that* is an act of profound reverberation.'

He said wistfully, 'I guess you've got a point there,' and emerged to tell Margaret.

She was wrathful. She was furious. She was vicious. 'A lady wrote 'em?' she cried. 'An old Jewish immigrant lady who never even made it to America?'

'My Tante Rivka,' he said bravely.

'Now Margaret,' I said. 'Don't be obtuse. The next book will be every bit as good as the ones that preceded it. The quality is exactly the same. He picked those poems at random out of a box and one's as good as another. They're all good. They're brilliant, you know that. The book won't be different so its reception won't be different. The profits will be the same.'

She screwed up a doubtful scowl. 'It'll be the last one. He says *he* can't write. There won't be any more after this.'

'The canon closes,' I agreed, 'when the poet dies.'

'This poet's dead all right,' she said, and threw him a spiteful laugh. Edmund Gate rubbed his glasses, sucked his cigarette, rented a room, and disappeared.

Margaret grappled in vain with the publisher. 'Why not *Virility* again? It was good enough for the other five. It's a selling title.'

'This one's by a woman,' he said. 'Call it *Muliebrity*, no one'll understand you.' The publisher was a wit who was proud of his Latin, but he had an abstract and wholesome belief in the stupidity of his readers.

The book appeared under the name *Flowers from Liverpool*. It had a pretty cover, the colour of a daisy's petal, with a picture of Tante Rivka on it. The picture was a daguerro-type that Edmund had kept flat at the bottom of the cigar box. It showed his aunt as a young woman in Russia, not very handsome, with large lips, a circular nose, and minuscule light eyes – the handle of what looked strangely like a pistol stuck out of her undistinguished bosom.

The collection itself was sublime. By some accident of the unplanned gesture the last poems left in Edmund Gate's cracked cigar box had turned out to be the crest of the poet's vitality. They were as clear and hard as all the others, but somehow rougher and thicker, perhaps more intellectual. I read and marvelled myself into shame – if I had believed I would dash his career by inducing him to drop his connection with it, I had been worse than misled. I had been criminal. Nothing could damage the career of these poems. They would soar and soar beyond petty revenges. If Shakespeare was really Bacon, what difference? If Edmund Gate was really Tante Rivka of Liverpool, what difference? Since nothing can betray a good poem, it is pointless to betray a bad poet.

With a pre-publication copy in my hand I knocked at his door. He opened it in his underwear: a stink came out of him. One lens was gone from his glasses.

'Well, here it is,' I said. 'The last one.'

He hiccuped with a mournful drunken spasm.

'The last shall be first,' I said with a grin of disgust; the smell of his room made me want to run.

'The first shall be last,' he contradicted, flagging me down with an old newspaper. 'You want to come in here, Edmund? Come in, sure.'

But there was no chair. I sat on the bed. The floor was splintered and his toenails scraped on it. They were long filthy crescents. I put the book down. 'I brought this for you to have first thing.'

He looked at the cover. 'What a mug on her.'

'What a mind,' I said. 'You were lucky to have known her.'

'An old nuisance. If not for her I'd still be what I was. If she didn't run out on me.'

'Elia,' I began; I had come to tell him a horror. 'The publisher did a little biographical investigation. They found where your aunt was living when she died. It seems,' I said, 'she was just what you've always described. Self-sufficient.'

'Always blah blah at me. Old nuisance. I ran out on her, couldn't stand it.'

'She got too feeble to work and never let on to a soul. They found her body, all washed clean for burial, in her bed. She'd put on clean linens herself and she'd washed herself. Then she climbed into the bed and starved to death. She just waited it out that way. There wasn't a crumb in the place.'

'She never asked me for anything,' he said.

'How about the one called "Hunger"? The one everybody thought was a battle poem?'

'It was only a poem. Besides, she was already dead when I got to it.'

'If you'd sent her something,' I said, 'you might have kept Edmund

Gate going a few years more. A hardy old bird like that could live to be a hundred. All she needed was bread.'

'Who cares? The stuff would've petered out sooner or later anyhow, wouldn't it? The death of Edmund Gate was unavoidable. I wish you'd go away, Edmund. I'm not used to feeling this drunk. I'm trying to get proficient at it. It's killing my stomach. My bladder's giving out. Go away.'

'All right.'

'Take that damn book with you.'

'It's yours.'

'Take it away. It's your fault they've turned me into a woman. I'm a man,' he said; he gripped himself between the legs; he was really very drunk.

All the same I left it there, tangled in his dirty quilt.

Margaret was in Mexico with a young client of hers, a baritone. She was arranging bookings for him in hotels. She sent back a photograph of him in a swimming pool. I sat in the clamorous nursery with the stockbroker and together we rattled through the journals, looking for reviews.

'Here's one. "Thin feminine art," it says.'

'Here's another. "A lovely girlish voice reflecting a fragile girlish soul: a lace valentine."'

'"Limited, as all domestic verse must be. A spinster's one-dimensional vision."'

'"Choked with female inwardness. Flat. The typical unimaginativeness of her sex."'

'"Distaff talent, secondary by nature. Lacks masculine energy."'

'"The fine womanly intuition of a competent poetess."'

The two youngest children began to yowl. 'Now, now Gatey boy,' said the stockbroker, 'now, now, Edmund. Why can't you be good? Your brothers and sisters are good, *they* don't cry.' He turned to me with a shy beam. 'Do you know we're having another?'

'No,' I said. 'I didn't know that. Congratulations.'

'She's the New Woman,' the stockbroker said. 'Runs a business all by herself, just like a man.'

'Has babies like a woman.'

He laughed proudly. 'Well, she doesn't do that one by herself, I'll tell you that.'

'Read some more.'

'Not much use to it. They all say the same thing, don't they? By the way, Edmund, did you happen to notice they've already got a new man in *The Centennial?* Poor Fielding, but the funeral was worthy of him. Your father would have wept if he'd been there.'

'Read the one in *The Centennial*,' I said.

'"There is something in the feminine mind which resists largeness and depth. Perhaps it is that a woman does not get the chance to sleep under bridges. Even if she got the chance, she would start polishing the piles. Experience is the stuff of art, but experience is not something God made woman for . . . " It's just the same as the others,' he said.

'So is the book.'

'The title's different,' he said wisely. 'This one's by a woman, they all point that out. All the rest of 'em were called *Virility*. What happened to that fellow, by the way? He doesn't come around.'

The babies howled down the ghost of my reply.

I explained at the outset that only last week I visited the grave of Edmund Gate, but I neglected to describe a curious incident that occurred on that spot.

I also explained the kind of camaraderie elderly people in our modern society feel for one another. We know we are declining together, but we also recognize that our memories are a kind of national treasury, being living repositories for such long-extinct customs as burial and intra-uterine embryo-development.

At Edmund Gate's grave stood an extraordinary person – a frazzled old woman, I thought at first. Then I saw it was a very aged man. His teeth had not been trans-rooted and his vision seemed faint. I was amazed that he did not salute me – like myself, he certainly appeared to be a centagenerian – but I attributed this to the incompetence of his eyes, which wore their lids like hunched capes.

'Not many folks around here nowadays,' I said. 'People keep away from the old Preserved Cemeteries. My view is these youngsters are morbid. Afraid of the waste. They have to use everything. We weren't morbid in our time, hah?'

He did not answer. I suspected it was deliberate.

'Take this one,' I said, in my most cordial manner, inviting his friendship. 'This thing right here.' I gave the little stone a good knock, taking the risk of arrest by the Outdoor Museum Force. Apparently no one saw. I knocked it again with the side of my knuckle. 'I actually knew this fellow. He was famous in his day. A big celebrity. That young

Chinese fellow, the one who just came back from flying around the edge of the Milky Way, well, the fuss they made over *him*, that's how it was with this fellow. This one was literary, though.'

He did not answer; he spat on the part of the stone I had touched, as if to wash it.

'You knew him too?' I said.

He gave me his back – it was shaking horribly – and minced away. He looked shrivelled but of a good size still; he was uncommonly ragged. His clothing dragged behind him as though the covering over the legs hobbled him; yet there was a hint of threadbare flare at his ankle. It almost gave me the sense that he was wearing an ancient woman's garment, of the kind in fashion seventy years ago. He had on queer old-fashioned woman's shoes with long thin heels like poles. I took off after him – I am not slow, considering my years – and slid my gaze all over his face. It was a kettle of decay. He was carrying a red stick – it seemed to be a denuded lady's umbrella (an apparatus no longer known among us) – and he held it up to strike.

'Listen here,' I said hotly, 'what's the matter with you? Can't you pass a companionable word? I'll just yell for the Museum Force, you and that stick, if you don't watch it—'

'I watch it,' he said. His voice burst up and broke like boiling water – it sounded vaguely foreign. 'I watch it all the time. That's my monument, and believe you me I watch it. I won't have anyone else watch it either. See what it says there? "I am a man." You keep away from it.'

'I'll watch what I please. You're no more qualified than I am,' I said.

'To be a man? I'll show you,' he retorted, full of malice, his stick still high. 'Name's Gate, same as on that stone. That's my stone. They don't make 'em any more. *You'll* do without.'

Now this was a sight: madness has not appeared in our society for over two generations. All forms of such illness have vanished these days, and if any pops up through some genetic mishap it is soon eliminated by Electromed Procedure. I had not met a madman since I was sixty years old.

'Who do you say you are?' I asked him.

'Gate, born Gatoff. Edmund, born Elia.'

This startled me: it was a refinement of information not on the monument.

'Edmund Gate's dead,' I said. 'You must be a literary historian to know a point like that. I knew him personally myself. Nobody's heard of him now, but he was a celebrated man in my day. A poet.'

'Don't tell *me*,' the madman said.

'He jumped off a bridge dead drunk.'

'That's what you think. That so, where's the body? I ask you.'

'Under that stone. Pile of bones by now.'

'I thought it was in the river. Did anybody ever pull it out of the river, hah? You've got a rotten memory, and you look roughly my age, boy. My memory is perfect: I can remember perfectly and I can forget perfectly. That's my stone, boy. I survived to see it. That stone's all there's left of Edmund Gate.' He peered at me as though it pained him. 'He's dead, y'know.'

'Then you can't be him,' I told the madman; genuine madmen always contradict themselves.

'Oh yes I can! I'm no dead poet, believe you me. I'm what survived him. He was succeeded by a woman, y'know. Crazy old woman. Don't tell *me*.'

He raised his bright stick and cracked it down on my shoulder. Then he slipped off, trembling and wobbling in his funny shoes, among the other monuments of the Preserved Cemetery.

He had never once recognized me. If it had really been Elia, he would certainly have known my face. That is why I am sure I have actually met a genuine madman for the first time in over forty years. The Museum Force at my request has made an indefatigable search of the Cemetery area, but up to this writing not so much as his pointed heel-print has been discovered. They do not doubt my word, however, despite my heavy age; senility has been eliminated from our modern society.

An Education

I. There are at least a couple of perfect moments in any life, and the one Una Meyer counted as second-best was a certain image of herself entering her college Latin class. It is a citified February morning. The classroom is in a great drab building, not really a skyscraper but high above the nearest church-tower, and the window looks out on the brick solemnity of an airshaft. A draught of worn cafeteria coffee slides by. Una is wearing a new long-sleeved dress with a patent-leather belt; the sleeves and the belt are somehow liberating and declare her fate to her. Besides, she is the only one in the class who can tell the difference between synecdoche and metonymy. One is the-part-for-the-whole, the other is the-sign-for-the-thing. Her body is a series of exquisitely strung bones. Her face has that double plainness of innocence and ordinariness. Her brain is deliciously loaded with Horace – wit, satire, immortality – and even more deliciously with Catullus – sparrows and lovers and a thousand kisses, and yet again a thousand, which no mean and jinxing spy shall ever see. Una has kissed no one but her parents, but she is an intellectual and the heiress of all the scholars who ever lived. The instructor's name is Mr Collie. He is Roger Ascham resurrected. He is violent with Mr Organski, who never prepares the lesson and can't manage case-endings. Mr Collie is terribly strict and terribly exacting. Everything must be rendered precisely. When he turns his back, Mr Organski spits in the air. The class shudders with indifference. 'You're late,' says Mr Collie in open joy. He never tolerates lateness in anyone else, but he can't conceal his delight at seeing Una in the doorway at last. He teaches only Una. *'Tell* Mr Organski, won't you, *why* he may not use the accusative case with the verb I've just taken the great trouble to conjugate for him on the blackboard? *Oblige* him, Miss Meyer, won't you?' Mr Organski patiently wipes the excess spit from his mouth. He is a foreigner and a veteran; he is a year older than Mr Collie and has a mistress, which would disgust Mr Collie if he knew. In spite of everything Mr Organski does not hate Una, who is now hiking up her eyeglasses by pushing on the nosepiece. He pities her because she is so skinny; she reminds him of a refugee survivor. 'Well it takes the genitive,' Una says, and thinks: If only the universe would stay as it is this moment! Only a tiny handful of very obscure verbs – who can remember them? – take the genitive. Una is of the elect who can remember. And she is dazzled – how poignantly she senses her stupendous and glorious fate! How tenderly she contemplates her mind!

That is the sort of girl Una Meyer was at eighteen.

At twenty-four she hadn't improved. By then she had a master's degree in Classics and most of a Ph.D. – the only thing left was to write the damn dissertation. Her subject was certain Etruscan findings in southern Turkey. Their remarkable interest lay in the oddity that all the goddesses seemed to be left-handed. Una, who was right-handed, felt she must be present at the dig – she was waiting for her Fulbright to come through. No one doubted it would, but all the same Una was positive she had deteriorated. It was summer. Her dissertation adviser and his wife Betty and sons Bruce and Brian had rented a cottage on Martha's Vineyard. The younger teachers had taken a house on Fire Island; no one had invited Una. The department office was empty most of the day, and a pneumatic drill in the street below roared and rattled the paper clips in the desk-drawers, so Una took to spending her afternoons in the college cafeteria. In six years the coffee had aged a bit – you could tell by the brittle staleness meandering through the cigarette smells – but never Una. She still thought of herself as likely to be damaged by caffeine, and she said she hated lipstick because it was savagery to paint oneself brighter than one was born, but mainly she was against coal tar.

And that was how she came to notice Rosalie. Rosalie was one of those serious blue-eyed fat girls, very short-fingered, who seem to have arrived out of their mothers' wombs with ten years' experience at social work. She wore her hair wrapped in a skimpy braid around her big head, which counted against her, but she was reading *Coming of Age in Samoa* in paperback, a good point in a place where all the other girls were either paring or comparing – nails or engagement rings as the case might be. It wasn't the engaged girls that made Una feel she had declined – what she felt for *them* was scorn. She was sure they would all marry nightgown salesmen or accountants from the School of Business Administration; not one of them would ever get to Turkey to study left-handed Etruscan goddesses. But all the same she was depressed. Her life struck her as very ordinary – nowadays practically everyone she was acquainted with could tell the difference between synecdoche and metonymy (that was what came of being a graduate student), but the sad thing was it no longer seemed important. That was her trouble: the importance of everything had fallen. And worse than that, she had a frightening secret – she was afraid she really didn't care enough about her dissertation subject. And she was afraid she would get dysentery in Turkey, even though she had already promised her mother to boil everything. She almost wished she was stupid and fit only to be engaged, so that she wouldn't have to win a Fulbright.

Rosalie, meanwhile, had come to page 95, and was gulping a lemonade without looking; when the straw gargled loudly she knew she had attained the end of her nourishment, and let go. The straw, though bitten, was a clean yellow. Una, whom the sight of lipstick on straws offended, decided Rosalie might be interesting to talk to.

'You realize Margaret Mead's a waste of time,' she began. 'There aren't any *standards* in cultural anthropology' – this was just to start the argument off – 'that's what's wrong with it.'

Rosalie showed no surprise at being addressed that way, out of the blue. 'That's the idea,' she said. 'That's the way it's supposed to be. Cultural relativity. Whatever is, is. What's wrong in New York can be right in Zanzibar.'

'I don't go for that,' Una said. 'That sounds pretty depraved. Take murder. Murder's wrong in any culture. I believe in the perfectibility of man.'

'So do I,' Rosalie said.

'Then your position isn't really logical, is it? I mean if you believe in the perfectibility of man you have to believe in that very standard of perfection all peoples aspire to.'

'Nobody's perfect,' Rosalie said, going sour.

'I disagree with that.'

'Well, name somebody who is.'

'That has nothing to do with it,' Una said in her most earnest style, 'just because I personally don't know anybody doesn't mean they don't exist.'

'They *can't* exist.'

'They might if they wanted to. They exist in theory. I'm a Platonist,' Una explained.

'I'm a *bezbozhnik*,' Rosalie said. 'That's Russian for atheist.'

Una was overwhelmed. 'Do you know Russian?'

'I have this pregnant friend who was studying it last year.'

'Say something else.'

'*Tovarichka*, I don't know anything else, I only know the names those two call me.'

'Two?' Una picked up. She was very good at picking up small points and turning them into jokes. 'You have *two* pregnant friends who speak Russian?'

'One's the husband.'

'Oh,' Una said, because nothing bored her more than married couples. 'How come you go around with people that old?'

'*She's* twenty-three and *he's* twenty-two.'

Una was impressed, not to say horrified. 'That's younger than *I* am. I mean that's *very* young to cage yourself up like that. I suppose they never had a chance to get any real education or anything?'

'Mary's a lawyer and Clement – well, if you're that way about Margaret Mead I won't tell you about Clement.'

'Tell!' Una said.

'Clement *studied* with Margaret Mead and got his master's in anthropology at Columbia, but then he suddenly got interested in religion – mysticism, really – and now he commutes to the Union Theological Seminary. They had to move up to Connecticut so Mary can start on her JSD at Yale Law School right after the baby comes. Actually' – Rosalie's stumpy forefinger scratched at *Coming of Age in Samoa* – 'this is Clement's book. He lent it to me about two months ago, but I haven't seen either of them for ages – I'm going up there this weekend and I wouldn't dare turn up without it. They're *wild* on people who borrow books and don't give them back. They've got this little card catalogue they keep, just like a library, and when you return a book they ask you *questions* about it, just to make sure you didn't borrow it for nothing.'

'So you're boning up!' Una concluded. She realized she was jealous. The part about the card catalogue thrilled her. 'They sound marvellous. I mean they sound really wonderful and delightful.'

'They're very nice,' Rosalie agreed coldly.

'What's their name? In case they get famous some day.' Una always took note of potential celebrity as a sort of investment, the way some people collect art. 'Their last name, I mean.'

'Chimes. Like what a bell does.'

'Chimes. That's beautiful.'

'It was legally changed from Chaims.'

'But isn't that Jewish?' Una asked. 'I thought you said Union Theological Sem—'

'They're emancipated. I'm bringing them a four-pound ham. You should hear Clement on "Heidegger and the Holocaust".'

'Heidegger and the *what*?'

'The Holy Ghost,' Rosalie said. 'Clement's awfully witty.'

II. The really perfect moment – the one that came just when Una had decided there were no new revelations to be had in the tired old world, and the one she promised herself she would remember forever and ever – happened on the shore of the State of Connecticut at half-past four in the afternoon. Now it is the very core of August. The sky is a speckless white cheek. Yards away the water fizzes up like soda-pop against a cosy rock in the shape of a sleeping old dog. A live young dog skids maniacally between the nibble-marks the tide has bitten into the sand. The dog's owners, a couple in their fifties, are packing up to go home. They stop for one last catch of a ball – it zooms over poor Spot's jaws, but in a second Clement has dropped *King Lear* and hypnotizes the ball: it seems to wait in air for him to rise and pluck it from the lip of the sun. 'Good *boy*,' says the man, 'damn good catch. Give 'er here.' Back and forth goes the ball between Clement and the stranger. The stranger's wife compliments Clement: 'You got a good build, sonny,' she says, 'only you ruin your looks with that hairy stuff. I got a picksher of my father, he wore one of them handlebars fifty years back. What's a young kid like you want with that? Take my advice, shave it off, sonny.' Clement returns to the blanket grinning – how forbearing he is with his inferiors! How graceful! He is a thick-thighed middle-sized young man who looks like the early Mark Twain; he is even beginning crinkles around his eyes, and he is egalitarian with kings and serfs. Una has been in Connecticut only an hour, but he is as comradely towards her as though they had been friends since spherical trigonometry. Mary is a bit cooler. There has been the smallest misunderstanding: the Chimeses were honestly under the impression that Rosalie said on the phone she was bringing a Turk. Mary expected a woman in purdah, and here is only bony Una in a bathing suit.

The Chimeses have had Indians, Chinese, Malayans, Chileans, Arabs (especially these: on the Israeli question they are pro-Arab); they have not yet had any Turks. Una is a disappointment, but since she doesn't know it, she continues in her rapture without a fault.

They go back to reading the play aloud. There are only three copies; Mary and Una share one. Una scarcely dares to peek at Mary, her voice is so dramatic, but she sees a little of her teeth, which are very large and unabashed, perfect teeth unlike anyone else's; cavities in Mary's teeth are inconceivable. The baby she is harbouring under her smock is also very large and unabashed, and Mary, to accommodate its arc, leans down hard on one elbow, like a mermaid. Mary is beautiful. Her nose is ideally made and her eyes have broad sceptical lids that close as slowly as garret shutters. Amazingly, a child's laugh leaps from her mouth. Una is embarrassed when her own turn comes, but then she is relieved – Rosalie doesn't act well at all. Rosalie plays Goneril, Una is Regan, Clement is Cordelia, Mary is King Lear. 'I prithee, daughter, do not make me mad,' Mary says to Rosalie, 'thou art a boil, a plague-sore, an embossed carbuncle,' and they all four screech with hilarity. Mary's giggle runs higher and lasts longer than anyone's. 'Mary went to a special drama school when she was ten,' Clement explains. 'Clement sings,' Mary informs Una. 'We ought to do a play with songs. He's got this marvellous baritone but you have to beg him.' 'Next time we'll do the *Beggar's Opera*,' Clement teases. A little wind comes flying over them, raising a veil of sand. 'Time to go home, you'll be cold, bunny,' Clement tells Mary. He stretches across fat Rosalie to kiss the pink heel of Mary's foot, and in the very next moment, when they all slap their Shakespeares down and tussle with the pockets in the sand as they scramble up, a brilliance is revealed to Una. All the world's gold occupies the sky. The cooling sun drops a notch lower. They head for the iron staircase that leads to the Chimeses' seaside apartment, and Una carries in her ribs a swelling secret. Her whole long-ago sense of illimitable possibility is restored to her. It is as though she has just swallowed Beauty. A charm of ecstasy has her in thrall. She has fallen in love with the Chimeses, the two of them together. Oh, the two of them together!

They were perfect. Everything about them was perfect. Una had never before seen so enchanting an apartment: it was exactly right, just what you would expect of a pair of intellectual lovers. Instead of pictures on the walls, there were two brightly crude huge rectangles of tapestry, with abstract designs in them. Clement had sewn them. On the inside of the bathroom door, where vain people stupidly hang mirrors, Mary had painted a Mexican-style mural, with overtones of Dali. And all along the walls, in the kitchen and the bedroom and the living room and even in the little connecting corridor, were rows and rows of bookshelves nailed together very serviceably by Clement. Clement could build a bookcase, Mary said, in two hours flat. Meanwhile Rosalie was in the kitchen checking on the ham, which they had left cooking all afternoon.

'Is it done?' Mary asked from the bathroom.

'I'd guess another fifteen minutes,' Rosalie said.

'Then I'm going to shower. You're next, Rosalie. Then Una. Then Clement.'

Una went prowling among the books. Regiments of treasure marched by. The Chimeses had the entire original New York edition of Henry James. They had Jones's life of Freud. They had Christmas Humphreys on Buddhism, *Memoirs of Hecate County*, four feet of Balzac, a volume of Sappho translated into Mandarin on the facing pages, and a whole windowsill's length of advanced mathematics. There were several histories of England and plenty of Fichte and Schelling. There was half a wall of French.

Between a copy of *Das Kapital* and a pale handbook called 'How to Become an Expert Electrician for Your Own Home Purposes in Just Thirty Minutes', Una discovered the card catalogue Rosalie had told her about. It was in a narrow green file box from Woolworth's. 'What a fabulous idea,' Una said, flipping through the cards. She adored anything alphabetical.

'We've only just started on our record collection. We've got about a thousand records and we're going to catalogue the whole shebang,' Clement said.

The bathroom door clattered. 'Your turn!' Mary yelled – Una had never known anyone to bathe so quickly. Out came Mary wrapped in a Chinese bathrobe, with her long dark hair pinned up. She smelled like a piney woods.

Rosalie said she didn't see the necessity of showering, she hadn't been on the beach an hour.

'You haven't improved a bit,' Mary complained. 'We *always* used to have to coax Rosalie to take baths.'

'In our other apartment,' Clement said.

'*My* apartment,' Rosalie growled from under the shower. Like Mary, she kept the door open.

'Rosalie was paying a lot less rent than we were, so we moved in with her,' Mary said. 'Up to two months ago we were all living together.'

'Rosalie's a pretty good cook,' Clement said, 'but *we* taught her how to do a salad. She used to cut things up piecemeal. First the lettuce, then the cucumbers—'

'Cucumber rinds have no nutritional value whatso*ever*,' Mary announced, 'but we keep them on for cosmetic purposes. Poor Rosalie, after we came up here she was left all alone with her chunks of piecemeal lettuce.'

'Her clumsy tomato-halves,' Clement said, 'her big pitted black ripe olives.'

'Poor Rosalie,' Rosalie called. 'She was left all alone with the hole in the closet door.'

'We put the loudspeaker for our hi-fi in it,' Clement told Una.

'They always cut holes in closet doors,' Rosalie called.

Una, who was very law-abiding, was privately awed at such a glamorous affront to landlords' rights. But when Rosalie came out of the shower Una hurried in after her, so that the Chimeses wouldn't think she was one of those girls who had to be coaxed to bathe.

After supper Clement asked Una what she would like to hear, and Una, a musical nitwit, timidly said *The Mikado*. 'Is that all right for you?' she wondered.

'Oh, we like everything,' Clement said. 'Bach, jazz, blues—'

'What you want to remember about the Chimeses,' Rosalie instructed, 'is that they're Renaissance men, they're nothing if not well-rounded.'

'Especially me,' said Mary. She tossed out one of her childlike giggles and suddenly sat down on the floor in frog-position and puffed very fast, like a locomotive, while Clement counted up to fifty. 'That's for painless childbirth. You anticipate the contractions,' he said, and put on *The Mikado*. Mary's legs rolled in the air. 'Listen, bunny, Una said she's going to help organize the record catalogue.'

Una flushed. She didn't remember saying it, but she *had* thought it – it was exactly what she hoped they would ask her to do. It was wonderful that Clement had guessed.

'Not me,' said Rosalie, and spread herself on the sofa. Una decided Rosalie was terrifically lazy and not very sociable, and to show the Chimeses *she* wasn't at all like that, she squatted right down on the floor next to Mary and prepared for business. Mary gave Una a pile of index cards and her own fountain pen, and Clement took the records out of their folders and read out the date of issuance, the Köchel number, and all sorts of complicated-sounding musical information Una had never before encountered.

'We're going to index by cross-reference,' Mary said. 'Composer's name by alphabet, name of piece by order of composition, and then a list of our personal record-numbers by order of date of purchase. That way we'll know whether they're scratchy because of being worn or because of difficulties in the system itself.'

Una hardly understood a word, but she went on gamely making notes, until Clement finally discovered she was no good for anything but alphabetizing.

'You could use her for your bibliographical index, she'd be fine for that,' Mary suggested. 'Do you know John Livingston Lowes's *The Road to Xanadu*? Well, Clement's doing something like that. He's working on the sources of Paul Tillich's thought.'

Una said that must be pretty interesting, but unless you were a mind-reader how could you find them out?

'I'm researching all the books he's ever read. It's a very intricate problem. I'm in constant correspondence with him.'

'You mean he sends you *letters*?' Una cried. 'Paul *Tillich*, the philosopher?'

'No, he communicates by carrier-pigeon. And it's Paul Tillich the president of the carpenters' union,' Clement said. 'My God, girl, you need educating.'

'Especially in library science,' Rosalie sneered from the sofa.

But Una was stirred. 'That's really *doing* something. It's thinking about the world. I mean it's really scholarship!'

'Don't you like what you're doing?' Clement asked.

'I don't. Oh, I don't. I'm sick to death of Latin and Greek and I don't give a damn about the Etruscan Aphrodite and I'm scared silly about getting a Turkish disease,' she burst out. 'Oh, I envy you two, I really do. You have a passion and you go right ahead with it, you're doing exactly what you want to do, you're right in the middle of being alive.'

Mary said gravely, 'You should never do what you don't want to do. You should never go against your own nature.'

'It's the same as going against God,' Clement said.

Rosalie tumbled off the sofa. 'Oh God. If we're on God again I'm going home.'

'I feel,' Clement said, 'that the teleological impulse in the universe definitely includes man.'

Rosalie turned up the Lord High Executioner's volume.

'The thing is,' Mary said, 'if you're going after your Ph.D. only for fashionable reasons or prestige reasons you should give it up.'

'I've got these fabulous recommendations,' Una said morosely. 'I'm probably going to *get* the damn Fulbright.'

'You should give it up,' Mary insisted.

Una had never considered this. It was logical, but it didn't occur to her that anyone ever took logic seriously enough to live by it. 'I'd have to do something else instead. I don't know what I'd do,' she argued.

'Find somebody and get married.' This was Rosalie, that traitor. She was no different from all those other girls who came down to the cafeteria to show off their new rings. Probably she wished she had one herself, but she was too fat, and no one would so much as blink at her. The only reason Rosalie didn't wear lipstick was that Mary didn't. The only reason Una had been attracted to Rosalie in the first place was that Rosalie had been reading Clement's book. What a fake! What a hypocrite! Rosalie was a toad in Chimeses' clothing. Una felt the strictest contempt for herself – she had let that sly girl take her in. She was astonished that the Chimeses could ever have endured living with Rosalie, she was so ordinary. She wondered that they hadn't dropped her long ago. It only proved how incredibly superior they were. They always looked for the right motives not to do a thing.

'Marriage is exactly *not* the point,' Clement snapped. Una could see he was just as impatient with Rosalie as she was, but he smothered his disgust in philosophy. 'It's not a question of externals, it's a question of internals. Going to Turkey is an external solution. Getting married is an external solution. But the problem *of* the Self requires a solution *for* the Self, you can see that, can't you?'

Una wasn't sure. 'But I wouldn't know what to *do*,' she wailed.

'In an existential dilemma it isn't action that's called for, it's *in*action. Nonaction. Stasis. Don't think about what you ought to do, think about what you ought *not* to do. – Come on, Rosalie, cut out the noise, lower that damn thing down. What I mean,' Clement said, 'is stop looking at the world in terms of your own self-gratification. It's God's world, not yours.'

'God knows it's not mine,' Rosalie said. She reduced Nanki-Poo's song to the size of an ant's – she seemed good-natured enough, but really she had no mind of her own: she did whatever anyone told her to do. 'If I owned the world Clement would've cut a hole in it by now.'

Una was shocked. Here was a fresh view! And it was true, it was true, she was too proud, she had always thought of her own gratification. Clement was so clever he could look right through her. But all the same she was a little flattered – she had never before been in an existential dilemma. 'I've always been very careerist,' she admitted. 'I guess the thing I've cared about most is getting some sort of recognition.'

'You won't get it in Turkey,' Mary warned, but her voice was now very kind.

'You'll get buried same as those left-handed Etruscans,' Clement said. This made Una laugh. Oh, they were perfect!

'Take my advice,' Rosalie said. 'Get your degree and be a teacher.'

'Rosalie means be like Rosalie,' Clement said.

'There's worse,' Rosalie said.

'I'll give it up,' Una said, but the momentousness of this was somehow lost, because Mary suddenly clapped the knot of her piled-up hair and shrieked 'Breakfast! Clement, what'll we do for breakfast? There's not a scrap.'

'I'll bicycle out to the market in the morning.'

'Oh, I'll go,' Una offered, charmed at the picture of herself pedalling groceries in the basket before her. It would almost make her one of them. 'I'm a very early riser.'

'There's not a scrap of cash either,' Mary said ruefully. 'Clement's scholarship money comes quarterly, and my scholarship money comes every month, but it doesn't start till the term starts. We were *counting* on Rosalie's bringing the ham, but I spent the last penny on tonight's baked beans.'

'It wasn't your fault, bunny. And it wasn't the beans that did it, it was the wine I bought day before yesterday. Hell with budgets anyhow – come on, let's have the wine!'

'Here's to Una Meyer,' Clement sing-songed, and Una glowed, because it was plain her cataclysmic avowal hadn't been overlooked after all. 'Drink to Una on the Brink.'

'Of disaster,' Rosalie purred.

'Of Selfhood,' Clement declared, and Una was nearly embarrassed with the pleasure of her importance. The wine was a rosé and seemed to blush for her. Mary poured it out in pretty little goblets, which she explained were the product of a brand-new African glass industry, and not only helped to make a budding economy viable, but were much cheaper than they looked. All at once the four of them were having a party. They switched off the record-player, and Clement, after only two or three pleas from Mary, sang a comic version of an old-time movie version of 'The Road to Mandalay'. He sounded exactly like a witty Nelson Eddy. Then he took down his guitar from its special hook next to the towel-rack in the bathroom and they all joined in on 'On Top of Old Smoky', 'Once I Wore My Apron Low', 'Jimmy Crack Corn', 'When I Was a Bachelor', and a lot of others, and by the time Clement carried in the folding cot for Una and Mary covered the sofa pillow with a clean pillowcase for Rosalie, Una was happier than she had ever been in her life, until a wonderful thing happened. It touched her so much she almost wept with sentiment. When all the lights were off and everyone was very still, Clement and Mary came softly out of their bedroom in their pyjamas, and, one by one, they kissed Una and Rosalie as though they had been their own dear children.

'Goodnight,' Mary whispered.

'Goodnight,' Una whispered back.

'Goodnight,' Clement said.

'Goodnight,' Rosalie said, but even in the dark, without seeing the sarcastic bulge of her neck, Una thought Rosalie sounded stubbornly unmoved.

'Rosalie honey,' Clement said tenderly, 'can you lend us five for breakfast?'

'All I've got's my trainfare back,' Rosalie said in the most complacent tone imaginable. Una was certain Rosalie was lying for her own malicious ends, whatever they could be.

'Oh, let *me*, please,' she cried, sitting upright very fast. 'Listen, Clement, where do you keep your bikes? I'll get everything the minute I'm up.'

'We wouldn't think of it,' Mary said in her steadfast way. 'It isn't just breakfast, you know, it's practically the whole week till Clement's cheque comes.'

No one was whispering now.

'Oh, *please*,' Una said. 'I'd really like to, honest. I mean before today you didn't know me from a hole in the wall—'

'In the door,' Rosalie crowed.

'—and you gave me all this marvellous hospitality and everything. It's only right.'

'Well,' Clement said – he seemed very stern, almost like a father – 'if you really want to. Only don't forget the eggs.'

'Oh, I won't,' Una promised, and could hardly fall asleep waiting for the next day of living in the Chimeses' aura to begin.

III. Early in the fall the Chimeses moved into New Haven proper, which was a relief for everyone, but for no one more than Una, who hadn't really minded nights on the sofa until they had had to put the crib right up against her feet. There was no other place for it. The Chimeses' seaside bedroom, though it had a romantic view of the waves, was only a cubicle with a window – there wasn't even a cranny with a dresser in it, much less a crib. In New Haven they found a downtown tenement that was cheap and by comparison almost spacious. In the new flat there were three bedrooms: one for the Chimeses', one was a study for Mary, and the one farthest from this, to keep the noise at a distance, was the baby's. Clement bought a second-hand screen and put it between Una's bed and the crib – 'to give the infant its privacy,' he joked.

The birth itself had been remarkable – all the nurses agreed the hospital had never had anyone to match Mary. She was over and done with it in an hour, and with hardly any fuss. Mary attributed this to having learned how to deal with the contractions, and Clement, who had turned more ebullient than ever, laughed and said Mary had practised with can't, won't, and ain't.

The baby, of course, was magnificent. It was unusually beautiful for a small infant and had long limbs. Mary had all along been indifferent to its sex, but Clement claimed he needed to free himself of potential incest-fantasies by releasing them into reality: he had wanted a girl from the start. Mary, Una, and Clement argued about names for days, and finally compromised on Christina, after the heroine of *The Princess Casamassima*. Christina, as a combination of two perfections, was exactly what Una had expected, and she looked at her as on some sacred object which she was not allowed to touch too often. But soon Mary decided that she had to spend more and more time in the law library, so she let Una wheel Christina around and around the streets near the university for a couple of hours every day.

Una had the time for it now: Clement had made up his mind not to finish his bibliographical index. His correspondence had waned, and to Una's surprise it turned out that the letters weren't really from Tillich, but from his secretary. Clement said this was just like all theologians:

their whole approach was evasive, you could see it right in their titles. *The Courage to Be*, Clement said, was a very ambiguous book, and if the *product* was that ambiguous, you could hardly follow up the sources, could you? He told Una he would have dropped the project as futile long ago if she hadn't taken such an interest in the way he went about it. In the beginning he spent hours typing involved letters on this or that point to obscure academics with names like Knoll or Creed, but after a while he discovered he could think better if he dictated and Una typed. Anyhow he was always having to run off and help Mary with the baby, or else he had to stop in the middle of a sentence to carry a big bundle of diapers to the laundromat. Gradually Una could complete his abandoned phrases without him. She got so good at this that the two of them had a little conspiracy: Una worked out the letters in Clement's style, all on her own, and Clement signed them. He often praised her, and said she could follow up leads even better than he could. Now and then he told her she wrote very well for a non-writer, and at those moments Una felt that maybe she wasn't an imposition on the Chimeses after all.

She worried about this a lot, even though they let her pay a good chunk of the rent – she had begged them so poignantly they couldn't refuse her. At first she had tried not to get in their way, and reminded them several times a day that if they regretted their invitation they shouldn't hesitate a wink in withdrawing it. She still couldn't believe that they actually *wanted* her to live with them. They were always comparing her to Rosalie and reminding themselves what a nasty temper Rosalie sometimes had. Rosalie used to like to sleep to the last minute, when she realized perfectly well that they *depended* on her for breakfast – at that time they'd both had very tough schedules, much tougher than that sluggard Rosalie's, and if they missed breakfast they wouldn't eat again until supper. They had a lot of other Rosalie stories, all terrible. Una determined to be as unlike Rosalie as possible – for instance, she took to preparing breakfast every day, even though Mary and Clement were both shocked at her zeal and told her it wasn't in the least bit necessary. But Mary observed that if Una was going to be up anyway, she might as well give Christina her seven o'clock bottle, which would mean Una's getting up only fifteen minutes earlier than she had to to make the breakfast. Sometimes it was three-quarters-of-an-hour earlier, but Una didn't mind – whenever she lifted Christina she felt she was holding treasure. She knew Christina would turn out to be extraordinary.

Besides, she wanted to be as useful as possible, considering how

Clement was sweating to get her some sort of sub-fellowship from the seminary. It was only fair, he said, now that she was doing practically half his work, even though it was the superficial half. He took the train to New York three days a week, and every time he returned it was with a solemn anger. 'They're trying to get me to believe their budget's closed,' he would say. Or, 'Damn them, they don't realize the calibre of what I'm *doing*. They say they don't give money for research assistants to anyone lower than associate professor. That's a lot of baloney. Don't worry about it, Una, we'll get something for you.' Una said it was all right – so far she still had some money in the bank account her grandmother had started for her: every year on Una's birthday or on holidays her grandmother had put in seventy-five dollars. Mary said it was a shame Una's grandmother was dead. 'People don't *need* grandmothers any more,' Clement said, 'they've got fellowships nowadays.' 'If Una were getting her Fulbright money right now, it would help,' Mary said in a voice a little more pinched than her usual one. 'If Una were getting her Fulbright money right now,' Clement noted, 'she'd be in Turkey, and where would *we* be? – Look, I'll beat them down somehow, don't you worry about the moolah, Una.'

Whenever the Chimeses mentioned her lost Fulbright – it *seemed* often, but it wasn't really – Una felt guilty. Just as she feared, she had won the thing, and her adviser came back from Martha's Vineyard with his wife and boys and flew into a fury. He called Una a fool and a shirker for saying she'd pass up a prize like that, and for what? It was only an honour and not life, Una said. He asked whether the real point wasn't that she was going off to be married like all of them. He said he was against women in universities anyhow; they couldn't be trusted to get on with their proper affairs. Her real trouble, he told her, was she didn't have the guts to settle down to hard work. Sometimes Una wondered whether any of this was true. She was busy with domestic details – washing up, making the beds, tending the baby (of course it wasn't *just* a baby), exactly like a married person. And even though helping Clement on top of all the rest wore her out, still that sort of thing didn't count as *work*, since she didn't really understand what it was he was getting at. Clement had explained that he couldn't take the time to show her the basic insight of his project, it was too complex for a philosophical novice, and without it she couldn't hope to get near the nerve of his idea. That was why, he reminded her, she mustn't expect more than a pittance of the sum he was demanding for her from the seminary.

But one day Clement stomped off the train and said he was never going back. They had suspended him.

'But why?' Una exclaimed. The first thought she had was that Clement had finally gone too far on her behalf. 'Is it on account of badgering them all the time? The money I mean,' she said in her shame.

'Don't be silly, it has nothing to do with you, why should it?'

'Haven't you noticed, Una?' Mary said. She wasn't a bit upset. 'Clement's been losing his faith. He's been intellectualizing about it too much – that's always the first sign.'

'I finally had to speak up in Systematic Dogmatics,' Clement said modestly. 'I told old Hodges today I didn't think he or any of them actually knew what the Gnostics were *after*. Well, he let on about it to the Dean, and the Dean called me in and asked whether I was really on the road to Damascus. "The fact is," I said, "I don't feel the present ministry's coming to grips with the problem of the *Trinity*, sir." And you know what the old baboon answers? "Suppose we respect those feelings for a year or two, Mr Chimes. If you're not at home with the Gnostics by then maybe you'd be better off among the *agnostics*." Very funny. I resigned then and there.'

'And about time,' Mary said.

'How humiliating!' Una cried. 'How awful!' But Clement was wearing a hurt look, and immediately she understood she had made a mistake. She was sure he was offended.

'You think too much about status. Society may look up to the ministry, but what I've gotten out of all this is that I don't look up to society.'

'You can't stand still in this world,' Mary put in. 'You have to shed your old skin every now and then.'

Una was abashed. She realized that living with the Chimeses hadn't profited her an iota. She was as uneducated as ever. She still jumped to false conclusions, and she still needed instruction in life-values.

'Not that Clement wasn't *perfectly* right to leave,' Una said quickly. It came out almost abject, and she could see Mary's teeth shine into forgiveness. Mary was so good! She was practically a saint. Just when you thought she was going to be terrifyingly severe, she turned around and gave you another chance to restore yourself to ordinary common sense.

'Fact is,' Clement said, 'I could never *be* part of the Establishment in any form. It's just something I've been avoiding coming face to face with. Actually I'm an anarchist.'

'Now watch it,' Mary said, giggling. 'Una'll think you're secretly manufacturing bombs in the bathroom.' The reason this was funny was that no place could have been less secret than the bathroom; Clement had taken off the door to make a desk for Mary's study.

'Let 'er think so, it's just what I intend to do.'

'Make a *bomb?*' Una squealed, though she didn't feel like it. Sometimes she acted straight man just to please them.

'Exactly. A bomb called *Social Cancer*.'

'Oh, a book,' Una said, since she knew Clement expected her to sound relieved. All the same she was really impressed.

'I intend to pillory the whole society from top to bottom in blank verse. It'll be an exposé of the rich and the poor, the common man and the intelligentsia – and a work of art besides. There hasn't been anything like it since Alexander Pope wrote *The Dunciad*,' Clement pointed out, 'and Pope wasn't that comprehensive in his conception.'

That night they celebrated Clement's new book, which he was going to start writing early the next morning. They wheeled Christina to the park and right in front of her carriage built a fire out of Clement's bibliographical index. Clement and Mary threw notebook after notebook into the fire, and Una was sad, because there were so many months of toil in them. She saw her own handwriting curl up and char – all the notes she had taken for Clement on Buber and Niebuhr and Bultmann and Karl Jaspers and Kierkegaard. She had read all those difficult philosophers for nothing.

'It's not as though you haven't been through this sort of thing yourself – you're always forgetting that,' Mary said. Mary was uncanny. She always knew when Una's thoughts were limping off in the wrong direction. 'You have to learn how to dispense with the past, even if outsiders say it shows personal instability. Remember the night we all drank to you? You were great that time about letting the Fulbright go,' Mary said, 'you were really one of us that night.' Una was stunned. Mary had never before given her such a compliment. Mary was not indiscriminate with compliments at all.

'That was different,' Una objected – inside herself she was wondering whether she should dare to take Mary's praise as a sign of moral improvement, but at the same time she was afraid Mary suspected her of thinking Clement unstable. If so, it was a shameful calumny, and Mary wanted Una to know it. 'I wasn't *burning* anything,' Una said feebly.

'Yes you were,' said witty Clement: 'your ships behind you!' He had hardly ever seemed more cheerful; it had happened all at once, and it was plain even to Una that he was glad to be rid of all that long theological drudgery, which had been worthless all the time, though of course it was only Una who hadn't realized it. At lunch the next day he was delightful; he joked right through his coffee and enunciated 'Excoriate the corrupt republic' at Christina in a comical falsetto until she screamed. 'You're taking her out, aren't you, Una? Brat can raise the dead.'

'Mary said not until three o'clock.' – Mary had gone off to the library at ten that morning. She was preparing a paper on the Jurisprudence of Domestic Relations. For an epigraph it had a quotation from Rousseau urging the mothers of France to nurse their own babies, but that was the only part Una could fathom; the rest of it was a forest of alien footnotes. 'Christina might be catching cold,' Una said. 'She sneezed a couple of times, so Mary thought she ought to stay in most of the day.' Una privately believed Mary was mistaken whenever she argued there was no inborn maternal instinct – Mary herself seemed to exemplify it admirably. She always knew exactly the right thing to do about Christina.

'Oh, what's the difference,' Clement said. 'She needs airing, doesn't she? Una, I'll *tell* you what you show, what you show is the definite effects of overprotectiveness in conjunction with a mother-fixation – it's a lot healthier for Christina to get a cold than a fixation, isn't it?' He waited for Una to appreciate this sally. 'Take her out now, there's a honey. Can't hear myself cerebrate with all the racket.'

It was true that Christina was still screaming, but Una couldn't help thinking she had been perfectly behaved before Clement had frightened her – Christina was far too young to understand Clement's humour. She went to fetch Christina's little woollen cap and booties.

'Besides,' Clement said, following Una into Christina's room, 'I haven't got much time. I figure I can just about get *into* the first chapter before six.'

'You haven't begun it?' Una said.

'Oh, I've *begun* it, I just haven't put it down on paper yet.'

'But I thought you'd already gotten to work on it,' Una said, a little discomposed. 'Wouldn't you be well into it by now?' Clement had locked himself up in Mary's study all morning, and Una had taken special pains to woo Christina's silence. She had played hushing games with her for three hours, and was heavy with weariness afterwards. Christina woke so early nowadays that Una never really got enough sleep.

'I didn't say I didn't get to work on it,' Clement gave out in his most complicated tone, the one that only pretended to pretend annoyance, but all the while was genuinely annoyed. 'I said I just hadn't committed it to paper yet. Actually, Una honey, the trouble with you is you don't understand the most fundamental thing about the Muse. As per tradition, she has to be *invoked*, you silly,' but he was so fresh-faced and wide awake that Una had the strangest idea. She hardly dared to articulate it, even to herself, but what she secretly wondered was whether Clement hadn't just gone back to sleep after breakfast. Not that she minded, of course.

'I know,' she said, 'Creation is a Many-Staged Process.'

Clement warmed to her at once after that. She was quoting one of his own mottoes, which he had painted on the kitchen canisters. Instead of FLOUR he had put 'Self-Discipline is Achievement', and instead of SUGAR (but the wet paint had dripped off the brush into the canister and they had to replace the whole five pounds), 'Art is Love'. The line about Creation was on the teabag can.

'But look,' Una said, to make it up to Clement for seeming to criticize his working-habits (not that she meant to, but for the moment she *had* forgotten about the Muse), 'you don't have to quit at six. I mean can't you work right through supper if you feel like it? Mary wouldn't mind, she'd just as soon eat in the commons anyhow. I can make you a sandwich – there's some baloney, I think – and you can have supper in the study. You don't have to *stop*.'

Clement smiled at her so luminously that Una was sure she had set everything to rights again. 'Well, to tell the truth, Una honey,' he began, 'you're still just a little bit obtuse, now aren't you? Is it your grandmother's shade that's going to pay for the baloney in my sandwich? Does it reach you what the condition of the writer is vis-à-vis a society economically structured against him?'

Christina's yells grew louder and her wriggles more unwieldy as Una tried to get the bootie on her foot. Her miniature arch was aristocratically high, but Una was too shocked by Clement's words to admire it. Still, his smile continued so brilliant that she thought the whole affair must be one of his jokes – he was right about how obtuse she was.

'Tell you what,' Clement offered, 'I'll put you straight on something. You want to hear the real reason I got bounced from the seminary? Lo, the greed of Una Meyer. You pushed just a little bit too far – not that I ever let on about it. But you know what they accused me of? Of trying to fatten up my scholarship *by unscrupulous methods*. I never told you that, and I wouldn't be mentioning it now if you weren't so thick—'

'Oh, Clement!' Una burst out. 'I had no idea. I'm so ashamed! I was afraid it was my fault, but you said—'

'Never mind,' Clement said. 'Don't worry about it. I think I've got a good book in me, maybe even a great one if I can get to finish it, and by hook or crook I'm *going* to finish it. Hook: I refer to the hooks they sell at the hardware counter in Woolworth's. Crook: I refer to the management of same – they're tight-fisted enough, they pay like thieves.'

'Clement, what do you *mean?*'

'It's not exactly a man's job, but for a philosopher it'll have to do. At least it's evenings – six to ten. I can write all day before I have to go, and what with Mary's law school money I guess we'll manage. Now listen, Una,' he said, 'I'll be candid with you. This house is a complex working hive. There isn't room for parasites. Visualize, if you will, the salt-shaker.'

'Work or Die,' Una said with a drying mouth. 'You're going to work in the *five and ten?*'

'Spinoza was a lens-grinder. Don't be so appalled. Lincoln split logs. Clement Chimes will sell hooks, locks, bolts, and all manner of chains, some of them metaphysically displayed around his neck.'

'Oh, Clement! It sounds awful! What's Mary say?'

'She says A, the work is beneath Clement, a view to which Clement heartily accedes, and B, we need the cash. That being the hard case, will you now please remove the fire-siren from the premises so I can get *some*thing done?'

'Clement,' Una said – meditatively she buttoned up Christina's sweater – 'if it takes you practically the whole day to get started—'

'To invoke the Muse,' Clement corrected.

'—and you only *really* begin about two or maybe three and you have to leave about five-thirty to get to the Woolworth's by six—'

'Congratulations. You're getting the point,' Clement said. 'Education is slowly setting in.'

'—it means you'll have only about two hours or so to do any work at all.'

'Insufficient and unfortunate,' Clement agreed.

'But what about *Social Cancer?*'

''Twill suffer remissions,' Clement said.

That evening, at great inconvenience to Mary, who had to rush home from the library to feed Christina and put her to bed, Una started her new job at the hardware counter in Woolworth's, and sold hooks, locks, bolts, and all manner of chains.

IV. One afternoon Una was wheeling Christina along her usual route in the streets around Yale, when she decided to try a block she had never walked on before. It led her through the campus and past some of the old buildings. The day was cold and she pushed the carriage stolidly, without looking ahead of her, until she finally pushed it right into the briefcase of a young man hurrying across the path. The bag fell open and an assortment of medical instruments lay scattered on the ground.

'Well, look who it is,' said the young man in an ugly accent. He bent to retrieve his stethoscope. 'Aunt? Babysitter? Unwed mother? None of the above?'

The voice was familiar. It was Mr Organski.

'What are you doing in New Haven?' Una yelped.

'Being diligent at my Latin, as usual.'

'You were terrible in Latin, you didn't go *on* with it!'

'I couldn't help it, they name diseases in it.'

'Oh, you're a doctor,' Una said, laughing and picking up a pair of clamps. From inside the carriage came a small sneeze.

'If I pass. So far I'm a pompous medical student. And you? Settled in New Haven? Married, I see.'

Una frowned. 'This is my friends' baby.'

'Aha. A spinster doing a good turn. You prefer a career?'

'Well,' Una said uncomfortably.

'I understand. In that case not another word. Classified information. You're a scientist with the government? They use the labs around here, I've heard. A cyclotronist perhaps. A supersonistician. In short you're not permitted to describe your work.'

'It's hardware,' Una muttered.

'Just as I thought. Missiles. The classicist who thinks up the tags? Titan. Nike. Mars. Don't tell me your latest, I couldn't bear the responsibility of knowing. What's the baby's tag?'

'Christina.'

'Unworthy of a warhead, better return her to the pad. Take her home anyhow. Christina has a cold.'

'She has this cough. Sometimes her eyes run,' Una admitted.

'Your friends are dangerous madmen, why do they let her out?'

'Well, she's awfully noisy—'

'A common disease of babyhood – *infanta clamorata* – which passes with the onset of confinement in a school building – *kindergartenia absentia*.'

'—and her father's writing a book.'

'Aha. A question of immortality. Christina shows symptoms of mortality, however. Look, I think I'm going your way. Where are you going?'

Mr Organski walked her home, but Una didn't invite him in. She explained she couldn't – Clement was working.

'And the female parent?'

'Studying jurisprudence.'

'A remarkable family.'

'It is,' Una said fervently.

'They've taken you in? How fortunate for you,' said Mr Organski.

'I know,' Una said.

'Yet your good fortune increases. You were born under a lucky star. This family of geniuses has taken you in but I, Organski, a failure at conjugation, am going to take you out. To the movies Saturday night, what do you say? Say thank you.'

'I can't,' Una said. 'Clement and Mary are going. We decided on it days ago – they're so busy they hardly ever get out, I just couldn't spoil it for them.'

'Aha,' said Mr Organski. 'Call me Boris. We'll arrange something else immediately.'

'What about your mistress?'

'My mistress?'

'You had one.'

'Didn't I just say I was a failure at conjugation? I disown and disavow all previous alliances, without promising not to look forward to others more successful. Now listen carefully. When are Clement and Mary going to have the pleasure of meeting me?'

'Well, they're both home at night, but they're usually working—'

'This will be a medical visit. About Christina.'

Una said humbly, 'I'm the one who takes care of her mostly. If she's sick it's really my fault.'

'Fine. Then you should be present at my lecture. Time, tomorrow night. Place, the crowded apartment of Clement and Mary and Christina and Una.'

'My job is at night,' Una demurred.

'Aha. Night manoeuvres of the hardware. Top secret. Don't tell me anything. If the government has to hide its rocket failures under cover of darkness I don't want to share in its humiliation.'

'It's *Woolworth's*,' Una said in exasperation.

'Thank God, an ordinary Latinist after all. *Tedium Woolworthiae*, a harmless temporary state. I offer you a consolation. I suggest, in view of my having solemnly disowned and disavowed my previous conduct, that you undertake to shape my present conduct. Praise your stars. I'm asking you to become my current mistress.'

Una giggled. It sounded just like Mary's giggle.

'I assume you lend a hand in paying your friends' rent?' Mr Organski said. 'Come and pay mine. My apartment is far less crowded.'

V. The Chimeses didn't like Boris at all. In the first place, he didn't think Christina was perfect. He implied, in fact, that she was much worse than perfect. He said she was malnourished and needed liquid vitamins and her left lung wasn't clear. He said he would have to come often until he was confident she was improving. He asked to see where she slept.

'The room is too small,' he insisted. 'And when you put a screen around the crib like that, how do you expect the poor baby to breathe?'

'The screen is to give Una privacy,' Mary said viciously.

'Take it out.'

'I don't see how one thin little piece of plastic could make any difference,' Clement said.

'Never mind the screen. I'm talking about the bed. Take out the bed.'

'It's Una's.'

'Well, all *right*,' Mary said, 'Una can sleep on the couch again. After all, she used to.'

'Maybe you'd better ask her if she minds,' Boris said.

'She won't mind.'

'She never minds anything.'

Boris said, 'That sort of person can be an awful bore.'

'As a matter of fact she is,' Mary said. 'She's the most obsequious person I've ever known.'

Boris gave a labial croak that was meant to sound sympathetic. 'Impedes intimacies, I would guess.'

'You're a bit on the patronizing side, aren't you?' said Mary.

'As a matter of fact,' Clement said, 'she does. Always underfoot.'

'She's only so-so with Christina, lets her howl.'

'An impediment indeed,' Boris said in his medical-student style, very grand. 'I suppose she cooks?'

'If you call it that. Slices baloney. Opens cans.'

'An adult should never sleep near a child,' Boris said firmly. 'She never gave it a thought. Is her intelligence low? I'm thinking of the kind of job she has – small metallic objects and so forth.'

'Not particularly low,' Clement said. 'Though I wouldn't call Una *imaginative*, bunny, would you? The thing is she won a Fulbright once.'

'Incredible.'

'Passed it up. It was stupid, she would've seen Turkey on it.'

'Mmm,' Boris said, 'interesting. A neighbouring land. I myself am originally from Bulgaria. Of course she's too thin. She has very small breasts.'

That night, when Una returned from the hardware counter – it was a whole hour later than usual – the Chimeses waylaid her in the living room and began to speak to her very sternly.

'You're not seeing the point. Listen, Una honey,' Clement said, 'that man is out for no good. He came sneaking around here when he knew you were out—'

'On purpose,' Mary said. 'Behind your back.'

'Don't confuse the issue, bunny. That's the least of it. The point is he came to try to set us against you, Una. That's the point.'

'It was plain as day that's what he was out for,' Mary told Una. 'I can't think what his motives could be.'

'No motive,' Clement said. 'The world is full of jealous people like that. They can't bear seeing close relationships, they just have to wreck them.'

'He's even trying to turn Christina against you,' Mary said. 'A *baby*, imagine. He thinks you contaminate her. He says you have to sleep somewhere else, for health reasons.'

'There wasn't an item he didn't criticize. He just wouldn't be satisfied until he got us to say nasty things about you. Not that he managed it.'

'It's written all over his face what he is,' Mary said.

'He even insulted your *looks*,' Clement said. 'He's one of these belittlers, I know that kind. Medical types tend to think they're little gods. He said you didn't have the sense to deal with sickness. As if anybody's sick.'

'If he keeps it up he'll frighten you off, Una, you'll be scared to go *near* Christina.'

'He's pretty damn self-important, that guy. He's just looking to assert some so-called authority.'

'Keep away from him,' Mary advised.

Una thought it was odd that they were talking about Boris, whom they had only just met, exactly the way they always talked about Rosalie. 'But I left him only ten minutes ago.'

'Boris?' the Chimeses chimed together.

'When I came out of the Woolworth's there he was at the door.'

'Waiting for you? He must've gone over right from here.'

'He never said a word. Sly,' Mary observed.

'We went to this place,' Una explained, 'for coffee. *He* had coffee,' she amended; 'I had cocoa.'

'You see? You see?' Mary said.

'She doesn't see,' Clement said. 'Una honey, *look* at it, it's right under your nose. He's trying to wreck things. Like Rosalie. Didn't Rosalie tell you not to move in with us? Didn't she? You can't deny it, we *knew* it, it would be just like her. You've never been sorry you came in halfies with us, have you?'

'Gosh no,' Una said gratefully, but the truth was she felt a little muddled. It was after midnight; she had sold four Phillips screwdrivers, three combination locks and an ordinary padlock, two cans of furniture polish, a wad of picture-wire, a tube of automobile touch-up, a bicycle chain, a pair of bicycle clips, a dozen boxes of thumbtacks, and one door-knob. She longed for bed.

'Stop,' Mary said. 'Not in there. You're not supposed to use up any more of Christina's oxygen.'

'Oh,' said Una, and sank down on the sofa. *Pang*, went the bad spring. Mary, whose figure was every bit as good now as before her pregnancy, had broken the spring while doing her Royal Canadian Women's Division Air Force Exercises on the sofa. She did them every evening, and was very diligent and disciplined about it; she followed them out of a book.

'You'd be dead wrong if you were sorry, Una, I mean that seriously. I'm being very sincere with you. The point is you're not the same person you used to be, is she, bunny?'

'She had these awfully conformist ideas, remember? Honest to God, Una, you were worse than Rosalie. Well, not *worse* really, but you acted just like Rosalie when we first knew her. Always mooning around us and toadying up. We couldn't *stand* it from her. I mean *there* was a type who had no individuality whatever. She didn't *believe* in individuality.'

'And when we told her about it – you know, open and candid – she just got fresher and fresher. Don't look so upset, Una honey, *you're* not like that. She wasn't educable. The thing about you, Una, you've improved a lot because you're educable. You're on the brink of maturity, you could find yourself, your true métier, any day now – I mean, look at Mary, if you want an example – and all it would take to throw you off is for a guy like Organski to come along right about now and give you the business and tell you you ought to be one of these little housewife-types—'

'He didn't say anything like that,' Una said slowly. Then, just as slowly, she yawned. She was really very tired. 'I nearly forgot. Here.' She held out a package. 'It's the liquid vitamins for Christina. Boris said they're awfully expensive if you have to buy them in the drugstore. He said when he left here he remembered where he could get a whole load of doctors' samples, you know, for free, and then he ran right over to the Woolworth's with them. That's what he met me for. To deliver them. I'm so collapsed I think I'll just sleep in my clothes. Could you shut the light off, please?'

Pang, went the spring, but Una didn't hear.

VI After that Boris took to meeting Una outside the Woolworth's every night. At first she was astonished to see him there, leaning against the display windows and reading one of his medical books, waiting for her to come out; but he appeared so regularly that after the second week she began to look for him almost hopefully. The other clerks laughed and called out at him, as they passed, names like Totem Pole and Cigar Store Indian, and asked if he thought the place would fall in if he weren't around all the time to hold it up, and Boris always bowed comically but heartily to the fattest girls. That, he told Una, was a lesson to her: only fat girls were worth paying attention to. His object, he explained, was to fatten her up before he made her his mistress.

They always went to the same sandwich shop and Boris always bought her two thick sandwiches.

'Eat, don't talk,' he said, and kept his head down among anatomical drawings until she was done. 'I don't call that finished,' he objected – that was if she left her crusts – and then he ordered her a chocolate malted milk, sometimes with an egg beaten into it. Meanwhile he studied and forgot his coffee until it was too cold to drink. He never took her home before midnight, but on the way – they always walked, even on the stormiest nights – he made up for his two hours' silence in the sandwich place by teasing without a stop. 'Now promise, tomorrow I want a weight report. Without shoes, please, and in the nude, and on a reliable scale, try the one in the drugstore. I once had a mistress who was all skin and bones, like you, an experience I hope never to repeat. The points of her elbows made pinholes right through my best sheets. You should see those sheets today. In time the holes expanded to the size of washbasins, but you don't get to marvel at this phenomenon until I can observe the effects of ten pounds more in the clavicle area. A clavicle should not have such exaggerated visibility. The skeletal structure of the human body is not for public display except in the medical laboratory. My bedroom is not *that* sort of laboratory, my dear,' but by then they were at the Chimeses' door.

'What'll I *tell* them?' Una whispered one night, in the middle of only her first sandwich.

'Eat, don't talk,' said Boris.

'Boris!'

'Five minutes more. Just be quiet, my sweet, until I've done my gall bladder and liver. Finish your crusts, there's a dear.'

'Boris, I've *already* told Clement and Mary an awful lie. I told them the hardware supervisor extended my time by one hour.'

Boris looked up from his book and scratched an ear. It happened to be Una's.

'Well, it was only because they're mad that I'm always getting home so late. I couldn't tell them it's for nothing. I *had* to lie.'

'Aha,' Boris said. 'Thank you. I'm obliged to you. To Miss Meyer, Mr Organski is nothing.'

'Oh, Boris! Just *listen*. First I told them I was working this one hour overtime, and so then they wanted to know where the extra money was. Then I had to say *something*, so I said it was just plain overtime, and there wasn't any pay for it. And they didn't believe me! And now they want to know where I *go* after work. I don't know what to tell them, Boris.'

'Naturally they haven't heard you're out with Organski? Naturally. "I'm out with nothing" doesn't sound convincing.'

'It's because I'm getting home too late, Boris. Really, couldn't we leave earlier? Couldn't we leave right now?'

'Before you've had your fortified malted milk? Never!'

'But it's ruining everything, I keep oversleeping. I overslept practically every morning this week and nobody got any breakfast, not even

Christina, and later on she howled for hours, and Clement was so mad he couldn't do his chapter, and Mary said she was sick to her stomach in the library the whole day. She gets that way on an empty stomach. It's because I'm getting home too late, Boris.'

'All right,' Boris said. 'We leave right now. Immediately. Will that satisfy you? It interferes with my studying, of course – that goes without saying – but if it satisfies you to interfere with my studying let's go. Organski's entire career may go up the flue, but Una Meyer must be satisfied. Mr and Mrs Chimes *told* me what a model of selfishness you are, I can't say I haven't been warned. Up with you. Come! Leave your crusts, please, we have no time for them. There will be no beverage tonight, madam,' he yelled to the waitress.

'Oh, Boris, stop!' Una wailed. 'I don't know *what* to do, honest I don't.'

'Abandon fantasy. Tell Clement and Mary you're out with your lover. Excuse me. Your *prospective* lover – I'm afraid you're still several pounds short of realization of the fact, my dear. If you expose our liaison, you see, it will perhaps hint to them that you have an adumbration of a chimera of a life of your own.'

'Boris, that's not the *point*,' Una said, refusing even to smile.

'Aha. Clement's phrase exactly. You've mastered his intonation to the life, my dear. He spoke those very words to me, in that very tone, this very evening.'

'You've seen *Clement*?' Una exclaimed.

'Only by chance. I intended to see Christina and he happened to be in the house. He was eating an apple at the time and comfortably reading the funnies. He said the funnies were not the point. Meanwhile I took a sampling of the poor child's sputum.'

'Oh. Then she's worse,' Una said.

'Dr Chichester's having a peep at her in the morning – obviously a good man, he recognized Organski's gifts and gave him an A. That was last term. This term Una Meyer does not permit Organski to study. Oh, there won't be a fee, don't look so wild-eyed. Actually there *is* something wrong with your eyes, now that I observe them.'

'What?' Una cried.

'They're half shut. Tell you what. Beginning tomorrow night, instead of fattening you here, I'll fatten you privately, in my own apartment. I have a little kitchen you'll find perfectly adequate for slicing baloney in. While I study you'll sleep. On one condition – that you avoid further puncturing my sheets with a randomly protruding bone. After which I'll walk you home.'

'That won't solve anything,' Una said gloomily.

'Ungrateful girl. Think of the Chimeses' going without breakfast! You'll have your duty sleep, won't you?'

'But what'll I tell Clement and Mary?'

'You'll tell them,' Boris said peacefully, 'the simple truth. That you were innocently slumbering in the bed of your lover.'

VII. Boris was right about his sheets. They were terribly ragged. And his apartment was a calamity. The lease was handed on from one generation of students to another, year after year, and though everyone always left something behind, no one ever took anything away. The two rooms were full of useless objects, and the grease on the stove was as high as a finger. There was a television set that didn't work, a vacuum cleaner ditto, and, right in the middle of the tiny kitchen, a bureau stuffed with old underwear.

'My goodness,' Una said, 'hasn't this place ever been swept at all?'

'Long, long ago, my sweet, but only by the primeval Flood,' Boris replied, and opened the refrigerator with a flourish. It was crammed with food.

'I feel awful,' Una said. 'I feel just so depressed about the whole thing, Boris, it's horrible. Clement and Mary are just sick about it.'

'Eat, don't talk,' Boris said. He settled himself at his desk. It stood at the foot of his unmade bed. The lamp had a red shade and his face looked pink under it. Una suddenly noticed how, when he lowered his head, the bulb of Boris's nose made a shadow over his mouth. He had a long, attractive nose, a bit thick at the tip, and long, stiff nostrils that stared downwards like an extra pair of eyes. It was as though everything he said was uttered under surveillance.

'Itt, dunt tuck,' Una mocked; she had begun not to mind his accent so much. 'Do you have any olives?' It was a third-hand taste; Una had acquired it from the Chimeses, who had acquired it from Rosalie.

'In the closet. No, not that one, look in the one with my raincoat. There's a jar in the right pocket.'

'I bet you spent the whole afternoon in the supermarket,' Una accused, 'and then you say you never get any time to study. These are green. Don't you have any black?'

'It doesn't matter, the fat content is nearly the same. Oleo your bread, my dear, always oleo your bread.'

'You can't imagine the atmosphere over there, Boris. Everybody's so upset. Clement's stopped work on his book. He doesn't think he'll ever finish it now, he says he's lost the thread. Boris?'

'No, dear, no conversation, please, I'm on the spleen tonight. The spleen is a very complicated organ.'

'Boris, how long will Christina have to stay in the hospital?'

'Till Chichester lets her out. I suppose you forgot your toothbrush?'

'I brought it,' Una said dejectedly. 'I'm positive it's my fault she got sick in the first place.'

'You're not a microscopic organism, my sweet. It can be proved incontrovertibly by the presence of your thirty-two teeth. Brush them, dear, and go to sleep right away or you won't wake up on time to go home. It's my duty to inform you that you're still five pounds avoirdupois short of spending the night.'

But when Una got into Boris's bed he left his desk and started kissing her. She was rather surprised, because she was pretty sure he couldn't have progressed very far into his spleen.

'My luck,' Boris said with his little croak. 'For a mistress I have to pick a reader of the expurgated versions. Listen, my sweet, your Catullus was bowdlerized – the villains suppressed everything profitable, especially the best verbs. Now, hold the principal parts *so*,' and he kissed her once more. And then Una was surprised all over again – it turned out she liked it. She liked it so much, in fact, that Boris finally had to give it up. 'I don't want to keep you awake, my dear, or you won't be able to say you slept in Organski's bed. Well, Una,' he finished, 'anyhow I can tell you you're educable.'

'That's what Clement and Mary always say,' Una boasted, but dolefully. 'Poor Mary. If Christina has to stay in the hospital for very long she won't get her thesis done on time. Dr Chichester told them they'd better *be* in the hospital every day till the danger's over. Mary might even lose her degree. It's awful, that little perfect angel, all of a sudden such a fever and everything,' and, rather earlier than they had expected to, they walked home to the Chimeses, in gloom over Christina.

When Una opened the door she saw a terrible sight. Clement and Mary were at war. Mary's left temple was bleeding. Clement's shirt was ripped across the back. Mary was dashing from room to room, spitting at things, and Clement ran after her. His shouts were violent and dirty.

Mary spat on the tapestries, she fled from bookcase to bookcase, spitting on the shelves. She pulled down *The Princess Casamassima* and began tearing out handfuls of pages. Her hair fell down over her neck and her teeth blazed with spittle. 'Damn it all,' Mary said, 'damn it all, *I* was away all day, *you* were the one who was always home—' 'Crap on you, you're supposed to be the goddam *mother*, aren't you?' 'Derelict! Psychotic! Theologian!' Mary screamed, and for a moment a subtleness crept across her face. Then she whirled and seized a pile of records, trying to smash them with her shoe, but they were plastic and wouldn't break, so instead she hurled them in a black rain at Clement. Clement rushed at her shins and threw her over. They rolled and squirmed, pounding at one another – Clement was weeping, and a grid of long bright scratches was slowly bubbling red on Mary's arm. 'Great, tag *me* with the blame, that's just the point, where *were* you, left her to a fool, a nincompoop, that girl doesn't know her thumb from her bum, an idiot—' 'That's right, that's right, you've hit it,' Mary yelled, 'I left her with an idiot, I left her with you!'

Una was too stupefied to speak. A fight! Clement and Mary! Perfection!

She slipped out the door and raced down the street. Boris was trudging under the lamplight a block ahead of her. She ran and ran and caught up with him at last.

'Boris! I want to go back with you.'

'Go home, Una.'

'Boris, they're killing each other—'

'Unlikely. I eavesdropped for a second or so before boredom set in. Then I left. Go home.'

'I can't go back there, Boris, they've *never* been like that. Boris, I want to stay with you tonight.'

'I'm in no mood to collect rent, Una, go home to your friends.'

'Boris,' Una pleaded, 'aren't you my friend? Be my friend, I can't go back there! They're crazy, they're insane, they're *attacking* each other—'

'Each other, no. An attack, yes. An attack of guilt. Go home, Una, they'll be all right,' Boris said sadly. 'Let me have a look at you. No lipstick, a convenience. Why don't you ever wear any?'

'I don't know,' Una said. 'Mary doesn't either.'

'Mary's teeth stick out, she looks better without it. You should wear it,' he said critically. He drew her away from the light and kissed her under a tree. It was a new kind of kiss.

'It wasn't like that in bed before,' Una said wonderingly.

'Go home,' Boris groaned, but it was half an hour before he let her go.

The house was quiet. A lava of wreckage spread everywhere. The Chimeses were waiting.

'About time,' Clement greeted her. 'Good morning, good morning.'

Mary lay on the sofa face down. 'We *saw* you come in before. We both saw you.'

'We saw you slink out,' Clement said. His chin was swollen and his moustache was a ruin. 'You came in and you slunk right out again. We saw the whole thing.'

'Christina's in the hospital and all Una Meyer can find to do is neck all night with a Bulgarian,' Mary rasped into the upholstery. She shifted and sat up, and the bad spring snapped like the note of a bassoon.

'I'll be frank with you,' Clement said. 'Open and candid. We've been talking you over, Una. We've analysed exactly what you've done.'

'We've analysed what you are.'

'An exploiter,' Clement said.

'Exploiter,' said Mary. 'Manipulator.'

'When we asked you to come in halfies with us it was for your sake. Build up your ego and so forth. The Sorcerer's Apprentice, it turned out.' Clement scowled. 'We never dreamed you'd take over.'

'You took over everything.'

'The whole damn house.'

'The books.'

'The john.'

'The records.'

'The refrigerator.'

'The baby,' Mary said. 'You had her out in the middle of blizzards, you were always practically suffocating her trying to shut her up—'

'She was abused,' Clement said. 'We depended on you and you abused the kid. You abused our good faith. You took over, that's all.'

Una stared at the floor. A hassock had burst in the battle and there were peculiar cloud-bits stirring like little roaming mice.

'A matter of neglect,' Mary said bitterly. 'It began with Organski. After he started hanging around you could never keep your mind on anything. We told you he was no good.'

'He's *good*,' Una said. 'If not for Boris nobody would ever've found out what was wrong with Christina, it would've been worse—'

'*Could* it be worse?' Mary asked.

'Never mind, bunny, don't try talking decency to her. He's set her against us, that's the point.'

Una felt obscurely startled; she tasted salt. Then a wetness heated her nose, and she realized she had been crying all along.

'Isn't it a bit late for theatricals?' Mary said. 'The least you can do is clean up the place. Clement's shirt's in little pieces.'

'One thing you managed to do, my God, Rosalie at her worst never could. You even set the two of us against each *other*. Compared to you Rosalie was a goddam saint.'

Una put her arms behind her. 'I know it's my fault. Boris said it wasn't. I mean about Christina. But it really is my fault, I know it is,' and went on silently discharging tears.

'Maudlin!' Mary cried. 'That's the worst thing about you, it's disgusting the way you like to go on like that, it's just masochism. She's so *humble* it's sickening, a born martyr, always got her neck stuck out for the persecutors. Look, if you want somebody to make you suffer, go find your pal Boris.'

'Boris is good,' Una repeated stupidly.

'He's not serious,' Clement said. 'These medical types never are. I know what you want out of him, but forget it. He's no damn good, whatever you say. Mary and I spotted it the first time we set eyes on him, but you knew better. You never listened to anything. We used to think something could be done with you, you could be salvaged, but the material turned out to be weak. You're in shreds, Una. That man will never marry you.'

'She'll get what she deserves from that man,' Mary said.

'If he's as good as she thinks he'll give it to her good,' Clement said; and because this was rather witty, Una saw him suddenly smile.

VIII. Early in the morning the Chimeses went to the hospital. Una couldn't go with them; they told her only the parents were allowed. She washed the breakfast dishes and scrubbed Mary's blood off the sofa and swept the living room and heaped together a pile of broken plunder. Then she tried to read a little. It seemed to her years had passed since she had read anything at all. No book could interest her. She mooned into the study, looking for Clement's manuscript.

There it was finally: under a mound of newspapers on the table he had made for Mary out of the bathroom door. The first page said

SOCIAL CANCER

A DIAGNOSIS IN VERSE

AND ANGER

By Clement Chimes, MA

There was no second page.

The day was long and tedious. Una could think of nothing worth doing. At six o'clock she would have to go back to the hardware counter, but there were hours before that. She walked out to Boris's, and of course he wasn't home.

A family of young cockroaches filed out of a crack between two boards and ducked their tall antennae over the sill. Una wished she had a key. Then she wished she could slide under the door like the cockroaches. She squatted on the floor in front of Boris's apartment and waited for his classes to be done. It grew dark in the corridor, and cold. 'Oh Lord, a visitation,' Boris muttered when he found her, and they nuzzled their way into bed and kissed there all afternoon. Una was late for work, but she felt warm and almost plump; her lips and cheeks and breasts and arms felt warm and golden. Boris's key was in her pocket.

The next evening the hardware supervisor gave her a warning for two latenesses in a row; it was easy to get girls these days, he said.

The Chimeses scarcely spoke to her. Their mood was strange. In the mornings they seemed to float out to the hospital, not with anxiety, but as though anxiety was over. They couldn't tell Una much about Christina. She was better, they murmured – she was definitely better. Boris, who kept in touch with Dr Chichester, said nothing. Una was encouraged. Everyone struck her as optimistic – more than that, almost happy. The Chimeses' relief was clear. Boris rolled her all over his bed, laughing. By the end of the week she was fired, but the Chimeses only looked docile when Una told them she would have no money towards the rent.

She talked and talked to Boris. She talked to him about the Chimeses' queer enchanted gratitude. Day after day they passed through the hospital waiting rooms like scheming honeymooners. Afterwards the nurses told how their heads were always close. They were noticed because they were beautiful and because they lived on candy bars. Their vigil left them not haggard but fresh and radiant. Una remembered how Mary had once, and more than once, praised the science of soil chemistry: it had more to contribute to the fortunes of the underdeveloped nations than bloodless jurisprudence could. And it came to her how Clement often spoke of travelling to a country where all the inhabitants practised a totally unfamiliar religion, and how he always ended by twitting Una for throwing away her chance at diving into Turkey and the Koran. All along Mary had been bored and Clement jealous. They were relieved. They were glad to be interrupted. Fate had marred their perfect dedication and they did not despair. A brilliance stirred them. They were ready for something new.

By the beginning of the Chimeses' second hospital week Boris and Una were lovers in earnest, and in the middle of that same week Christina died. The sight of a small box handed down into a small ditch made Una think of a dog burying a bone. The young rabbi wore a crumpled bow tie. At the graveside he celebrated all students and intellectuals who do not neglect the duty of procreation – plainly it was his first funeral, and after it the Chimeses sold their books and left New Haven, and Una never saw them again.

IX. Sometimes she thought she read about them. A headline would say WOMAN JOINS PEACE CORPS TO GIVE HUSBAND SOME PEACE; it would be about a girl who went to Tanganyika while her husband sat home in the quiet to write a novel about corruption in the banking business, and Una would hunt down the column avidly to see the names, but it was always about someone else. Or she would hear of a couple adopted by an Indian tribe and living right on the reservation, teaching the elders Hochdeutsch and solid geometry – it wasn't Clement and Mary, though. Once she got wind of a young man who had left his wife, a beautiful and dark-haired agronomist working in Burma, to enter a Buddhist monastery, and she was positive this at last must be the Chimeses, repaired and reconverted by fresh educations. But when the story was finally printed in *Time*, the remarkable pair turned out to be Soviet citizens; they hailed from Pinsk.

'Forget about them,' Boris said, but she never could. She was always expecting the Chimeses to jump out at her from a newspaper, already famous.

'I've got their *card* catalogue, haven't I? What if they want to reconstitute their library some day? They'll need it.'

'They're no good,' Boris said.

'That's what they used to say about you.'

'Two rights don't make a wrong.'

'Ha ha,' Una sneered. 'They *were* wrong in one thing. They swore you'd never marry me.'

Boris sighed. 'After all they had a point.'

'No they didn't. They meant you'd never *want* to.'

'I want to, Una,' Boris said, and he asked her to marry him for the thousandth time. 'Why not? Why not? I don't see why you won't say yes. Really, Una, what're you worrying about? Everything would be just the same as it is now.'

'You're embarrassed,' Una accused. 'You're ashamed. Everybody knows about us and you can't stand it.'

'That caps it. Now look. Let's go over it again, all right? *I'm* not the one who cares; the hospitals do. How do you think I'm going to get a decent internship anywhere? In a first-class clinic? Who's going to take me? Enough is enough. Let's get married, Una.'

'Don't talk about everything being the same,' Una said. 'Everything's different already. *You're* not the same.'

'Neither are you. You're a lot dumber than you used to be. And a bit of a shrew. You don't have a thought in your head any more. You fuss over grease, you fuss over dust—'

'I'm not as educated as you are,' Una said meanly. 'I gave up my education for the sake of the Phillips screwdriver and the Yale lock.'

'I told you not to go back to that idiotic job.'

'Who paid the bill to have the place fumigated? Who paid for the kitchen paint? And I notice you don't mind eating,' Una said. 'You're more interested in eating than you are in me anyhow. You always were. The only thing you ever liked about me was watching me eat.'

'It's a lot less agonizing than watching you cook. Shrew,' Boris said, 'let's get married.'

'No.'

'Why the hell not? Finally and rationally, what've you got against it?'

'There's no education in it!' Una yelled.

'I don't want a mistress,' Boris said, 'I want a wife.'

In the end – but this was years later, and how it came about, what letters were written, how often and how many, who introduced whom: all this was long forgotten – Boris did get a wife. When Una visited the Organskis ten years after their marriage, Boris was unrecognizable, except for the length of his nose; Una thought to herself that he looked like a long-nosed hippopotamus. His little boy, though only seven years old, seemed more like the medical student she remembered; he was arrogant and charming, and kept her laughing. Mrs Organski was herself deliciously fat – but then she had always been fat, even in girlhood. She was newly widowed when Una got the idea that she would do nicely for Boris. Boris was now a psychiatrist. He had never stopped writing her his complicated, outrageous letters; he said he had finally come to understand that she was suffering from an ineradicable marriage-trauma. She had already been married vicariously; she had *lived* the Chimeses' marriage, she continued to believe in its perfection, and she was afraid she would fail to duplicate it. Now and again he offered to marry her in spite of everything.

Una finished her Ph.D. at a midwestern university; her old adviser and his wife and sons telegraphed an orchid. Her dissertation topic was 'The Influence of the Greek Middle Voice on Latin Prosody', and it required no travel, foreign or internal. By a horrid coincidence she joined the faculty of a small college in Turkey, New York. All her colleagues were invincibly domesticated. They gave each other little teas and frequent dinner parties. Occasionally they invited some of the more intelligent teachers from the high school that bordered the campus. One of these turned out to be a Mrs Orenstein, who taught social studies. Una and Mrs Orenstein fell into one another's arms, and left the party early to reminisce in privacy. Mrs Orenstein chafed her short fingers and told how Mr Orenstein, a popular phys. ed. teacher, had been killed six months before in a terrible accident in the gym. Demonstrating a belly grind, he slipped off the parallel bars. The rest of the night they talked about the Chimeses. Mrs Orenstein had heard from someone that Clement had become a dentist; an accountant from someone else; but she didn't know whether either was true. There was a rumour that Mary was with the State Department; another that Mary had become a nun and Clement a pimp for the Argentinian consul's brother-in-law. What was definite was that they lived in Washington; maybe they lived in Washington; they were both teaching astronomy at UCLA; they had no children; they had six girls and a boy; Mary was in prison; Clement was dead.

Finally Mrs Orenstein asked Una why she had never married. Una thought the question rude and deflected it: 'If you ever want to get married again, Rosalie, I have just the person. He'd like everything about you. Clement and Mary always used to say you were a good cook anyhow.'

'I hated them,' Rosalie said. 'I hate them right now when I think about them, don't you?'

'I don't know,' Una said. 'I used to, but Boris mixed me up about them years ago. Just before I met Boris I was really hating them. I was a rotten hypocrite in those days. Then the baby died and they blamed me, so I started feeling sorry for them. The more Boris showed them up for selfish and shallow and all that, and not awfully bright after all, the more I began to see that they *had* something anyhow. I mean they kept themselves intact. They had *that*.'

Rosalie snorted. 'Anybody could see right through them.'

'Well, what of it?' Una said. 'It didn't matter. You could see through them and they were wonderful all the same, just *because* you could see through them. They were like a bubble that never broke, you could look right through and they kept on shining no matter what. They're the only persons I've ever known who stayed the same from start to finish.'

'I don't follow any of that,' Rosalie said. 'Who's this Boris?'

Una laughed furiously. 'Rosalie, Rosalie, aren't you listening? Boris is your second husband.'

She waited a decade before she dared to visit them; she was forty-two years old. She had trouble with her gums, had lost some teeth, and wore movable bridges. 'Has anybody ever heard anything about the Chimeses?' No one had.

'Ding dong,' said the new Organski daughter, and everyone smiled.

Oddly enough the visit was a success. She observed the Organskis' marriage. They had a full and heavy table, and served three desserts: first pudding, then fruit, then cake and tea. The two children would plainly never turn out to be extraordinary. Boris's accent was as bad as ever. Rosalie let the dust build; she quarrelled with all her cleaning women. The house held no glory and no wars.

Rosalie asked Una to come again, and she accepted, but only with her lips. Inwardly she refused. It wasn't that she any longer resented imperfection, but it seemed to her unendurable that her education should go on and on and on.

From a Refugee's Notebook

Redactor's Comment: These fragments, together with the above unprepossessing title, were found (in a purple-covered spiral tablet of the kind used by university students of an earlier generation and in another country behind a mirror in a vacant room-for-rent on West 106th Street, New York City. The author, of European or perhaps South American origin, remains unidentified.

I. Freud's room

Not long ago they turned Freud's house in Vienna into a museum, but few visitors come. It is even hard to know it is there: the big hotels don't list it on their bulletin boards, no one thinks of it as part of the tourist circuit. If you want to find it, the only place to ask is at the police station.

I have not been there myself (I do not go to any land which once suckled the Nazi boot), but I have dreamed over photographs of those small rooms where Sigmund Freud wrote his treatises and met with his patients and kept, in a glass case, his collection of ancient stone animals and carved figurines. There is a picture of Freud sitting at his desk, looking downwards through dark-rimmed perfectly round lenses at a manuscript; behind him is the shining case with a good-sized camel, wood or stone, on top of it, and a great Grecian urn to the side. There are a wall of books, a vase of pussy willows, and on every shelf and surface cups, goblets, beasts, and hundreds of those strange little gods.

The museum, I suppose, is clear now of all that Egyptian debris, unless somehow it has all been brought back to fill the emptiness of the refugee's rooms.

In another of these famous photographs there is a curious juxtaposition. The picture is divided exactly in two by a lamp pole. On the left there is the crowd of stone godlets, on the right the couch on which Freud's patients lay during analysis. The wall behind the couch is covered by a Persian carpet hung in lieu of a tapestry; the couch itself is draped, in a heavy, ugly way, by another carpet hiding a hump of bolster beneath it and wearing a soft flat velveteen pillow as a kind of depressed beret. The very centre of the picture is occupied by the low plush armchair in which Freud himself sat. The arms of the chair look worn, the whole small space seems cramped by so many objects, so many picture frames dangling in clumsy disorder up and down and across the wall behind the armchair and the couch. In one of the frames, under glass, the flanks of a greyhound dog glimmer. All this, of course, is what we have come to think of as Victorian clutter, and one pities the housemaid who came timidly in with her perilous duster. Yet if you take a second look, there is no clutter. Everything in the room is necessary: the couch and the gods. Even the slim dog who runs and yelps on the wall.

Especially the gods. The gods, the gods!

It is not the juxtaposition you suppose. What you are thinking is this: these primitive stone things, ranged like small determined marchers on shelves and tables (is it not amazing how many of them have one foot thrust forward, like the men who marched afterwards in Vienna, or is it simply that the sculptor requires this posture for balance, else his god would shatter?) – these stone things, then, represent the deep primitive grain of the mind Freud sought. The woman or man on the couch was an archaeological enterprise – layer after layer to be spaded and sifted through, ever so delicately as archaeologists do, with feather brush, like the maid who slips in every morning to touch the top of each stone head with a sculptor's tender fear of despoiling the very matter the god-spirit has entrusted to him.

(The German word for matter is excellent, and illumines our English usage: *der Stoff*. Stuff. As in: the stuff of the universe. The wonder of the term is its thinginess. The awesome little gods in Freud's consulting room are matter, stuff, crumbs of rock; rubble.)

No, the juxtaposition I am thinking of is not merely the tangency of primitive with primitive. It is something else. The proliferation of gods, in mobs and bevies, the carpets with their diamond and flower figures, their languid tassels drooping down, the heavy figured table shawl with even longer fringes, over which a handful of gods blindly parade, the varnished brown wood frames, the vases curved and straight-sided, the libation cups standing dry, the burdensome tomes with their oppressive squatness mimicking pyramids – it is the room of a king.

The breath of this room drones with dreams of a king who lusts to become a god absolute as stone. The dreams that rise up from couch and armchair mix and braid in the air: the patient recounts her dream of a cat, signifying the grimness of a bad mother, and behind this dream, lurking in the doctor, is the doctor's dream. The gods walking over the long-fringed table shawl have chosen their king.

Respected reader: if I seem to be saying that Sigmund Freud wished to be a god, do not mistake me. I am no poet, and despise metaphors. I am a literal-minded person. I have no patience with figures of speech. Music is closed to me, and of art I have seen little. I have suffered the harsh life of a refugee and have made my living in bolts of cloth. I am familiar with texture: I can, with eyes shut, tell you which is rayon and which silk, which the genuine wool and which the synthetic, which pure nylon and which graduated towards cotton, which the coarse lace and which the fine. My whole bent is towards the tangible and the palpable. I know the difference between what is there and what is not there; between the empty and the full. I have nothing to do with make-believe.

I tell you that Sigmund Freud wished to become a god.

Some few men in history have wished it and would, but for mortality, have achieved it – some by tyranny: the Pharaohs indisputably, and also that Louis who was Sun King of France. Some by great victories: Napoleon and Hannibal. Some by chess: those world masters who murder in effigy the potent queens of their imaginings. Some by novel-writing: that conquistador Tolstoy who used only himself, costumed and dyed, under other names, and his aunties and his brothers and his poor wife Sonya (pragmatic and sensible like myself). Some by medicine and dentistry, wizardries of prosthesis and transplantation.

But others scheming to become gods utilize another resource altogether. Kings, generals, chess masters, surgeons, even those who wreak immense works of imagination – their resources are ultimately their sanity; their sobriety; their bourgeois probity. (Bourgeois? The sacred monarchs too? Yes; to live a decent life in dynastic Egypt, with food not likely to fester, clean drains, and comfortable beds, it was necessary to own ten thousand slaves.) The notion of the mad genius is a foolish and false commonplace. Ambition sniffs out the grain of logic and possibility. Genius summons up not grotesqueries but verisimilitudes: the lifelike, the anti-magical. Whoever seeks to become an earthly god must follow the earth itself.

Some few do not. At least two have not. The inventor of the Sabbath – call him Moses if you wish – declared the cycle of the earth null. What do the birds, the worms their prey, the corn in the field, men and animals who sleep and wake up hungry, know of a Sabbath, this arbitrary call to make a stop in the diurnal rhythm, to move consciously apart from the natural progression of days? It is only God, standing apart from nature, who tells nature to cease, who causes miracles, who confounds logic.

After Moses, Freud. They are not alike. What the Sabbath and its emanations sought to suppress, Freud meant to reveal: everything barbarous and dreadful and veiled and terror-bearing: the very tooth and claw. What the roiling half-savage village Christianity of the Dark Ages called Hell, Freud called Id, which he similarly described as a 'cauldron'. And just as the village priest with a gift for the drama of fright peopled Hell with this and that demon, Beelzebub, Eblis, Apollyon, Mephisto, those curiously-named assistants or doubles of Satan, so Freud peopled the Unconscious with the devils of Id and Ego and Superego, potent dancing ghosts who cavort unrecorded in our anatomies while we pretend they are not there. And this too is to go against the diurnal rhythm of things. Nature does not stop to suspect itself of daily subterfuge. Inventing such a stop, Freud imposed on all our surface coherencies a Sabbath of the soul.

Which is to moon over the obvious: Freud was lured by what was clearly not 'sane'. The draw of the irrational has its own deep question: how much is research, how much search? Is the scientist, the intelligent physician, the sceptical philosopher who is attracted to the irrational, himself a rational being? How explain the attraction? I think of that majestic scholar of Jerusalem sitting in his university study composing, with bookish distance and objectivity, volume after volume on the history of Jewish mysticism . . . is there an objective 'scientific interest' or is all interest a snare? And Freud: is the student of the dream-life – that subterranean grotto all drowned and darkling, torn with the fury of anguish and lust – is the student of the dream-life not himself a lovesick captive of it? Is the hidden cauldron not an enticement and a seduction to its inventor? Is the doctor of the Unconscious not likely to be devoured by his own creation, like that rabbi of Prague who constructed a golem?

Or, to say it even more terribly: it may be that the quarry is all the time in the pursuer.

[Here the first fragment ends.]

II. The Sewing Harems

It was for a time the fashion on the planet Acirema for the more sophisticated females to form themselves into Sewing Harems. Each Sewing Harem would present itself for limited rental, in a body, to a rich businessman capable of housing it in a suitably gracious mansion or tasteful duplex apartment or roomy ranch or luxurious penthouse. Prices ran high. The typical Sewing Harem could be had for a little over seventy-five thousand dollars, but hiring one of these groups was splendidly prestigious, and was worth sacrificing foreign travel for, a new car, or even college for one's children.

What the Sewing Harems sewed was obvious. Do not visualize quilting bees, samplers, national flags.

What I have failed to mention so far is that the atmosphere of this planet contained a profusion of imperva molecules, which had the property of interacting with hormonal chemistry in such a way as to allow the women of that place to sew their own bodies with no anguish whatsoever. Imperva molecules had been present only since the last ice age, and their inherent volatility offered no guarantee that they could withstand the temperature assaults of the next ice age; but since no one was predicting a new ice age, and since the last one had been over for at least a hundred million years, no immediate atmospheric peril was anticipated.

Once rented, the Sewing Harem would incarcerate itself in comfortable chambers, feast abundantly but privately, and rest prodigiously. After a day or so of hungerless inactivity, the sewing would begin.

There was considerable virtuosity in the style of stitches, but the most reliable, though not the most aesthetic, was the backstitch, which consists of two, sometimes three, running stitches, the final one repeated over upon itself. One woman would sew another, with the most cooperative cheerfulness imaginable, though occasionally an agile woman – an athlete or acrobat or dancer – managed, with fastidious poise, in exquisite position, to sew herself.

There was, as I have explained, no anguish in the flesh. Still, there was the conventional bleeding while the needle penetrated again and again, and the thread, whatever colour was used, had to be tugged along swollen by wet blood, so that the whole length of it was finally dyed dark red. Healing took the usual week or so, and then the man who had leased the Sewing Harem was admitted to try whatever licentious pleasure his fancy and theirs could invent – except, of course, bodily entry. Inaccessibility increased wit, discrimination, manoeuvrability, and intellectuality on both sides.

The terms of the rental did not allow for snipping open stitches.

At the close of the rental period (between three and six months), a not insignificant number of the women would have become pregnant. How this could have happened I leave to the reader's nimble imagination, but surely in several instances stitches had been opened in defiance of contractual obligations, and perhaps even with the complicity and connivance of the women in question.

The terms of rental further stipulated that should any children be born to any of the women as a consequence of the activity of the leasing period, said children would be held in common by all the women: each one, equal with every other, would be designated as mother.

Now it should be immediately evident that all of this was far, far less than ordinary custom. The lighthearted hiring of Sewing Harems was practised in a number of the great cities of that planet, but could be found hardly at all in the underdeveloped countries. The formation of Sewing Harems – or so it was charged by the Left and the Right – was the fad of the self-indulgent and the irrepressibly reckless. Not altogether so: since after the period of the lease expired, the members of each Sewing Harem, in their capacity as equal mothers, often attempted to remain together, and to continue as a serious social body, in order to raise its children intelligently.

Given the usual temperamental difficulties, the peregrinations of restless individuals, the nomadic habits of the group as a whole, and the general playfulness (their own word being the more ironic 'frivolousness') of the membership, a Sewing Harem was frequently known to disband not many years after the nearly simultaneous birth of its children.

But the chief reason for the dissolution of a Sewing Harem was jealousy over the children. The children were few, the mothers many. Each child was everyone's child in the mind of the community, but by no means in the mind of the child. At first the babies were kept together in a compound, and all the mothers had equal access to them for dandling, rocking, and fondling. But of course only the mothers who could breastfeed were at all popular with the babies, since the theorists of these societies, who had a strong and authoritative caucus, frowned on bottles. Consequently, the mothers who had not experienced parturition, and who had no breast-milk, were avoided by the babies, and soon the community of mothers began to be divided into those the babies preferred and those the babies shunned; or, into milkers and non-milkers; or, into elite mothers and second-class mothers.

Somehow, even after the children were weaned, the original classifications persisted, causing depression among the second-class mothers.

As the children grew older, moreover, it was discovered that they *interrupted*. By now, several of the second-class mothers, feeling disappointed, had gone off to join other Sewing Harems just then in the process of putting themselves out for rental. And only these defeated mothers, by virtue of being no longer on the scene, were not interrupted. All the rest were. It was found that the children interrupted careers, journeys, appointments, games, telephone calls, self-development, education, meditation, sexual activity, and other enlightened, useful, and joyous pursuits. But since the children were all being brought up with the highest self-expectations, they believed themselves to be ('as indeed you are,' the mothers told them) in every way central to the community.

They believed this, in spite of their understanding that, morally and philosophically, they had no right to exist. Morally: each one had been conceived by breach of contract. Philosophically: each one had been born to a mother theoretically committed to the closure of the passage leading to the womb. In brief, the children knew that they were the consequence of unpredictable deviations from a metaphysical position; or, to state it still more succinctly, the fruit of snipped stitches.

That the children interrupted the personal development of the mothers was difficulty enough. In a less dialectical community, there might have been a drive towards comfortable if imperfect solutions. But these were (as it ought by now to be radiantly clear) no ordinary women. Ordinary women might have taken turns in caring for the children, or hired men and other women for this purpose, or experimented with humane custodial alternatives. A Sewing Harem, however, was a community of philosophers. And just as bottle-feeding had been condemned as an inferior compromise, so now were the various permutations of day-care proposals scorned. Each child was regarded as the offspring not simply of a single philosopher, but of a community of philosophers; hence not to be subjected to rearing by hirelings, or by any arrangement inferior to the loftiest visions of communal good.

As for taking turns, though it might be fair, it was inconceivable: just as each child was entitled to the highest self-expectation without compromise, so was each philosopher entitled to the highest self-development without compromise or interruption.

The children as they grew not only interrupted the mothers; they interfered with the mothers' most profound ideals. The blatant fact of the birth of a large group of children hindered ecological reform, promoted pollution, and frustrated every dramatic hope of rational population reduction. In short, the presence of the children was anti-progressive. And since not only joy and self-development, but also friendship and truth, were the dearest doctrines of a Sewing Harem, the children were made to understand that, in spite of their deserving the highest self-expectations, they represented nevertheless the most regressive forces on the planet.

It is hardly necessary to note, given the short life of any novelty, that by the time the children became adults, the fad of the Sewing Harems had virtually died out (excepting, now and then, an occasional nostalgic revival). Not surprisingly, the term 'Harem' itself was by now universally repudiated as regressive and repugnant, despite the spirited voluntarism and economic self-sufficiency of the original societies. But the historic influence of those early societies was felt throughout the planet.

Everywhere, including the most backward areas, women were organizing themselves for sewing, with the result, of course, that there were fewer and fewer natural mothers and more and more adoptive mothers. The elitist distinctions observed by the founding groups no longer pertained, and were, in fact, reversed by the overwhelming vote of the underdeveloped countries. Devotion to egalitarian principles put the sewn majority in the saddle; and since the majority were adoptive mothers, or women whose lives were peripheral to children, or women who had nothing to do with children at all, natural motherhood (though it continued to be practised, with restraint, in all circles except the very literary) was little noticed and less remarked on, neither as neurosis nor as necessity. It was neither patronized nor demeaned, and it was certainly not persecuted. It was not much on anyone's mind.

It goes without saying that society at large instantly improved. The planet took on a tidier appearance: more room for gardens and trees, a diminution of garbage and poverty, fewer smoky factories, highways decently uncrowded for a holiday drive. In the international sphere, matters were somewhat less satisfactory, at least in the view of the men and women who ran the planet. Though the wicked remained dominant, as always, it was not much worthwhile making wars any more, since in any conflict it is preferable that vast and vaster quantities of lives be butchered, and the numbers of young soldiers available for losing the bottom halves of their torsos went on diminishing.

To put it as briefly and delightfully as possible: the good (those self-respecting individuals who did not intend to waste their years) had greater opportunities to add to their goodness via self-improvement and self-development, the wicked were thwarted, and the planet began to look and smell nicer than anyone had ever expected.

And all this was the legacy of a handful of Sewing Harems which had once been dismissed as a self-indulgent ideological fad.

Meanwhile, something rather sad had happened, though it applied only to a nearly imperceptible minority and seldom drew anyone's constructive attention.

The children of the Sewing Harems had become pariahs. How this occurred is of not much interest: whether they were regarded as a laughing-stock anachronism, the spawn of geishas, scions of an anti-quated and surely comical social contrivance, the very reminder of which was an embarrassment to the modern temper; whether they were taken as the last shameful relic of an aggressively greedy entrepreneurial movement; whether they were scorned as personalities mercilessly repressed by the barbaric extremes of the communal impulse; whether they were damned as the offspring of the pornographic imagination; whether they were jeered at as the deformed cubs of puritanical bluestockings; whether all of these or none, no one can rightly say.

Sociologists with enough curiosity to look into the origins of the sect pointed, predictably, to their upbringing: they were taught that they were at the root of the planet's woes, and yet they were taught that they had earned not one, but many, mothers. As a consequence of the first teaching, they fulfilled themselves as irrational demons and turned themselves into outcasts. As a consequence of the second teaching, they idolized motherhood.

You will have noticed that I have referred to these unfortunates as a 'sect'. This is exactly true. They were content to marry only one another; or, perhaps, no one else was content to marry any of *them*. Since numbers of them had the same father, or the same natural mother, or both, they were already afflicted with the multitudinous ills of inbreeding, and their fierce adherence to endogamy compounded these misfortunes. They had harelips, limps, twisted jaws and teeth, short arms, diseases of the blood, hereditary psychoses; some were wretchedly strabismic, others blind or deaf. They were an ugly, anxious, stern-minded crew, continually reproducing themselves.

Any woman of the sect who sewed herself they would kill; but this was generally unheard of among them, since sewing was their most ferocious taboo. Male babies born in any way sexually deformed were admitted to early surgery, but female babies born with unusually small or sealed vaginas were fed cyanide. The only remaining resemblance to the gaily lucid and civilizing Sewing Harems from which these savages derived was their prohibition of bottle-feeding.

They were organized into strong family units, and emphasized family orderliness and conventionality. All this was within the tribe. Otherwise they were likely to be criminals – members of the sect were frequently convicted of having murdered sewn women. If they had any gift at all, it was for their indulgence in unusual art forms. They had a notorious talent for obscene stonecutting.

Worst of all was their religious passion. They had invented a Superior Goddess: a single unimaginative and brutish syllable of three letters, two of them identical, formed her name – ingenious nonetheless, since it was a palindrome, pronounced identically whether chanted forward or backward. The goddess was conceived as utterly carnal, with no role other than to nurture the urge to spawn; under her base auspices the tribe spewed forth dozens of newborn savages in a single day.

In addition to murdering sewn women, the descendants of the Sewing Harems were guilty of erecting religious statuary on highways in the dead of night. These appeared in the likenesses of immense round gate-pillars, which, looming without warning in the blaze of day where there had been nothing the evening before, were the cause of multiple bloody traffic accidents. The best were carved out of enormous rocks quarried no one knew where, hauled on trucks, and set in place by cranes. The cheapest were made of concrete, mixed on the spot, and left to dry behind sawhorses hung with bright rags. In police reports these structures were usually described as mammary replicas; in actuality they had the shapes of huge vulvae. Sometimes the corpse of a sewn woman, stinking of some foul incense, a shiny magazine picture of an infant nailed into her thigh, would be found between the high walls of the two horrendous labia.

I have already remarked that these primitives did not number significantly in the general population (though they were disproportionately present in the prison population). They were pests, rather than a pestilence, and their impact on the planet would without doubt have continued negligible had the imperva molecules not suddenly begun first to deteriorate in the skies, and then to disintegrate entirely. All this was inexplicable; until now every firm scientific expectation was that no such dissolution could occur except under the climatic threat of a new ice age. Such a comment was always taken for a joke. In point of fact it remained a joke. There were no extraordinary atmospheric upheavals; the normal temperature of the planet was undisturbed.

But it became of course impossible for women to sew themselves as casually, uncomplicatedly, and joyfully as they had been capable of doing for immemorial generations – ever since, in fact, that planet's version of Eden: a humane Eden, incidentally, which had passed on no unkind-nesses or encumbrances, whether to women or to men.

And because of irresistible advances in technology, the vulval thread had been so improved (composed of woven particles of infertels encased in plastic, it could now withstand blood-dye) that the stitches could not be undone, except by the most difficult and dangerous surgery, which the majority eschewed, because of the side effects of reversed infertels when they are burst. The treacherous stitch-snipping of the Sewing Harems, so long a subject of mockery and infamy among those who admired both progress and honest commitment, was all at once seen to be a lost treasure of the race.

Nearly all of the sewn women remained sewn until their deaths.

And the pariahs, the only source of mothers, bred like monkeys in their triumph, until the great stone vulvae covered the planet from end to end, and the frivolous memory of the Sewing Harems was rubbed away, down to the faintest smear of legend.

[Here ends the second fragment.]

Helping T. S. Eliot Write Better

(Notes Towards a Definitive Bibliography)

It is not yet generally known to the world of literary scholarship that an early version of T. S. Eliot's celebrated poem, 'The Love Song of J. Alfred Prufrock', first appeared in *The New Shoelace*, an impoverished publication of uncertain circulation located on East Fifteenth Street in New York City. Eliot, then just out of Harvard, took the train down from Boston carrying a mottled manila envelope. He wore slip-on shoes with glossy toes. His long melancholy cheeks had the pallor associated in those days with experimental poets.

The New Shoelace was situated on the top floor of an antique factory building. Eliot ascended in the elevator with suppressed elation; his secret thought was that, for all he knew, the young Henry James, fastidiously fingering a book review for submission, might once have entered this very structure. The brick walls smelled of old sewing-machine oil. The ropes of the elevator, visible through a hole in its ceiling, were frayed and slipped occasionally; the car moved languidly, groaning. On the seventh floor Eliot emerged. The deserted corridor, with its series of shut doors, was an intimidating perplexity. He passed three with frosted glass panels marked by signs: BIALY'S WORLDWIDE NEEDLES; WARSHOWER WOOL TRADING CORP.; and MEN. Then came the exit to the fire escape. *The New Shoelace*, Eliot reasoned, must be in the opposite direction. MONARCH BOX CO.; DIAMOND'S LIGHTING FIXTURES – ALL NEW DESIGNS; MAX'S THIS-PLANET-ONLY TRAVEL SERVICE; YANKELO-WITZ'S ALL-COLOR BRAID AND TRIM; LADIES. And there, at the very end of the passage, tucked into a cul-de-sac, was the office of *The New Shoelace*. The manila envelope had begun to tremble in the young poet's grip. Behind that printed title reigned Firkin Barmuenster, editor.

In those far-off days, *The New Shoelace*, though very poor, as its shabby furnishings readily attested, was nevertheless in possession of a significant reputation. Or, rather, it was Firkin Barmuenster who had the reputation. Eliot was understandably cowed. A typist in a fringed scarf sat huddled over a tall black machine, looking rather like a recently oppressed immigrant out of steerage, swatting the keys as if they were flies. Five feet from the typist's cramped table loomed Firkin Barmuenster's formidable desk, its surface hidden under heaps of butter-spotted manuscript, odoriferous paper bags, and porcelain-coated tin mugs chipped at their rims. Firkin Barmuenster himself was nowhere to be seen.

The typist paused in her labours. 'Help you?'

'I am here,' Eliot self-consciously announced, 'to offer something for publication.'

'F. B. stepped out a minute.'

'May I wait?'

'Suit yourself. Take a chair.'

The only chair on the horizon, however, was Firkin Barmuenster's own, stationed forbiddingly on the other side of the awe-inspiring desk. Eliot stood erect as a sentry, anticipating the footsteps that at last resounded from the distant terminus of the corridor. Firkin Barmuenster, Eliot thought, must be returning from the door marked MEN. Inside the manila envelope in Eliot's fevered grasp 'The Love Song of J. Alfred Prufrock' glowed with its incontrovertible promise. One day, Eliot felt sure, it would be one of the most famous poems on earth, studied by college freshmen and corporate executives on their way up. Only now there were these seemingly insurmountable obstacles: he, Tom Eliot, was painfully young, and even more painfully obscure; and Firkin Barmuenster was known to be ruthless in his impatience with bad writing. Eliot believed in his bones that 'Prufrock' was not bad writing. He hoped that Firkin Barmuenster would be true to his distinction as a great editor, and would be willing to bring out Eliot's proud effort in the pages of *The New Shoelace*. The very ink-fumes that rose up out of the magazine excited Eliot and made his heart fan more quickly than ever. Print!

'Well, well, what have we here?' Firkin Barmuenster inquired, settling himself behind the mounds that towered upwards from the plateau of his desk, and reaching into one of the paper bags to extract a banana.

'I've written a poem,' Eliot said.

'We don't mess with any of those,' Firkin Barmuenster growled. 'We are a magazine of opinion.'

'I realize that,' Eliot said, 'but I've noticed those spaces you sometimes leave at the bottom of your articles of opinion, and I thought that might be a good place to stick in a poem, since you're not using that space for anything else anyhow. Besides,' Eliot argued in conciliatory fashion, 'my poem also expresses an opinion.'

'Really? What on?'

'If you wouldn't mind taking half a second to look at it—'

'Young man,' Firkin Barmuenster barked rapidly, 'let me tell you the kind of operation we run here. In the first place, these are modern times. We're talking 1911, not 1896. What we care about here are up-to-date issues. Politics. Human behaviour. Who rules the world, and how. No wan and sickly verses, you follow?'

'I believe, sir,' Eliot responded with grave courtesy, 'that I own an entirely new Voice.'

'Voice?'

'Experimental, you might call it. Nobody else has yet written this way. My work represents a revolt from the optimism and cheerfulness of the last century. Dub it wan and sickly if you will – it is, if you don't mind my blowing my own horn' – but here he lowered his eyes to prove to Firkin Barmuenster that he was aware of how painfully young, and painfully obscure, he was – 'an implicit declaration that poetry must not only be found *through* suffering, but can find its own material only *in* suffering. I insist,' he added even more shyly, 'that the poem should be able to see beneath both beauty and ugliness. To see the boredom, and the horror, and the glory.'

'I like what you say about the waste of all that white space,' Firkin Barmuenster replied, growing all at once thoughtful. 'All right, let's have a look. What do you call your jingle?'

'"The Love Song of J. Alfred Prufrock".'

'Well, that won't do. Sit down, will you? I can't stand people standing, didn't my girl tell you that?'

Eliot looked around once again for a chair. To his relief, he spied a high stool just under the single grimy window, which gave out onto a bleak airshaft. A stack of back issues of *The New Shoelace* was piled on it. As he gingerly removed them, placing them with distaste on the sooty sill, the cover of the topmost magazine greeted Eliot's eye with its tedious headline: MONARCHY VS. ANARCHY – EUROPE'S POLITICAL DILEMMA. This gave poor Tom Eliot a pang. Perhaps, he reflected fleetingly, he had brought his beloved 'Prufrock' to the wrong crossroads of human aspiration. How painfully young and obscure he felt! Still, a novice must begin somewhere. Print! He was certain that a great man like Firkin Barmuenster (who had by then finished his banana) would sense unusual new talent.

'Now, Prudecock, show me your emanation,' Firkin Barmuenster demanded, when Eliot had dragged the stool over to the appropriate spot in front of the editor's redoubtable desk.

'Prufrock, sir. But I'm Eliot.' Eliot's hands continued to shake as he drew the sheets of 'Prufrock' from the mottled manila envelope.

'Any relation to that female George?' Firkin Barmuenster freely associated companionably, so loudly that the fringed typist turned from her clatter to stare at her employer for a single guarded moment.

'It's *Tom*,' Eliot said; inwardly he burned with the ignominy of being so painfully obscure.

'I like that. I appreciate a plain name. We're in favour of clarity here. We're straightforward. Our credo is that every sentence is either right or wrong, exactly the same as a sum. You follow me on this, George?'

'Well,' Eliot began, not daring to correct this last slip of the tongue (Freud was not yet in his heyday, and it was too soon for the dark significance of such an error to have become public knowledge), 'actually it is my belief that a sentence is, if I may take the liberty of repeating myself, a kind of Voice, with its own suspense, its secret inner queries, its chancy idiosyncrasies and soliloquies. Without such a necessary view, one might eunuchize, one might neuter—'

But Firkin Barmuenster was already buried in the sheets of 'Prufrock'. Eliot watched the steady rise and fall of his smirk as he read on and on. For the first time, young Tom Eliot noticed Barmuenster's style of dress. A small trim man lacking a moustache but favoured with oversized buff teeth and grizzled hair the colour of ash, Barmuenster wore a checkered suit of beige and brown, its thin red pinstripe running horizontally across the beige boxes only; his socks were a romantic shade of robin's egg blue, and his shoes, newly and flawlessly heeled, were maroon with white wing-tips. He looked more like a professional golfer down on his luck than a literary man of acknowledged stature. Which, Eliot mused, was more representative of Barmuenster's intellectual configuration – his sartorial preferences or the greasy paper bags under his elbows? It was impossible to decide.

Firkin Barmuenster kept reading. The typist went on smacking imaginary flies. Eliot waited.

'I confess,' Firkin Barmuenster said slowly, raising his lids to confront the pallid face of the poet, 'that I didn't expect anything this good. I like it, my boy, I like it!' He hesitated, gurgling slightly, like a man who has given up pipe-smoking once and for all. And indeed, Eliot spied two or three well-chewed abandoned pipes in the tumbler that served as pencil-holder; the pencils, too, were much bitten. 'You know our policy on fee, of course. After we get finished paying Clara and the rent and the sweeping up and the price of an occasional banana, there's not much left for the writer, George – only the glory. I know that's all right with you, I know you'll understand that what we're chiefly interested in is preserving the sanctity of the writer's text. The text is holy, it's holy writ, that's what it is. We'll set aside the title for a while, and put our minds to it later. What's the matter, George? You look speechless with gratitude.'

'I never hoped, sir – I mean, I *did* hope, but I didn't think—'

'Let's get down to business, then. The idea is excellent, first-rate, but there's just a drop too much repetition. You owned up to that yourself a minute ago. For instance, I notice that you say, over here,

> In the room the women come and go
> Talking of Michelangelo,

and then, over *here*, on the next page, you say it again.'

'That's meant to be a kind of *refrain*,' Eliot offered modestly.

'Yes, *I* see that, but our subscribers don't have *time* to read things twice. We've got a new breed of reader nowadays. Maybe back, say, in 1896 they had the leisure to read the same thing twice, but our modern folks are on the run. I see you're quite addicted to the sin of redundancy. Look over here, where you've got

> "I am Lazarus, come back from the dead,
> Come back to tell you all, I shall tell you all"—
> If one, settling a pillow by her head,
>> Should say: "That is not what I meant at all;
>> That is not it, at all."

Very nice, but that reference to the dead coming back is just too iffy. I'd drop that whole part. The pillow, too. You don't need that pillow; it doesn't do a thing *for* you. And anyhow you've said "all" four times in a single place. That won't do. It's sloppy. And who uses the same word to make a rhyme? Sloppy!' Barmuenster iterated harshly, bringing his fist down heavily on the next banana, peeled and naked, ready for the eating. 'Now this line down here, where you put in

No! I am not Prince Hamlet, nor was meant to be,

well, the thing to do about that is let it go. It's no use dragging in the Bard every time you turn around. You can't get away with that sort of free ride.'

'I thought,' Eliot murmured, wondering (ahead of his time) whether banana-craving could somehow be linked to pipe-deprivation, 'it would help show how Prufrock feels about himself—'

'Since you're saying he *doesn't* feel like Hamlet, why put Hamlet *in*? We can't waste words, not in 1911 anyhow. Now up here, top of the page, you speak of

> *a pair of ragged claws*
> *scuttling across the floor of silent seas.*

Exactly what kind of claws are they? Lobster claws? Crab? Precision, my boy, precision!'

'I just meant to keep it kind of general, for the atmosphere—'

'If you *mean* a crustacean, *say* a crustacean. At *The New Shoelace* we don't deal in mere metonymy.'

'Feeling is a kind of meaning, too. Metaphor, image, allusion, lyric form, melody, rhythm, tension, irony, above all the objective correlative—' But poor Tom Eliot broke off lamely as he saw the older man begin to redden.

'Tricks! Wool-pullers! Don't try to tell Firkin Barmuenster about the English language. I've been editing *The New Shoelace* since before you were born, and I think by now I can be trusted to know how to clean up a page of words. I like a clean page, I've explained that. I notice you have a whole lot of question marks all over, and they go up and down the same ground again and again. You've got *So how should I presume?* and then you've got *And how should I presume?* and after that you've got *And should*

I presume? You'll just have to decide on how you want that and then keep to it. People aren't going to make allowances for you forever, you know, just because you're painfully young. And you shouldn't put in so many question marks anyhow. You should use nice clean declarative sentences. Look at this, for instance, just look at what a mess you've got here—

> *I grow old . . . I grow old . . .*
> *I shall wear the bottoms of my trousers rolled.*
>
> *Shall I part my hair behind? Do I dare to eat a peach?*
> *I shall wear white flannel trousers and walk upon the beach.*
> *I have heard the mermaids singing, each to each.*

That won't *do* in a discussion of the ageing process. There you go repeating yourself again, and then that question business cropping up, and "beach" and "each" stuck in just for the rhyme. Anybody can see it's just for the rhyme. All that jingling gets the reader impatient. Too much baggage. Too many *words*. Our new breed of reader wants something else. Clarity. Straightforwardness. Getting to the point without a whole lot of nervous distraction. Tell me, George, are you serious about writing? You really want to become a writer some day?'

The poet swallowed hard, the blood beginning to pound in his head. 'It's my life,' he said simply.

'And you're serious about getting into print?'

'I'd give my eye-teeth,' admitted Tom.

'All right. Then you leave it to me. What you need is a good clean job of editing. Clara!' he called.

The fringed typist glanced up, as sharply as before.

'Do we have some white space under any of next issue's articles?'

'Plenty, F. B. There's a whole slew of white at the bottom of that piece on Alice Roosevelt's new blue gown.'

'Good. George,' the editor pronounced, holding out his viscid hand in kindness to the obscure young poet, 'leave your name and address with Clara and in a couple of weeks we'll send you a copy of yourself in print. If you weren't an out-of-towner I'd ask you to come pick it up, to save on the postage. But I know what a thrill real publication in a bona fide magazine is for an aspiring novice like yourself. I recollect the days of my own youth, if you'll excuse the cliché. Careful on the elevator – sometimes the rope gets stuck on that big nail down on the fifth floor, and you get a bounce right up those eye-teeth of yours. Oh, by the way – any suggestions for the title?'

The blood continued to course poundingly in young Tom Eliot's temples. He was overwhelmed by a bliss such as he had never before known. Print! 'I really think I still like "The Love Song of J. Alfred Prufrock",' his joy gave him the courage to declare.

'Too long. Too oblique. Not apropos. Succinctness! You've heard of that old maxim, "So that he who runs may read"? Well, my personal credo is: *So that he who shuns may heed.* That's what *The New Shoelace* is about. George, I'm about to put you on the map with all those busy folks who shun versifying. Leave the title to me. And don't you worry about that precious Voice of yours, George – the text is holy writ, I promise you.'

Gratefully, Tom Eliot returned to Boston in high glee. And within two weeks he had fished out of his mailbox the apotheosis of his tender years: the earliest known publication of 'The Love Song of J. Alfred Prufrock'.

It is a melancholy truth that nowadays every company president can recite the slovenly unedited opening of this justly famous item—

> *Let us go then, you and I,*
> *When the evening is spread out against the sky*
> *Like a patient etherized upon a table;*
> *Let us go, through certain half-deserted streets,*
> *The muttering retreats*
> *Of restless nights in cheap hotels, etc.*

—but these loose and wordy lines were not always so familiar, or so easily accessible. Time and fate have not been kind to Tom Eliot (who did, by the way, one day cease being painfully young): for some reason the slovenly unedited version has made its way in the world more successfully during the last ninety years than Barmuenster's conscientious efforts at perfection. Yet the great Firkin Barmuenster, that post-fin-de-siècle editor renowned for meticulous concision and passionate precision, for launching many a new literary career, and for the improvement of many a flaccid and redundant writing style, was – though the fact has so far not yet reached the larger reading public – T. S. Eliot's earliest supporter and discoverer.

For the use of bibliographers and, above all, for the delectation of poetry lovers, the complete text of 'The Love Song of J. Alfred Prufrock' as it appeared in *The New Shoelace* of 17 April 1911 follows:

THE MIND OF MODERN MAN
by George Eliot

(Editor's Note: A new contributor, Eliot is sure to be heard from in the future. Out of respect for the author's fine ideas, however, certain purifications have been made in the original submission on the principle that, in the Editor's words, GOOD WRITING KNOWS NO TRICKS, SO THAT HE WHO SHUNS MAY HEED.)

On a high-humidity evening in October, shortly after a rainfall, a certain nervous gentleman undertakes a visit, passing through a bad section of town. Arriving at his destination, the unhappy man overhears ladies discussing an artist well-known in history (Michelangelo Buonarroti, 1475–1564, Italian sculptor, painter, architect and poet). Our friend contemplates his personal diffidence, his baldness, his suit and tie, and the fact that he is rather underweight. He notes with some dissatisfaction that he is usually addressed in conventional phrases. He cannot make a decision. He believes his life has not been well-spent; indeed, he feels himself to be no better than a mere arthropod (of the shelled aquatic class, which includes lobsters, shrimps, crabs, barnacles, and wood lice). He has been subjected to many social hours timidly drinking tea, for, though he secretly wishes to impress others, he does not know how to do so. He realizes he is an insignificant individual, with a small part to play in the world. He is distressed that he will soon be eligible for an old age home, and considers the advisability of a fruit diet and of permitting himself a greater relaxation in dress, as well as perhaps covering his bald spot. Thus, in low spirits, in a markedly irrational frame of mind, he imagines he is encountering certain mythological females, and in his own words he makes it clear that he is doubtless in need of the aid of a reliable friend or kindly minister. (As are, it goes without saying, all of us.)

Usurpation (Other People's Stories)

Occasionally a writer will encounter a story that is his, yet is not his. I mean, by the way, a writer of *stories*, not one of these intelligences that analyse society and culture, but the sort of ignorant and acquisitive being who moons after magical tales. Such a creature knows very little: how to tie a shoelace, when to go to the store for bread, and the exact stab of a story that belongs to him, and to him only. But sometimes it happens that somebody else has written the story first. It is like being robbed of clothes you do not yet own. There you sit, in the rapt hall, seeing the usurper on the stage caressing the manuscript that, in its deepest turning, was meant to be yours. He is a transvestite, he is wearing your own hat and underwear. It seems unjust. There is no way to prevent him.

You may wonder that I speak of a hall rather than a book. The story I refer to has not yet been published in a book, and the fact is I heard it read aloud. It was read by the author himself. I had a seat in the back of the hall, with a much younger person pressing the chair-arms on either side of me, but by the third paragraph I was blind and saw nothing. By the fifth paragraph I recognized my story – knew it to be mine, that is, with the same indispensable familiarity I have for this round-flanked left-side molar my tongue admires. I think of it, in all that waste and rubble amid gold dental crowns, as my pearl.

The story was about a crown – a mythical one, made of silver. I do not remember its title. Perhaps it was simply called 'The Magic Crown'. In any event, you will soon read it in its famous author's new collection. He is, you may be sure, very famous, so famous that it was startling to see he was a real man. He wore a conventional suit and tie, a conventional haircut and conventional eyeglasses. His whitening moustache made him look conventionally distinguished. He was not at all as I had expected him to be – small and astonished, like his heroes.

This time the hero was a teacher. In the story he was always called 'the teacher', as if how one lives is what one is.

> The teacher's father is in the hospital, a terminal case. There is no hope. In an advertisement the teacher reads about a wonder-curer, a rabbi who can work miracles. Though a rational fellow and a devout sceptic, in desperation he visits the rabbi and learns that a cure can be effected by the construction of a magical silver crown, which costs nearly five hundred dollars. After it is made the rabbi will give it a special blessing and the sick man will recover. The teacher pays and in a vision sees a glowing replica of the marvellous crown. But afterwards he realizes that he has been mesmerized.

> Furiously he returns to the rabbi's worn-out flat to demand his money. Now the rabbi is dressed like a rich dandy. 'I telephoned the hospital and my father is still sick.' The rabbi chides him – he must give the crown time to work. The teacher insists that the crown he paid for be produced. 'It cannot be seen,' says the rabbi, 'it must be believed in, or the blessing will not work.'

> The teacher and the rabbi argue bitterly. The rabbi calls for faith, the teacher for his stolen money. In the heart of the struggle the teacher confesses with a terrible cry that he has really always hated his father anyway. The next day the father dies.

With a single half-archaic word the famous writer pressed out the last of the sick man's breath: he 'expired'.

Forgive me for boring you with plot-summary. I know there is nothing more tedious, and despise it myself. A rabbi whose face I have not made you see, a teacher whose voice remains a shadowy moan: how can I burn the inside of your eyes with these? But it is not my story, and therefore not my responsibility. I did not invent any of it.

From the platform the famous writer explained that the story was a gift, he too had not invented it. He took it from an account in a newspaper – which one he would not tell: he sweated over fear of libel. Cheats and fakes always hunt themselves up in stories, sniffing out twists, insults, distortions, transfigurations, all the drek of the imagination. Whatever's made up they grab, thick as lawyers against the silky figurative. Still, he swore it really happened, just like that – a crook with his crooked wife, calling himself rabbi, preying on gullible people, among them educated men, graduate students even; finally they arrested the fraud and put him in jail.

Instantly, the famous writer said, at the smell of the word 'jail', he knew the story to be his.

This news came to me with a pang. The silver crown given away free, and where was I? I who am pocked with newspaper-sickness, and hunch night after night (it pleases me to read the morning papers after midnight) catatonically fixed on shipping lists, death columns, lost wallets, maimings, muggings, explosions, hijackings, bombs, while the unwashed dishes sough thinly all around.

It has never occurred to me to write about a teacher; and as for rabbis, I can make up my own craftily enough. You may ask, then, what precisely in this story attracted me. And not simply attracted: seized me by the lung and declared itself my offspring – a changeling in search of its natural mother. Do not mistake me: had I only had access to a newspaper that crucial night (the *Post*, the *News*, the *Manchester Guardian*, *St Louis Post-Dispatch*, *Boston Herald-Traveler*, ah, which, which? and where was I? in a bar? never; buying birth control pills in the drugstore? I am a believer in fertility; reading, God forbid, a *book*?), my own story would have been less logically decisive. Perhaps the sick father would have recovered. Perhaps the teacher would not have confessed to hating his father. I might have caused the silver crown to astonish even the rabbi himself. Who knows what I might have sucked out of those swindlers! The point is I would have fingered out the magical parts.

Magic – I admit it – is what I lust after. And not ordinary magic, which is what one expects of pagan peoples; their religions declare it. After all, half the world asserts that once upon a time God became a man, and moreover that whenever a priest in sacral ceremony wills it, that same God-man can climb into a little flat piece of unleavened bread. For most people nowadays it is only the *idea* of a piece of bread turning into God – but is that any better? As for me, I am drawn not to the symbol, but to the absolute magic act. I am drawn to what is forbidden.

Forbidden. The terrible Hebrew word for it freezes the tongue – *asur*; Jewish magic. Trembling, we have heard in Deuteronomy the No that applies to any slightest sniff of occult disclosure: how mighty is Moses, peering down the centuries into the endlessness of this allure! Astrologists, wizards and witches: *asur*. The Jews have no magic. For us bread may not tumble into body. Wine is wine, death is death.

And yet with what prowess we have crept down the centuries after amulets, and hidden countings of letters, and the silver crown that heals: so it is after all nothing to marvel at that my own, my beloved, subject should be the preternatural – everything anti-Moses, all things blazing with their own wonder. I long to be one of the ordinary peoples, to give up our agnostic God whom even the word 'faith' insults, who cannot be imagined in any form, whom the very hope of imagining offends, who is without body and cannot enter body . . . oh, why can we not have a magic God like other peoples?

Some day I will take courage and throw over being a Jew, and then I will make a little god, a silver godlet, in the shape of a crown, which will stop death, resurrect fathers and uncles; out of its royal points gardens will burst. That story! Mine! Stolen! I considered: was it possible to leap up on the stage with a living match and burn the manuscript on the spot, freeing the crown out of the finished tale, restoring it once more to a public account in the press? But no. Fire, even the little humble wobble of a match, is too powerful a magic in such a place, among such gleaming herds. A conflagration of souls out of lust for a story! I feared so terrible a spell. All the same, he would own a carbon copy, or a photographic copy: such a man is meticulous about the storage-matter of his brain. A typewriter is a volcano. Who can stop print?

If I owned a silver godlet right now I would say: Almighty small Crown, annihilate that story; return, return the stuff of it to me.

A peculiar incident. Just as the famous writer came to the last word – 'expired' – I saw the face of a goat. It was thin, white, blurry-eyed; a scraggly fur beard hung from its chin. Attached to the beard was a transparent voice, a voice like a whiteness – but I ought to explain how I came just then to be exposed to it. I was leaning against the wall of that place. The fading hiss of 'expired' had all at once fevered me; I jumped from my seat between the two young people. Their perspiration had dampened the chair-arms, and the chill of their sweat, combined with the hotness of my greed for this magic story which could not be mine, turned my flesh to a sort of vapour. I rose like a heated gas, feeling insubstantial, and went to press my head against the cold side wall along the aisle. My brain was all gas, it shuddered with envy. Expired! How I wished to write a story containing that unholy sound! How I wished it was I who had come upon the silver crown. . . . I must have looked like an usher, or in some fashion a factotum of the theatre, with my skull drilled into the wall that way.

In any case I was taken for an official: as someone in authority who lolls on the job.

The goat-face blew a breath deep into my throat.

'I have stories. I want to give him stories.'

'*What* do you want?'

'Him. Arrange it, can't you? In the intermission, what d'you say?'

I pulled away; the goat hopped after me.

'How? When?' said the goat. 'Where?' His little beard had a tremor. 'If he isn't available here and now, tell me his mailing address. I need criticism, advice, I need help—'

We become what we are thought to be; I became a factotum.

I said pompously, 'You should be ashamed to pursue the famous. Does he know you?'

'Not exactly. I'm a cousin—'

'*His* cousin?'

'No. That rabbi's wife. She's an old lady, my mother's uncle was her father. We live in the same neighbourhood.'

'What rabbi?'

'The one in the papers. The one he swiped the story from.'

'That doesn't oblige him to read you. You expect too much,' I said. 'The public has no right to a writer's private mind. Help from high places doesn't come like manna. His time is precious, he has better things to do.' All this, by the way, was quotation. A famous writer – not this one – to whom I myself sent a story had once stung me with these words; so I knew how to use them.

'Did he say you could speak for him?' sneered the goat. 'Fame doesn't cow me. Even the famous bleed.'

'Only when pricked by the likes of you,' I retorted. 'Have you been published?'

'I'm still young.'

'Poets before you died first and published afterwards. Keats was twenty-six, Shelley twenty-nine, Rimbaud—'

'I'm like these, I'll live forever.'

'Arrogant!'

'Let the famous call me that, not you.'

'At least I'm published,' I protested; so my disguise fell. He saw I was nothing so important as an usher, only another unknown writer in the audience.

'Do *you* know him?' he asked.

'He spoke to me once at a cocktail party.'

'Would he remember your name?'

'Certainly,' I lied. The goat had speared my dignity.

'Then take only one story.'

'Leave the poor man alone.'

'*You* take it. Read it. If you like it – look, only if you like it! – give it to him for me.'

'He won't help you.'

'Why do you think everyone is like you?' he accused – but he seemed all at once submerged, as if I had hurt him. He shook out a vast envelope, pulled out his manuscript, and spitefully began erasing something. Opaque little tears clustered on his eyelashes. Either he was weeping or he was afflicted with pus. 'Why do you think I don't deserve some attention?'

'Not of the great.'

'Then let me at least have yours,' he said.

The real usher just then came like a broom. Back! Back! Quiet! Don't disturb the reading! Before I knew it I had been swept into my seat. The goat was gone, and I was clutching the manuscript.

The fool had erased his name.

That night I read the thing. You will ask why. The newspaper was thin, the manuscript fat. It smelled of stable: a sort of fecal stink. But I soon discovered it was only the glue he had used to piece together parts of corrected pages. An amateur job.

If you are looking for magic now, do not. This was no work to marvel at. The prose was not bad, but not good either. There are young men who write as if the language were an endless bolt of yard goods – you snip off as much as you need for the length of fiction you require: one turn of the loom after another, everything of the same smoothness, the texture catches you up nowhere.

I have said 'fiction'. It was not clear to me whether this was fiction or not. The title suggested it was: 'A Story of Youth and Homage'. But the narrative was purposefully inconclusive. Moreover, the episodes could be interpreted on several 'levels'. Plainly it was not just a story, but meant something much more, and even that 'much more' itself meant much more. This alone soured me; such techniques are learned in those hollowed-out tombstones called Classes in Writing. In my notion of these things, if you want to tell a story you tell it. I am against all these masks and tricks of metaphor and fable. That is why I am attracted to magical tales: they mean what they say; in them miracles are not symbols, they are conditional probabilities.

The goat's story was realistic enough, though self-conscious. In perfectly ordinary, mainly trite, English it pretended to be incoherent. That, as you know, is the fashion.

I see you are about to put these pages down, in fear of another plot-summary. I beg you to wait. Trust me a little. I will get through it as painlessly as possible – I promise to abbreviate everything. Or, if I turn out to be long-winded, at least to be interesting. Besides, you can see what risks I am taking. I am unfamiliar with the laws governing plagiarism, and here I am, brazenly giving away stories that are not rightfully mine. Perhaps one day the goat's story will be published and acclaimed. Or perhaps not: in either case he will recognize his plot as I am about to tell it to you, and what furies will beat in him! What if, by the time *this* story is published, at this very moment while you are reading it, I am on my back in some filthy municipal dungeon? Surely so deep a sacrifice should engage your forgiveness.

Then let us proceed to the goat's plot:

An American student at a yeshiva in Jerusalem is unable to concentrate. He is haunted by worldly desires; in reality he has come to Jerusalem not for Torah but out of ambition. Though young and unpublished, he already fancies himself to be a writer worthy of attention. Then why not the attention of the very greatest?

It happens that there lives in Jerusalem a writer who one day will win the most immense literary prize on the planet. At the time of the story he is already an old man heavy with fame, though of a rather parochial nature; he has not yet been to Stockholm – it is perhaps two years before the Nobel Prize turns him into a mythical figure. ['Turns him into a mythical figure' is an excellent example of the goat's prose, by the way.] But the student is prescient, and fame is fame. He composes a postcard:

> There are only two
> religious writers in the world.
> You are one and I am
> the other. I will come to visit you.

It is true that the old man is religious. He wears a skullcap, he threads his tales with strands of the holy phrases. And he cannot send anyone away from his door. So when the student appears, the old writer invites him in for a glass of tea, though homage fatigues him; he would rather nap.

The student confesses that his own ambitiousness has brought him to the writer's feet: he too would wish one day to be revered as the writer himself is revered.

—I wish, says the old writer, I had been like you in my youth. I never had the courage to look into the face of anyone I admired, and I admired so many! But they were all too remote; I was very shy. I wish now I had gone to see them, as you have come to see me.

—Whom did you admire most? asks the student. In reality he has no curiosity about this or anything else of the kind, but he recognizes that such a question is vital to the machinery of praise. And though he has never read a word the old man has written, he can smell all around him, even in the old man's trousers, the smell of fame.

—The Rambam, answers the old man. – Him I admired more than anyone.

—Maimonides? exclaims the student. – But how could you visit Maimonides?

—Even in my youth, the old man assents, the Rambam had already been dead for several hundred years. But even if he had not been dead, I would have been too shy to go and see him. For a shy young man it is relieving to admire someone who is dead.

—Then to become like you, the student says meditatively, it is necessary to be shy?

—Oh yes, says the old man. – It is necessary to be shy. The truest ambition is hidden in shyness. All ambitiousness is hidden. If you want to usurp my place you must not show it, or I will only hang to it all the more tightly. You must always walk with your head down. You must be a true *ba'al ga'avah*.

—A *ba'al ga'avah?* cries the student. – But you contradict yourself! Aren't we told that the *ba'al ga'avah* is the man whom God most despises? The self-righteous self-idolator? It's written that him alone God will cause to perish. Sooner than a murderer!

It is plain that the young man is in good command of the sources; not for nothing is he a student at the yeshiva. But he is perplexed, rattled. – How can I be like you if you tell me to be a *ba'al ga'avah*? And why would you tell me to be such a thing?

—The *ba'al ga'avah*, explains the writer, is a supplanter: the man whose arrogance is godlike, whose pride is like a tower. He is the one who most subtly turns his gaze downwards to the ground, never looking at what he covets. I myself was never cunning enough to be a genuine *ba'al ga'vah*; I was always too timid for it. It was never necessary for me to feign shyness, I was naturally like that. But you are not. So you must invent a way to become a genuine *ba'al ga'avah*, so audacious and yet so ingenious that you will fool God and will live.

The student is impatient. – How does God come into this? We're talking only of ambition.

—Of course. Of *serious* ambition, however. You recall: 'All that is not Torah is levity.' This is the truth to be found at the end of every incident, even this one. —You see, the old man continues, my place can easily be taken. A blink, and it's yours. I will not watch over it if I forget that someone is after it. But you must make me forget.

—How? asks the student, growing cold with greed.

—By never coming here again.

—It's a joke!

—And then I will forget you. I will forget to watch over my place. And then, when I least look for it to happen, you will come and steal it. You will be so quiet, so shy, so ingenious, so audacious, I will never suspect you.

—A nasty joke! You want to get rid of me! It's mockery, you forget what it is to be young. In old age everything is easier, nothing burns inside you.

But meanwhile, inside the student's lungs, and within the veins of his wrists, a cold fog shivers.

—Nothing burns? Yes; true. At the moment, for instance, I covet nothing more lusty than my little twilight nap. I always have it right now.

—They say (the student is as cold now as a frozen path, all his veins are paths of ice), they say you're going to win the Nobel Prize! For literature!

—When I nap I sleep dreamlessly. I don't dream of such things. Come, let me help you cease to covet.

—It's hard for me to keep my head down! I'm young, I want what you have, I want to be like you!

Here I will interrupt the goat's story to apologize. I would not be candid if I did not confess that I am rewriting it; I am almost making it my own, and that will never do for an act of plagiarism. I don't mean only that I have set it more or less in order, and taken out the murk. That is only by the way. But, by sticking to what one said and what the other answered, I have broken my promise; already I have begun to bore you. Boring! Oh, the goat's story was boring! Philosophic stories make excellent lullabies.

So, going on with my own version (I hate stories with ideas hidden in them), I will spring out of paraphrase and invent what the old man does.

Right after saying 'Let me help you cease to covet', he gets up and, with fuzzy sleepy steps, half-limps to a table covered by a cloth that falls to the floor. He separates the parts of the cloth, and now the darkness underneath the table takes him like a tent. In he crawls, the flaps cling, his rump makes a bulge. He calls out two words in Hebrew: *ohel shalom!* and backs out, carrying with him a large black box. It looks like a lady's hat box.

'An admirer gave me this. Only not an admirer of our own time. A predecessor. I had it from Tchernikhovsky. The poet. I presume you know his work?'

'A little,' says the student. He begins to wish he had boned up before coming.

'Tchernikhovsky was already dead when he brought me this,' the old man explains. 'One night I was alone, sitting right there – where you are now. I was reading Tchernikhovsky's most famous poem, the one to the god Apollo. And quite suddenly there was Tchernikhovsky. He disappointed me. He was a completely traditional ghost, you could see right through him to the wall behind. This of course made it difficult to study his features. The wall behind – you can observe for yourself – held a bookcase, so where his nose appeared to be I could read only the title of a Tractate of the Mishnah. A ghost can be seen mainly in outline, unfortunately, something like an artist's charcoal sketch, only instead of the blackness of charcoal, it is the narrow brilliance of a very fine white light. But what he carried was palpable, even heavy – this box. I was not at all terror-stricken, I can't tell you why. Instead I was bemused by the kind of picture he made against the wall – 'modern', I would have called it then, but probably there are new words for that sort of thing now. It reminded me a little of a collage: one kind of material superimposed on another kind which is utterly different. One order of creation laid upon another. Metal on tissue. Wood on hide. In this case it was a three-dimensional weight superimposed on a line – the line, or luminous congeries of lines, being Tchernikhovsky's hands, ghost hands holding a real box.'

The student stares at the box. He waits like a coat eager to be shrunk.

'The fact is,' continues the old writer, 'I have never opened it. Not that I'm not as inquisitive as the next mortal. Perhaps more so. But it wasn't necessary. There is something about the presence of an apparition which satisfies all curiosity forever – the deeper as well as the more superficial sort. For one thing, a ghost will tell you everything, and all at once. A ghost may *look* artistic, but there is no finesse to it, nothing indirect or calculated, nothing suggesting *raffinement*. It is as if everything gossamer had gone simply into the stuff of it. The rest is all grossness. Or else Tchernikhovsky himself, even when alive and writing, had a certain clumsiness. This is what I myself believe. All that pantheism and earth-worship! That pursuit of the old gods of Canaan! He thickened his tongue with clay. All pantheists are fools. Likewise trinitarians and gnostics of every kind. How can a piece of creation be its own Creator?

'Still, his voice had rather a pretty sound. To describe it is to be obliged to ask you to recall the sound of prattle: a baby's purr, only shaped into nearly normal cognitive speech. A most pleasing combination. He told me that he was reading me closely in Eden and approved of my stories. He had, he assured me, a number of favourites, but best of all he liked a quite short tale – no more than a notebook sketch, really – about why the Messiah will not come.

'In this story the Messiah is ready to come. He enters a synagogue and prepares to appear at the very moment he hears the congregation recite the "I believe". He stands there and listens, waiting to make himself visible on the last syllable of the verse "I believe in the coming of the Messiah, and even if he tarry I will await his coming every day". He leans against the Ark and listens, listens and leans – all the time he is straining his ears. The fact is he can hear nothing: the congregation buzzes with its own talk – hats, mufflers, business, wives, appointments, rain, lessons, the past, next week ... the prayer is obscured, all its syllables are drowned in dailiness, and the Messiah retreats; he has not heard himself summoned.

'This, Tchernikhovsky's ghost told me, was my best story. I was at once suspicious. His baby-voice hinted at ironies, I caught a tendril of sarcasm. It was clear to me that what he liked about this story was mainly its climactic stroke: that the Messiah is prevented from coming. I had written to lament the tarrying of the Messiah; Tchernikhovsky, it seemed, took satisfaction exactly in what I mourned. "Look here," he tinkled at me – imagine a crow linked to a delicious little gurgle, and the whole sense of it belligerent as a prizefighter and coarse as an old waiter – "now that I'm dead, a good quarter-century of deadness under my dust, I've concluded that I'm entirely willing to have you assume my eminence. For one thing, I've been to Sweden, pulled strings with some deceased but still influential Academicians, and arranged for you to get the Nobel Prize in a year or two. Which is beyond what I ever got for myself. But I'm aware this won't interest you as much as a piece of eternity right here in Jerusalem, so I'm here to tell you you can have it. You can" – he had a babyish way of repeating things – "assume my eminence."

'You see what I mean about grossness. I admit I was equally coarse. I answered speedily and to the point. I refused.

'"I understand you," he said. "You don't suppose I'm pious enough, or not pious in the right way. I don't meet your yeshiva standards. Naturally not. You know I used to be a doctor, I was attracted to biology, which is to say to dust. Not spiritual enough for you! My Zionism wasn't of the soul, it was made of real dirt. What I'm offering you is something tangible. Have some common sense and take it. It will do for you what the Nobel Prize can't. Open the box and put on whatever's inside. Wear it for one full minute and the thing will be accomplished."'

'For God's sake, what *was* it?' shrieks the student, shrivelling into his blue city-boy shirt. With a tie: and in Jerusalem! (The student is an absurdity, a crudity. But of course I've got to have him; he's left over from the goat's story, what else am I to do?)

'Inside the box,' replies the old writer, 'was the most literal-minded thing in the world. From a ghost I expected as much. The whole idea of a ghost is a literal-minded conception. I've used ghosts in my own stories, naturally, but they've always had a real possibility, by which I mean an ideal possibility: Elijah, the True Messiah. . . .'

'For God's sake, the box!'

'The box. Take it. I give it to you.'

'What's in it?'

'See for yourself.'

'Tell me first. Tchernikhovsky told *you*.'

'That's a fair remark. It contains a crown.'

'What kind of crown?'

'Made of silver, I believe.'

'*Real* silver?'

'I've never looked on it, I've explained this. I *refused* it.'

'Then why give it to me?'

'Because it's meant for that. When a writer wishes to usurp the place and power of another writer, he simply puts it on. I've explained this already.'

'But if I wear it I'll become like Tchernikhovsky—'

'No, no, like me. Like me. It confers the place and power of the giver. And it's what you want, true? To be like me?'

'But this isn't what you advised a moment ago. *Then* you said to become arrogant, a *ba'al ga'avah*, and to conceal it with shyness—'

(Quite so. A muddle in the plot. That was the goat's story, and it had no silver crown in it. I am still stuck with these leftovers that cause seams and cracks in my own version. I will have to mend all this somehow. Be patient. I will manage it. Pray that I don't bungle it.)

'Exactly,' says the old writer. 'That's the usual way. But if you aren't able to feign shyness, what is necessary is a short cut. I warned you it would demand audacity and ingenuity. What I did not dare to do, you must have the courage for. What I turned down you can raise up. I offer you the crown. You will see what a short cut it is. Wear it and immediately you become a *ba'al ga'avah*. Still, I haven't yet told you how I managed to get rid of Tchernikhovsky's ghost. Open the box, put on the crown, and I'll tell you.'

The student obeys. He lifts the box onto the table. It seems light enough, then he opens it, and at the first thrust of his hand into its interior it disintegrates, flakes off into dust, is blown off at a breath, consumed by the first alien molecule of air, like something very ancient removed from the deepest clay tomb and unable to withstand the corrosive stroke of light.

But there, in the revealed belly of the vanished box, is the crown.

It appears to be made of silver, but it is heavier than any earthly silver

– it is heavy, heavy, heavy, dense as a meteorite. Puffing and struggling, the student tries to raise it up to his head. He cannot. He cannot lift even a corner of it. It is weighty as a pyramid.

'It won't budge.'

'It will after you pay for it.'

'You didn't say anything about payment!'

'You're right. I forgot. But you don't pay in money. You pay in a promise. You have to promise that if you decide you don't want the crown you'll take it off immediately. Otherwise it's yours forever.'

'I promise.'

'Good. Then put it on.'

And now lightly, lightly, oh so easily as if he lifted a straw hat, the student elevates the crown and sets it on his head.

'There. You are like me. Now go away.'

And oh so lightly, lightly, as easily as if the crown were a cargo of helium, the student skips through Jerusalem. He runs! He runs into a bus, a joggling mob crushed together, everyone recognizes him, even the driver: he is praised, honoured, young women put out their hands to touch his collar, they pluck at his pants, his fly unzips and he zips it up again, oh fame! He gets off the bus and runs to his yeshiva. Crowds on the sidewalk, clapping. So this is what it feels like! He flies into the yeshiva like a king. Formerly no one blinked at him, the born Jerusalemites scarcely spoke to him, but now! It is plain they have all read him. He hears a babble of titles, plots, characters, remote yet familiar – look, he thinks, the crown has supplied me with a ready-made bibliography. He reaches up to his head to touch it: a flash of cold. Cold, cold, it is the coldest silver on the planet, a coldness that stabs through into his brain. Frost encases his brain, inside his steaming skull he hears more titles, more plots, names of characters, scholars, wives, lovers, ghosts, children, beggars, villages, candlesticks – what a load he carries, what inventions, what a teeming and a boiling, stories, stories, stories! His own; yet not his own. The Rosh Yeshiva comes down the stairs from his study: the Rosh Yeshiva, the Head, a bony miniaturized man grown almost entirely inwards and upwards into a spectacular dome, a brow shaped like the front of an academy, hollowed-out temples for porticoes, a resplendent head with round dead-end eyeglasses as denying as bottle-bottoms and curl-scribbled beard and small attachments of arms and little antlike legs thin as hairs; and the Rosh Yeshiva, who has never before let fall a syllable to this obscure tourist-pupil from America, suddenly cries out the glorious blessing reserved for finding oneself in the presence of a sage: Blessed are You, O God, Imparter of wisdom to those who fear Him! And the student in his crown understands that there now cleave to his name sublime parables interpreting the divine purpose, and he despairs, he is afraid, because suppose he were obliged to write one this minute? Suppose these titles clamouring all around him are only empty pots, and he must fill them up with stories? He runs from the yeshiva, elbows out, scattering admirers and celebrants, and makes for the alley behind the kitchen – no one ever goes there, only the old cats who scavenge in the trash barrels. But behind him – crudely sepulchral footsteps, like thumps inside a bucket, he runs, he looks back, he runs, he stops – Tchernikhovsky's ghost! From the old writer's description he can identify it easily. 'A mistake,' chimes the ghost, a pack of bells, 'it wasn't for you.'

'What!' screams the student.

'Give it back.'

'What!'

'The crown,' pursues the baby-purr voice of Tchernikhovsky's ghost. 'I never meant for that old fellow to give it away.'

'He said it was all right.'

'He tricked you.'

'No he didn't.'

'He's sly sly sly.'

'He said it would make me just like him. And I am.'

'No.'

'Yes!'

'Then predict the future.'

'In two years, the Nobel Prize for Literature!'

'For him, not for you.'

'But I'm *like* him.'

'"Like" is not the same as the same. You want to be the same? Look in the window.'

The student looks into the kitchen window. Inside, among cauldrons, he can see the roil of the students in their caps, spinning here and there, in the pantry, in the Passover dish closet even, past a pair of smoky vats, in search of the fled visitor who now stares and stares until his concentration alters seeing; and instead of looking behind the pane, he follows the light on its surface and beholds a reflection. An old man is also looking into the window; the student is struck by such a torn rag of a face. Strange, it cannot be Tchernikhovsky: he is all web and wraith; and anyhow a ghost has no reflection. The old man in the looking-glass window is wearing a crown. A silver crown!

'You see?' tinkles the ghost. 'A trick!'

'I'm old!' howls the student.

'Feel in your pocket.'

The student feels. A vial.

'See? Nitroglycerin.'

'What is this, are you trying to blow me up?'

Again the small happy soaring of the infant's grunt. 'I remind you that I am a physician. When you are seized by a pulling, a knocking, a burning in the chest, a throb in the elbow-crook, swallow one of these tablets. In coronary insufficiency it relaxes the artery.'

'Heart failure! Will I die? Stop! I'm young!'

'With those teeth? All gums gone? That wattle? Dotard! Bag!'

The student runs; he remembers his perilous heart; he slows. The ghost thumps and chimes behind. So they walk, a procession of two, a very old man wearing a silver crown infinitely cold, in his shadow a ghost made all of lit spider-thread, giving out now and then with baby's laughter and odd coarse curses patched together from Bible phrases; together they scrape out of the alley onto the boulevard – an oblivious population there.

'My God! No one knows me. Why don't they know me here?'

'Who should know you?' says Tchernikhovsky.

'In the bus they yelled out dozens of book titles. In the streets! The Rosh Yeshiva said the blessing for seeing a sage!'

But now in the bus the passengers are indifferent; they leap for seats; they snore in cosy spots standing up, near poles; and not a word. Not a gasp, not a squeal. Not even a pull on the collar. It's all over! A crown but no king.

'It's stopped working,' says the student, mournful.

'The crown? Not on your life.'

'Then you're interfering with it. You're jamming it up.'

'That's more like the truth.'

'Why are you following me?'

'I don't like misrepresentation.'

'You mean you don't like magic.'

'They're the same thing.'

'Go away!'

'I never do that.'

'*He* got rid of you.'

'Sly sly sly. He did it with a ruse. You know how? He refused the crown. He took it but he hid it away. No one ever refused it before. Usurper! Coveter! *Ba'al ga'avah!* That's what he is.'

The student protests, 'But he *gave* me the crown. "Let me help you cease to covet," that's exactly what he said, why do you call him *ba'al ga'avah?*'

'And himself? *He's* ceased to covet, is that it? That's what you think? You think he doesn't churn saliva over the Nobel Prize? Ever since I told him they were speculating about the possibility over at the Swedish Academicians' graveyard? Day and night that's all he dreams of. He loves his little naps, you know why? To sleep, perchance to dream. He imagines himself in a brand-new splendiferous bow tie, rear end trailing tails, wearing his skullcap out of public arrogance, his old wife up there with him dressed to the hobbledorfs – in Stockholm, with the King of Sweden! That's what he sees, that's what he dreams, he can't work, he's in a fever of coveting. You think it's different when you're old?'

'I'm not old!' the student shouts. A wilful splinter, he peels himself from the bus. Oh, frail, his legs are straw, the dry knees wrap close like sheaves, he feels himself pouring out, sand from a sack. Old!

Now they are in front of the writer's house. 'Age makes no matter,' says the ghost, 'the same, the same. Ambition levels, lust is unitary. Lust you can always count on. I'm not speaking of the carnal sort. Carnality's a brevity – don't compare wind with mountains! But lust! Teetering on the edge of the coffin there's lust. After mortality there's lust, I guarantee you. In Eden there's nothing but lust.' The ghost raps on the door – with all his strength, and his strength is equal to a snowflake. Silence, softness. 'Bang on the thing!' he commands, self-disgusted; sometimes he forgets he is incorporeal.

The student obeys, shivering; he is so cold now his three or six teeth clatter like chinaware against a waggling plastic bridge anchored in nothing, his ribs shake in his chest, his spine vibrates without surcease. And what of his heart? Inside his pocket he clutches the vial.

The old writer opens up. His fists are in his eyes.

'We woke you, did we?' gurgles Tchernikhovsky's ghost.

'You!'

'Me,' says the ghost, satisfied. '*Ba'al ga'avah!* Spiteful! You foisted the crown on a kid.'

The old writer peers. 'Where?'

The ghost sweeps the student forward. 'I did him the service of giving him long life. Instantly. Why wait for a good thing?'

'I don't want it! Take it back!' the student cries, snatching at the crown on his head; but it stays on. 'You said I could give it back if I don't want it any more!'

Again the old writer peers. 'Ah. You keep your promise. So does the crown.'

'What do you mean?'

'It promised you acclaim. But it generates this pest. Everything has its price.'

'Get rid of it!'

'To get rid of the ghost you have to get rid of the crown.'

'All right! Here it is! Take it back! It's yours!'

The ghost laughs like a baby at the sight of a teat. 'Try and take it off then.'

The student tries. He tears at the crown, he flings his head upwards, backwards, sideways, pulls and pulls. His fingertips flame with the ferocious cold.

'How did *you* get rid of it?' he shrieks.

'I never put it on,' replies the old writer.

'No, no, I mean the ghost, how did you get rid of the ghost!'

'I was going to tell you that, remember? But you ran off.'

'You sent me away. It was a trick, you never meant to tell.'

The ghost scolds: 'No disputes!' And orders, 'Tell now.'

The student writhes; twists his neck; pulls and pulls. The crown stays on.

'The crown loosens,' the old writer begins, 'when the ghost goes. Everything dissolves together—'

'But *how?*'

'You find someone to give the crown to. That's all. You simply pass it on. All you do is agree to give away its powers to someone who wants it. Consider it a test of your own generosity.'

'Who'll want it? Nobody wants such a thing!' the student shrieks. 'It's stuck! Get it off! Off!'

'*You* wanted it.'

'Prig! Moralist! *Ba'al ga'avah!* Didn't I come to you for advice? Literary advice, and instead you gave me this! I wanted help! You gave me metal junk! Sneak!'

'Interesting,' observes the ghost, 'that I myself acquired the crown in exactly the same way. I received it from Ibn Gabirol. Via ouija board. I was sceptical about the method but discovered it to be legitimate. I consulted him about some of his verse-forms. To be specific, the problem of enjambment, which is more difficult in Hebrew than in some other languages. By way of reply he gave me the crown. Out of the blue it appeared on the board – naked, so to speak, and shining oddly, like a fish without scales. Of course there wasn't any ghost attached to the crown then. I'm the first, and you don't think I *like* having to materialize thirty minutes after someone's put it on? What I need is to be left in peace in Paradise, not this business of being on call the moment someone—'

'Ibn Gabirol?' the old writer breaks in, panting, all attention. Ibn Gabirol! Sublime poet, envied beyond envy, sublimeness without heir, who would not covet the crown of Ibn Gabirol?

'He said *he* got it from Isaiah. The quality of ownership keeps declining apparently. That's why they have me on patrol. If someone unworthy acquires it – well, that's where I put on my emanations and dig in. Come on,' says the ghost, all at once sounding American, 'let's go.' He gives the student one of his snowflake shoves. 'Where you go, I go. Where I go, you go. Now that you know the ropes, let's get out of here and find somebody who deserves it. Give it to some goy for a change. "The righteous among the Gentiles are as judges in Israel." My own suggestion is Oxford, Mississippi, Faulkner, William.'

'Faulkner's dead.'

'He is? I ought to look him up. All right then. Someone not so fancy. Norman Mailer.'

'A Jew,' sneers the student.

'Can you beat that. Never mind, we'll find someone. Keep away from the rot of Europe – Kafka had it once. Maybe a black. An Indian. Spic maybe. We'll go to America and look.'

Moistly the old writer plucks at the ghost. 'Listen, this doesn't cancel the Prize? I still get it?'

'In two years you're in Stockholm.'

'And me?' cries the student. 'What about me? What happens to me?'

'You wear the crown until you get someone to take it from you. Blockhead! Dotard! Don't you *listen*?' says the ghost: his accent wobbles, he elides like a Calcuttan educated in Paris.

'No one wants it! I told you! Anyone who really needs it you'll say doesn't deserve it. If he's already famous he doesn't need it, and if he's unknown you'll think he degrades it. Like me. Not fair! There's no *way* to pass it on.'

'You've got a point.' The ghost considers this. 'That makes sense. Logic.'

'So get it off me!'

'However, again you forget lust. Lust overcomes logic.'

'Stop! Off!'

'The King of Sweden,' muses the old writer, 'speaks no Hebrew. That will be a difficulty. I suppose I ought to begin to study Swedish.'

'Off! Off!' yells the student. And tugs at his head, yanks at the crown, pulling, pulling, seizing it by the cold points. He throws himself down, wedges his legs against the writer's desk, tumbling after leverage; nothing works. Then methodically he kneels, lays his head on the floor, and methodically begins to beat the crown against the wooden floor. He jerks, tosses, taps, his white head in the brilliant crown is a wild flashing hammer; then he catches at his chest; his knuckles explode; then again he beats, beats, beats the crown down. But it stays stuck, no blow can knock it free. He beats. He heaves his head. Sparks spring from the crown, small lightnings leap. Oh, his chest, his ribs, his heart! The vial, where is the vial? His hands squirm towards his throat, his chest, his pocket. And his head beats the crown down against the floor. The old head halts, the head falls, the crown stays stuck, the heart is dead.

'Expired,' says the ghost of Tchernikhovsky.

Well, that should be enough. No use making up any more of it. Why should I? It is not my story. It is not the goat's story. It is no one's story. It is a story nobody wrote, nobody wants, it has no existence. What does the notion of a *ba'al ga'avah* have to do with a silver crown? One belongs to morals, the other to magic. Stealing from two disparate tales I smashed their elements one into the other. Things must be brought together. In magic all divergences are linked and locked. The fact is I forced the crown onto the ambitious student in order to punish.

To punish? Yes. In life I am, though obscure, as generous and reasonable as those whom wide glory has sweetened; earlier you saw how generously and reasonably I dealt with the goat. So I am used to being taken for everyone's support, confidante, and consolation – it did not surprise me, propped there against that wall in the dark, when the goat begged me to read his story. Why should he not? My triumph is that, in my unrenown, everyone trusts me not to lie. But I always lie. Only on paper I do not lie. On paper I punish, I am malignant.

For instance: I killed off the student to punish him for arrogance. But it is really the goat I am punishing. It is an excellent thing to punish him. Did he not make his hero a student at the yeshiva, did he not make him call himself 'religious'? But what is that? What is it to be 'religious'? Is religion any different from magic? Whoever intends to separate them ends in proving them to be the same.

The goat was a *ba'al ga'avah*! I understood that only a *ba'al ga'avah* would dare to write about 'religion'.

So I punished him for it. How? By transmuting piety into magic.

Then – and I require you to accept this with the suddenness I myself experienced it: *as if by magic* – again I was drawn to look into the goat's story; and found, on the next-to-last page, an address. He had rubbed out (I have already mentioned this) his name; but here was a street and a number:

618 Herzl Street
Brooklyn, NY

6   A street fashioned – so to speak – after the Messiah. Here I will halt you once more to ask you to take no notice of the implications of the goat's address. It is an aside worthy of the goat himself. It is he, not I, who would grab you by the sleeve here and now in order to explain exactly who Theodor Herzl was – oh, how I despise writers who will stop a story dead for the sake of showing off! Do you care whether or not Maimonides (supposing you had ever heard of that lofty saint) tells us that the messianic age will be recognizable simply by the resumption of Jewish political independence? Does it count if, by that definition, the Messiah turns out to be none other than a Viennese journalist of the last century? Doubtless Herzl was regarded by his contemporaries as a *ba'al ga'avah* for brazening out, in a modern moment, a Hebrew principality. And who is more of a *ba'al ga'avah* than the one who usurps the Messiah's own job? Take Isaiah – was not Isaiah a *ba'al ga'avah* when he declared against observance – 'I hate your feasts and your new moons' – and in the voice, no less, of the Creator Himself?

But thank God I have no taste for these notions. Already you have seen how earnestly my mind is turned towards hatred of metaphysical speculation. Practical action is my whole concern, and I have nothing but contempt for significant allusions, nuances, buried effects.

Therefore you will not be astonished at what I next undertook to do. I went – ha! – to the street of the Messiah to find the goat.

It was a place where there had been conflagrations. Rubble tentatively stood: brick on brick, about to fall. One remaining configuration of wall, complete with windows but no panes. The sidewalk underfoot stirred with crumbs, as of sugar grinding: mortar reduced to sand. A desert flushed over tumbled yards. Lintels and doors burned out, foundations squared like pebbles on a beach: in this spot once there had been cellars, stoops, houses. The smell of burned wood wandered. A civilization of mounds – who had lived here? Jews. There were no buildings left. A rectangular stucco fragment – of what? synagogue maybe – squatted in a space. There was no Number 18 – only bad air, light flying in the gape and gash where the fires had driven down brick, mortar, wood, mothers, fathers, children pressing library cards inside their pockets – gone, finished.

And immediately – as if by magic – the goat!

'You!' I hooted, exactly as, in the story that never was, the old writer had cried it to Tchernikhovsky's shade.

'You've read my stuff,' he said, gratified. 'I knew you could find me easy if you wanted to. All you had to do was want to.'

'Where do you live?'

'Number 18. I knew you'd want to.'

'There isn't any 18.'

He pointed. 'It's what's left of the shul. No plumbing, but it still has a good kitchen in the back. I'm what you call a squatter, you don't mind?'

'Why should I mind?'

'Because I stole the idea from a book. It's this story about a writer who lives in an old tenement with his typewriter and the tenement's about to be torn down—'

The famous author who had written about the magic crown had written that story too; I reflected how some filch their fiction from life, others filch their lives from fiction. What people call inspiration is only pilferage. 'You're not living in a tenement,' I corrected, 'you're living in a synagogue.'

'What used to be. It's a hole now, a sort of cave. The Ark is left, though, you want to see the Ark?'

I followed him through shards. There was no front door.

'What happened to this neighbourhood?' I said.

'The Jews went away.'

'Who came instead?'

'Fire.'

The curtain of the Ark dangled in charred shreds. I peered inside the orifice which had once closeted the Scrolls: all blackness there, and the clear sacrificial smell of things that have been burned.

'See?' he said. 'The stove works. It's the old wood-burning kind. For years they didn't use it here, it just sat. And now – resurrection.' Ah: the clear sacrificial smell was potatoes baking.

'Don't you have a job?'

'I write, I'm a writer. And no rent to pay anyhow.'

'How do you drink?'

'You mean *what*.' He held up a full bottle of Schapiro's kosher wine. 'They left a whole case intact.'

'But you can't wash, you can't even use the toilet.'

'I pee and do my duty in the yard. Nobody cares. This is freedom, lady.'

'Dirt,' I said.

'What's dirt to Peter is freedom to Paul. Did you like my story? Sit.'

There was actually a chair, but it had a typewriter on it. The goat did not remove it.

'How do you take a bath?' I persisted.

'Sometimes I go to my cousin's. I told you. The rabbi's wife.'

'The rabbi from this synagogue?'

'No, he's moved to Woodhaven Boulevard. That's Queens. All the Jews from here went to Queens, did you know that?'

'*What* rabbi's wife?' I blew out, exasperated.

'I *told* you. The one with the crown. The one they wrote about in the papers. The one *he* lifted the idea of that story from. A rip-off that was, my cousin ought to sue.'

Then I remembered. 'All stories are rip-offs,' I said. 'Shakespeare stole his plots. Dostoevsky dug them out of the newspaper. Everybody steals. *The Decameron*'s stolen. Whatever looks like invention is theft.'

'Great,' he said, 'that's what I need. Literary talk.'

'What did you mean, you knew I would want to come? – Believe me, I didn't come for literary talk.'

'You bet. You came because of my cousin. You came because of the crown.'

I was amazed: instantly it coursed in on me that this was true. I had come because of the crown; I was in pursuit of the crown.

I said: 'I don't care about the crown. I'm interested in the rabbi himself. The crown-blesser. What I care about is the psychology of the thing.'

This word – 'psychology' – made him cackle. 'He's in jail, I thought you knew that. They got him for fraud.'

'Does his wife still have any crowns around?'

'One.'

'Here's your story,' I said, handing it over. 'Next time leave your name in. You don't have to obliterate it, rely on the world for that.'

The pus on his eyelids glittered. 'Alex will obliterate the world, not vice versa.'

'How? By bombing it with stories? The first anonymous obliteration. The Flood without a by-line,' I said. 'At least everything God wrote was publishable. Alex what?'

'Goldflusser.'

'You're a liar.'

'Silbertsig.'

'Cut it out.'

'Kupferman. Bleifischer. Bettler. Kenigman.'

'All that's mockery. If your name's a secret—'

'I'm lying low, hiding out, they're after me because I helped with the crowns.'

I speculated, 'You're the one who made them.'

'No. She did that.'

'Who?'

'My cousin. The rabbi's wife. She crocheted them. What he did was go buy the form – you get it from a costume loft, stainless steel. She used to make these little pointed sort of *gloves* for it, to protect it, see, and the shine would glimmer through, and then the customer would get to keep the crown-cover, as a sort of guarantee—'

'My God,' I said, 'what's all that about, why didn't *she* go to jail?'

'Crocheting isn't a crime.'

'And you?' I said. 'What did you do in all that?'

'Get customers. Fraudulent solicitation, that's a crime.'

He took the typewriter off the chair and sat down. The wisp of beard wavered. 'Didn't you like my story?' he accused. The pages were pressed with an urgency between his legs.

'No. It's all fake. It doesn't matter if you've been to Jerusalem. You've got the slant of the place all wrong. It doesn't matter about the yeshiva either. It doesn't matter if you really went to see some old geezer over there, you didn't get anything right. It's a terrible story.'

'Where do you come off with that stuff?' he burst out. 'Have *you* been to Jerusalem? Have *you* seen the inside of a yeshiva?'

'No.'

'So!'

'I can tell when everything's fake,' I said. 'What I mean by fake is raw. When no one's ever used it before, it's something new under the sun, a whole new combination, that's bad. A real story is whatever you can predict, it has to be familiar, anyhow you have to know how it's going to come out, no exotic new material, no unexpected flights—'

He rushed out at me: 'What you want is to bore people!'

'I'm a very boring writer,' I admitted; out of politeness I kept from him how much his story, and even my own paraphrase of it, had already bored me. 'But in *principle* I'm right. The only good part in the whole thing was explaining about the *ba'al ga'avah*. People hate to read foreign words, but at least it's ancient wisdom. Old, old stuff.'

Then I told him how I had redesigned his story to include a ghost.

He opened the door of the stove and threw his manuscript in among the black-skinned potatoes.

'Why did you do that?'

'To show you I'm no *ba'al ga'avah*. I'm humble enough to burn up what somebody doesn't like.'

I said suspiciously, 'You've got other copies.'

'Sure. Other potatoes too.'

'Look,' I said, riding malice, 'it took me two hours to find this place, I have to go to the yard.'

'You want to take a leak? Come over to my cousin's. It's not far. My cousin's lived in this neighbourhood sixty years.'

Furiously I went after him. He was a crook leading me to the house of crooks. We walked through barrenness and canker, a ruined city, store-windows painted black, one or two curtained by gypsies, some boarded, barred, barbed, old newspapers rolling in the gutter, the sidewalks speckled with viscous blotch. Overhead a smell like kerosene, the breath of tenements. The cousin's toilet stank as if no one had flushed it in half a century; it had one of those tanks high up, attached to the ceiling, a perpetual drip running down the pull chain. The sink was in the kitchen. There was no soap; I washed my hands with Ajax powder while the goat explained me to his cousin.

'She's interested in the crown,' he said.

'Out of business,' said the cousin.

'Maybe for her.'

'Not doing business, that's all. For nobody whatsoever.'

'I'm not interested in buying one,' I said, 'just in finding out.'

'Crowns is against the law.'

'For healing,' the goat argued, 'not for showing. She knows the man who wrote that story. You remember about that guy, I told you, this famous writer who took—'

'Who took! Too much fame,' said the cousin, 'is why Saul sits in jail. Before newspapers and stories we were left in peace, we helped people peacefully.' She condemned me with an oil-surfaced eye, the colourless slick of the ripening cataract. 'My husband, a holy man, him they put in jail. Him! A whole year, twelve months! A man like that! Brains, a saint—'

'But he fooled people,' I said.

'In helping is no fooling. Out, lady. You had to pee, you peed. You needed a public facility, very good, now out. I don't look for extra customers for my toilet bowl.'

'Goodbye,' I said to the goat.

'You think there's hope for me?'

'Quit writing about ideas. Stay out of the yeshiva, watch out for religion. Don't make up stories about famous writers.'

'Listen,' he said – his nose was speckled with pustules of lust, his nostrils gaped – 'you didn't like that one, I'll give you another. I've got plenty more, I've got a crateful.'

'What are you talking,' said the cousin.

'She knows writers,' he said, 'in person. She knows how to get things published.'

I protested, 'I can hardly get published myself—'

'You published something?' said the cousin.

'A few things, not much.'

'Alex, bring Saul's box.'

'That's not the kind of stuff,' the goat said.

'Definitely. About expression I'm not so concerned like you. What isn't so regular, anyone with a desire and a pencil can fix it.'

The goat remonstrated, 'What Saul has is something else, it's not *writing*—'

'With connections,' said the cousin, 'nothing is something else, everything is writing. Lady, in one box I got my husband's entire holy life work. The entire theory of healing and making the dead ones come back for a personal appearance. We sent maybe to twenty printing houses, nothing doing. You got connections, I'll show you something.'

'Print,' I reminded her, 'is what you said got the rabbi in trouble.'

'Newspapers. Lies. False fame. Everything with a twist. You call him rabbi, who made from him a rabbi? The entire world says rabbi, so let it be rabbi. There he sits in jail, a holy man what did nothing his whole life to harm. Whatever a person asked for, this was what he gave. Whatever you wanted to call him, this was what he became. Alex! Take out Saul's box, it's in the bottom of the dresser with the crown.'

'The crown?' I said.

'The crown is nothing. What's something is Saul's brain. Alex!'

The goat shut his nostrils. He gave a snicker and disappeared. Through the kitchen doorway I glimpsed a sagging bed and heard a drawer grind open.

He came back lugging a carton with a picture of tomato cans on it. On top of it lay the crown. It was gloved in a green pattern of peephole diamonds.

'Here,' said the cousin, 'is Saul's ideas. Listen, that famous writer what went to steal from the papers – a fool. If he could steal what's in Saul's brain, what would he need a newspaper? Read!' She dipped a fist into a hiss of sheets and foamed up a sheaf of them. 'You'll see, the world will rush to put in print. The judge at the trial – I said to him, look in Saul's box, you'll see the truth, no fraud. If they would read Saul's papers, not only would he not sit in jail, the judge with hair growing from his ears they would throw out!'

I looked at the goat; he was not laughing. He reached out and put the crown on my head.

It felt lighter than I imagined. It was easy to forget you were wearing it.
I read:

Why does menkind not get what they wish for? This is an easy solution. He is used to No. Always No. So it comes he is afraid to ask.

'The power of positive thinking,' I said. 'A philosopher.'

'No, no,' the cousin intervened, 'not a philosopher, what do philosophers know to heal, to make real shadows from the dead?'

Through thinning threads of beard the goat said, 'Not a philosopher.'
I read:

Everything depends what you ask. Even you're not afraid to ask, plain asking is not sufficient. If you ask in a voice, there got to be an ear to listen in. The ear of Ha-shem, King of the Universe. (His Name we don't use it every minute like a shoelace.) A Jew don't go asking Ha-shem for inside information, for what reason He did this, what ideas He got on that, how come He let happen such-and-such a pogrom, why a good person loved by one and all dies with cancer, and a lousy bastard he's rotten to his partner and cheats and plays the numbers, this fellow lives to 120. With questions like this don't expect no replies, Ha-shem don't waste breath on trash from fleas. Ha-shem says, My secrets are My secrets, I command you what you got to do, the rest you leave to Me. This is no news that He don't reveal His deepest business. From that territory you get what you deserve, silence.

'What are you up to?' said the goat.
'Silence.'
'Ssh!' said the cousin. 'Alex, so let her read in peace!'

For us, not one word. He shuts up, His mouth is locked. So how come G-d conversed in history with Adam, with Abraham, with Moses? All right, you can argue that Moses and Abraham was worth it to G-d to listen to, what they said Ha-shem wanted to hear. After all they fed Him back His own ideas. An examination, and already they knew the answers. Smart guys, in the whole history of menkind no one else like these couple of guys. But with Adam, new and naked with no clothes on, just when the whole world was born, was Adam different from me and you? What did Adam know? Even right from wrong he didn't know yet. And still G-d thought, to Adam it's worthwhile to say a few words, I'm not wasting my breath. So what was so particular about Adam that he got Ha-shem's attention, and as regards me and you He don't blink an eye? Adam is better than me and you? We don't go around like a nudist colony, between good and lousy we already know what's what, with or without apples. To me and you G-d should also talk!

'You're following?' the cousin urged. 'You see what's in Saul's brain? A whole box full like this, and sits in jail!'

But when it comes wishes, when it comes dreams, who says No? Who says Ha-shem stops talking? Wishes, dreams, imaginations – like fishes in the head. Ha-shem put in Joseph's head two good dreams, were they lies? The truth and nothing but the truth! QED. To Adam Ha-shem spoke one way, and when He finishes with Moses he talks another way. In a dream, in a wish. That *epikoros* Sigmund Freud, he also figured this out. Whomever says Sigmund Freud stinks from sex, they're mistaken. A wish is the voice, a dream is the voice, an imagination is the voice, all is the voice of Ha-shem the Creator. Naturally a voice is a biological thing, who says No? Whatsoever happens inside the human is a biological thing.

'What are you up to?' the goat asked again.
'Biology.'
'Don't laugh: A man walked in here shaking all over, he walked out OK, I saw it myself.'
The cousin said mournfully, 'A healer.'
'I wrote a terrific story about that guy, I figured what he had was cystic fibrosis, I can show you—'
'There isn't any market for medical stories,' I said.
'This was a miracle story.'
'There are no miracles.'
'That's right!' said the cousin. She dug down again into the box. 'One time only, instead of plain writing down, Saul made up a story on this subject exactly. On a yellow piece paper. Aha, here. Alex, read aloud.'
The goat read:

One night in the middle of dim stars Ha-shem said, No more miracles! An end with miracles, I already did enough, from now on nothing.

So a king makes an altar and bows down. 'O Ha-shem, King of the Universe, I got a bad war on my hands and I'm taking a beating. Make a miracle and save the whole country.' Nothing doing, no miracle.

Good, says Ha-shem, this is how it's going to be from now on.

So along comes the Germans, in the camp they got a father and a little son maybe twelve years old. And the son is on the list to be gassed tomorrow. So the father runs around to find a German to bribe, G-d knows what he's got to bribe him with, maybe his wife's diamond ring that he hid somewhere and they didn't take it away yet. And he fixes up the whole thing, tomorrow he'll bring the diamond to the German and they'll take the boy off the list and they won't kill him. They'll slip in some other boy instead and who will know the difference?

Well, so that could be the end, but it isn't. All day after everything's fixed up, the father is thinking and thinking, and in the middle of the night he goes to an old rabbi that's in the camp also, and he tells the rabbi he's going to save his little son.

And the rabbi says, 'So why come to me? You made your decision already.' The father says, 'Yes, but they'll put another boy in his place.' The rabbi says, 'Instead of Isaac, Abraham put a ram. And that was for G-d. You put another child, and for what? To feed Moloch.' The father asks, 'What is the law on this?' 'The law is, Don't kill.'

The next day the father don't bring the bribe. And his eyes don't never see his beloved little child again. Well, so that could be the end, but it isn't. Ha-shem looks at what's happening, here is a man what didn't save his own boy so he wouldn't be responsible with killing someone else. Ha-shem says to Himself, I made a miracle anyhow. I blew in one man so much power of My commandments that his own flesh and blood he lets go to Moloch, so long he shouldn't kill. That I created even one such person like this is a very great miracle, and I didn't even notice I was doing it. So now positively no more.

And after this the destruction continues, no interruptions. Not only the son is gassed, but also the father, and also the boy what they would have put in his place. And also and also and also, until millions of bones of alsos goes up in smoke. About miracles Ha-shem don't change his mind except by accident. So the question menkind has to ask their conscience is this: If the father wasn't such a good commandment-keeper that it's actually a miracle to find a man like this left in the world, what could happen instead? And if only one single miracle could slip through before G-d notices it, which one? Suppose this father didn't use up the one miracle, suppose the miracle is that G-d will stop the murderers altogether, suppose! Instead: nothing doing, the father on account of one kid eats up the one miracle that's lying around loose. For the sake of one life, the whole world is lost.

But on this subject, what's written in our holy books? What the sages got to say? The sages say different: If you save one life only, it's like the whole world is saved. So which is true? Naturally, whatever's written is what's true. What does this prove? It proves that if you talk miracle, that's when everything becomes false. Men and women! Remember! No stories from miracles! No stories and no belief!

'You see?' said the cousin. 'Here you have Saul's theories exactly. Whoever says miracles, whoever says magic, tells a lie. On account of a lie a holy man sits in a cage.'

'And the crown?' I asked.

She ignored this. 'You'll help to publish. You'll give to the right people, you'll give to connections—'

'But why? Why do you need this?'

'What's valuable you give away, you don't keep it for yourself. Listen, is the Bible a secret? The whole world takes from it. Is Talmud a secret? Whatever's a lie should be a secret, not what's holy and true!'

I appealed to the goat. He was licking his fingertips. 'I can't digest any of this—'

'You haven't had a look at Saul,' he said, 'that's why.'

The cousin said meanly, 'I saw you put on her the crown.'

'She wants it.'

'The crown is nothing.'

'She wants it.'

'Then show her Saul.'

'You mean in prison?' I said.

'In the bedroom on the night table.'

The goat fled. This time he returned carrying a small gilded tin frame. In it was a snapshot of another bearded man.

'Look closely.'

But instead of examining the photograph, I all at once wanted to study the goat's cousin. She was one of those tiny twig-thin old women who seem to enlarge the more you get used to their voices. It was as if her whine and her whirr were a pump, and pumped her up; she was now easily as tall as I (though I am myself not very tall) and expanding curiously. She was wearing a checked nylon housedress and white socks in slippers, above which bulged purplish varicose nodules. Her eyes were terribly magnified by metal-rimmed lenses, and looked out at me with the vengefulness of a pair of greased platters. I was astonished to see that a chromium crown had buried itself among the strings of her wandering hairs: having been too often dyed ebony, they were slipping out of their follicles and onto her collarbone. She had an exaggerated widow's peak and was elsewhere a little bit bald.

The goat too wore a crown.

'I thought there was only one left,' I objected.

'Look at Saul, you'll see the only one.'

The man in the picture wore a silver crown. I recognized him, though the light was shut off in him and the space of his flesh was clearly filled.

'Who is this?' I said.

'Saul.'

'But I've seen him!'

'That's right,' the cousin said.

'Because you wanted to,' said the goat.

'The ghost I put in your story,' I reminded him, 'this is what it looked like.'

The cousin breathed. 'You published that story?'

'It's not even written down.'

'Whose ghost was it?' asked the goat.

'Tchernikhovsky's. The Hebrew poet. A *ba'al ga'avah*. He wrote a poem called "Before the Statue of Apollo". In the last line God is bound with leather thongs.'

'Who binds him?'

'The Jews. With their phylacteries. I want to read more,' I said.

The two of them gave me the box. The little picture they set on the kitchen table, and they stood over me in their twinkling crowns while I splashed my hands through the false rabbi's stories. Some were already browning at the margins, in ink turned violet, some were on lined school paper, written with a ball-point pen. About a third were in Yiddish; there was even a thin notebook all in Russian; but most were pressed out in pencil in an immigrant's English on all kinds of odd loose sheets, the insides of old New Year greeting cards, the backs of cashiers' tapes from the supermarket, in one instance the ripped-out leather womb of an old wallet.

Saul's ideas were:

sorcery, which he denied.

levitation, which he doubted.

magic, which he sneered at.

miracles, which he denounced.

healing, which he said belonged in hospitals.

instant cures, which he said were fancies and delusions.

the return of deceased loved ones, which he said were wishful hallucinations.

the return of dead enemies, which ditto.

plural gods, which he disputed.

demons, which he derided.

amulets, which he disparaged and repudiated.

Satan, from which hypothesis he scathingly dissented.

He ridiculed everything. He was a rationalist.

'It's amazing,' I said, 'that he looks just like Tchernikhovsky.'

'What does Tchernikhovsky look like?' one of the two crowned ones asked me; I was no longer sure which.

'I don't know, how should I know? Once I saw his picture in an anthology of translations, but I don't remember it. Why are there so many crowns in this room? What's the point of these crowns?'

Then I found the paper on crowns:

You take a real piece mineral, what kings wear. You put it on, you become like a king. What you wish, you get. But what you get you shouldn't believe in unless it's real. How do you know when something's real? If it lasts. How long? This depends. If you wish for a Pyramid, it should last as long like a regular Pyramid lasts. If you wish for long life, it should last as long like your own grandfather. If you wish for a Magic Crown, it should last as long like the brain what it rests on.

I interrupted myself: 'Why doesn't he wish himself out of prison? Why didn't he wish himself out of getting sentenced?'

'He lets things take their course.'

Then I found the paper on things taking their course:

From my own knowledge I knew a fellow what loved a woman, Beylinke, and she died. So he looked and looked for a twin to this Beylinke, and it's no use, such a woman don't exist. Instead he married a different type altogether, and he made her change her name to Beylinke and make love on the left side, like the real Beylinke. And if he called Beylinke! and she forgot to answer (her name was Ethel) he gave her a good knock on the back and one day he knocked hard into the kidney and she got a growth and she died. And all he got from his forcing was a lonesome life.

Everything is according to destiny, you can't change nothing. Not that anybody can know what happens before it happens, not even Ha-shem knows which dog will bite which cat next week in Persia.

'Enough,' said one of the two in the crowns. 'You read and you took enough. You ate enough and you drank enough from this juice. Now you got to pay.'
'To pay?'
'The payment is, to say thank you what we showed you everything, you take and you publish.'
'Publishing isn't the same as Paradise.'
'For some of us it is,' said one.
'She knows from Paradise!' scoffed the other.
They thrust the false rabbi's face into my face.
'It isn't English, it isn't even coherent, it's inconsistent, it's crazy, nothing hangs together, nobody in his right mind would—'
'Connections you got.'
'No.'
'That famous writer.'
'A stranger.'
'Then somebody else.'
'There's no one. I can't make magic—'
'*Ba'al ga'avah!* You're better than Saul? Smarter? Cleverer? You got better ideas? You, a nothing, they print, and he sits in a box?'
'I looked up one of your stories. It stank, lady. The one called "Usurpation". Half of it's swiped, you ought to get sued. You don't know when to stop. You swipe other people's stories and you go on and on, on and on, I fell asleep over it. Boring! Long-winded!'
The mass of sheets pitched into my lap. My fingers flashed upwards: there was the crown, with its crocheted cover, its blunted points. Little threads had gotten tangled in my hair. If I tugged, the roots would shriek. Tchernikhovsky's paper eyes looked frightened. Crevices opened on either side of his nose and from the left nostril the grey bone of his skull poked out, a cheekbone like a pointer.
'I don't have better ideas,' I said. 'I'm not interested in ideas, I don't care about ideas. I hate ideas. I only care about stories.'

'Then take Saul's stories!'

'Trash. Justice and mercy. He tells you how to live, what to do, the way to think. Righteousness fables, morality tales. Didactic stuff. Rabbinical trash,' I said. 'What I mean is *stories*. Even you,' I said to the goat, 'wanting to write about writers! Morality, mortality! You people eat yourself up with morality and mortality!'

'What else should a person eat?'

Just then I began to feel the weight of the crown. It pressed unerringly into the secret tunnels of my brain. A pain like a grief leaped up behind my eyes, up through the temples, up, up, into the marrow of the crown. Every point of it was a spear, a nail. The crown was no different from the bone of my head. The false rabbi Tchernikhovsky tore himself from the tin prison of his frame and sped to the ceiling as if gassed. He had bluish teeth and goblin's wings made of brown leather. Except for the collar and cravat that showed in the photograph, below his beard he was naked. His testicles were leathery. His eyeballs were glass, like a doll's. He was solid as a doll; I was not so light-headed as to mistake him for an apparition. His voice was as spindly as a harpsichord: 'Choose!'

'Between what and what?'

'The Creator or the creature. God or god. The Name of Names or Apollo.'

'Apollo,' I said on the instant.

'Good,' he tinkled, 'blessings,' he praised me, 'flowings and flowings, streams, brooks, lakes, waters out of waters.'

Stories came from me then, births and births of tellings, narratives and suspenses, turning-points and palaces, foam of the sea, mermen sewing, dragons pullulating out of quicksilver, my mouth was a box, my ears flowed, they gushed legends and tales, none of them of my own making, all of them acquired, borrowed, given, taken, inherited, stolen, plagiarized, usurped, chronicles and sagas invented at the beginning of the world by the offspring of giants copulating with the daughters of men. A king broke out of the shell of my left eye and a queen from the right one, the box of my belly lifted its scarred lid to let out frogs and swans, my womb was cleft and stories burst free of their balls of blood. Stories choked the kitchen, crept up the toilet tank, replenished the bedroom, knocked off the goat's crown, knocked off the cousin's crown, my own crown in its coat contended with the vines and tangles of my hair, the false rabbi's beard had turned into strips of leather, into whips, the whips struck at my crown, it slid to my forehead, the whips curled round my arm, the crown sliced the flesh of my forehead.

At last it fell off.

The cousin cried out her husband's name.

'Alex,' I called to the goat: the name of a conqueror, Aristotle's pupil, the arrogant god-man.

In the hollow streets which the Jews had left behind there were scorched absences, apparitions, usurpers. Someone had broken the glass of the kosher butcher's abandoned window and thrown in a pig's head, with anatomical tubes still dripping from the neck.

When we enter Paradise there will be a cage for story-writers, who will be taught as follows:

All that is not Law is levity.

But we have not yet ascended. The famous writer has not. The goat has not. The false rabbi has not; he sits out his year. A vanity press is going to bring out his papers. The bill for editing, printing, and binding will be $1,847.45. The goat's cousin will pay for it from a purse in the bottom bowel of the night table.

The goat inhabits the deserted synagogue, drinking wine, littering the yard with his turds. Occasionally he attends a public reading. Many lusts live in his chin-hairs, like lice.

Only Tchernikhovsky and the shy old writer of Jerusalem have ascended. The old writer of Jerusalem is a fiction; murmuring psalms, he snacks on leviathan and polishes his Prize with the cuff of his sleeve. Tchernikhovsky eats nude at the table of the nude gods, clean-shaven now, his limbs radiant, his youth restored, his sex splendidly erect, the discs of his white ears sparkling, a convivial fellow; he eats without self-restraint from the celestial menu, and when the Sabbath comes (the Sabbath of Sabbaths, which flowers every seven centuries in the perpetual Sabbath of Eden), as usual he avoids the congregation of the faithful before the Footstool and the Throne. Then the taciturn little Canaanite idols call him, in the language of the spheres, kike.

The Butterfly
and the
Traffic Light

... the moth for the star.

– Shelley

Jerusalem, that phoenix city, is not known by its street-names. Neither is Baghdad, Copenhagen, Rio de Janeiro, Camelot, or Athens; nor Peking, Florence, Babylon, St Petersburg. These fabled capitals rise up ready-spired, story-domed and filigreed; they come to us at the end of a plain, behind hill or cloud, walled and moated by myths and antique rumours. They are built of copper, silver, and gold; they are founded on milk-white stone; the bright thrones of ideal kings jewel them. Balconies, parks, little gates, columns and statuary, carriage-houses and stables, attics, kitchens, gables, tiles, yards, rubied steeples, brilliant roofs, peacocks, lapdogs, grand ladies, beggars, towers, bowers, harbours, barbers, wigs, judges, courts, and wines of all sorts fill them. Yet, though we see the shimmer of the smallest pebble beneath the humblest foot in all the great seats of legend, still not a single street is celebrated. The thoroughfares of beautiful cities are somehow obscure, unless, of course, we count Venice: but a canal is not really the same as a street. The ways, avenues, plazas, and squares of old cities are lost to us, we do not like to think of them, they move like wicked scratches upon the smooth enamel of our golden towns; we have forgotten most of them. There is no beauty in cross-section – we take our cities, like our wishes, whole.

It is different with places of small repute or where time has not yet deigned to be an inhabitant. It is different especially in America. They tell us that Boston is our Jerusalem; but, as anyone who has ever lived there knows, Boston owns only half a history. Honour, pomp, hallowed scenes, proud families, the Athenaeum and the Symphony are Boston's;

but Boston has no tragic tradition. Boston has never wept. No Bostonian has ever sung, mourning for his city, 'If I do not remember thee, let my tongue cleave to the roof of my mouth' – for, to manage his accent, the Bostonian's tongue is already in that position. We hear of Beacon Hill and Back Bay, of Faneuil market and State Street: it is all cross-section, all map. And the State House with its gilt dome (it counts for nothing that Paul Revere supplied the bottom-most layer of gold leaf: he was businessman, not horseman, then) throws back furious sunsets garishly, boastfully, as no power-rich Carthage, for shame, would dare. There is no fairy mist in Boston. True, its street-names are notable: Boylston, Washington, Commonwealth, Marlborough, Tremont, Beacon; and then the Squares, Kenmore, Copley, Louisburg, and Scollay – evidence enough that the whole, unlike Jerusalem, has not transcended its material parts. Boston has a history of neighbourhoods. Jerusalem has a history of histories.

The other American towns are even less fortunate. It is not merely that they lack rudimentary legends, that their names are homely and unimaginative, half ending in burg and half in ville, or that nothing has ever happened in them. Unlike the ancient capitals, they are not infixed in our vision, we are not born knowing them, as though, in some earlier migration, we had been dwellers there: for no one is a stranger to Jerusalem. And unlike even Boston, most cities in America have no landmarks, no age-enshrined graveyards (although death is famous everywhere), no green park to show a massacre, poet's murder, or high marriage. The American town, alas, has no identity hinting at immortality; we recognize it only by its ubiquitous street-names: sometimes Main Street, sometimes High Street, and frequently Central Avenue. Grandeur shuns such streets. It is all ambition and aspiration there, and nothing to look back at. Cicero said that men who know nothing of what has gone before them are like children. But Main, High, and Central have no past; rather, their past is now. It is not the fault of the inhabitants that nothing has gone before them. Nor are they to be condemned if they make their spinal streets conspicuous, and confer egregious lustre and false acclaim on Central, High, or Main, and erect minarets and marquees indeed as though their city were already in dream and fable. But it is where one street in particular is regarded as the central life, the high spot, the main drag, that we know the city to be a pre-natal trace only. The kiln of history bakes out these prides and these divisions. When the streets have been forgotten a thousand years, the divine city is born.

In the farm-village where the brewer Buldenquist had chosen to establish his Mighty College, the primitive commercial artery was called, not surprisingly, 'downtown', and then, more respectably, Main Street, and then, rather covetously looking to civic improvement, Buldenquist Road. But the Sacred Bull had dedicated himself to the foundation and perpetuation of scientific farming, and had a prejudice against putting money into pavements and other citifications. So the town fathers (for by that time the place *was* a town, swollen by the boarding houses and saloons frequented by crowds of young farm students) – the town fathers scratched their heads for historical allusions embedded in local folklore, but found nothing except two or three old family scandals, until one day a travelling salesman named Rogers sold the mayor an 'archive' – a wrinkled, torn, doused, singed, and otherwise quite ancient-looking holographic volume purporting to hold the records and diaries of one Colonel Elihu Bigghe. This rather obscure officer had by gratifying coincidence passed through the neighbourhood during the war with a force of two hundred, the document claimed, encountering a skirmish with the enemy on the very spot of the present firehouse – the 'war' being, according to some, the Civil War, and in the positive authority of others, one of the lesser Indian Wars – in his private diary Bigghe was not, after all, expected to drop hints. At any rate, the skirmish was there in detail – one hundred or more of the enemy dead; not one of ours; ninety-seven of theirs wounded; our survivors all hale but three; the bravery of our side; the cowardice and brutality of the foe; and further pious and patriotic remarks on Country, Creator, and Christian Charity. A decade or so after this remarkable discovery the mayor heard of Rogers' arrest, somewhere in the East, for forgery, and in his secret heart began to wonder whether he might not have been taken in: but by then the Bigghe diaries were under glass in the antiseptic-smelling lobby of the town hall, schoolchildren were being herded regularly by their teachers to view it, boring Fourth of July speeches had been droned before the firehouse in annual commemoration, and most people had forgotten that Bigghe Road had ever been called after the grudging brewer. And who could blame the inhabitants if, after half a hundred years, they began to spell it Big Road? For by then the town had grown into a city, wide and clamorous.

*

For Fishbein it was an imitation of a city. He claimed (not altogether correctly) that he had seen all the capitals of Europe, and yet had never come upon anything to match Big Road in name or character. He liked to tell how the streets of Europe were 'employed', as he put it: he would people them with beggars and derelicts – 'they keep their cash and their beds in the streets'; and with crowds assembled for riot or amusement or politics – 'in Moscow they filled, the revolutionaries I mean, three troikas with White Russians and shot them, the White Russians I mean, and let them run wild in the street, the horses I mean, to spill all the corpses' (but he had never been to Moscow); and with travellers determined on objective and destination – 'they use the streets there to go from one place to another, the original design of streets, *n'est-ce pas?*' Fishbein considered that, while a city exists for its own sake, a street is utilitarian. The uses of Big Road, on the contrary, were plainly secondary. In Fishbein's view Big Road had come into being only that the city might have a conscious centre – much as the nucleus of a cell demonstrates the cell's character and maintains its well-being ('although,' Fishbein argued, 'in the cell it is a moot question whether the nucleus exists for the sake of the cell or the cell for the sake of the nucleus: whereas it is clear that a formless city such as this requires a centrality from which to learn the idea of form'). But if the city were to have modelled itself after Big Road, it would have grown long, like a serpent, and unreliable in its sudden coilings. This had not happened. Big Road crept, toiled, and ran, but the city nibbled at this farmhouse and that, and spread and spread with no pattern other than exuberance and greed. And if Fishbein had to go to biology or botany or history for his analogies, the city was proud that it had Big Road to stimulate such comparisons.

Big Road was different by day and by night, weekday and weekend. Daylight, sunlight, and even rainlight gave everything its shadow, winter and summer, so that every person and every object had its Doppelgänger, persistent and hopeless. There was a kind of doubleness that clung to the street, as though one remembered having seen this and this and this before. The stores, hung with signs, had it, the lazy-walking old women had it (all of them uniformly rouged in the geometric centres of their cheeks like victims of some senile fever already dangerously epidemic), the traffic lights suspended from their wires had it, the air dense with the local accent had it.

This insistent sense of recognition was the subject of one of Fishbein's favourite lectures to his walking companion. 'It's America repeating itself! Imitating its own worst habits! Haven't I seen the same thing everywhere? It's a simultaneous urbanization all over, you can almost hear the coxswain crow, "Now all together, boys!" This lamppost, I saw it years ago in Birmingham, that same scalloped bowl teetering on a wrought-iron stick. At least in Europe the lampposts look different in each place, they have individual characters. And this traffic light! There's no cross-street there, so what do they want it for in such a desert? I'll tell you: they put it up to pretend they're a real city – to tease the transients who might be naïve enough to stop for it. And that click and buzz, that flash and blink, why do they all do that in just the same way? Repeat and repeat, nothing meaningful by itself. . . .'

'I don't mind them, they're like abstract statues,' Isabel once replied to this. 'As though we were strangers from another part of the world and thought them some kind of religious icon with a red and a green eye. The ones on poles especially.'

He recognized his own fancifulness, coarsened, laboured, and made literal. He had taught her to think like this. But she had a distressing disinclination to shake off logic; she did not know how to ride her intuition.

'No, no,' he objected, 'then you don't know what an icon is! A traffic light could never be anything but a traffic light. What kind of religion would it be which had only one version of its deity – a whole row of identical icons in every city?'

She considered rapidly. 'An advanced religion. I mean a monotheistic one.'

'And what makes you certain that monotheism is "advanced"? On the contrary, little dear! It's as foolish to be fixed on one God as it is to be fixed on one idea, isn't that plain? The index of advancement is flexibility. Human temperaments are so variable, how could one God satisfy them all? The Greeks and Romans had a god for every personality, the way the Church has a saint for every mood. Savages, Hindus, and Roman Catholics understand all that. It's only the Jews and their imitators who insist on a rigid unitarian God – I can't think of anything more unfortunate for history: it's the narrow way, like God imposing his will on Job. The disgrace of the fable is that Job didn't turn to another god, one more germane to his illusions. It's what any sensible man would have done. And then wouldn't the boils have gone away of their own accord? The Bible states clearly that they were simply a psychogenic nervous disorder – isn't that what's meant by "Satan"? There's no disaster that doesn't come of missing an imagination: I've told you that before, little dear. Now the Maccabean War, for instance, for an altogether unintelligible occasion! All Antiochus the Fourth intended – he was Emperor of Syria at the time – was to set up a statue of Zeus on the altar of the Temple of Jerusalem, a harmless affair – who would be hurt by it? It wasn't that Antiochus cared anything for Zeus himself – he was nothing if not an agnostic: a philosopher, anyway – the whole movement was only to symbolize the Syrian hegemony. It wasn't worth a war to get rid of the thing! A little breadth of vision, you see, a little imagination, a little *flexibility*, I mean – there ought to be room for Zeus *and* God under one roof. . . . That's why traffic lights won't do for icons! They haven't been conceived in a pluralistic spirit, they're all exactly alike. Icons ought to differ from one another, don't you see? An icon's only a mask, that's the point, a representational mask which stands for an idea.'

'In that case,' Isabel tried it, 'if a traffic light were an icon it would stand for two ideas, stop and go—'

'Stop and go, virtue and vice, logic and law! Why are you always on the verge of moralizing, little dear, when it's a fever, not morals, that keeps the world spinning! Are masks only for showing the truth? But no, they're for hiding, they're for misleading, too. . . . It's a maxim, you see: one mask reveals, another conceals.'

'Which kind is better?'

'Whichever you happen to be wearing at the moment,' he told her.

Often he spoke to her in this manner among night crowds on Big Road. Sometimes, too argumentative to be touched, she kept her hands in her pockets and, unexpectedly choosing a corner to turn, he would wind a rope of hair around his finger and draw her leashed after him. She always went easily; she scarcely needed to be led. Among all those night walkers the two of them seemed obscure, dimmed-out, and under a heat-screened autumn moon, one of those shimmering country-moons indigenous to midwestern America, he came to a kind of truce with the street. It was no reconcilement, nothing so friendly as that, not even a cessation of warfare, only of present aggression. To come to terms with Big Road would have been to come to terms with America. And since this was impossible, he dallied instead with masks, and icons, and Isabel's long brown hair.

After twilight on the advent of the weekend the clutter of banners, the parades, the caravans of curiously outfitted convertibles vanished, and the students came out to roam. They sought each other with antics and capers, brilliantly tantalizing in the beginning darkness. Voices hung in the air, shot upwards all along the street, and celebrated the Friday madness. It was a grand posture of relief: the stores already closed but the display-windows still lit, and the mannequins leaning forward from their glass cages with leers of painted horror and malignant eyeballs; and then the pirate movie letting out (this is 1949, my hearties), and the clusters of students flowing in gleaming rows, like pearls on a string, past posters raging with crimson seas and tall-masted ships and black-haired beauties shrieking, out of the scented palace into drugstores and ice-cream parlours. Sweet, sweet, it was all sweet there before the shops and among the crawling automobiles and under the repetitious street lamps and below the singular moon. On the sidewalks the girls sprouted like tapestry blossoms, their heads rising from slender necks like woven petals swaying on the stems. They wore thin dresses, and short capelike coats over them; they wore no stockings, and their round bare legs moved boldly through an eddy of rainbow skirts; the swift white bone of ankle cut into the breath of the wind. A kind of greed drove Fishbein among them. 'See that one,' he would say, consumed with yearning, turning back in the wake of the young lasses to observe their gait, and how the filaments of their dresses seemed to float below their arms caught in a gesture, and how the dry sparks of their eyes flickered with the sheen of spiders.

And he would halt until Isabel too had looked. 'Are you envious?' he asked, 'because you are not one of them? Then console yourself.' But he saw that she studied his greed and read his admiration. 'Take comfort,' he said again. 'They are not free to become themselves. They are different from you.' 'Yes,' Isabel answered, 'they are prettier.' 'They will grow corrupt. Time will overwhelm them. They have only their one moment, like the butterflies.' 'Looking at butterflies gives pleasure.' 'Yes, it is a kind of joy, little dear, but full of poison. It belongs to the knowledge of rapid death. The butterfly lures us not only because he is beautiful, but because he is transitory. The caterpillar is uglier, but in him we can regard the better joy of becoming. The caterpillar's fate is bloom. The butterfly's is waste.'

They stopped, and around them milled and murmured the girls in their wispy dresses and their little cut-off capes, and their yellow hair, whitish hair, tan hair, hair of brown-and-pink. The lithe, O the ladies young! It was all sweet there among the tousled bevies wormy with ribbon streamers and sashes, mock-tricked with make-believe gems, gems pinned over the breast, on the bar of a barrette, aflash even in the rims of their glasses. The alien gaiety took Fishbein in; he rocked in their strong sea-wave. From a record shop came a wild shiver of jazz, eyes unwound like coils of silk and groped for other eyes: the street churned with the laughter of girls. And Fishbein, arrested in the heart of the whirlpool, was all at once plunged again into war with the street and with America, where everything was illusion and all illusion led to disillusion. What use was it then for him to call O lyric ladies, what use to chant O languorous lovely November ladies, O lilting, lolling, lissome ladies – while corrosion sat waiting in their ears, he saw the maggots breeding in their dissolving jewels?

Meanwhile Isabel frowned with logic. 'But it's only that the caterpillar's future is longer and his fate farther off. In the end he will die too.' 'Never, never, never,' said Fishbein; 'it is only the butterfly who dies, and then he has long since ceased to be a caterpillar. The caterpillar never dies. Neither to die nor to be immortal, it is the enviable state, little dear, to live always at the point of beautiful change! That is what it means to be extraordinary – when did I tell you that?—' He bethought himself. 'The first day, of course. It's always best to begin with the end – with the image of what is desired. If I had begun with the beginning I would have bored you, you would have gone away. . . . In my ideal kingdom, little dear, everyone, even the very old, will be passionately in the process of guessing at and preparing for his essential self. Boredom will be unnatural, like a curse, or unhealthy, like a plague. Everyone will be extraordinary.'

'But if the whole population were extraordinary,' Isabel objected, 'then nobody would be extraordinary.'

'Ssh, little dear, why must you insist on dialectics? Nothing true is ever found by that road. There are millions of caterpillars, and not one of them is intended to die, and they are all of them extraordinary. *Your* aim,' he admonished, as they came into the darkened neighbourhood beyond Big Road, 'is to avoid growing into a butterfly. Come,' he said, and took her hand, 'let us live for that.'

A Mercenary

Stanislav Lushinski, a Pole and a diplomat, was not a Polish diplomat. People joked that he was a mercenary, and would sell his tongue to any nation that bargained for it. In certain offices of the glass rectangle in New York he was known as 'the PM' – which meant not so much that they considered him easily as influential as the Prime Minister of his country (itself a joke: his country was a speck, no more frightening than a small wart on the western – or perhaps it was the eastern – flank of Africa), but stood, rather, for Paid Mouthpiece.

His country. Altogether he had lived in it, not counting certain lengthy official and confidential visits, for something over fourteen consecutive months, at the age of nineteen – that was twenty-seven years ago – en route to America. But though it was true that he was not a native, it was a lie that he was not a patriot. Something in that place had entered him, he could not shake out of his nostrils the musky dreamy fragrance of nights in the capital – the capital was, as it happened, the third-largest city, though it had the most sophisticated populace. There, his colleagues claimed, the men wore trousers and the women covered their teats.

The thick night-blossoms excited him. Born to a flagstoned Warsaw garden, Lushinski did not know the names of flowers beyond the most staid dooryard sprigs, daisies and roses, and was hardly conscious that these heaps of petals, meat-white, a red as dark and boiling as an animal's maw, fevered oranges and mauves, the lobe-leafed mallows, all hanging downwards like dyed hairy hanged heads from tall bushes at dusk, were less than animal. It was as if he disbelieved in botany, although he believed gravely enough in jungle. He felt himself native to these mammalian perfumes, to the dense sweetness of so many roundnesses, those round burnt hills at the edge of the capital, the little round brown mounds of the girls he pressed down under the trees – he, fresh out of the roil of Europe; they, secret to the ground, grown out of the brown ground, on which he threw himself, with his tongue on their black-brown nipples, learning their language.

He spoke it not like a native – though he was master of that tangled clot of extraordinary inflections scraped on the palate, nasal whistles, beetle-clicks – but like a preacher. The language had no written literature. A century ago a band of missionaries had lent it the Roman alphabet and transcribed in it queer versions of the Psalms, so that

thou satest in the throne judging right

came out in argot:

god squat-on-earth-mound
tells who owns
accidentally-decapitated-by-fallen-tree-trunk
deer,

and it was out of this Bible, curiously like a moralizing hunting manual, the young Lushinski received his lessons in syntax. Except for when he lay under a cave of foliage with a brown girl, he studied alone, and afterwards (he was still only approaching twenty) translated much of Jonah, which the exhausted missionaries had left unfinished. But the story of the big fish seemed simple-minded in that rich deep tongue, which had fifty-four words describing the various parts and positions of a single rear fin. And for 'prow' many more: 'nose-of-boat-facing-brightest-star', or star of middle dimness, or dimmest of all; 'nose-of-boat-fully-invisible-in-rain-fog'; half-visible; quarter-visible; and so on. It was an observant, measuring, meticulous language.

His English was less given to sermonizing. It was diplomat's English: which does not mean that it was deceitful, but that it was innocent before passion, and minutely truthful about the order of paragraphs in all previous documentation.

He lived, in New York, with a mistress: a great rosy woman, buxom, tall and talkative. To him she was submissive.

In Geneva – no one could prove this – he lived on occasion with a strenuous young Italian, a coppersmith, a boy of twenty-four, red-haired and lean and not at all submissive.

His colleagues discovered with surprise that Lushinski was no bore. It astounded them. They resented him for it, because the comedy had been theirs, and he the object of it. A white man, he spoke for a black country: this made a place for him on television. At first he came as a sober financial attaché, droning economic complaints (the recently expelled colonial power had exploited the soil by excessive plantings; not an acre was left fallow; the chief crop – jute? cocoa? rye? Lushinski was too publicly fastidious ever to call it by its name – was thereby severely diminished, there was famine in the south). And then it was noticed that he was, if one listened with care, inclined to obliqueness – to, in fact, irony.

It became plain that he could make people laugh. Not that he told jokes, not even that he was a wit – but he began to recount incidents out of his own life. Sometimes he was believed; often not.

In his office he was ambitious but gregarious. His assistant, Morris Ngambe, held an Oxford degree in political science. He was a fat-cheeked, flirtatious young man with a glossy bronze forehead, perfectly rounded, like a goblet. He was exactly half Lushinski's age, and sometimes, awash in papers after midnight, their ties thrown off and their collars undone, they would send out for sandwiches and root beer (Lushinski lusted after everything American and sugared); in this atmosphere almost of equals they would compare boyhoods.

Ngambe's grandfather was the brother of a chief; his father had gone into trade, aided by the colonial governor himself. The history and politics of all this was murky; nevertheless Ngambe's father became rich. He owned a kind of assembly-line consisting of many huts. Painted gourds stood in the doorways like monitory dwarfs; these were to assure prosperity. His house grew larger and larger; he built a wing for each wife. Morris was the eldest son of the favourite wife, a woman of intellect and religious attachment. She stuck, Morris said, to the old faith. A friend of Morris's childhood – a boy raised in the missionary school, who had grown up into a model book-keeper and dedicated Christian – accused her of scandal: instead of the Trinity, he shouted to her husband (his employer), she worshipped plural gods; instead of caring for the Holy Spirit, she adhered to animism. Society was progressing, and she represented nothing but regression: a backslider into primitivism. The village could not tolerate it, even in a female. Since it was fundamental propriety to ignore wives, it was clear that the fellow was crazy to raise a fuss over what one of a man's females thought or did. But it was also fundamental propriety to ignore an insane man (in argot the word for 'insane' was, in fact, 'becoming-childbearer', or, alternatively, 'bottom-hole-mouth'), so everyone politely turned away, except Morris's mother, who followed a precept of her religion: a female who has a man (in elevated argot 'lord') for her enemy must offer him her loins in reconciliation. Morris's mother came naked at night to her accuser's hut and parted her legs for him on the floor. Earlier he had been sharpening pencils; he took the knife from his pencil-pot (a gourd hollowed-out and painted, one of Morris's father's most successful export items) and stabbed her breasts. Since she had recently given birth (Morris was twenty years older than his youngest brother), she bled both blood and milk, and died howling, smeared pink. But because in her religion the goddess Tanake declares before five hundred lords that she herself became divine through having been cooked in her own milk, Morris's mother, with her last cry, pleaded for similar immortality; and so his father, who was less pious but who had loved her profoundly, made a feast. While the governor looked the other way, the murderer was murdered; Morris was unwilling to describe the execution. It was, he said in his resplendent Oxonian voice, 'very clean'. His mother was ceremonially eaten; this accomplished her transfiguration. Her husband and eldest son were obliged to share the principal sacrament, the nose, 'emanator-of-wind-of-birth'. The six other wives – Morris called each of them Auntie – divided among them a leg steamed in goat's milk. And everyone who ate at that festival, despite the plague of gnats that attended the day, became lucky ever after. Morris was admitted to Oxford; his grandfather's brother died at a very great age and his father replaced him as chief; the factory acquired brick buildings and chimneys and began manufacturing vases both of ceramic and glass; the colonial power was thrown out; Morris's mother was turned into a goddess, and her picture sold in the villages. Her name had been Tuka. Now she was Tanake-Tuka, and could perform miracles for devout women, and sometimes for men.

Some of Ngambe's tales Lushinski passed off as his own observations of what he always referred to on television as 'bush life'. In the privacy of his office he chided Morris for having read too many Tarzan books. 'I have only seen the movies,' Ngambe protested. He recalled how in London on Sunday afternoons there was almost nothing else to do. But he believed his mother had been transformed into a divinity. He said he often prayed to her. The taste of her flesh had bestowed on him simplicity and geniality.

From those tedious interviews by political analysts Lushinski moved at length to false living rooms with false 'hosts' contriving false conversation. He felt himself recognized, a foreign celebrity. He took up the habit of looking caressingly into the very camera with the red light alive on it, signalling it was sensitive to his nostrils, his eyebrows, his teeth and his ears. And under all that lucid theatrical blaze, joyful captive on an easy chair between an imbecile film reviewer and a cretinous actress, he began to weave out a life.

Sometimes he wished he could write out of imagination: he fancied a small memoir, as crowded with desires as with black leafy woods, or else sharp and deathly as a blizzard; and at the same time very brief and chaste, though full of horror. But he was too intelligent to be a writer. His intelligence was a version of cynicism. He rolled irony like an extra liquid in his mouth. He could taste it exactly the way Morris tasted his mother's nose. It gave him powers.

He pretended to educate. The 'host' asked him why he, a white man, represented a black nation. He replied that Disraeli too had been of another race, though he led Britain. The 'host' asked him whether his fondness for his adopted country induced him to patronize its inhabitants. This he did not answer; instead he hawked up into the actress's handkerchief – leaning right over to pluck it from her decolletage where she had tucked it – and gave the 'host' a shocked stare. The audience laughed – he seemed one of those gruff angry comedians they relished.

Then he said: 'You can only patronize if you are a customer. In my country we have no brothels.'

Louisa – his mistress – did not appear on the programmes with him. She worried about his stomach. 'Stasek has such a very small stomach,' she said. She herself had oversized eyes, rubbed blue over the lids, a large fine nose, a mouth both large and nervous. She mothered him and made him eat. If he ate corn she would slice the kernels off the cob and warn him about his stomach. 'It is very hard for Stasek to eat, with his little stomach. It shrank when he was a boy. You know he was thrown into the forest when he was only six.'

Then she would say: 'Stasek is generous to Jews but he doesn't like the pious ones.'

They spoke of her as a German countess – her last name was preceded by a 'von' – but she seemed altogether American, though her accent had a fake melody either Irish or Swedish. She claimed she had once run a famous chemical corporation in California, and truly she seemed as worldly as that, an executive, with her sudden jagged gestures, her large hands all alertness, her curious attentiveness to her own voice, her lips painted orange as fire. But with Lushinski she could be very quiet. If they sat at some party on opposite sides of the room, and if he lifted one eyebrow, or less, if he twitched a corner of his mouth or a piece of eyelid, she understood and came to him at once. People gaped; but she was proud. 'I gave up everything for Stanislav. Once I had three hundred and sixty people under me. I had two women who were my private secretaries, one for general work, one exclusively for dictation and correspondence. I wasn't always the way you see me now. When Stasek tells me to come, I come. When he tells me to stay, I stay.'

She confessed all this aloofly, and with the panache of royalty. On official business he went everywhere without her. It was true his stomach was very flat. He was like one of those playing-card soldiers in *Alice in Wonderland*: his shoulders a pair of neat thin corners, everything else cut along straight lines. The part in his hair (so sleekly black it looked painted on) was a clean line exactly above the terrifying pupil of his left eye. This pupil measured and divided, the lid was as cold and precise as the blade of a knife. Even his nose was a rod of machined steel there under the live skin – separated from his face, it could have sliced anything. Still, he was handsome, or almost so, and when he spoke it was necessary to attend. It was as if everything he said was like that magic pipe in the folktale, the sound of which casts a spell on its hearers' feet and makes the whole town dance madly, willy-nilly. His colleagues only remembered to be scornful when they were not face to face with him; otherwise, like everybody else, they were held by his mobile powerful eyes, as if controlled by silent secret wheels behind, and his small smile that was not a smile, rather a contemptuous little mock-curtsey of those narrow cheeks, and for the moment they believed anything he told them, they believed that his country was larger than it seemed and was deserving of rapt respect.

In New York Morris Ngambe had certain urban difficulties typical of the times. He was snubbed and sent to the service entrance (despite the grandeur of his tie) by a Puerto Rican elevator man in an apartment house on Riverside Drive, he was knocked down and robbed not in Central Park but a block away by a gang of seven young men wearing windbreakers reading 'Africa First, Harlem Nowhere' – a yellow-gold cap covering his right front incisor fell off, and was aesthetically replaced by a Dr Korngelb of East Forty-ninth Street, who substituted a fine white up-to-date acrylic jacket. Also he was set upon by a big horrible dog, a rusty-furred female chow, who, rising from a squat, having defecated in the middle of the sidewalk, inexplicably flew up and bit deep into Morris's arm. Poor Morris had to go to Bellevue outclinic for rabies injections in his stomach. For days afterwards he groaned with the pain. 'This city, this city!' he wailed to Lushinski. 'London is boring but at least civilized. New York is just what they say of it – a wilderness, a jungle.' He prayed to his mother's picture, and forgot that his own village at home was enveloped by a rubbery skein of grey forest with all its sucking, whistling, croaking, gnawing, perilously breathing beasts and their fearful eyes luminous with moonlight.

But at other times he did not forget, and he and Lushinski would compare the forests of their boyhoods. That sort of conversation always made Morris happy: he had been gifted with an ecstatic childhood, racing with other boys over fallen berries, feeling the squush of warm juice under his swift toes, stopping to try the bitter taste of one or two; and once they swallowed sour flies, for fun, and on a dare. But mostly there were games – so clever and elaborate he wondered at them even now, who had invented them, and in what inspired age long ago: concealing games, with complicated clue-songs attached, and quiet games with twigs of different sizes from different kinds of bark, requiring as much concentration as chess; and acrobatic games, boys suspended upside down from branches to stretch the muscles of the neck, around which, one day, the great width of the initiation-band would be fitted; and sneaking-up games, mimicking the silence of certain deer-faced little rodents with tender flanks who streaked by so quickly they could be perceived only as a silver blur. And best of all, strolling home after a whole dusty day in the bright swarm of the glade, insects jigging in the slotted sunbeams and underfoot the fleshlike fever-pad of the forest floor; and then, nearing the huts, the hazy smell of dusk beginning and all the aunties' indulgent giggles; then their hearts swelled: the aunties called them 'lord'; they were nearly men. Morris – in those days he was Mdulgo-kt'dulgo ('prime-soul-born-of-prime-soul') – licked the last bit of luscious goat-fat from his banana leaf and knew he would one day weigh in the world.

Lushinski told little of his own forest. But for a moment its savagery wandered up and down the brutal bone of his nose.

'Wolves?' Morris asked; in his forest ran sleek red jackals with black swaths down their backs, difficult to trap but not dangerous if handled intelligently, their heads as red as some of these female redheads one saw taking big immodest strides in the streets of London and New York. But wolves are northern terrors, Slavic emanations, spun out of snow and legends of the Baba Yaga.

'Human wolves,' Lushinski answered, and said nothing after that. Sometimes he grew sullen all at once, or else a spurt of fury would boil up in him; and then Morris would think of the chow. It had never been determined whether the chow was rabid or not. Morris had endured all that wretchedness for nothing, probably. Lulu (this was Louisa: a name that privately disturbed Morris – he was ashamed to contemplate what these two horrid syllables denoted in argot, and prayed to his mother to help him blot out the pictures that came into his thoughts whenever Lushinski called her on the telephone and began with – O Tanake-Tuka! – 'Lulu?') – Lulu also was sometimes bewildered by these storms which broke out in him: then he would reach out a long hard hand and chop at her with it, and she would remember that once he had killed a man. He had killed; she saw in him the power to kill.

On television he confessed to murder:

Once upon a time, long ago in a snowy region of the world called Poland, there lived a man and his wife in the city of Warsaw. The man ruled over a certain palace – it was a bank – and the woman ruled over another palace, very comfortable and rambling, with hundreds of delightful story-books behind glass doors in mahogany cases and secret niches to hide toy soldiers in and caves under chairs and closets that mysteriously connected with one another through dark and enticing passageways – it was a rich fine mansion on one of the best streets in Warsaw. This noble and blessed couple had a little son, whom they loved more than their very lives, and whom they named Stanislav. He was unusually bright, and learned everything more rapidly than he could be taught, and was soon so accomplished that they rejoiced in his genius and could not get over their good luck in having given life to so splendid a little man. The cook used to bring him jigsaw puzzles consisting of one thousand pieces all seemingly of the same shape and colour, just for the marvel of watching him make a picture out of them in no time at all. His father's chauffeur once came half an hour early, just to challenge the boy at chess; he was then not yet five, and the manoeuvres he invented for his toy soldiers were amusingly in imitation of the witty pursuits of the chessboard. He was already joyously reading about insects, stars, and trolley cars. His father had brought home for him one evening a little violin, and his mother had engaged a teacher of celebrated reputation. Almost immediately he began to play with finesse and ease.

In Stanislav there was only one defect – at least they thought it a defect – that grieved his parents. The father and mother were both fair, like a Polish prince and a Polish princess; the mother kept her golden hair plaited in a snail-like bun over each pink ear, the father wore a sober grey waistcoat under his satiny pink chin. The father was ruddy, the mother rosy, and when they looked into one another's eyes, the father's as grey as the buttery grey cloth of his vest, the mother's as clamorously blue as the blue chips of glass in her son's kaleidoscope, they felt themselves graced by God with such an extraordinary child, indeed a prodigy (he was obsessed by an interest in algebra) – but, pink and ruddy and golden and rosy as they were, the boy, it seemed, was a gypsy. His hair was black with a slippery will of its own, like a gypsy's, his eyes were brilliant but disappointingly black, like gypsy eyes, and even the skin of his clever small hands had a dusky glow, like gypsy skin. His mother grew angry when the servants called him by a degrading nickname – Ziggi, short for *Zigeuner*, the German word for gypsy. But when she forbade it, she did not let slip to them that it was the darkness she reviled, she pretended it was only the German word itself; she would not allow German to be uttered in that house – German, the language of the barbarian invaders, enemies of all good Polish people.

All the same, she heard them whisper under the stairs, or in the kitchen: *Zigeuner*; and the next day the Germans came, in helmets, in boots, tanks grinding up even the most fashionable streets, and the life of the Warsaw palaces, the fair father in his bank, the fair mother under her rose-trellis, came to an end. The fair father and the fair mother sewed *zloty* in their underclothes and took the dark child far off into a peasant village at the edge of the forest and left him, together with the money to pay for it, in the care of a rough but kind-hearted farmer until the world should right itself again. And the fair blessed couple fled east, hoping to escape to Russia: but on the way, despite fair hair and pale eyes and aristocratic manners and the cultivated Polish speech of city people with a literary bent, they were perceived to be non-Aryan and were roped to a silver birch at the other end of the woods and shot.

All this happened on the very day Stanislav had his sixth birthday. And what devisings, months and months ahead of time, there had been for that birthday! Pony rides, and a clown in a silken suit, and his father promising to start him on Euclid. . . . And here instead was this horrid dirty squat-necked man with a bald head and a fat nose and such terrible fingers with thick horny blackened nails like angle irons, and a dreadful witchlike woman standing there with her face on fire, and four children in filthy smocks peering out of a crack in a door tied shut with a rubber strap.

'He's too black,' said the witch. 'I didn't know he'd be a black one. You couldn't tell from the looks of *them*. He'll expose us, there's danger in it for us.'

'They paid,' the man said.

'Too black. Get rid of him.'

'All right,' said the man, and that night he put the boy out in the forest. . . .

But now the 'host' interrupted, and the glass mouth of the television filled up with a song about grimy shirt collars and a soap that could clean them properly. 'Ring around the collar,' the television sang, and then the 'host' asked, 'Was that the man you killed?'

'No,' Lushinski said. 'It was somebody else.'

'And you were only six?'

'No,' Lushinski said, 'by then I was older.'

'And you lived on your own in the forest – a little child, imagine! – all that time?'

'In the forest. On my own.'

'But how? How? You were only a child!'

'Cunning,' Lushinski said. It was all mockery and parody. And somehow – because he mocked and parodied, sitting under the cameras absurdly smiling and replete with contradictions, the man telling about the boy, Pole putting himself out as African, candour offering cunning – an uneasy blossom of laughter opened in his listeners, the laughter convinced: he was making himself up. He had made himself over, and now he was making himself up, like one of those comedians who tell uproarious anecdotes about their preposterous relatives. 'You see,' Lushinski said, 'by then the peasants wanted to catch me. They thought if they caught me and gave me to the Germans there would be advantage in it for them – the Germans might go easy on the village, not come in and cart away all the grain without paying and steal the milk – oh, I was proper prey. And then I heard the slaver of a dog: a big sick bulldog, I knew him, his name was Andor and he had chewed-up genitals and vomit on his lower jaw. He belonged to the sexton's helper who lived in a shed behind the parish house, a brute he was, old but a brute, so I took a stick when Andor came near and stuck it right in his eye, as deep as I could push it. And Andor comes rolling and yowling like a demon, and the sexton's helper lunges after him, and I grab Andor – heavy as a log, heavy as a boulder, believe me – I grab him and lift him and smash him right down against the sexton's helper, and he's knocked over on his back, by now Andor is crazy, Andor is screeching and sticky with a river of blood spilling out of his eye, and he digs his smelly teeth like spades, like spikes, like daggers, into the old brute's neck—'

All this was comedy: Marx Brothers, Keystone cops, the audience is elated by its own disbelief. The bulldog is a dragon, the sexton's helper an ogre, Lushinski is only a story-teller, and the 'host' asks, 'Then that's the man you killed?'

'Oh no, Jan's Andor killed Jan.'

'Is it true?' Morris wanted to know – he sat in the front row and laughed with the rest – and began at once to tell about the horrid chow on East Ninetieth Street; but Lulu never asked this. She saw how true. Often enough she shook him out of nightmares, tears falling from his nostrils, his tongue curling after air with hideous sucking noises. Then she brought him hot milk, and combed down his nape with a wet hand, and reminded him he was out of it all, Poland a figment, Europe a fancy, he now a great man, a figure the world took notice of.

He told no one who the man was – the man he killed: not even Lulu. And so she did not know whether he had killed in the Polish forest, or in the camp afterwards when they caught him, or in Moscow where they took him, or perhaps long afterwards, in Africa. And she did not know whether the man he killed was a gypsy, or a Pole, or a German, or a Russian, or a Jew, or one of those short brown warriors from his own country, from whom the political caste was drawn. And she did not know whether he had killed with his hands, or with a weapon, or through some device or ruse. Sometimes she was frightened to think she was the mistress of a murderer; and sometimes it gladdened her, and made her life seem different from all other lives, adventurous and poignant; she could pity and admire herself all at once.

He took Morris with him to Washington to visit the Secretary of State. The Secretary was worried about the threatened renewal of the northern tribal wars: certain corporate interests, he explained in that vapid dialect he used on purpose to hide the name of the one furious man whose fear he was making known, who had yielded his anxiety to the Secretary over a lunch of avocado salad, fish in some paradisal sauce, wine-and-mushroom-scented roast, a dessert of sweetened asparagus mixed with peppered apricot liqueur and surrounded by a peony-pattern of almond cakes – certain corporate interests, said the Secretary (he meant his friend), were concerned about the steadiness of shipments of the single raw material vital to the manufacture of their indispensable product; the last outbreak of tribal hostility had brought the cutting in the plantations to a dead halt; the shippers had nothing to send, and instead hauled some rotted stuff out of last year's discarded cuttings in the storehouses; it wouldn't do, an entire American industry depended on peace in that important region; but when he said 'an entire American industry', he still meant the one furious man, his friend, whose young third wife had been at the luncheon too, a poor girl who carried herself now like a poor girl's idea of a queen, with hair expensively turned stiff as straw, but worth looking at all the same. And so again he said 'that important region'.

'You know last time with the famine up there,' the Secretary continued, 'I remember twenty years or so ago, before your time, I was out in the Cameroon, and they were at each other's throats over God knows what.'

Morris said, 'It was the linguistic issue. Don't think of "tribes", sir; think of nations, and you will comprehend better the question of linguistic pride.'

'It's not a matter of comprehension, it's a matter of money. They wouldn't go to the plantations to cut, you see.'

'They were at war. There was the famine.'

'Mr Ngambe, you weren't born then. If they had cut something, there wouldn't have been famine.'

'Oh, that crop's not edible, sir,' Morris protested: 'it's like eating rope!'

The Secretary did not know what to do with such obtuseness; he was not at all worried about a hunger so far away which, full of lunch, he could not credit. His own stomach seemed a bit acid to him, he hid a modest belch. 'God knows,' he said, 'what those fellows eat—'

But 'Sir,' said Lushinski, 'you have received our documents on the famine in the south. The pressure on our northern stocks – believe me, sir, they are dwindling – can be alleviated by a simple release of Number Three grain deposits, for which you recall we made an appeal last week—'

'I haven't gotten to the Number Threes, Mr Lushinski. I'll look them over this weekend, I give you my word. I'll put my staff right on it. But the fact is, if there's an outbreak—'

'Of cholera?' said Morris. 'We've had word of some slight cholera in the south already.'

'I'm talking about war. It's a pity about the cholera, but that's strictly internal. We can't do anything about it, unless the Red Cross . . . Now look here, we can't have that sort of interference again with cutting and with shipments. We can't have it. There has got to be a way—'

'Negotiations have begun between the Dt' and the Rundabi,' Morris said; he always understood when Lushinski wished him to speak, but he felt confused, because he could feel also that the Secretary did not wish him to speak and was in fact annoyed with him, and looked to Lushinski only. All at once bitterness ran in him, as when the Puerto Rican elevator man sent him to the service entrance: but then it ebbed, and he admonished himself that Lushinski was his superior in rank and in years, a man the Prime Minister said had a heart like a root of a tree in his own back yard. This was a saying derived from the Dt' proverb: the man whose heart is rooted in his own garden will betray your garden, but the man whose heart is rooted in your garden will take care of it as if it were his own. (In the beautiful compressed idiom of the Prime Minister's middle-region argot: *bl'kt pk'ralwa, bl'kt duwam pk'ralwi.*)

And so instead of allowing himself to cultivate the hard little knob of jealousy that lived inside his neck, in the very spot where he swallowed food and drink, Morris reminded himself of his patriotism – his dear little country, still more a concept than a real nation, a confederacy of vast and enviously competitive families, his own prestigious tribe the most prominent, its females renowned for having the sleekest skin, even grandmothers' flesh smooth and tight as the flesh of panthers. He considered how inventiveness and adaptability marked his father and all his father's brothers, how on the tribe-god's day all the other families had to bring his great-uncle baskets of bean-flour and garlic buds, how on that day his great-uncle took out the tall tribe-god from its locked hut, and wreathed a garland of mallows on its *lulu*, and the females were shut into the tribe-god's stockade, and how at the first star of night the songs from the females behind the wall heated the sky and every boy of fourteen had his new bronze collar hitched on, and then how, wearing his collar, Morris led out of the god's stockade and into the shuddering forest his first female of his own, one of the aunties' young cousins, a pliant little girl of eleven. . . .

In New York there were dangerous houses, it was necessary to be married to be respectable, not to acquire a disease, in New York it was not possible for an important young man to have a female of his own who was not his wife; in London it was rather more possible, he had gone often to the bedsitter of Isabel Oxenham, a cheerful, bony, homely young woman who explained that being a Cockney meant you were born within the sound of Bow Bells and therefore she was a Cockney, but in New York there was prejudice, it was more difficult, in this Lushinski could not be his model. . . . Now he was almost listening to the Secretary, and oh, he had conquered jealousy, he was proud that his country, so tender, so wise, so full of feeling, could claim a mind like Lushinski's to represent it! It was not a foreign mind, it was a mind like his own, elevated and polished. He heard the Secretary say 'universal', and it occurred to him that the conversation had turned philosophical. Instantly he made a contribution to it; he was certain that philosophy and poetry were his only real interests: his strengths.

'At bottom,' Morris said, 'there is no contradiction between the tribal and the universal. Remember William Blake, sir: "To see a world in a grain of sand"—'

The Secretary had white hair and an old, creased face; Morris loathed the slender purple veins that made flower-patterns along the sides of his nose. The ugliness, the defectiveness, of some human beings! God must have had a plan for them if He created them, but since one did not understand the plan, one could not withhold one's loathing. It was not a moral loathing, it was only aesthetic. 'Nationalism,' Morris said, 'in the West is so very recent: a nineteenth-century development. But in Africa we have never had that sort of thing. Our notion of nationhood is different, it has nothing political attached to it; it is for the dear land itself, the customs, the rites, the cousins, the sense of family. A sense of family gives one a more sublime concept: one is readier to think of the Human Family,' but he thanked his mother that he was not related to this old, carmine-coloured, creased and ugly man.

On the way back to New York in the shuttle plane Lushinski spoke to him like a teacher – avoiding English, so as not to be overheard. 'That man is a peasant,' he told Morris. 'It is never necessary to make conversation with peasants. They are like their own dogs or pigs or donkeys. They only know if it rains. They look out only for their own corner. He will make us starve if we let him.' And he said, using the middle-region argot of the Prime Minister, 'Let him eat air,' which was, in that place, a dark curse, but one that always brought laughter. In spite of this, and in spite of the funny way he pronounced *hl'tk*, 'starve', aspirating it (*hlt'k*) instead of churning it in his throat, so that it came out a sort of half-pun for 'take-away-the-virginity-of', Morris noticed again that whenever Lushinski said the word 'peasant' he looked afraid. The war, of course, happened. For a week the cables flew. Lushinski flew too, to consult with the Prime Minister; he had letters from the Secretary, which he took with him to burn in the Prime Minister's ashtray. Morris remained in New York. One evening Lulu telephoned, to invite him to supper. He heard in her voice that she was obeying her lover, so he declined.

The war was more than fifty miles north of the capital. The Prime Minister's bungalow was beaten by rain; after the rain, blasts of hot wind shook the shutters. The leaves, which had been turned into cups and wells, dried instantly. Evaporation everywhere sent up steam and threads of rainbows. The air-conditioners rattled like tin pans. One by one Lushinski tore up the Secretary's letters, kindling them in the Prime Minister's ashtray with the Prime Minister's cigarette lighter – it was in the shape of the Leaning Tower of Pisa. Then he stoked them in the Prime Minister's ashtray with the Prime Minister's Japanese-made fountain pen. Even indoors, even with the air-conditioners grinding away, the sunlight was dense with scents unknown in New York: rubber mingled with straw and tar and monkey-droppings and always the drifting smell of the mimosas. The Prime Minister's wife (he pretended to be monogamous, though he had left off using this one long ago) – rather, the female who had the status of the Prime Minister's wife – went on her knees to Lushinski and presented him with a sacerdotal bean-flour cake.

The war lasted a second week; when the Prime Minister signed the cease-fire, Lushinski stood at his side, wearing no expression at all. From the Secretary came a congratulatory cable; Lushinski read it under those perfumed trees, heavy as cabbage-heads, smoking and smoking – he was addicted to the local tobacco. His flesh drank the sun. The hills, rounder and greener than any other on the planet, made his chest blaze. From the aeroplane – now he was leaving Africa again – he imagined he saw the tarred roofs of the guerrilla camps in the shadows of the hills; or perhaps those were only the dark nests of vultures. They ascended, and through the window he fixed on the huge silver horn of the jet, and under it the white cloud-meadows.

In New York the Secretary praised him and called him a peacemaker.

Privately Lushinski did not so much as twitch, but he watched Morris smile. They had given the Secretary air to eat! A month after the 'war' – the quotation marks were visible in Lushinski's enunciation: what was it but a combination of village riots and semistrikes? only two hundred or so people killed, one of them unfortunately the Dt' poet L'duy – the price of the indispensable cuttings rose sixty per cent, increasing gross national income by two thirds. The land was like a mother whose breasts overflow. This was Morris's image: but Lushinski said, 'She has expensive nipples, our mother.' And then Morris understood that Lushinski had made the war the way a man in his sleep makes a genital dream, and that the Prime Minister had transfigured the dream into wet blood.

The Prime Minister ordered a bronze monument to commemorate the dead poet. Along the base were the lines, both in argot and in English,

The deer intends,	*Kt'ratalwo*
The lion fulfils.	*Mnep g'trpa*
Man the hunter	*Kt'bl ngaya wiba*
Only chooses sides.	*Gagl gagl mrpa.*

The translation into English was Lushinski's. Morris said worshipfully, 'Ah, there is no one like you,' and Lulu said, 'How terrible to make a war just to raise prices,' and Lushinski said, 'For this there are many precedents.'

To Morris he explained: 'The war would have come in any case. It was necessary to adjust the timing. The adjustment saved lives' – here he set forth the pre-emptive strategy of the Rundabi, and how it was foiled: his mouth looked sly, he loved tricks – 'and simultaneously it accomplished our needs. Remember this for when you are Ambassador. Don't try to ram against the inevitable. Instead, tinker with the timing.' Though it was after midnight and they were alone in Morris's office – Lushinski's was too grand for unofficial conversation – they spoke in argot. Lushinski was thirstily downing a can of Coca-Cola and Morris was eating salted crackers spread with apple butter. 'Will I be Ambassador?' Morris asked. 'One day,' Lushinski said, 'the mother will throw me out.' Morris did not understand. 'The motherland? Never!' 'The mother,' Lushinski corrected, 'Tanake-Tuka.' 'Oh, never!' cried Morris, 'you bring her luck.' 'I am not a totem,' Lushinski said. But Morris pondered. 'We civilized men,' he said (using for 'men' the formal term 'lords,' so that his thought ascended, he turned eloquent), 'we do not comprehend what the more passionate primitive means when he says "totem".' 'I am not afraid of words,' Lushinski said. 'You are,' Morris said.

Lulu, like Morris, had also noticed a word which made Lushinski afraid. But she distinguished intelligently between bad memories and bad moods. He told her he was the century's one free man. She scoffed at such foolery. 'Well, not the only one,' he conceded. 'But more free than most. Every survivor is free. Everything that can happen to a human being has already happened inside the survivor. The future can invent nothing worse. What he owns now is recklessness without fear.'

This was his diplomat's English. Lulu hated it. 'You didn't die,' she said. 'Don't be pompous about being alive. If you were dead like the others, you would have something to be pompous about. People call them martyrs, and they were only ordinary. If you were a martyr, you could preen about it.'

'Do you think me ordinary?' he asked. He looked just then like a crazy man burning with a secret will; but this was nothing, he could make himself look any way he pleased. 'If I were ordinary I would be dead.'

She could not deny this. A child strung of sticks, he had survived the peasants who baited and blistered and beat and hunted him. One of them had hanged him from the rafter of a shed, by the wrists. He was four sticks hanging. And his stomach shrank and shrank, and now it was inelastic, still the size of a boy's stomach, and he could not eat. She brought him a bowl of warm farina, and watched him push the spoon several times into the straight line of his mouth; then he put away the spoon; then she took his head down into her lap, as if it were the head of a doll, and needed her own thoughts to give it heat.

He offered her books.

'Why should I read all this? I'm not curious about history, only about you.'

'One and the same,' he said.

'Pompous,' she told him again. He allowed her only this one subject. 'Death,' she said. 'Death, death, death. What do you care? *You* came out alive.' 'I care about the record,' he insisted. There were easy books and there were hard books. The easier ones were stories; these she brought home herself. But they made him angry. 'No stories, no tales,' he said. 'Sources. Documents only. Politics. This is what led to my profession. Accretion of data. There are no holy men of stories,' he said, 'there are only holy men of data. Remember this before you fall at the feet of anyone who makes romances out of what really happened. If you want something liturgical, say to yourself: *what really happened.*' He crashed down on the bed beside her an enormous volume: it was called *The Destruction*. She opened it and saw tables and figures and asterisks; she saw train-schedules. It was all dry, dry. 'Do you know that writer?' she asked; she was accustomed to his being acquainted with everyone. 'Yes,' he said, 'do you want to have dinner with him?' 'No,' she said.

She read the stories and wept. She wept over the camps. She read a book called *Night*; she wept. 'But I can't separate all that,' she pleaded, 'the stories and the sources.'

'Imagination is romance. Romance blurs. Instead count the numbers of freight trains.'

She read a little in the enormous book. The title irritated her. It was a lie. 'It isn't as if the whole *world* was wiped out. It wasn't like the Flood. It wasn't *mankind*, after all, it was only one population. The Jews aren't the whole world, they aren't mankind, are they?'

She caught in his face a prolonged strangeness: he was new to her, like someone she had never looked at before. 'What's the matter, Stasek?' But all at once she saw: she had said he was not mankind.

'Whenever people remember mankind,' he said, 'they don't fail to omit the Jews.'

'An epigram!' she threw out. 'What's the good of an epigram! Self-conscious! In public you make jokes, but at home—'

'At home I make water,' and went into the bathroom.

'Stasek?' she said through the door.

'You'd better go read.'

'Why do you want me to know all that?'

'To show you what you're living with.'

'I know who I'm living with!'

'I didn't say *who*, I said *what*.'

The shower water began.

She shouted, 'You always want a bath whenever I say that word!'

'Baptism,' he called. 'Which word? Mankind?'

'Stasek!' She shook the knob; he had turned the lock. 'Listen, Stasek, I want to tell you something. Stasek! I want to say something *important*.'

He opened the door. He was naked. 'Do you know what's important?' he asked her.

She fixed on his member; it was swollen. She announced, 'I want to tell you what I hate.'

'I hope it's not what you're staring at,' he said.

'History,' she said. 'History's what I hate.'

'Poor Lulu, some of it got stuck on you and it won't come off—'

'Stasek!'

'Come wash it away, we'll have a tandem baptism.'

'I know what *you* hate,' she accused. 'You hate being part of the Jews. You hate that.'

'I am not part of the Jews. I am part of mankind. You're not going to say they're the same thing?'

She stood and reflected. She was sick of his satire. She felt vacuous and ignorant. 'Practically nobody knows you're a Jew,' she said. '*I* never think of it. You always make me think of it. If I forget it for a while you give me a book, you make me read history, three wars ago, as remote as Attila the Hun. And then I say that word' – she breathed, she made an effort – 'I say *Jew*, and you run the water, you get afraid. And then when you get afraid you *attack*, it all comes back on you, you attack like an animal—'

Out of the darkness came the illusion of his smile: oh, a sun! She saw him beautifully beaming. 'If not for history,' he said, 'think! You'd still be in the *Schloss:*, you wouldn't have become a little American girl, you wouldn't have grown up to the lipstick factory—'

'Did you leave the drain closed?' she said suddenly. 'Stasek, with the shower going, how stupid, now look, the tub's almost ready to overflow—'

He smiled and smiled: 'Practically nobody knows you're a princess.'

'I'm *not*. It's my great-aunt – oh for God's sake, there it goes, over the side.' She peeled off her shoes and went barefoot into the flood and reached to shut off the water. Her feet streamed, her two hands streamed. Then she faced him. 'Princess! I know what it is with you! The more you mock, the more you mean it, but I know what it is! You want little stories, deep gossip, you want to pump me and pump me, you have a dream of royalty, and you know perfectly well, you've known it from the first *minute*, I've told and told how I spent the whole of the war in school in England! And then you say nonsense like "little American girl" because you want that too, you want a princess and you want America and you want Europe and you want Africa—'

But he intervened. 'I don't want Europe,' he said.

'Pompous! Mockery! You want everything you're not, *that's* what it's about! Because of what you are!' She let herself laugh; she fell into laughter like one of his audiences. 'An African! An African!'

'Louisa' – he had a different emphasis now: 'I am an African,' and in such a voice, all the sinister gaming out of it, the voice of a believer. Did he in truth believe in Africa? He did not take her there. Pictures swam in her of what it might be – herons, plumage, a red stalk of bird-leg in an unmoving pool, mahogany nakedness and golden collars, drums, black bodies, the women with their hooped lips, loin-strings, yellow fur stalking, dappled, striped . . . the fear, the fear.

He pushed his nakedness against her. Her hand was wet. Always he was cold to Jews. He never went among them. In the Assembly he turned his back on the ambassador from Israel; she was in the reserved seats, she saw it herself, she heard the gallery gasp. All New York Jews in the gallery. She knew the word he was afraid of. He pressed her, he made himself her master, she read what he gave her, she, once securely her own mistress, who now followed when he instructed and stayed when he ordered it, she knew when to make him afraid.

'You Jew,' she said.

Without words he had told her when to say those words; she was obedient and restored him to fear.

Morris, despite his classical education, had no taste for Europe. No matter that he had studied 'political science' – he turned it all into poetry, or, at the least, psychology; better yet, gossip. He might read a biography but he did not care about the consequences of any life. He remembered the names of Princess Margaret's dogs and it seemed to him that Hitler, though unluckily mad, was a genius, because he saw how to make a whole people search for ecstasy. Morris did not understand Europe. Nevertheless he knew he was superior to Europe, as people who are accustomed to a stable temperature are always superior to those who must live with the zaniness of the seasons. His reveries were attuned to a steady climate – summer, summer. In his marrow the crickets were always rioting, the mantises always flashing: sometimes a mantis stood on a leaf and put its two front legs one over the other, like a good child.

Lushinski seemed to him invincibly European: Africa was all light, all fine scent, sweet deep rain and again light, brilliance, the cleansing heat of shining. And Europe by contrast a coal, hellish and horrible, even the snows dark because humped and shadowy, caves, paw-prints of wolves, shoe-troughs of fleeing. In Africa you ran for joy, the joyous thighs begged for fleetness, you ran into veld and bush and green. In Europe you fled, it was flight, you ran like prey into shadows: Europe the Dark Continent.

Under klieg lights Lushinski grew more and more polished; he was becoming a comic artist, he learned when to stop for water, when to keep the tail of a phrase in abeyance. Because of television he was invited to talk everywhere. His stories were grotesque, but he told them so plausibly that he outraged everyone into nervous howls. People liked him to describe his student days in Moscow, after the Russian soldiers had liberated him; they liked him to tell about his suitcase, about his uniform.

He gave very little. He was always very brief. But they laughed. 'In Moscow,' he said, 'we lived five in one room. It had once been the servant's room of a large elegant house. Twenty-seven persons, male and female, shared the toilet; but we in our room were lucky because we had a balcony. One day I went out on the balcony to build a bookcase for the room. I had some boards for shelves and a tin of nails and a hammer and a saw, and I began banging away. And suddenly one of the other students came flying out onto the balcony: "People at the door! People at the door!" There were mobs of callers out there, ringing, knocking, yelling. That afternoon I received forty-six orders in three hours, for a table, a credenza, endless bookshelves, a bed, a desk, a portable commode. They thought I was an illegal carpenter working out in the open that way to advertise: you had to wait months for a State carpenter. One of the orders – it was for the commode – was from an informer. I explained that I was only a student and not in business, but they locked me up for hooliganism because I had drawn a crowd. Five days in a cell with drunkards. They said I had organized a demonstration against the regime.

'A little while afterwards the plumbing of our communal toilet became defective – I will not say just how. The solid refuse had to be gathered in buckets. It was unbearable, worse than any stable. And again I saw my opportunity as a carpenter. I constructed a commode and delivered it to the informer – and oh, it was full, it was full. Twenty-seven Soviet citizens paid tribute.'

Such a story made Morris uncomfortable. His underwear felt too tight, he perspired. He wondered why everyone laughed. The story seemed to him European, uncivilized. It was something that could have happened but probably did not happen. He did not know what he ought to believe.

The suitcase, on the other hand, he knew well. It was always reliably present, leaning against Lushinski's foot, or propped up against the bottom of his desk, or the door of his official car. Lushinski was willing enough to explain its contents: 'Several complete sets of false papers,' he said with satisfaction, looking the opposite of sly, and one day he displayed them. There were passports for various identities – English,

French, Brazilian, Norwegian, Dutch, Australian – and a number of diplomas in different languages. 'The two Russian ones,' he boasted, 'aren't forgeries,' putting everything back among new shirts still in their wrappers.

'But why, why?' Morris said.

'A maxim. Always have your bags packed.'

'But why?'

'To get away.'

'Why?'

'Sometimes it's better where you aren't than where you are.'

Morris wished the Prime Minister had heard this; surely he would have trusted Lushinski less. But Lushinski guessed his thought. 'Only the traitors stay home,' he said. 'In times of trouble only the patriots have false papers.'

'But now the whole world knows,' Morris said reasonably. 'You've told the whole world on television.'

'That will make it easier to get away. They will recognize a patriot and defer.'

He became a dervish of travel: he was mad about America and went to Detroit and to Tampa, to Cincinnati and to Biloxi. They asked him how he managed to keep up with his diplomatic duties; he referred them to Morris, whom he called his "conscientious blackamoor'. Letters came to the consulate in New York accusing him of being a colonialist and a racist. Lushinski remarked that he was not so much that as a cyclist, and immediately – to prove his solidarity with cyclists of every colour – bought Morris a gleaming ten-speed two-wheeler. Morris had learned to ride at Oxford, and was overjoyed once again to pedal into a rush of wind. He rode south on Second Avenue; he circled the whole Lower East Side. But in only two days his bike was stolen by a gang of what the police designated as 'teen-age black male perpetrators'. Morris liked America less and less.

Lushinski liked it more and more. He went to civic clubs, clubs with animal names, clubs with Indian names; societies internationalist and jingoist; veterans, pacifists, vegetarians, feminists, vivisectionists; he would agree to speak anywhere. No Jews invited him; he had turned his back on the Israeli ambassador. Meanwhile the Secretary of State withdrew a little, and omitted Lushinski from his dinner list; he was repelled by a man who would want to go to Cincinnati, a place the Secretary had left forever. But the Prime Minister was delighted and cabled Lushinski to 'get to know the proletariat' – nowadays the Prime Minister often used such language: he said 'dialectic', 'collective', and 'Third World'. Occasionally he said 'peoples', as in 'peoples' republic'. In a place called Oneonta, New York, Lushinski told about the uniform: in Paris he had gone to a tailor and asked him to make up the costume of an officer. 'Of which nationality, sir?' 'Oh, no particular one.' 'What rank, sir?' 'High. As high as you can imagine.' The coat was long, had epaulets, several golden bands on the sleeves, and metal buttons engraved with the head of a dead monarch. From a toy store Lushinski bought ribbons and medals to hang on its breast. The cap was tall and fearsomely military, with a strong bill ringed by a scarlet cord. Wearing this concoction, Lushinski journeyed to the Rhineland. In hotels they gave him the ducal suite and charged nothing, in restaurants he swept past everyone to the most devoted service, at airports he was served drinks in carpeted sitting rooms and ushered on board, with a guard, into a curtained parlour.

'Your own position commands all that,' Morris said gravely. Again he was puzzled. All around him they rattled with hilarity. Lushinski's straight mouth remained straight; Morris brooded about impersonation. It was no joke (but this was years and years ago, in the company of Isabel Oxenham) that he sought out Tarzan movies: Africa in the Mind of the West. It could have been his thesis, but it was not. He was too inward for such a generality: it was his own mind he meant to observe. Was he no better than that lout Tarzan, investing himself with a chatter not his own? How long could the ingested, the invented, foreignness endure? He felt himself – himself, Mdulgo-kt'dulgo, called Morris, dressed in suit and tie, his academic gown thrown down on a chair twenty miles north of this cinema – he felt himself to be self-duped, an impersonator. The film passed (jungle, vines, apes, the famous leap and screech and fisted thump, natives each with his rubber spear and extra's face – janitors and barmen), it was a confusion, a mist. His thumb climbed Isabel's vertebrae: such a nice even row, up and down like a stair. The children's matinée was done, the evening film commenced. It was in Italian, and he never forgot it, a comedy about an unwilling impostor, a common criminal mistaken for a heroic soldier: General della Rovere.

The movie made Isabel's tears fall onto Morris's left wrist.

The criminal, an ordinary thug, is jailed; the General's political enemies want the General put away. The real General is a remarkable man, a saint, a hero. And, little by little, the criminal acquires the General's qualities, he becomes selfless, he becomes courageous, glorious. At the end of the movie he has a chance to reveal that he is not the real General della Rovere. Nobly, he chooses instead to be executed in the General's place, he atones for his past life, a voluntary sacrifice. Morris explained to Isabel that the ferocious natives encountered by Tarzan are in the same moral situation as the false General della Rovere: they accommodate, they adapt to what is expected. Asked to howl like men who inhabit no culture, they howl. 'But they have souls, once they were advanced beings. If you jump into someone else's skin,' he asked, 'doesn't it begin to fit you?'

'Oi wouldn now, oi hev no ejucytion,' Isabel said.

Morris himself did not know.

All the same, he did not believe that Lushinski was this sort of impersonator. A Tarzan perhaps, not a della Rovere. The problem of sincerity disturbed and engrossed him. He boldly asked Lushinski his views.

'People who deal in diplomacy attach too much importance to being believed,' Lushinski declaimed. 'Sincerity is only a manoeuvre, like any other. A quantity of lies is a much more sensible method – it gives the effect of greater choice. Sincerity offers only one course. But if you select among a great variety of insincerities, you're bound to strike a better course.'

He said all this because it was exactly what Morris wanted to hear from him.

The Prime Minister had no interest in questions of identity. 'He is not a false African,' the Prime Minister said in a parliamentary speech defending his appointment, 'he is a true advocate.' Though vainglorious, this seemed plausible enough; but for Morris, Lushinski was not an African at all. 'It isn't enough to be *politically* African,' Morris argued one night; 'politically you can assume the culture. No one can assume the cult.' Then he remembered the little bones of Isabel Oxenham's back. 'Morris, Morris,' Lushinski said, 'you're not beginning to preach Negritude?' 'No,' said Morris; he wanted to speak of religion, of his mother; but just then he could not – the telephone broke in, though it was one in the morning and not the official number, rather his own private one, used by Louisa. She spoke of returning to her profession; she was too often alone. 'Where are you going tomorrow?' she asked Lushinski. Morris could hear the little electric voice in the receiver. 'You say you do it for public relations,' she said, 'but why really? What do they need to know about Africa in Shaker Heights that they don't know already?' The little electric voice forked and fragmented, tiny lightnings in her lover's ear.

The next day a terrorist from one of the hidden guerrilla camps in the hills shot the Prime Minister's wife at a government ceremony with many Westerners present; he had intended to shoot the Prime Minister. The Prime Minister, it was noted, appeared to grieve, and ordered a bubble-top for his car and a bulletproof vest to wear under his shirt. In a cable he instructed Lushinski to cease his circulation among the American proletariat. Lulu was pleased. Lushinski began to refuse invitations, his American career was over. In the Assembly he spoke – 'with supernal,' Morris acknowledged, 'eloquence' – against terrorism; though their countries had no diplomatic relations, and in spite of Lushinski's public snub, the Israeli ambassador applauded, with liquid eyes. But Lushinski missed something. To address an international body representing every nation on the planet seemed less than before; seemed limiting; he missed the laughter of Oneonta, New York. The American provinces moved him – how gullible they were, how little they knew, or would ever know, of cruelty's breadth! A country of babies. His half-year among all those cities had elated him: a visit to an innocent star: no sarcasm, cynicism, innuendo grew there; such nice church ladies; a benevolent passiveness which his tales, with their wily spikes, could rouse to nervous pleasure.

Behind Lushinski's ears threads of white hairs sprang; he worried about the Prime Minister's stability in the aftermath of the attack. While the representative from Uganda 'exercised', Lushinski sneered, 'his right of reply' – 'The distinguished representative from our sister-country to the north fabricates dangerous adventures for make-believe pirates who exist only in his fantasies, and we all know how colourfully, how excessively, he is given to whimsy' – Lushinski drew on his pad the head of a cormorant, with a sack under its beak. Though there was no overt resemblance, it could pass nevertheless for a self-portrait.

In October he returned to his capital. The Prime Minister had a new public wife. He had replenished his ebullience, and no longer wore the bulletproof vest. The new wife kneeled before Lushinski with a bean-flour cake. The Prime Minister was sanguine: the captured terrorist had informed on his colleagues, entire nests of them had been cleaned out of four nearby villages. The Prime Minister begged Lushinski to allow him to lend him one of his younger females. Lushinski examined her and accepted. He took also one of Morris's sisters, and with these two went to live for a month alone in a white villa on the blue coast.

Every day the Prime Minister sent a courier with documents and newspapers; also the consular pouch from New York.

Morris in New York: Morris in a city of Jews. He walked. He crossed a bridge. He walked. He was attentive to their houses, their neighbourhoods. Their religious schools. Their synagogues. Their multitudinous societies. Announcements of debates, ice cream, speeches, rallies, delicatessens, violins, felafel, books. Ah, the avalanche of their books!

Where their streets ended, the streets of the blacks began. Mdulgo-kt'dulgo in exile among the kidnapped – cargo-Africans, victims with African faces, lost to language and faith; impostors sunk in barbarism, primitives, impersonators. Emptied-out creatures, with their hidden knives, their swift silver guns, their poisoned red eyes, christianized, made not new but neuter, fabricated: oh, only restore them to their inmost selves, to the serenity of orthodoxy, redemption of the true gods who speak in them without voice!

Morris Ngambe in New York. Alone, treading among traps, in jeopardy of ambush, with no female.

And in Africa, in a white villa on the blue coast: the Prime Minister's gaudy pet, on a blue sofa before an open window, smoking and smoking, under the breath of the scented trees, under the sleek palms of a pair of young females, smoking and caressing – snug in Africa, Lushinski.

In Lushinski's last week in the villa, the pouch from New York held a letter from Morris.

The letter:

A curious note concerning the terrorist personality. I have just read of an incident which took place in a Jerusalem prison. A captive terrorist, a Japanese who had murdered twenty-nine pilgrims at the Tel Aviv airport, was permitted to keep in his cell, besides reading matter, a comb, a hairbrush, a nailbrush, and a fingernail clippers. A dapper chap, apparently. One morning he was found to have partially circumcised himself. His instrument was the clippers. He lost consciousness and the job was completed in the prison hospital. The doctor questioned him. It turned out he had begun to read intensively in the Jewish religion. He had a Bible and a text for learning the Hebrew language. He had begun to grow a beard and earlocks. Perhaps you will understand better than I the spiritual side of this matter.

You recall my remarks on culture and cult. Here is a man who wishes to annihilate a society and its culture, but he is captivated by its cult. For its cult he will bleed himself.

Captivity leading to captivation: an interesting notion.

It may be that every man at length becomes what he wishes to victimize.

It may be that every man needs to impersonate what he first must kill.

Lushinski recognized in Morris's musings a lumpy parroting of *Reading Gaol* mixed with – what? Fanon? Genet? No; only Oscar Wilde, sentimentally epigrammatic. Oscar Wilde in Jerusalem! As unlikely as the remorse of Gomorrah. Like everyone the British had once blessed with Empire, Morris was a Victorian. He was a gentleman. He believed in civilizing influences; even more in civility. He was besotted by style. If he thought of knives, it was for buttering scones.

But Lushinski, a man with the nose and mouth of a knife, and the body of a knife, understood this letter as a blade between them. It meant a severing. Morris saw him as an impersonator. Morris uncovered him; then stabbed. Morris had called him a transmuted, a transfigured, African. A man in love with his cell. A traitor. Perfidious. A fake.

Morris had called him Jew.

—Morris in New York, alone, treading among traps, in jeopardy of ambush, with no female. He knew his ascendancy. Victory of that bird-bright forest, glistening with the bodies of boys, over the old terror in the Polish woods.

Morris prayed. He prayed to his mother: down, take him down, bring him something evil. The divine mother answers sincere believers: O Tanake-Tuka!

And in Africa, in a white villa on the blue coast, the Prime Minister's gaudy pet, on a blue sofa before an open window, smoking and smoking, under the breath of the scented trees, under the shadow of the bluish snow, under the blue-black pillars of the Polish woods, under the breath of Andor, under the merciless palms of peasants and fists of peasants, under the rafters, under the stone-white hanging stars of Poland – Lushinski.

Against the stones and under the snow.

Bloodshed

Bleilip took a Greyhound bus out of New York and rode through icy scenes half-urban and half-countrified until he arrived at the town of the hasidim. He had intended to walk, but his coat pockets were heavy, so he entered a loitering taxi. Though it was early on a Sunday afternoon he saw no children at all. Then he remembered that they would be in the yeshivas until the darker slant of the day. Yeshivas not yeshiva: small as the community was, it had three or four schools, and still others, separate, for the little girls. Toby and Yussel were waiting for him and waved his taxi down the lumpy road above their half-built house – it was a new town, and everything in it was new or promised: pavements, trash cans, septic tanks, newspaper stores. But just because everything was unfinished, you could sniff rawness, the opened earth meaty and scratched up as if by big animal claws, the frozen puddles in the basins of ditches fresh-smelling, mossy.

Toby he regarded as a convert. She was just barely a relative, a third or fourth cousin, depending on how you counted, whether from his mother or from his father, who were also cousins to each other. She came from an ordinary family, not especially known for its venturesomeness, but now she looked to him altogether uncommon, freakish: her bun was a hairpiece pinned on, over it she wore a bandanna (a *tcheptichke*, she called it), her sleeves stopped below her wrists, her dress was outlandishly long. With her large red face over this costume she almost passed for some sort of peasant. Though still self-reliant, she had become like all their women.

She served him orange juice. Bleilip, feeling his bare bald head, wondered whether he was expected to say the blessing, whether they would thrust a headcovering on him: he was baffled, confused, but

Yussel said, 'You live your life and I'll live mine, do what you like,' so he drank it all down quickly. Relief made him thirsty, and he drank more and more from a big can with pictures of sweating oranges on it – some things they bought at a supermarket like all mortals.

'So,' he said to Toby, 'how do you like your *shtetl*?'

She laughed and circled a finger around at the new refrigerator, vast-shouldered, gleaming, a presence. 'What a village we are! A backwater!'

'State of mind,' he said, 'that's what I meant.'

'Oh, state of mind. What's that?'

'Everything here feels different,' was all he could say.

'We're in pieces, that's why. When the back rooms are put together we'll seem more like a regular house.'

'The carpenter,' Yussel said, 'works only six months a year – we got started with him a month before he stopped. So we have to wait.'

'What does he do the rest of the year?'

'He teaches.'

'He teaches?'

'He trades with Shmulka Gershons. The other half of the year Shmulka Gershons lays pipes. Six months *Gemara* with the boys, six months on the job. Mr Horowitz the carpenter also.'

Bleilip said uncertainly, meaning to flatter, 'It sounds like a wonderful system.'

'It's not a *system*,' Yussel said.

'Yussel goes everywhere, a commuter,' Toby said: Yussel was a salesman for a paper-box manufacturer. He wore a small trimmed beard, very black, black-rimmed eyeglasses, and a vest over a rounding belly. Bleilip saw that Yussel liked him – he led him away from Toby and showed him the new hot air furnace in the cellar, the gas-fired hot water tank, the cinder blocks piled in the yard, the deep cuts above the road where the sewer pipes would go. He pointed over a little wooded crest – they could just see a bit of unpainted roof. 'That's our yeshiva, the one our boys go to. It's not the toughest, they're not up to it. They weren't good enough. In the other yeshiva in the city they didn't give them enough work. Here,' he said proudly, 'they go from seven till half-past six.'

They went back into the house by the rear door. Bleilip believed in instant rapport and yearned for closeness – he wanted to be close, close. But Yussel was impersonal, a guide, he froze Bleilip's vision. They passed through the bedrooms and again it seemed to Bleilip that Yussel was a real-estate agent, a bureaucrat, a tourist office. There were a few shelves of books – holy books, nothing frivolous – but no pictures on the walls, no radio anywhere, no television set. Bleilip had brought with him, half-furtively, a snapshot of Toby taken eight or nine years before: Toby squatting on the grass at Brooklyn College, short curly hair with a barrette glinting in it, high socks and loafers, glimpse of panties, wispy blouse blurred by wind, a book with its title clear to the camera: Political Science. He offered this to Yussel: 'A classmate.' Yussel looked at the wall. 'Why do I need an image? I have my wife right in front of me every morning.' Toby held the wallet, saw, smiled, gave it back. 'Another life,' she said.

Bleilip reminded her, 'The joke was which would be the bigger breakthrough, the woman or the Jew—' To Yussel he explained, 'She used to say she would be the first lady Jewish President.'

'Another life, other jokes,' Toby said.

'And this life? Do you like it so much?'

'Why do you keep asking? Don't you like your own life?'

Bleilip liked his life, he liked it excessively. He felt he was part of society-at-large. He told her, without understanding why he was saying such a thing, 'Here there's nothing to mock at, no jokes.'

'You said we're a village,' she contradicted.

'That wasn't mockery.'

'It wasn't, you meant it. You think we're fanatics, primitives.'

'Leave the man be,' Yussel said. He had a cashier's tone, guide counting up the day's take, and Bleilip was grieved, because Yussel was a survivor, everyone in the new town, except one or two oddities like Toby, was a survivor of the death-camps or the child of a survivor. 'He's looking for something. He wants to find. He's not the first and he won't be the last.' The rigid truth of this – Bleilip had thought his purposes darkly hidden – shocked him. He hated accuracy in a survivor. It was an affront. He wanted some kind of haze, a nostalgia for suffering perhaps. He resented the orange juice can, the appliances, the furnace, the sewer pipes. 'He's been led to expect saints,' Yussel said. 'Listen, Jules,' he said, 'I'm not a saint and Toby's not a saint and we don't have miracles and we don't have a rebbe who works miracles.'

'You have a rebbe,' Bleilip said; instantly a wash of blood filled his head.

'He can't fly. What we came here for was to live a life of study. Our own way, and not to be interrupted in it.'

'For the man, not the woman. You, not Toby. Toby used to be smart. Achievement goals and so forth.'

'Give the mother of four sons a little credit too, it's not only college girls who build the world,' Yussel said in a voice so fair-minded and humorous and obtuse that Bleilip wanted to knock him down – the first lady Jewish President of the United States had succumbed in her junior year to the zealot's private pieties, rites, idiosyncrasies. Toby was less than lucid, she was crazy to follow deviants, not in the mainstream even of their own tradition. Bleilip, who had read a little, considered these hasidim actually christologized: everything had to go through a mediator. Of their popular romantic literature he knew the usual bits and pieces, legends, occult passions, quirks, histories – he had heard, for instance, about the holiday the Lubavitcher hasidim celebrate on the anniversary of their master's release from prison: pretty stories in the telling, even more touching in the reading – poetry. Bleilip, a lawyer though not in practice, an ex-labour consultant, a fund-raiser by profession, a rational- ist, a *mitnagid* (he scarcely knew the word), purist, sceptic, enemy of fresh revelation, enemy of the hasidim! – repelled by the sects themselves, he was nevertheless lured by their constituents. Refugees, survivors. He supposed they had a certain knowledge the unscathed could not guess at.

He said: 'Toby makes her bed, she lies in it. I didn't come expecting women's rights and God knows I didn't come expecting saints.'

'If not saints then martyrs,' Yussel said.

Bleilip said nothing. This was not the sort of closeness he coveted – he shunned being seen into. His intention was to be a benefactor of the feelings. He glimpsed Yussel's tattoo-number (it almost seemed as if Yussel just then lifted his wrist to display it) without the compassion he had schemed for it. He had come to see a town of dead men. It spoiled Bleilip's mood that Yussel understood this.

At dusk the three of them went up to the road to watch the boys slide down the hill from the yeshiva. There was no danger: not a single car, except Bleilip's taxi, had passed through all day. The snow was a week old, it was coming on to March, the air struck like a bell-clapper, but Bleilip could smell through the cold something different from the smell of winter. Smoke of woodfire seeped into his throat from somewhere with a deep pinyness that moved him: he had a sense of farness, clarity, other lands, displaced seasons, the brooks of a village, a foreign bird piercing. The yeshiva boys came down on their shoe-soles, one foot in front of the other, lurching, falling, rolling. A pair of them tobogganed past on a garbage-can lid. The rest jostled, tumbled, squawked, their yarmulkas dropping from their heads into the snow like gumdrops, coins, black inkwells. Bleilip saw hoops of haloes wheeling everywhere, and he saw their ear-curls leaping over their cheeks, and all at once he penetrated into what he took to be the truth of this place – the children whirling on the hillside were false children, made of no flesh, it was a crowd of ghosts coming down, a clamour of white smoke beat on the road. Yussel said, 'I'm on my way to *mincha*, want to come?' Bleilip's grandfather, still a child but with an old man's pitted nose, appeared to be flying towards him on the lid. The last light of day split into blue rays all around them; the idea of going for evening prayer seemed natural to him now, but Bleilip, privately elated, self-proud, asked, 'Why, do you need someone?' – because he was remembering what he had forgotten he knew. Ten men. He congratulated his memory, also of his grandfather's nose, thin as an arrow – the nose, the face, the body, all gone into the earth – and he went on piecing together his grandfather's face, tan teeth that gave out small clicks and radiated stale farina, shapely grey half-moon eyes with fleshy lids, eyebrows sparse as a woman's, a prickly whiskbroom of a moustache whiter than cream. Yussel took him by the arm: 'Pessimist, joker, here we never run short, a *minyan* always without fail, but come, anyhow you'll hear the rebbe, it's our turn for him.' Briefly behind them Bleilip saw Toby moving into the dark of the door, trailed by two pairs of boys with golden earlocks: he felt the shock of that sight, as if a beam of divinity had fixed on her head, her house. But in an instant he was again humiliated by the sting of Yussel's eye— 'She'll give them supper,' he said merely, 'then they have homework.' 'You people make them work.' 'Honey on the page is only for the beginning,' Yussel said, 'afterwards comes hard learning.'

Bleilip accepted a cap for his cold-needled skull and they toiled on the ice upwards towards the schoolhouse: the rebbe gave himself each week to a different *minyan*. When Bleilip reached for a prayer-shawl inside a cardboard box Yussel thumbed a No at him, so he dropped it in again. No one else paid him any attention. Through the window the sky deepened; the shouts were gone from the hill. Yussel handed him a *sidur*, but the alphabet was jumpy and strange to him: it needed piecing together, like his grandfather's visage. He stood up when the others did. Then he sat down again, fitting his haunches into a boy's chair. It did not seem to him that they sang out with any special fervour, as he had read the hasidim did, but the sounds were loud, cadenced, earnest. The leader, unlike the others a mutterer, was the single one wearing the fringed shawl – it made a cave for him, he looked out of it without mobility of heart. Bleilip turned his stare here and there into the tedium – which was the rebbe? He went after a politician's face: his analogy was to the mayor of a town. Or a patriarch's face – the father of a large family. They finished *mincha* and herded themselves into a corner of the room – a long table (three planks nailed together, two sawhorses) covered by a cloth. The cloth was grimy: print lay on it, the backs of old *sidurim*, rubbing, shredding, the backs of the open hands of the men. Bleilip drew himself in; he found a wooden folding chair and wound his legs into the rungs, away from the men. It stunned him that they were not old, but instead mainly in the forties, plump and in their prime. Their cheeks were blooming hillocks above their beards; some wore yarmulkas, some tall black hats, some black hats edged with fur, some ordinary fedoras pushed back, one a workman's cap. Their mouths especially struck him as extraordinary – vigorous, tender, blessed. He marvelled at their mouths until it came to him that they were speaking another language and that he could follow only a little of it: now and then it was almost as if their words were visibly springing out of their mouths, like flags or streamers. Whenever he understood the words the flags whipped at him, otherwise they collapsed and vanished with a sort of hum. Bleilip himself was a month short of forty-two, but next to these pious men he felt like a boy; even his shoulder blades weakened and thinned. He made himself concentrate: he heard *azazel*, and he heard *kohen gadol*, they were knitting something up, mixing strands of holy tongue with Yiddish. The noise of Yiddish in his ear enfeebled him still more, like Titus's fly – it was not an everyday language with him, except to make cracks with, jokes, gags. . . . His dead grandfather hung from the ceiling on a rope. Wrong, mistaken, impossible, uncharacteristic of his grandfather! – who died old and safe in a Bronx bed, mischief-maker, eager aged imp. The imp came to life and swung over Bleilip's black corner. Here ghosts sat as if already in the World-to-Come, explicating Scripture. Or whatever. Who knew? In his grandfather's garble the hasidim (refugees, dead men) were crying out Temple, were crying out High Priest, and the more Bleilip squeezed his brain towards them, the more he comprehended. Five times on the tenth day of the seventh month, the Day of Atonement, the High Priest changes his vestments, five times he lowers his body into the ritual bath. After the first immersion garments of gold, after the second immersion white linen, and wearing the white linen he confesses his sins and the sins of his household while holding on to the horns of a bullock. Walking eastwards, he goes from the west of the altar to the north of the altar, where two goats stand, and he casts lots for the goats: one for the Lord, one for Azazel, and the one for the Lord is given a necklace of red wool and will be slaughtered and its blood caught in a bowl, but first the bullock will be slaughtered and its blood caught in a bowl; and once more he confesses his sins and the sins of his household, and now also the sins of the children of Aaron, this holy people. The blood of the bullock is sprinkled eight times, both upwards and downwards, the blood of the goat is sprinkled eight times, then the High Priest comes to the goat who was not slaughtered, the one for Azazel, and now he touches it and confesses the sins of the whole house of Israel, and utters the name of God, and pronounces the people cleansed of sin. And Bleilip, hearing all this through the web of a language gone stale in his marrow, was scraped to the edge of pity and belief, he pitied the hapless goats, the unlucky bullock, but more than this he pitied the God of Israel, whom he saw as an imp with a pitted nose dangling on a cord from the high beams of the Temple in Jerusalem, winking down at His tiny High Priest – now he leaps in and out of a box of water, now he hurries in and out of new clothes like a quick-change vaudevillian, now he sprinkles red drops up and red drops down, and all the while Bleilip, together with the God of the Jews, pities these toy children of Israel in the Temple long ago. Pity upon pity. What God could take the Temple rites seriously? What use does the King of the Universe have for goats? What, leaning on their dirty tablecloth – no vestments, altars, sacrifices – what do these survivors, exemptions, expect of God now?

All at once Bleilip knew which was the rebbe. The man in the work-cap, with a funny flat nose, black-haired and red-bearded, fist on mouth, elbows sunk into his lap – a self-stabber: in all that recitation, those calls and streamers of discourse, this blunt-nosed man had no word: but now he stood up, scratched his chair backwards, and fell into an ordinary voice. Bleilip examined him: he looked fifty, his hands were brutish, two fingers missing, the nails on the others absent. A pair of muscles bunched in his neck like chains. The company did not breathe and gave him something more than attentiveness. Bleilip reversed his view and saw that the rebbe was their child, they gazed at him with the possessiveness of faces seized by a crib, and he too spoke in that mode, as if he were addressing parents, old fathers, deferential, awed, guilty.

And still he was their child, and still he owed them his guilt. He said: 'And what comes next? Next we read that the *kohen gadol* gives the goat fated for Azazel to one of the *kohanim*, and the *kohen* takes it out into a place all bare and wild, with a big cliff in the middle of it all, and he cuts off a bit of the red wool they had put on it, and ties it onto a piece of rock to mark the place, and then he drives the goat over the edge and it spins down, down, down, and is destroyed. But in the Temple the worship may not continue, not until it is known that the goat is already given over to the wilderness. How can they know this miles away in the far city? All along the way from the wilderness to Jerusalem, poles stand up out of the ground, and on top of every pole a man, and in the hand of every man a great shawl to shake out, so that pole flies out a wing to pole, wing after wing, until it comes to the notice of the *kohen gadol* in the Temple that the goat has been dashed into the ravine. And only then can the *kohen gadol* finish his readings, his invocations, his blessings, his beseechings. In the neighbourhood of Sharon often there are earthquakes: the *kohen gadol* says: let their homes not become their graves. And after all this a procession, no, a parade, a celebration, all the people follow the *kohen gadol* to his own house, he is safe out of the Holy of Holies, their sins are atoned for, they are cleansed and healed, and they sing how like a flower he is, a lily, like the moon, the sun, the morning star among clouds, a dish of gold, an olive tree. . . . That, gentlemen, is how it was in the Temple, and how it will be again after the coming of Messiah. We learn it' – he tapped his book – 'in *Mishna Yoma, Yoma* – Targum for Day, *yom hakipurim*, but whose is the atonement, whose is the cleansing? Does the goat for Azazel atone, does the *kohen gadol* cleanse and hallow us? No, only the Most High can cleanse, only we ourselves can atone. Rabbi Akiva reminds us: "Who is it that makes you clean? Our Father in Heaven." So why, gentlemen, do you suppose the Temple was even then necessary, why the goats, the bullock, the blood? Why is it necessary for all of this to be restored by Messiah? These are questions we must torment ourselves with. Which of us would slaughter an animal, not for sustenance, but for an idea? Which of us would dash an animal to its death? Which of us would not feel himself to be a sinner in doing so? Or feel the shame of Esau? You may say that those were other days, the rituals are obsolete, we are purer now, better, we do not sprinkle blood so readily. But in truth you would not say so, you would not lie. For animals we in our day substitute men. What the word Azazel means exactly is not known – we call it wilderness, some say it is hell itself, demons live there.

But whatever we mean by "wilderness", whatever we mean by "hell", surely the plainest meaning is *instead of*. Wilderness instead of easeful places, hell and devils instead of plenitude, life, peace. Goat instead of man. Was there no one present in the Temple who, seeing the animals in all their majesty of health, shining hair, glinting hooves, timid nostrils, muscled like ourselves, gifted with tender eyes no different from our own, the whole fine creature trembling – was there no one there when the knife slit the fur and skin and the blood fled upwards who did not feel the splendour of the living beast? Who was not in awe of the miracle of life turned to carcass? Who did not think: *how like that goat I am! The goat goes, I stay, the goat instead of me*. Who did not see in the goat led to Azazel his own destiny? Death takes us too at random, some at the altar, some over the cliff. . . . Gentlemen, we are this moment so to speak in the Temple, the Temple devoid of the Holy of Holies – when the Temple was destroyed it forsook the world, so the world itself had no recourse but to pretend to be the Temple by mockery. In the absence of Messiah there can be no *kohen gadol*, we have no authority to bless multitudes, we are not empowered, we cannot appeal except for ourselves, ourselves alone, in isolation, in futility, instead we are like the little goats, we are assigned our lot, we are designated for the altar or for Azazel, in either case we are meant to be cut down. . . . O little fathers, we cannot choose, we are driven, we are not free, we are only *instead of*: we stand *instead of*, instead of choice we have the yoke, instead of looseness we are pointed the way to go, instead of freedom we have the red cord around our throats, we were in villages, they drove us into camps, we were in trains, they drove us into showers of poison, in the absence of Messiah the secular ones made a nation, enemies bite at it. All that we do without Messiah is in vain. When the Temple forsook the world, and the world presumed to mock the Temple, everyone on earth became a goat or a bullock, he-animal or she-animal, all our prayers are bleats and neighs on the way to a forsaken altar, a teeming Azazel. Little fathers! How is it possible to live? When will Messiah come? You! You! Visitor! You're looking somewhere else, who are you not to look?'

He was addressing Bleilip – he pointed a finger without a nail.

'Who are you? Talk and look! Who!'

Bleilip spoke his own name and shook: a schoolboy in a schoolroom. 'I'm here with the deepest respect, Rabbi. I came out of interest for your community.'

'We are not South Sea islanders, sir, our practices are well known

since Sinai. You don't have to turn your glance. We are not something
new in the world.'

'Excuse me, Rabbi, not new – unfamiliar.'

'To you.'

'To me,' Bleilip admitted.

'Exactly my question! Who are you, what do you represent, what are
you to us?'

'A Jew. Like yourselves. One of you.'

'Presumption! Atheist, devourer! For us there is the Most High, joy,
life. For us trust! But you! A moment ago I spoke your own heart for you,
emes?'

Bleilip knew this word: truth, true, but he was only a visitor and did
not want so much: he wanted only what he needed, a certain piece of
truth, not too big to swallow. He was afraid of choking on more. The
rebbe said, 'You believe the world is in vain, *emes?*'

'I don't follow any of that, I'm not looking for theology—'

'Little fathers,' said the rebbe, 'everything you heard me say, everything
you heard me say in a voice of despair, emanates from the liver of this
man. My mouth made itself his parrot. My teeth became his beak. He
fills the study-house with a black light, as if he keeps a lump of radium
inside his belly. He would eat us up. Man he equates with the goats. The
Temple, in memory and anticipation, he considers an abattoir. The world
he regards as a graveyard. You are shocked, Mister Bleilip, that I know
your kidneys, your heart? Canker! Onset of cholera! You say you don't
come for "theology", Mister Bleilip, and yet you have a particular
conception of us, *emes?* A certain idea.'

Bleilip wished himself mute. He looked at Yussel, but Yussel had his
eyes on his sleeve-button.

'Speak in your own language, please' – Bleilip was unable to do
anything else – 'and I will understand you very well. Your idea about us,
please. Stand up!'

Bleilip obeyed. That he obeyed bewildered him. The crescents of faces
in profile on either side of him seemed sharp as scythes. His yarmulka
fell off his head but, rising, he failed to notice it – one of the men quickly
clapped it back on. The stranger's palm came like a blow.

'Your idea,' the rebbe insisted.

'Things I've heard,' Bleilip croaked. 'That in the Zohar it's written how
Moses coupled with the Shekhina on Mount Sinai. That there are books
to cast lots by, to tell fortunes, futures. That some Rabbis achieved

levitation, hung in air without end, made babies come in barren women, healed miraculously. That there was once a Rabbi who snuffed out the Sabbath light. Things,' Bleilip said, 'I suppose legends.'

'Did you hope to witness any of these things?'

Bleilip was silent.

'Then let me again ask. Do you credit any of these things?'

'Do you?' asked Bleilip.

Yussel intervened: 'Forbidden to mock the rebbe!'

But the rebbe replied, 'I do not believe in magic. That there are influences I do believe.'

Bleilip felt braver. 'Influences?'

'Turnings. That a man can be turned from folly, error, wrong choices. From misery, evil, private rage. From a mistaken life.'

Now Bleilip viewed the rebbe; he was suspicious of such hands. The hands a horror: deformity, mutilation: caught in what machine? – and above them the worker's cap. But otherwise the man seemed simple, reasoned, balanced, after certain harmonies, sanities, the ordinary article, no mystic, a bit bossy, pedagogue, noisy preacher. Bleilip, himself a man with a profession and no schoolboy after all, again took heart. A commonplace figure. People did what he asked, nothing more compli-cated than this – but he had to ask. Or tell, or direct. A monarch perhaps. A community needs to be governed. A human relationship: of all words Bleilip, whose vocabulary was habitually sociological, best of all liked 'relationship'.

He said, 'I don't have a mistaken life.'

'Empty your pockets.'

Bleilip stood without moving.

'Empty your pockets!'

'Rabbi, I'm not an exercise, I'm not a demonstration—'

'Despair must be earned.'

'I'm not in despair,' Bleilip objected.

'To be an atheist is to be in despair.'

'I'm not an atheist, I'm a secularist,' but even Bleilip did not know what he meant by this.

'Esau! For the third time: empty your pockets!'

Bleilip pulled the black plastic thing out and threw it on the table. Instantly all the men bent away from it.

'A certain rebbe,' said the rebbe very quietly, 'believed every man should carry two slips of paper in his pockets. In one pocket should be written: "I am but dust and ashes." In the other: "For my sake was the world created." This canker fills only one pocket, and with ashes.' He picked up Bleilip's five-and-ten gun and said 'Esau! Beast! Lion! To whom did you intend to do harm?'

'Nobody,' said Bleilip out of his shame. 'It isn't real. I keep it to get used to. The feel of the thing. Listen,' he said, 'do you think it's easy for me to carry that thing around and keep on thinking about it?'

The rebbe tried the trigger. It gave out a tin click. Then he wrapped it in his handkerchief and put it in his pocket. 'We will now proceed with *ma'ariv*,' he said. 'The study hour is finished. Let us not learn more of this matter. This is Jacob's tent.'

The men left the study table and took up their old places, reciting. Bleilip, humiliated (the analogy to a teacher confiscating a forbidden toy was too exact), still excited, the tremor in his groin worse, was in awe before this incident. Was it amazing chance that the rebbe had challenged the contents of his pockets, or was he a seer? At the conclusion of *ma'ariv* the men dispersed quickly; Bleilip recognized from Yussel's white stare that this was not the usual way. He felt like an animal they were running from. He intended to run himself – all the way to the Greyhound station – but the rebbe came to him. 'You,' he said (*du*, as if to an animal, or to a child, or to God), 'the other pocket. The second one. The other side of your coat.'

'What?'

'Disgorge.'

So Bleilip took it out. And just as the toy gun could instantly be seen to be a toy, all tin glint, so could this one be seen for what it was: monstrous, clumsy and hard, heavy, with a scarred trigger and a barrel that smelled. Dark, no gleam. An actuality, a thing for use. Yussel moaned, dipping his head up and down. 'In my house! Stood in front of my wife with it! With two!'

'With one,' said the rebbe. 'One is a toy and one not, so only one need be feared. It is the toy we have to fear: the incapable—'

Yussel broke in, 'We should call the police, rebbe.'

'Because of a toy? How they will laugh.'

'But the other! This!'

'Is it capable?' the rebbe asked Bleilip.

'Loaded, you mean? Sure it's loaded.'

'Loaded, you hear him?' Yussel said. 'He came as a curiosity-seeker, rebbe, my wife's cousin, I had no suspicion of this—'

The rebbe said, 'Go home, Yussel. Go home, little father.'

'Rebbe, he can shoot—'

'How can he shoot? The instrument is in my hand.'

It was. The rebbe held the gun – the real one. Again Bleilip was drawn to those hands. This time the rebbe saw. 'Buchenwald,' he said. 'Blocks of ice, a freezing experiment. In my case only to the elbow, but others were immersed wholly and perished. The fingers left are toy fingers. That is why you have been afraid of them and have looked away.'

He said all this very clearly, in a voice without an opinion.

'Don't talk to him, rebbe!'

'Little father, go home.'

'And if he shoots?'

'He will not shoot.'

Alone in the schoolhouse with the rebbe – how dim the bulbs, dangling on cords – Bleilip regretted that because of the dishonour of the guns. He was pleased that the rebbe had dismissed Yussel. The day (but now it was night) felt full of miracles and lucky chances. Thanks to Yussel he had gotten to the rebbe. He never supposed he would get to the rebbe himself – all his hope was only for a glimpse of the effect of the rebbe. Of influences. With these he was satisfied. He said again, 'I don't have a mistaken life.'

The rebbe enclosed the second gun in his handkerchief. 'This one has a bad odour.'

'Once I killed a pigeon with it.'

'A live bird?'

'You believers,' Bleilip threw out, 'you'd cut up those goats all over again if you got the Temple back!'

'Sometimes,' the rebbe said, 'even the rebbe does not believe. My father when he was the rebbe also sometimes did not believe. It is characteristic of believers sometimes not to believe. And it is characteristic of unbelievers sometimes to believe. Even you, Mister Bleilip – even you now and then believe in the Holy One, Blessed Be He? Even you now and then apprehend the Most High?'

'No,' Bleilip said; and then: 'Yes.'

'Then you are as bloody as anyone,' the rebbe said (it was his first real opinion), and with his terrible hands put the bulging white handkerchief on the table for Bleilip to take home with him, for whatever purpose he thought he needed it.

Shots

I came to photography as I came to infatuation – with no special talent for it, and with no point of view. Taking pictures – when *I* take them, I mean – has nothing to do with art and less to do with reality. I'm blind to what intelligent people call 'composition', I revile every emanation of 'grain', and any drag through a gallery makes me want to die. As for the camera as *machine* – well, I know the hole I have to look through, and I know how to press down with my finger. The rest is thingamajig. What brought me to my ingenious profession was no idea of the Photograph as successor to the Painting, and no pleasure in darkrooms, or in any accumulation of clanking detritus.

Call it necrophilia. I have fallen in love with corpses. Dead faces draw me. I'm uninformed about the history of photography – 1832, the daguerreotype, mercury vapour; what an annoyance that so blatant a thing as picture-taking is considered worth applying a history to! – except to understand how long a past the camera has, measured by a century-old length of a woman's skirt. People talk of inventing a time machine, as if it hadn't already been invented in the box and shutter. I have been ravished by the last century's faces, now motes in their graves – such lost eyes, and noses, and mouths, and earlobes, and dress-collars: my own eyes soak these up; I can never leave off looking at anything brown and brittle and old and decaying at the edges.

The autumn I was eleven I found the Brown Girl. She was under a mound of chestnut-littered leaves near five tall trash barrels in a corner of the yard behind the Home for the Elderly Female Ill. Though the old-lady inmates were kept confined to a high balcony above the browning grass of their bleak overgrown yard, occasionally I would see some witless half-bald refugee shuffling through a weed-sea with stockings rolled midway down a sinewy blue calf engraved by a knotted garter. They scared me to death, these sticks and twigs of brainless ancients, rattling their china teeth and howling at me in foreign tongues, rolling the bright gems of their mad old eyes inside their nearly visible crania. I used to imagine that if one of these fearful witches could just somehow get beyond the gate, she would spill off garters and fake teeth and rheumy eye-whites and bad smells and stupid matted old flesh, and begin to bloom all plump and glowing and ripe again: Shangri-La in reverse.

What gave me this imagining was the Brown Girl. Any one of these pitiful decaying sacks might once have been the Brown Girl. If only someone had shot a kind of halt-arrow through the young nipples of the Brown Girl at the crest of her years, if only she had been halted, arrested, stayed in her ripeness and savour!

The Brown Girl lived. She lay in a pile of albums dumped into the leaves. It seemed there were hundreds of her: a girl in a dress that dropped to the buttons of her shoes, with an arched bosom and a hint of bustle, and a face mysteriously shut: you never once saw her teeth, you never once saw the lips in anything like the hope of a smile; laughter was out of the question. A grave girl; a sepia girl; a girl as brown as the ground. She must have had her sorrows.

Gradually (to my eyes suddenly) I saw her age. It wasn't that the plain sad big-nosed face altered: no crinkles at the lids, no grooves digging out a distinct little parallelogram from nostril-sides to mouth-ends – or, if these were in sight, they weren't what I noticed. The face faded out – became not there. The woman turned to ghost. The ghost wore different clothes now, too familiar to gape at. The fingers were ringless. The eyes whitened off. Somehow for this melancholy spinster's sake the first rule of the box camera was always being violated: not to put the sun behind your subject. A vast blurred drowning orb of sun flooded massively, habitually down from the upper right corner of her picture. Whoever photographed her, over years and years and years, meant to obliterate her. But I knew it was no sun-bleach that conspired to efface her. What I was seeing – what I *had* seen – was time. And not time on the move, either, the illusion of stories and movies. What I had seen was time as stasis, time at the standstill, time at the fix; the time (though I hadn't yet reached it in school) of Keats's Grecian urn. The face faded out because death was coming: death the changer, the collapser, the witherer; death the bleacher, blancher, whitener.

*

The truth is, I'm looked on as a close-mouthed professional, serious about my trade, who intends to shut up and keep secrets when necessary. I repel all 'technical' questions – if someone wants to discuss the make of my camera (it's Japanese), or my favourite lens, or some trick I might have in developing, or what grade of paper I like, I'll stare her down. Moonings on Minor White's theories I regard as absolutely demeaning. I have a grasp on what I am about, and it isn't any of that.

What it is, is the Brown Girl. I kept her. I kept her, I mean, in a pocket of my mind (and one of her pictures in the pocket of my blouse); I kept her because she was dead. What I expect you to take from this is that I *could* keep her *even though* she was dead. I wasn't infatuated by her (not that she was the wrong sex: infatuation, like any passion of recognition, neglects gender); she was too oppressed and brown and quiet for that. But it was she who gave me the miraculous hint: a hint derived from no science of mechanics or physics, a rapturous hint on the other side of art, beyond metaphor, deep in the wonderfully literal. What she made me see was that if she wasn't a girl any more, if she wasn't a woman any more, if she was very likely not even a member of the elderly female ill any more (by the time her photos fell among the leaves, how long had she been lying under them?), still I *had* her, actually and physically and with the certainty of simple truth. I could keep her, just as she used to be, because someone had once looked through the bunghole of a box and clicked off a lever. Whoever had desultorily drowned her in too much sun had anyhow given her a monument two inches wide and three inches long. What happened then was here now. I had it in the pocket of my blouse.

Knowing this – that now will become then, that huge will turn little – doesn't cure. I walk around the wet streets with a historian now, a tenured professor of South American history: he doesn't like to go home to his wife. Somehow it always rains when we meet, and it's Sam's big blue umbrella, with a wooden horse's head for a handle, that preoccupies me this instant. Which is strange: he hasn't owned it for a whole year. It was left in a yellow garish coffee shop on the night side of a street you couldn't trust, and when Sam went back, only ten minutes later, to retrieve it, of course it wasn't there.

At that time I didn't care about one thing in Sam's mind. I had to follow him, on assignment, all through a course of some public symposia he was chairing. We had – temporarily – the same employer. His college was setting up a glossy little booklet for the State Department to win South American friends with: I had to shoot Sam on the podium with Uruguayans, Sam on the podium with Brazilians, Sam on the podium with Peruvians, and so forth. It was a lacklustre job – I had just come, not so long ago, from photographing an intergalactic physicist whose bravest hope was the invention of an alphabet to shoot into the kindergartens of the cosmos – so it was no trouble at all not to listen to the speeches while I shot the principals. Half the speeches were in Portuguese or Spanish, and if you wanted to you could put on earphones anywhere in the hall and hear a simultaneous translation. The translator sat at the squat end of the long symposium table up on the stage with Sam and the others, but kept his microphone oddly close to his lips, like a kiss, sweat sliding and gleaming along his neck – it seemed he was tormented by that bifurcated concentration. His suffering attracted me. He didn't count as one of the principals – the celebrity of the day (now it was night, the last of the dark raining afternoon) was the vice-consul of Chile – but I shot him anyhow, for my own reasons: I liked the look of that shining sweat on his bulging Adam's apple. I calculated my aim (I'm very fast at this), shot once, shot again, and was amazed to see blood spring out of a hole in his neck. The audience fell apart – it was like watching an anthill after you've kicked into it; there was a spaghetti of wires and police; the simultaneous translator was dead. It made you listen for the simultaneous silence of the principal speaker, but the Chilean vice-consul only swerved his syllables into shrieks, with his coat over his head; he was walked away in a tremor between two colleagues suddenly sprouting guns. A mob of detectives took away my film; it was all I could do to keep them from arresting my camera. I went straight to Sam – it was his show – to complain. 'That's *film* in there, not bullets.' 'It's evidence now,' Sam said. 'Who wanted to do that?' I said. 'God knows,' Sam said; 'they didn't do what they wanted anyhow,' and offered six political possibilities, each of which made it seem worthwhile for someone to do away with the Chilean vice-consul. He found his umbrella under the table and steered me out. The rain had a merciless wind in it, and every glassy sweep of it sent fountains spitting upwards from the pavement. We stood for a while under his umbrella (he gripping the horse's head hard enough to whiten his knuckles) and watched them carry the simultaneous translator out. He was alone on a stretcher; his duality was done, his job as surrogate consummated. I reflected how quickly vertical becomes horizontal. 'You knew him,' I said.

'Only in a public way. He's been part of all these meetings.'

'So have I,' I said.

'I've watched you watching me.'

I resisted this. 'That's professional watching. It's more like stalking. I always stalk a bit before I shoot.'

'You talk like a terrorist,' Sam said, and began a history of South American conspiracy, which group was aligned with whom, who gave asylum, who withheld it, who the Chilean vice-consul's intimates across several borders were, at this instant plotting vengeance. He had exactly the kind of mentality – cumulative, analytical – I least admired, but since he also had the only umbrella in sight, I stuck with him. He was more interested in political factionalism – he had to get everything sorted out, and his fascination seemed to be with the victims – than in his having just sat two feet from a murder. 'My God,' I said finally, 'doesn't the power of inaccuracy impress you? It could've been you on that stretcher.'

'I don't suppose *you* ever miss your target,' he said.

'No,' I said, 'but I don't shoot to kill.'

'Then you're not one of those who want to change the world,' he said, and I could smell in this the odour of his melancholy. He was a melancholic and an egotist; this made me a bit more attentive. His umbrella, it appeared, was going to pilot him around for miles and miles; I went along as passenger. We turned at last into a coffee shop – this wasn't the place he lost the horse's head in – and then turned out again, heated up, ready for more weather. 'Don't you ever go home?' I asked him.

'Don't you?'

'I live alone.'

'I don't. I hate my life,' he said.

'I don't blame you. You've stuffed it up with South American facts.'

'Would you like North American facts better?'

'I can't take life in whole continents,' I protested.

'The thing about taking it in continents is that you don't have to take it face by face.'

'The faces are the best part.'

'Some are the worst,' Sam said.

I looked into his; he seemed a victim of factionalism himself, as if you become what you study. He had rather ferocious eyes, much too shiny, like something boiling in a pot – the ferocity made you think them black, but really they were pale – and black ripe rippled hair and unblemished orderly teeth, not white but near-white. 'Which faces are the worst?'

'Now I'll go home,' he said.

The murder had cut short the series of symposia; the South Americans scattered, which was too bad – they were Sam's source of vitality. But it never occurred to either of us that we might not meet again officially, and often enough we did – he on a platform, myself with camera. Whether this meant that all the magazine people I knew – the ones who were commissioning my pictures – were all at once developing a fevered concern for South American affairs (more likely it was for terrorism) is a boring question. I know *I* wasn't. I never wanted to listen to Sam on the subjects he was expert in, and I never did. I only caught what I thought of as their 'moans' – impure and simmering and winnowing and sad. The sounds that came through his microphone were always intensely public: he was, his audience maintained – loyalists, they trotted after him from speech to speech – a marvellous generalist. He could go from predicting the demand for bauxite to tracing migrations of Indian populations, all in a single stanza. He could connect disparate packets of contemporary information with a linking historic insight that took your breath away. He was a very, very good public lecturer; all his claque said so. He could manage to make anyone (or everyone but me) care about South America. Still, I had a little trick in my head as he declaimed and as I popped my flashbulbs, not always at him – more often at the distinguished sponsors of the event. I could tell they were distinguished from the way they dragged me up to the dais to photograph them – it showed how important they were. Sometimes they wanted to be photographed just before Sam began, and sometimes, with their arms around him, when he was just finished, themselves grinning into Sam's applause. All the while I kept the little trick going.

The little trick was this: whatever he said that was vast and public and South American, I would simultaneously translate (I hoped I wouldn't be gunned down for it) into everything private and personal and secret. This required me to listen shrewdly to the moan behind the words – I had to blot out the words for the sake of the tune. Sometimes the tune would be civil or sweet or almost jolly – especially if he happened to get a look at me before he ascended to his lectern – but mainly it would be narrow and drab and resigned. I knew he had a wife, but I was already thirty-six, and who didn't have a wife by then? I wasn't likely to run into them if they didn't. Bachelors wouldn't be where I had to go, particularly not in public halls gaping at the per capita income of the interior villages of the Andes, or the future of Venezuelan oil, or the fortunes of the last Paraguayan bean crop, or the differences between the centrist parties in Bolivia and Colombia, or whatever it was that kept Sam ladling away at his tedious stew. I drilled through all these sober-shelled facts into their echoing gloomy melodies: and the sorrowful sounds I unlocked from their casings – it was like breaking open a stone and finding the music of the earth's wild core boiling inside – came down to the wife, the wife, the wife. That was the tune Sam was moaning all the while: wife wife wife. He didn't like her. He wasn't happy with her. His whole life was wrong. He was a dead man. If I thought I'd seen a dead man when they took that poor fellow out on that stretcher, I was stupidly mistaken; *he* was ten times deader than that. If the terrorist who couldn't shoot straight had shot *him* instead, he couldn't be more riddled with gunshot than he was this minute – he was smoking with his own death.

In the yellow garish coffee shop he went on about his wife – he shouldn't be telling me all this, my God, what the hell did he think he was doing; he was a fool; he was a cliché; he was out of a cartoon or an awful play; he was an embarrassment to himself and to me. It was either a trance or a seizure. And then he forgot his umbrella, and ran back after it, and it was gone. It wouldn't have had, necessarily, to be a desperate thief who stole his horse's head that night; it might easily have been a nice middle-class person like ourselves. A nice middle-class person especially would have hated to be out in such a drenching without a shred of defence overhead – Sam charged on into gales of cold rain, and made me charge onwards too: for the first time he had me by the hand. I wouldn't let him keep it, though – I had to bundle my camera under my coat.

'How long are we going to walk in this?' I said.

'We'll walk and walk.'

'I've got to go home or I'll soak my equipment,' I complained.

'I'm not going home.'

'Don't you ever go home?'

'My whole life is wrong,' he said.

We spilled ourselves into another coffee place and sat there till closing. My shoes were seeping and seeping. He explained Verity: 'I admire her,' he said. 'I esteem her, you wouldn't believe how I esteem that woman. She's a beautiful mother. She's strong and she's bright and she's independent and there's nothing she can't do.'

'Now tell her good points,' I said.

'She can fix a car. She always fixes the car. Puts her head into the hood and fixes it. She builds furniture. We live in a madhouse of excess property – she built every stick of it. She saws like a madwoman. She *sews* like a madwoman – I don't mean just *clothes*. She sews her own clothes and the girls' clothes too. What I mean is she *sews* – bedspreads and curtains and upholstery, even *car* upholstery. And she's got a whole budding career of her own. I've made her sound like a bull, but she's really very delicate at whatever she does – she does plates, you know.'

'Licence plates?'

'She's done *some* metalwork – her minor was metallurgy – but what I'm talking about is ceramics. Porcelain. She does painted platters and pots and pitchers and sells them to Bloomingdale's.'

'She's terrific,' I said.

'She's terrific,' he agreed. 'There's nothing she can't do.'

'Cook?'

'My God, *cook*,' he said. 'French, Italian, Indian, whatever you want. And bakes. Pastries, the difficult stuff, crusts made of cloud. She's a domestic genius. We have this big harp – hell, it was busted, a skeleton in a junk shop, so she bought it cheap and repaired it – she plays it like an angel. You think you're in heaven inside that hell. She plays the piano, too – classics, ragtime, rock. She's got a pretty nice singing voice. She's good at basketball – she practically never misses a shot. Don't ask me again if I admire her.'

I asked him again if he admired her.

'I'm on my knees,' he groaned. 'She's a goddamn goddess. She's powerful and autonomous and a goddam genius. Christ,' he said, 'I hate my life.'

'If I had someone like that at home,' I said, 'I'd never be out in the rain.'

'She could abolish the weather if she wanted to, only she doesn't want to. She has a terrific will.'

I thought this over and was surprised by my sincerity: 'You ought to go home,' I told him.

'Let's walk.'

After that we met more or less on purpose. The South American fad wore off – there was a let-up in guerrilla activity down there – and it got harder to find him in public halls, so I went up to his college now and then and sat in on his classes, and afterwards, rain or shine, but mostly rain, we walked. He told me about his daughters – one of them was nearly as terrific as Verity herself – and we walked with our arms hooked. 'Is something happening here?' I inquired. 'Nothing will ever happen here,' he said. We had a friend in common, the editor who'd assigned me to photographing that intergalactic physicist I've mentioned; it turned out we were asked, Sam with Verity, myself as usual, to the editor's party, in honour of the editor's ascension. There were some things the editor hadn't done which added immensely to his glory; and because of all the things he hadn't done they were making him vice-chancellor of Sam's college. I did justice to those illustrious gaps and omissions: I took the host, now majestic, and his wife, their children, their gerbil, their maid. I shot them embedded in their guests. I dropped all those pictures behind me like autumn leaves. I hadn't brought my usual Japanese spy, you see; I'd carried along a tacky Polaroid instead – instant development, a detective story without a detective, ah, I disliked that idea, but the evening needed its jester. I aimed and shot, aimed and shot, handing out portraits deciduously. Verity had her eye on all this promiscuity; she was blonde and capacious and maybe capricious; she seemed without harm and without mercy.

'You're the one who shot the simultaneous translator,' she said.

'Judicial evidence,' I replied.

'Now let me,' she said, 'ask you something about your trade. In photography, do you consistently get what you expect?'

I said: 'It's the same as life.'

Verity expressed herself: 'The viewfinder, the viewfinder!'

'I always look through that first,' I admitted.

'And then do you get what you see? I mean can you predict exactly, or are you always surprised by what comes out?'

'I can never predict,' I told her, 'but I'm never surprised.'

'That's fatalism,' Verity said. Her voice was an iron arrow; she put her forefinger into my cheek as humbly as a bride. 'Talk about shots, here's a parting one. You take a shot at Sam, no expectations. He's not like life. He's safe. He's *good*.'

He was safe and he was good: Sam the man of virtue. She knew everything exactly, even when everything was nothing she knew it exactly, she was without any fear at all; jealousy wasn't in her picture; she was more virtuous than he was, she was big, she had her great engine, she was her own cargo. And you see what it is with infatuation: it comes on you as quick as a knife. It's a bullet in the neck. It gets you from the outside. One moment you're in your prime of health, the next you're in anguish. Until then – until I had the chance to see for myself how clear and proud his wife was – Sam was an entertainment, not so entertaining after all. Verity was the Cupid of the thing, Verity's confidence the iron arrow that dragged me down. She had her big foot on her sour catch. I saw in her glow, in her sureness, in her pride, in her tall ship's prow of certitude, the plausibility of everything she knew: he'd have to go home in the end.

But the end's always at the end; in the meantime there's the meantime.

How to give over these middle parts? I couldn't see what I looked like, from then on, to Sam: all the same I had my automatic intelligence – light acting on a treated film. I was treated enough; Verity had daubed me. Since I was soaked in her solution, infatuation took, with me, a mechanical form – if you didn't know how mechanical it was, you would have imagined it was sly. I could listen now to everything Sam said. Without warning, I could *follow* him; I discovered myself in the act of wanting more. I woke up one morning in a fit of curiosity about the quantity of anthracite exports on the Brazilian littoral. I rooted in hard-to-find volumes of Bolivar's addresses. I penetrated the duskier hells of the public library and boned up on every banana republic within reach. It was astounding: all at once, and for no reason – I mean for *the* reason – Sam interested me. It was like walking on the lining of his brain.

On the South American issue he was dense as a statue. He had never noticed that I hadn't paid attention to his subject before; he didn't notice that I was attentive now. His premise was that everyone alive without exception was all the time infatuated with the former Spanish Empire. On *my* subject, though, Sam was trying; it was because of Verity; she had made him ambitious to improve himself with me.

'Verity saw at that party,' he said, 'that you had the kind of camera that gets you the picture right away.'

'Not exactly right away. You have to wait a minute,' I corrected.

'Why don't you use a camera like that all the time? It's magic. It's like a miracle.'

'Practical reasons of the trade. The farther you are from having what you think you want, the more likely you are to get it. It's just that you have to wait. You really have to *wait*. What's important is the waiting.'

Sam didn't get it. 'But it's *chemistry*. The image is already on the film. It's the same image one minute later or two months later.'

'You're too miracle-minded even for a historian,' I admonished him. 'It's not like that at all. If you have a change of heart between shooting your picture and taking it out of the developer, the picture changes too.' I wanted to explain to him how, between the exposure and the solution, history comes into being, but telling that would make me bleed, like a bullet in the neck, so I said instead, 'Photography is *literal*. It gets what's *there*.'

Meanwhile the rain is raining on Sam and me. We meet in daylight now, and invent our own occasions. We hold hands, we hook arms, we walk through the park. There is a mole on his knuckle which has attached itself to my breathing; my lungs grasp all the air they can. I want to lay my tears on the hairs of his fingers. Because of the rain, the daylight is more like twilight; in this perpetual half of dusk, the sidewalks a kind of blackened purple, like fallen plums, we talk about the past and the future of the South American continent. Verity is in her house. I leave my camera behind too. Our faces are rivers, we walk without an umbrella, the leaves splash. When I can't find Sam on my own, I telephone Verity; she stops the motor of her sewing machine and promises to give him the message when he returns. He comes flying out to meet me, straight from his Committee on Inter-American Conditions; I'm practically a colleague now, and a pleasure to talk to about Ecuadorian peonage. He tells me he's never had a mistress and never will; his wife is too remarkable. I ask him whether he's ever walked in a summer rain this way with anyone else. He admits he has; he admits it hasn't lasted. 'The rain hasn't lasted? Or the feeling?' He forgets to answer. I remember that *he* is only interested; it's I who feel. We talk some more about the native religions still hiding out in the pampas; we talk about the Jewish gauchos in nineteenth-century Argentina. He takes it all for granted. He doesn't realize how hard I've had to study. A big leaf like a pitcher overturns itself all over our heads, and we make a joke about Ponce de León and the Fountain of Youth. I ask him then if he'll let me take his picture in the park, under a dripping linden tree, in a dangerous path, so that I can keep him forever, in case it doesn't last.

I see that he doesn't understand. He doesn't understand: unlike me, he's not under any special spell, he's not in thrall to any cult. That's the rub always – infatuation's unilateral or it doesn't count as real. I think he loves me – he may even be 'in love' – but he's not caught like me. He'd never trace my life over as I've traced over his brain waves. He asks me why I want to shoot him under the linden tree. I tell him the truth I took from his wife: virtue ravishes me. I want to keep its portrait. I am silent about the orphaned moment we're living in now, how it will leave us. I feel, I feel our pathos. We are virtue's orphans. The tree's green shoots are fleeting; all green corrupts to brown. Sam denies that he's a man of virtue. It's only his guilt about Verity: she's too terrific to betray.

He consents to having his picture taken in the sopping park if I agree to go home with him afterwards.

I say in my amazement, 'I can't go home with you. She's there.'

'She's always there.'

'Then how can I go home with you?'

'You have to *see*. It's all been too obscure. I want you to know what I know.'

'I know it, you've told me. You've told and told.'

'You have to get the smell of it. Where I am and how I live. Otherwise you won't believe in it. You won't know it,' he insists. 'Such cosy endurances.'

'You endure them,' I said.

'Yesterday,' he said, 'she brought home a box of old clothes from the Salvation Army. From a thrift shop. From an old people's home, who knows where she got it from. Pile of rags. She's going to sew them into God's bright ribbons. A patchwork quilt. She'll spin straw into gold, you'll see.'

'She's terrific.'

'She's a terrific wife,' he says.

We walk to my place, pick up my camera – I stop to grab my light meter for the rain's sake – and walk crosstown to the park again. I shoot Sam, the man of virtue, under the dripping linden tree. Although I am using my regular equipment, it seems to me the picture's finished on the spot. It's as if I roll it out and fix it then and there. Sam has got his back against the bark, and all the little wet leaves lick down over his bumpy hair. He resembles a Greek runner resting. His face is dappled by all those heart-shaped leaves, and I know that all the rest of my life I'll regret not having shot him in the open, in a field. But my wish for now is to speckle him and see him darkle under the rainy shade of a tree. It comes to me that my desire – oh, my desire! it stings me in the neck – is just now not even for Sam's face: it's for the transitoriness of these thin vulnerable leaves, with their piteous veins turned upwards towards a faintness of liverish light.

We walk the thirty-one blocks, in the quickening rain, to his place. It's only a four-room apartment, but Verity's made a palace of it. Everything plain is converted into a sweetness, a furriness, a thickness of excess. She weaves, she knits. She's an immense spider building out of her craw. The floors are piled with rugs she's woven, the chairs with throws she's knitted. She's cemented up a handy little fireplace without a flue; it really works, and on a principle she invented herself. She's carpentered all the bookcases – I catch the titles of the four books Sam's written; he's a dignitary and a scholar, after all – and overhead there wafts and dazzles the royal chandelier she found in the gutter and refurbished. Each prism slid through her polishing and perfecting fingers. Verity resurrects, Verity's terrific – you can't avoid thinking it. She's got her big shoulders mounted over her sewing machine in the corner of the living room, hemming brown squares. 'It's weird, you wouldn't believe it,' she says, '*all* the stuff in this box they gave me is brown. It's good rich fabric, though – a whole load of clothes from dead nuns. You know what happened? A convent dissolved, the young nuns broke their vows and ran to get married.'

'That's *your* story,' Sam says.

Verity calls her daughter – only one of the girls is at home, the other is away at college. Clearly this one isn't the daughter that's so much like Verity. She has a solemn hard flank of cheek, and no conversation. She carries out a plate of sliced honey cake and three cups of tea; then she hides herself in her bedroom. A radio is in there; gilded waves of Bach tremble out of it. I look around for Verity's harp.

'Hey, let's dress you up,' Verity says out of her teacup; she's already downed a quantity of cake. 'There's stuff in that box that would just fit you. You've got a waist like our girls. I wish *I* had a waist like that.' I protest; I tell her it's too silly. Sam smoulders with his sour satisfaction, and she churns her palms inside the box like a pair of oars. She pulls out a long skirt, and a blouse called a bodice, and another blouse to wear under that, with long sleeves. Sam pokes my spine and nudges me into the girl's bedroom, where there's a tall mirror screwed into the back of the door. I look at myself.

'Period piece!' says Verity.

I'm all in brown, as brown as leaves. The huge high harp, not gold as I imagined it but ivory, is along the wall behind me. I believe everything Sam has told about the conquistadores. I believe everything he's told about Verity. He's a camera who never lies. His wet hair is black as olives. He belongs to his wife, who's terrific. She's put a nun's bonnet on herself. She has an old-fashioned sense of fun – the words come to me out of, I think, Louisa May Alcott: she likes costume and dress-up. Soon she will have us guessing riddles and playing charades. They are a virtuous and wholesome family. The daughter, though her look is bone, is fond of Bach; no junk music in such a household. They are sweeter than the whole world outside. When Sam is absent the mother and her daughter climb like kittens into a knitted muff.

I shoot Verity wearing the nun's bonnet.

'Look at *you!*' she cries.

I return to the mirror to see. I am grave; I have no smile. My face is mysteriously shut. I'm suffering. Lovesick and dreamsick, I'm dreaming of my desire. I am already thirty-six years old, tomorrow I will be forty-eight years old, and a crafty parallelogram begins to frame the space between my nose and mouth. My features are very distinct – I will live for years and years before they slide out of the mirror. I'm the Brown Girl in the pocket of my blouse. I reek of history. If, this minute, I could glide into a chemical solution, as if in a gondola, splashed all over and streaming with wet silver, would the mirror seize and fix me, like a photographic plate? I watch Sam's eyes, poached and pale and mottled with furious old civilizations, steaming hatred for his wife. I trip over the long drapery of my nun's hem. All the same I catch up my camera without dropping it – my ambassador of desire, my secret house with its single shutter, my chaste aperture, my dead infant, husband of my bosom. Their two heads, hers light, his black, negatives of each other, are caught side by side in their daughter's mirror. I shoot into their heads, the white harp behind. Now they are exposed. Now they will stick forever.

Levitation

A pair of novelists, husband and wife, gave a party. The husband was also an editor; he made his living at it. But really he was a novelist. His manner was powerless; he did not seem like an editor at all. He had a nice plain pale face, likeable. His name was Feingold.

For love, and also because he had always known he did not want a Jewish wife, he married a minister's daughter. Lucy too had hoped to marry out of her tradition. (These words were hers. 'Out of my tradition,' she said. The idea fevered him.) At the age of twelve she felt herself to belong to the people of the Bible. ('A Hebrew,' she said. His heart lurched, joy rocked him.) One night from the pulpit her father read a Psalm; all at once she saw how the Psalmist meant *her*; then and there she became an Ancient Hebrew.

She had huge, intent, sliding eyes, disconcertingly luminous, and copper hair, and a grave and timid way of saying honest things.

They were shy people, and rarely gave parties.

Each had published one novel. Hers was about domestic life; he wrote about Jews.

All the roil about the State of the Novel had passed them by. In the evening after the children had been put to bed, while the portable dishwasher rattled out its smell of burning motor oil, they sat down, she at her desk, he at his, and began to write. They wrote not without puzzlements and travail; nevertheless as naturally as birds. They were devoted to accuracy, psychological realism, and earnest truthfulness; also to virtue, and even to wit. Neither one was troubled by what had happened to the novel: all those declarations about the end of Character and Story. They were serene. Sometimes, closing up their notebooks for the night, it seemed to them that they were literary friends and lovers, like George Eliot and George Henry Lewes.

In bed they would revel in quantity and murmur distrustingly of theory. 'Seven pages so far this week.' 'Nine-and-a-half, but I had to throw out four. A wrong tack.' 'Because you're doing first person. First person strangles. You can't get out of their skin.' And so on. The one principle they agreed on was the importance of never writing about writers. Your protagonist always has to be someone *real*, with real work-in-the-world – a bureaucrat, a banker, an architect (ah, they envied Conrad his shipmasters!) – otherwise you fall into solipsism, narcissism, tedium, lack of appeal-to-the-common-reader; who knew what other perils.

This difficulty – seizing on a concrete subject – was mainly Lucy's. Feingold's novel – the one he was writing now – was about Menachem ben Zerach, survivor of a massacre of Jews in the town of Estella in Spain in 1328. From morning to midnight he hid under a pile of corpses, until a 'compassionate knight' (this was the language of the history Feingold relied on) plucked him out and took him home to tend his wounds. Menachem was then twenty; his father and mother and four younger brothers had been cut down in the terror. Six thousand Jews died in a single day in March. Feingold wrote well about how the mild winds carried the salty fragrance of fresh blood, together with the ashes of Jewish houses, into the faces of the marauders. It was nevertheless a triumphant story: at the end Menachem ben Zerach becomes a renowned scholar.

'If you're going to tell about how after he gets to be a scholar he just sits there and *writes*,' Lucy protested, 'then you're doing the Forbidden Thing.' But Feingold said he meant to concentrate on the massacre, and especially on the life of the 'compassionate knight'. What had brought him to this compassion? What sort of education? What did he read? Feingold would invent a journal for the compassionate knight, and quote from it. Into this journal the compassionate knight would direct all his gifts, passions, and private opinions.

'Solipsism,' Lucy said. 'Your compassionate knight is only another writer. Narcissism. Tedium.'

They talked often about the Forbidden Thing. After a while they began to call it the Forbidden City, because not only were they (but Lucy especially) tempted to write – solipsistically, narcissistically, tediously, and without common appeal – about writers, but, more narrowly yet, about writers in New York.

'The compassionate knight,' Lucy said, 'lived on the Upper West Side of Estella. He lived on the Riverside Drive, the West End Avenue, of Estella. He lived in Estella on Central Park West.'

The Feingolds lived on Central Park West.

In her novel – the published one, not the one she was writing now – Lucy had described, in the first person, where they lived:

> By now I have seen quite a few of those West Side apartments. They have mysterious layouts. Rooms with doors that go nowhere – turn the knob, open: a wall. Someone is snoring behind it, in another apartment. They have made two and three or even four and five flats out of these palaces. The toilet bowls have antique cracks that shimmer with moisture like old green rivers. Fluted columns and fireplaces. Artur Rubinstein once paid rent here. On a gilt piano he raced a sonata by Beethoven. The sounds went spinning like mercury. Breathings all lettered now. Editors. Critics. Books, old, old books, heavy as centuries. Shelves built into the cold fireplace; Freud on the grate, Marx on the hearth, Melville, Hawthorne, Emerson. Oh God, the weight, the weight.

Lucy felt herself to be a stylist; Feingold did not. He believed in putting one sentence after another. In his publishing house he had no influence. He was nervous about his decisions. He rejected most manuscripts because he was afraid of mistakes; every mistake lost money. It was a small house panting after profits; Feingold told Lucy that the only books his firm respected belonged to the accountants. Now and then he tried to smuggle in a novel after his own taste, and then he would be brutal to the writer. He knocked the paragraphs about until they were as sparse as his own. 'God knows what you would do to mine,' Lucy said; 'bald man, bald prose.' The horizon of Feingold's head shone. She never showed him her work. But they understood they were lucky in each other. They pitied every writer who was not married to a writer. Lucy said: 'At least we have the same premises.'

Volumes of Jewish history ran up and down their walls; they belonged to Feingold. Lucy read only one book – it was *Emma* – over and over again. Feingold did not have a 'philosophical' mind. What he liked was event. Lucy liked to speculate and ruminate. She was slightly more intelligent than Feingold. To strangers he seemed very mild. Lucy, when silent, was a tall copper statue.

They were both devoted to omniscience, but they were not acute enough to see what they meant by it. They thought of themselves as children with a puppet theatre: they could make anything at all happen, speak all the lines, with gloved hands bring all the characters to shudders or leaps. They fancied themselves in love with what they called 'imagination'. It was not true. What they were addicted to was counterfeit pity, and this was because they were absorbed by power, and were powerless.

They lived on pity, and therefore on gossip: who had been childless for ten years, who had lost three successive jobs, who was in danger of being fired, which agent's prestige had fallen, who could not get his second novel published, who was *persona non grata* at this or that magazine, who was drinking seriously, who was a likely suicide, who was dreaming of divorce, who was secretly or flamboyantly sleeping with whom, who was being snubbed, who counted or did not count; and towards everyone in the least way victimized they appeared to feel the most immoderate tenderness. They were, besides, extremely 'psychological': kind listeners, helpful, lifting hot palms they would gladly put to anyone's anguished temples. They were attracted to bitter lives.

About their own lives they had a joke: they were 'secondary-level' people. Feingold had a secondary-level job with a secondary-level house. Lucy's own publisher was secondary-level; even the address was Second Avenue. The reviews of their books had been written by secondary-level reviewers. All their friends were secondary-level: not the presidents or partners of the respected firms, but copy editors and production assistants; not the glittering eagles of the intellectual organs, but the wearisome hacks of small Jewish journals; not the fiercely cold-hearted literary critics, but those wan and chattering daily reviewers of film. If they knew a playwright, he was off-off-Broadway in ambition and had not yet been produced. If they knew a painter, he lived in a loft and had exhibited only once, against the wire fence in the outdoor show at Washington Square in the spring. And this struck them as mean and unfair; they liked their friends, but other people – why not they? – were drawn into the deeper caverns of New York, among the lions.

New York! They risked their necks if they ventured out to Broadway for a loaf of bread after dark; muggers hid behind the seesaws in the playgrounds, junkies with knives hung upside down in the jungle gym.

Every apartment a lit fortress; you admired the lamps and the locks, the triple locks on the caged-in windows, the double locks and the police rods on the doors, the lamps with timers set to make burglars think you were always at home. Footsteps in the corridor, the elevator's midnight grind; caution's muffled gasps. Their parents lived in Cleveland and St Paul, and hardly ever dared to visit. All of this: grit and unsuitability (they might have owned a snowy lawn somewhere else); and no one said their names, no one had any curiosity about them, no one ever asked whether they were working on anything new. After half a year their books were remaindered for eighty-nine cents each. Anonymous mediocrities. They could not call themselves forgotten because they had never been noticed.

Lucy had a diagnosis: they were, both of them, sunk in a ghetto. Feingold persisted in his morbid investigations into Inquisitional autos-da-fé in this and that Iberian marketplace. She herself had supposed the inner life of a housebound woman – she cited *Emma* – to contain as much comedy as the cosmos. Jews and women! They were both beside the point. It was necessary to put aside pity; to look to the centre; to abandon selflessness; to study power.

They drew up a list of luminaries. They invited Irving Howe, Susan Sontag, Alfred Kazin, and Leslie Fiedler. They invited Norman Podhoretz and Elizabeth Hardwick. They invited Philip Roth and Joyce Carol Oates and Norman Mailer and William Styron and Donald Barthelme and Jerzy Kosinski and Truman Capote. None of these came; all of them had unlisted numbers, or else machines that answered the telephone, or else were in Prague or Paris or out of town. Nevertheless the apartment filled up. It was a Saturday night in a chill November. Taxis whirled on patches of sleet. On the inside of the apartment door a mound of rainboots grew taller and taller. Two closets were packed tight with raincoats and fur coats; a heap of coats smelling of skunk and lamb fell tangled off a bed.

The party washed and turned like a sluggish tub; it lapped at all the walls of all the rooms. Lucy wore a long skirt, violet-coloured, Feingold a lemon shirt and no tie. He looked paler than ever. The apartment had a wide centre hall, itself the breadth of a room; the dining room opened off it to the left, the living room to the right. The three party-rooms shone like a triptych: it was as if you could fold them up and enclose everyone into darkness. The guests were free-standing figures in the niches of a cathedral; or else dressed-up cardboard dolls, with their drinks, and their costumes all meticulously hung with sashes and draped collars and little capes, the women's hair variously bound, the men's sprouting and spilling: fashion stalked, Feingold moped. He took in how it all flashed, manhattans and martinis, earrings and shoe-tips – he marvelled, but knew it was a falsehood, even a figment. The great world was somewhere else. The conversation could fool you: how these people talked! From the conversation itself – grains of it, carried off, swallowed by new eddyings, swirl devouring swirl, every moment a permutation in the tableau of those free-standing figures or dolls, all of them afloat in a tub – from this or that hint or syllable you could imagine the whole universe in the process of ultimate comprehension. Human nature, the stars, history – the voices drummed and strummed. Lucy swam by blank-eyed, pushing a platter of mottled cheeses. Feingold seized her: 'It's a waste!' She gazed back. He said, 'No one's here!' Mournfully she rocked a stump of cheese; then he lost her.

He went into the living room: it was mainly empty, a few lumps on the sofa. The lumps wore business suits. The dining room was better. Something in formation: something around the big table: coffee cups shimmering to the brim, cake cut onto plates (the mock-Victorian rosebud plates from Boots's drug store in London: the year before their first boy was born Lucy and Feingold saw the Brontës' moors; Coleridge's house in Highgate; Lamb House, Rye, where Edith Wharton had tea with Henry James; Bloomsbury; the Cambridge stairs Forster had lived at the top of) – it seemed about to become a regular visit, with points of view, opinions; a discussion. The voices began to stumble; Feingold liked that, it was nearly human. But then, serving round the forks and paper napkins, he noticed the awful vivacity of their falsetto phrases: actors, theatre chatter, who was directing whom, what was opening where; he hated actors. Shrill puppets. Brainless. A double row of faces around the table; gurgles of fools.

The centre hall – swept clean. No one there but Lucy, lingering.

'Theatre in the dining room,' he said. 'Junk.'

'Film. I heard film.'

'Film too,' he conceded. 'Junk. It's mobbed in there.'

'Because they've got the cake. They've got all the food. The living room's got nothing.'

'My God,' he said, like a man choking, 'do you realize *no one came*?'

The living room had – had once had – potato chips. The chips were gone, the carrot sticks eaten, of the celery sticks nothing left but threads. One olive in a dish; Feingold chopped it in two with vicious teeth. The business suits had disappeared. 'It's awfully early,' Lucy said; 'a lot of people had to leave.' 'It's a cocktail party, that's what happens,' Feingold said. 'It isn't *exactly* a cocktail party,' Lucy said. They sat down on the carpet in front of the fireless grate. 'Is that a real fireplace?' someone inquired. 'We never light it,' Lucy said. 'Do you light those candlesticks ever?' 'They belonged to Jimmy's grandmother,' Lucy said, 'we never light them.'

She crossed no-man's-land to the dining room. They were serious in there now. The subject was Chaplin's gestures.

In the living room Feingold despaired; no one asked him, he began to tell about the compassionate knight. A problem of ego, he said: compassion being superconsciousness of one's own pride. Not that he believed this; he only thought it provocative to say something original, even if a little muddled. But no one responded. Feingold looked up. 'Can't you light that fire?' said a man. 'All right,' Feingold said. He rolled a paper log made of last Sunday's *Times* and laid a match on it. A flame as clear as a streetlight whitened the faces of the sofa-sitters. He recognized a friend of his from the seminary – he had what Lucy called 'theological' friends – and then and there, really very suddenly, Feingold wanted to talk about God. Or, if not God, then certain historical atrocities, abominations: to wit, the crime of the French nobleman Draconet, a proud Crusader, who in the spring of the year 1247 arrested all the Jews of the province of Vienne, castrated the men, and tore off the breasts of the women; some he did not mutilate, and only cut in two. It interested Feingold that Magna Carta and the Jewish badge of shame were issued in the same year, and that less than a century afterwards all the Jews were driven out of England, even families who had been settled there seven or eight generations. He had a soft spot for Pope Clement IV, who absolved the Jews from responsibility for the Black Death. 'The plague takes the Jews themselves,' the Pope said. Feingold knew innumerable stories about forced conversions, he felt at home with these thoughts, comfortable, the chairs seemed dense with family. He wondered whether it would be appropriate – at a cocktail party, after all! – to inquire after the status of the seminary friend's agnosticism: was it merely that God had stepped out of history, left the room for a moment, so to speak, without a pass, or was there no Creator to begin with, nothing had been created, the world was a chimera, a solipsist's delusion?

Lucy was uneasy with the friend from the seminary; he was the one who had administered her conversion, and every encounter was like a new stage in a perpetual examination. She was glad there was no Jewish catechism. Was she a backslider? Anyhow she felt tested. Sometimes she spoke of Jesus to the children. She looked around – her great eyes wheeled – and saw that everyone in the living room was a Jew.

There were Jews in the dining room too, but the unruffled, devil-may-care kind: the humorists, the painters, film reviewers who went off to studio showings of *Screw on Screen* on the eve of the Day of Atonement. Mostly there were Gentiles in the dining room. Nearly the whole cake was gone. She took the last piece, cubed it on a paper plate, and carried it back to the living room. She blamed Feingold, he was having one of his spasms of fanaticism. Everyone normal, everyone with sense – the humanists and humorists, for instance – would want to keep away. What was he now, after all, but one of those boring autodidacts who spew out everything they read? He was doing it for spite, because no one had come. There he was, telling about the blood-libel. Little Hugh of Lincoln. How in London, in 1279, Jews were torn to pieces by horses, on a charge of having crucified a Christian child. How in 1285, in Munich, a mob burned down a synagogue on the same pretext. At Eastertime in Mainz two years earlier. Three centuries of beatified child martyrs, some of them figments, all called 'Little Saints'. The Holy Niño of LaGuardia. Feingold was crazed by these tales, he drank them like a vampire. Lucy stuck a square of chocolate cake in his mouth to shut him up. Feingold was waiting for a voice. The friend from the seminary, pragmatic, licked off his bit of cake hungrily. It was a cake sent from home, packed by his wife in a plastic bag, to make sure there was something to eat. It was a guaranteed no-lard cake. They were all ravenous. The fire crumpled out in big paper cinders.

The friend from the seminary had brought a friend. Lucy examined him: she knew how to give catechisms of her own, she was not a novelist for nothing. She catechized and catalogued: a refugee. Fingers like long wax candles, snuffed at the nails. Black sockets: was he blind? It was hard to tell where the eyes were under that ledge of skull. Skull for a head, but such a cushioned mouth, such lips, such orderly expressive teeth. Such a bone in such a dry wrist. A nose like a saint's. The face of Jesus. He whispered. Everyone leaned over to hear. He was Feingold's voice: the voice Feingold was waiting for.

'Come to modern times,' the voice urged. 'Come to yesterday.' Lucy was right: she could tell a refugee in an instant, even before she heard any accent. They all reminded her of her father. She put away this insight (the resemblance of Presbyterian ministers to Hitler refugees) to talk over with Feingold later: it was nicely analytical, it had enough mystery to satisfy. 'Yesterday,' the refugee said, 'the eyes of God were shut.' And Lucy saw him shut his hidden eyes in their tunnels. 'Shut,' he said, 'like iron doors' – a voice of such nobility that Lucy thought immediately of that eerie passage in Genesis where the voice of the Lord God walks in the Garden in the cool of the day and calls to Adam, 'Where are you?'

They all listened with a terrible intensity. Again Lucy looked around. It pained her how intense Jews could be, though she too was intense. But she was intense because her brain was roiling with ardour, she wooed mind-pictures, she was a novelist. *They* were intense all the time; she supposed the grocers among them were as intense as any novelist; was it because they had been Chosen, was it because they pitied themselves every breathing moment?

Pity and shock stood in all their faces.

The refugee was telling a story. 'I witnessed it,' he said, 'I am the witness.' Horror; sadism; corpses. As if – Lucy took the image from the elusive wind that was his voice in its whisper – as if hundreds and hundreds of Crucifixions were all happening at once. She visualized a hillside with multitudes of crosses, and bodies dropping down from big bloody nails. Every Jew was Jesus. That was the only way Lucy could get hold of it: otherwise it was only a movie. She had seen all the movies, the truth was she could feel nothing. That same bulldozer shovelling those same sticks of skeletons, that same little boy in a cap with twisted mouth and his hands in the air – if there had been a camera at the Crucifixion Christianity would collapse, no one would ever feel anything about it. Cruelty came out of the imagination, and had to be witnessed by the imagination.

All the same, she listened. What he told was exactly like the movies. A grey scene, a scrubby hill, a ravine. Germans in helmets, with shining tar-black belts, wearing gloves. A ragged bundle of Jews at the lip of the ravine – an old grandmother, a child or two, a couple in their forties. All the faces stained with greyness, the stubble on the ground stained grey, the clothes on them limp as shrouds but immobile, as if they were already under the dirt, shut off from breezes, as if they were already stone. The refugee's whisper carved them like sculptures – there they stood, a shadowy stone asterisk of Jews, you could see their nostrils, open as skulls, the stony round ears of the children, the grandmother's awful twig of a neck, the father and mother grasping the children but strangers to each other, not a touch between them, the grandmother cast out, claiming no one and not claimed, all prayerless stone gums. There they stood. For a long while the refugee's voice pinched them and held them, so that you had to look. His voice made Lucy look and look. He pierced the figures through with his whisper. Then he let the shots come. The figures never teetered, never shook: the stoniness broke all at once and they fell cleanly, like sacks, into the ravine. Immediately they were in a heap, with random limbs all tangled together. The refugee's voice like a camera brought a German boot to the edge of the ravine. The boot kicked sand. It kicked and kicked, the sand poured over the family of sacks.

Then Lucy saw the fingers of the listeners – all their fingers were stretched out.

The room began to lift. It ascended. It rose like an ark on waters. Lucy said inside her mind, 'This chamber of Jews.' It seemed to her that the room was levitating on the little grains of the refugee's whisper. She felt herself alone at the bottom, below the floorboards, while the room floated upwards, carrying Jews. Why did it not take her too? Only Jesus could take her. They were being kidnapped, these Jews, by a messenger from the land of the dead. The man had a power. Already he was in the shadow of another tale: she promised herself she would not listen, only Jesus could make her listen. The room was ascending. Above her head it grew smaller and smaller, more and more remote, it fled deeper and deeper into upwardness.

She craned after it. Wouldn't it bump into the apartment upstairs? It was like watching the underside of an elevator, all dirty and hairy, with dust-roots wagging. The black floor moved higher and higher. It was getting free of her, into loftiness, lifting Jews.

The glory of their martyrdom.

Under the rising eave Lucy had an illumination: she saw herself with the children in a little city park. A Sunday afternoon early in May. Feingold has stayed home to nap, and Lucy and the children find seats on a bench and wait for the unusual music to begin. The room is still levitating, but inside Lucy's illumination the boys are chasing birds. They run away from Lucy, they return, they leave. They surround a pigeon. They do not touch the pigeon; Lucy has forbidden it. She has read that city pigeons carry meningitis. A little boy in Red Bank, New Jersey, contracted sleeping sickness from touching a pigeon: after six years, he is still asleep. In his sleep he has grown from a child to an adolescent; puberty has come on him in his sleep, his testicles have dropped down, a benign blond beard glints mildly on his cheeks. His parents weep and weep. He is still asleep. No instruments or players are visible. A woman steps out onto a platform. She is an anthropologist from the Smithsonian Institution in Washington, DC. She explains that there will be no 'entertainment' in the usual sense; there will be no 'entertainers'. The players will not be artists; they will be 'real peasants'. They have been brought over from Messina, from Calabria. They are shepherds, goatherds. They will sing and dance and play just as they do when they come down from the hills to while away the evenings in the taverns. They will play the instruments that scare away the wolves from the flock. They will sing the songs that celebrate the Madonna of Love. A dozen men file onto the platform. They have heavy faces that do not smile. They have heavy dark skins, cratered and leathery. They have ears and noses that look like dried twisted clay. They have gold teeth. They have no teeth. Some are young; most are in their middle years. One is very old; he wears bells on his fingers. One has an instrument like a butter churn: he shoves a stick in and out of a hole in a wooden tub held under his arm, and a rattling screech spurts out of it. One blows on two slender pipes simultaneously. One has a long strap, which he rubs. One has a frame of bicycle bells; a descendant of the bells the priests used to beat in the temple of Minerva.

The anthropologist is still explaining everything. She explains the 'male' instrument: three wooden knockers; the innermost one lunges up and down between the other two. The songs, she explains, are mainly erotic. The dances are suggestive.

The unusual music commences. The park has filled with Italians – greenhorns from Sicily, settled New Yorkers from Naples. An ancient people. They clap. The old man with the bells on his fingers points his dusty shoe-toes and slowly follows a circle of his own. His eyes are in trance, he squats, he ascends. The anthropologist explains that up-and-down dancing can also be found in parts of Africa. The singers wail like Arabs; the anthropologist notes that the Arab conquest covered the southernmost portion of the Italian boot for two hundred years. The whole chorus of peasants sings in a dialect of archaic Greek; the language has survived in the old songs, the anthropologist explains. The crowd is laughing and stamping. They click their fingers and sway. Lucy's boys are bored. They watch the man with the finger-bells; they watch the wooden male pump up and down. Everyone is clapping, stamping, clicking, swaying, thumping. The wailing goes on and on, faster and faster. The singers are dancers, the dancers are singers, they turn and turn, they are smiling the drugged smiles of dervishes. At home they grow flowers. They follow the sheep into the deep grass. They drink wine in the taverns at night. Calabria and Sicily in New York, sans wives, in sweat-blotched shirts and wrinkled dusty pants, gasping before strangers who have never smelled the sweetness of their village grasses!

Now the anthropologist from the Smithsonian has vanished out of Lucy's illumination. A pair of dancers seize each other. Leg winds over leg, belly into belly, each man hopping on a single free leg. Intertwined, they squat and rise, squat and rise. Old Hellenic syllables fly from them. They send out high elastic cries. They celebrate the Madonna, giver of fertility and fecundity. Lucy is glorified. She is exalted. She comprehends. Not that the musicians are peasants, not that their faces and feet and necks and wrists are blown grass and red earth. An enlightenment comes on her: she sees what is eternal: before the Madonna there was Venus; before Venus, Aphrodite; before Aphrodite, Astarte. The womb of the goddess is garden, lamb, and babe. She is the river and the waterfall. She causes grave men of business – goatherds are men of business – to cavort and to flash their gold teeth. She induces them to blow, beat, rub, shake and scrape objects so that music will drop out of them.

Inside Lucy's illumination the dancers are seething. They are writhing. For the sake of the goddess, for the sake of the womb of the goddess, they are turning into serpents. When they grow still they are earth. They are from always to always. Nature is their pulse. Lucy sees: she understands: the gods are God. How terrible to have given up Jesus, a man like these, made of earth like these, with a pulse like these, God entering nature to become god! Jesus, no more miraculous than an ordinary goatherd; is a goatherd miracle? Is a leaf? A nut, a pit, a core, a seed, a stone? Everything is miracle! Lucy sees how she has abandoned nature, how she has lost true religion on account of the God of the Jews. The boys are on their bellies on the ground, digging it up with sticks. They dig and dig: little holes with mounds beside them. They fill them with peach pits, cherry pits, cantaloupe rinds. The Sicilians and Neapolitans pick up their baskets and purses and shopping bags and leave. The benches smell of eaten fruit, running juices, insect-mobbed. The stage is clean.

The living room has escaped altogether. It is very high and extremely small, no wider than the moon on Lucy's thumbnail. It is still sailing upwards, and the voices of those on board are so faint that Lucy almost loses them. But she knows which word it is they mainly use. How long can they go on about it? How long? A morbid cud-chewing. Death and death and death. The word is less a human word than an animal's cry; a crow's. Caw caw. It belongs to storms, floods, avalanches. Acts of God. 'Holocaust,' someone caws dimly from above; she knows it must be Feingold. He always says this word over and over and over. History is bad for him: how little it makes him seem! Lucy decides it is possible to become jaded by atrocity. She is bored by the shootings and the gas and the camps, she is not ashamed to admit this. They are as tiresome as prayer. Repetition diminishes conviction; she is thinking of her father leading the same hymns week after week. If you said the same prayer over and over again, wouldn't your brain turn out to be no better than a prayer wheel?

In the dining room all the springs were running down. It was stale in there, a failed party. They were drinking beer or Coke or whisky-and-water and playing with the cake crumbs on the tablecloth. There was still some cheese left on a plate, and half a bowl of salted peanuts. 'The impact of Romantic Individualism,' one of the humanists objected. 'At the Frick?' 'I never saw that.' 'They certainly are deliberate, you have to say that for them.' Lucy, leaning abandoned against the door, tried to tune in. The relief of hearing atheists. A jacket designer who worked in Feingold's art department came in carrying a coat. Feingold had invited her because she was newly divorced; she was afraid to live alone. She was afraid of being ambushed in her basement while doing laundry. 'Where's Jimmy?' the jacket designer asked. 'In the other room.' 'Say goodbye for me, will you?' 'Goodbye,' Lucy said. The humanists – Lucy saw how they were all compassionate knights – stood up. A puddle from an overturned saucer was leaking onto the floor. 'Oh, I'll get that,' Lucy told the knights, 'don't think another thought about it.'

Overhead Feingold and the refugee are riding the living room. Their words are specks. All the Jews are in the air.

At Fumicaro

Frank Castle knew everything. He was an art critic; he was a book critic; he wrote on politics and morals; he wrote on everything. He was a journalist, both in print and weekly on the radio; he had 'sensibility', but he was proud of being 'focused'. He was a Catholic; he read Cardinal Newman and François Mauriac and Étienne Gilson and Simone Weil and Jacques Maritain and Evelyn Waugh and Graham Greene. He reread *The Heart of the Matter* a hundred times, weeping (Frank Castle could weep) for poor Scobie. He was a parochial man who kept himself inside a frame. He had few Protestant and no Jewish friends. He said he was interested in happiness, and that was why he liked being Catholic; Catholics made him happy.

Fumicaro made him happy. To get there he left New York on an Italian liner, the *Benito Mussolini*. Everything about it was talkative but excessively casual. The schedule itself was casual, and the ship's engines growled in the slip through a whole day before embarkation. Aboard, the passageways were packed with noisy promenaders – munchers of stuffed buns with their entrails dripping out (in all that chaos the dock pedlars had somehow pushed through), quaffers of coloured fizzy waters.

At the train station in Milan he found a car, at an exorbitant rate, to take him to Fumicaro. He was already hours late. He was on his way to the Villa Garibaldi, established by a Chicago philanthropist who had set the place up for conferences of a virtuous nature. The Fascists interfered, but not much, and out of a lazy sense of duty; so far, only a convention of lepidopterists had been sent away. One of the lepidopterists had been charged with supplying information, not about butterflies, to gangs of anti-Fascists in their hideouts in the hills around Fumicaro.

There were wonders all along the road: dun brick houses Frank Castle had thought peculiar only to certain neighbourhoods in the Bronx, each with its distinctive four-sided roof and, in the dooryard of each, a fig tree tightly mummified in canvas. It was still November, but not cold, and the banks along the spiralling mountain route were rich with purple flowers. As they ascended, the driver began to hum a little, especially where the curves were most hair-raising, and when a second car came hurtling into sight from the opposite direction in a space that seemed too narrow even for one, Frank Castle believed death was near; and yet they passed safely and climbed higher. The mountain grew more and more decorous, sprouting antique topiary and far flecks of white villas.

In the Villa Garibaldi the three dozen men who were to be his colleagues were already at dinner, under silver chandeliers; there was no time for him to be taken to his room. The rumbling voices put him off a bit, but he was not altogether among strangers. He recognized some magazine acquaintances and three or four priests, one of them a public charmer whom he had interviewed on the radio. After the conference – it was called 'The Church and How It is Known', and would run four days – almost everyone was planning to go on to Rome. Frank Castle intended to travel to Florence first (he hoped for a glimpse of the portrait of Thomas Aquinas in the San Marco), and then to Rome, but on the fourth day, entirely unexpectedly, he got married instead.

After dinner there was a sluggish session around the huge conference board in the hall next to the dining room – Frank Castle, who had arrived hungry, now felt overfed – and then Mr Wellborn, the American director, instructed one of the staff (a quick hollow-faced fellow who had waited on Frank Castle's table) to lead him down to the Little Annexe, the cottage where he was to sleep. It was full night now; there was a stone terrace to cross, an iron staircase down, a pebbled path weaving between lofty rows of hedges. Like the driver, the waiter hummed, and Frank Castle looked to his footing. But again there was no danger – only strangeness, and a fragrance so alluring that his nostrils strained after it with appetite. The entrance to the Little Annexe was an engaging low archway. The waiter set down Frank Castle's suitcase on the gravel under the arch, handed him a big cold key, and pointed upwards to a circular flight of steps. Then he went humming away.

At the top of the stairs Frank Castle saw a green door, but there was no need for the key – the door was open; the lamp was on. Disorder; the bed unmade, though clean sheets were piled on a chair. An empty wardrobe; a desk without a telephone; a bedside cabinet, holding the lit gooseneck; a loud clock and a flashlight; the crash of water in crisis. It was the sound of a toilet flushing again and again. The door to the toilet gaped. He went in and found the chambermaid on her knees before it, retching; in four days she would be his wife.

He was still rather a young man, yet not so young that he was unequal to suddenness. He was thirty-five, and much of his life had flowered out of suddenness. He did not exactly know what to do, but he seized a washcloth, moistened it with cold water at the sink, and pressed it against the forehead of the kneeling woman. She shook it off with an animal sound.

He sat on the rim of the bathtub and watched her. He did not feel especially sympathetic, but he did not feel disgust either. It was as if he were watching a waterfall – a thing belonging to nature. Only the odour was unnatural. Now and then she turned her head and threw him a wild look. *Condemn what thou art, that thou mayest deserve to be what thou art not*, he said to himself; it was St Augustine. It seemed right to him to think of that just then. The woman went on vomiting. A spurt of colourless acrid liquid rushed from her mouth. Watching serenely, he thought of some grand fountain where dolphins, or else infant cherubim, spew foamy white water from their bottomless throats. He saw her shamelessly: she was a solid little nymph. She was the coarse muse of Italia. He recited to himself, *If to any man the tumult of the flesh were silenced, silenced the phantasies of earth, waters, and air, silenced, too, the poles.*

She reached back with one hand and grasped the braid that lay along her neck. Her nape, bared, was running with sweat, and also with tears that trailed from the side of her mouth and around. It was a short robust neck, like the stem of a mushroom.

'Are you over it?' he said.

She lifted her knees from the floor and sat back on her heels. Now that she had backed away from it, he could see the shape of the toilet bowl. It was, to his eyes, foreign-looking: high, much taller than the American variety, narrow. The porcelain lid, propped upright, was bright as a mirror. The rag she had been scrubbing it with was lost in her skirt.

Now she began to hiccup.

'Is it over?'

She leaned her forehead along the base of the washstand. The light was not good – it had to travel all the way from the lamp on the table in the bedchamber and through the door, dimming as it came; nevertheless her colour seemed high. Surely her lips were swollen; they could not have been intended to bulge like that. He believed he understood just how such a face ought to be composed. With her head at rest on the white pillar of the sink, she appeared to him (he said these words to himself slowly and meticulously, so clarified and prolonged was the moment for him) like an angel seen against the alabaster column that upholds the firmament. Her hiccups were loud, frequent; her shoulders jerked, and still the angel did not fall.

She said, '*Le dispiace se mi siedo qui? Sono molto stanca.*'

The pointless syllables – it was his first day in Italy – made him conscious of his stony stare. His own head felt stone: was she a Medusa? – those long serpents of her spew. It occurred to him that, having commenced peacefully enough, he was far less peaceful now. He was, in fact, staring with all his might, like a statue, a stare without definition or attachment, and that was foolish. There was a glass on a shelf over the sink. He stood up and stepped over her feet (the sensation of himself as great stone arch-of-triumph darkening her body) and filled the glass with water from the tap and gave it to her.

She drank as quickly as a child, absorbed. He could hear her throat race and shut on its hinge, and race again. When the glass was empty she said, '*Molto gentile da parte sua. Mi sento così da ieri. È solo un piccolo problema.*' All at once she saw how it was for him: he was a foreigner and could not understand. Recognition put a smoke of anxiety over her eyes. She said loudly, '*Scusi,*' and lapsed into a brevity of English as peculiar as any he had ever heard, surprising in that it was there at all: 'No belief!' She jumped up on her thick legs and let her braid hang. '*Ho vomitato!*' she called – a war cry roughened by victorious good humour. The rag separated itself from the folds of her big skirt and slid to the floor, and just then, while he was contemplating the density of her calves and the marvel of their roundness and heaviness, she seemed as he watched to grow lighter and lighter, to escape from the fine aspiring weight that had pulled her up, and she fell like the rag, without a noise.

Her lids had slapped down. He lifted her and carried her – heaved her – onto the bed and felt for her pulse. She was alive. He had never before been close to a fainted person. If he had not seen for himself how in an instant she had shut herself off, like a faucet turned, he would have been certain that the woman he had set down on the naked grey mattress, without sheets, was asleep.

The night window was no better than a blind drawn to: no sight, no breath, no help. Only the sweet grassy smells of the dark mountainside. He ran halfway down the spiral stone staircase and then thought, Suppose, while I am gone, the woman dies. She was only the chambermaid; she was a sound girl, her cheeks vigorous and plump; he knew she would not die. He locked the door and lay down beside her in the lamplight, riding his little finger up and down her temple. It was a marvel and a luxury to be stretched out there with her, unafraid. He assured himself she would wake and not die.

He was in a spiritual condition. He had been chaste for almost six months – demandingly pure, even when alone, even inside his secret mind. His mind was a secret cave, immaculately swept and spare. It was an initiation. He was preparing himself for the first stages of a kind of monasticism. He did not mean that he would go off and become a monk in a monastery: he knew how he was of the world. But he intended to be set apart in his own privacy: to be strong and transcendent, above the body. He did not hope to grow into a saint, yet he wanted to be more than ordinary, even while being counted as 'normal'. He wanted to possess himself first, so that he could yield himself, of his own accord, to the forces of the spirit.

Now here was his temptation. It seemed right – foreordained – that he would come to Italy to be lured and tempted. The small rapture versus the greater rapture – the rapture in the body and the rapture in God, and he was for the immensity. Who would not choose an ocean, with its heaven-tugged tides, over a single drop? He looked down at the woman's face and saw two wet black drops, each one an opened eye.

'Do you feel sick again? Are you all right?' he said, and took away his little finger.

'No belief! No belief!'

The terrible words, in her exhausted croak, stirred him to the beginning of a fury. What he had done, what he had endured, to be able to come at last to belief! And a chambermaid, a cleaner of toilets, could cry so freely against it!

'No belief! *Ho vomitato*, no belief!'

He knew her meaning: she was abashed, shame punched out her tears, she was sunk in absurdity and riddle. But still it shook him – he turned against her – because every day of his life he had to make this same pilgrimage to belief all over again, starting out each dawn with the hard crow's call of no belief.

'No belief! No belief!' she croaked at him.

'Stop that.'

She raised herself on her wrist, her arm a bent pole. 'Signore, *mi scusi*, I make the room—'

'Stay where you are.'

She gestured at the pile of sheets on the chair, and fell back again.

'Do they know you're sick? Does Mr Wellborn know?'

She said laboriously, 'I am two day sick.' She touched her stomach and hiccuped. 'I am not sick two day like now.'

He could not tell from this whether she meant she was better or worse. 'Do you want more water?'

'Signore, *grazie*, no water.'

'Where do you stay?' He did not ask where she lived; he could not imagine that she lived anywhere.

Her look, still wet, trailed to the window. 'In the town.'

'That's all the way down that long road I drove up.'

'*Si.*'

He reflected. 'Do you always work so late?'

'Signore, in this morning when I am sick I no make the room, I come back to make finish the room. I make finish over there all the room' – her eyes jumped in the direction of the Villa – 'only the Signore's room I no make.'

He let out his breath: a wind so much from the well of his ribs that it astonished him. 'They don't know where you are.' He was in awe of his own lung. 'You can stay here,' he said.

'Oh, Signore, *grazie*, no—'

'Stay,' he said, and elevated his little finger. Slowly, slowly, he dragged it across her forehead. A late breeze, heavy with the lazy fragrance of some alien night-bloomer, had cooled her. He tasted no heat in the tiny salted cavern between her nose and mouth. The open window brought him the smell of water; during the taxi's climb to the Villa Garibaldi he had scarcely permitted himself a glimpse of old shining Como, but now his nostrils were free and full: he took in the breath of the lake while again letting out his own. He unbuttoned his shirt and wiped every cranny of her face with it, even inside her ears; he wiped her mushroom neck. He had worn this shirt all the way from Leghorn, where the *Benito Mussolini* had docked, to Milan, and from the train station in Milan to Fumicaro. He had worn it for twenty hours. By now it was dense with the exhalations of Italy, the sweat of Milan.

*

When he spoke of Milan she pushed away his shirt. Her mother, she told him, lived in Milan. She was a maid at the Hotel Duomo, across from the cathedral. Everyone called her Caterina, though it wasn't her name. It was the name of the last maid, the one who got married and went away. They were like that in Milan. They treated the maids like that. The Duomo was a tourist hotel; there were many Americans and English; her mother was quick with foreign noises. Her mother's English was very good, very quick; she claimed to have learned it out of a book. An American had given her his bilingual dictionary to keep, as a sort of tip.

In Milan they were not kind. They were so far north they were almost like Germans or Swiss. They cooked like the Swiss, and they had cold hearts like the Germans. Even the priests were cold. They said ordinary words so strangely: they accused Caterina of a mischief called 'dialect', but the mischief was theirs, not hers. Caterina had a daughter, whom she had left behind in Calabria. The daughter lived with Caterina's old mother, but when the daughter was thirteen Caterina summoned her north to Milan, to work in the hotel. The daughter's name was Viviana Teresa Accenno, and it was she who now lay disbelieving in Frank Castle's bed in the Little Annexe of the Villa Garibaldi. Viviana at thirteen was very small, and looked no more than nine or ten. The manager of the Duomo did not wish to employ her at all, but Caterina importuned, so he put the girl into the kitchen to help the under-chefs. She washed celery and broccoli; she washed the grit out of spinach and lettuce. She reached with the scrub brush, under the stove and behind it, crevices where no one else could fit. Her arm then was a little stick for poking. Unlike Caterina, she hardly ever saw any Americans or English. Despite the bilingual dictionary, Viviana did not think that her mother could read anything at all – it was only that Caterina's tongue was so quick. Caterina kept the dictionary at the bottom of her wardrobe; sometimes she picked it up and cradled it, but she never looked into it. Still, her English was very fine, and she tried to teach it to Viviana. Viviana could make herself understood, she could say what she had to, but she could never speak English like Caterina.

Because of her good English Caterina became friends with the tourists. They gave her presents – silk scarves, and boxes made of olivewood, with celluloid crucifixes resting on velveteen inside, all the useless things tourists are attracted to – and in return she took parties out in the evenings; often they gave her money. She led them to out-of-the-way restaurants in neighbourhoods they would never have found on their own, and to a clever young cobbler she was acquainted with, who worked in a shoe factory by day but measured privately for shoes at night. He would cut the leather on a Monday and have new shoes ready on a Wednesday – the most up-to-date fashions for the ladies, and for the gentlemen Oxfords as sober and sturdy as anyone could wish. His prices were as low as his workmanship was splendid. The tourists all supposed he stole the leather from the factory, but Caterina guaranteed his probity and assured them this could not be. His jacket pockets were heavy with bits of leather of many shapes, and also straps and buckles, and tiny corked flacons of dye.

Caterina had all these ways of pleasing tourists, but she would not allow Viviana to learn any of them. Every Easter she made Viviana go back to spend a whole week with the grandmother in Calabria, and when Viviana returned, Caterina had a new Easter husband. She had always had a separate Milan husband, even when her Calabria husband, Viviana's father, was alive. It was not bigamy, not only because Caterina's Calabria husband had died long ago but also because Caterina had never, strictly speaking, been married in the regular way to the Milan husband. It wasn't that Caterina did not respect the priests; each day she went across the street and over the plaza to the cathedral to kneel in the nave, as broad as a sunless grassless meadow. The floor was made holy by the bones of a saint shut up in a box in front of the altar. All the priests knew her, and tried to persuade her to marry the Easter husband, and she always promised that very soon she would. And they in turn promised her a short cut: if only she showed good will and an honest faith, she could become a decent wife overnight. But she did not, and Viviana at length understood why: the Easter husband kept changing heads. Sometimes he had one head, sometimes another, sometimes again the first. You could not marry a husband who wore a different head all the time. Except for the heads, the Easter husband was uniformly very thin, from his Adam's apple all the way down to his fancy boots. One Easter he wore the cobbler's head, but Caterina threw him out. She said he was a thief. A silver crucifix she had received as a present from a Scottish minister was missing from the bottom of the wardrobe, though the bilingual dictionary was still there. But the cobbler came back with the news that he had a cousin in Fumicaro, where they were looking for maids for the American villa there; so Caterina decided to send her daughter, who was by now sixteen and putting flesh on her buttocks. For an innocent, Caterina said, the money was safer than in Milan.

And just then the grandmother died; so Caterina and Viviana and the cobbler all travelled down to Calabria for the funeral. That night, in the grandmother's tiny house, Viviana had a peculiar adventure, though as natural as rain; it only felt peculiar because it had never happened before – she had always trusted that some day it would. The cobbler and Caterina were crumpled up together in the grandmother's shabby bed; Caterina was awake, sobbing; she explained how she was a dog at loose in the gutters, she belonged nowhere, she was a woman without a place, first a widow, now an orphan and the mother of an orphan. The highfalutin priests in the cathedral could not understand how it was for a widow of long standing. If a widow of long standing, a woman used to making her own way, becomes a wife, they will not let her make her own way any more, she will be poorer as a poor man's wife than as a widow. What can priests, those empty pots, those eunuchs, know of the true life of a poor woman? Lamenting, Caterina fell asleep, without intending to; and then the cobbler with his bony shadow slipped out from the grandmother's bed and circled to the corner where Viviana slept, though now she was as wide awake as could be, in her cot near the stove, a cot dressed up during the day in a rosy fringed spread. It had crocheted pillow covers patterned with butterflies that the grandmother had let Viviana hold at night, like dolls. Viviana's lids were tight. She felt the saint's bones had risen from their northern altar and were sliding towards her in the dark. Caterina kept on clamorously breathing through the tunnel of her throat, and Viviana squeezed her shut eyes down on the butterflies. If she pressed them for five minutes at a time, their wings would appear to flutter. She could make their wings stir just by pressing down on them. It seemed she was making the cobbler shudder now as he moved, in just that same way; her will was surely against it, and yet he was shuddering close to the cot. He had his undershirt on, and his bony-faced smile, and he shivered, though it was only September and the cabbage-headed trees in her grandmother's yard were luxuriant in Calabrian warmth.

After this she came to Fumicaro to work as a chambermaid at the Villa Garibaldi; she had not told her mother a thing about where the cobbler had put his legs and his arms, and not only because he had shown her the heavy metal of his belt. The cobbler was not to blame; it was her mother's mourning that was at fault, because if Caterina had not worn herself out with mourning the cobbler would have done his husband business in the regular way, with Caterina; and instead he had to do it with Viviana. All men have to do husband business, even if they are not regular husbands; it is how men are. How you are also, Signore, an American, a tourist.

It was true. In less than two hours Frank Castle had become the lover of a child. He had carried her into his bed and coaxed her story from her, beginning with his little finger's trip across her forehead. Then he had let his little finger go riding elsewhere, and elsewhere, riding and riding, until her sweat returned, and he began to sweat himself; the black night window was not feeding them enough air. Air! It was like trying to breathe through a straw. He drew the key from the door and steered her, both of them barefoot, down the curling stairs, and walked with her out onto the gravel, through the arch. There was no moon, only a sort of gliding whitish mist low to the ground, and transitory; sometimes it was there, sometimes not. At the foot of the invisible hill, below the long hairy slope of mountainside, Como stretched like a bit of black silk nailed down. A galaxy prickled overhead, though maybe not: lights of villas high up, chips of stars – in such a blackness it was impossible to know the difference. Earth and sky were without distinction. She pointed far out, to the other side of the lake: nothingness. Yet there, she said, stood the pinkish palace of Il Duce, filled with seventy-five Fascist servants, and a hundred soldiers who never slept.

After breakfast, at the first meeting of the morning, a young priest read a paper. It seemed he had forgotten the point of the conference – public relations – and was speaking devoutly, liturgically. His subject was purity. The flesh, he said, is holy bread, like the shewbread of the Israelites, meant to be consecrated for God. To put it to use for human pleasure alone is defilement. The words inflamed Frank Castle: he had told Viviana to save his room for last and to wait for him there in the afternoon. At four o'clock, after the day's third session, while the others went down the mountain – the members of the conference had been promised a ride across Como in a motor launch – he climbed to the green door of the Little Annexe and once again took the child into his bed.

He knew he was inflamed. He felt his reason had been undermined, like a crazy man's. He could not get enough of this woman, this baby. She came to him again after dinner; then he had to attend the night session, until ten; then she was in his bed again. She was perfectly well. He asked her about the nausea. She said it was gone, except very lightly, earlier that day; she was restored. He could not understand why she was yielding to him this way. She did whatever he told her to. She was only afraid of meeting Guido, Mr Wellborn's assistant, on her way to the Little Annexe: Guido was the one who kept track of which rooms were finished, and which remained, and in what order. Her job was to make the beds and change the towels and clean the floors and the tub. Guido said the Little Annexe must be done first. It was easy for her to leave the Little Annexe for last – it had only two rooms in it, and the other was empty. The person who was to occupy the empty room had not yet arrived. He had sent no letter or telegram. Guido had instructed Viviana to tend to the empty room all the same, in case he should suddenly make his appearance. Mr Wellborn was still expecting him, whoever it was.

On the third day, directly after lunch, it was Frank Castle's turn to speak. He was, after all, he said, only a journalist. His paper would be primarily neither theological nor philosophical – on the contrary, it was no more than a summary of a series of radio interviews he had conducted with new converts. He would attempt, he said, to give a collective portrait of these. If there was one feature they all had in common, it was what Jacques Maritain characterized as 'the impression that evil was truly and substantially someone'. To put it otherwise, these were men and women who had caught sight of demons. Let us not imagine, Frank Castle said, that – at the start – it is the love of Christ that brings souls into the embrace of Christ. It is fear; sin; evil; true cognizance of the Opposer. The corridor to Christ is at bottom the Devil, just as Judas was the necessary corridor to redemption.

He read for thirty minutes, finished to a mainly barren room, and thought he had been too metaphorical; he should have tried more for the psychological – these were modern men. They all lived, even the priests, along the skin of the world. They had cleared out, he guessed, in order to walk down the mountain into the town in the brightness of midday. There was a hot-chocolate shop, with pastry and picture postcards of Fumicaro: clusters of red tiled roofs, and behind them, like distant ice-cream cones, the Alps – you could have your feet in Italy and your gaze far into Switzerland. Around the corner from the hot-chocolate place, he heard them say, there was a little box of a shop, with a tinkling bell, easily overlooked if you didn't know about it. It was down an alley as narrow as a thread. You could buy leather wallets, and ladies' pocketbooks, also of leather, and shawls and neckties labelled *seta pura*. But the true reason his colleagues were drawn down to the town was to stand at the edge of

Como. Glorious disc of lake! It had beckoned them yesterday. It beckoned today. It summoned eternally. The bliss of its flat sun-shot surface; as dazzling as some huge coin. The room had emptied out towards it; he was not offended, not even discontented. He had not come to Fumicaro to show how clever he could be (nearly all these fellows were clever), or how devout; he knew he was not devout enough. And not to discover new renunciations, and not to catch the hooks the others let fly. And not even to be tested. He was beyond these trials. He had fallen not into temptation but into happiness. Happy, happy Fumicaro! He had, he saw, been led to Fumicaro not for the Church – or not directly for the Church, as the conference brochure promised – but for the explicit salvation of one needful soul.

She was again waiting for him. He was drilled through by twin powers: the power of joy, the power of power. She was obedient, she was his own small nun. The roundness of her calves made him think of loaves of round bread, bread like domes. She asked him – it was in a way remarkable – whether his talk had been a success. His 'talk'. A 'success'. She was alert, shrewd. It was clear she had a good brain. Already she was catching on. Her mind skipped, it was not static; it was a sort of burr that attached itself to whatever passed. He told her his paper had not been found interesting. His listeners had drifted off to look at Como. Instantly she wanted to take him there – not through the town, with its lures for tourists, but down an old stone road, mostly overgrown, back behind the Villa Garibaldi, to the lake's unfrequented rim. She had learned about it from some of the kitchen staff. He was willing, but not yet. He considered who he was; where he was. A man on fire. He asked her once more if she was well. Only a little in the morning not, she said. He was not surprised; he was prepared for it. She had missed, she said, three bleedings. She believed she might be carrying the cobbler's seed, though she had washed herself and washed herself. She had cleaned out her insides until she was as dry as a saint.

She lay with her head against his neck. Her profile was very sharp. He had seen her head a hundred times before, in museums: the painted walls of Roman villas. The oversized eyes with their black oval shine, like a pair of olives, the nose broad but so splendidly symmetrical, the top lip with its two delectably lifted points. Nevertheless she was mysteriously not handsome. It was because of her caste. She was a peasant's child. Her skin was a marvel – as if a perpetual brownish shadow had dropped close against it, partly translucent. A dark lens stretched over her cheeks, through which he saw, minutely, the clarity of her youth. He thought she was too obedient; she had no pride. Meekness separated her from beauty. She urged her mouth on his neck and counted: *Settembre, Ottobre, Novembre*, all without the bleeding.

He began to explain the beginning of his plan: in a week or two she would see New York.

'New York! No belief!' She laughed – and there was her gold tooth! – and he laughed too, because of his idiocy, his recklessness; he laughed because he had really lost his reason now and was giving himself over to holy belief. She had been disclosed to him, and on her knees; it followed that he had been sent. Her laughter was all youth and clarity and relief – what she had escaped! Deliverance. His was clownishness: he was a shaman. And recognition: he was a madman, driven like a madman or an idiot.

'You're all right,' he said. 'You'll be all right.'

She went on laughing. 'No belief! No belief! *Dio, Dio!*' She laughed out the comedy of her entanglements: a girl like herself, who has no husband, and goes three bleedings without bleeding, will be, she said, 'finish' – she had seized the idiom out of the air. There was no place for her but the ditch. There would never be a regular husband for her – not in Fumicaro, not in Milan, not at home in Calabria, not anywhere on any piece of God's earth inhabited by the human family. No one would touch her. They would throw her into the ditch. She was in hell. Finish. God had commanded the American signore to pull her out from the furnace of hell.

He explained again, slowly (he was explaining it to himself), in a slow voice, with the plainest words he could muster, that he would marry her and take her home with him to America. To New York.

'New York!' She *did* believe him; she believed him on the instant. Her trust was electric. The beating of her belief entered his rib cage, thrashing and plunging its beak into his spine. He could not help himself: he was his own prisoner, he was inside his own ribs, pecking there. 'New York!' she said. For this she had prayed to the Holy Bambino. Oh, not for New York, she had never prayed for America, who could dream it!

No belief: he would chain himself to a rock and be flung into the sea, in order to drown unbelief.

Therefore he would marry Viviana Teresa Accenno. It was his obeisance. It was what had brought him to Italy; it was what had brought him to the Little Annexe of the Villa Garibaldi. There were scores of poor young women all over Italy – perhaps in Fumicaro itself – in her position. He could not marry them all. Her tragedy was a commonplace. She was a noisy aria in an eternal opera. It did not matter. This girl was the one he had been led to. Now the power travelled from him to her; he felt the pounding of her gratitude, how it fed her, how it punished him, how she widened herself for him, how stalwart she was, how nervy! He was in her grip, she was his slave; she had the vitality of her surrender. For a few moments it made her his master.

He did not return to the salons and chandeliers of the Villa Garibaldi that day – not for the pre-dinner session or for the after-dinner session; and not for dinner either. From then on everything went like quicksilver. Viviana ran to find Guido, to report that she was short of floor wax; he gave her the key to the supplies closet, which was also the wine cellar. Easeful Fumicaro, where such juxtapositions reigned! She plucked a flask of each: wax and wine. Mr Wellborn blinked at such pilfering; it kept the staff content. It was only Guido who was harsh. Still, it was nothing at all for her to slip into the kitchen and spirit away a fat fresh bread and a round brick of cheese. They trod on ivy that covered the path under the windows of the grand high room that held the meadow-long conference board. Frank Castle could hear the cadenced soughing of the afternoon speaker. The sun was low but steady. She took him past enormous bricked-up arches, as tall as city apartment buildings. In the kitchen, where they were so gullible, they called it the Roman aqueduct, but nobody sensible supposed that Romans had once lived here. It was *stupido*, a tale for children. They say about the Romans that they did not have God; the priests would not let them linger in holy Italy if they did not know Jesus, so they must have lived elsewhere. She did not doubt that they had once existed, the Romans, but elsewhere. In Germany, maybe in Switzerland. Only never in Italy. The Pope of those days would never have allowed infidels to stay in such a place as Fumicaro. Maybe in Naples! Far down, under their feet, they could descry a tiny needle: it was the bell tower of the ancient church in Fumicaro. Frank Castle had already inquired about this needle. It had been put there in the twelfth century. Wild irises obscured the stone road; it wound down and down, and was so spare and uneven that they had to go single file. They met no one. It was all theirs. He had a sense of wingedness: how quickly they came to the lip of Como. The lake was all gold. A sunball was submerged in it as still as the yolk of an egg, and the red egg on the horizon also did not move. They encamped in a wilderness – thorny bushes and a jumble of long-necked, thick-speared grasses.

The wine was the colour of light, immaculately clear, and warm, and wonderfully sour. He had never before rejoiced in such a depth of sourness – after you swallowed some and contemplated it, you entered the second chamber of the sourness, and here it was suddenly apple-like. Their mouths burst into orchards. They were not hungry; they never broke off even a crumb of the bread and cheese; of these they would make a midnight supper, and in the early morning he would pay something to the milk driver, who would carry them as far as he could. The rest of the trip they would go by bus, like ordinary people. Oh, they were not ordinary! And in Milan Viviana would tell Caterina everything – everything except about where the cobbler had put his legs and his arms; she would not mention the cobbler at all – and Caterina would lead them across the plaza into the cathedral, and the priests would marry them in the short-cut way they had always promised for Caterina and her Easter husband.

It was nearly night. Como had eaten the red egg; it was gone. Streaks of white and pink trailed over water and sky. There was still enough light for each to see the other's face. They passed the bottle of wine between them, back and forth, from hand to hand, stumbling upwards, now and then wandering wide of the path – the stones were sometimes buried. A small abandoned shrine blocked the way. The head was eroded, the nose chipped. 'This must be a Roman road,' he told her. 'The Romans built it.'

'No belief!' It was becoming their life's motto.

The air felt miraculously dense, odorous with lake and bush. It could almost be sucked in, it was so liquidly thick. They spiralled higher, driving back the whiplike growth that snapped at their eyes. She could not stop laughing, and that made him start again. He knew he was besotted.

Directly in front of them the grasses appeared to part. Noises: rustle and flutter and an odd abrasive sound – there was no mistake, the bushes were moving. The noises ran ahead with every step they took; the disturbance in the bushes and the growling scrape were always just ahead. He thought of the malcontents who were said to have their hiding places in the mountains – thugs; he thought of small mountain beasts that might scramble about in such a space – a fox? He was perfectly ignorant of the usual habitat of foxes.

Then – in what was left of the dusk – he caught sight of a silhouette considerably' bigger and less animate than a fox. It was a squarish thing kicking against the vegetation and scudding on the stones. It looked to be attached to a pallid human shape, broad but without glimmer, also in silhouette.

'Hello?' said an elderly American voice. 'Anybody back there speak English?'

'Hello,' Frank Castle called.

The square thing was a suitcase.

'Damn cab let me off at the bottom. Said he wouldn't go up the hill in the dark. Didn't trust his brakes. Damn lazy thieving excuse – I paid him door to door. This can't be the regular way up anyhow.'

'Are you headed for the Villa Garibaldi?'

'Three days late to boot. You mixed up in it? Oh, it just stirs my blood when they name a bed to sleep in after a national hero.'

'I'm mixed up in it. I came on the *Benito Mussolini*,' Frank Castle said.

'Speaking of never getting a night's sleep. So did I. Didn't see you aboard. Didn't see anyone. Stuck to the bar. Not that I can see you now, getting pitch black. Don't know where the hell I am. Dragging this damn thing. Is that a kid with you? I'll pay him to lug my bag.'

Frank Castle introduced himself, there on the angle of the mountainside, on the Roman road, in the tunnelling night. He did not introduce Viviana. All his life it would be just like that. She crept back off the bit of path into the thornbushes.

'Percy Nightingale,' the man said. 'Thank you kindly, but never mind, if the kid won't take it, I'll carry it myself. Damn lazy types. How come you're on the loose, they haven't corralled you for the speeches?'

'You've missed mine.'

'Well, I don't like to get to these things too early. I can sum up all the better if I don't sit through too many speeches – I do a summing-up column for the *All-Parish Wick*. Kindles Brooklyn and Staten Island. What've I missed besides you?'

'Three days of inspiration.'

'Got my inspiration in Milan, if you want the truth. Found a little inn with a bar and had myself a bender. Listen, you've got to see the *Last Supper* – it's just about over. Peeling. They stick the paint back down somehow, but I give it no more'n fifty years. And for God's sake don't skip the unfinished *Pietà* – arms and legs in such a tangle you wouldn't believe. Extra legs stuck in. My God, what now?' They had come flat out against a wall.

Viviana jumped into the middle of the stone road and zigzagged leftwards. An apparition of battlements: high box hedges. Without any warning they had emerged right under the iron staircase abutting the kitchen of the Villa Garibaldi.

Climbing, the man with the suitcase said, 'The name's familiar. Haven't I heard you on the radio, WJZ, those interviews with convicts?'

'Converts.'

'I know what I said.'

Viviana had evaporated.

'Are you the one Mr Wellborn's expecting?'

'Mister who?'

'Wellborn,' Frank Castle said. 'The director. You'd better go to his office first. I think we're going to be neighbours.'

'Love thy neighbour as thyself. He doesn't sound like a Wop.'

'He's a Presbyterian from New Jersey.'

'Myself, I'm a specialist. Not that I ever got my degree. I specialize in Wops and Presbyterians. Ad hoc and à la carte. We all have to make a living.'

In his cups, Frank Castle thought. Then he remembered that he was drunk himself. He dug into his pocket and said with patient annoyance, 'You know you can still catch the night session if you want. Here, take my programme. It lists the whole conference. They were handing these out after Mass on the first day.'

Percy Nightingale said, 'After Mass? Liturgy giving birth to jargon. The sublime giving birth to what you'd damn well better be late arriving at.'

But it was too dark to read.

In the Little Annexe, behind the green door, Frank Castle began to pack. The wine had worn off. He wondered whether his stupefying idea – his idiocy – would wear off. He tested his will: was it still firm? He had no will. He had no purpose. He did not know what he was thinking. He was not thinking of a wedding. He felt infinitely bewildered. He stood staring at his shirts. Had Viviana run down the mountain again, into Fumicaro, to fetch her things from her room? They had not planned that part. Somehow he took it for granted that she had no possessions, or that her possessions did not matter, or were invisible. He saw that he had committed the sin of heroism, which always presumes that everyone else is unreal, especially the object of rescue. She was the instrument of his carnality, the occasion of his fall; no more than that, though that was too much. He had pushed too far. A stranger, a peasant's child. He was no more capable of her salvation than of his own.

The doorknob turned. He hardly understood what he would say to her. After all she was a sort of prostitute, the daughter of a sort of prostitute. He did not know exactly what these women were – the epiphenomena, he supposed, of the gradual movement, all over the world, of the agricultural classes to the city. He was getting his reason back again. She, on her side, was entirely reasonable. An entrapment. Such women are always looking for free tickets to the New World. She had planted herself in his room – just his luck – to pretend sickness. All right, she hadn't pretended; he could see it wasn't pretence. All the more blatant. A scheme; a pit; a noose. With her bit of English she had examined the conference lists and found her eligible prey: an unmarried man. The whole roster were married men – it was only the priests and himself. So she had done her little research. A sensible girl who goes after what she wants. He was willing to give her some money, though God was his witness he didn't have so much that he could take on an extended programme of philanthropy – his magazine, the *Sacral Review*, was making good his expenses. All the same he had to pinch. It was plain to him that she had never expected him to redeem the impulse of his dementia. It was his relief – the relief he felt in coming to his senses – that she had all along meant to exploit. Relief and the return of sanity were what he had to pay for. Mild enough blackmail. He wrenched his head round.

There stood Nightingale, anxiously jubilating and terrifically white. He had, so far, been no more than an old man's voice in the night, and to the extent that a voice represents a soul, he had falsified, he had misrepresented utterly. He was no older than Frank Castle, and it was not only that he was alarmingly indistinct – his ears were blanched; his mouth was a pinkish line; his eyes, blue over-rinsed to a transparency, were humps in a face as flat as zinc. He was almost blotted out. His look was a surprise: white down to his shoes, and immensely diffident. His shirt was white, his thighs were white, his shoes the same, and even shyer; he was self-effacing. He had already taken off his pants – he was without dazzle or glare. Washed out to a Celtic pallor. Frank Castle was unsure, with all this contradiction between words and appearance, where to put his confidence.

'You're right. Neighbours,' Nightingale said. 'You can have your programme back, I've got the glory of my own now. It's a wonder *any*one shows up for these things. It puts the priests to sleep, not that you can tell the difference when they're awake. I don't mind myself forgoing the pleasure' – he shook open the little pamphlet – 'of, get this, *Approaches to Bigotry. The Church and the Community, North, East, South, West. The Dioceses of Savannah, Georgia, and Denver, Colorado, Compared. Parish or Perish.* My God, I wish I could go to bed.'

'No one's forcing you to attend,' Frank Castle said.

'You bet they're not. If I sum up better by turning up late, I sum up best if I don't turn up at all. Listen, I like a weight on me when I sleep. No matter what the climate or the weather, put me in the tropics, I've got to have plenty of blankets on me. I told them so in the office – they're sending the chambermaid. Not that she isn't taking her own sweet time. No wonder, godforsaken place they've stuck us in, way down here. The rest get to sleep like princes in the palace. I know about me, I always get the short straw, but what's your crime, you're not up at the big house? Hey, you packing?'

Was he really packing? There were his shirts in a mound, folded and waiting to be folded, and his camera; there was his open suitcase.

'Not that I blame you, running off. Three days of it should do anyone.' Nightingale tossed the pamphlet on the bed. 'You've paid your dues. Especially if you got to stick in your two cents with the speechifying – what on?'

Footsteps on the circling stairs. Heavy goat hops. Viviana, obscured by blankets. She did not so much as glance in.

'Interviews with convicts,' Frank Castle said.

Nightingale guffawed – the pouncing syllables of a hawk, the thread of the lips drawn covertly in. A hider. Recklessness at war with panic. Mistrusting the one, Frank Castle believed in the other. Panic. 'What's your fix on these fellows? Cradle Catholics in my family since Adam, if not before, but I got my catechism from Father Leopold Robin.'

'Never heard of him.'

'Wouldn't expect you to. Né Rabinowitz.'

Frank Castle felt himself heat up. The faintest rise of vertigo. It was stupid to give in to peculiar sensations just because Viviana hadn't looked in the door. He said, 'Would you mind asking the chambermaid' – the word tugged at his tongue, as if it had fallen into something glutinous – 'to stop by when she's finished? They haven't changed my towels—'

'A whole speech on seeing the light? That's what you did? Too pious for me.'

'Scientific. I put in the statistics. Enough to please even a specialist. How many converts per parish, what kinds of converts, from what kinds of backgrounds.'

But he was listening to the small sounds in the next room.

Nightingale said, 'Clare Boothe Luce. There's your trophy.'

'We get all sorts these days. Because of the ascent of the Devil. Everyone's scared of the Devil. The rich and the poor. The soft and the arrogant—'

'And who's the Devil? You one of these fellows think Adolf's the new Satan? At least he holds off against the Commies.'

'I'm willing to think you're the Devil,' Frank Castle said.

'You're a touchy one.'

'Well, the Devil's in all of us.'

'Touchy and pious – I told you pious. You wouldn't think it would take a year to drop two blankets on a bed! All right, I'll send you that girl.' He took two steps into the corridor and turned back. 'This Father Robin wore the biggest crucifix you ever saw. Maybe it only looked that big – I was just a kid. But that's how it is with those convicts – they're self-condemned, so they take their punishment more seriously than anybody. It gives me the willies when they come in hotter'n Hades. They act like a bunch of goddam Holy Rollers with lights in their sockets. Show me a convert, I'll show you a fellow out to get even with someone. They're killers.'

'Killers?'

'They kill the old self for the sake of the new self. Conversion,' Nightingale said, 'is revenge.'

'You're forgetting Christ.'

'Oh Jesus God. I never forget Christ. Why else would I end up in this goddam shack in this godforsaken country? Maybe the Fascists'll make something out of these Wops yet. Put some spine in 'em. You want that girl? I'll get you that girl.'

Left to himself, Frank Castle dropped his head into his hands. With his eyes shut, staring into the flesh of his lids, he could see a whirligig of gold flecks. He had met a man and instantly despised him. It seemed to him that everyone here, not counting the handful of priests, was a sham – mountebanks all. And, for that matter, the priests as well. Public-relations types. Journalists, editors. In an older time these people would have swarmed around the marketplace selling indulgences and hawking pigs' hair.

The chambermaid came in. She was a fleshless uncomprehending spindly woman of about forty, perspiring at the neck, with ankles like balloons. There was a purple mark in the middle of her left cheek. 'Signore?' she said.

He went into the toilet and brought out a pair of fresh bath towels. 'I won't need these. I'm leaving. You might as well do whatever you want with them.' She shook her head and backed away. He had already taken it in that she would not be able to follow a word. And anyhow his charade made no sense. Still, she accepted the towels with a maddening docility; she was no different from Viviana. Any explanation, or no explanation, was all the same to these creatures. He said, 'Where's the other maid who always comes?'

The woman stared.

'Viviana,' he said.

'Ah! *L'altra cameriera*.'

'Where is she?'

With the towels stuck firmly under one armpit, she lifted her shoulders and held out her palms; then shut the door smartly behind her. A desolation entered him. He decided to attend the night session.

The meadow-long conference board had grown slovenly. Notebooks, squashed paper balls, pencils without points, empty pitchers and dirty cups, an exhausted coffee urn, languid eyeglasses lying with their earpieces askew, here and there a leg thrown up on the table: formality had vanished, decay was crawling through. The meeting was well under way; the speaker was annunciating Pascal. It was very like a chant – he had sharp tidy hand gestures, a grocer slicing cheese. '"Not only do we understand God only through Jesus Christ, but we understand ourselves only through Jesus Christ. We understand life and death only through Jesus Christ. Outside Jesus Christ we do not know what life is, nor death, nor God, nor ourselves." These words do not compromise; they do not try to get along with those who are indifferent to them, or with those who would laugh at them. They are neither polite nor gentle. They take their stand, and their stand is eternal and absolute. Today the obligation of Catholic public relations is not simply to defend the Church, though there is plenty of that to be done as well. In America especially we live with certain shadows, yet here in the mountains and valleys of Fumicaro, in glorious Italy, the Church is a serene mother, and it is of course easy to forget that she is troubled elsewhere. Elsewhere she is defamed as the refuge of superstition. She is accused of unseemly political advantages.

She is assaulted as a vessel of archaism and as an enemy of the scientific intelligence. She is pointed to as an institution whose whole raison d'être is the advance of clerical power. Alas, the Church in her true soul, wearing her Heavenly garments, is not sufficiently understood or known.

'All this public distortion is real enough, but our obligation is even more fundamental than finding the right lens of clarification to set over the falsifying portrait. The need to defend the Church against the debasement of the ignorant or the bigoted is, how shall we call it, a mere ripple in the sacred river. Our task as opinion-makers – and we should feel no shame over this phrase, with all its American candour, for are we not Americans at an American colloquy, though we sit here charmed by the antiquity of our surroundings? – our task, then, is to show the timelessness of our condition, the applicability of our objectifying vision even to flux, even to the immediate instant. We are to come with our high banner inscribed Eternity, and demonstrate its pertinence in the short run; indeed, in the shortest run of all, the single life, the single moment. We must let flower the absolute in the concrete, in the actual rise and fall of existence. Our aim is transmutation, the sanctification of the profane.'

It was impossible to listen; Nightingale was right. Frank Castle sank down into some interior chamber of mind. He was secretive; he knew this about himself. It was not that he had habits of concealment, or that, as people say, he kept his own counsel. It was instead something akin to sensation, an ache or a bump. Self-recognition. Every now and then he felt the jolt of who he was and what he had done. He was a man who had invented his own designations. He was undetermined. He was who he said he was. No one, nothing, least of all chance, had put him in his place. Like Augustine, he interpreted himself, and hotly. Oh, hotly. Whereas this glacial propagandist, reciting his noble text, bleating out 'absolute' and 'concrete' and 'transmutation', had fallen into his slot like a messenger from fate. Once fallen, fixed. Rooted. A stalactite.

Far behind the speaker, just past the lofty brass-framed doorway – a distance of several pastures, a whole countryside – a plump little figure glimmered. Viviana! There she was; there she stood. You would need a telescope to bring her close. Even with his unaccoutred eye, Frank Castle noticed how nicely she was dressed: if he had forgotten that she might have possessions, here was something pleasant – though it was only a blouse and skirt. She was clutching an object, he could not make out what. The blouse had a bright blue ribbon at the neck, and long sleeves. It might have been the ribbon, or the downward flow of the sleeves, or even the skirt, red as paint, which hung lower than he was used to – there was a sudden propriety in her. The wonderful calves were hidden: those hot domes he had only that afternoon drawn wide apart. Her thighs, too, were as hot and heavy as corn bread. Across such a space her head, remote and even precarious, was weighted down, like the laden head of a sunflower. She was absorbed by the marble floor tiles of the Villa Garibaldi. She would not come near. She eclipsed herself. She was a bit of shifting reflection.

He wondered if he should wait the speaker out. Instead he got up – every step a crash – and circled the table's dishevelled infinity. No one else moved. He was a scandal. Under the chandelier the speaker stuck to his paper. Frank Castle had done the same the day before, when they had all walked out on him for a ride across Como. Now here he was deserting, the only one to escape. It was almost ten o'clock at night; the whole crew of them had been up since eight. One had made a nest of his rounded arms and was carefully, sweetly, cradling his face down into it. Another was propped back with his mouth open, brazenly asleep, something between a wheeze and a snuffle puffing intermittently out.

In the hall outside he said, 'You've changed your clothes.'

'We go Milano!'

She was in earnest then. Her steady look, diverted downwards, was patient, docile. He did not know what to make of her; but her voice was too high. He set an admonitory finger over his own mouth. 'Where did you disappear to?'

'I go, I put' – he watched her labour after the words; excitement throttled her – '*fiore. Il santo!* To make *un buon viaggio.*'

He was clear enough about what a *santo* was. 'A saint? Is there a saint here?'

'You see before, in the road. You see him,' she insisted. She held up a metal cylinder. It was the flashlight from his bedside cabinet in the Little Annexe. 'Signore, come.'

'Do you have things? You're taking things?'

'*La mia borsa, una piccola valigia.* I put in the Signore's room.'

They could not stand there whispering. He followed where she led. She took him down the mountainside again, along the same half-buried road, to a weedy stone stump. It was the smothered little shrine he had noticed earlier. It grew right up out of the middle of the path. The head, with its rotted nose, was no more than a smudge. Over it, as tall as his hipbone, a kind of stone umbrella, a shelter like an upside-down U, or a fragment of vertical bathtub, seemed to be turning into a mound of wild ivy. Spiking out of this dense net was the iris Viviana had stuck there.

'San Francesco!' she said; the kitchen staff had told her. Such hidden old saints were all over the hills of Fumicaro.

'No,' Frank Castle said.

'*Molti santi*. You no belief? Look, Signore. San Francesco.'

She gave him the flashlight. In its white pool everything had a vivid glaze, like a puppet stage. He peered at the smudge. Goddess or god? Emperor's head, mounted like a milestone to mark out sovereignty? The chin was rubbed away. The torso had crumbled. It hardly looked holy. Depending on the weather, it might have been as old as a hundred years, or a thousand; two thousand. Only an archaeologist could say. But he did not miss how the flashlight conjured up effulgence. A halo blazed. Viviana was on her knees in the scrub; she tugged him down. With his face in leaves he saw the eroded fragment of the base, and, half sunken, an obscure tracing, a single intact word: 'DELEGI.' I chose; I singled out. Who chose, what or who was singled out? Antiquity alone did not enchant him: the disintegrating image of some local Roman politico or evanescent godlet. The mighty descend to powder and leave chalk on the fingertips.

Her eyes were shut; she was now as she had been in her small faint, perfectly ordered; but her voice was crowded with intense little mutterings. She was at prayer.

'Viviana. This isn't a saint.'

She stretched forward and kissed the worn-away mouth.

'You don't know *what* it is. It's an old pagan thing.'

'San Francesco,' she said.

'No.'

She turned on him a smile almost wild. The thing in the road was holy to her. It had a power; she was in thrall to sticks and stones. '*Il santo*, he pray for us.' In the halo of the flashlight her cheeks looked oiled and sleek and ripe for biting. She crushed her face down into the leaves beside his own – it was as if she read him and would consent to be bitten – and said again, 'Francesco.'

He had always presumed that sooner or later he would marry. He had spiritual ambition; yet he wanted to join himself to the great protoplasmic heave of human continuity. He meant to be fruitful: to couple, to procreate. He could not be continent; he could not sustain purity; he was not chaste. He had a terrible impulsiveness; his fall with Viviana was proof enough. He loved the priests, with their parched lip-corners and glossy eyes, their enigmatic loins burning for God. But he could not become like them; he was too fitful. He had no humility. Sometimes he thought he loved Augustine more than God. *Imitatio Dei*: he had come to Christ because he was secretive, because Jesus lived, though hiddenly. Hence the glory of the thousand statues that sought to make manifest the reticent Christ. Sculptors, like priests, are least of all secretive.

Often it had seemed to Frank Castle that, marriage being so open a cell, there was no one for him to marry. Wives were famous for needing explanations. He could not imagine not being married to a bookish sort – an 'intellectual' – but also he feared this more than anything. He feared a wife who could talk and ask questions and analyse and inquire after his history. Sometimes he fancied himself married to a rubber doll about his own size. She would serve him. They would have a rubber child.

A coldness breathed from the ground. Already hoarfrost was beginning to gather – a blurry veil over the broken head in the upended tub.

He said, 'Get up.'

'Francesco.'

'Viviana, let's go.' But he hung back himself. She was a child of simple intuitions, a kind of primitive. He felt how primitive she was. She was not a rubber doll, but she would keep clear of the precincts of his mind. This gladdened him. He wondered how such a deficiency could make him so glad.

She said for the third time, 'Francesco.' He understood finally that she was speaking his name.

They spent the night in his room in the Little Annexe. At six the milk driver would be grinding down from the kitchen lot past the arch of the Little Annexe. They waited under a brightening sunrise. The mist was fuming free of the mountainside; they could see all the way down to Como. Quietly loitering side by side with the peasant's child, again Frank Castle felt himself slowly churning into chaos: half an hour ago she had stretched to kiss his mouth exactly as she had stretched to kiss the mouth of the pagan thing fallen into the ground. He was mesmerized by the strangeness he had chosen for himself: a whole life of it. She was holding his hand like an innocent; her fingers were plaited into his. And then, out of the blue, as if struck by a whirlwind, they were not. She tore herself from him; his fingers were ripped raw; it seemed like a seizure of his own skin; he lost her. She had hurled herself nearly out of sight. Frank Castle watched her run – she looked flung. She ran into the road and down the road and across, behind the high hedges, away from the bricked-up vaults of the Roman aqueduct.

Percy Nightingale was descending from those vaults. Under his open overcoat a pair of bare bluish-white knees paraded.

'Greetings,' he called, 'from a practised insomniac. I've been examining the local dawn. They do their dawns very nicely in these parts, I'll give 'em *that*. What detritus we travellers gather as we move among the realms – here you are with two bags, and last night I'm sure I saw you with only one. You don't happen to have any extra booze in one of those?' He stamped vaguely round in an uneven try at a circle. 'Who was that rabbit who fled into the bushes?'

'I think you scared it off,' Frank Castle said.

'The very sight of me? It's true I'm not dressed for the day. I intend to pull on my pants in time for breakfast. You seem to be waiting for a train.'

'For the milk driver.'

'Aha. A slow getaway. You'd go quicker with the booze driver. I'd come along for kicks with the booze driver.'

'The fact of the matter,' Frank Castle said in his flattest voice, 'is that you've caught me eloping with the chambermaid.'

'What a nice idea. Satan, get thee behind me and give me a push. Long and happy years to you both. The scrawny hag with the pachyderm feet and the birthmark? She made up my bed very snugly – I'd say she's one of the Roman evidences they've got around here.' He pointed his long chin upwards towards the aqueduct. 'Since you didn't invite me to the exhumation, I won't expect to be invited to the wedding. Believe it or not, here's your truck.'

Frank Castle picked up Viviana's bag and his own and walked out into the middle of the road, fluttering his green American bills; the driver halted.

'See you in the funny papers,' Nightingale yelled.

He sat in the seat next to the driver's and turned, his face to the window. The road snaked left and then left again: any moment now a red-skirted girl would scuttle out from behind a dip in the foliage. He tried to tell this to the driver, but the man only chirped narrowly through his country teeth. The empty steel milk cans on the platform in the back of the truck jiggled and rattled; sometimes their flanks collided – a robust clang like cymbals. It struck him then that the abyss in his belly was his in particular: it wasn't fright at being discovered and judged that had made her bolt but practical inhibition – she was canny enough, she wasn't about to run off with a crazed person. Lust! He had come to his senses yesterday, though only temporarily; she had come to hers today, and in the nick of time. After which it occurred to him that he had better look in his wallet. Duped. She had robbed him and escaped. He dived into his pocket.

Instantly the driver's open palm was I under his nose.

'I paid you. *Basta*, I gave you *basta*.'

The truck wobbled perilously around a curve, but the hand stayed.

'Good God! Keep hold of the wheel, can't you? We'll go off the road!'

He shook out a flood of green bills onto the seat. Now he could not know how much she had robbed him of. He did not doubt she was a thief. She had stolen cheese from the kitchen and wine from a locked closet. He thought of his camera. It would not surprise him if she had bundled it off in a towel or a pillowcase in the night. Thievery had been her motive from the beginning. Everything else was ruse, snare, distraction, flimflam; she was a sort of gypsy, with a hundred tricks. He would never see her again. He was relieved. The freakishness of the last three days stung him; he grieved. Never again this surrender to the inchoate; never again the abyss. A joke! He had almost eloped with the chambermaid. Damn Nightingale!

They rattled – sounding now like a squad of carillons – into Fumicaro. Here was the promenade; here was the hot-chocolate shop; here was the church with its bell tower; here was morning-dazzled Como – high and pure the light that rose from it. 'Autobus,' he commanded the driver. He had spilled enough green gold to command. The country teeth showed the bliss of the newly rich. He was let out at an odd little turn of gossipy street, which looked as if it had never in all its existence heard tell of a bus; and here – 'No belief!' – was Viviana, panting hard. She could not catch her breath, because of the spy. A spy had never figured in their fears, God knows! A confusion and a danger. The spy would be sure to inform Guido, and Guido would be sure to inform Mr Wellborn, or, worse yet, the cobbler's cousin, who, as it happened, was Guido's cousin, too, only from the other side of the family. And then they would not let her go. No, they would not! They would keep her until her trouble became visible and ruinous, and then they would throw her into the ditch. The spy was an untrustworthy man. He was the man they had met on the hill, who took her for a boy. He was the man in the empty room of the Little Annexe. The other *cameriera* had told her that on top of all the extra blankets she had brought him he had put all the towels there were, and then, oh! he pulled down the curtains and piled them on top of the towels. And he stood before the other *cameriera* shamelessly, without his *pantaloni*! And so what could she do? She flew down the secret stone path, she flew right past San Francesco without stopping, to get to the autobus piazza before the milk driver.

Droplets of sweat erupted in a phalanx on her upper lip. She gave him the sour blink of an old woman; he glimpsed the Calabrian grandmother, weathered by the world's suspiciousness. 'You think I no come?'

He would not tell that he thought she had stolen.

'No belief!' Out tumbled her hot laugh, redolent of his bed in the Little Annexe. 'When *questo bambino* finish' – she pressed the cushion of her belly – 'you make new *bambino*, OK?'

In Milan that evening (his fourth in Italy), in a cramped cold chapel in the cathedral, within sight of the relic, they were married by a priest who was one of Caterina's special friends.

Caterina herself surprised him: she was dressed like a businesswoman. She wore a black felt hat with a substantial brim; she was substantial everywhere. Her head was set alertly on a neck that kept turning, as if wired to a generator; there was nothing she did not take in with her big powerful shining eyes. He felt that she took *him* in, all in a gulp. Her arm shot out to smack Viviana, because Viviana, though she had intended to continue not to tell about the cobbler, on her wedding day could not dissemble. The arm drew back. Caterina would not smack Viviana in front of a tourist, an American, on her wedding day. She was respectful. Still, it was a slander – the cobbler did not go putting seeds into the wombs of innocent girls. Twisting her neck, Caterina considered the American.

'Three days? You are friend of my Viviana three days, Signore?' She tapped her temple, and then made circles in the air with her forefinger. 'For what you want to marry my Viviana if you no put the seed?'

He knew what a scoundrel he seemed. The question was terrifying; but it was not meant for him. They went at it, the mother and the daughter, weeping and shrieking, in incomprehensible cascades: it was an opera, extravagant with drama, in a language he could not fathom. All this took place in Caterina's room in the Hotel Duomo, around the corner from a linen closet as capaciously fitted with shelves as a library; he sat in a chair face to face with the wardrobe in which the bilingual dictionary was secreted. The door was at his right hand – easy enough to grab the knob and walk away. For nearly an hour he sat. The two barking mouths went on barking. The hands clenched, grasped, pushed. He felt detached, distant; then, to his amazement, at a moment of crescendo, when the clamour was at its angriest, the two women fell into each other's embrace. Implausible as it was, preposterous as it was, Caterina was sending Viviana to America. *Un colpo di fulmine! Un fulmine a ciel sereno!*

Just before the little ceremony, the priest asked Frank Castle how he would feel about a baby that was – as he claimed – not his. Frank Castle could not think what to say. The priest was old and exhausted. He spoke of sin as of an elderly dog who is too sick to be companionable – yet you are used to him, you can't do without him, you can't bring yourself to get rid of him. The wedding ring was Caterina's.

Frank Castle exchanged his return ticket for two others on the *Stella Italiana*, sailing for New York in ten days. It was all accident and good luck: someone had cancelled. There were two available places. That left time for the marriage to be accorded a civil status: the priest explained to Caterina that though in the eyes of God Viviana was now safe, they had to fetch a paper from the government and get it stamped. This was the law.

There was time for Milan. It was very queer: Viviana had been brought to this northern treasure-city as a girl of thirteen and still did not know where the *Last Supper* was. Caterina knew; she even knew who had made it. 'Leonardo da Vinci,' she recited proudly. But she had never seen it. She took Viviana away to shop for a trousseau; they bought everything new but shoes, because Viviana was stubborn. She refused to go to the cobbler. '*Ostinata!*' Caterina said, but a certain awe had begun to creep into her fury. Viviana had found an American husband who talked on the radio in New York! Il Duce talked on the radio, too, and they could hear him as far away as America. Viviana a bride! Married, and to a tourist! These were miracles. Someone, Caterina said, had kissed a saint.

The *Last Supper* was deteriorating. It had to be looked at from behind a velvet rope. Viviana said it was a pity the camera hadn't yet been invented when Our Lord walked the earth – a camera would get a *much* better picture of Our Lord than the one in the flaking scene on the wall. Frank Castle taught her how to use his camera, and she snapped him everywhere; they snapped each other. They had settled into Caterina's room, but they had to come and go with caution, so that the manager would not know. It cost them nothing to stay in Caterina's room. Caterina did not say where she went to sleep; she said she had many friends who would share. When Viviana asked her who they were, Caterina laughed. 'The priests!' she said. All over the Duomo, Frank Castle was treated with homage, as a person of commercial value. He was an American with an Italian wife. In the morning they had coffee in the dining room. The waiter gave his little bow. Viviana was embarrassed. At the Villa Garibaldi she had deferred to the waiters; no one was so low as the *cameriera*. It made her uncomfortable to be served. Frank Castle told her she was no longer a *cameriera*; soon she would be an American. Unforgiving, she confided that Caterina had gone to stay with the cobbler.

He took her – it was still Nightingale's itinerary – to see the unfinished *Pietà* in a castle with bartizans and old worn bricks; schoolchildren ran in and out of the broad grassy trench that had once been the moat, but Viviana was unmoved. It was true that she admired the lustre of Our Lady's perfect foot, as polished as the marble flagging of the Villa Garibaldi; the rest was mainly rough rock. She thought it ridiculous to keep a thing like that on display. Our Lord didn't have a face. The Virgin didn't have a face. They looked like two ghouls. And this they called religion! What sense was it that the *muratore* who made it was famous – his sprawling Jesus was no more beautiful or *sacro* than a whitewashed wall falling down. And without a face! She let Frank Castle take her picture in her new bird-speckled dress in front of all that rubble, and meanwhile she described the statue of Our Lady that had stood on a shelf in her own plain room at Fumicaro. The Madonna's features were perfect in every detail – there were even wonderfully tiny eyelashes glued on, made of actual human hair. And all in the nicest brightest colours, the eyes a sweet blue, the cheeks rosy. The Holy Bambino was just as exact. He had a tiny belly button with a blue rhinestone in it, to match Our Lady's blue robe, and under his gauzy diaper he even had a lacquered penis that showed through, the colour of a human finger, though much tinier. He had tiny celluloid fingernails! A statue like that, Viviana said, is *molto sacro* – she had kneeled before it a thousand times. She had cried penitential floods because of the bleeding that did not come. She had pleaded with Our Lady for intercession with the Holy Bambino, and the Holy Bambino had heard her prayer. She had begged the Holy Bambino, if He could not make the bleeding come, to send a husband, and He had sent a husband.

They walked through rooms of paintings: voluptuous Titians; but Frank Castle was startled only by the solidity of Viviana. Ardour glowed in her. He had arrived in Italy with two little guidebooks, one for Florence and one for Rome, but he had nothing for Milan. Viviana herself was unmapped. Everything was a surprise. He could not tell what lay around the corner. He marvelled at what he had done. On Monday, at Fumicaro, Augustine and philosophy; on Thursday, the chattering of a brown-eyed bird-speckled simple-minded girl. His wife. His little peasant wife, a waif with a baby inside her! All his life he would feel shame over her. To whom could he show her without humiliation?

Her ignorance moved and elevated him. He thought of St Francis rejoicing in the blows and ridicule of a surly innkeeper: *Willingly and for the love of Christ let me endure pains and insults and shame and want, inasmuch as in all other gifts of God we may not glory, since they are not ours but God's.* Frank Castle understood he would always be mocked because of this girl; he went on snapping his camera at her. How robust she was, how gleaming, how happy! She was more hospitable to God than anyone who hoped to find God in books. She gave God a home everywhere – in old Roman tubs, in painted wooden dolls: it did not matter. Sticks and stones. He saw that no one had taught her to clean under her fingernails. He puzzled over it: she was the daughter of a trader in conveniences, she was herself a kind of commodity; she believed herself fated, a vessel for anyone's use. He had married shame. Married! It was what he had done. But he felt no remorse; none. He was exhilarated – to have had the courage for such a humbling!

In front of them, hanging from a crossbar, was a corpse made of oak. It was the size of a real man, and had the head of a real man. It wore a wreath made of real brambles, and there were real holes in its body, with real nails beaten into them.

Viviana dropped to the floor and clasped her hands.

'Viviana, people don't pray here.'

Her mouth went on murmuring.

'You don't *do* that in a place like this.'

'*Una chiesa,*' she said.

'People don't pray in museums.' Then it came to him that she did not know what a museum was. He explained that the pictures and statues were works of art. And he was married to her! 'There aren't any priests,' he said.

She shot him a look partly comical and partly shocked. Even priests have to eat, she protested. The priests were away, having their dinner. Here it was almost exactly like the *chiesa* at Fumicaro, only more crowded. At the other *chiesa*, where they kept the picture of the *Last Supper*, there were also no priests to be seen, and did that prove it wasn't a *chiesa*? Caterina had always told her how ignorant tourists were. Now she would have to put in an extra prayer for him, so that he could feel more sympathy for the human hunger of priests.

She dipped her head. Frank Castle circled all around the medieval man of wood. Red paint, dry for seven centuries, spilled from the nail holes. Even the back of the figure had its precision: the draw of muscles stretching in fatigue. The carver had not stinted anywhere. Yet the face was without a grain of pious inspiration. It was as if the carver had cared only for the carving itself, and not for its symbol. The man on the crossbar was having his live body imitated, and that was all. He was a copy of the carver's neighbour perhaps, or else a cousin. When the carving was finished, the neighbour or cousin stepped down, and together he and the carver hammered in the nails.

The nails. Were they for pity? They made him feel cruel. He reflected on their cruelty – a religion with a human corpse at the centre, what could that mean? The carver and his model, beating and beating on the nails.

In the streets there were all at once flags, and everywhere big cloth posters of Il Duce flapping on the sides of buildings. Il Duce had a frog's mouth and enormous round Roman eyes. Was it a celebration? He could learn nothing from Viviana. Some of the streets were miraculously enclosed under a glass dome. People walked and shopped in a greenish undersea twilight. Masses of little tables freckled the indoor sidewalks. Mobs went strolling, all afternoon and all night, with an exuberance that stunned him. All of Milan was calling out under glass. They passed windows packed with umbrellas, gloves, shoes, pastries, silk ties, marzipan. There was the cathedral itself, on a giant platter, made all of white marzipan. He bought a marzipan goose for Viviana, and from a pedlar a little Pinocchio on a string. Next to a bookstore, weaving in and out of the sidewalk coffee-drinkers – 'Turista? Turista?' – boys were handing out leaflets in French and English. Frank Castle took one and read: 'Only one of my ancestors interests me: there was a Mussolini in Venice who killed his wife who had betrayed him. Before fleeing he put two Venetian *scudi* on her chest to pay for her funeral. This is how the people of Romagna are, from whom I descend.'

They rode the elevator to the top of the cathedral and walked over the roofs, among hundreds of statues. Behind each figure stood a dozen others. There were saints and martyrs and angels and gryphons and gargoyles and Romans; there were Roman soldiers whose decorated sword handles and buskins sprouted the heads of more Roman soldiers. Viviana peered out through the crenellations at the margins of the different roofs, and again there were hundreds of sculptures; thousands. The statues pullulated. An army of carvers had swarmed through these high stones, century after century, striking shape after amazing shape. Some were reticent, some ecstatic. Some were motionless, some flew. It was a dream of proliferation, of infinity: of figures set austerely inside octagonal cupolas, and each generative flank of every cupola itself lavishly friezed and fructified; of limbs erupting from limbs; of archways efflorescing; of statues spawning statuary. What had looked, from the plaza below, like the frothiest lacework or egg-white spume here burst into solidity, weight, shadow and dazzlement: a derangement of plenitude tumbling from a bloated cornucopia.

A huge laughter spurted out of Frank Castle's lung. On the hot copper roof he squatted down and laughed.

'What? What?' Viviana said.

'You could be here years and years,' he said. 'You would never finish! You would have to stay up in the air your whole life!'

'What?' she said. 'What I no finish?'

He had pulled out his handkerchief and was pummelling his wet eyes. 'If – if—' But he could not get it out.

'What? What? Francesco—'

'If – suppose—' The laughter felt like a strangulation; he coughed out a long constricted breath. 'Look,' he said, 'I can see you falling on your goddam knees before every goddam *one* of these! Viviana,' he said, 'it's a *chiesa*! The priests aren't eating dinner! The priests are down below! Under our feet! You could be up here,' he said – now he understood exactly what had happened at Fumicaro; he had fixed his penance for life – 'a thousand years!'

Actors

Matt Sorley, born Mose Sadacca, was an actor. He was a character actor and (when they let him) a comedian. He had broad, swarthy, pliant cheeks, a reddish widow's peak that was both curly and balding, and very bright teeth as big and orderly as piano keys. His stage name had a vaguely Irish sound, but his origins were Sephardic. One grandfather was from Constantinople, the other from Alexandria. His parents could still manage a few words of the old Spanish spoken by the Jews who had fled the Inquisition, but Matt himself, brought up in Bensonhurst, Brooklyn, was purely a New Yorker. The Brooklyn that swarmed in his speech was useful to him. It got him parts.

Sometimes he was recognized in the street a day or so following his appearance on a television lawyer series he was occasionally on call for. These were serious, mostly one-shot parts requiring mature looks. The pressure was high. Clowning was out, even in rehearsals. Matt usually played the judge (three minutes on camera) or else the father of the murder victim (seven minutes). The good central roles went to much younger men with rich black hair and smooth flat bellies. When they stood up to speak in court, they carefully buttoned up their jackets. Matt could no longer easily button his. He was close to sixty and secretly melancholy. He lived on the Upper West Side in a rent-controlled apartment with a chronic leak under the bathroom sink. He had a reputation for arguing with directors; one director was in the habit of addressing him, rather nastily, as Mr Surly.

His apartment was littered with dictionaries, phrase books, compendiums of scientific terms, collections of slang, encyclopaedias of botany, mythology, history. Frances was the one with the steady income. She worked for a weekly crossword-puzzle magazine, and by every Friday had to have composed three new puzzles in ascending order of complexity. The job kept her confined and furious. She was unfit for deadlines and tension; she was myopic and suffered from eye-strain. Her neck was long, thin, and imperious, with a jumpy pulse at the side. Matt had met her, right out of Tulsa, almost twenty years ago on the tiny stage of one of those downstairs cellar theatres in the Village – the stage was only a clearing in a circle of chairs. It was a cabaret piece, with ballads and comic songs, and neither Matt nor Frances had much of a voice. This common deficiency passed for romance. They analysed their mutual flaws endlessly over coffee in the grimy little café next door to the theatre. Because of sparse audiences, the run petered out after only two weeks, and the morning after the last show Matt and Frances walked downtown to City Hall and were married.

Frances never sang onstage again. Matt sometimes did, to get laughs. As long as Frances could stick to those Village cellars she was calm enough, but in any theatre north of Astor Place she faltered and felt a needlelike chill in her breasts and forgot her lines. And yet her brain was all storage. She knew words like 'fenugreek', 'kermis', 'sponson', 'gibberel-lin'. She was angry at being imprisoned by such words. She lived, she said, behind bars; she was the captive of a grid. All day long she sat fitting letters into squares, scrambling the alphabet, inventing definitions made to resemble conundrums, shading in the unused squares. 'Grid and bear it,' she said bitterly, while Matt went out to take care of ordinary household things – buying milk, picking up his shirts from the laundry, taking his shoes to be resoled. Frances had given up acting for good. She didn't like being exposed like that, feeling nervous like that, shaking like that, the needles in her nipples, the numbness in her throat, the cramp in her bowel. Besides, she was embarrassed about being near-sighted and hated having to put in contact lenses to get through a performance. In the end she threw them in the trash. Offstage, away from audiences, she could wear her big round glasses in peace.

Frances resented being, most of the time, the only breadwinner. After four miscarriages she said she was glad they had no children, she couldn't imagine Matt as a father – he lacked gumption, he had no get-up-and-go. He thought it was demeaning to scout for work. He thought work ought to come to him because he was an artist. He defined himself as master of a Chaplinesque craft; he had been born into the line of an elite tradition. He scorned props and despised the way some actors relied on cigarettes to move them through a difficult scene, stopping in the middle of a speech to light up. It was false suspense, it was pedestrian. Matt was a purist. He was contemptuous of elaborately literal sets, rooms that looked like real rooms. He believed that a voice, the heel of a hand, a hesitation, the widening of a nostril could furnish a stage. Frances wanted Matt to hustle for jobs, she wanted him to network, bug his agent, follow up on casting calls. Matt could do none of these things. He was an actor, he said, not a goddam pedlar.

It wasn't clear whether he was actually acting all the time (Frances liked to accuse him of this), yet, even on those commonplace daytime errands, there was something exaggerated and perversely open about him: an unpredictability leaped out and announced itself. He kidded with all the store help. At the Korean-owned vegetable stand, the young Mexican who was unpacking peppers and grapefruits hollered across to him, 'Hey, Matt, you in a movie now?' For all its good will, this question hurt. It was four years since the last film offer, a bit part with Marlon Brando, whom Matt admired madly, though without envy. The part bought Matt and Frances a pair of down coats for winter, and a refrigerator equipped with an ice-cube dispenser. But what Matt really hoped for was getting back onstage. He wanted to be in a play.

At the shoe-repair place his new soles were waiting for him. The proprietor, an elderly Neapolitan, had chalked 'Attore' across the bottom of Matt's well-worn slip-ons. Then he began his usual harangue: Matt should go into opera. 'I wouldn't be any good at it,' Matt said, as he always did, and flashed his big even teeth. Against the whine of the rotary brush he launched into 'La donna è mobile'. The shoemaker shut off his machine and bent his knees and clapped his hands and leaked tears down the accordion creases that fanned out from the corners of his eyes. It struck Matt just then that his friend Salvatore had the fairy-tale crouch of Geppetto, the father of Pinocchio; the thought encouraged him to roll up the legs of his pants and jig, still loudly singing. Salvatore hiccuped and roared and sobbed with laughter.

Sometimes Matt came into the shop just for a shine. The shoemaker never let him pay. It was Matt's trick to tell Frances (his awful deception, which made him ashamed) that he was headed downtown for an audition, and wouldn't it be a good idea to stop first to have his shoes buffed? The point was to leave a decent impression for next time, even if they didn't hire you this time. 'Oh, for heaven's sake, buy some shoe polish and do it yourself,' Frances advised, but not harshly; she was pleased about the audition.

Of course there wasn't any audition – or, if there was, Matt wasn't going to it. After Salvatore gave the last slap of his flannel cloth, Matt hung around, teasing and fooling, for half an hour or so, and then he walked over to the public library to catch up on the current magazines. He wasn't much of a reader, though in principle he revered literature and worshipped Shakespeare and Shaw and Oscar Wilde. He looked through *The Atlantic* and *Harper's* and *The New Yorker*, all of which he liked; *Partisan Review, Commentary*, magazines like that, were over his head.

Sitting in the library, desultorily turning pages, he felt himself a failure and an idler as well as a deceiver. He stared at his wristwatch. If he left this minute, if he hurried, he might still be on time to read for Lionel: he knew this director, he knew he was old-fashioned and meanly slow – one reading was never enough. Matt guessed that Lionel was probably a bit of a dyslexic. He made you stand there and do your half of the dialogue again and again, sometimes three or four times, while he himself read the other half flatly, stumblingly. He did this whether he was seriously considering you or had already mentally dismissed you: his credo was fairness, a breather, another try. Or else he had a touch of sadism. Directors want to dominate you, shape you, turn you into whatever narrow idea they have in their skulls. To a director an actor is a puppet – Geppetto with Pinocchio. Matt loathed the ritual of the audition; it was humiliating. He was too much of a pro to be put through these things, his track record ought to speak for itself, and why didn't it? Especially with Lionel; they had both been in the business for years. Lionel, like everyone else, called it 'the business'. Matt never did.

He took off his watch and put it on the table. In another twenty minutes he could go home to Frances and fake it about the audition: it was the lead Lionel was after, the place was full of young guys, the whole thing was a misunderstanding. Lionel, believe it or not, had apologized for wasting Matt's time.

'Lionel apologized?' Frances said. Without her glasses on, she gave him one of her naked looks. It was a way she had of avoiding seeing him while drilling straight through him. It made him feel damaged.

'You never went,' she said. 'You never went near that audition.'

'Yes, I did. I did go. That shit Lionel. Blew my whole day.'

'Don't kid me. You didn't go. And Lionel's not a shit, he's been good to you. He gave you the uncle part in *Navy Blues* only three years ago. I don't know why you insist on forgetting that.'

'It was junk. Garbage. I'm sick of being the geezer in the last act.'

'Be realistic. You're not twenty-five.'

'What's realistic is if they give me access to my range.'

And so on. This was how they quarrelled, and Matt was pained by it: it wasn't is if Frances didn't understand how much he hated sucking up to directors, waiting for the verdict on his thickening fleshy arms, his round stomach, his falsely grinning face, his posture, his walk, even his voice. His voice he knew passed muster: it was like a yo-yo, he could command it to tighten or stretch, to torque or lift. And still he had to submit to scrutiny, to judgment, to prejudice, to whim. He hated having to be obsequious, even when it took the form of jolliness, of ersatz collegiality. He hated lying. His nose was growing from all the lies he told Frances.

On the other hand, what was acting if not lying? A good actor is a good impostor. A consummate actor is a consummate deceiver. Or put it otherwise: an actor is someone who falls into the deeps of self-forgetfulness. Or still otherwise: an actor is a puppeteer, with himself as puppet.

Matt frequently held forth in these trite ways – mostly to himself. When it came to philosophy, he didn't fool anybody, he wasn't an original.

'You got a call,' Frances said.

'Who?' Matt said.

'You won't like who. You won't want to do it, it doesn't fit your range.'

'For crying out loud,' Matt said. 'Who was it?'

'Somebody from Ted Silkowitz's. It's something Ted Silkowitz is doing. You won't like it,' she said again.

'Silkowitz,' Matt groaned. 'The guy's still in diapers. He's sucking his thumb. What's he want with me?'

'That's it. He wants you and nobody else.'

'Cut it out, Frances.'

'See what I mean? I know you, I knew you'd react like that. You won't want to do it. You'll find some reason.' She pulled a tissue from inside the sleeve of her sweater and began to breathe warm fog on her lenses. Then she rubbed them with the tissue. Matt was interested in bad eyesight – how it made people stand, the pitch of their shoulders and necks. It was the kind of problem he liked to get absorbed in. The stillness and also the movement. If acting was lying, it was at the same time mercilessly and mechanically truth-telling. Watching Frances push the earpieces of her glasses back into the thicket of her hair, Matt thought how pleasing that was, how quickly and artfully she did it. He could copy this motion exactly; he drew it with his tongue on the back of his teeth. If he looked hard enough, he could duplicate anything at all. Even his nostrils, even his genitals, had that power. His mind was mostly a secret from him – he couldn't run it, it ran him, but he was intimate with its nagging pushy heat.

'It's got something to do with Lear. Something about King Lear,' Frances said. 'But never mind, it's not for you. You wouldn't want to play a geezer.'

'Lear? What d'you mean, Lear?'

'Something like that, I don't know. You're supposed to show up tomorrow morning. If you're interested,' she added; he understood how sly she could be. 'Eleven o'clock.'

'Well, well,' Matt said, 'good thing I got my shoes shined.' Not that he believed in miracles, but with Silkowitz anything was possible: the new breed, all sorts of surprises up their baby sleeves.

Silkowitz's building was off Eighth Avenue, up past the theatre district. The neighbourhood was all bars, interspersed with dark little slots of Greek luncheonettes; there was a sex shop on the corner. Matt, in suit and tie, waited for the elevator to take him to Silkowitz's office, on the fifth floor. It turned out to be a cramped two-room suite: a front cubicle for the receptionist, a boy who couldn't have been more than nineteen, and a rear cubicle for the director. The door to Silkowitz's office was shut.

'Give him a minute. He's on the phone,' the boy said. 'We've run into a little problem with the writer.'

'The writer?' Matt said stupidly.

'She died last night. After we called you about the Lear thing.'

'I thought the writer died a long time ago.'

'Well, it's not *that* Lear.'

'Matt Sorley,' Silkowitz yelled. 'Come on in, let's have a look. You're the incarnation of my dream – I'm a big fan, I love your work. Hey, all you need is the Panama hat.'

The hat crack was annoying; it meant that Silkowitz was familiar mainly with one of Matt's roles on that television lawyer show – it was his signature idiosyncrasy to wear a hat in court until the judge reprimanded him and made him take it off.

Matt said, 'The writer's *dead*?'

'We've got ourselves a tragedy. Heart attack. Passed away in intensive care last night. Not that she's any sort of spring chicken. Marlene Miller-Weinstock, you know her?'

'So there's no play,' Matt said: he was out of a job.

'Let me put it this way. There's no playwright, which is an entirely different thing.'

'Never heard of her,' Matt said.

'Right. Neither did I, until I got hold of this script. As far as I know she's written half a dozen novels. The kind that get published and then disappear. Never wrote a play before. Face it, novelists can't do plays anyhow.'

'Oh, I don't know,' Matt said. 'Gorky, Sartre, Steinbeck Galsworthy. Wilde.' It came to him that Silkowitz had probably never read any of these old fellows from around the world. Not that Matt had, either, but he was married to someone who had read them all.

'Right,' Silkowitz conceded. 'But you won't find Miller-Weinstock on that list. The point is what I got from this woman is raw. Raw but full of bounce. A big look at things.'

Silkowitz was cocky in a style that was new to Matt. Lionel, for all his arrogance, had an exaggerated courtly patience that ended by stretching out your misery, Lionel's shtick was to keep you in suspense. And Lionel had a comfortingly, ageing face, with a firm deep wadi slashed across his forehead, and a wen hidden in one eyebrow. Matt was used to Lionel – they were two old horses, they knew what to expect from each other. But here was Silkowitz with his baby face – he didn't look a lot older than that boy out there – and his low-hung childishly small teeth under a bumpy tract of exposed fat gums: here was Silkowitz mysteriously dancing around a questionable script by someone freshly deceased. The new breed, they didn't wait out an apprenticeship, it was drama school at Yale and then the abrupt ascent into authority, reputation, buzz. The sureness of this man, sweatshirt and jeans, pendant dangling from the neck, a silver ring on his thumb, hair as sleek and flowing as a girl's – the whole thick torso glowing with power. Still a kid, Silkowitz was already on his way to Lionel's league: he could make things happen. Ten years from now the scruffy office would be just as scruffy, just as out of the way, though presumably more spacious; the boy out front would end up a

Hollywood agent, or else head out for the stock exchange in a navy blazer with brass buttons. Lionel left you feeling heavy, superfluous, a bit of an impediment. This Silkowitz, an enthusiast, charged you up: Matt had the sensation of an electric wire going up his spine, probing and poking his vertebrae.

'Look, it's a shock,' Silkowitz said. 'I don't feel good about it, but fact is I never met the woman. Today was supposed to be the day. Right this instant, actually. I figured, first organize the geriatric ward, get the writer and the lead face to face. Well, no sweat, we've still got her draft and we've still got our lead.'

'Lead,' Matt said; but 'geriatric', quip or no, left him sour.

'Right. The minute I set eyes on the script I knew you were the one. As a matter of fact,' Silkowitz said, flashing a pair of clean pink palms, 'I ran into Lionel the other night and he put me on to you.'

These two statements struck Matt as contradictory, but he kept his mouth shut. He had his own scenario, Silkowitz scouting for an old actor and Lionel coming up with Matt: 'Call Sorley. Touchy guy, takes offence at the drop of a hat, but one hundred per cent reliable. Learns his lines and shows up.' Showing up being nine-tenths of talent.

Matt was businesslike. 'So you intend to do the play without the writer.'

'We don't need the writer. It's enough we've got the blueprint. As far as I'm concerned, theatre's a director's medium.'

Oh, portentous: Silkowitz as infant lecturer. And full of himself. If he could do without the writer, maybe he could do without the actor?

Silkowitz handed Matt an envelope. 'Photocopy of the script,' he said. 'Take it home. Read it. I'll call you, you'll come in again, we'll talk.'

Matt hefted the envelope. Thick, not encouraging. In a way Silkowitz was right about novelists doing plays. They overwrite, they put in a character's entire psychology, from birth on: a straitjacket for an actor. The actor's job is to figure out the part, to feel it out. Feather on feather, tentative, gossamer. The first thing Matt did was take a black marking pen and cross out all the stage directions. That left just the dialogue, and the dialogue made him moan: monologues, soliloquies, speeches. Oratory!

'Never mind,' Frances said. 'Why should *you* care? It's work, you wanted to work.'

'It's not that the idea's so bad. A version of a classic.'

'So what's the problem?'

'I can't do it, that's the problem.'

Naturally he couldn't do it. And he resented Silkowitz's demand that he trek all the way down to that sex-shop corner again – wasn't the telephone good enough? Silkowitz threw out the news that he couldn't proceed, he couldn't think, except in person: he was big on face to face. As if all that counted was his own temperament. With a touch of spite Matt was pleased to be ten minutes late.

A young woman was in the outer cubicle.

'He's waiting for you,' she said. 'He's finishing up his lunch.'

Matt asked where the boy was.

Silkowitz licked a plastic spoon and heaved an empty yogurt cup into a waste-basket across the room. 'Quit. Got a job as assistant stage manager in some Off Off. So, what d'you say?'

'The part's not for me. I could've told you this straight off on the phone. The character's ten years older than I am. Maybe fifteen.'

'You've got plenty of time to grow a beard. It'll come in white.'

'I don't know anything about the background here, it's not my milieu.'

'The chance of a lifetime,' Silkowitz argued. 'Who gets to play Lear, for God's sake?'

Matt said heavily, bitterly, 'Yeah. The Lear of Ellis Island. Just off the boat.'

'That's the ticket,' Silkowitz said. 'Think of it as a history play.'

Matt sat there while Silkowitz, with lit-up eyes, lectured. A history riff for sure. Fourth, fifth generation, steerage troubles long ago strained out of his blood – it was all a romance to little Teddy Silkowitz. Second Avenue down at Twelfth, the old Yiddish theatre, the old feverish plays. Weeping on the stage, weeping in all the rows. Miller-Weinstock ('May she rest in peace,' Silkowitz put in) was the daughter of one of those pioneer performers of greenhorn drama; the old man, believe it or not, was still alive at ninety-six, a living fossil, an actual breathing known-to-be-extinct duck-billed dodo. That's where she got it from – from being his daughter. Those novels she turned out, maybe they were second-rate, who knows? Silkowitz didn't know – he'd scarcely looked at the handful of reviews she'd sent – and it didn't matter. What mattered was the heat that shot straight out of her script, like the heat smell of rusted radiators knocking in worn-out five-storey tenements along Southern Boulevard in the thirties Bronx, or the whiff of summer ozone at the trolley-stop snarl at West Farms. It wasn't those Depression times that fired Silkowitz – it wasn't that sort of recapturing he was after. Matt was amazed – Matt who worshipped nuance, tendril, shadow, intimation, instinct, Matt who might jig for a shoemaker but delivered hints and shadings to the proscenium, Matt who despised exaggeration, caricature, going over the top, Matt for whom the stage was holy ground. . . . And what did little Teddy Silkowitz want?

'Reversal,' Silkowitz said. 'Time to change gears. The changing of the guard. Change, that's what! Where's the overtness, the overture, the passion, the emotion? For fifty, sixty years all we've had is mutters, muteness, tight lips, and, God damn it, you can't hear their voices, all that Actors Studio blather, the old religion, so-called inwardness, a bunch of Quakers waiting for Inner Light – obsolete! Dying, dead, finished! Listen, Matt, I'm talking heat, muscle, human anguish. Where's the theatrical *noise*? The big speeches and declamations? All these anaemic monosyllabic washed-out two-handers with their impotent little climaxes. Matt, let me tell you my idea, and I tell it with respect, because I'm in the presence of an old-timer, and I want you to know I know my place. But we're in a new era now, and someone's got to make that clear—' Silkowitz's lantern eyes moved all around his cubicle; it seemed to Matt they could scald the paint off the walls. 'This is what I'm for. Take it seriously. My idea is to restore the old lost art of melodrama. People call it melodrama to put it down, but what it is is open feeling, you see what I mean? And the chance came out of the blue! From the daughter of the genuine article!'

Matt said roughly (his roughness surprised him), 'You've got the wrong customer.'

'Look before you leap, pal. Don't try to pin that nostalgia stuff on me. The youthful heart throbbing for grandpa's world. That's what you figure, right?'

'Not exactly,' Matt fibbed.

'That's not it, honest to God. It's the largeness – big feelings, big cries. Outcries! The old Yiddish theatre kept it up while it was dying out everywhere else. Killed by understatement. Killed by abbreviation, downplaying. Killed by sophistication, modernism, psychologizing, Stanislavsky, all those highbrow murderers of the Greek chorus, you see what I mean? The Yiddish Medea. The Yiddish Macbeth! Matt, it was *big*!'

'As far as I'm concerned,' Matt said, 'the key word here is old-timer.'

'There aren't many of your type around,' Silkowitz admitted. 'Look, I'm saying I really want to do this thing. The part's yours.'

'A replay of the old country, that's my type? I was doing Eugene O'Neill before you were born.'

'You've read the script, it's in regular English. American as apple pie. Lear on the Lower East Side! We can make that the Upper West Side. And those daughters – I've got some great women in mind. We can update everything, we can do what we want.'

'Yeah, we don't have the writer to kick around.' Matt looked down at his trouser cuffs. They were beginning to fray at the crease; he needed a new suit. 'I'm not connected to any of that. My mother's father came from Turkey and spoke Ladino.'

'A Spanish grandee, no kidding. I didn't realize. You look—'

'I know how I look,' Matt broke in. 'A retired pants presser.' He wanted to play Ibsen, he wanted to play Shaw! Henry Higgins with Eliza. Something grand, aloof, cynical; he could do Brit talk beautifully.

Silkowitz pushed on. 'Lionel says he's pretty sure you're free.'

Free. The last time Matt was on a stage (television didn't count) was in Lionel's own junk play, a London import, where Matt, as the beloved missing uncle, turned up just before the final curtain. That was more than three years ago; by now four.

'I'll give it some thought,' Matt said.

'It's a deal. Start growing the beard. There's only one thing. A bit of homework you need to do.'

'Don't worry,' Matt said. 'I know how the plot goes. Regan and Goneril and Cordelia. I read it in high school.'

But it wasn't Shakespeare Silkowitz had in mind: it was Eli Miller the nonagenarian. Silkowitz had the old fellow's address at a 'senior residence'. Probably the daughter had mentioned its name, and Silkowitz had ordered his underling – the boy, or maybe the girl – to look it up. It was called the Home for the Elderly Children of Israel, and it was up near the Cloisters.

'Those places give me the creeps,' Matt complained to Frances. 'The smell of pee and the zombie stare.'

'It doesn't have to be like that. They have activities and things. They have social directors. At that age maybe they go for blue material, you never know.'

'Sure,' Matt said. 'The borscht belt revived and unbuckled. You better come with me.'

'What's the point of that? Silkowitz wants you to get the feel of the old days. In Tulsa we didn't *have* the old days.'

'Suppose the guy doesn't speak English? I mean just in case. Then I'm helpless.'

So Frances went along; Tulsa notwithstanding, she knew some attenuated strands of household Yiddish. She was a demon at languages anyhow; she liked to speckle her tougher crosswords with 'cri de cœur', 'Mitleid', 'situación difícil'. She had once studied ancient Greek and Esperanto.

A mild January had turned venomous. The air slammed their foreheads like a frozen truncheon. Bundled in their down coats, they waited for a bus. Icicles hung from its undercarriage, dripping black sludge. The long trip through afternoon dusk took them to what seemed like a promontory; standing in the driveway of the Home for the Elderly Children of Israel, they felt like a pair of hawks surveying rivers and roads and inch-tall buildings. 'The Magic Mountain,' Frances muttered as they left the reception desk and headed down the corridor to Room 1-A: Eli Miller's digs.

No one was there.

'Let's trespass,' Frances said. Matt followed her in. The place was overheated; in two minutes he had gone from chill to sweat. He was glad Frances had come. At times she was capable of an unexpected aggressiveness. He saw it now and then as she worked at her grids, her lists of synonyms, her trickster definitions. Her hidden life inside those little squares gave off an electric ferocity. She was prowling all around 1-A as if it was one of her boxes waiting to be solved. The room was cryptic enough: what was it like to be so circumscribed – a single dresser crowded with tubes and medicines, a sagging armchair upholstered in balding plush, a bed for dry bones – knowing it to be your last stop before the grave? The bed looked more like a banquet table, very high, with fat carved legs; it was covered all over with a sort of wrinkly cloak, heavy maroon velvet tasselled at the corners – a royal drapery that might have been snatched from the boudoir of a noblewoman of the Tsar's court. A child's footstool stood at the bedside.

'He must be a little guy,' Frances said. 'When you get old you start to shrink.'

'Old-timer,' Matt spat out. 'Can you imagine? That's what he called me actually.'

'Who did?'

'That twerp Silkowitz.'

Frances ignored this. 'Get a look at that bedspread or whatever it is. I'd swear a piece of theatre curtain. And the bed! Stage furniture. Good God, has he read all this stuff?'

Every space not occupied by the dresser, the chair, and the bed was tumbled with books. There were no shelves. The books rose up from the floorboards in wobbly stacks, with narrow aisles between. Some had fallen and lay open like wings, their pages pulled from their spines.

'German, Russian, Hebrew, Yiddish. A complete set of Dickens. Look,' Frances said. '*Moby-Dick!*'

'In the atrium they told me visitors,' said a voice in the doorway. It was the brassy monotone of the almost-deaf, a horn bereft of music. Frances hiked up her glasses and wiped her right hand on her coat: *Moby-Dick* was veiled in grime.

'Mr Miller?' Matt said.

'Bereaved, sir. Eli Miller is bereaved.'

'I heard about your daughter. I'm so sorry,' Matt said; but if this was going to be a conversation, he hardly knew how to get hold of it.

The old man was short, with thick shoulders and the head of a monk. Or else it was Ben-Gurion's head: a circle of naked scalp, shiny as glass, and all around it a billowing ring of pearl-white hair, charged with static electricity. His cheeks were a waterfall of rubbery creases. One little eye peeped out from the flow, dangerously blue. The other was sealed into its socket. You might call him ancient, but you couldn't call him frail. He looked like a butcher. He looked like a man who even now could take an axe to a bull.

He went straight to the stepstool, picked it up, and tossed it into the corridor, it made a brutal clatter.

'When I go out they put in trash. I tell them, Eli Miller requires no ladders!' With the yell of the deaf he turned to Frances: 'She was a woman your age. What, you're fifty? Your father, he's living?'

'He died years ago,' Frances said. Her age was private; a sore point.

'Naturally. This is natural, the father should not survive the child. A very unhappy individual, my daughter. Divorced. The husband flies away to Alaska and she's got her rotten heart. A shame, against nature – Eli Miller, the heart and lungs of an elephant! Better a world filled with widows than divorced.' He curled his thick butcher's arm around Frances's coat collar. 'Madam, my wife if you could see her you would be dumbstruck. She had unusually large eyes and with a little darkening of the eyelids they became larger. Big and black like olives. Thirty-two years she's gone. She had a voice they could hear it from the second balcony, rear row.'

Matt caught Frances's look: it was plain she was writing the old fellow off. *Not plugged in,* Frances was signalling, *nobody home upstairs, lost his marbles.* Matt decided to trust the better possibility: a bereaved father has a right to some indulgence.

'There's real interest in your daughter's play,' he began; he spoke evenly, reasonably.

'An ambitious woman. Talent not so strong. Whoever has Eli Miller for a father will be ambitious. Eli Miller's talent, this is another dimension. What you see here' – he waved all around 1-A – 'are remnants. Fragments and vestiges! *The Bewildered Bridegroom,* 1924!' He pinched a bit of the maroon velvet bedspread and fingered its golden tassel. 'From the hem of Esther Borodovsky's dress hung twenty-five like this! And four hundred books on the walls of Dr Borodovsky! That's how we used to do it, no stinginess! And who do you think played the Bridegroom? Eli Miller! The McKinley Square Theatre, Boston Road and 169th, they don't forget such nights, whoever was there they remember!'

Matt asked, 'You know your daughter wrote a play? She told you?'

'And not only the Bridegroom! Othello, Macbeth, Polonius. Polonius the great philosopher, very serious, very wise. Jacob Adler's Shylock, an emperor! Thomashefsky, Schwartz, Carnovsky!'

'Matt,' Frances whispered, 'I want to leave *now.*'

Matt said slowly, 'Your daughter's play is getting produced. I'm *in* it. I'm an actor.'

The old man ejected a laugh. His dentures struck like a pair of cymbals; the corona of his magnetic hair danced. 'Actor, actor, call yourself what you want, only watch what you say in front of Eli Miller! My daughter, first it's *romanen,* now it's a play! Not only is the daughter taken before the father but also the daughter is mediocre. Always mediocre. She cannot ascend to the father! Eli Miller the pinnacle! The daughter climbs and falls. Mediocre!'

'Matt, let's go,' Frances growled.

'And this one?' Again the old man embraced her, Frances recoiled. 'This one is also in it?'

'Here,' Matt said, and handed Eli Miller one of Teddy Silkowitz's cards. 'If you want to know more, here's the director.' He stopped; he thought better of what he was about to say. But he said it anyway: 'He admires your daughter's work.'

'Eli Miller's Polonius, in the highest literary Yiddish, sir! Standing ovations and bravo every night. Every matinée. Three matinées a week, that's how it was. Bravo bravo. By the time she's born, my daughter, it's after the war, 1948, it's finishing up, it's practically gone. Gone – the whole thing! After Hitler, who has a heart for tragedy on a stage? Anyhow no more actors, only movie stars. Please, sir, do me a favour and name me no names, what is it, who is it, who remembers? But Eli Miller and Esther Borodovsky, also Dr Borodovsky, whoever was there they remember!'

'With or without you,' Frances warned, 'I'm going.'

Matt hung on. 'Your daughter's play,' he said, 'is out of respect for all that. For everything you feel.'

'What are you saying? I know what she is! My daughter, all her life she figures one thing, to take away Eli Miller's soul. This is why God makes her mediocre, this is why God gives her a rotten heart, this is why God buries the daughter before the father!'

They left him with tears running out of the one blue eye.

'I think you incited him,' Frances said. 'You just went ahead and provoked him.' They were huddled in the bus shelter, out of the wind. It was five o'clock and already night.

Matt said, 'An old actor, maybe he was acting.'

'Are you kidding?' Frances said; hunched inside the bulk of her coat, she was shivering.

'You're always telling me I do that.'

'Do what?'

'Act all the time.'

'Oh, for Pete's sake,' Frances said. 'Why did you make me come anyhow? My toes are numb.'

Late in February, on a day of falling snow, rehearsals began. Silkowitz had rented a cellar in a renovated old factory building in the West Forties, in sight of the highway and the river. The space had a stage at one end and at the other a sort of stockade surrounding a toilet that occasionally backed up. The ceiling groaned and shuddered. A far-off piano thumped out distracting rhythms: there was a dance studio directly overhead. The cast was smaller than Matt had expected – the three female roles had been reduced to two. Silkowitz had spent the last month reviewing the script, and was still not satisfied. No sooner did Matt learn the movements of a scene than the director had second thoughts and rearranged the blocking. To Matt's surprise, the boy who had been in Silkowitz's office was there, presiding over a notebook; Silkowitz had brought him back to be stage manager. Matt calculated that the kid had six weeks' experience.

Silkowitz had put himself in charge of secrets. Each rehearsal session felt like a cabal from which the actors were excluded. Strangers came and went, carrying portfolios. Silkowitz never introduced any of them. 'This is going to be a tight job, nothing extraneous. I believe in collaboration with all my heart, but just remember that collaboration runs through me,' he announced. And another time: 'My intention is to clot the curds.' It was a tyranny that outstripped even Lionel's. The veneer was on the shabby side, but there was a stubborn complacency beneath. Matt, who had his own ideas and liked to cavil, was disinclined to argue with Silkowitz. The director would stop him mid-sentence to murmur against a wall with one of those coming and going unknowns: it was a discussion of the set, or some question about the lighting; or there would be a cassette to listen to. The house was already booked, Silkowitz reported – a two-hundred-and-ninety-nine-seater west of Union Square – and he had nailed down a pair of invisible backers, whom he did not name. Silkowitz had a reputation for working fast: what seemed important yesterday no longer mattered today. He scarcely listened when Matt began to tell about the visit to Eli Miller. 'Good, good,' he replied, 'right,' and turned away to look over someone's swatch of cloth. It was as if he had never insisted on the journey to the Home for the Elderly Children of Israel.

At the end of each day's rehearsal, the director sat on the edge of the stage and drew the actors around him in a half-circle and gave them his notes. And then came the daily exhortation: what he wanted from them all, he said, was more passion, more susceptibility. He wanted them to be drinking metaphorical poison; he wanted them to pour out blood and bile and bitter gall.

'Especially you, Matt. You're under-playing again. Forget that less-is-more business, it's crap! More energy! We've got to hear the thunder-clap.'

Matt's throat hurt. He was teaching himself to howl. He had abandoned all his customary techniques: his vocal cords seemed perplexed by these new uses. He felt his chest fill with a curious darkness. In the morning, before taking the subway down to rehearsal, he tramped through the blackening snow to the public library and found a warm spot near a radiator and fell into *King Lear*, the original. He saw how those selfish women were stripping the old guy to the bone – no wonder he howls!

He was heading back to the subway when it occurred to him that it was weeks since he had stepped into the shoe-repair shop.

Salvatore did not know him.

'Hey, Salvatore!' Matt called in that stagy roar Silkowitz liked, and attempted an abbreviated version of his little comic jig. But in his clumsy buckled-up snow boots he could only stamp.

Salvatore said over the noise of his machines, 'You got shoes to fix, Mister?'

'What's the matter with *you*?' Matt said.

'*Il attore!*'

The trouble was the beard, the shoemaker said. Who could see it was his friend Matteo? What was the beard *for*? Had he gone into opera after all? With the beard he looked one hundred years old. This frightened Matt. Just as Silkowitz had predicted, Matt's whiskers had grown in stark white: he was passing for an old-timer in earnest.

And it was true: in a way he *had* gone into opera. Marlene Miller-Weinstock's primal voices still reverberated, even with Silkowitz's changes. His changes were logistical: he had moved the locale, updated the era, and accommodated the names of the characters to contemporary ears. Marlene Miller-Weinstock's play was a kind of thirties costume drama, and Silkowitz had modernized it. That was all. The speeches were largely unaltered. Grandiloquence! There were no insinuations or intimations, none of those shrewd hesitations that Matt loved to linger over. His gods were ellipsis and inference. Hers were bombast and excitation. Matt's particular skill was in filling in the silent spaces: he did it with his whole elastic face, and in the stance of his legs – a sceptical tilt of knee, an ironical angle of heel. But Marlene Miller-Weinstock's arias left no room for any play of suggestion or uncertainty. Fury ruled; fury and conviction and a relentless and fiery truth. It came to Matt that fury *was* truth; it amazed him that this could be so. His actor's credo had always been the opposite: glimmer and inkling are truth, hint and intuition are truth; nuance is essence. What Marlene Miller-Weinstock was after was malevolence, rage, even madness: vehemence straight out; shrieks blasted from the whirlwind's bowel. She was all storm. In the gale's wild din – inside all that howling – Matt was learning how to hear the steady blows of some interior cannon. The booms were loud and regular: it was his own heartbeat.

Those two women with him on that dusty little ill-lit stage – he felt apart from them, he saw them as moving shadows of himself. He felt apart from the men, one of whom he had worked with before, under Lionel's direction. And in the darkened margins of the place, on folding chairs along the wall, here was the boy with his notebook, and Silkowitz next to him, faintly panting, kicking his foot up and down as if marching to an unheard band. But Matt had pushed through a vestibule of embarrassment (it was shame over being made to howl) into some solitary chamber, carpeted and tapestried; it was as if he had broken through a membrane, a lung, behind which a sudden altar crouched, covered with Eli Miller's heavy tasselled bedspread. In this chamber Matt listened to his heartbeat. He understood that it wasn't Silkowitz who had led him here. Silkowitz was a literalist, a sentimentalist, a theorist – one of these, or all. Mainly he was flashy. Silkowitz's bets were on the future. He had nothing to do with this voluptuous clamour, Matt inside the gonging of his own rib cage, alone and very large; terrifyingly huge there on that dusty ill-lit stage. Marlene Miller-Weinstock had drawn him in. Or her father had. Inside his howl, Matt was beginning to believe the father's accusation: the daughter had taken hold of the father in order to copy his soul.

Silkowitz was pleased. 'You've got it together,' he told Matt. 'Stick with Matt,' he said to the others. He praised Matt for being everywhere at once, like a rushing ghost; for looking into the women's eyes with a powerful intimacy beyond naturalism; for what he called 'symbolic stature' and 'integration into the scene'. All this puzzled Matt. He hated the lingo. It wasn't what he was feeling, it wasn't what he was doing. He had no consciousness of being part of a company. He wasn't serving the company, whatever Silkowitz might think. He was in pursuit of his grand howl. He wanted to go on living inside it. When rehearsals were over he kept to himself and hurried to the subway.

Ten days before the opening, Silkowitz moved the cast to the theatre. It was a converted movie house; the stage was undersized but workable. To get to the men's dressing room you had to go through a narrow airless tunnel with great rusted pipes sweating overhead. The place was active, swarming. The boy with the notebook kept on checking his lists and schedules; he seemed professional enough. Wires crisscrossed the floor. Taped music travelled in phantom waves between scenes. Big wooden shapes materialized, pushed back and forth along the apron. Silkowitz had a hand in everything, running from corner to corner, his long girlish hair rippling, the silver thumb ring reddening in the light of the 'Exit' sign whenever he glided past it

Frances had decided to attend these final days of rehearsal. Silkowitz made no objection. She came hauling a tote bag, and settled into the next-to-last row, laying out her dictionaries and references and pencils on the seats around her. She worked quietly, but Matt knew she was attentive and worried. He was indifferent to her inspections and judgments; he was concentrating on his howl. She mocked it as rant, but it didn't trouble her that Matt had departed from his usual style – he was doing his job, he was giving the director what he wanted. What it meant was a paycheque. And by now Matt couldn't claim, either, that Silkowitz was egging him on. The director was taking in whatever Matt was emitting. He was emitting a sea of lamentation. Frances dumped her papers back into the tote and listened. Matt was standing downstage, alone, in profile, leaning forward like a sail in a wind, or like the last leaf of a wintry tree. He looked wintry himself. It was the day's concluding run-through; the rest of the cast had left. Matt was doing his solo scene near the end of the second act. His big belly had mostly sunk. Lately he had no appetite. He was never hungry. His beard had lengthened raggedly; a brownish-yellowish tinge showed at the tips. He seemed mesmerized, suffering. He was staring ahead, into the dark of the wings.

He turned to Silkowitz. 'Someone's out there,' he said.

'There shouldn't be,' Silkowitz said. 'Lily's kid's sick, she went home. And anyhow her cue brings her in the other way. Is that electrician still working back there?' he called to the boy with the notebook.

'Everyone's gone,' the boy called back.

Matt said hoarsely, 'I thought I saw someone.' He had let his hair grow down to meet the beard. His eyes were birdlike, ringed with creases.

'OK, call it a day. You're not the only one who's dead tired,' Silkowitz said. 'Go get some sleep.'

On the way to the subway, Frances beside him, Matt brooded. 'There was a guy out there. He was coming from the men's toilet, I saw him.'

'It's the neighbourhood. Some creep wandered in.'

'He was there yesterday, too. In the middle of that same speech. I think someone's hiding out.'

'Where? In the men's toilet?'

'Ever since we got to the theatre. I saw him the first day.'

'You never said anything.'

'I wasn't sure he was there.'

He was sorry he had spoken at all. It was not something he wanted to discuss with Frances. She had ridiculed his howl; she told him it was rant, he was only ranting. The ignorance, the obtuseness! He was seized, dissolved, metamorphosed. His howl had altered him: the throat widens and becomes a highway for spectres, the lungs an echo chamber for apparitions. His howl had floated him far above Frances, far above Silkowitz. Silkowitz and Lionel, what did it matter? They were the same, interchangeable, tummlers and barkers, different styles, what did it matter? Silkowitz was attracted to boldness and colour, voices as noisy as an old music hall; he was as helpless as Frances to uncover what lay in the cave of the howl. As for the actors, Matt saw them as automatons; he was alone, alone. Except for the man who was hiding out, lurking, gazing.

'My God, Matt,' Frances exploded, 'you're hallucinating all over the place. It's enough you've started to *look* the part, you don't have to go crazy on top of it. Don't expect me there again, I'm keeping away, I've got my deadlines anyhow.'

That night her grids sprouted 'urus', 'muleta', 'athanor', 'nystagmic', 'mugient'. She worked into the dawn and kept her head down. Occasionally she stopped to polish her lenses. Matt knew her to be inexorably logical.

The day before dress rehearsal, Matt brought his shoes in for a shine. Salvatore seemed wary. Matteo, he said, no longer looked one hundred years old; he looked two hundred.

'You know,' Matt said carefully – he had to whisper now to preserve his howl – 'there's something better than opera.'

Salvatore said there was nothing better than opera. What could be better than opera? For the first time he let Matt pay for his shine.

Dress rehearsal went well, though a little too speedily. The man in the wings had not returned. Silkowitz sat with the cast and gave his last notes. He did not address Matt. Odours of coffee and pastries wafted, and with unexpected lust Matt devoured a bagel spread with cream cheese. He understood himself to be in possession of a deep tranquillity. All around him there was nervous buffoonery, witticisms, unaccountable silliness; it was fruition, it was anticipation. The director joined in, told jokes, teased, traded anecdotes and rumours. A journalist, a red-haired woman from the *Times*, arrived to interview Silkowitz. He had hired an industrious publicist; there had been many such journalists. This one had just come from speaking to Lionel, she said, to cover the story from another angle: how, for instance, a more traditional director might view the goings-on down near Union Square. Lionel had responded coolly: he was a minimalist; he repudiated what he took to be Teddy Silkowitz's gaudy post-modern experimentalism. Would he show up at the opening? No, he thought not.

'He'll be here,' Silkowitz told the interviewer. The little party was breaking up. 'And don't I know what's bugging him. He used to do this sort of thing himself. He was a child actor at the old Grand Theatre downtown.'

'Oh, come on. Lionel's an Anglophile.'

'I read up on it,' Silkowitz assured her. 'In 1933 he played the boy Shloymele in *Mirele Efros*. God forbid anybody should find out.'

The cast, packing up to go home, laughed; wasn't this one of Silkowitz's show-biz gags? But Matt was still contemplating the man in the wings. He had worked himself up to unhealthy visions. It was likely that Frances was right; at least she was sensible. Someone had sneaked in from the street. A homeless fellow sniffing out a warm corner to spend the night. A drunk in need of a toilet. Or else a stagehand pilfering cigarettes on the sly. A banner, a rope, an anything, swaying in the narrow wind that blew through a crack in the rafters. Backstage – deserted at the end of a day, inhabited by the crawling dark.

On the other hand, he knew who it was; he knew. It was the old guy. It was Eli Miller, come down on the M-4 bus from his velvet-curtained bed in the Home for the Elderly Children of Israel.

Lionel would keep his word. He would stay away. Matt had his own thoughts about this, on a different track from Silkowitz's. Matt as Lear! Or a kind of Lear. Lionel had never given Matt the lead in anything; he was eating crow. Naturally he wouldn't put in an appearance. Thanks to Marlene Miller-Weinstock – swallowing her father's life, vomiting out a semblance of Lear – it was a case of Matt's having the last laugh.

In the clouded dressing-room mirror, preparing during intermission for the second act, he thickened his eyebrows with paint and white gum and spilled too much powder all over his beard – the excesses and accidents of opening night. He stepped out of his newly polished shoes to stand on bare feet and then pulled on his costume: a tattered monkish robe. Sackcloth. A tremor shook his lip. He examined the figure in the mirror. It was himself, his own horrifying head. He resembled what he remembered of Job – diseased, cut down, humiliated. The shoemaker if he could see him would add another hundred years.

The first act had survived the risks. Silkowitz had all along worried that the audience, rocked by the unfamiliar theatricality – the loudness, the broadness, the brazenness, the bigness – would presume something farcical. He was in fear of the first lone laugh. A shock in the serpent's tail pulses through to its tongue. An audience is a single beast, a great vibrating integer, a shifting amoeba without a nucleus. One snicker anywhere in its body can set off convulsions everywhere, from the orchestra to the balcony. Such were the director's sermons, recounting the perils ahead; Matt habitually shut out these platitudes. And more from that cornucopia – think of yourselves, Silkowitz lectured them all, as ancient Greek players on stilts, heavily, boldly masked; the old plays of Athens and the old plays of Second Avenue are blood cousins, kin to kin. Power and passion! Passion and power!

Were they pulling it off? During the whole first act, a breathing silence.

Sweating, panting his minor pant, Silkowitz came into the dressing room. Matt turned his back. A transgression. An invasion. Where now was that sacred stricture about the inviolability of an actor's concentration in the middle of a performance, didn't that fool Silkowitz know better? A rip in the brain. Matt was getting ready to lock it up – his brain; he was goading it into isolation, into that secret chamber, all tapestried and tasselled. He was getting ready to enter his howl, and here was Silkowitz, sweating, panting, superfluous, what was he doing here, the fool?

'Your wife said to give you this.' Silkowitz handed Matt a folded paper. He recognized it as a sheet from the little spiral pad Frances always carried in her pocketbook. It was her word-collector.

'Not now. I don't want this now.' The fool!

'She insisted,' Silkowitz said, and slid away. He looked afraid; for the first time he looked respectful. Matt felt his own force; his howl was already in his throat. What was Frances up to? Transgression, invasion!

He read: 'metamerism', 'oribi', 'glyptic', 'enatic' – all in Frances's compact, orderly fountain-pen print. But an inch below, in rapid pencil: *Be advised I saw him. He's here.*

She had chosen her seat herself, in the next-to-last row, an aerie from which to spot the reviewers and eavesdrop on the murmurs, the sighs, the whispers. She meant to spy, to search out who was and wasn't there.

Aha: then Lionel was there. He was in the audience. He had turned up after all – out of rivalry. Out of jealousy. Because of the buzz. To get the lay of Silkowitz's land. An old director looking in on a young one: age, fear, displacement. They were saying Lionel was past it; they were saying little Teddy Silkowitz, working on a shoestring out of a dinky cell over a sex shop, was cutting-edge. So Lionel was out there, Lionel who made Matt audition, who humiliated him, who stuck him with the geezer role, a bit part in the last scene of a half-baked London import.

As flies to wanton boys are we to the gods; they kill us for their sport.

Unaccommodated man is no more but such a poor, bare, fork'd animal as thou art.

Lear on the heath – now let Lionel learn what a geezer role could be, and Matt in it!

Lionel wasn't out there. He would not come for Silkowitz; he would not come for Matt. Matt understood this. It was someone else Frances had seen.

He made his second-act entrance. The set was abstract, filled with those cloth-wrapped wooden free forms that signified the city. Silkowitz had brought the heath to upper Broadway. But no one laughed, no one coughed. It was Lear all the same, daughter-betrayed, in a storm, half mad, sported with by the gods, a poor, bare, forked animal, homeless, shoeless, crying in the gutters of a city street on a snowy night. The fake snow drifted down. Matt's throat let out its unholy howl; it spewed out old forgotten exiles, old lost cities, Constantinople, Alexandria, kingdoms abandoned, refugees ragged and driven, distant ash heaps, daughters unborn, Frances's wasted eggs and empty uterus, the wild, roaring cannon of a human heartbeat.

A noise in the audience. Confusion; another noise. Matt moved downstage, blinded, and tried to peer through the lights. A black silhouette was thudding up the middle aisle, shrieking. Three stairs led upwards to the apron; up thudded the silhouette. It was Eli Miller in a threadbare cape, waving a walking stick.

'This is not the way! This is not the way!' Eli Miller yelled, and slammed his stick down again and again on the floor of the stage. 'Liars, thieves, corruption! In the mother tongue, with sincerity, not from such a charlatan like this!' He thudded towards Matt; his breath was close. It smelled of farina. Matt saw the one blue eye, the one dead eye.

'Jacob Adler, *he* could show you! Not like this! Take Eli Miller's word for it, this is not the way! You weren't there, you didn't see, you didn't hear!' With his old butcher's arm he raised his stick. 'People,' he called, 'listen to Eli Miller, they're leading you by the nose here, it's charlatanism! Pollution! Nobody remembers! Ladies and gentlemen, my daughter, she wasn't born yet, mediocre! Eli Miller is telling you, this is not the way!'

Back he came to Matt. 'You, you call yourself an actor? You with the rotten voice? Jacob Adler, this was a thunder, a rotten voice is not a thunder! Maurice Schwartz, the Yiddish Art Theatre, right around the corner it used to be, there they did everything beautiful, Gordin, even Herzl once, Hirschbein, Leivick, Ibsen, Molière. Lear! And whoever was there, whoever saw Jacob Adler's Lear, what they saw was not of this earth!'

In a tide of laughter the audience stood up and clapped – a volcano of applause. The laughter surged. Silkowitz ran up on the stage and hauled the old man off, his cape dithering behind him, his stick in the air, crying Lear, Lear. Matt was still loitering there in his bare feet, watching the wavering cape and the bobbing stick, when the curtain fell and hid him in the dark. Many in the audience, Frances informed him later, laughed until they wept.

What Happened to the Baby?

When I was a child, I was often taken to meetings of my Uncle Simon's society, the League for a Unified Humanity. These meetings, my mother admitted, were not suitable for a ten-year-old, but what was she to do with me? I could not be left alone at night, and my father, who was a detail man for a pharmaceutical company, was often away from home. He had recently been assigned to the south-west: we would not see him for weeks at a time. To our ears, places like Arizona and New Mexico might as well have been far-off planets. Yet Uncle Simon, my mother told me proudly, had been to even stranger regions. Sometimes a neighbour would be called in to look after me while my mother went off alone to one of Uncle Simon's meetings. It was important to go, she explained, if only to supply another body. The hall was likely to be half empty. Like all geniuses, Uncle Simon was— 'so far', she emphasized – unappreciated.

Uncle Simon was not really my uncle. He was my mother's first cousin, but out of respect, and because he belonged to an older generation, I was made to call him uncle. My mother revered him. 'Uncle Simon,' she said, 'is the smartest man you'll ever know.' He was an inventor, though not of mundane things like machines, and it was he who had founded the League for a Unified Humanity. What Uncle Simon had invented, and was apparently still inventing, since it was by nature an infinite task, was a wholly new language, one that could be spoken and understood by everyone alive. He had named it GNU, after the African deer that sports two curved horns, each one turned towards the other, as if striving to close a circle. He had travelled all over the world, picking up roots and discarding the less-common vowels. He had gone to Turkey and China and many countries in South America, where he interviewed Indians and wrote down, in his cryptic home-made notation, the sounds they spoke. In Africa, in a tiny Xhosa village nestled in the wild, he was inspired by observing an actual yellow-horned gnu. And still, with all this elevated foreign experience, he lived, just as we did, in a six-storey walk-up in the East Bronx, in a neighbourhood of small stores, many of them vacant. In the autumn the windows of one of these stores would all at once be shrouded in dense curtains. Gypsies had come to settle in for the winter. My mother said it was the times that had emptied the stores. My father said it was the Depression. I understood it was the Depression that made him work for a firm cruel enough to send him away from my mother and me.

Unlike my mother, my father did not admire Uncle Simon. 'That panhandler,' he said. 'God only knows where he finds these suckers to put the touch on.'

'They're cultured Park Avenue people,' my mother protested. 'They've always felt it a privilege to fund Simon's expeditions.'

'Simon's expeditions! If you ask me, in the last fifteen years he's never gotten any farther than down the street to the public library to poke his nose in the *National Geographic*.'

'Nobody's asking, and since when are you so interested? Anyhow,' my mother said, 'it's not Simon who runs after the money, it's *her*.'

'Her', I knew, was Uncle Simon's wife, Essie. I was not required to call her aunt.

'She dresses up to beat the band and flatters their heads off,' my mother went on. 'Well, someone's got to beg, and Simon's not the one for that sort of thing. Who's going to pay for the hall? Not to mention his research.'

'Research,' my father mocked. 'What're you calling research? Collecting old noises in order to scramble them into new noises. Why doesn't he go out and get a regular job? A piece of work, those two – zealots! No, I've got that wrong, he's the zealot, and she's the fawning ignoramus. Those idiot jingles! Not another penny, Lily, I'm warning you, you're not one of those Park Avenue suckers with money to burn.'

'It's only for the annual dues—'

'The League for Scrambling Noises. Ten bucks down the sewer.' He put on his brown felt fedora, patted his vest pocket to check for his train ticket, and left us.

'Look how he goes away angry,' my mother said, 'and all in front of a child. Vivian dear, you have to understand. Uncle Simon is ahead of his time, and not everyone can recognize that. Daddy doesn't now, but some day he surely will. In the meantime, if we don't want him to come home angry, let's not tell that we've been to a meeting.'

Uncle Simon's meetings always began the same way, with Uncle Simon proposing a newly minted syllable, explaining its derivation from two or three alien roots, and the membership calling out their opinions. Mostly these were contentious, and there were loud arguments over whether it was possible for the syllable in question to serve as a verb without a different syllable attached to its tail. Even my mother looked bored during these sessions. She took off her wool gloves and then pulled them on again. The hall was unheated, and my feet in their galoshes were growing numb. All around us a storm of furious fingers holding lit cigarettes stirred up haloes of pale smoke, and it seemed to me that these irritable shouting men (they were mostly men) detested Uncle Simon almost as much as my father did. How could Uncle Simon be ahead of his time if even his own League people quarrelled with him?

My mother whispered, 'You don't have to be upset, dear, it's really all right. It's just their enthusiasm. It's what they have to do to decide, the way scientists do experiments, try and try again. We're sitting right in the middle of Uncle Simon's laboratory. You'll see, in the end they'll all agree.'

It struck me that they would never all agree, but after a while the yelling ebbed to a kind of low communal grumbling, the smoke darkened, and the next part of the meeting, the part I liked best (or disliked least) commenced. At the front of the hall, at the side, was a little platform, broad enough to accommodate one person. Two steps led up to it, and Uncle Simon's wife mounted them and positioned herself. 'The opera star,' my mother said into my ear. Essie was all in yellow silk, with a yellow silk rose at her collarbone, and a yellow silk rose in her greying hair. She had sewn this dress herself, from a tissue-paper pattern bought at Kresge's. She was a short plump flat-nosed woman who sighed often; her blackly gleaming pumps with their thin pedestals made her look, I thought, like Minnie Mouse. Her speaking voice too was mouselike, too soft to carry well, and there was no microphone.

'"Sunshine Beams,"' she announced. 'I will first deliver my poem in English, and then I will render it in the lovely idiom of GNU, the future language of all mankind, as translated by Mr Simon Greenfeld.'

It was immediately plain that Essie had designed her gown to reflect her recitation:

> *Sunshine Beams*
> *If in your most radiant dreams*
> *You see the yellow of sunshine beams,*
> *Then know, O Human Race all,*
> *That you have heard the call*
> *Of Humanity Unified.*
> *So see me wear yellow with pride!*
> *For it means that the horns of the gnu are meeting at last,*
> *and the Realm of Unity has come to pass!*

'Yellow horn, yellow horn, each one towards his fellow horn' was the refrain, repeated twice.

'The opera star and the poetess,' my mother muttered. But then something eerie happened: Essie began to sing, and the words, which even I could tell were silly, were transmuted into reedlike streams of unearthly sounds. I felt shivery all over, and not from the cold. I was not unused to the hubbub of foreign languages: a Greek-speaking family lived across the street, the greengrocer on the corner was Lebanese, and our own building vibrated with Neapolitan and Yiddish exuberances. Yet what we were hearing now was something altogether alien. It had no affinity with anything recognizable. It might just as well have issued from the mouths of mermaids at the bottom of the sea.

'Well?' my mother said. 'How beautiful, didn't I tell you? Even when it comes out of *her*.'

The song ended in a pastel sheen, like the slow decline of a sunset.

Uncle Simon held up his hand against the applause. His voice was hoarse and high-pitched and ready for battle. 'For our next meeting,' he said, 'the programme will feature a GNU rendition, by yours truly, of Shelley's "To A Skylark", to be set to music by our own songbird, Esther Rhoda Greenfeld, so please everyone be sure to mark the date . . .'

But the hall was in commotion. A rocking boom was all at once erupting from the mostly empty rear rows, drowning Uncle Simon out. Three men and two women were standing on their chairs and stamping their feet, drumming faster and faster. This was, I knew, no more unexpected than Essie's singing and Uncle Simon's proclamations. It burst out at the close of nearly every meeting, and Uncle Simon revelled in the clamour. These were his enemies and rivals; but no, he had no rivals, my mother informed me afterwards, and he took it as a compliment that those invaders, those savages, turned up at all, and that they waited until after Essie had finished. They waited in order to ridicule her, but what was their ridicule if not envy? They were shrieking out some foolish babble, speaking in tongues, pretending a parody of GNU, and when they went off into their customary chanting, wasn't that the truest sign of their defeat, of their envy?

'ZA-men-hof! ZA-men-hof!' Uncle Simon's enemies were howling. They jumped off their seats and ran down the aisle towards the podium, bawling right into Uncle Simon's reddening face.

'Esper-ANto! Esper-ANto! ZA-men-hof!'

'We'd better leave,' my mother said, 'before things get rough.' She hurried me out of the hall without stopping to say goodnight to Uncle Simon. I saw that this would have been impossible anyhow. He had his fists up, and I wondered if his enemies were going to knock him down. He was a small man, and his near-sighted eyes were small and frail behind their fat lenses. Only his ridged black hair looked robust, scalloped like the sand when the tide has run out.

Though I had witnessed this scene many times in my childhood, it was years before I truly fathomed its meaning. By then my father had, according to my mother, 'gone native': he had fallen in love with the south-west and was bringing back hand-woven baskets from New Mexico for my mother's rubber plants, and toy donkeys made of layers of coloured crêpe paper for me. I was in my late teens when he persuaded my mother to move to Arizona. 'Ludicrous,' she complained. 'I'll be a fish out of water out there. I'll be cut off from everything.' She worried especially about what would happen to Uncle Simon, who was now living alone downtown, in a room with an icebox and a two-burner stove hidden behind a curtain. That Essie! A divorce! It was a scandal, and all of it Essie's doing: no one in our family had ever before succumbed to such shame. She had accused Uncle Simon of philandering.

'What a viper that woman is,' my mother said. 'And all on top of what she did to the baby.' She was filling a big steamer trunk with linens and quilts. The pair of creases between her eyebrows tightened. 'God knows how those people out there think. As far as they're concerned, I could just as well be a greenhorn right off the boat. I'd rather die than live in such a place, but Daddy says he's up for a raise if he sticks to the territory.'

I had heard about the baby nearly all my life. Uncle Simon and Essie had not always been childless. Their little girl, eleven months old and already walking, had died before I was born. Her name was Henrietta. They had gone to South America on one of Uncle Simon's expeditions – in those days Essie went everywhere with him. 'She never used to let him out of her sight,' my mother recounted. 'She was always jealous. Suspicious. She expected Simon to be no better than she was, that's the truth. You know she was already pregnant at the wedding, so she was grateful to him for marrying her. As well she should be, considering that who knows whose baby it was, maybe Simon's, maybe not. If you ask me, not. She'd had a boyfriend who had hair just like Simon's, black and wiry. The baby had a headful of black curls. The poor little thing caught one of those diseases they have down there, in Peru or Bolivia, one of those places. Leave it to Essie, would any normal mother drag a baby through a tropical swamp?'

'A swamp?' I asked. 'The last time you told about the baby it was a desert.'

'Desert or swamp, what's the difference? It was something you don't come down with in the Bronx. The point is Essie killed that child.'

I was happy that the move to the south-west did not include me. I had agitated to attend college locally, chiefly to escape Arizona. My father had paid for a year's tuition at NYU, and also for half the rent of a walk-up on Avenue A that I shared with another freshman, Annette Sorenson. The toilet was primitive – it had an old-fashioned pull chain and a crack in the overhead tank that leaked brown sludge. The bathtub was scored with reddish stains that could not be scrubbed away, though Annette went at it with steel wool and bleach. She cried nearly every night, not from homesickness but from exasperation. She had come from Briar Basin to NYU, she confided, because it was located in Greenwich Village. ('Briar Basin, Minnesota,' she said; she didn't expect me to know that.) She was on the lookout for bohemia, and had most of Edna St Vincent Millay's verse by heart. She claimed she had discovered exactly which classroom Thomas Wolfe had once taught in. She explored the nearby bars, but legend eluded her. Her yearnings were commonplace in that neighbourhood: she wanted to act some day, and in the meantime she intended to inhale the atmosphere. She was blonde and large all over. Her shoulder blades were a foot and a half apart and her wrist-bones jutted like crab apples. I thought of her as a kind of Valkyrie. She boasted, operatically, that she wasn't a virgin.

I took Annette with me to visit Simon. I had long ago dropped the 'Uncle'; I was too old for that. My mother's letters were reminding me not to neglect him. A twenty-dollar bill was sometimes enclosed, meant for delivery to Simon. I knew my father believed the money was for me; now and then he would add an admonitory line. Essie was still living in the old apartment in the Bronx, supporting herself well enough. She had a job in a men's clothing store and sat all day in a back room doing alterations, letting out seams and shortening sleeves. I suspected that Simon was on the dole. It seemed unlikely, after all this time, that he was still being shored up by his Park Avenue idealists.

'Is your uncle some sort of writer?' Annette asked as we climbed the stairs. The wooden steps creaked tunefully; the ancient layers of paint on the banisters were thickly wrinkled. I had told her that Simon was crazy about words. 'I mean really crazy,' I said.

Simon was sitting at a bridge table lit by a goose-neck lamp. A tower of dictionaries was at his left. A piece of questionable-looking cheese lay in a saucer on his right. In between was a bottle of ink. He was filling his fountain pen.

'My mother sends her love,' I said, and handed Simon an envelope with the twenty-dollar bill folded into a page torn from my Modern History text. Except for a photograph of a zeppelin, it was blank. My father's warning about how not to be robbed in broad daylight was always to keep your cash well swaddled. 'Otherwise those Village freaks down there will sure as shooting nab it,' he wrote at the bottom of my mother's letter. But I had wrapped the money mostly to postpone Simon's humiliation: maybe, if only for a moment, he would think I was once again bringing him one of my mother's snapshots of cactus and dunes. She had lately acquired a box camera; in order not to be taken for a greenhorn, she was behaving like a tourist. At that time I had not yet recognized that an occasional donation might not humiliate Simon.

He screwed the cap back on the ink bottle and looked Annette over. 'Who's this?'

'My room-mate. Annette Sorenson.'

'A great big girl, how about that. Viking stock. You may be interested to know that I've included a certain uncommon Scandinavian diphthong in my work. Zamenhof didn't dare. He looked the other way. He didn't have the nerve.' Behind his glasses Simon was grinning. 'Any friend of my niece Vivian I intend to like. But never an Esperantist. You're not an Esperantist, are you?'

This, or something like it, was his usual opening. I had by now determined that Essie was right: Simon was a flirt, and something more. He went for the girls. Once he even went for me: he put out a hand and cupped my breast. Then he thought better of it. He had, after all, known me from childhood; he desisted. Or else, since it was January, and anyhow I was wearing a heavy wool overcoat, there wasn't much of interest worth cupping. For my part, I ignored it. I was eighteen, with eyes in my head, beginning to know a thing or two. I had what you might call an insight. Simon coveted more than the advancement of GNU.

On my mother's instructions I opened his icebox. A rancid smell rushed out. There was a shapeless object green at the edges – the other half of the cheese in his saucer. The milk was sour, so I poured it down the toilet. Simon was all the while busy with his spiel, lecturing Annette on the evil history of Esperanto and its ignominious creator and champion, Dr Ludwig Zamenhof of Bialystok, Poland.

'There they spoke four languages, imagine that! Four lousy languages! And this is what inspires him? Four languages? Did he ever go beyond European roots? Never! The man lived inside a puddle and never stepped out of it. Circumscribed! Small! Narrow!'

'I'll be right back,' I called out from the doorway, and went down to the grocery on the corner to replenish Simon's meagre larder. I had heard this grandiose history too many times: how Simon alone had ventured into the genuinely universal, how he had roamed far beyond Zamenhof's paltry horizons into the vast tides of human speech, drawing from these a true synthesis, a compact common language unsurpassed in harmony and strength. Yet tragically eclipsed – eclipsed by Zamenhof's disciples, those deluded believers, those adorers of a false messiah! An eye doctor, that charlatan, and look how he blinds all his followers: Germanic roots, Romance roots, and then he stops, as if there's no India, no China, no Russia, no Arabia! No Aleutian islanders! Why didn't the fellow just stick to the polyglot Yiddish he was born into and let it go at that? Did he ever set foot twenty miles past Warsaw? No! Then why didn't he stick to Polish? An eye doctor who couldn't see past his own nose. *Hamlet* in Esperanto, did you ever hear of such chutzpah?

And so on: Esperanto, a fake, a sham, an injustice!

As I was coming up the stairs, carrying bread and milk and eggs in the straw-handled Indian bag my mother had sent as a present for Simon, I heard Annette say, 'But I never knew Esperanto even *existed*,' and I saw that Simon had Annette's hand in his. He was circling her little finger with a coarse thumb that curved backwards like a twisted spoon. She didn't seem to mind.

'You shouldn't call him crazy,' she protested. 'He's only disappointed.' By then we were already in the street. She looked up at Simon's fourth-floor window. It flashed back at her like a signal: it had caught the late sun. I noticed that she was holding a white square of paper with writing on it.

'What's that?'

'A word he gave me. A brand-new word that no one's ever used before. He wants me to learn it.'

'Oh my God,' I said.

'It means "enchanting maiden", isn't that something?'

'Not if maiden's supposed to be the same as virgin.'

'Cut it out, Vivian, just stop it. He thinks I can help.'

'You? How?'

'I could recruit. He says I could get young people interested.'

'I'm young people,' I said. 'I've never been interested, and I've had to listen to Simon's stuff all my life. He bores me silly.'

'Well, he told me you take after your father, whatever that means. A prophet is without honour in his own family, that's what he said.'

'Simon isn't a prophet, he's a crank.'

'I don't care what he is. You don't get to meet someone like that in Minnesota. And he even wears sandals!'

It seemed she had found her bohemian at last. The sandals were another of my mother's presents. Like the photos of the cactus and the dunes, they were intended as souvenirs of distant Arizona.

After that, though Annette and I ate and slept within inches of each other, an abyss opened between us. There had never been the chance of a friendship. I was serious and diligent, she was not. I attended every class. Annette skipped most of hers. She could spurt instant tears. I was resolutely dry-hearted. Besides, I had my suspicions of people who liked to show off and imagined they could turn into Katharine Cornell, the famous actress. Annette spoke of 'thespians' and 'theatre folk', and began parading in green lipstick and black stockings. But even this wore off after a time. She was starting to take her meals away from our flat. She kept a secret notebook with a mottled cover, bound by a strap connected to a purple sash tied around her waist. I had nothing to say to her, and when in a month or so she told me she had decided to move out ('I need to be with my own crowd,' she explained), I was altogether relieved.

I was also troubled. I was afraid to risk another room-mate: would my father agree to shouldering the full rent? I put this anxiety in a letter to Arizona; the answer came, unexpectedly, from my father, and not, as usual, in a jagged postscript below my mother's big round slanted Palmer-method penmanship. The extra money, he said, wouldn't be a problem. 'Believe it or not,' he wrote, 'your mother thinks she's a rich woman, she's gone into business! There she was, collecting beaded belts and leather dolls, and God only knows what other cheap junk people like to pick up out here, and before I can look around, she's opened up this dinky little gift shop, and she's got these gullible out-of-staters paying good dollars for what costs your mother less than a dime. Trinkets! To tell the truth, I never knew she had this nonsense in her, and neither did she.'

This time it was my mother who supplied the postscript – but I observed it had a later date, and I guessed she had mailed the letter without my father's having seen her addendum. It was a kind of judicial rider: she had put him in the dock. 'I don't know why your dad is so surprised,' she complained in a tone so familiar that I could almost hear her voice in the sprawl of her handwriting. 'I've always had an artistic flair, whether or not it showed, and I don't much appreciate it when your dad puts me down like that, just because he's disillusioned with being stuck out here. He says he's sick and tired of it and misses home, but I don't, and my gallery is already beginning to look like a success, it's all authentic Hopi work! But that's the way your dad is – anywhere there's culture and ambition, he just has to put it down. For years he did it to Simon, and now he's doing it to me. And Vivian dear, speaking of Simon, he ought to be eating his greens. I hope you're remembering to bring him a salad now and then.' A fifty-dollar bill dropped out of the envelope.

That my mother was writing to me without my father's knowledge did not disturb me. It was of a piece with her long-ago attempts to conceal our attendance at Simon's old meetings. But I felt the heat of my guilt: I had neglected Simon, I hadn't looked in on him for . . . I hardly knew how many weeks it might have been. Weeks, surely; two months, three? I resented those visits; I resented the responsibility my mother had cursed me with. Simon was worse than a crank and a bore. He was remote from my youth and my life. I thought of him as a bad smell, like his icebox.

But I obediently chopped up lettuce and cucumber and green peppers, and poured a garlic-and-oil dressing over all of it. Then, with the fifty-dollar bill well wrapped in waxed paper and inserted into a folded piece of cardboard with a rubber band around it, I went to see Simon.

Two flights below the landing that led to his place I could already hear the commotion vibrating out of it: an incomprehensible clamour, shreds of laughter, and a strangely broken wail that only vaguely passed for a chant. The door was open; I looked in. A mob of acolytes was swarming there – no, not swarming after all: in the tiny square of Simon's parlour, with its sofa-bed in one corner and its makeshift pantry, a pair of wooden crates, in the other, there was hardly a clear foot of space to accommodate a swarming. Yet what I saw through a swaying tangle of elbows and legs had all the buzz and teeming of a hive: a squatting, a slouching, a splaying, a leaning, a curling up, a lying down. And in the centre of this fleshy oscillation, gargling forth the syllables of GNU, stood Annette. She stood like a risen tower, solid as bricks. She seemed to be cawing – croaking, crackling, chirring – though in the absence of anything intelligible, how was it possible to tell? Were these the sounds and cadences of the universal tongue? I could not admit surprise: from the start Annette had been so much my unwanted destiny. What else could she be now, having materialized here, in the very bosom of GNU? Or, if she wasn't to be *my* destiny, she intended to be Simon's. She was resurrecting his old meetings – it was plain from the spirit of the thing that this wasn't the first or the last. Anyhow it was flawed. No enemies lurked among these new zealots (they were mostly female), if they were zealots at all.

At that time there were faddists of various persuasions proliferating up and down the Village, anarchists who dutifully went home every night to their mother's kitchens, a Hungarian monarchist with his own following, free-verse poets who eschewed capital letters, cultists who sat rapturously for hours in orgone boxes, cloudy Swedenborgians, and all the rest. These crazes never tempted me; my early exposure to Simon's fanatics had been vaccination enough. As for where Annette had fetched this current crew, I supposed they were picked up from the looser margins of her erstwhile theatre crowd. There were corroboratory instances, here and there, of black stockings and green lipstick. And no Esperantists. Zamenhof was as alien to these recruits as – well, as GNU had been two months ago. Not one of them would have been willing to knock Simon down.

Annette lifted her face from her mottled notebook. All around her the wriggling knots of torsos turned inert and watchful.

'Oh my God, it's Vivian,' she said. 'What're you doing here? Can't you see we're in the middle of something?'

'I'm just bringing a green salad for my uncle—'

'Little Green Riding Hood, how sweet. She's not his actual *niece*,' Annette explained to the mob. 'She doesn't give a hoot about his work. Hey, Viv, you don't think we'd let a man like that starve? And if you want to know what a real green salad looks like, here's a green salad.' She swooped to the floor and swept up a large straw basket (yet another of my mother's souvenirs) heaped with verdant dollars. 'This week's dues,' she told me.

I surveyed the bodies at my feet, sorting among them. 'Where is he?'

'Simon? Not here. Thursday's his day away, but he gave us the new words last time, so we carry on. We do little dialogues, we're getting the hang of it. We're his pioneers,' she declaimed: Katharine Cornell to the hilt.

'And then it'll spread all over,' a voice called out.

'There, you see?' Annette said. 'Some people understand. Poor Viv's never figured it out. Simon's going against the Bible, he's an atheist.'

'Is that what he tells you?'

'You are *such* a dope,' she spat out. 'The Tower of Babel's why he got to thinking about GNU in the first place, isn't it? So that things would go back to the way they were. The way it was before.'

'Before what? Before they invented lunatic asylums? Look,' I said, 'as far as I'm concerned Simon's not exactly right in the head, so I'm supposed to—' But I broke off shamefacedly. 'I have to watch out for him, he's sort of my responsibility.'

'As far as you're concerned? How far is that? How long's it been since you showed up anyhow?'

Annette, I saw, was shrewder than I could ever hope to be. She was stupid and she was earnest. The stupidity would last, the earnestness might be fleeting, but the combination ignited a volcanic purposefulness: she had succeeded in injecting a bit of living tissue into Simon's desiccated old fossil. She was a first-rate organizer. I wondered how much of that weekly green salad she took away with her. And why not? It was a commission on dues. It was business.

'Where *is* he?' I insisted. I was still holding the bowl of cut vegetables, and all at once discovered a tremor in my hands: from fury, from humiliation.

'He went to visit a family member. That's what he said.'

'A family member? There aren't any around here, there's only me.'

'He goes every Thursday, I guess to see his wife.'

'His ex-wife. He's been divorced for years.'

'Well, *he* didn't want that divorce, did he? He's a man who *likes* being affectionate – maybe not to you. He gives back what he's given, that's why, and believe me he doesn't need you to turn up with your smelly old veggies once in a blue moon.' Behind her the mob was breaking up. It was distracted, it was annoyed, it was impatient, it was uprooted, it was stretching its limbs. It was growling, and not in the universal tongue. 'Just look what you've done,' Annette accused, 'barging in like that. We were doing so beautifully, and now you've broken the spell.'

Circumspectly, I wrote the news to my mother. I had been to Simon's flat, I said, and things were fine. They were boiling away. His old life had nicely recommenced: he had a whole new set of enthusiasts. His work was reaching the next generation; he even had an agent to help him out. I did not tell her that I hadn't in fact *seen* Simon, and I didn't dare hint that he might be courting Essie again: wasn't that what Annette had implied? Nor did I confess that I had unwrapped the fifty-dollar bill and kept it for myself. I had no right to it; it couldn't count as a commission. I had done nothing for Simon. I had failed my mother's charge.

My mother's reply was long in coming. In itself this was odd enough: I had expected an instant happy outcry. With lavish deception I had depicted Simon's triumphant renewal, the future of GNU assured, crowds of mesmerized and scholarly young people streaming to his lectures – several of which, I lied, were held in the Great Hall of Cooper Union, at the very lectern Lincoln himself had once sanctified.

And it was only Annette, it was only the Village revolving on its fickle wheel: soon the mob would be spinning away to the next curiosity.

But my mother was on a wheel of her own. She was whirling on its axle, and Simon was lately at the distant perimeter. Her languorously sweeping Palmer arches were giving way to crabbed speed. She was out of time, she informed me, she had no time, no time at all, it was good to hear that Simon was doing well, after all these years he was finally recovered from that fool Essie, that witch who had always kept him down, but so much was happening, happening so fast, the gallery was flooded with all these tourists crazy for crafts, the place was wild, she was exhausted, she'd had to hire help, and meanwhile, she said, your father decided to retire, it was all to the good, she needed him in the gallery, and yes, he had his little pension, that was all right, never mind that it was beside the point, there was so much stock and it sold so fast that she'd had to buy the building next door to store whatever came in, and what came in went out in a day, and your father, can you imagine, was keeping the books and calling himself Comptroller, she didn't care what he called himself, they were importing like mad, all these kachina dolls from Japan, they certainly *look* like the real thing, the customers don't know the difference anyhow . . .

It seemed she was detaching herself from Simon. The kachinas had freed her. I was not sorry that I had deceived her; hadn't she taught me how to deceive? For my part, I had no desire to look after Simon. He was hokum. He was snake oil. What may have begun as a passion had descended into a con. Simon's utopia was now no more than a Village whim, and Annette its volatile priestess. But what had Essie, sewing out her old eyes in the lint-infested back room of a neighbourhood haberdashery, to do with any of it – on Thursdays or any other day? She had thrown him out, and for reason. I surmised that along with Simon's infidelities she had thrown out her fidelity to GNU. How many strapping young Annettes had he cosseted over the decades?

I did not go back to Simon's place. I did what I could to chuck him out of my thoughts – but there were reminders and impediments. My mother in her galloping prosperity had taken to sending large cheques. The money was no longer for Simon, she assured me; I had satisfied her that he was launched on what, in my telling, was a belated yet flowering career. The money was for me: for tuition and rent and textbooks, of course, but also for new dresses and shoes, for the movies, for treats. With each cheque – they were coming now in scrappy but frequent maternal rushes – Simon poked a finger in my eye. He invaded, he abraded, he gnawed. I began to see that I would never be rid of him. Annette and her mob would drop him. He would fall from her eagle's claws directly into my unwilling hands. And still I would not go back.

Instead I went down into the subway at Astor Place (where, across a broad stretch of intersection, loomed my lie: the venerable red brick of Cooper Union), and headed for the Bronx and Essie. I found her where time had left her, in apartment 2-C on the second floor of the old walk-up. It was not surprising that she did not recognize me. We had last met when I was twelve and a half; emulating my mother, I had been reliably rude.

'You're who?' She peered warily through the peephole. On my side I saw a sad brown eye startled under its drooping hood.

'It's Vivian,' I said. 'Lily and Dan's daughter. From down the block.'

'They left the neighbourhood years ago. I don't know where they went. Ask somebody else.'

'Essie, it's *Vivian*,' I repeated. 'My mother used to take me to hear Uncle Simon.'

She let me in then, and at the same time let out the heavy quick familiar sigh I instantly recognized: as if some internal calipers had pinched her lung. She kept her look on me fixedly yet passively, like someone sitting in a movie house, waiting for the horses on the screen to rear up.

'How about that, Simon's cousin's kid,' she said. 'Your mother never liked me.'

'Oh no, I remember how she admired your singing—'

'She admired Simon. She thought he was the cat's pyjamas. Like every other female he ever got near, the younger the better. I wouldn't put it past him if he had some girlie in his bed right now, wherever he is.'

'But he comes to see you, and he wouldn't if he didn't want to be' – I struggled for the plainest word – 'together. Reconciled, I mean. At his age. Now that he's . . . older.'

'He comes to see me? Simon?' The horses reared up in her eyes. 'Why would he want to do that after all this time?'

I had no answer for this. It was what I had endured an hour or more in the subway to find out. If Simon could be restored to Essie, then – as Annette had pronounced – things would go back to the way they once were. The Tower of Babel had nothing to do with it; it was rather a case of Damocles' sword, Simon's future dangling threateningly over mine. I wanted him back in the Bronx. I wanted him reinstalled in 2-C. I wanted Essie to claim him.

Her rooms had the airless smell of the elderly. They were hugely overfurnished – massive, darkly oiled pieces, china figurines on every surface. A credenza was littered with empty bobbins and crumpled-up tissue paper. An ancient sewing machine with a wrought-iron treadle filled half a wall; the peeling bust of a mannequin was propped against it. In the bedroom a radio was playing; through spasms of static I heard fragments of opera. Though it was a mild Sunday afternoon in early May, all the windows were shut – despite which, squads of flies were licking their feet along the flanks of the sugar bowl. The kitchen table (Essie had led me there) was covered with blue-flowered oilcloth, cracked in places, so that the canvas lining showed through. I waved the flies away. They circled just below the ceiling for an idling minute, then hurled themselves against the panes like black raindrops. The smell was the smell of stale changelessness.

Essie persisted, 'Simon hasn't been here since God knows how long it is. Since the divorce. He never comes.'

'Not on Thursdays?' The question hung in all its foolishness. 'I heard he goes to visit family, so I thought—'

'I'm not Simon's family, not any more. I told you, I haven't seen him in years. Where would you get an idea like that?'

'From . . . his assistant. He has an assistant now. A kind of manager. She sets up his meetings.'

'His manager, his assistant, that's what he calls them. Then he goes out and diddles them. And how come he's still having those so-called meetings? Who's paying the bills?' She coughed out a disordered laugh that was half a viscous sigh. 'Those famous Park Avenue philanthropists?'

The laugh was too big for her body. Her bones had contracted, leaving useless folds of puckered fallen skin. Her hands were horribly veined.

'Listen, girlie,' she said, 'Simon doesn't come, nobody comes. I do a fitting for a neighbour, I sew up a hem, I put in a pocket, that's who comes. A bunch of the old Esperantists used to show up, this was when Simon left, but then it stopped. By now they're probably dead. The whole thing is dead. It's a wonder Simon isn't dead.'

The flies had settled back on the sugar bowl. I stood up to go. Nothing could be clearer: there would be no reconciliation. 2-C would not see Simon again.

But Essie was pulling at my sleeve. 'Don't think I don't know where he goes anyhow. Maybe not Thursdays, who could figure Thursdays, but every week he goes there. He always goes there, it never stops.'

'Where?'

I asked it reluctantly. Was she going to plummet me into a recitation of Simon's history of diddlings? Did she think me an opportune receptacle for an elderly divorcée's sour old grievances?

'Why should I tell you where? What have you got to do with any of it? Simon never told your mother, he never told anyone, so why should I tell *you*? Sit down,' she commanded. 'You want something to drink? I've got Coca-Cola.'

The bottle had been opened long ago. The glass was smudged. I felt myself ensnared by a desolate hospitality. Having got what I came for – or not having got it – I wanted to hear nothing more.

But she had my arm in her grip. 'At my time of life I'm not still squatting down there in the back room of somebody's pants store, you understand? I've got my own little business, I do my fittings right here in my own dining room. The point is I'm someone who can make a living. I could always make a living. My God, your mother was gullible! What wouldn't she believe, she swallowed it all.'

My mother gullible? She who was at that very hour gulling her tourists into buying Pueblo artefacts factory-made in Japan?

'If you mean she believed in Simon—'

'She believed everything.' She released me then, and sank into a deflecting whisper. 'She believed what happened to the baby.'

So it was not simple grievance that I took from Essie that afternoon. It was broader and deeper and wilder and stranger. And what she was deflecting – what she was repudiating as trivia and trifle, as pettiness and quibble – was Simon and his diddlings. He had his girlies – his assistants, his managers – and for all she cared, staring me down, wasn't I one of them? No, he wouldn't go so far as his cousin's kid, and even if he did, so what? It hardly interested her anyhow that I was his cousin's kid, the offspring of a simple-minded woman, an imbecile who would believe anything, who swallowed it all, a chump for any hocus-pocus . . .

'Lily had her kid,' she said – torpidly, as though reciting an algebraic equation – 'she had *you*, and by then what did I have? An empty crib, and then nothing, nothing, empty—'

When I left Essie four hours later, I knew what had happened to the baby. At Astor Place I ascended, parched and hungry, from the subway's dark into the dark of nine o'clock: she had offered me nothing but that stale inch of Coke. Instead she had talked and talked, loud and low, in her mouselike whisper, too often broken into by her big coarse bitter croak of a laugh. It *was* a joke, she assured me, it was a joke and a trick, and now I would know what a gullible woman my mother was, how easy it was to deceive her; how easy it was to trick the whole world. She clutched at me, she made me her muse, she gave me her life. She made me *see*, and why? Because her child was dead and I was not, or because my mother was a gullible woman, or because there were flies in the room? Who could really tell why? I had fallen in on her out of the blue, out of the ether, out of the past (it wasn't *my* past, I hadn't come to be anyone's muse, I had only come to dispose of Simon): I was as good, for giving out her life, as a fly on the wall. And did I want her to sing? She could still sing some stanzas in GNU, she hadn't forgotten how.

I did not ask her to sing. She had hold of me with her fingernails in my flesh, as if I might escape. She drew me back, back, into her young womanhood, when she was newly married to Simon, with Retta already two months in the womb and Simon in his third year at City College, far uptown, dreaming of philology, that funny-sounding highfalutin stuff (as if a boy from the Bronx could aspire to such goings-on!), unready for marriage and fatherhood, and seriously unwilling. And that was the first of all the jokes, because finally the other boy, the one from Cincinnati who was visiting his aunt (the aunt lived around the corner), and who met Essie in the park every night for a week, went home to Ohio . . . She didn't tell Simon about that other boy, the curly-haired boy who pronounced all his 'r's the midwestern way; even under the wedding canopy Simon had no inkling of the Ohio boy. He believed only that he was behaving as a man should behave who has fathered a child without meaning to. It was the first of all the jokes, the first of all the tricks, but the joke was on herself too, since she was just as much in the dark as anyone: was Retta's papa the Ohio boy, or Simon? Simon had to leave school then, and went to work as a salesman in a men's store on East Tremont Avenue. Essie had introduced him to her boss; she was adept with a needle, and had already been shortening trousers and putting in pleats and letting out waists for half a year.

Their first summer they did what in those days all young couples with new babies did. They fled the burning Bronx sidewalks, they rented a *kochaleyn* in the mountains, in one of those Catskill bungalow colonies populated by musty one-room cottages set side by side, no more than the width of a clothes line between them. Every cottage had its own little stove and icebox and tiny front porch. The mothers and babies spent July and August in the shade of green leaves, among wild tiger lilies as orange as the mountain sunsets, and the fathers came up from the city on weekends, carrying bundles of bread and rolls and oily packets of pastries and smoked whitefish. It was on one of these weekends that Essie decided to tell Simon the joke about the baby, it was so much on her mind, and she thought it would be all right to tell him now because he liked the baby so much, he was mad about Retta, and the truth is the truth, so why not? She had been brought up to tell the truth, even if sometimes the truth is exactly like a joke.

But he did not take it as a joke. He took it as a trick, and for the next two weeks he kept away. Essie, alone with her child and humiliated, went wandering through the countryside, discovering who her neighbours were, and what sort of colony they'd happened into. All the roads were plagued by congregations of wasps, and once the baby, pointing and panting, spied a turtle creeping in the dust. They followed the turtle across the road, and found a community of Trotskyites, beyond which, up the hill, were the Henry George people, and down towards the village a nest of Tolstoyans. Whoever they were, they all had tears in their clothes, they all required mending, they all wanted hand-made baby dresses, they all had an eye on styles for the fall, and Essie's summertime business was under way.

When Simon returned, out of sorts, Essie informed him that in the interim she had taken in fifty-four dollars and twenty-five cents, she could get plenty more if only she had a sewing machine, and besides all that, there was a peculiar surprise that might interest him: next door on one side, next door on the other, and all around, behind them and in front of them – why hadn't she noticed it sooner? but she was preoccupied with the baby, and now with the sewing – their neighbours were chattering in a kind of garble. Sometimes it sounded like German, sometimes like Spanish (it never sounded like Yiddish), and sometimes like only God knows what. Groups of them were gathering on the little porches, which were no more than leaky wooden lean-tos; they seemed to be studying; they were constantly exchanging comments in their weird garble. They even spoke the weird garble to their older children, who rolled their eyes and answered in plain English.

Which was how Simon fell in among the Esperantists. Bella was one of them. She lived four cottages down, and had a little boy a month or two older than Retta. Julius, her husband, turned up only rarely; his job, whatever it was, kept him at work even on weekends. Bella ordered a dimity blouse and a flowered skirt (dirndl was the fashion) and came often to sit with Essie while she diligently sewed. The two babies, with their pull-toys and plush bears, prattled and crowed at their feet. It was a pleasant time altogether, and Simon, when he arrived from the city, seeing the young women sweetly side by side with their children crawling all around them, seemed no longer out of sorts. He was silent now about Essie's deception, if it *was* a deception, because, after all, Essie herself wasn't certain, and the boy from Ohio was by now only a moment's vanished vapour. Besides, Retta's pretty curls were as black and billowy as Simon's own, and Essie was earning money, impressively more than Simon would ever make selling men's underwear in the Bronx. One August afternoon he arranged to have a second-hand sewing machine delivered to the cottage. Essie jumped up and kissed him, she was so pleased; it was as if the sleek metal neck of the sewing machine had restored them to each other.

After that Essie's orders increased, and on Saturday and Sunday mornings, while she worked her treadle, Simon went round to one porch or another, happy in the cenacle of the Esperantists. They were eager for converts, of course, and he wanted nothing so much as to be converted. Of all of them, Bella was the most advanced. She was not exactly their leader, but she was an expert teacher, and actually had in her possession a letter of praise from Lidia Zamenhof, Zamenhof's own daughter and successor. Bella had sent her a sonnet in fluent Esperanto; Lidia replied that Bella's ingenuity in creating rhyming couplets in the new language exceeded even that of Ludwig Zamenhof himself. There was nothing concerning Esperanto that Bella did not know; she knew, for instance, that the Oomoto religion in Japan held Esperanto to be a sacred language and Zamenhof a god. Zamenhof a god! Simon was entranced; Essie thought he envied Bella even more than he was inspired by her. Also, she felt a little ashamed. It was all those outlandish words Simon loved, he was possessed by them, words had always been his *ambition*, and on account of his wife and the child whose hair was as black and thick as his own he had been compelled to surrender words for a life of shirts and ties, boxer shorts and suspenders.

So when Bella asked Essie to take charge of her little boy for just two hours that evening – perhaps he could be put to bed together with Retta, and Bella would come to fetch him afterwards – Essie gladly took the child in her arms, and stroked his warm silky nape, and did the same with Retta, whose nape was every bit as silky, and sang both babies to sleep, while Simon walked with Bella through the grassy dusk to be tutored in the quiet of her porch. An electric cord led indoors; there was a lamp and a table and a bottle of citronella to ward off the mosquitoes and (the point of it all) Bella's weighty collection of Esperanto journals.

It was more than the two hours Bella had promised (it was closer to five, and the crickets had retired into their depth-of-night silence) when she and Simon returned. Simon had under his arm a fat packet of Bella's journals, borrowed to occupy his empty weekday evenings in the city; but it was Bella, not Simon, who explained this. Essie had fallen into a doze in the old stained armchair next to the big bed – Simon and Essie's marital bed – where she had set the babies down, nestled together under one blanket. Retta's crib was too narrow for the two of them; they lay head to head, their round foreheads nearly touching, breathing like a single organism. Bella looked down at her sleeping boy, and murmured that it was a pity to take him out into the cold night air, he was so snug, why wake him, and could she leave him there until morning? She would arrive early to carry him off, and in the meantime wasn't Essie comfortable enough right where she was, in that nice chair, and Simon wouldn't mind a cushion on the floor, would he, it would only be for a few more hours . . .

Bella went away, and it was as if she had plotted to keep Simon from Essie that night. But surely this was a worthless imagining: settling into his cushion at Essie's feet, Simon was fixed with all the power and thirst of his will on Bella's journals; he intended to study them until he could rival Bella, he meant to pursue and conquer the language that was to be humanity's salvation, the structure of it, its strange logic and beauty, and already tonight, he said, he had made a good beginning – and then, without a sign, in the middle of it all, he sent out a soft snore, a velvety vibrating hum. Haplessly alert now, Essie tried not to follow her thoughts. But the night was long, there was so much left of it, and the mountain chill crept round her shoulders, and except for the private voice inside her, a voice that nagged with all its secret confusions, there was nothing to listen to – only one of the babies turning, and Simon's persistent dim hum. She went on listening, she wasn't the least bit drowsy, she forced her eyelids shut and they clicked wide again, of their own accord, like a mechanical doll's. Simon's hum – was it roughening into a wheeze, or something more brutish than a wheeze? A spiralling unnatural noise; an animal being strangled. But the animal noise wasn't coming from Simon, it was hurtling out of one of the babies – a groaning, and then a yowling – good God, was it Retta? No, no, not Retta, it was Bella's boy! She leaped up to see what was the matter: the child's face was mottled, purple and red, his mouth leaked vomit, he was struggling to breathe. . . . She touched his head. It was wildly hot: a tropical touch.

'Simon!'

She pummelled him awake.

'There's something wrong, you have to get down to the village right away, you have to get to the doctor's, the boy's sick—'

'It's the middle of the night, Essie, for God's sake! Bella's coming for the kid first thing, and maybe by then it'll pass—'

'Simon, I'm telling you, he's *sick*—'

In those unaccoutred years none of the *kochaleyns* had a telephone, and few of the families owned cars. On Friday evenings the husbands, Simon among them, made their way up the mountainside from the train station by means of the one ancient village taxi, or else they trudged with their suitcases and their city bundles along the mile of dusty stone-strewn road, between high weedy growths, uphill to the colonies of cottages. The village itself was only a cluster of stores on either side of the train station, and a smattering of old houses inhabited by the year-round people. The doctor was one of these. His office was in his front parlour.

'Go!' Essie cried. Then she thought of the danger to Retta, so close to the feverish child, and seized her and nearly threw her, sobbing, and awakened now by the excitement, into her crib; but the thin little neck under the moistly knotted curls was cool.

'I ought to stop at Bella's, don't you think, and let her know—'

'No, no, don't waste a minute, what's the point, what can she do? Oh listen to him, you've got to hurry, the poor thing can't catch his breath—'

'It's Bella's kid, she'll know what to do,' he urged. 'It's happened before.'

'What makes you think that?'

'Bella told me. She said it in Esperanto actually, when we were working on it last week—'

'Never mind that gibberish, just go and get the doctor!'

Gibberish. She had called the universal language, the language of human salvation, gibberish.

He started down the road to the village: it meant he had to pass Bella's cottage. Her windows were unlit, and he went on. But a few yards beyond her door, he stopped and turned back – how perverse it seemed, how unreasonable, it wasn't right not to tell the mother, and probably the kid would get better anyhow, it was a long walk down the mountain in the dark and cold of the country night, Essie had hurried him out without so much as a sweater, and why wake the poor doctor, a doctor needs his sleep even more than ordinary people, why not hold off till morning, a decent hour, wasn't the main thing to let Bella know?

And here, waiting and waiting, was Essie, with the boy folded in her lap; she kept him there, in the big armchair, lifting him at times (how heavy he was!) to pace from one wall of the narrow room to the other. Now and then she wiped the soles of his feet with a dampened cloth, until he let out a little shudder – almost, it seemed, of satisfaction. But mainly she stood at the window, her wrists aching from the child's weight, watching the sky alter from an opaque square of black to a ghostly pinkish stripe. Retta had long since grown quiet: she lay in the tranquil ruddiness of waxworks sleep, each baby fist resting beside an ear. And finally the white glint of morning struck the windowsill and lit the walls; and at half-past eight the doctor came, together with Simon and Bella. He had driven them both up from the village in his Ford. The child was by now perfectly safe, he said, there was nothing the matter that he wouldn't get over, and wasn't the mother told repeatedly not to feed him milk? Her son was clearly allergic to milk, and still she had forgotten, and put some in his pudding.

'You know your boy's had these episodes before,' the doctor said, peevishly, 'and he may have them again. Because, dear lady, you don't *listen*.'

And Bella, apologizing, said, 'It's a good thing anyhow we didn't drag you out of your bed at three o'clock in the morning, the way some people would have—'

Essie knew what 'some people' meant, but who was 'we'?

'While I'm here,' the doctor said, 'I suppose I ought to have a look at the other one.'

'She's fine,' Essie said. 'She slept through the rest of the night like an angel. Just look, she's still asleep—'

The doctor looked. He shook Retta. He picked up her two fists; they fell back.

'Good God,' the doctor said. 'This child is dead.'

They buried her on the outskirts of a town fifteen miles to the west, in a small non-sectarian cemetery run by an indifferent undertaker who sold them a dog-sized coffin. There was no ceremony; no one came, no one was asked to come. A private burial, a secret burial. In the late afternoon a workman dug out a cavity in the dry soil; down went the box. Simon and Essie stood alone at the graveside and watched as the shovelfuls of earth flew, until the ground was level again. Then they left the *kochaleyn* and for the rest of the summer rented a room not far from the cemetery. Simon went every day to sit beside the grave. At first Essie went with him; but after a while she stayed away. How he wailed, how he hammered and yammered! She could not endure it: too late, that spew, too late, his shame, his remorse, his disgrace: if only he'd gone earlier for the doctor . . . if only he hadn't stopped to see Bella . . . if only he hadn't told her the kid's all right, there's no emergency, my wife exaggerates, morning's time enough to bring the doctor . . . if only he hadn't knocked on Bella's door, if only she hadn't let him in!

In her flat whisper Essie said, 'What happened to the baby, maybe it wouldn't have happened—'

She understood that Simon had become Bella's lover that night. She was silent when she saw him carry out Bella's journals and set them afire. The smell of Esperanto burning remained in his clothes for days afterwards.

She did not know what the doctor could have done; she knew only that he hadn't been there to do it.

Summer after summer they returned to the town near the cemetery, far from all the *kochaleyns* that were scattered along the pebbly dirt roads in those parts, and settled into the top floor of a frame house owned by a deaf old widower. Simon never went back to his job in the men's store, but Essie kept busy at her sewing machine. She placed a two-line advertisement in the 'Personals' column of the local paper – 'Seamstress, Outfits Custom-Made' – and had more orders than ever. Simon no longer sat by the little grave every day; instead, he turned his vigil into a sabbath penance, consecrating one night each week to mourning. Their first year it was Saturday – it was on a Saturday night that Retta had died. The following year it was Tuesday: Simon had burned Bella's journals on a Tuesday evening. Always, whatever the day and whatever the year and whatever the weather, he walked out into the midnight dark, and lingered there, among the dim headstones, until daybreak. Essie had no use for this self-imposed ritual. It was made-up, it was another kind of gibberish out there in the night. She scorned it: what did it mean, this maundering out to the cemetery to talk to the wind? He had deceived her with Bella, he had allowed Retta to die. Essie never spoke of Retta; only Simon spoke of her. He remembered her first steps, he remembered her first words, he remembered how she had pointed with her tiny forefinger at this and that beast at the zoo. 'Tiger,' she said. 'Monkey,' she said. And when they came to the yellow-horned gnu, and Simon said 'gnu', Retta, mistaking it for a cow, blew out an elongated 'Moo'. And how Simon and Essie had laughed at that! Retta was dead; Simon was to blame, he had deceived her with Bella, and what difference now if he despised Bella, if he had made a bonfire of Bella's journals, if he despised everything that smacked of Bella, if he despised Esperanto, and condemned it, and called it delusion and fakery – what difference all of that, if Retta was dead?

It was not their first summer, but the next, when Simon was setting aside Tuesdays to visit his shrine ('His shrine,' Essie said bitterly to herself), that he began writing letters to Esperanto clubs all over the city, all over the world – nasty letters, furious letters. 'Zamenhof, your false idol! Your god!' he wrote. 'Why don't you join the Oomoto, you fools!'

This was the start of Simon's grand scheme – the letters, the outcries, the feverish heaps of philological papers and books with queer foreign alphabets on their spines. Yet in practice it was not grand after all; it was remarkably simple to execute. Obscure lives inspire no inquisitiveness. If your neighbour tells you he was born in Pittsburgh when he was really born in Kalamazoo, who will trouble to search out his birth certificate? As for solicitous – or prying – relations, Essie had been motherless since childhood, and her father had remarried a year after her own marriage to Simon. Together with his new wife he ran a hardware store in Florida; he and Essie rarely corresponded. Simon himself had been reared in the Home for Jewish Orphans: his only living connection was his cousin Lily – gullible Lily, silly Lily! The two of them, Simon and Essie, were as rootless as dandelion spores. They had to account to no one, and though Simon continued jobless, there was money enough, as long as Essie's treadle purred. She kept it purring: her little summertime business spread to half a dozen towns nearby, and her arrival in May was regularly greeted by a blizzard of orders for the following autumn. She changed her ad to read 'Get Set for Winter Warmth in Summer Heat', and had an eye out for the new styles in woollen jackets and coats. She bought, at a discount, discarded pieces of chinchilla and learned to sew fur collars and linings. And all the while Simon was concocting GNU. He named it, he said, in memory of Retta at the zoo; and besides, it announced itself to the ear as New – only see how it superseded and outshone Esperanto, that fake old carcass!

In the fall of each year they moved back to the Bronx. By now Essie owned two sewing machines. 'My city Singer and my country Singer,' she liked to say, and in the winter worked her treadle as tirelessly as in the summer, while Simon went out proselytizing. He printed up flyers on yellow paper, with long rows of sponsors – lists that were anonymous but for their golden Park Avenue addresses – and tacked them on telephone poles.

It was not surprising, Essie thought, that GNU could attract its earliest adherents – all the kochaleyns come home for the winter, and more: the Trotskyites, the Henry George people, the Tolstoyans, the classical music

lovers who went to the free concerts at Lewisohn Stadium, the Norman
Thomas loyalists, the Yiddish Bundists, the wilder Hebraists, the evolving
Thomas Merton mystics, the budding young Taoists and Zen Buddhists,
the ageing humanists and atheists, the Ayn Rand enthusiasts . . . and,
most dangerously, the angry Esperantists. But after the first few
meetings, too many of Simon's would-be converts fell away, drastically,
the merely inquisitive to begin with, the rest out of boredom, or
resentment over dues, or because the rental hall was unheated (the
stinginess of those Park Avenue donors!), or because the accustomed
messianisms they had arrived with were more beguiling than Simon's
ingrown incantations.

'What these people need to keep them interested,' Simon argued, 'is
entertainment. If it's a show they want, Essie, let's give them a show, how
about it?'

So Essie was recruited to sing. She had not immediately agreed; the
idea of it repelled her, but only until she perceived the use of it; the ruse
of it. She was already complicit in Simon's scheme – give your little finger
to the devil, and he'll take your whole arm. And even the little finger was
not so spare: no matter what Simon's yellow flyers boasted, it was Essie's
industry at her two sewing machines that paid for the rental hall. Well
then, all right, she'd sing! It turned out, besides, that she had a way with
a rhyme. Her rhymes were inconsequential ditties, private mockeries –
the latest of her mockeries: the Park Avenue philanthropists were the
first of her inventions. As for her singing voice, it had no range, and she
was nearly breathless at the close of a long verse, but she poured into it
the fury and force of her ridicule, and her ridicule had the sound of
conviction. She put herself in the service of Simon's gibberish – why
not, why not? Retta was dead, Simon was to blame! Her performances
in the cold hall – the costume, the patter, the ditties – were her own
contraption, her secret derision, her revenge for what happened to the
baby.

And still Simon's meetings shrank and shrank, until only the
quarrelsome diehards remained, and Simon's enemies, the Esperantists.

'Jealousy!' he said. 'Because I've outdone them, I've finished them off.
And it's Bella who's sending them, it's got to be Bella, who else?'

But it was Essie. She knew where they were, she knew how to find
them: she had helped Simon with all those letters calling them fools, she
had written their names on the envelopes. Slyly, clandestinely, she
summoned them, and they were glad to come, and stand on chairs, and

stomp and chant and shriek and pound and threaten. Simon, that usurper, with his shabby home-made mimicry of the real thing, had called them fools! They were pleased to shout him down, and some were even pleased to put up their fists in defence of the sole genuine original universal language, Zamenhof's! Essie herself gave the signal: when she ended those nonsensical couplets, when she hopped off the little podium, the assault began.

She let it go on, winter after winter, with the summer's expeditions to look forward to. From a second-hand bookshop she bought herself a world atlas, and instructed Simon in latitudes and longitudes, all those remote wadis and glaciers and canyons and jungles and steppes he was to explore from May through August (she always with him on every trek, never mind how hazardous), all for the purpose of uncovering fresh syllables to feed and fatten his GNU – while here they sat, the two of them, from May through August, lapping up their suppers of bananas-and-sour-cream at the kitchen counter, half of which held Essie's faithful Singer, on the top floor of the deaf old widower's decaying house.

She let it go on, the meetings winter after winter in the city, in the summers hidden away in their mountain townlet close to Retta's grave. She let it go on until it was enough, until her mockery was slaked, until the warring Esperantists had left him sufficiently bruised to satisfy her. There was more to it than spite, the almost carnal relishing of spite, the gloating pleasure of punishing Simon with his own stick. It was the fantastical stick itself: Essie's trickster apparatus, the hoax of those exotic wanderings, when all the world – simple-minded, credulous world! – believed them to be . . . where? Wherever Dravido-Munda, Bugi, Veps, Brihol, Khowa, Oriya, Ilokano, Mordvinian, Shilha, Jagatai, Tipur, Yurak, and all other swarming tongues, were spoken. From May through August, Essie's atlas marked out these shrewdly distant regions; and on a Tuesday, or a Sunday, or any chosen day of the week, Simon moaned out his gibberish beside Retta's grave in the misty night air.

It did not take long for Annette and her crowd to tire of GNU. They cleared out, I learned afterwards, on one of those Thursdays that took Simon conveniently away: there were no goodbyes. When I went to see him again, he was alone. This time, and all the times that followed, I was not prodded by my mother. Her mind was on business; she trusted that Simon was still, as she put it, *blooming*, and I did not disabuse her. She too, she reported, was blooming like mad – it was no longer economical to import the kachinas, so she had gone into producing them on her own. She'd bought up a bit more property, and had a little factory buzzing away, which made not only replicas of the dolls, but all sorts of other Indian artefacts, leather purses, beaded belts. Many of these she had designed herself ('I do have this flair,' she reminded me), and to tell the truth, they were an improvement on the raw-looking native stuff. My father wrote often, asking when I was coming out for a visit, since from my mother's point of view a trip to New York was out of the question: they had their hands full, the business was so demanding. I answered with commonplace undergraduate complaints – I had too many papers overdue, catching up would consume the winter break, and as for vacation later in the year, I was intending to take courses all summer long.

I was becoming an easy liar. My papers were not overdue. I was reluctant to witness my mother's pride in turning out fakes.

The cheques she continued to send (with my father's signature over 'Comptroller' in print) grew bigger and bigger. I cashed them and gave the money to Simon. He took it sadly, idly, without protest. He was unshaven and wore his sandals on bare feet. His toenails were overgrown and as thick as oyster shells. His breath was bad; he had an abscess on a molar that sometimes tormented him and sometimes receded. I begged him to see a dentist. Little by little I had begun to look after him. I tipped the grocery boy and hired the janitor to take a brush to the toilet bowl. He had given up those fruitless hours among alien lexicons; but every Thursday he put on his worn city hat, with its faded grosgrain ribbon, and locked the door of his flat and did not return until late the next afternoon. I imagined him in a rattling train headed upstate, towards a forgotten town in the Catskills; I imagined him kneeling in the dark in damp grass alongside a small stone marker. I went so far as to conjecture what Thursday might commemorate to a mind as deluded as Simon's: suppose it was on a Thursday that Essie had confessed her doubts about the baby; suppose it was on a Thursday that Simon first heard about the curly-haired boy from Cincinnati – then the grieving guilty mourner at the graveside might not be a father at all, but only the man Essie had gulled into marriage long ago. If he did not know which one he was, the father or the dupe, why should he not be half mad?

And what if everything Essie had confided was a fickle fable, myself (like those flies to her sugar bowl) lured into it, a partner to Simon's delusions?

The sophomore term began. One morning on my way to class I saw, across the street, Annette and two young men. The men were dressed in grey business suits and striped ties and had conventional short haircuts. All three were carrying leather briefcases. Annette herself looked less theatrical than I remembered her, though I could not think why. She wore a silk scarf and sober shoes with sharp little heels.

'Hey, Viv,' she called. 'How's your uncle nowadays?'

Unwillingly, I crossed the street.

'Tim. John. My old room-mate,' she introduced me. Close up, I noticed the absence of lipstick. 'Is Simon OK? I have to tell you, he changed my life.'

'You wrecked his.'

'Well, you were right, maybe I took him too seriously. But I got something out of it. I'm in the School of Commerce now. I've switched to accounting, I'm a finance major.'

'Just like Katharine Cornell.'

'No, really, I have this entrepreneurial streak. I figured it out just from running Simon's meetings.'

'Sure, all that green salad,' I said, and walked off.

I did not honestly believe that Annette had wrecked Simon's life. It was true that her defection had left him depleted, but some inner deterioration, from a source unknown to me, was gnawing at him. Perhaps it was age: he was turning into a sick old man. The tooth abscess, long neglected, had affected his heart. He suffered from repeated fits of angina and for relief swallowed handfuls of nitroglycerin. He implored me to visit more often; there were no more Thursdays away. I had come to suspect these anyhow – was it conceivable after so many decades that he would still be looking to set his thin haunches on the hard ground of a graveyard, and in icy winter to boot? Had there been, instead, a once-a-week lover? One of those girlies he diddled? Or Bella, secretly restored? He had no lover now. When he put out a hand to me, it was no longer an attempt to feel for my breast. He hoped for comfort, he wanted to hold on to warmth. The old man's hand that took mine was bloodlessly cold.

I loitered with him through tedious afternoons. I brought him petit-fours and tins of fancy tea. While he dozed over his cup, I emptied the leaves out of their gilt canister and filled it with hundred-dollar bills: froth and foam of my mother's fraudulent prosperity. I tried to wake him into alertness: I asked why he had stopped working on GNU.

'I haven't stopped.'

'I don't see you *doing* it—'

'I think about it. It's in my head. But lately . . . well, what good does it do, you can't beat the Esperantists. Zamenhof, that swindler, he had it all sewed up long ago, he cornered the market.' He blinked repeatedly; he had acquired a distracting twitch. 'Is Lily getting on all right out there? I remember how she hated to go. You know,' he said, 'your mother was always steadfast. The only one who was steadfast was my cousin Lily.'

Some weeks after this conversation I went to see Essie; it would be for the last time.

'Simon's dead,' I told her.

'Simon? How about that.' She took it in with one of her shallow breathy sighs, and all at once blazed up into rage. 'Who made the arrangements? Who! Was it you? If he's buried *there*, next to Retta, I swear I'll have him dug up and thrown out!'

'It's all right, my mother took care of it. On the telephone, long distance, from Arizona. He's over in Staten Island, my parents own some plots.'

'Lily took care of it? Well, at least that, *she* doesn't know where Retta is. She thinks it was Timbuctoo, what happened to the baby. I've told you and told you, your silly mother never knew a thing—'

The apartment had its familiar smell. I had done what I came for, and was ready to leave. But I noticed, though the mannequin still kept its place against the wall, that the sewing machine was gone.

'I got rid of it. I sold it,' she said. 'I saved up, I've got plenty. There never was a time when I couldn't make a living, no matter what. Even after the divorce. But people came in those days, it was like a condolence call. I don't suppose anyone's coming now.'

I said lamely, 'I'm here.'

'Lily's kid, why should I care? I mean the Esperanto people, they're the ones who came. Because they saw I was against Simon. Some of them brought flowers, can you believe it?'

'If you were against him,' I said, 'why did you go along with everything?'

'I told you why. To get even.'

'A funny way of getting even, if you did just what he wanted.'

'My God, the apple doesn't fall far from the tree, just like your mother, blind as a bat. You don't think I'd let anybody know my own husband managed to kill off my own child right in my own bed, do you?'

She was all zigzag and contradiction: she had taken revenge on Simon;

she had protected him. She was both sword and shield. Was this what an improvisational temperament added up to? I was certain now that no word Essie uttered could be trusted.

She had little more to say about Simon, and there was little more she cared to hear. But before I left she pushed her brownish face, wrinkled as a walnut, into mine, and told me something I have never forgotten.

'Listen,' she said, 'that goddamn universal language, you want to know what it is? Not that crazy Esperanto, and not Simon's gibberish either. I'll tell you, but only if you want to know.'

I said I did.

'Everyone uses it,' she said. 'Everyone, all over the world.'

And was that it really, what Essie gave out just then in her mercurial frenzied whisper? Lie, illusion, deception, she said – was that it truly, the universal language we all speak?